THE Myatheira
CHRONICLES

Volume I

THE VOR'SHAI:
From the Ashes

MELISSA GRZANKA

ISBN: 0692654119
ISBN 13: 9780692654118

Website: www.myatheirachronicles.com
Facebook: www.facebook.com/myatheirachronicles
Cover Art & Photography: Keith Heptinstall
Cover Model: Michaela Miller

Prologue

eyna could sense the panic in her mother's movements with every step they took toward the back of the house. She wanted to ask her what was wrong, but she'd been instructed to remain silent, in fear of drawing attention to them from something, but what, she couldn't be sure. Her mother held her, clutched tightly to her chest, glancing over her shoulder nervously to make sure nothing was following.

Upon reaching the cloak room, her mother pulled open the door to a closet there, her fingers fumbling over the latch of a large trunk settled on the floor inside. She could see the difficulty her mother was having while holding her. Not wanting to be a burden, Leyna slipped quietly out of her grasp, keeping close to her legs in fear of becoming separated. She wasn't sure what was wrong, but the fear in her mother's eyes was all she needed to see to know something bad was happening. She watched her mother's hands as they easily opened the latch, lifting the lid while motioning for Leyna to get inside.

"Come on, Leyna. I need you to hide in here until mommy says you can come out, okay?" her mother whispered. Her voice shook, unshed tears glistening in the corners of her eyes. Leyna gave no argument to her request, grabbing onto the edge of the trunk with her hands to pull herself inside, her mother's arms helping to boost her up.

Leyna's heart jumped in fear at the sight of her mother starting to tug the lid down once again. She didn't want to be left in the dark. The trunk was small, confining, impossible to move around in without the risk of hitting her head on something. Her eyes gazed up at her mother, desperate for her to change her mind about the hiding place. "Mommy, please don't shut it," she pleaded. "I don't want to be in the dark."

Bringing her index finger to her lips, her mother hushed her, pulling the lid down further while guiding Leyna's head inside the trunk to prevent it from getting hit by the heavy top. They jumped at the sound of something crashing within the house. To her ears, it was like splintering wood, though from where they were, it was too hard to tell exactly what it was. Turning back to Leyna, her mother shook her head, whispering sadly as she lowered the lid into place. "Stay here, baby. You will be safe in here."

The light disappeared altogether with the soft click of the lid settling into the frame. She hated the darkness. It was frightening to her young mind, feeling cut off from everything. Muffled by the thick casing of the trunk, she could hear the closet door sliding shut, adding to the isolation she already felt. With a whimper, she laid down on her side, curling her legs up to her chest protectively. All she could do was wait for her mother to return. She said she would. Otherwise, how would she know when it was okay for her to come out?

She could hear the sound of glass shattering. Footsteps shook the foundation from somewhere outside her confinement, grunts and shouts followed by loud pounding against the walls in the hallway. Deeper in the house, someone screamed, the voice so shrill that she couldn't recognize the source. It seemed too high to be her mother's. Thinking of the other children in the house, she tightened her grip around her legs, trying not to let the frightened tears escape her eyes. *Did mom put Reina in a box, too? She's afraid of the dark. . .*

Through the darkness of her hiding place, the screaming continued, echoing in Leyna's head. Fear held her motionless, unable to move. Her eyes were open wide in wait of the light that would come again when her mother lifted the lid for her to escape. Eventually the clamor eased, the house filled with a silence almost more disconcerting than the screams she'd listened to for so long. Mother would be coming soon. She just had to lie there quietly like she was told. Time crawled by, her stomach aching for food. What was taking her so long?

After what felt like hours of silence, her heart leapt in her chest at the sudden realization that she could hear someone crying nearby. It was a faint noise. Barely audible from where she was hidden away. She was unconvinced that it wasn't her imagination running wild the way a nine year old mind tended to do. But the sound persisted, rising and falling with the passing time.

Her body was growing anxious to be free. The fear of her mother having forgotten her there was suffocating, her throat tightening with the desire to lie there and cry, while her muscles became restless, yearning to move around without the restrictive walls holding her in place. She maneuvered her body around inside, ducked down to place her hands over her head. The lid was heavier than she expected. It bore down on her despite her efforts. Lips pursed in determination, she lay down on her back, pushing up with her legs to kick at it with all her strength.

Very little light filtered through the small opening she created. Her tiny legs trembled under the strain of the weight, not long enough to push the lid all the way up. Her thoughts filled with panic at the possibility of being trapped inside this awful box forever. She brought her legs back to her chest, braced for one final heave, her arms positioned to allow herself to pull her body up quickly if she was successful. With a determined cry, she threw all of her weight into her legs, taking advantage of the brief moment as an opportunity to escape presented itself. Arms up, she pushed her head through the opening. She tried to jump through, but the closet door blocked her from being able to throw herself to the ground. There wasn't enough space. Before she could get her body through, she felt the heavy lid fall hard on top of her back.

The pain was excruciating, all the air being pushed from her lungs upon impact. Slumped over the edge, she started to cry, giving in to the mixture of fear and pain that overwhelmed her small body. Her own predicament distracted her from the weeping sound she heard while inside the trunk. At that moment she could hear nothing but the sound of her own sobs echoing off the walls of the tiny closet.

Through her tears, she saw the door suddenly open. Her own saliva nearly choked her in fear of who might be there. Reflexively, she coughed to clear her throat, staring in awe at the sight of a young girl standing there, her chubby face muddied and tear-streaked. Her long hair was disheveled; one of the two little barrettes clipped on either side of her head dangled uselessly from only a few strands which held it in place. "Reina," Leyna gasped, holding her arms out frantically to the young girl. "I'm stuck."

The girl's hands were shaking. Leyna grabbed onto them, trying to pull herself free from the trunk's mouth, feeling the heavy edge dig into her skin with every inch of her body she managed to slip through. She could think of nothing but getting out. The pain didn't matter. Gritting her teeth, she forced herself to keep going through the torturous endeavor. Arching her back, she used the last of her strength to push the lid upward, the locking mechanism raking down the center of her spine as she threw her legs over the side, tumbling down to the floor in a heap.

She laid there on her stomach, feeling the dampness of blood soaking into the material at the back of her dress. The house around her was in shambles. Portraits had been torn down, the canvases shredded to completely mar the painted faces, chunks of the walls splintered and broken to leave behind gaping holes along the hallway.

Slowly, she pushed her way to her feet. She grimaced at the pain in her back, more aware of it now than she'd been throughout her escape. Reina clutched at her hand desperately, following at Leyna's side as she made her way down the hall toward the front room. The condition of the house grew worse with every step they took. All of the furniture was overturned, the dining room table broken into pieces and scattered about the floor. Blood could be seen, smeared and splattered, across the walls, bodies of unfamiliar men lying in grotesque heaps.

Everything felt surreal, as if she'd fallen asleep in her hiding place and was trapped in a nightmare from which she couldn't awaken. She could hear Reina start to weep softly beside her, drawing her attention away from the bloodied corpses lying at her feet. Gently, she shielded Reina's eyes from the sight, moving out of the room to guide her to the hallway from where they'd come.

"Reina, can you stay here for me? I'm going to find Mother," Leyna whispered. A sinking feeling started to build in her stomach, making everything seem far more real than she wanted to believe. Nervously, she glanced over her shoulder. Had something moved? Frozen, she held Reina still, listening intently for any signs of something else inside the house with them. Content with the silence, she helped Reina step into the closet, watching her settle herself on the floor next to the trunk where Leyna had been hidden. She couldn't ask her to get inside it. The thought was too cruel to even consider.

Satisfied that Reina wouldn't move, Leyna hurried back in the direction of the bodies. She shuffled around the floor from figure to figure, trying to make out the faces of them all. Who were these men? None of them resembled anyone she'd seen before. They were dressed like soldiers, though the color of their uniforms was all wrong from what she'd seen when the military had been in town for a parade. She stared down at one of the men, a trickle of blood dripping from his mouth onto the leather of his armor. Bile rose in her throat at the sight of him. Falling to her knees, her stomach began to retch in disgust, dry heaving from the lack of food in her system, unable to stop. The image was too much. She needed to get away from the gruesome scene around her and find her mother. Mother would know what to do. Everything would be fine if she could just figure out where she went. Maybe she was hiding, too.

Clambering to her feet, she stumbled onward toward the front of the house. Near the front door, she caught sight of a woman lying on the floor, her long black hair fanned out about her face, spatters of blood staining her pale skin. She didn't want to admit the truth of who it was, but there was no denying it. The woman's elegantly pointed ears protruded from under the mass of black hair. Deep blue eyes gazed life-lessly up at the ceiling, the internal energy within her no longer creating the soft glow around the iris Leyna was used to seeing there; the thin white fabric of her dress covered in blood, torn in various places across her chest and abdomen. Her face was bruised and beaten, her lips turning a soft shade of blue from the death which had settled over her.

Mumbling quietly, Leyna shook the still form of the woman, tears forming in her eyes once again. "Mother, wake up," she sobbed, her lips trembling in grief. Lying over her mother's chest, she wept into the crimson-stained fabric of her dress, her arms wrapped around her in a tight embrace. She knew very little about death. In her child-like mind, she hoped her mother would simply awaken with her urging and return the hug, telling her everything would be alright. But she remained unmoving; her skin cold to the touch.

Through her tears, she could hear footsteps moving across the floor behind her, too heavy to be those of little Reina. Fearfully, she lifted her head from her mother's dress to see who approached, her shrill scream filling the room at the sight of a man coming toward her. He was dressed in the same armor as the corpses in the dining room, his arm raised with his sword at the ready. Leyna scrambled backward on her hands, trying to get to her feet, her legs frantically running about the room to find a place to hide. The man's eyes were set on her. Anywhere she found, he would see her. There had to be somewhere else for her to get away from him.

If she went too deep into the house, she risked the armed man's attention being drawn to where Reina sat hidden in the closet. She needed something closer, out of the way, but he was on her heels, his long strides easily keeping up with her frantic pace. Moving toward the hall, she found the door to Reina's father's study, ducking inside just as the man swung the blade of his sword downward, narrowly missing her.

There was no time to close the door. Her eyes scanned the area for somewhere to take cover, spotting a narrow opening at the bottom of a table near the desk in the back of the room. It was just large enough for her to slide under. Sweat mixed with the blood on her hands, the moist surface of her palms slipping over the floor while she tried to push herself further under the table and against the wall. The man's footsteps were already inside the room, his face appearing where he knelt down next to the opening.

"Get out here, you little brat!"

Hunching her shoulders, Leyna rolled her stomach against the wall, desperate to put as much distance between her and the man as possible. She could hear the metal of his sword scratch against the floor, his arm waving wildly through the small gap to strike at her. There wasn't enough room for her to get away. A sharp twinge of pain erupted along her back, setting her into a panic, the sword slicing at her skin, swipe after swipe.

Unable to reach her sufficiently, the man took to pulling at the table, the legs creaking across the floor over her head. His progress was halted at the arrival of someone else to the room. Leyna's screams trailed off, curious to see who had come to her rescue, but too afraid to move from where she lay pressed against the wall. The sound of clashing swords caught her attention. Someone was fighting him. Maybe Mother woke up after all? It was a foolish notion. One she wanted too badly to cling to. A sickening crunch ended the fight abruptly, the man's body landing on the floor in front of the table with a heavy thud. After a moment, his face slid away, replaced by the familiar eyes of Reina's older sister, Nasha.

"Leyna, come out. We need to leave," she stated calmly. Her arm stretched out to Leyna, beckoning her to take it. Accepting her hand, Leyna allowed the girl to pull her from under the table and back to her feet. "Where is Reina? Is she still here?"

Leyna nodded, aware of the painful grimace over the girl's young features. Her upper body was slouched, her hands blood-covered from a wound in her side. "Nasha, what's wrong?" she asked innocently, heeding the girl's urging to move closer to the door. "What's happening?"

"These men killed Father. If they know you are still alive, they will most likely kill you, too. Now come. Show me where Reina is. We need to get you both out of here before he wakes up."

With hurried steps, Leyna moved away from the girl, making her way to where she'd left Reina. What if she wasn't there? The thought quickened her pace to the door, afraid of opening it to find the closet empty. To her relief, Reina was still sitting there, knees hugged tightly to her chest, rocking back and forth. Quickly, she grabbed her under the arms, lifting Reina up. The position was awkward under Reina's weight. Both girls were nearly the same size, her mass causing Leyna to stumble back. "Nasha said we have to leave," she groaned, taking a few steps for balance before lowering Reina to her feet. She was too heavy to be carried, and the strain only served to stretch the wounds on her back.

Leyna snatched a cloak from a hook in the closet, wrapping it over Reina's shoulders to secure it in place. It was a few sizes too big, the bottom dragging along the floor with every step they took. Upon reaching the back door, Leyna motioned for Reina to stop, waiting for Nasha to reach them. They couldn't go anywhere without her. It was too dangerous.

Nasha appeared at the end of the hallway, her face pale and drawn from loss of blood. She stumbled about drunkenly as she approached them, her steps uneven, barely able to hold herself up long enough to reach the girls before collapsing to her knees, the strength in her body finally giving out. "Do you remember the way to the boats, Leyna? The ones to the mainland?" Her bloodied fingers fumbled over a coin pouch, struggling to slip it over Leyna's slender wrist.

"I don't want to carry it," Leyna argued, shaking her hand to try and slide free of the pouch. Nasha grabbed her hand, pressing it firmly with her own to keep her from moving.

"You don't have a choice." Nasha's voice was strained from the effort it took to speak. She stared deeply into Leyna's eyes, the desperation in them sending a cold chill down Leyna's spine. With a heavy heart, she realized what Nasha was saying. Her energy was fading fast. It took all her strength just to hold her head up. "Take Reina to the boats. These coins are all I can find, but they will be enough to pay the dock workers and get you some food. Can you do this for me?"

Before Leyna could answer, Nasha's hand reached out to the handle on the door, pulling it open to let a cool breeze filter into the room. She didn't want to do what was being asked of her. There had to be some way Nasha could come with them. "Nasha, come on," she begged. "Get up. Reina is too heavy for me to carry."

A final breath escaped Nasha's body, her fingers slipping away from the door handle as she slumped to the floor, leaving the two girls in absolute silence. Fear gripped at Leyna's heart again to see her lying there. It would be so easy to just sit down and cry. To mourn the loss of her mother and everyone else she'd considered family for the better part of her young life. But now wasn't the time for that. She needed to take care of Reina; to get her away from the macabre sights inside the house.

Turning Reina away from her sister's body, Leyna pushed her through the door, checking to make sure the coin pouch was still attached to her wrist. Feeling the weight of it, she began to lead Reina into the rapidly deepening darkness of the night, praying the light of the moon would be enough to guide them to the docks.

Chapter One

"Never take your eyes off your opponent," the teacher lectured, lunging forward at Leyna with a flat-tipped wooden sword. Parrying it away, she tried to maneuver around him, feeling the sweat dripping into her eyes. The heat of the sun was unbearable in the heavy armor she wore, her throat parched from the rigorous exercise.

Gracefully ducking to the side, she evaded the teacher's next strike, poking the tip of her own sword against his back triumphantly. Stepping away from him, she made sure she was out of range for any further attacks, watching him cautiously until he turned to face her with a smile. "Very good," he nodded, moving his sword across his body in a sharp salute. "You're getting much better."

"That's why I'm here," she shrugged, returning his salute respectfully. Grabbing onto her practice helmet with a firm hold, she pulled it from her head, shaking her long black hair loose over her shoulders. The air from the training yard felt good against her face, cooling her warm skin. She didn't mind the dust particles that filled her nose from the dry ground. All she cared about was the breeze, trying to ease her body before it overheated.

"Have you had any luck finding a job?" he asked. His arm reached out to take the sword from Leyna's hand with a smile. "I know there aren't very many around here and you said your income from helping teach wasn't enough for you and the child."

Shaking her head, Leyna gave a soft sigh, lowering her eyes to the ground sadly. "I have been trying, but no one will hire me. They all know how young I am. No one wants to bring on a child. It looks bad for business."

"You're what? Fifteen?" he asked curiously, pulling a flask from his belt. Tipping it up to his lips, he took a drink, basking in the hot rays of the sun. His skin was deeply tanned from exposure to the elements, his hair a shocking mass of white in contrast to his complexion. His soft blue eyes looked her over carefully, appraising her appearance with a critical gaze. "That's a fine age for my people. You Vor'shai will never make sense to me."

Leyna tapped her fingertips idly over the metal of her helmet still clutched in her hand, shrugging her shoulders dismissively. She knew that as a simple human race, his culture was far too different from her own, leaving a gap between them that she'd found common with all of his kind. The life span of the Vor'shai people was known to far exceed the limitations of so many others, their secret rumored to be hidden within the magic which coursed through their bodies. Due to the extensiveness of their physical life, their maturing process was much slower than that of the humans, drawing out their childhood state.

At the age of fifteen, she was still considered a child among her people. Although it was customary for a Vor'shai to be kept from society until such an age they were deemed adult, Leyna had found herself thrust out on her own, forced to find her way in a world that was less than accepting of her. Schooling was difficult to come by and she counted her blessings every day that her teacher had agreed to take her in, granting her an education which otherwise would have been denied to her.

"I hear the military in Siscal is in need of soldiers. I was contemplating attempting acceptance into the ranks there," Leyna replied absently, following her teacher into the much needed shade of the school. A series of racks had been set up near the door, allowing a place for students to put their armor after each training session. Locating the one designated for her, she arranged her helmet at the top, tugging on it to make sure it was securely in place.

Her teacher went to work on his chest armor, pulling it carefully over his head to situate it on the rack with the rest. While tying it in place, he glanced over to Leyna with uncertainty, his eyes searching her expression as if expecting her to admit she'd been speaking in jest. "You can't possibly be serious," he chuckled. His hand patted at the armor contentedly before making his way back over to her. "If you can't even get a job cleaning the stables around here, what makes you think Siscal will allow you into the military?"

"And what makes you think I have to tell them my age?" she shrugged, winking deviously at him. "Blaise, you've said it yourself, in the past, that I can keep up with the best of the warriors here in Carpaen. Would the armies in Siscal be any different that they would require such far superior fighters?"

"Leyna, it's different," he sighed, his shoulders drooping in defeat. She could see the frantic look in his eyes while he struggled to find the right words to deter her from the idea. "Carpaen isn't at war. If you joined the military here, they would provide you with the training you needed. If you go to Siscal they would toss you into a unit and you'd be on the battlefield before you could even blink."

"But the military here won't accept me. They know me; and they know how young I am." A frown passed over Leyna's slender features, all traces of her lighthearted humor dissipating with the seriousness of her tone. "My options are limited. There is nothing else I can do."

Blaise stared back at her, his eyes alone speaking of his discontent. Unable to bear his disheartened gaze any longer, Leyna brushed past him down the hallway, making her way further into the school. She could hear the sound of his footsteps following her, loudly echoing off the stone walls. "And what if they find out you lied to them? How do you think they would react to that slight?"

She came to a stop in the middle of the hall, pursing her lips together at the sound of Blaise's voice. It was something she'd contemplated herself when considering her options. Lying to any government could hold severe consequences, though she couldn't be honest with anyone if she had any hope of making a living. For years, she'd spent her time scraping every coin she could find, picking up any odd job that would offer her something more. It just wasn't enough.

Her first year in Carpaen, she and Reina slept in the streets until she managed to beg enough money from the shoppers in the market. Eventually they were able to pay for a room at the cheapest inn she could find in the slums. When she came to the academy in the city of Eykanua, it had been to beg for work from the administrators. If Blaise hadn't taken pity on her and brought her in as his student, she and Reina would've been back out on the streets with nothing. But he'd taken her in, teaching her the ways of military combat and fighting for her to be able to work as an assistant to him in his classes. The time Leyna spent in the streets was all she needed to know that she had to do something to prevent Reina from ever having to live that way again. It didn't matter what the risk was to her; even if it meant going off to war in a country she'd never seen with her own eyes.

"They will just have to not find out, then," she said quietly, rubbing the tip of her ear thoughtfully. Blaise's footsteps grew nearer as he made his way to her side, his expression reminding her of a father preparing to lecture a child. Before he could speak, she held up her hand to cut him off, shaking her head vehemently. "Do not try to talk me out of it. I have already managed to save up enough money for a horse and enough food to take along with me on the journey."

"This will never work, Leyna," Blaise argued, lightly pushing her hand back down to look her in the eye. "You may be able to talk like an adult, but you don't look like one. If there are *any* Vor'shai people in Siscal's military, they will call your bluff instantly upon seeing your face."

Hanging her head shamefully, she stared down at her ragged dress, the hem of it frayed from wear. Oversized for her small figure, the material draped past her feet, dragging on the ground with every step she took. The fabric was stained from mud and dust gathered in the training courtyard, its appearance unsightly, holes worn through the sleeves. Folding her arms across her abdomen she tried to hide it from view, her discomfort evident in her hunched posture. "My age is only noticeable because I look like a vagrant. If I am able to present myself with a bit of dignity, I may have a chance at fooling them."

The sound of Blaise's defeated sigh reached her ears. "You are too stubborn for me to think I could change your mind," he frowned, tilting Leyna's chin upward with his hand. "Promise me you will at least tell me when you plan to leave so that I might be able to help you."

"By the week's end. I have already spoken with the administrators and they have granted me leave," she replied calmly, shifting her head away from Blaise's touch. Of all the people in Carpaen she'd come to know, it was Blaise she'd dreaded telling about her plans the most, knowing he wouldn't agree with her decision. Despite her young age, his affection for her it had been a poorly guarded secret throughout the students at the academy. Though he had not spoken of it, she'd been made aware through the rumors, causing a feeling of awkwardness when near him. There was no doubt in her mind going into the conversation that he would take it the hardest of anyone; she simply hoped she could use whatever persuasive abilities she possessed to convince him that he had no say in the matter.

"You've already spoken with the administrators? How long have you been planning this?" he demanded, reaching out for her again. With a sharp gesture, she pushed his arm away, stepping back to place distance between them.

"Several months now," Leyna stated defiantly. She could see the hurt in his eyes. At her dismissive behavior, his expression contorted into anger, quickly working to regain his composure. He stared at her in disbelief, making a move as if to close the gap between them before thinking better of it.

Other students started to filter into the hallway, their curious gazes watching with growing interest at the scene. It was difficult to ignore the burning eyes of the onlookers anxiously awaiting what would happen next. Running her fingers through her hair she turned away from him, her feet carrying her toward the front of the academy with determined strides, throwing her final words over her shoulder. "I will not discuss the matter with you any further."

She was grateful for the silence in response, assuring her Blaise had chosen not to follow. *The nerve of him*; she thought in frustration, her fists clenched tightly at her sides. *If I had known he would assume he had any rights over my life because he took me in, I never would have accepted. . .*

The anger slowly waned at her own thoughts, realizing she was lying to herself. Without Blaise, there was no way to know where she and Reina would be now; if they would even still be alive. She owed their lives to him and yet she couldn't help but feel he was asking too much of her. Respect would dictate her to be in his debt; but honor argued that she was not obligated to offer her life to him. She was heir to a noble family of the great Vor'shai. It would bring more disgrace upon her to become romantically involved with a human than if she lived as a pauper surviving on bread crumbs and dressing in rags. *Not far from how I am living now. . .*

Stepping through the heavy doors at the entrance of the academy, she immediately felt the unbearable heat from the sun bearing down on her face once again. The street was filled with horses and crowds of people hurrying along to the markets. Day was soon to become night, the merchants due to begin packing up their wares within a couple of hours. She could feel the hot gravel under her feet, burning her skin through the holes worn in the fabric of her slippers. The soles were peeling and worthless; the shoes serving as more of a decoration than actually acting in their intended function.

Cries from the local beggars filled her ears as she made her way further into the heart of the poorer section of town. The buildings were dilapidated, paint peeling from the weathered exteriors while the roofs sagged with age. Reaching the door of the inn, she cringed at the sound of the creaking hinges. From behind the desk the clerk glanced up from her paperwork with an apathetic gaze, barely acknowledging Leyna's presence before returning to her business.

The floor boards on the stairs groaned loudly under the weight of Leyna's steps, announcing her presence despite her attempts to keep quiet. Hurrying down the hallway, she kept her eyes cast downward, finding her way to her room quickly while fumbling with the key. Silently, she slipped inside, closing the door behind her, double checking to make sure the latch was securely in place.

"Reina, I'm home!" she called out, looking around the room curiously. At the sound of her voice she watched a little blonde-haired head pop up from the other side of the bed, a pair of green eyes opening excitedly. Scurrying over the blankets, the girl ran up to Leyna, wrapping her arms around her tightly.

Returning the gesture, Leyna patted her on the back, forcing a smile through the sadness she felt to see the young girl. She cared for her the way she would have cared for a sister, if she had one. The difference in their racial heritage meant little to Leyna after so many years. Reina was the closest thing to family she had left. She was of Mialan descent, her skin remaining fair even through the exposure to the sun for so many years in Carpaen. The similarities of the Mialans to the Vor'shai could be seen easily between the two girls, the points of Reina's ears less sharp than those of Leyna's, though still noticeable from under her tangled mass of hair.

Lifting Reina into her arms, Leyna carried her across the floor, setting her down carefully on the bed. "Oh, you're getting too big," she chuckled, lowering herself onto the mattress beside her. "In another year, I'm not sure I'll still be able to pick you up."

"I'm not that big," Reina stated innocently, kicking her feet out to bounce down on the bed playfully. Reaching her hands out to Reina's stomach, Leyna began to tickle her, a warmth flooding her senses at the sound of her laughter.

She hated the thought of leaving Reina behind in Eykanua. There was no other option for her, if she intended to leave, but the idea tore at her very insides. The question she faced was who would care for Reina while she was away. Although Reina was a year older than Leyna had been after her mother's death, she wasn't sure if she would be capable of caring for herself if left alone. She could think of no one else with whom she would trust such a responsibility; and the orphanage seemed too desolate of a place for a girl like her.

Unable to hide the distant look in her eyes, Leyna bowed her head forward, hoping to conceal her face from Reina. She didn't want her to know the troubled thoughts that filled her head, afraid they would worry her young mind. It was all too much for a girl so small. *Her time should be spent with toys and fresh air, not struggling to find money in the putrid streets of this decaying town.*

A gentle tug on the sleeve of her tattered dress pulled Leyna from her thoughts, her lips turning upward into a smile at the sight of Reina curled up by her side. "Leyna, why do you have to leave?" Reina asked quietly, snuggling against her. "I don't want you to go."

"I have to, sweetie," Leyna frowned, gently twirling Reina's blonde locks around her finger, holding her tight. "The innkeeper has decided to raise our rent and I don't make enough money at the academy to pay for it. If I stay here, we will end up on the streets again and I couldn't bear to see that happen."

"But you said the orphanage would have kids we could play with. We could both go there," Reina pouted, her lower lip sticking out pathetically. "Then you wouldn't have to go to work all the time. You could stay and play with me."

Leyna ruffled the young girl's hair, leaning forward to give her a kiss on the forehead. "I am too old for the orphanage. They will accept you, but I am beyond the age of entry now. I think you will like it there while I am away. And when the war in Siscal is over, I could come get you and you could live with me in the north."

"Could we have a big house and eat chocolate every day?" Reina asked excitedly, shifting on the bed to stare at her happily. Unable to resist a smile, Leyna laughed softly, pulling Reina to her in a tight hug.

"Of course we will. And you can have ice cream for breakfast every morning and a new dress every week for you to dirty while you play," she smiled, tapping the tip of Reina's nose. Reina's face wrinkled up with a giggle, her body squirming free of Leyna's arms.

"I hope the war gets over soon, then," she said absently, ducking back down beside the bed where she'd been when Leyna first arrived home. "What if the kids at the orphanage are mean to me?"

Slowly rising from the bed, Leyna watched Reina playing with a tattered old doll, one of the arms nearly torn completely from its body with the stuffing poking out of the seam. The painted smile on its face was worn almost entirely away, its eyes staring out like little dots on a wooden ball, no longer discernable as to what they'd originally been. "They won't be mean to you," she assured her. "They will love you; just so long as you share your toys and treat them all nicely."

A familiar pain in her stomach caused her to hunch over uncomfortably, breathing deeply to ease the discomfort. It had been two days since she'd eaten last, her meals from the academy being the only source of food she could bring home to Reina. Grimacing, she realized she'd left the school without stopping by the lunchroom, leaving her with nothing to feed either one of them. She cursed under her breath, making her way toward the door, thinking desperately how she could manage something for Reina to eat. They had no coin to spare. Her only option was to go back and face the students at the academy again.

"Reina, honey, I need to run back to the academy and then we'll have dinner, okay?" she smiled forcefully, unhooking the latch on the door. From somewhere on the other side of the bed she could hear a mumble from Reina, her words unintelligible as she continued to play with her doll. Not wanting to distract her, Leyna slipped quietly into the hallway, dragging her feet dejectedly along the floor and back out into the street toward the school.

She barely recognized herself in the reflection staring back at her in the mirror, cosmetics outlining the unique shape of her eyes. Their deep blue color shone brilliantly against the soft tan of her skin, the presence of the Vor'shai energy strengthening their glow like tiny sapphire lights sparkling inside the iris. Her borrowed dress hung somewhat awkwardly off her slender form, the curves not quite fitting to her own. The lace lining the neckline stuck out across her chest, tailored to fit the matured body of the human girl who loaned it to her. Pressing it down against her skin with a sigh she looked around the room, hoping to find something with which she could use to fill it in.

"The shoes might be a little big, but I'm sure we can stuff some cloth in the toes and you'll hardly know the difference," a young human girl smiled, offering out a dainty pair of silver high-heeled slippers. Leyna accepted them graciously, looking them over in awe. The fabric was well-sewn, putting her ragged old shoes to shame with their design.

Bending forward, she slipped the shoes onto her feet, her toes sliding down into the tip, leaving a large gap between the back of the shoe and her heel. With a careful step she tried to move forward, nearly walking right out of them. "I think they're more than a little big," she sighed. The human girl chuckled to herself, grabbing up a bolt of grey fabric from the table.

Carefully, she dragged a pair of scissors across a line of the fabric, separating two sections from the rest. Folding them into tiny squares, she knelt down at Leyna's feet, placing a piece in the toes of each shoe before sliding them back on her to see how they fit. "The goal is to make you look older and more mature. Bigger is fine, as long as we can compensate for the difference well enough to make it look believable. How is that?"

"Strange," Leyna laughed uncomfortably, moving about the room with cautious steps. "I feel like I will fall over at any moment."

"Well, don't do that. We aren't finished yet," the girl giggled, moving over to stop Leyna from walking. Turning her, she tugged at the neckline, her brow furrowed in concentration. She grabbed up the bolt of fabric once again, going to work cutting out several more pieces, tossing the scissors absently down to the floor at their feet.

Leyna inhaled nervously at the feeling of the girl stuffing the pieces of fabric into her corset, uncertain about the idea of altering her appearance to such a degree. The more they added, the more difficult it would be to keep up the façade until her own body managed to fill itself in.

Stepping back to admire her work, the young girl nodded in approval, guiding Leyna over to the mirror once again. Leyna blinked in surprise, speechless at the sight, a soft smile passing over her lips. The padding filled out the excess material of the bodice, boosting her just enough to make it look like a natural fit. The silver fabric of the dress still hung awkwardly around her waist, the fancy skirt barely brushing the floor from where it dragged before, lifted by the slight heel of her shoes.

"I have a belt somewhere that might make the waistline look a little less – lacking," the girl smiled. Her long legs carried her over to a large wooden wardrobe on the other side of the room. Leyna watched her, jealous of her figure. If she had legs like hers, there wouldn't be any need to stuff anything. Pulling open the doors, the girl began to rifle through the contents, pausing occasionally to look at something before continuing her search.

Entranced by the transformation that had taken place with herself, Leyna's confidence started to rebuild with every second she spent admiring her reflection. She was convinced she was capable of pulling off such a masquerade. It would take some work, but it wouldn't be impossible. No one should be seeing her unclothed anyway to know that any of it was fake. "Cady, I am forever in your debt for this. You are far too kind," she smiled, twirling around in front of the mirror.

"Don't thank me yet," the girl mumbled, distracted by something inside the wardrobe. "You still have to convince everyone that all this stuffing is really you. I can't help you with that."

Moving away from the drawers, she carried a silver belt over to Leyna, holding it out against the fabric of the dress to see how it looked. The polished surface shimmered in the light of the sun as it filtered through the window, revealing the fine craftsmanship of the design. Each link had been carefully entwined with the next, creating a delicate pattern of chainwork from end to end. Wrapping it around Leyna's waist, she connected the links together, leaving a long strand to dangle off to one side.

"Perfect," Leyna beamed, smoothing out the folds of the skirt. "I can barely notice the looseness." Pressing the sides of the dress with her hands, she gazed distractedly at her thin waistline, wishing there was some way to make her hips look more defined, while at the same time knowing such a thing would be ridiculous. *They will hardly notice your lack of curves when you get into the military armor. This is only necessary to get myself signed on.*

"You look good with cosmetics. You should take some with you and wear them regularly. It makes you look much older." Licking her finger, Cady wiped off a smear of eye liner from Leyna's cheek, looking her over with a scrutinizing gaze. "Looking like this, you'll have those military men eating out of your hand in no time."

She shifted her shoulders back, wrapping the cloak around her, never taking her eyes off the mirror while securing the clasp in place. It wasn't the finest quality of material, but it was good enough to serve the purpose she needed it for. The price tag had been the most important thing, and she'd managed to convince the merchant to lower the cost into a range she could afford. "I hope you're right," she sighed, turning around to face her friend. "It is about time for me to head off. How do I look?"

"Like the next recruit of the Siscalian military," Cady smiled, wrapping her arms around Leyna in a warm hug. "You promise me you'll be careful. We're all worried about you."

"Don't be. Regardless of what happens; this will be a dream come true for me. I am getting a chance to see the world." Squeezing Cady gently, Leyna pulled back, looking her friend over with a smile. "I only wish you could come with me. This trip will be awful by myself."

Cady chuckled quietly, shaking her head in disagreement. "I would be terrible company, and an even more terrible soldier. Trust me; you'll be so focused on getting through the desert on the eastern end of the country that you'll hardly notice you're alone."

"I hope you're right," Leyna nodded, stepping toward the door. Her entire body was filled with nervous excitement about the trip, anxious to see the world yet fearful she would lose her way. The terrain of the desert was known to be difficult to traverse, the endless expanse of sand drawing out in all directions as far as the eye could see. Many tales of lost travelers had been told over the years. Most people no longer dared make the journey without first traveling north to Tanispa, adding several days to the trip. The desert was the quickest route – and the most perilous.

"Take care of yourself. I promise to write." With a final wave she stepped out of the dormitory door, unsteady on her feet from the awkwardness of the heels on her shoes. Keeping along the back of the building, she hoped to avoid notice by the other students, not wanting to draw attention to herself that would alert Blaise to her presence. She didn't have the patience to handle his attempts at convincing her not to leave. Her mind was already far away with thoughts of escaping the wretched heat of Carpaen and his unwanted affections.

Her horse was still saddled and hitched to a post near the street. Hands trembling, she fumbled over her packs, making sure her food and water was still where she'd left it. Tucking her map into the front compartment of her bag, she hoisted herself up onto the horse, struggling to settle into the saddle. It felt out of place to ride in such a fashion, her legs straddling its back. At the academy, they stressed the preference for women to ride sidesaddle. Any other way was considered unladylike, but to make the trip in such a dainty manner was out of the question. The unbalanced position would make it more difficult to perform a hasty escape if it became necessary.

She'd said her farewells to Reina earlier that morning on the orphanage steps, her pouting lips still vivid in Leyna's mind. Although she seemed sad to see Leyna go, she'd also been looking forward to playing with the other children, her innocent thoughts not wrapping around the seriousness of their situation. Her happiness was all that mattered, however, and the fact that she had others to take care of her and keep her company was enough to calm Leyna's aching heart at leaving her behind. In defense of her own actions, she argued it was not deserting Reina to leave her in the care of the orphanage. The idea wasn't to leave her there forever. When circumstances allowed, she would come back for her. It was just a matter of saving up enough money to make it possible.

It was at least a three day ride to the Siscalian border from Carpaen, requiring her to set up camp for the evening in the desert. Continuing to travel through the night was too risky. To do so increased the chances of veering off course without the position of the sun to guide her in the right direction, the landscape too barren and open, nothing setting one path apart from the next. She glanced up at the sky, seeing the sun already sinking from its peak. It would take her until morning to reach the main stretch of the desert, allowing her to ride throughout the night along the road, shaving nearly an entire day's ride from her journey.

Anxious to be away from the city, she dug her heels into the horse's sides, calling out for it to move. It started at a slower pace, weaving through the curves of the streets until she reached the less densely populated outskirts, snapping the reins to pick up speed.

The feeling of the wind on her face was a welcome relief from the afternoon sun beating down on her from up above. The air was arid and dust-filled; a constant reminder of the dreadful landscape. Rain was a rarity, making crops difficult to grow around the city, while the dryness made it easy for a weary traveler to experience dehydration if they weren't cautious of how they rationed their water.

When the sun finally set, Leyna could already feel the tug of fatigue on her body. Sleep had been impossible the night before, eluding her despite her attempts to welcome it. Images of the life she prayed for in Siscal haunted her vision like dreams to her waking mind. She'd never been there before; the only pictures of it she had to go by were drawings from books in the library of the academy.

Wiping her eyes tiredly, she tried to focus on the road ahead. The horse's pace had slowed, the steady sound of its hooves on the ground echoing through the emptiness surrounding her, hypnotic in its rhythm. Trees were becoming scarcer with every mile, slowly giving way to the desert. As the sun began to peek back over the horizon, she brought the horse to a halt, climbing down to stretch her legs in hopes of regaining her senses from the overwhelming need to lay down and fall asleep in the warm sand.

The light of day changed everything about the endless expanse of land. From where she stood at the side of her horse, she could see no end in sight, the heat of the sun already starting to warm her face. Uncertain of what sort of obstacles lie ahead, she dug through her bags for the protection of her sword, her fingers wrapping naturally around the thick leather of her scabbard. She strapped it around her waist, paying little attention to the lack of fashion it held against her dress, caring only that it would be readily accessible if she had need of it.

Restless to get moving again, she struggled against the height of her horse, straining the muscles in her arms to lift back up into the saddle. Every moment seemed to increase the temperature, sweat dripping from her brow. She was desperate for any respite from the heat. Urging the horse on, she snapped the reins, grateful for the sensation of the wind in her hair, still warm, though granting a slight relief from the dryness.

As the sun started to set, she became increasingly aware of the outline of the mountains starting to take shape in the distance. With the quickly fading light, the air began to cool for the evening, minimal, but enough to make it more bearable. Bringing the horse to a stop, she lowered herself down into the sand, lying back to gaze up at the sky. Her head reeled from exhaustion. Her thoughts were cloudy and jumbled. It felt wonderful to lie there, her muscles relaxing into the warm ground. She could feel her eyelids growing heavy, though she knew she couldn't allow herself to sleep quite yet.

Groggily, she climbed back to her feet, stumbling over her high heels in the soft sand. Why had she chosen to wear them so soon? A flat sole would have been more convenient for the ride. *That shows how clearly I was thinking about things.*

From inside her travel pack, she pulled out a small pan, pouring water into it from her canteen. Patting her horse gently on the neck, she placed the pan on the ground in front of it, watching it lap up the liquid greedily.

She stared off into the distance, trying to picture in her mind what Siscal would look like on the other side of the mountains. They appeared so close and yet were so far away. Their massive silhouette blocked out the entirety of the horizon beyond them, creating a wall between her and her destination. The sudden feeling of something sliding over her foot caused her to jump in surprise, crying out at the sight of a tiny snake slithering across her shoe. Kicking her foot wildly, she sent the creature soaring through the air, landing in the sand with a soft thud some distance away.

A shiver coursed through her while watching the snake skitter at an angle across the ground. Still feeling a tingle where it touched her, she shook her foot again to rid herself of the sensation. "Yuck, yuck, yuck," she muttered disgustedly, snatching up the empty water pan. Waving it to the side, she shook out the last few remaining droplets before stuffing it back into her travel pack.

It took significantly more effort than before to get back onto the horse, her muscles trembling and fatigued. The thought of lying down on the sand with the snake brought a harsh shudder over her body. Somehow it managed to make the idea of sleep seem less enticing to her aching limbs.

With her newfound desire to keep moving, she weighed her options carefully, recognizing the danger in attempting the final stretch in the dark. Every argument was laid to rest with the promise of the mountains still visible in the distance, acting as a guiding point to help her in her way. The cooler air made the journey more comfortable. It would be easier to tolerate the desert without the intensity of the heat. She didn't want to sleep. Every step forward brought her closer to a new life, creating possibilities that would allow her to make something of herself. It was worth the risk. The faster she could make it to those mountains, the better.

Her wandering mind distracted her throughout the night. She was oblivious to the slight change in the terrain, the sand giving way to heavier gravel. An occasional tree jutted up from the ground, the height of the mountains growing more intimidating at her approach. At the soft light of the sun brightening the area around her, she was surprised to see how far she had traveled, the landscape beginning to slope upward with a steady incline into the mountains.

Excitement welled up inside her at the realization that she had made it through the desert to the border of Siscal, the wretched heat of Carpaen now behind her. She could feel her horse struggling against her directions. It was no doubt exhausted from the long journey. Speaking gently, she tried to urge it forward, snapping the reins to push it faster. It did nothing but shake its head in irritation. Though the speed wasn't the same as its refreshed pace from when they started the trip, it moved steadily up the incline of the trail, dragging its hooves along the rocks.

From somewhere in the mountains she could hear a strange howl echo through the air, sending shivers down her spine. The unfamiliar terrain made her uneasy, uncertain of what wildlife inhabited the area. Everything was far different from that of Carpaen.

The shifting climate between warm and cold created a much more livable environment for many species not seen back home.

She slowed her pace, hoping the horse's hooves would cease their loud clattering over the hard ground. Her eyes darted from side to side, vigilant for any sign of the creature that made the noise. The air was eerily silent, devoid of even a flutter of the wind in the leaves of the trees. Through the quiet, she suddenly caught the sound of rocks scattering about the road from behind her. Turning her head, she cried out in surprise, breath catching in her throat at the sight of a large beast lumbering toward her.

Its eyes glowed yellow even through the bright light of the late morning sun shining down from above. Brown fur covered its body, the lithe figure resembling a large cat while the face was contorted into a shape she had never seen before. The snout protruded grotesquely, sharpened fangs overlapping its blackened lips. Each digit of its paws extended beyond that of the beasts she was accustomed to, the claws arching to a sharp point where it connected with the ground on every step it took.

The beast remained on all fours while approaching her until it was nearly ready to strike, rising onto its hind legs to an impressive height, towering above her. Crying out in panic, she thought to push her horse forward, finding it already jolted into motion at a brisk pace around the mountainside. The uneven ground made it difficult for the horse to keep its footing, forced to decrease its speed to keep from falling. Glancing over her shoulder, she could see the foul beast gaining on her again, the horse no match for its agile form.

Options scarce, she tried to force the horse to one side, urging it off the clear path that wound through the mountains and onto a small wilderness trail worn into the grass. The steepness of the incline intimidated it, its head shaking violently as it tried to maneuver away. With a ferocious snarl, the beast leapt into the air toward her, the impact of its body with her own pushing the breath from her chest. Feeling her fingers ripped from the reins, she tumbled to the ground, tucking her shoulder to cushion her fall. Gracefully, she rolled over and back onto her feet, instinctively reaching for the scabbard at her side.

Thoughts raced through her tired head, eyes searching the beast desperately for an opening that might expose a weakness. She knew running would be futile without the help of her horse. Her own feet would never carry her fast enough to escape. Drawing her sword, she clutched it with both hands, heart racing with frightened excitement.

Now is the time to see if you are really cut out for this, she told herself sternly. Her eyes opened wide at the sight of the creature rising back onto its hind legs, swiping its front claws at her with amazing precision. The motions of its body seemed almost too well executed for any normal animal, a hint of intelligence twinkling from its glowing eyes. Narrowly avoiding the blow, Leyna ducked out of the way, the power of the creature's momentum carrying it past her in a rush.

In a fluid motion, it turned around, growling deep in its throat while beginning a slow circling motion around her. Tightening her grip on her sword, she moved with it, trying to conceal the fear she felt inside, conveying an image of confidence to the beast. Its movements were cold and calculating, sizing her up with every step. With a powerful burst of motion it lunged toward her, stretching its claws in preparation to strike, teeth bared. She bent to the side easily to avoid the blow, dragging her blade along its flank.

It wasted no time in regaining its lost ground, twisting sharply to face her again. Effortlessly, it took to the air, leaping forward to where she was still recovering from her last strike. Gripping the hilt of her sword with both hands, she thrust it forward, cringing at the sickening crunch of metal piercing through the flesh of the beast.

The weight of its body pushed her backward, sending her falling flat onto her back. Sharpened rocks jutted up from the ground, pressing into her skin uncomfortably. For several moments she lay there, listening, afraid of hearing its heavy breath. It landed a few feet away, the area around her silent once again as it had been before. Inhaling deeply, she gazed up at the sky, whispering a silent prayer of thanks to the gods that she was still alive.

Lifting her upper body from the ground, she sat up quickly, brushing the dirt from her arms. A glint of light caught her eye in her peripheral vision, drawing her attention to her sword, still protruding from the blood-covered fur where it struck its mark. Her eyes settled on it calmly, watching the abdomen of the creature for any sign of movement that would alert her to any danger of it returning to its feet. Satisfied with the stillness, she rose to her feet, dusting herself off absentmindedly.

Her shoulders bowed at the realization that her horse was no longer within sight. The thought of being stranded in the mountains with such unnatural beasts caused her to shudder. Pursing her lips, she tried to ease her frustration by taking determined strides over to the corpse of the beast. Wrapping her fingers tightly around the hilt of her sword, she pulled upward with all of her strength, wrinkling her nose at the soft squish of the blade slicing through its skin. "I would feel bad for killing you, but you cost me my horse, you wretched thing," she frowned, resisting the urge to kick the corpse in fear of damaging her shoes.

Suddenly reminded of her borrowed wardrobe, she began to quickly pat herself down, checking to make sure all of the extra padding was still in place where Cady positioned it. Adjusting her corset, she gave a sigh of relief before feeling the coolness of the mountain breeze blowing over one of her feet, her heart sinking in her chest. Tugging up her skirt, she cursed under her breath, her toes wiggling in the dirt while her eyes scoured the area for her lost shoe.

She could see no sign of it anywhere, her gaze falling curiously back to the beast. This couldn't be happening. Rolling her eyes heavenward, she dropped down to her knees, positioning her hands under the belly of the corpse. With a strong heave she tried to roll it over, the weight feeling heavier than she expected, even after having felt its force knock her from her horse. It took several tries to make any progress in moving it, a smile passing over her lips at the sight of a piece of silver fabric becoming visible from underneath the body. Renewing her efforts, she tried to roll the creature the rest of the way over, grunting under the strain.

As she succeeded in freeing her shoe, she heard a sharp scrape of metal come from behind her, followed almost instantly by a pathetic wail that chilled her to the core. A loud thud brought a sudden halt to the noise, her heart pounding wildly in her chest in fear of what she would find if she turned toward the sound. Rising slowly, she drew in a deep breath, her body shifting uncomfortably to leave the corpse of the beast at her back.

There, two yards away, lay a second animal like the one she'd just fought, the hilt of a large sword sticking from the brown fur on its back. A man stood over it, his eyes surveying the body of the beast to ascertain if it was dead. "Annoying creatures they are, really," the man said calmly, his voice low and fluid in a language Leyna hadn't heard spoken since before her mother was killed. His words were in the graceful Vor'shai tongue, their meaning not reaching her at first in her surprise at the sound. "They tend to travel in pairs. You always have to be prepared for their mate."

Leyna stood frozen in awe of the man, his strong slender hands easily drawing the sword from the creature's back. Clearing the blade of any blood that remained with a hard shake, he slid it confidently into his sheath. His eyes glowed a bright silver, reflecting the internal energy inherent in the Vor'shai race. His hair was cut short, the thick black locks lying somewhat haphazardly atop his head from the mountain wind. The paleness of his skin contrasted his dark hair, a common trait among their people, reassuring her that he must reside somewhere outside of the desert.

"I apologize," he spoke again, his voice thickly accented as he utilized the language more widely used throughout Carpaen. "It may have been presumptuous of me to assume you spoke the language. The color of your skin leads me to believe you are from one of the Carpaen cities on the southern border of the desert. You are a good ways from home, if that is the case – and alone, which is even more peculiar."

Shaking her head to clear her mind of the initial shock at his presence, Leyna felt her cheeks flush with warmth in embarrassment at her behavior. She could only imagine what a fright she must look to him, despite the pains she had endured in hopes of appearing more mature upon her arrival. After sleep deprivation and a journey through the desert, it made her efforts with her appearance seem like the naïve work of an inexperienced con-artist. "I am sorry," she stated slowly, searching in her mind for the words in her native tongue. Though the language remained constantly at the back of her memory, it felt odd to speak it again after so many years.

"Ah, you do have a voice. I was beginning to think I had stumbled upon a mute," the man smiled, looking her over carefully where she continued to stand in a daze. "Are you quite alright? I cannot tell if you have been injured, or if you are in shock. I suppose I can see where an unexpected attack by one of these beasts could cause such."

"Oh, no – no, I am fine. I just..." Leyna found herself at a loss for words, fatigue overwhelming her senses. She tried to focus on the man, not wanting to give the impression that she was a witless child lost in the mountains; though it was exactly what she was. With the quickly dissipating adrenaline from her limbs, exhaustion threatened with renewed force, causing her to sway somewhat on her feet. "I have not slept in at least three days and I fear the intolerable heat of the sun may have left me a good bit dehydrated; but aside from that, I am in good health."

"You look so young to be traveling on your own," the man mused, offering his hand to help her back out onto the main path.

Once free of the weeds, she became aware again of her missing shoe, feeling the rocks poking up at the bottom of her foot. Heaving a dejected sigh, she bowed her head forward, her stance somewhat skewed from the difference in height between her feet. "I was blessed with youthful looks, it would seem. I get accused of being too young quite frequently, but I am fully capable of handling myself."

"Of course," the man nodded. Following her eyes he caught a glimpse of her bare foot from under the dust covered hem of her dress, immediately turning his attention to search the area for her missing shoe. "So, does this youthful yet perfectly capable woman have a name?"

"She does. And her shoe is somewhere near the corpse of one of those creatures," Leyna sighed, taking a step forward to help him in his search. She could feel the tall weeds brushing against her legs from under her skirt, her uneven gait causing her to lope across the ground toward the beast she'd killed. "Do these things have a name that the people here call them?" she asked. Before she could reach the creature, she watched the man bend over to retrieve her shoe, the tiny swatch of material fluttering from inside the toe down to the ground.

Leyna watched the fabric come to rest in the grass, mortified by the sight of it in the presence of this strange man. She tried to ignore it, her manner nonchalant as he handed it over to her, sweeping his hand down to gather up the material from his feet and offering it to her with a curious smile. She could feel the pointed tips of her ears burning with humiliation, reaching out to accept the items from his hands without meeting his eye. With a mumbled thank you, she turned away from him, stuffing the fabric back into the shoe.

"I do not claim to understand ladies' fashion. I assume that must have something to do with a new style?" he chuckled, moving around her toward the path once again. "You still have not told me your name."

"A new style, yes," she muttered, sliding the shoe onto her foot. Making sure it was comfortably in place, she took a couple of steps to test it before turning around to face him. "You never told me what you call these beasts."

The smile on the man's lips seemed to widen at her remark, his arms folding casually across his chest. "I believe I asked you your name before you inquired about the beasts."

"Fair enough," she sighed, rubbing her eyes with her hands, her vision blurring as she tried to direct her attention toward the man. "I am Leyna. Who are you?"

"Well, first things first," he chuckled quietly, motioning for her to come back to the road. Looking around, she realized she was still standing among the weeds, her legs moving her quickly toward the well-traveled path. "The natives here call these ghereac. It is believed the name translated into something at one point. Language has evolved so drastically since the land was first discovered that even the high scholars consider the word to be merely gibberish now."

Unsteady on her feet, Leyna looked over her shoulder at the two corpses before glancing back to the road. "Perhaps it translates to 'the beast that frightens off your horse and leaves you stranded in the middle of nowhere.'" Shielding her eyes from the sun with her hand, she gazed off in the direction she last saw her horse, finding nothing in the distance which would imply its presence.

While she was speaking, she became suddenly aware of the man's eyes as he did a double take toward her, a look of concern passing over his features. With a single stride he was to her, his hand reaching out for the side of her head. She recoiled reflexively from his fingers, her eyes opening wide in disbelief. "What are you doing?"

"I am going to ask you some questions — a few of which I already know the answer to, but I must ask them anyway to hear your response," he replied calmly. Raising his hands defensively in front of him, he took a step back, placing a slight distance between them. "How are you feeling? Does your head hurt?"

Thrown off by his line of questioning, Leyna stared at him in confusion, trying to register the meaning of his words. Her vision started to blur again, her hand lifting shakily to her right temple. "My head aches, yes. I am merely tired. I should find a location to set up camp and rest."

Extending her arms out to her sides for balance, she gazed absently down at the ground. She knew the words she intended to speak in response, though the sound of them had not been as she expected. Her voice was shaky, her speech somewhat slurred in her attempts to utilize the old language of her childhood. She was vaguely aware of the man at her side again, his arm wrapping around her to keep her from falling. Taking advantage of her distraction, he lifted her hair from the side of her neck, frowning deeply at what he saw there.

Lightly touching the back of her head, he drew his hand away, holding it out for Leyna to see. Through her foggy vision she could see what looked to be blood covering his fingertips, the sight of it bringing a wave of nausea over her. "That was only two questions," she mumbled. Tilting her head up to stare at him, she squinted her eyes, the light of the sky making it difficult to focus on his features. Her brow rose inquisitively. Distracted, she forgot what they'd been discussing. "You never told me your name... I asked you your name before you – did you ask me something?"

"For now, you can call me Thade; and the rest of my questions are irrelevant," he replied, lifting her easily into his arms. Carefully, he placed her into the saddle of a large horse, its white body perfectly brushed and tended. With a gentle hand, he rested her fingers over the mane, closing them around the hair and nodding to her, trying to catch her gaze directly with his own. "Leyna, I need you to try and stay awake for me a little bit longer and keep a good hold on Aine. There is a military camp not far from here. I will be able to better assess your wound when we get there."

Awake. The word bounced around in her head, her conscious mind barely aware the man was still speaking. *I want to sleep.* She wasn't certain if she had said the words out loud, hearing them over and over again mentally. In the distance she could hear the sound of the man's voice, repeating her name, quieter and quieter, until it disappeared altogether, the world around her giving in to the glorious darkness of sleep.

Chapter Two

An excruciating pain throbbed in Leyna's head as she opened her eyes, slowly regaining consciousness. It hurt to open them, the dim light causing her to wince. She could hear people bustling around, their words making little sense to her confused mind.

Lifting her hand to her head, she groaned. Her throat was dry, her body gritty from her journey through the desert. She paid no attention to it while on her trip; though now she was fully aware of the discomfort, wishing she could find a means to wash the dirt away.

"Leyna? Leyna, can you hear me?"

Someone snapped their fingers from somewhere to her left. Peeking through one eye, she strained to look in the direction of the sound, a blurry outline of a person coming into view at her side. As her mind gradually started to focus from her slumber, she recognized the familiar face of the man that saved her from the beast in the mountains, his glowing silver eyes staring down upon her now with concern.

He held two long slender fingers out in front of her, positioning them directly within her line of sight. "How many fingers do you see?"

"Two," she coughed, grimacing at the strain on the muscles in her head and neck. Though still sensitive to the light, her eyes were beginning to register her surroundings, finding herself to be in a large tent of sorts. Men were coming and going through a flap at the far end, dressed in full military uniform. Their clothes were a dark blue fabric, some decorated with gold stripes around their arms while others were simple and unadorned. From her experience, she believed the stripes to denote a higher status, but her lack of familiarity with Siscalian culture made it hard to know for sure.

With a sharp flick of his wrist, the man signaled one of the uniformed soldiers to come closer, motioning toward where Leyna was lying on a small cot. "Commander Vanyin, could you fetch some water for this poor woman? She must be absolutely parched."

"Yes, Captain," the uniformed man responded sharply with a stern salute, his shoulders drawn back proudly. Leyna was surprised to discover his appearance was also that of the Vor'shai people, his eyes shining a brilliant shade of grey. His black hair was long, tied back to keep it from falling in his face. The pointed tips of his ears were distinct against his dark hair with his fair complexion, the deep color of his uniform serving only to make him appear paler than he already was.

He was gone for only a few moments before he returned with a tin in his hand, holding it out to Leyna with a smile. She accepted it gratefully, tilting her head up to gulp it down in almost a single swallow. Staring down into the empty tin, she willed for there to be more water, watching the bottom of the cup as if she could somehow make more liquid appear magically inside it.

She felt someone tugging on the tin in her hand, her head snapping upward to stare hard into the man's grey eyes. Her fingers remained clenched around it, unwilling to let it go. The sound of the man's soft laughter under his breath caught her attention, his voice calm as he gently pried her hands from the cup. "It's alright, miss. I'm going to get you some more. I promise, I will bring it right back."

Warmth rushed to her face, adding a soft red hue to her sickly pallor. Slowly she used her hands to lift her upper body, weakly sitting up to face the man who brought her here. "Captain?" she murmured, distinctly aware of the prestigious title the commander used to address him. For the first time, she became aware of the uniform he wore, several pins and badges decorating the left breast of his jacket. Flustered with her lack of coherent memories, she racked her brain to recall his name, feeling as though she should know it, but finding it eluding her attempts. "I apologize; I feel so foolish. I cannot remember your name, if you ever told it to me at all."

"I expected as much," he nodded, leaning forward to check the dressings wrapped around the side of Leyna's neck and up to the base of her skull. "You suffered a good concussion. I saw you strike your head on the ground, but I did not realize at first that there must have been quite a rock there as well. Your strange behavior seemed a bit too extreme to be mere fatigue."

"I must have acted like such a fool," Leyna frowned. She remained perfectly still until the man had moved away from her neck, twisting from her waist to glance up at him curiously. "Please, I must ask you forgive me if I behaved disrespectfully. If my memory serves me, then I recall it was your turn to tell me your name before I lost my senses completely."

Leaning back in his chair casually, the man placed his hands behind his head. "Your memory is intact, then. That is a good sign."

Leyna watched him patiently, waiting for him to give a name in response to her question. Her brow furrowed in confusion at his silence, uncertain of exactly what he was thinking as he returned her gaze, looking her over appraisingly. "Or – perhaps it is disrespectful to speak of your first name. Shall I simply call you Captain?"

"By the gods, no," he chuckled, nodding politely to the commander as he returned with more water. Leaning forward, he watched Leyna accept the tin and drink it down thirstily. "That title is only required to be used by the members of my unit. Everyone else is free to call me by my first name."

"Well, that is helpful," Leyna smirked, handing the empty tin back to the commander. She dabbed at the corners of her mouth with her hand, making sure none of the water had escaped her lips.

Her eyes followed the man as he stood up, his height exaggerated by the low lying cot she rested on. "I was thinking we could try our introductions again. I know I have been calling you by a name, but I would hate to learn I am incorrect and that you misspoke due to the delirium of your injury."

"Goodness, I hope my speech was not so scattered that such a thing would be considered. In any event, you have been saying my name correctly. Leyna Evantine, if you are hoping for me to be more specific," she replied calmly. Biting her tongue, she scolded herself for her brazen mannerisms. She couldn't believe she was behaving in such a way toward a man of his rank while, on the same token, she wasn't sure why he was tolerating it with such a lighthearted demeanor.

At the sound of her family name, his smile faded somewhat, his eyes briefly taking on a distant gaze before focusing back on her. "I am Captain Thade Imri of the Siscalian military. I am charged with the protection of the western and southern borders of Siscal, up to the Carpaen desert and the Tanispan forests. It is a pleasure to meet you, Miss Evantine."

With a formal bow he lowered his eyes to the floor. Leyna found herself in awe at the fortune which she had stumbled upon, barely able to contain her excitement at the opportunity presenting itself to her. When she left Carpaen, she was at a loss for how she would even approach the military command to inquire about admission to the lower ranks. Fortune instead had smiled upon her, bringing the military to her.

"It seems the gods favor me, for you are exactly who I was hoping to speak with upon arrival to Siscal," she smiled, folding her hands neatly over her lap. Nervously twiddling her thumbs, she tried to think of how best to word her request, not wanting to sound inexperienced despite the impression she feared to have already made.

"Me?" Thade asked curiously, straightening the front of his uniform idly with his hand. "I am not sure I would call that knock on your head to be favor, but if you were seeking to speak with me – well, I am anxious to hear what you crossed that damnable desert just to discuss."

Lightly brushing her fingers over the dressings on her neck, she stared off into the distance, preparing herself for the worst. Her biggest fear was to find she had come so far only to be turned away like had happened so many other places back home. Straightening her shoulders, she held her chin out proudly, her voice calm and steady as she spoke. "As it turns out, Captain, I was on my way to Siscal to apply for admission into the military. I am a trained fighter and was the assistant to the combat training department instructor of the Carpaen academy prior to coming here. It is my hope that you may have an opening."

"Well, that certainly was not what I was expecting." Thade's eyes drifted over to the commander, his brow rising inquisitively. A silent exchange passed between the two of them, their body language impossible for Leyna to decipher. She watched them hopefully, praying their decision would be to her benefit.

"We don't see very many women aspiring to military goals," the commander said suddenly, directing his comment to Leyna's hopeful gaze. "It is not that the women here do not know how to fight, but merely that they have no desire to crawl around in the mud and surround themselves with blood and gore."

Defensively, she shook her head at him, surprised it was her gender which piqued their interest rather than her age. She'd never been faced with any obstacles regarding her sex, leaving her at a loss at how to argue. "My stomach is like iron. I assure you I would not place my fellow soldiers in danger over a retching fit at the sight of a little blood. I give you my word that I am just as strong a fighter as any of the men at the academy."

Thade's quiet laughter distracted her from the commander, her eyes shifting to him questioningly. Noticing her gaze, he coughed awkwardly, repressing his amusement. "No, I don't doubt that," he chortled. After a moment his smile disappeared, a thoughtful expression crossing his features. "Your behavior is certainly not the dainty upbringing of the women around Siscal, which is a definite plus in arguing your point. My hesitation comes in your youth. After watching you fight that ghereac, I cannot disagree with your assessment of being capable of handling yourself. I merely am forced to look at the big picture."

With a snap of his fingers, he made a gesture toward the commander, who quickly retrieved a scroll from a nearby table, placing it hastily into Thade's hand. He appeared contemplative while reading over the words written there, pondering aloud quietly to himself. "Yes, I think this will work," he mused, rolling the scroll back up and handing it to the commander. "We could use another scout. There should be no combat required of that position, but it is important nonetheless. Once we've been able to observe you for a while, possibly even giving you some advanced training, we will see about moving you up to the soldiering ranks. Does that sound agreeable to you?"

"Quite so, Captain," Leyna smiled. Her heart felt as though it might burst from her chest, the fluttering sensation distracting her from the discomfort in her head. She could think of nothing but Reina back home at the orphanage. It stung her deep to know she had left Reina there in such a miserable place; but everything seemed to be working out for the best. It would only be a matter of time before she was able to return to Carpaen and bring Reina to Siscal with her.

"Excellent," Thade nodded, offering her his hand. "Our next scout will be taking place in a couple of days. That should be plenty of time for you to get rested up and back in shape."

Leyna clasped Thade's outstretched hand in her own, his fingers wrapping around hers completely until her tiny palm was obscured by his hand. Holding it there, he stared down at it, turning her arm over curiously to glance at her wrist without removing his grip. She swallowed hard at his searching gaze, afraid of what he might say about her slight form. Her bones were not yet fully matured, her limbs still appearing frail like that of a child. A hint of some understanding flickered in the depths of his silver eyes, his hand slowly releasing its hold on hers.

She sat in silence, speechless by his strange behavior. She wasn't sure what words would be appropriate; something that wouldn't draw unwanted attention to her unease. Her situation was precarious, and she knew it. The slightest mistake could cost her everything, and she wasn't willing to take such a risk.

"It will be a task to find a uniform that will fit your small frame. And we are fresh out of skirts, so I hope you have no qualms about dressing yourself in trousers," Thade's voice broke through the silence, cutting the tension in the air between them. Giving him a sharp nod, Leyna lowered herself back down onto the cot, the pain in her head flaring up once again.

"I will find a way to make them fashionable, I am sure," she mumbled, covering her eyes with her hand. The pain eased at the absence of light, her body longing to return to its slumber. Listening intently, she could hear the sound of Thade's footsteps moving away from her, his voice giving a soft order to the commander before disappearing into the distance. Content that she had managed to survive her first encounter, she allowed her mind to drift, giving in to the comfort of sleep that overtook her.

Leyna gazed proudly at her reflection in the mirror. Everything about the uniform was too big for her, though it mattered little. All she could see was her dream coming true from under the extra fabric and clunky boots. Cady's method of stuffing shoes helped bring her boots to a more comfortable fit while the leather armor laced over her chest and midsection made any further scheming unnecessary. She spent the prior evening working to hem the wrists and pant legs to fit her more appropriately. The last thing she wanted was to risk stumbling over her own feet while on the scout. She was happy that the dark blue material matched her complexion well, the hat a bit more stylish with its tiny brim. The ensemble was somewhat oversized, but at least she looked fashionable.

"Well, Soldier, are you about ready?" the commander announced, stepping through the flap of the tent. Jumping to attention, Leyna nodded, quickly catching herself to give an awkward salute. The stern expression on the commander's face eased at the sight of her, his lips curling into a gentle smile. "Relax, dear," he chuckled, moving across the room to where she was standing. "This scout is less formal than you might think."

"That may be so, Commander, but I should still maintain proper etiquette…"

"Please —" he cut in, holding his hand up to stop her from speaking. "We are kin. Call me Feolan when we are not in the presence of other soldiers. It helps keep my ego in check."

A smile tugged at the corners of Leyna's mouth, uncertain of whether or not it would be acceptable. Once she heard Feolan's casual laughter, she gave in to the smile, a rush of relief coming over her at the release of the tension built up inside her. "I was not sure if you were serious…"

"Even if I wasn't, how could I be angry with you? You look like a little girl playing dress up in daddy's uniform," he grinned, patting her once on the shoulder.

Leyna's smile instantly faded at his words. She didn't know what to expect from him, afraid he may be using some form of trickery to discover her secret. The men she was surrounded by now were not like those whom she'd become accustomed to at the academy. They were trained to discern tactics and secrets of their enemies. Her ruse seemed hardly clever enough to slip past them. "I am not a child," she stated calmly. She kept her gaze locked steadily on Feolan's, hoping her unshaken demeanor would help to back her words.

"Oh, of course," Feolan nodded, his smile slowly disappearing from his gentle features. "Either way, we have all been instructed by the Captain that we are to treat you like one of the men. Failure to do so holds consequences I doubt any of them will want to risk. Our only concern is for you. If you are to be treated like one of the men, then you will have to act like one of the men — there will be no easing up on any of our training on your behalf. Thade, however, seems extremely confident that you will be fine."

"That is reassuring," she mumbled. A feeling of dread washed over her at the thought, worried she wouldn't be able to keep up with their rigorous routines. She held no false ideas that the academy was anything like the real military. It was a means of basic training, and nothing more. She knew her physical strength was severely lacking. Her only hope was that her size would compensate with increased speed and agility the others didn't possess.

Absently tying her hair back, she made sure it was out of her face, tucking the stray strands behind her pointed ears. Snatching her hat up from off its hook, she situated it on her head, checking it briefly in the mirror to make sure it was straight. *I can't be looking like a slob...*

The armor was heavier than what she was used to. It weighed down her upper body, making it more difficult to maneuver. She was thankful she'd been allowed to keep her own sword, granting her the advantage of having a lighter weapon than those of the other soldiers.

"There will be four of us on the scout today. I should brief you before we head out," Feolan announced, motioning for her to have a seat on a makeshift chair nearby. "The Captain will be going. You will also be accompanied by a fellow scout, a Mialan man by the name of Teagan, and myself. We received intelligence a few days ago that the enemy is planning an attack. We know they will be traveling from the south, so we need to determine a good location to set up our troops to cut them off without them becoming aware of our position."

Sitting stiffly in the chair, Leyna watched Feolan intently. His movements and manner of speaking were captivating, much the same way as she'd felt about Thade. The Vor'shai people were scarce in Carpaen, most of them avoiding the hotter climates. Because of this, she had little experience with them, her earlier memories faded due to her young age when she'd last been among her own kind. Seeing them again reminded her of her mother, reviving her memory in Leyna's soul.

"What do we know about our enemy? I hate to admit that I have little knowledge of the situation here in Siscal," she inquired curiously, anxious at the opportunity to learn more. Knowledge would make her more useful to the unit, and it was the one thing she knew she lacked.

Feolan paced the floor slowly, his hands clasped lightly behind his back. "We face the delusional people of Namorea. The Namirens, however, also have the Sanarik people on their side. We find them to be a larger concern. They are crafty and they fall hard in battle. While the Namirens prefer traditional attacks, the Sanarik utilize trickery, setting traps and whatnot. We know a new wave has landed off the coastline of Carpaen, taking advantage of the wasteland there to make camp before making their way across the border."

"They make their base in Carpaen, and the Carpaens have nothing to say about this?" she asked in disbelief, shivering uncomfortably at the thought of how possible it would have been for her to have accidentally stumbled upon them during her journey here. It was frightening to think what might have happened to her. An unsuspecting prey.

"Carpaen has made it very clear that they are hoping to remain neutral through this. More importantly, though — they aren't aware it's occurring. The closest civilization outside the desert is so far away that the Carpaens are oblivious to the fact that their "neutral ground" is being taken advantage of. I also doubt they would be willing to trek their army across the desert to stop them."

At the sound of the tent flap opening, Leyna raised her eyes to see who had arrived, climbing swiftly to her feet at the sight of Thade standing there. To his left stood another young male, whom she assumed was the other scout Feolan mentioned to be Teagan. His light brown hair was tied back behind his shoulders, his somewhat slanted, gold-colored eyes glancing over to Leyna curiously before averting his gaze to Feolan. "We should be heading out before it gets much later. I want to make sure we are back at camp before nightfall." Thade's tone was more commanding than Leyna was used to, realizing she'd never actually seen him while in the role of Captain.

Without argument she made her way over to him, following behind Feolan obediently. Seeing her there, Thade gave a courteous nod, turning away to lead them back outside the tent. They bypassed the horses, continuing out of the camp on foot. She struggled to keep up with their quick pace, her shorter legs unable to carry her the same distance as the lengthened strides of the men. Her armor hindered her progress further, her lungs feeling as though they would explode from the exertion.

Once out of view of the camp and deeper into the mountains, their pace slowed, allowing her an opportunity to catch her breath while making up the ground between them that she had lost. Teagan's eyes moved over to her as she stumbled up to his side, her cheeks red from her hasty steps. "This is your first scout. You must be excited," he mused, quickly shifting his eyes away.

"I think determined might be a better word to describe it," she exhaled, finding her breath still lost to her. Continuing to speak, her words were broken by attempts to take in air, gradually easing with the slower pace. "I think many of the men don't believe I can handle myself. I view this as an opportunity to show them I can keep up with anyone here."

"You won't find any harsh feelings among the people here. It's the Siscalian men you have to be wary of," Teagan stated flatly, his eyes staring straight ahead at the backs of Thade and Feolan. "You see, the soldiers of Siscal are lacking in comparison to the Tanispan and Mialan militaries, but they will argue that to their dying day. Truth be told, my grandmother could probably run circles around them."

Leyna could see Thade's shoulders shaking with quiet laughter in front of them. "In all fairness, Teagan, your grandmother is still in her prime. That hardly seems a fair comparison."

"My grandmother's grandmother then. Either way, it serves my point," Teagan shrugged, the leather of his armor creaking with the motion. "I doubt you would disagree, in any case."

"Regardless of whether I agree or not, they are still the soldiers we fight alongside, therefore we must do what we can to ensure they are the absolute best, or Siscal will have no chance at victory." Thade's tone was light yet dismissive, a hidden meaning buried within it which requested their conversation to cease. They were further into the mountains now, their direction completely lost to Leyna. Everything looked so similar. It was impossible to tell one mountain from another, the twisting paths taking them outside the main road.

She followed them silently, dreading the walk back to camp. A nagging fear lingered in the back of her mind that they had covered too much ground to be able to retrace their steps before nightfall. They pressed on further, weaving along the paths deeper into the wilderness. The trees were quickly becoming the most prominent thing along the terrain, a final trail leading them directly into the depths of a forest covering the entire side of the mountain they were scouting.

Feolan and Thade could be heard mumbling comments to one another up ahead, their hands motioning toward different things along the trail. Without the detailed knowledge of their enemy, she felt worthless in assisting to find a means of setting up any sort of ambush. The area felt too obvious for a trap, making it seem the worst possible place to attempt cutting them off. They would be sure to expect something. Catching them off guard here would be impossible. If anything, she feared they would come upon an ambush themselves if the Sanarik were as devious as Feolan described them to be.

Her eyes surveyed the landscape; uneasy by the number of places where an enemy could take cover in preparation for an assault. The trees were denser, creating a thick wall of branches and limbs to hide among. To her dismay, even the ground was covered by layers of grass and wildflowers, concealing the underlying soil which might have alerted them to fresh tracks in the area. Vines hung from the higher branches, seemingly out of place for the region. The change in breeds of foliage reminded Leyna just how close to the Tanispan forests they were.

A queasy feeling started to build in the pit of her stomach, stopping her in her tracks. With an appraising gaze, she swept over the area, searching for anything that might appear out of place.

Up ahead she could see Thade continuing forward, moving deeper into the forest. In front of them stood a large tree of some unknown species, its trunk massive in comparison to the others around it. Several vines draped from all levels of its branches, drawing her attention to where they brushed the ground. A single vine disappeared under the leaves at the base while the others remained visible at their place of rest.

Following the ground from the location of the submerged vine, she found a similar one connecting to another large tree in a direct line from the first, creating a suspicious design between them. "Captain, wait," she called out, hoping to catch him before he ventured much closer.

The three men were unaware of her lagging behind, turning to face her in confusion. Quickly, she maneuvered her way over to them, her eyes still focused on the ground in front of Thade's feet.

"Leyna, what is it?" Feolan asked, squinting his eyes at her odd behavior.

Ignoring his questioning gaze, she placed her arm across Thade's chest, urging him to take a step back. He gave no resistance to the pressure, moving out of her way to allow her closer to the tree. Keeping as light on her toes as she could manage in her heavy boots, she slipped over the leaves to stand at the base of the trunk, leaning forward to point at the vine with her index finger. "I have significantly less military experience than anyone else here, and even less experience with the set up of the land in Siscal – however, I think this would be suspicious in any landscape."

"Good catch," she heard Teagan mutter in fascination, bending forward to dislodge a rock from the ground at his feet. Brushing away the dirt, he tossed it up in the air casually, testing its weight in his hand. "What kind of trap do you think it is? I have a few ideas, none of which would be pleasant."

With careful steps Thade made his way over to Leyna's side, squatting down to get a better look at the vine she gestured at. He clucked his tongue in disappointment, glancing up at Feolan solemnly. "This is not a good sign. If they have found their way into the woods, it will be difficult to tell where they are or how close to the camp they are moving."

Giving his rock another small toss in the air, Teagan stared contemplatively at the ground in front of them. "Maybe they saw us coming and set this to try and intercept our path."

"Not likely," Leyna replied, trying not to laugh at the ridiculousness of his theory. "If it is a trap, it is too well-constructed to have been a throw-together attempt. It is here to intercept something, yes, but not necessarily us."

"The girl has a point. The question is how long has this been here, and even more disconcerting would be determining if they are still in the vicinity, watching us even now," Feolan frowned, following the line over to the tree opposite where Leyna and Thade had positioned themselves. "If they are still nearby, they could be advancing on us as we speak."

"I say we should spring it. That would either draw them out or chase them away with our presence," Teagan suggested confidently. He took a step forward, Leyna's heart nearly bursting from her chest at the sight of his feet coming to stop just along the ground where the leaves grew to a thicker cover.

Rising fluidly to his feet, Thade made a commanding grunt, the sound startling Leyna as she tried to calm her already quickened pulse. "Such a foolish notion." Thade shook his head irritably at Teagan. He rolled his eyes heavenward to gaze up at the canopy of branches and leaves overhead. "The Sanarik do not run from their opponents. Their honor requires them to stand and fight, regardless of how hopeless their odds may be; which in this case, I would have to assume the odds to be in their favor."

Leyna placed her hand firmly over the heavy leather of the armor covering her chest, drawing in several deep breaths to calm her labored breathing. She thought hard over their situation, fearing a confrontation with the enemy so unexpectedly. They had not come prepared to fight, leaving them at a severe disadvantage outside of mere numbers. "My theory is —" she started, pausing at the realization that it may not be appropriate for her to speak. Closing her mouth, she shifted her gaze curiously to Thade, hoping for some signal which would tell her whether to continue or be silent.

Lowering his eyes from the sky, he looked over to her expectantly, tilting his head to one side. She exhaled in relief, flashing a nervous smile before speaking again. "If they were watching us, it seems they would have attacked already, after seeing the trap failed. Springing it would only draw attention to us that we don't want. I say we attempt to disable it, familiarize ourselves with its structure and intent, then continue on carefully to see if we can find any signs which would indicate approximately how recently they were here."

"I was thinking the same," Thade nodded approvingly, motioning for Leyna to step away from the tree. Bending forward, he drew a knife from inside his right boot, turning it to inspect the blade in the light. "Feolan, if you can get that side — we have to make sure we cut it evenly. Do not pull on it, or we risk springing it unintentionally."

Leyna watched them both nervously, afraid of the slightest mistake which could result in disaster for them. She was impressed by their steady hands. Her own trembled uncontrollably, fingers fidgeting with anticipation. They made the cut with a single precise motion, leaving them both standing with an end of the long vine in their hands.

Once the vines were disconnected from the trees, Thade gave a hand signal to Feolan, motioning for him to step back. They moved together simultaneously, pulling the vine taut while lifting it from the ground. Leyna felt her body jerk in surprise as the leaves in front of her seemed to disappear, the ground opening up to reveal a wide pit dug out between the two trees. The vine had been a support for the branches holding up the leaves which concealed the gaping hole. A clever ruse to disguise such a potentially treacherous trap.

Taking a moment to compose herself, she couldn't help but think of Teagan's earlier theory, rolling her eyes in amusement at the shallow line of thought he displayed. "Yes, this certainly was arranged specifically for us," she muttered sarcastically, unable to prevent a smirk from crossing over her lips. He looked back to her crossly, his brow furrowed.

"How was I supposed to know it was a giant pit? I assumed it was some sort of live trap designed to wrap around our feet and hang us from the trees," he frowned. Leyna shrugged sympathetically in his direction, already losing interest in him. His thought processes had proven to be on the overconfident and impulsive side, striking her as dangerous to their group.

She kept close to Thade as he made his way around the other side of the massive trunk, discarding the useless vine he now clutched in his hands. On his lead, Feolan did the same, taking cautious steps around the tree across from them to meet on the other side. Unable to fight back her curiosity, Leyna peered over the edge of the pit, amazed by the depth of the hole. It was nearly three times her own height, guaranteed to have left them vulnerable to any attack which could have followed them if they had fallen prey to such trickery.

A gentle pressure on her shoulder pulled her eyes away from the trap, lifting up to see Thade motioning for her to keep moving. "I cannot have you falling in, Leyna; best to keep your distance."

Nodding her head in acknowledgement, she fell into step behind him, immediately aware of their change in approach. The casual pace from before had been replaced by more wary steps, their eyes on constant watch for any other traps which might be set to catch them off guard.

They had covered more ground than she expected, finding her stomach still unsettled by their current surroundings. The trees remained just as dense as they had been near the pit, every turn granting the perfect position for an enemy to lie in wait without being seen.

The light overhead was fading quickly, the day giving in to the coming night. By now there was no chance of them making it back to camp before dark. To this point, they'd found nothing which would lead them to suspect the Sanarik were nearby. The pit trap seemed an oddity in the middle of the woods; possibly left behind from a much earlier attack that had already been foiled.

When Thade announced they would be setting up camp for the night, the sick feeling in her stomach worsened. Not so much in fear of the Sanarik, but in disappointment that they would be lying in the open, without cover against the elements or whatever creatures might lurk amongst the trees. She said nothing to argue the decision. There was nothing to argue. The only option was to walk in utter blindness once the sun had set, and to do so would be foolish, possibly fatal. Without the light, any further traps would be perfectly concealed. A camp was the most logical idea.

Only a mild comfort came to her at the decision to keep someone on watch throughout the night. First watch would go to Thade and then Feolan would take over until morning. They were the best fighters of the four, if not the only ones. Although she was trained, Leyna couldn't hope to defend them all while they slept. She wasn't skilled enough for such an important task. Teagan had yet to do anything to display any skill with the blade. It was easy to assume he believed himself a master. Leyna had strong doubts he could even stand up to her limited abilities if they ever had reason to fight each other.

No campfire could be created for warmth amidst the cold evening air. After all her years in Eykanua, so close to the desert, Leyna wasn't used to the chill. The evenings had always been less warm, but never to the same degree the mountains held. Their bags contained only the necessary provisions; food, water, and salves in case of unexpected wounds. No blankets or pillows or tents. To the others, this was normal. It only took a matter of minutes for Feolan and Teagan to find a comfortable spot in the leaves and soil to drift off into dreaming.

A crackling twig shot like a firework through the silence of the woods. Leyna lay frozen amongst the leaves, too afraid to move in fear of drawing attention to their presence. Time dragged by slowly until the stillness returned long enough to reassure her that it was nothing. There couldn't possibly be anything out there other than wild animals, and they were more than capable of handling simple beasts.

The ground was too uncomfortable to find a position which would allow her to even consider sleep. It bumped awkwardly, placing her body at unnatural angles. With a sharp exhale, she sat up, wrapping her arms tightly around her knees to pull her legs into her chest. Memories of living on the streets of Carpaen flooded her head. The constant fear of waking up and never knowing where she was, or if the few belongings they owned would still be there when they opened their eyes. The worst scum of the city crawled out of the crevices when the sun went down, making the streets a dangerous place to be. It required a sharp ear and fast reflexes to avoid the drunks and thieves lurking in the shadows. Even more so, it required a keen mind to circumvent the tricks of the scoundrels seeking to take advantage of such young girls. Some men paid heavy loads of coin for young slaves.

Footsteps approached from somewhere nearby, their pace too slow and yet too fast to be those of an enemy. Resting her chin on her knees, she waited for the person to announce their presence, praying silently for it to be any of the men other than Teagan. His personality grated on her nerves. He was older than her by several years, though his mind seemed more on the level of Reina. She felt he required babysitting rather than being of any use to the military. He was a liability; unless they were able to train him in the art of common sense.

"You can sleep, you know. Feolan and I will take turns on watch. There is no sense in you wearing yourself out again after just recovering from the last time."

Thade's voice came as a relief. He was an intelligent man. She liked that about him. He carried the authority that required respect while yet the sensibility toward others which brought that regard naturally. Her body remained still. She was hesitant to respond, not wanting to risk waking the others with their chatter. "I have never really slept well outside."

His eyes stared at her through the darkness, though without the light of a fire, she wondered how well he could really see her. Her tiny frame was nothing more than a slight bump in the terrain. She wasn't even sure how he noticed her move at all.

"Really? You seem like the type of girl who doesn't mind the outdoors."

Leyna's mouth opened in response to his statement, her words catching in her throat, much to her relief. She wanted to tell him everything. To explain to him about the months she spent homeless in the streets, sleeping in any hole that might conceal her from the despicable sorts roaming at night. Even to tell him of the strange men who killed her mother and chased her from her home in Mialan, forcing her into such a life. It was a terrible idea, though. Anything that brought attention to her age would be too great a risk. Hearing that she had been an orphan would only spark more questions in a mind as sharp as Thade's. It was bad enough she feared he already suspected her secret. Why he hadn't confronted her about it remained a mystery.

"I do like the outdoors. Just not — sleeping there. It... well, my mind wanders and I start thinking I am hearing noises."

Another crack of a twig sounded again; closer this time than last. Thade was aware of it as well. She could almost hear his muscles tense, his head snapping alertly in the direction of the noise. Fluidly, he rose to his feet with his hand securely gripping the hilt of his sword at his side. "Stay here."

Even as the words were spoken, Leyna shot up to her feet in a single movement. Her own sword was still at her hip. Although she knew it foolish to attempt, she readied herself to draw the blade, prepared for a blind attack. At the academy she'd been one of the best at blind fighting. The difference between the situations was the intentions of her attacker. While Blaise aimed to simply get within range of her, she knew anything in the woods now would be striving for a much more gruesome goal.

"You don't listen very well," Thade whispered. She couldn't tell if it was respect or irritation she heard in his tone. It was too soft to tell.

In a blatant disregard of his order to stay back, she moved up to his side, her body at the ready toward the shadows. "You're right, I don't. I promise I'll work on that. Perhaps tomorrow."

Something small glinted from behind one of the trees, disappearing into the cover of the surrounding darkness. An eye. There was no mistaking the sight, though the shape was different from any other eye Leyna had ever seen. It was small and round, sitting close to the ground. The creature couldn't be more than five feet tall, if even, though it could've been kneeling. There was no way of knowing for sure until it revealed itself again, if it chose to.

Whoever it was, their approach had been far stealthier than any animal. It led her to believe if it wished to not be seen, it would easily make it so. Not wanting to draw attention to her awareness of its location, she bumped Thade's bicep with her shoulder, leaning her head forward across his chest to motion at the area it had come from. The metal of Thade's blade could be heard scraping the edges of his sheath as he drew it, the sound sending shivers through Leyna's spine. A simple scout. No fighting, they told her. Safe. Nothing about a war was safe. She should have known better. And yet she had. It was why she'd brought her own sword instead of the one they provided her.

Eyes would do little to help her in the heavy darkness. Most of the moonlight was prevented from breaking through the treetops due to the thick canopy, eliminating majority of the only source of light they could have possibly relied on. Taking Thade's lead, she drew her own sword from its sheath, gripping it tightly in both hands. Her breathing slowed. Survival relied on her ability to utilize her other senses outside of her vision. Scent and sound. As long as her eyes were open, her mind instinctively tried to strain them in the impossible blackness. *Close them. Remember your training. It's just like being back at the academy, only more necessary that you succeed. Real life offers no second chances for failure.*

Obedient to her own mental commands, she allowed her eyelids to fall closed, listening intently to the sounds around them. Thade was motionless, creating no disturbance which would hinder or distract her. Even his breath was silent as death, making her wonder if he was still breathing at all.

There in the trees she could hear something. The slow draw of a sword from a thick case of some kind. It didn't sound like the leather of their own sheaths, but there was no doubt in her mind what it was. A soft breeze made it hard to pinpoint the exact location of the noise. The first was quickly followed by another, and then another. Each one equally as slow and precise as the first, the movement perfectly controlled with the intention of muffling their preparations.

Wake the others. The thought rattled through her brain despite the arguments her mind tried to silence it with. She couldn't leave Thade's side. Any sudden movement would set off the attack prematurely. If that happened, it would give their enemies an even greater advantage than they already had, and would leave her unprepared to assist Thade in the defense.

A musty smell wafted across her nostrils, nearly gagging her with its intensity. She kept her eyes closed, not wanting to open them in case doing so dampened her other senses. Just hearing the sound wasn't enough to grant her a visual image of their foe. Opening her eyes would only hinder her until the enemy was within range of her sword.

The odor thickened, filling the air around them until it was an almost unbearable stench. A soft crackle of leaves could barely be made out, seeming to come from all angles. Her shoulders tensed; her back straightening. She didn't realize she was holding her breath until she felt the overwhelming desire for oxygen burning in her lungs. Cringing from the smell as she inhaled, she readied herself for the attack, her entire body tingling along her right side. Something was there. It was moving quickly, and it was already closer than she anticipated.

In a single swift motion, she pivoted to her right, lifting her sword across her chest and over her head. Metal clashing against metal filled the woods, echoing through the trees with an eerie clang. This was it. There was no turning back now. The enemy had made their move. All they could do was hope they were not outnumbered by much.

With the silence broken, Leyna let out a yell, pushing her attacker back with all of her strength. The shrill tone of her voice caused her assailant to flinch unexpectedly.

Unable to force her eyes to remain closed any longer, she allowed them to open, gasping in surprise at the sight of the creature in front her before almost choking on the heavy odor invading her senses. It appeared to be a man. The face was hairy and mud covered, the facial hair grown to lengths that caused it to blend into the darkness of the black clothes it was wearing. Its eyes were the same as she'd seen from behind the trees, abnormally small and round, set disproportionately in its wide features. It was over a foot shorter than her, though at least twice as wide, outweighing her significantly in mass. Although it was large, it was strong — and it was more skilled with a sword than any of the opponents she'd taken on during her days at the academy.

In the back of her head she was aware of Thade facing a second attacker. She'd lost track of him at her side, separating them with the darkness until all she could hear was the sound of his sword clashing with another. It was enough to assure her he was still alive. She just wasn't sure where.

Coherent thoughts attempted to break through her concentration. Her body burned at every joint from the exertion of the battle. Though she tried to formulate a plan of action, her focus on the movement was too extreme. Parry. Block. Thrust. The attacks were endless. Her assailant was barely winded, moving with the same speed as when he first entered into the fight. She couldn't keep going at such a pace for much longer.

The clanging of other swords seemed to cease, her ears filled with nothing but the noise of her own blade against her enemy's. Water built up in the corners of her eyes. She struggled to keep moving, fighting through the exhaustion threatening her. Life was the only thing that mattered now. If she gave in to the ache of the fatigue, she would die. Her opponent cared little about her age. All that mattered to him was whether she was still moving. Until one of them no longer was, the strikes would continue.

Without a light source, determining a weakness in her foe was next to impossible. He was quick, though she doubted his agility to be anywhere near her own. Their difference in size would be her best card to play. Muscle couldn't win it for her. He could overpower her easily if she wasn't careful. *Play to your strengths.* It was what Blaise ingrained in her mind every day in practice. *If you can move, then move.* She could move. It was her only option.

Dipping under his arm while he swung, she maneuvered around to his back side, forcing him to spin around to face her. She blocked a few more strikes before ducking around him again, thrusting her sword forward into his back. It met resistance from his armor. She hadn't accounted for the possibility of that. In practice the strikes never had need to penetrate the skin to be declared the victor. But this wasn't practice.

When she attempted to pull her sword back, she was met with even more resistance, the strength of her opponent's body flinging her backward with the sharpness of his movement. The pain angered him. She could hear the blood lust in his labored breathing. His steps were harder and more powerful than before. Her feet lifted completely from the ground, fingers sliding off the hilt of her weapon. While she felt her back connect with the heavy branches of a fallen tree, all she could think about was the horrible disadvantage she'd placed herself in. She couldn't block his strikes with her bare hands. Without a sword, she was doomed.

She gripped the branches of the tree tightly in her hands, lifting her body up onto the top of the trunk. Kicking out with her foot she could hear the crack of wood breaking, separating a large branch from where it connected to the tree. Again and again she struck until the splintering wood gave way. She could already hear her opponent approaching again. Even in the darkness he could trace her by the sound she was making.

Grabbing up the heavy branch, she waited until she could hear his footsteps nearly to the tree. With impressive speed she extended her foot out, using her opponent's own momentum against him with the strike. The heel of her boot connected sharply with his face. She could feel the bones crack under her foot. His pained growl echoed through the branches around her, his legs stumbling backward in disorientation.

To get up the power she required to manage the heavy branch, she kept it gripped in both hands, spinning her body around to gather speed. The impact jarred her. He was closer than she expected, already recovering from her initial strike. The second blow left her teeth tingling. Another thud on the ground nearby signaled her that something had fallen other than the branch she'd been holding. Based on the groan, she gave in to the hope that it was her enemy. Getting him off his feet was essential. As long as she was standing and he was not, she could find a way to use that to her advantage.

She heard the branch land, her hands instinctively reaching for it in the darkness. Securing it back in her grasp, she pushed forward to where the other sound had come from. Not wanting to take any chances, she brought it downward in front of her. It met a brief interference from her enemy's sword, his arms coming up in an attempt to block the incoming blow.

The blade wasn't strong enough to cut through the wood. Her arms lacked in control to maneuver the branch back up again, forced to allow it to finish its motion. A sickening gurgle erupted from under it. It was unmistakable. The sound of someone choking. But what could he be choking on? She didn't want to get close enough to find out.

Voices were calling her name somewhere in the distance. She wished they would stop. She needed the silence to hear her opponent. There was nothing moving in the leaves around her. It was unnerving. There should be something. Anything. Some indication of his attempts to regain his footing. He was most likely angrier now than he'd been before.

Still, there was nothing. Hands trembling, she slowly followed the line of the branch closer to the end. Every step unsettled her stomach even more. She took a step and then paused, listening. Each movement forward was met with nothing but silence. *Did he move? Is he not even here?*

Her foot connected with something on the ground. It felt like a hand, though under the thick sole of her boot she couldn't tell for sure. Nudging forward with her toes she prodded at whatever it was, discovering it to be heavy and unmoving. Cautiously, she lowered the branch to allow her a better look at the object.

In horror, she stepped away from it. The tiny round eyes gazed up at her, the light she'd seen in them before having dissipated into nothing but a cold, empty stare. Straining her eyes, she grimaced at the sight of her enemy lying there. His head was disconnected from the rest of his body, resting at an awkward angle amongst the leaves on the ground. Though she couldn't see it, she could feel the blood seeping over the grass under where her hand reached out, sticky to the touch.

She recoiled from the sensation. A miscalculated block by her enemy had been his downfall. Decapitated by the blade of his own sword under the weight of her strike. He must not have been prepared. He was strong enough to have pushed it away with his hands.

The need to vomit sent her reeling backward, her hand covering her mouth in disgust. She'd killed a man. Not just a beast in the wild, but a living man. She wasn't ready for that feeling. The thought of killing was so much different from the reality of actually having followed through. There was blood on her hand that didn't belong to her. It belonged to the life she'd claimed which now lay motionless, bleeding out onto the ground.

Protruding from the man's stomach was what appeared to be some metal object. Her sword. He landed on her sword when he fell. It had still been embedded into the soft tissue of his back where she'd left it. She dropped to her knees, wiping frantically on the leaves to rid her skin of the sickening substance that covered it. No tears fell. She felt no remorse for the death, only for the fact that it was on her head. She'd passed the final judgment on this man. But he'd passed the same judgment on her. In the end, it was to be one of them. The gods would have taken a soul that night, regardless of who had fallen. It was destiny. And she couldn't question the gods.

After several long moments she became aware again of the voices calling out her name. They sounded almost frantic, in a strange masculine way. The words came too close together to be a calm call for a response. They were desperate for some sound that would indicate her location. But she didn't want to give it. Not yet. She had to compose herself before they found her. A soldier couldn't cringe every time they took a life. The thought of being so hardened to death was almost as frightening to her as the death itself.

She clutched at her stomach, fighting back nausea. She refused to throw up. Everything hit her at once. The relief that she survived combined with the guilt for having taken the life of another and the exhaustion which overwhelmed her. Her joints ached, the adrenaline slowly fading away, leaving her drained of her energy.

Her sword. She wanted it back. She couldn't let it rot away with the corpse that had fallen on it. Getting back to her feet was a challenge, her knees trembling weakly under the weight of her upper body. The branch felt heavier now than it had before. It confused her how she was even able to lift it in the first place. Her only means of moving it was to drag it away, shuddering as it raked across the corpse.

Kneeling at the side of her fallen foe, she pushed with the last of the strength she could manage. Despite his weight, he was easier to move than the ghereac. It was odd how he'd fallen harder than such a monstrous beast, yet he was nothing in comparison to its size. Once she had the body rolled onto its stomach, she stepped up onto its back. She would need a good base in order to remove her blade from where it was lodged. He didn't make the sturdiest of surfaces, but she had little choice if she wanted to retrieve her sword.

Oh, what a sight she must be. It was embarrassing to consider what the others would think. She had won, though. She was the victor, regardless of how much of a struggle it was for her to regain her weapon. Yet all she could think of was getting it back before the men found her. Tightening her grip on the hilt, she started to pull upward, feeling it resist at first before eventually giving in to her persistence. She'd been prepared for a harder go of it, practically falling backward from the extra force she put into her attempt.

She took her time stepping down from atop the body. Energy was failing her. The simple motion of lifting her sword to clean it was too much, leaving her arm dangling limply at her side with the tip of her blade pointed down into the leaves. Dirt and blood caked to her skin. Everything had happened so fast; she wasn't entirely sure whether the blood was hers or her enemy's.

Her name still echoed through the trees. Had she really traveled so far from the others? Their calls were more insistent than before, repeating in quick succession. They were drawing nearer. She could hear their footsteps rustling through the leaves somewhere to her left. A soft glow of light filtered into the area, slowly illuminating the body of the man she'd killed.

The sight of it was even more gruesome than she expected. Nausea welled up in her throat once again, threatening to make her sick if she didn't look away. If she was ever going to get used to such a lifestyle, she couldn't avoid the sight of the body. There would be plenty more corpses where that one came from.

It was Thade's voice that finally pulled her from her reverie. Shock. It had to be what was causing her strange behavior. Words couldn't form on her lips to respond despite her thought processes telling her she should speak. What could she possibly say? "Leyna? By the gods, you gave me quite a fright."

Where was that light coming from? It hurt her eyes at first until Thade lowered his hand, the glow dimming with the motion. He was creating it somehow, manipulating it around his palm, allowing just enough light to see her face. Inhaling deeply, she tried to regain her senses. She needed to say something. Anything. Whatever it would take to appear like a mature fighter rather than a frightened child who had just realized the harsh truth of the reality she'd rushed into.

"There is no need to be frightened about me. As you can see, I am barely scratched."

The calmness of her tone was disconcerting, even to herself. It matched none of the thoughts in her head, still reeling from the kill. The fact that she was somehow collected on the outside made her feel as though her mind and body were two separate entities. "That light – how are you doing that?"

"This?" he lifted his hand up for her to see, flattening his palm. His movements were nonchalant, but there was something about them which led her to believe he was distracted. He was almost too calm. Too casual. "Surely you know such an easy manipulation of energy. It was one of the first things my family taught me."

Energy. Yes, the Vor'shai magic. It made sense, yet it only brought more frustration to her heart. Her mother died before she could learn anything of that magic. There was a whole side to her own people she was blocked from because of that fateful day. Her future had been so bright and then was ripped out from underneath her without giving her a chance to fight for it all those years ago. It seemed a disgrace that she lacked even the simple knowledge of her people. A pure Vor'shai trapped in the upbringing of a Mialan and Carpaen mutt.

Before she could respond, Feolan's voice interrupted her. It was a welcome sound. She was afraid of having to admit out loud her failure as a Vor'shai. She relied on these men to respect her and she couldn't guarantee their respect would continue if she told them anything. Her past had to remain a mystery to them all. They could never know; at least not any time soon.

"Oh, Captain – you found her. How did she get all the way over here?"

Both men could see the body of the man lying there. The light from Thade's hand was enough to illuminate its mutilated form. Leyna couldn't stand to look at it any longer. Taking advantage of the opportunity to turn away, she moved past Thade in the direction from which he had come. Their packs had to be over there. She just wanted to get back to their things so she could lie down. No more answers to unwanted questions. They didn't need to know anything about her other than that she could fight, and she had shown them that.

"Leyna, is that you?"

Oh, Teagan, not now. Why did he have to speak? Even more curious, why was he still so far back near their original camp? "Yes, it's me," she muttered. He was the last person she wanted to carry on a conversation with. She wasn't worried about him figuring out her secrets. He wasn't bright enough to be a concern. The worry was that he wouldn't know when to shut up, and her words might be overheard by the others. No, she couldn't talk to him either. She couldn't talk to anyone.

Gently cleaning the blade of her sword, she slid it easily into her sheath. There wouldn't be any more need for it that night. Only a few hours remained before the sky would start to lighten again and they would be on their way back to the main camp. Another attack was unlikely, but not impossible. If those men had been of the Sanarik, they would tend to lean toward the unexpected. Maybe sleep wasn't such a good idea after all.

She could hear the others coming through the trees, finally tiring of observing the corpse she'd left behind. "Back to sleep everyone," Thade announced, his tone authoritative, yet low to avoid drawing any further attention to their location. "I will continue the watch until morning. As soon as the sun is up, we will be moving back to camp, so I suggest you rest."

As the light faded from his hand, Leyna could see his eyes looking at her closely. Pretending not to notice, she settled herself down onto the leaves, curling up into a ball for warmth. The armor made it more difficult. It was bulky and uncomfortable, but she didn't mind. As long as she was unable to relax, she was guaranteed to remain awake. There would be plenty of other opportunities for rest. She would take advantage of those when they arose. Until then, she would remain vigilant.

Chapter Three

Days quickly turned into weeks for Leyna, soon starting to roll over into years. She had spent her sixteenth birthday silently sitting around the mountain camp, listening to the men share their war stories. Feolan urged her to tell the story of their successful battle against the Sanarik, hoping to open her up from the shell she'd sunk into after that night in the woods. They managed to head off the attack they had been scouting to plan against. The mission had been a success and earned her a spot as an actual soldier under Feolan's command.

She'd forgotten about her seventeenth birthday until it was already passed. They'd been in battle against the Namirens throughout the entire week, the endless days of fighting blending together. Remembering something so trivial as a birthday had been impossible. It wasn't until she heard the date of their return to central Siscal that she realized it had been forgotten.

Eighteen. This marked another year for her. Another year she had managed to keep her secret, and another day to reminisce about her days with Reina. Reina would be twelve now. She had to wonder if the little girl even still remembered her. Letters had been sent to the orphanage on a few occasions, but no response was ever received. Leyna eased her mind by assuring herself the replies had been lost in transit, unable to find her while she was in the field.

Music filled the air of the tavern, giving a jovial feeling to such a dismal place. It was dirty. Not a place for a young girl to be, especially not one as young as her. The bar keep wouldn't think to throw her out, though. She wore the uniform of the home military and the music was played in her honor. It was her party she attended amongst the filth, but not because of the sentimental memory of the day of her birth. After two years of service, she was being promoted to first lieutenant under Feolan. For the first time she would be placed in charge of her own unit of soldiers to keep watch over in battle. Men taking orders from a child. Even through her melancholy thoughts, she couldn't help but find a mild amusement in the truth.

"Your first drink is on me!" The grin on Teagan's face was just as irritating as usual, if not more so. He did so love his booze. Any occasion to celebrate, he was the first to the tavern with coin in hand. It had become his goal to get her to drink, and she constantly was forced to turn him down. The scent of the drink was hardly appetizing to her.

"I much prefer the tea, but thank you."

Shoving a mug into her hands, Teagan patted her on the back, ushering her away from the bar over to the table where he and several others were seated. Her nose wrinkled up at the smell. "How are we supposed to get you drunk at your own party if you won't drink?"

"You could always just not try to get her drunk," Feolan chuckled, sliding over on the seat to make room for Leyna to sit next to him. "There is no rule that states a person has to be completely out of their wits just because the celebration is in their honor."

"Thank you, Feolan." Slipping into the booth next to him, Leyna nodded her head approvingly to Feolan's comment, hoping Teagan would ease up on her, knowing that not everyone wished to see her inebriated.

There was no chance of him being so sensible. To him it was all about the alcohol. It wasn't a party without the drinks. "Just one. You don't have to get drunk. Just humor me and at least taste that."

A woman came by the table, passing out drinks to the men seated there. She was tall for a Siscalian woman, her long blonde hair hanging loose over her shoulders. Most people of Siscalian descent were somewhat shorter than the Vor'shai, their bodies more compact. Her fingers were shorter, having to press hard against the sides of the large round mugs in order to keep them from slipping out of her hands.

Leyna watched her place a mug in front of Thade, his eyes barely acknowledging the waitress's presence despite the hooting and hollering of the others. While the men leaned forward to catch a glimpse of her low neckline, she seemed to be trying to catch Thade's attention, bumping him nonchalantly with her arm as she leaned back across the table. "Oh, I'm so sorry, sir…"

"Do not worry about it," he waved dismissively, oblivious to her attempts at flirting. "If you could – I would like to buy a cup of tea for the lady here."

Teagan booed him loudly from where he stood outside the booth next to Leyna, still pushing the mug in Leyna's hands closer to her lips. "Don't encourage her, Captain."

Struggling against Teagan's insistent hands, she managed to maneuver the mug away from him, nearly spilling it down the front of her before getting it flat on the table. She heaved a sigh of contained frustration, her eyes shifting over to Thade curiously. "If it will get this animal here off my back… What is it that you are drinking? It looks far more pleasant than whatever this substance is that Teagan is trying to poison me with."

Thade tilted his drink to one side, peering into it thoughtfully before offering it to her over the table. "It is the house special wine. Not the best I have ever tasted, but certainly not the worst."

She accepted the drink, inhaling deeply of it. The scent was much more agreeable than the ale Teagan insisted she try. Slowly, she raised the glass to her lips. It felt foreign to her tongue, thicker than she expected. The taste was quite strong, filling her senses with a mixture of flavors she'd never experienced in a single beverage before. It was more bitter than anything else. Not wanting to reveal her distaste, she scrunched up her nose in feigned thoughtfulness, pretending to ponder over the flavor.

The waitress returned to the table, batting her eyes flirtatiously at Thade as she sat the cup of tea down on the table in front of him. Noticing his drink in Leyna's hand, the woman's smile faded somewhat. "Can I get you another glass of wine?"

He barely nodded to her in response, his eyes focused on Leyna curiously as the men at the table began to chant for her to chug. Bracing herself for the rush of the strong liquid, she tipped her head back, pouring it into her mouth. She gave no pause to her gulps until the last drop had fallen from the glass, her hand placing it firmly down on the table in front of her.

Almost immediately, another drink was pushed toward her. This one smelled even stranger than the last. She didn't know what it was, but the chant had started again, urging her to drink it. Taking the challenge, she tilted the mug back, practically choking on the disgusting fluid that came from it. She couldn't take any more. The after taste was unbearable, her mouth sticky and warm from the alcohol.

Thade gently pressed the cup of tea across the table toward her with his fingertips. "If you are going to chug anything else, it should be this."

She accepted the cup gratefully, lifting it to her lips in hopes of ridding her mouth of the horrible taste left behind from the last drink. She was afraid to ask what it had been. The flavor had been less potent than that of the wine, but it was significantly less tolerable. "How do you men drink that stuff? It is absolutely awful."

The tea soothed the lingering taste only mildly. She could hear the men laughing at her comment, their attention distracted once again by the return of the waitress. By now she was frustrated by Thade's disinterest, setting the glass in front of him with a lack of grace which nearly sloshed it over the edge of the cup. His eyebrow rose curiously to look up at her, seeming to see her for the first time – and unimpressed by her manners.

"Can I get you men anything else?"

Leyna ignored the inappropriate responses of the other men, her eyes gazing down into the familiar liquid of her cup. It was still warm to the touch. Her hands pressed against it, thankful for the comforting feel of it against her skin.

At first she felt nothing from the drinks she'd consumed. Her senses were unaffected, her thoughts still coherent and rational. She had just started to relax into the idea that she was in the clear from its effects when it hit her. Mild at first. A simple feeling of lightheadedness, going away almost as quickly as it had come. She was vaguely aware of Teagan still at her side, continuously offering her another drink.

The situation was slowly slipping out of her control. The dizziness was increasing, her vision hindered by several bright spots of light dancing across the faces of the men around her. Why was this feeling so sought after? It was absolutely miserable. Voices around her were hollow, their words no longer making any sense. She was only somewhat aware that certain comments were being directed at her, lost to the distractions of her head.

A sudden splash falling down the front of her shirt pulled her from her scattered thoughts, her hands clumsily wiping at the liquid soaking into the fabric. Thade and Feolan were instantly on their feet, their hollow voices scolding Teagan for something. She couldn't understand what. All she could think of was getting away from the table. The smell of ale perfumed from her drenched top, adding to the discomfort already starting to build in her stomach.

Standing did nothing to ease the spinning room. It only intensified it. She wasn't sure she would be able to maintain her footing, but she somehow managed it, her shoulder slamming into Teagan hard as she moved past him. His hand flailed about wildly in his own attempts to keep on his feet, almost striking her in the face. Her thoughts were slow and sluggish, her arm reaching out to push Teagan backward before she could think better of the action. In the back of her mind, she could hear the other men laughing. Teagan was on the floor now, holding out his hand to her. He wanted her to help him up? Why would she do that? He was an imbecile and a drunk. He could lay there all night for all she cared.

She stepped over him, ignoring his slurred request for help. Her clothes reeked of his drink. She didn't know how she was going to fix it, but she knew she had to try. Drenched in alcohol was not how she anticipated spending her birthday. It didn't seem right. She hadn't left Reina at that dismal orphanage just so she could move away and party. It wasn't fair to her.

Clear your head. How long could this awful feeling last? Nothing she did made it go away. The room continued to spin around her, sounds muffled to her ears. How she managed to find her way to the bathroom was a mystery, but there she was. Surrounded on all sides by the worst filth of the tavern. Did they ever clean this place? The stench wasn't quite strong enough to overpower the smell of ale still wafting up to her nostrils from her own shirt. She wasn't sure which scent was worse.

If she'd been able to think clearly, she wouldn't have let her hands touch the basin, but she found herself leaning over it. She needed something to help hold her up so she wouldn't fall onto the floor, which was even more disgusting. The sink seemed the lesser of the two evils. A film of muck covered the ground, its origins too gross to even want to consider. The water in the basin wasn't much better. It was nothing more than a large bowl filled with stagnant water. She didn't want to think of how many people had placed their hands in it — and even worse, what had been on their hands when they touched it. Even her confused mind wasn't disoriented enough to possess her to splash the disgusting liquid on her face.

"Leyna?"

Oh, go away. She didn't want to talk to anyone right now. She just wanted to stand there for a few minutes and wallow in her own misery. That was too difficult to do when someone was standing there watching her.

It took too much effort to lift her head. A clicking noise told her someone had locked the door. Odd. It was a male voice that had spoken. Why would a man come into the ladies' room and lock the door? They were segregated for a reason. Society frowned upon any instance of men and women being alone in a single room together.

"What do you want?" She didn't know what else to ask. "You do realize this is the ladies' room, right? We can't lock everyone out."

"It is the ladies' room in a tavern. Aside from the barmaids, there is maybe one other woman in the whole place, not counting you. She can wait."

Thade. She didn't want him to see her in her condition. It took all her focus just to straighten her back, removing her hands from the grimy sink. The room wasn't spinning at the moment, which was a welcome surprise. *Maybe it's wearing off.*

"I'm fine, really."

"You have not seemed fine all evening," he replied calmly. He was unfazed by her dismissive tone, the sound of his footsteps coming closer filling Leyna's ears. "Truthfully, you have come across as distracted by something. Is everything alright? Disregarding the ale dripping down the front of you, that is."

"I don't have anything to change into." She knew it didn't answer his question, but she didn't care. It was the first logical sentence that formed in her head.

Thade's eyes were watching her closely, taking in every detail. It made her uncomfortable to think they were in such a tiny room, alone. Something felt inappropriate about it, but her mind couldn't quite put a finger on what that something was. He was the Captain and she was a soldier under his authority. There was nothing out of the ordinary with that... Except for the fact that she was drunk. The alcohol had been much too potent, and her body was far too underdeveloped to handle such an amount so quickly and on an empty stomach.

Slowly, she turned to face him, afraid to meet his eyes. She was embarrassed. She was making a fool out of herself in her altered state of mind. If only she'd done the smart thing and continued to decline the drinks. What had she been thinking? Fitting in wasn't worth this.

Thade's expression was more sympathetic than scolding. His fingers were already halfway down his uniform jacket, unfastening the gold buttons which held it together. Through her unfocused eyes, Leyna tried to figure out what he was doing, confused by his actions. Noticing her questioning stare, he shrugged his shoulders nonchalantly. "These uniforms have so many pieces to them. You can wear my shirt and no one would even have to know. This jacket covers me well enough as it is."

"No, I am not going to ask you to give me the shirt off your own back just because I was too stupid…"

"You are not asking me for the shirt off my back. I am offering it. And you will accept it. Please." It sounded like an order coming from him, yet his tone remained gentle. She couldn't deny her appreciation at the gesture. It would allow her to go back out and face everyone again with at least some amount of dignity after what she'd done.

All she could think about was Teagan lying there on the floor. She'd pushed him down. Why in the world had she done that? He deserved it, but she had been out of her wits to follow through with it. She wondered how angry he would be when she returned to the table.

Thade didn't give her an opportunity to decline his offer. It didn't sink in right away until she saw him slide his jacket off, draping it over the handle on the door to keep it from touching the ground. Each button on his shirt took him only a moment to undo, easily allowing him to slip his arms from it. She initially didn't intend to stare, her eyes gazing at him without really seeing him. It was when his shirt had been fully removed that she felt her heart skip bashfully at the sight of him.

The muscles in his upper body were surprisingly well-defined, having been concealed from view under the heavy fabric of his uniform she was so used to seeing him in. Despite his slender build, his stomach was perfectly toned, his chest and shoulders broader than she expected. He was like a flawlessly chiseled statue there before her, his muscular arm holding the shirt out to her expectantly.

When she realized she was staring, she lowered her eyes to the floor, her hand still clumsy from the alcohol as she tried to take the shirt from his hand. Without thinking, she turned away from him, fumbling with her own ale soaked shirt to pull it off.

"Leyna, you can wait until I leave to…"

Thade's voice cut off sharply, reminding her of his presence still in the room with her. It was already too late. Her shirt was in her hand, dangling from her fingers onto the floor. She didn't even care about the filth it was touching. Her face flushed with embarrassment at the thought of having just removed her shirt in front of him. She was thankful she'd at least had the sense to turn around.

Out of nowhere she felt something against her back, causing her to jump unexpectedly. Thade was behind her, his fingertips brushing the sensitive skin. Scars. She had forgotten they were there. What a sight they must be to behold. Very rarely did she ever pay them mind anymore. After the attack on her mother, she'd spent many hours trying to see them in any mirror she could find, making sure the wounds were healing properly. They hadn't had enough coin to seek an actual doctor to tend them.

Flashes shot through her confused mind, jarring her back to reality. She could see the tiny opening under the table in Reina's father's study. Her heart raced again with the fear that had gripped her while she slid underneath it, trying to press herself against the wall to escape the sword of her attacker. Each slice of the blade carved a line into her back, connecting at different points and angles. A single line crossed them all from one side to the other, a deeper gouge near the center from the locking mechanism on the trunk her mother had hidden her in.

She flinched away from Thade's touch, pressing his shirt over her chest to keep her concealed from view. "What are you doing?" she gasped. It was unlike him to approach her in such a way. She could only imagine the confusion in his mind at the sight of the marks. There was no way to lie about how she received them. He'd been present during almost every battle she fought since arriving in Siscal. Thade would never believe she sustained the injuries so recently.

"Who did this to you?" he asked quietly, stepping away from her to a more suitable distance. He seemed embarrassed for having reacted the way he did. She could hear him turning away to face the door, giving her more privacy to slip her arms through the shirt, her fingers quickly fastening the buttons into place.

Turning back to face him, she folded her arms over her chest. She wanted to be angry with him. A part of her wanted to chastise him for touching her without her permission. She couldn't bring herself to do it. He'd shown her so much kindness since she met him that it was impossible to accuse him of mistreatment. The touch had been far from menacing and she knew he was the most trustworthy of all the men she'd met in the military. He would never take advantage of her, but at the moment she felt nothing but a boiling anger inside at the rush of emotions carried back into the front of her mind at the reminder of that horrible night.

She refused to cry. Crying would only show more weakness on top of that which she'd already shown with her drunkenness. The alcohol made her emotions difficult to control, shifting between rage and depression. She was angry at Teagan for having poured his drink down the front of her. She didn't even remember how it happened, but she felt it could have been avoided if he'd treated her with more respect. At the memory of Reina, she felt her throat contract, fighting back the urge to burst into tears. No. She couldn't do that. If she allowed that to occur, she risked exposing her secret through her weeping and that just wouldn't do.

"Leyna?" Thade's voice snapped her from her thoughts again. "I am sorry. I should not have…"

"No, don't," she cut him off. She could hear the anger in her voice, even though she didn't intend to direct it at him. There was no directing anything in her frame of mind. She wasn't in control of herself. "Please don't ask any questions. I'm in no condition to be answering them."

Thade slowly turned back to her, his eyes lowered to the floor until he was certain she was covered. His own jacket was only partially done up, the neckline remaining open near the top to reveal his chest from underneath. "You are upset about something, and I wish to know what it is that troubles you. We are not here speaking under official military rules, I am speaking to you as a friend. You can tell me."

"Tell you what, exactly? That it's my birthday and while I'm sitting here in this dirt hole drenched in booze, there is a young girl trapped in an orphanage in Carpaen who is counting on me and I'm letting her down?" She cursed under her breath. Damn that alcohol. She told herself specifically to say nothing and yet the words fell from her mouth against her will. *It was a good run, at least. Maybe there will be another military in need of my skills…*

Her back still tingled along the scar where Thade had touched. Uncrossing her arms, she reached her hand behind her, rubbing gently at the area. Through the thinner material of Thade's undershirt, she could feel the raised skin easily under her fingers. Those scars were her downfall in more ways than one. They not only were remnants of the end of her childhood, but they were now possibly the end of her chance at a future. *Stupid.* Why couldn't she have kept her mouth shut?

He was staring at her. That couldn't be a good sign. She could almost see the questions in his eyes. Their bright silver glow burned into her own, his lips pursed together tightly. He was holding something back. "Your birthday? Why did you not say something? We could have celebrated it appropriately."

"Appropriately?" What exactly was appropriately? Certainly not drinking in a tavern with a group of drunken men. "I prefer not to celebrate my birthday. That is why I have made no mention of it. Ever. And I hope it remains unknown to anyone."

"Could you perhaps humor me, before I conveniently forget that it is your birthday, and tell me how old you are today?"

There it was. The exact question she'd been dreading since she had first come up with the crazy idea to come to Siscal. The question that could ruin everything. She was smart enough to talk her way out of it. If only the alcohol wasn't still affecting her thought processes. "You would dare ask a woman her age?" she laughed. "How many women do you honestly think would willingly answer such a question?"

"Vor'shai women? Plenty," he nodded calmly, standing firm in wait of a response. Why couldn't he have gotten drunk with the others? If his mind had been hindered by the same intoxication as her own, the task might have been far easier to succeed in. His sober thoughts were too sharp for her clumsy attempts at subterfuge.

She stood there silently, her jaw agape in hopes that some clever means of evading the question would fall from her lips just as unexpectedly as the words that put her in this predicament in the first place. Nothing came. All she could do was deny him a response, which would only get her so far before he managed to find a way to pull it from her. "Age really matters little to our people. I fail to see why it is so important for you to know."

"This girl in the Carpaen orphanage – how old is she?"

"Twelve, I think." That was an innocent answer. It could do little to incriminate her while still giving the illusion that she was cooperating.

"Is this girl your daughter?"

"No."

"Are you married?"

"No."

"Widow?"

"No, and why does that matter?" she huffed, feeling her heart flutter wildly in her chest. There was no escaping his questions. He was suspicious, even more now than she assumed him to be before. Her refusal to answer would do nothing to quell that. "The girl at the orphanage is a sister — of sorts. The closest to one I could possibly have, at least. I left her in Eykanua to come here and join the military."

She could see Thade's face soften at her reply, his eyes dimming slightly. "You're an orphan?" The words came so quietly from his mouth that she was uncertain whether he was speaking to her or himself. "Did something happen with your family which caused those marks on your back?"

Frustration welled up inside her. She didn't want to admit anything. All that time she spent training with the military, working her way up to the promotion they were supposed to be there celebrating, and to end like this. Forced to speak of her mother, whom she had not breathed a word of in over two years. The memories were almost too painful to bear. "My mother was murdered, alright? Is that what you wanted to hear? Men came into our home and slaughtered her and the little girl's father... and sister. They tried to kill me, but she and I escaped. I don't know why, and I don't know who, and I don't want to talk about it because none of it is really any of your business."

"But it is my business. Anything involving the soldiers in this military is my duty to know," he said softly, reaching his hand out to gently touch her shoulder. She could hear the pain in his voice. Remorse for having pushed her to speak of such a delicate matter. His eyes were still filled with unanswered questions, but he remained quiet for a moment, giving her a chance to calm her anger. "I could order you to tell me your age. You know that."

All of the anger dissipated from her at his words, replaced with a strong pleading desire to make him change his mind. She stared up at him, wide-eyed and desperate. It was all she could do to keep from clinging to his jacket and begging him not to do it. "You wouldn't... would you?"

He held her gaze steady, their eyes burning into one another's. She could see no malice there, only the sympathetic look of a man left in a position he didn't want to be in. His job required him to be forceful, but something prevented him from exercising his command. "I will not, no."

"What? Why not?" Hearing her voice speak the question out loud caused her to cringe, scolding herself again for having consumed the drinks set in front of her. If she got through this, she was never drinking again.

Thade looked at her curiously, the corner of his mouth curling into a soft smile. She knew how silly her words must sound after her insistence for him to leave the topic be. "There are two reasons why I will not ask you." His voice was calm, devoid of the accusatory tone she would have expected under such circumstances. "One, is that if you answered and your response placed you anywhere within the possible ages I fear it would, then I would be forced to remove you from the unit – and I, for some reason, cannot bring myself to do that to you. It seems important to you, and on top of that, you fight better than at least half the men. I would be a fool to discharge one of our best soldiers."

"And what is reason number two?" she asked quietly, a wash of pride filling her at his compliment. She couldn't be sure he intended it to be so flattering, but it meant the world to her for him to say it.

"I have a great deal of respect for you, Leyna. I want you to know that." His tone was more serious now than it had been before, his eyes watching her with an almost sad-dened stare. "If your age is even close to what I suspect, then I can see where the posi-tion I would be putting you in by forcing you to tell me would lead you to lie; and I am not certain I could take the disappointment of hearing such a noble soldier lie to me."

"I have no desire to lie to you," she whispered, shaking her head solemnly at his unwavering gaze. "But I also have no desire to tell you the answer you request of me."

Nodding his head, Thade stepped away, straightening his back uncomfortably. "Then I will consider it a non-issue and allow you to continue as you were. I only ask that someday, years down the road when this war is over and Siscal is at peace once again, that you will find a way to tell me the truth. I already fear the gods may never forgive me for letting you get away with this."

The relief she felt was overwhelming. Why he was so willing to help her, she didn't know. She was too afraid to ask in case he might change his mind. It would be something she would have to remember to ask whenever the time came where she revealed her secret to him. Until then, she could only be thankful for his mercy. "I promise I will tell you – when the time is appropriate."

"Then that is all I can possibly ask of you, other than to keep up the good work. Do not let those men push you around. You are better than they are. You just may not know it yet."

A thump came from outside the door, causing them both to jump in surprise. Her head was starting to sober up, cleared by the grimness of their conversation. Just to think of how easily she could have lost everything. She owed Thade something more than a simple "thank you" could ever possibly be worth. He was risking his own neck for her without asking anything in return other than a promise of honesty. She could never lie to him.

In a fluid movement he grabbed onto the latch, flipping it over to unlock the door. As he pulled on it, Teagan stumbled forward, his balance lost to the shifting of the wood he'd been leaning against. Eavesdropping. The man had no respect for the privacy of others.

His drunken laughter filled the tiny room, a clumsy finger waggling deviously at Leyna. She knew how it must look to such a shallow mind, her standing there in Thade's shirt with his jacket only half buttoned. She'd overheard enough of the inappropriate stories and comments passed around by the men when discussing women. The last thing she wanted was for any rumors to be floating about. "You're a drunken fool, Teagan. And you owe me a shirt."

"The Captain's looks to fit you just fine," he laughed, stumbling forward to poke at one of her buttons. Slapping his hand away, she glared at him, finding it difficult to even be angry with him when he looked so pathetic. It was hard to hate a man who was too dense to create a rational line of thought which might make him understand why his behavior was unacceptable. The alcohol removed what little bit of sense he might have had left.

His hand extended toward her again, his eyes glassy and unfocused. Drawing back, she clenched her fist, striking him square in the face with her knuckles. The crack of his nose filled the room around them, followed quickly by the dull thud of his body connecting with the floor at her feet. He was out cold.

"Leave him there," Thade chuckled, casually fastening the last of the buttons on his jacket. "Maybe we can salvage what is left of this party while he sobers up on the floor."

It was a relief to no longer have to travel by foot with the soldiers, lugging the heavy packs on their backs. As first lieutenant, she had the honor of riding at Feolan's side, leading the unit through the roads up to the northern regions of Siscal. The Siscalian General had requested them to meet. He was concerned of an impending attack, rumored to be the largest wave the Namiren had hit with since the war started. Having met with little success with the southern borders, they were aiming at the north, expecting they wouldn't be quite so prepared in the more barren mountains of the country.

They'd already been on the road for three days, the morning sun in the sky marking the fourth and final day for the journey. The paths were becoming thinner and less traveled, weeds growing up in spots along the way. Fewer towns inhabited the area, the landscape less desirable for civilization. The mountains were taller, temperatures resting several degrees colder than the southern border at all times of the year, while the winter months brought even more bitter winds and snow.

Leyna could already feel the drop in temperature, thankful for the longer sleeves on her lieutenant's jacket. Her hair was done up tightly underneath her cap, allowing a biting breeze to brush over the skin of her neck. "You said the Captain is meeting us with two other units in Velorum at the base of the mountains?"

"Yes. It's a small town, but it will act as a central point for all units to meet rather than having to search everyone out in the mountains," Feolan nodded. His eyes constantly surveyed the area, taking note of every detail. It was new territory for most of them, their comfort left behind once they moved out of the main city of Siscal.

They had ridden most of the way in silence. Neither of them wanted to risk distraction in fear of losing their way through the unfamiliar roads. Leyna kept pace with Feolan, looking over to him occasionally. He had a proud air about him, his posture on his horse reminding her of Thade. Regal. Perfectly poised for anything that might come their way. It seemed a strange quality for military men to carry themselves in that fashion. In comparison to the rest of them, they stood out easily, even when not wear-ing their uniforms to denote superior status.

The sun was already lowering in the sky when they finally came upon a break in the trees, opening into a valley at the base of the mountain range. Smaller farm houses came into view, smoke rising from the chimneys. They looked so cozy. It brought back memories to Leyna of the days when she had a home, her family waiting inside for her with a warm meal on the table. She found it hard to imagine ever having it again.

Keeping her eyes on the road, she pushed the thoughts from her mind, not wanting to bring herself down with depressing things. She had to keep positive. There had been much favor granted her by the gods since that day in Mialan. They saw her safely to Siscal and settled her quite comfortably into the military. They could have just as easily had her thrown from it those few months back on her birthday when her foolish-ness nearly cost her everything. Instead, they only smiled upon her more. She couldn't dwell on the negatives in the past. It would make her appear ungrateful.

"Alright, men – and women... we will make camp here outside town." The sol-diers broke formation at Feolan's direction, moving off the road into a large open field. "Keep things back off the road a decent ways. The lieutenant and I are going to con-tinue on to meet with the Captain. We'll have further instructions when we return." He paused there for a moment to make sure they did as they were told before motioning for Leyna to follow, pointing his horse toward the road into town.

Town was closer than Leyna anticipated. They arranged camp only a couple miles out, giving a safe distance while yet keeping them close enough in case anything were to happen.

Only a few people could be seen on the streets, hurrying quickly through the cold to get to their destinations. Noise could be heard from a tavern off to their left. Cheerful music wafted through the air from the windows, mingled with hoots and hollers of the men inside. Directing his horse to the hitch beside the building, Feolan dismounted, securing the animal in place. "I will be right back. I would much rather have us not go in there if we don't have to. Let me just make sure the other commander isn't already here."

Leyna nodded to him in agreement. She wasn't going to argue his logic. The last place she wanted to be was inside a tavern. Especially one that was completely foreign to them. She didn't know enough about the types of people it drew in to know how safe of an environment it would be for a young girl. Her only protection would be her uniform, if they even respected the military this far into the mountains.

Climbing down off her saddle, she went to work tying the rope to the post. Aside from the clatter coming from the tavern, the rest of the area was silent, giving it the appearance of a ghost town. The cold sent a shiver down her spine, her arms wrapping around her body for warmth. It felt good to be off her horse. The blood in her legs had settled into her feet after sitting for so long, making her knees stiff and awkward. She started a slow pace back and forth across the gravel road, anxiously awaiting Feolan to exit the tavern doors.

A sudden jarring pain erupted in her back, causing her to stumble forward in surprise. Barely managing to keep her balance, she spun around to face whatever struck her, blinking in confusion at the figure standing there before her. The face was masked by a long hooded cloak, pulled down to conceal the features. Even the eyes could hardly be seen, their outline nothing but a dull glow from under the thick fabric. The figure was tall, resembling the body structure of a Vor'shai rather than any Siscalian native. A dark aura enveloped the masculine hands, hovering eerily just over the skin up to the wrists.

Quickly regaining her senses, she prepared herself to fight, her fists clenched tightly. The figure held no weapon. She found it odd someone would attack an armed soldier with nothing but their hands. He came at her with incredible speed, maneuvering fluidly around her. She tried to block the incoming blows, finding her own arms too slow to avoid them. Each strike met its target easily, sending her tumbling to the ground onto her back.

He was on top of her before her body landed. His palm rested flat on her chest, pressing down firmly at the base of her sternum. She reached her own hand up to grip his neck, digging her fingers into the soft flesh. A rush of cold filled her from the inside out. His hand. It felt like ice through her clothing, chilling her to the bone. Breath was no longer possible. It caught in her throat painfully with every attempt. Her eyes rolled back in her head, lashes fluttering unnaturally. The chill slowly turned into a pressure surrounding her chest, pulling upward toward the man's palm as if he were drawing her very soul from her body.

She kept her grip on his neck, unwilling to release her hold. Around her arm, the black aura she'd seen around the man's hands began to creep over her own skin, bathing her in a blanket of shadows. *What is happening to me?* The breathlessness increased until her lungs burned, her free hand flailing wildly at the man's head. Strained choking sounds emitted from her throat. She couldn't last much longer without air – and the man showed no sign of stopping whatever it was he was doing.

A bright flash of light erupted from out of the corner of Leyna's eye. It slammed into the cloaked man on top of her, knocking him hard to the ground. She clawed at her chest, desperate for air, still unable to catch a breath. The black aura remained over her. Through her confusion she couldn't be sure what she was seeing there in front of her. Feolan. It looked to be him, bright lights dancing around her vision. He was struggling with the cloaked figure. Strange sounds reached her ears from where they landed, crackling like electricity between each strike they traded back and forth.

Air. She needed air. Her fingers clutched at her chest and neck, the movements quickly becoming sluggish until her hands fell still at her sides.

A face came into view overhead. The eyes glowed a soft grey, staring down at her in concern. She thought she heard a voice. The face was saying something. What was he saying? She couldn't hear anything anymore. Just as consciousness failed her, a sudden jolt jerked her awake, air flooding into her lungs in a desperate gulp. Her back arched from the sensation, eyes open wide, staring blindly up into the remaining light of the sky.

She was only somewhat aware of the pressure of a hand on her chest, resting over the base of her sternum where the man had been. The pressure of another hand was against her back, holding her shoulders up off the ground. "Come on, Leyna. Come back to me. Breathe."

The clattering of horse hooves sounded across the empty road. She couldn't see who was approaching, but even through her clouded thoughts she recognized the noise. Feolan was holding her. The pressure of his hand against her chest was helping her to breathe, fighting back whatever had cut off the air from her lungs. Black shadows still lingered over her skin, slowly edging away as a soft grey glow spread over her from Feolan's touch.

"Feolan, what happened?" Thade's voice called out, coming closer to them at a surprising speed. It had been his horse she'd heard, coming from the other side of town. She wanted to know the answer to his question. Nothing made sense at that moment, her mind reeling over the events of the past few minutes. Magic. It had been some form of magic, but it was different from anything she witnessed Thade and Feolan use. It had been dark and foreboding, almost seeming to draw the life directly from her body.

She could feel Feolan's hand patting her on the back, urging her to sit up. "Ven'shal. I don't know where he came from. I went in to look for you or Commander Laoter and when I came out, he was on top of her."

Ven'shal. She'd heard that word before. Something her mother told her when she was just a young girl. Evil. That was the word her mother used to describe them. She wished she could remember what else she'd been told, but the details were hazy in her mind. She'd been too young at the time.

"Leyna, can you hear me?" Thade asked, bending forward to look at her closely. Using his fingers, he gently pulled up her eyelids, searching each eye individually. She flinched at the cold air reaching her eyes, blinking rapidly to push the feeling away.

"Yes, I hear you," she coughed. Rubbing her chest uncomfortably, she looked over to the body of the cloaked man lying on the ground. He was motionless. Not even a gentle rise and fall of his breath could be seen from under the heavy fabric. "Is it dead? Please tell me it's dead."

Feolan and Thade carefully helped her to her feet, making sure she was steady before moving their hands away. Feolan remained at her side as he guided her over to the body, nudging it with the toe of his boot in disgust. "This is your true enemy in this world, and don't ever let anyone tell you otherwise."

The hood had fallen away from the face, revealing a grotesque image of a man. The eyes were dark and dull, staring lifelessly up into the sky. His skin was shriveled and ashen with old age, stretched taut over his skull, making him look more like a wrinkled skeleton than a living creature. The ears came to a point like those of the Vor'shai. He resembled their people in every way outside of his eyes. Had she not heard Feolan call it something else, she would have believed him to be a kinsman.

There was no doubt he was dead upon looking at him. The dark aura had dissipated, leaving him an empty shell of the man he once was. "Ven'shal," she whispered. "I don't understand."

"She's not ready to be fighting them." Worry was evident in Thade's voice, his head shaking dejectedly toward the ground. "Let us hope this was a simple individual incident rather than a sign that they have sided with the Namirens. If they have…"

"If they have, then we will have to plead with Queen Vorsila to send the Tanispan military to aid us. We'll know soon enough," Feolan sighed, rubbing Leyna's shoulder comfortingly. The words and names being spoken brought vague flashes of memories in Leyna's mind. Tiny details she once knew but was too young at the time to realize how important they were.

Pressing her fingertips against her temples, Leyna let out a heavy sigh, turning around to face the two men still standing silently there in the street. "I think I would rather chance the tavern than remain out here to wait for Commander Laoter."

"I agree," Feolan nodded, pushing the body with his foot until it was lying face down in the gravel. "While we are inside, we can tell them to send someone out for the trash."

Chapter Four

Loud shouting echoed through the halls of the small home. Grandpa was always angry when he came to visit. There was always something that wasn't to his liking, something he claimed would cost them favor with the Queen. All he cared about was the Queen. As long as the family was in her good graces, he had all the wealth and power he could ever hope for.

She didn't understand what he was angry about this time. Something about her father. Leyna could hear him screaming at her mother about a disgrace to the family. What was a disgrace? That word sounded funny to her young ears. "Did you not think I would find out? It is the talk of the entire city! Everyone whispering about our family behind our backs at court. Is that what you wanted? Are you satisfied?"

"Father, you are the one who married me to that Ven'shal scum. You know Aviden had already asked for my hand in marriage before you decided to get in the way."

"Damir is a very well-respected man. If you can find proof he is working with the Ven'shal, it would raise our status among the people for having exposed a traitor. I fail to see how any of this is as terrible as you claim — unless Damir finds out his wife has been lying to him and his daughter is actually the child of another man."

None of it made any sense. Ven'shal. Disgrace. She wished they would stop yelling. Her father was due home at any time and he hated when things weren't in order. Grandpa had kept mother distracted. Dinner wasn't even on the fire yet.

"And if I do prove him to be a traitor, what would you have done if Leyna was actually his child? You would have her murdered. There is no way for this situation to have been any better. Either way, you will find it to be a disgrace to the family just so you can disown me as your daughter and pass the family line on to Priel like you wanted to do before I was even born."

Footsteps pounded down the hall toward where Leyna was sitting, smoothing out the folds of her doll's dress. It was her favorite doll. She'd had it since she was born, keeping it by her side at all times. Wherever she went, the doll was right there with her, its tiny painted mouth and eyes watching everything happily. Some of the stuffing had started to show through the fabric of the body, but she didn't care. She had plenty of little dresses for it to wear to cover the tears in the seams.

Her grandpa appeared in the doorway, his blue eyes glowing brightly in his anger. The tips of his pointed ears were bright red, lips pressed together tightly. With a solid grip he lifted her up from the floor by her arm. She winced in pain, grabbing for her doll as she lost her hold on it, her hands reaching out wildly to where it landed on the floor while her grandpa carried her over to her mother.

"Sarayi, I'll have you know that this child will never be considered a part of my family. Do you understand that?"

"Father, let her go. You are going to hurt her."

"I don't care!" he shouted, dropping her harshly to the ground at her mother's feet. Her lower lip trembled for a moment, preparing to let out a cry at the pain from where her head hit the floor. It went away quickly. She thought to cry anyway, but changed her mind, not wanting to anger her grandpa any further than he already was. "If you can do something useful for the family and find proof that Damir is a traitor, then I might consider continuing to accept you as my daughter. Until then, you are an embarrassment. I don't ever want to see this thing again."

Bending forward, her grandfather slapped Leyna hard across her cheek. She immediately began crying, more from fear than pain. Her grandpa was a scary man. Even her mother was afraid of him. He had raised their family up to where they were because of his strength. No man in Tanispa had ever dared to cross him and gotten away with it. His family was no different from anyone else. They did as he said, or they suffered the consequences.

Her mother quickly lifted Leyna from the floor, holding her close to her chest. "Get out," she hissed at him, the anger in her voice causing Leyna's cries to grow louder. She'd never heard her mother sound like that before. It was frightening.

The door slammed hard behind her grandpa as he left, rattling the paintings on the wall. Her mother stood there silently, bouncing Leyna gently to ease her crying. The skin on her cheek stung from her grandpa's hand, tingling uncomfortably despite the length of time that had passed since he struck her. "Mommy, what is Ven'shal?"

"The Ven'shal are evil, sweetie. They use their tainted magic to maim and kill everything around them."

"You think Daddy is evil?" The innocence in her voice caused tears to form in her mother's eyes.

Shaking her head, her mother lightly brushed her thumb under Leyna's eyes, wiping away the tears lingering there. "No, darling. Your father is a good man. A loyal Vor'shai. I want you to always remember that — even if someone tries to tell you differently."

"Leyna? Were you listening?"

Blinking her eyes, Leyna gave an apologetic glance at Feolan, embarrassed for having been caught daydreaming. They were prepared for an attack, lying in wait of the sun to set before the enemy would come marching through the trees. Soldiers were stationed all throughout the mountains, armed and ready for whatever the night would bring. Leyna hoped their intelligence had been correct and that they were in the right place. The southern borders had been left with only a handful of fighters while the main units traveled north.

"I'm sorry. I was thinking about something."

"You asked me about the Ven'shal and then I lost you. Everything okay?"

"Of course," she smiled. The last thing she wanted to do was let on that anything was bothering her. "I am still curious about them, though. Since we have plenty of time before we have to sit here in silence. Might as well talk about something."

Feolan looked her over curiously, clearly aware she was hiding something, but making no attempt to draw it out of her. His eyes stared into hers as if trying to decipher the answer from their depths. "I was under the impression they covered that part of history in the classes at the academy in Carpaen. Didn't you say you attended there?"

Leyna sighed helplessly, shifting her legs underneath her where she was sitting. "I trained in combat and assisted the instructor while he taught the new students, but I didn't attend other classes there, no."

"Oh." Feolan's expression revealed his confusion. It was uncommon for a child to be part of a school without participating in the general classes. Especially a female child. Although the combat courses were available to them, they tended to lean more toward the other studies, focusing on history and writing. Most families preferred it that way, in order to keep their daughters safe from the violence. The Vor'shai were very protective of their daughters. Among those of the higher status families, the daughters were the link to the family heritage. A child's mother could never be in question, therefore making the female the most reliable to determine the family line.

"It's a long story. But with my rigorous training schedule, I missed out on the history lesson about the Ven'shal... among other topics."

"Well, most notably, the Vor'shai and the Ven'shal were at war for years. This was centuries ago, mind you. Back when Queen Vorsila's mother was still on the throne in Tanispa." Feolan's voice was thoughtful, contemplating his own words before speaking them. "You don't know about the magic, either, do you?"

Idly playing with a piece of grass, she shook her head, avoiding his questioning gaze. She hated admitting to her ignorance. The humiliation felt less overwhelming when she didn't have to look into his eyes. "My mother died when I was nine and I never really knew my father. Even at the time of my mother's death, we were living in Mialan. There was little opportunity for me to learn anything."

"That is nothing to be ashamed of, Leyna," Feolan replied calmly, plucking the blade of grass from her hands to get her attention. She looked up at him hesitantly. He was still watching her, a sympathetic expression on his sharp features. With an understanding smile he handed it back to her, sliding his leather gloves from his slender hands. "The Vor'shai people have been blessed with a strong internal magic. We can utilize it to accomplish almost anything, but the methods can interfere with the outcome. It should only be used for honorable reasons; else we start to fall like the Ven'shal."

Leyna carefully laid the blade of grass back down on the ground, her eyes locked on Feolan. "I don't get it. So the Ven'shal and the Vor'shai are the same?"

"Not quite," he chuckled. Rubbing his hands together quickly he pulled them apart, letting his palms hover a few inches away from the other. "Physically, we are essentially the same. Our bodies are almost interchangeable. It is the energy inside that makes us different. The Vor'shai rely on life and everything around us on this planet of Myatheira to utilize our magic. We can access most anything in nature through the power inside of us. The Ven'shal, on the other hand, are what we would call tainted. The negative energy flow inside them warps the things that they do. Where the Vor'shai recognize death as a part of life, the Ven'shal don't cower from the darker aspects of the magic."

"None of that made sense to me, just so you know," Leyna sighed, following the motions of Feolan's hands with her eyes. She could almost hear the energy humming between his palms, a soft light radiating in the space between them.

"Look at it this way." Sitting up straight, Feolan situated himself on his knees. On the ground in front of him, he pointed to a wildflower still budding with new life. "If you can visualize things as either light or dark, our magic would be considered light. This flower, for instance. It is alive and very much a part of the system of nature around us." Gently, he cupped his palms around the flower, the soft glow Leyna had seen before now slowly enveloping the bud. Before her eyes it started to bloom, the petals opening up with a brilliant violet hue. "We can add to that life – even bend it to our own will in some situations. But we never destroy. Not that we aren't capable of destruction with our magic, but the Vor'shai are very strict on how the power is used."

"And the Ven'shal... they would be considered the dark magic?" she asked, still in wonder at the sight of the beautiful flower cupped in Feolan's hands.

Moving his hands away, Feolan took Leyna's hand in his, lightly sliding off one of her gloves. "In a sense, yes. You see, the initial energy is the same but, generations ago, they learned to utilize it in a different way. The Vor'shai consider it sorcerous what they do. To us, once the life seeps away from something, the energy is returned to nature where it came. Magic should no longer be allowed to touch it. The Ven'shal, they specialize in death. Their magic is grotesque. Use of that magic is forbidden among the Vor'shai, but not impossible. A Vor'shai who uses it will show signs of the dark energy until it takes them over."

From where his hands made contact with hers, Leyna could feel the thrum of energy flowing between them. It was exciting to her. After so many years, she finally felt the power flooding through her veins. Feolan directed his own energy through her hand, letting it course over her and back to his other awaiting palm, creating a circuit with both of their bodies. "The Vor'shai and Ven'shal were content to co-exist all those years ago. Occasionally, they would even come to each other for help, given the differences in things each were able to do. A Ven'shal could do little to manipulate life, so they many times would have to come to the Vor'shai, though it was frowned upon for a Vor'shai to seek out the Ven'shal for assistance."

"If they were so content to let the other live peacefully, why did they go to war?"

"That is the complicated part," Feolan frowned, releasing his hold on her hand. All at once the energy ceased to flow between them, though the thrum of it still tingled over every inch of her arms and legs. Sliding her other glove off, he used his own hands to press her palms together, holding them there tightly. "The Ven'shal at the time were led by a very powerful man by the name of Arcastus. Queen Vorsila's mother, Queen Nalashi, was on at least tolerable terms with Arcastus. They agreed to disagree with each other's beliefs. Until Mescavis."

Leyna's hands were starting to feel strange. Her palms were growing increasingly warm where they were pressed together, held firmly in place by Feolan's hands. Gently, he took his fingers and wrapped them over her wrists, guiding her hands to slide back and forth. "Mescavis was a well-known Vor'shai of some significant power. He lost his wife to an illness and was devastated by her passing. He began warping his own magic, trying to find a way to restore the life to her extinguished body, disregarding the rules of leaving the deceased to rest. His attempts became more and more obscene, twisting the corpse into a hideous deformity of what she once was. Realizing he was failing, he took what was left of her decaying body to Arcastus and begged for him to help. Even Arcastus didn't want to touch what Mescavis had done to his poor wife."

"It sounds like the Ven'shal had their limits, at least," Leyna mused. The warmth was building even stronger between her hands with every pass until Feolan released her wrists, positioning her palms to face each other the way he had done with his own not long before. As he pulled away from her completely, she felt the thrum of energy passing between her own hands, pushing against her palms like two opposite magnets forcing the other away.

"They did, possibly. But when Arcastus refused to help him, Mescavis murdered Arcastus with his perverted magics. He had fallen beyond redemption into the sorcery he created by carelessly mixing the Vor'shai energy with that of the Ven'shal. The Ven'shal took the slaughter of their great leader as a direct insult. They gathered up an army of grotesque composition, their own soldiers, mingled with abominations of corpses they had reanimated from their graves; and they marched on the city of Sivaeria, where the Queen lived. Queen Nalashi attempted to send men to negotiate and explain that it was an act of only one man and not her entire kingdom, but the bodies of the messengers were sent back to her repeatedly. The Vor'shai were left with no other alternative than to fight."

There, between her hands, a soft blue light materialized, strengthening the charge of energy bouncing back and forth between her palms. Excitement filled every part of her at the sight. She had done it. She could see the energy – her own energy – right there before her eyes. After so long, she'd started to think it didn't exist inside her. But there it was. Feolan had somehow awakened it from wherever it had lain dormant for over eighteen years.

"After nearly a decade of fighting, the Vor'shai finally won... but not without cost. Their military was severely depleted and the cities of Tanispa had been ravaged. Queen Nalashi forced the Ven'shal from Tanispa, sending them into hiding in fear of being taken captive and executed for the horrible crimes they committed throughout the war. The Ven'shal behaved unscrupulously. The scars left by their wicked magic can still be seen all throughout Tanispa. No one really knows where they crawled off to. I imagine they are scattered all across the provinces and countries, hiding their faces from the public eye. They should be well aware of the fact that the Vor'shai have not forgotten what they are capable of."

Thinking back, Leyna tried to summon the memories from all those years ago when she and her mother still lived in Tanispa. She could hear her mother's voice still pleading with her grandfather, insisting that someone had been Ven'shal. Her father? But that couldn't be possible. Her mother insisted her father had been a loyal Vor'shai. So then what had been such a disgrace? Someone had been working with the Ven'shal – "I think I can safely assume that any Vor'shai caught affiliating themselves with a Ven'shal even now would be considered traitors to our people?"

"Of the highest degree," Feolan nodded. That explained some of it. Someone had been a traitor and her grandfather wanted to use their exposure to benefit himself. Oh, why couldn't she remember anything else? The names, everything, it was all a haze to her. Maybe in time it would start to make more sense. Until then, she would just have to try and get by with what few memories she still had of her mother.

Out of curiosity, she lowered her hands to the ground, separating them just enough to place another budding flower between her palms. She knew Feolan was watching her. Willing her to succeed in her attempts. She wasn't quite sure how he'd done it, but it seemed easy enough to mimic. Picture the flower. See it blooming there in her hands.

The blue aura slowly worked its way over the bud. Nothing happened at first. The flower stem wobbled under the transfer of energy, rocking from side to side with no sign of opening its petals at her command. Relaxing her shoulders, she closed her eyes, envisioning the flower coming to life. She could still see the way the bud had opened to Feolan's gentle guidance, revealing its inner beauty. She could do it. She knew she could. It was just a matter of…

"Well done," Feolan applauded, his lips displaying a proud smile as Leyna opened her eyes. Glancing down to her hands, she saw the flower still resting between her palms, the soft blue light gradually pulling open the petals. Not quite as fluid as Feolan's had been, but it was working. That was all that mattered.

When the last petal pulled itself from the bud, she drew her hands back, beaming excitedly at her accomplishment. It wasn't much in the grand scheme of things, but it was a big deal to her. The energy was within her. It would only be a matter of time, and dedicated practice, before she would be able to utilize the magic the way she'd seen Feolan and Thade do so many times before.

A cracking noise came from somewhere in the distance. Instantly, Feolan and Leyna were on their stomachs, ducking down out of view of the main path. Feolan lifted his arm up, giving a warning signal to the other soldiers scattered in hiding around the woods. In silence, they waited. Leyna at first counted two sets of footsteps, quickly multiplying into more than she could decipher. Their pace was too brisk for them to be attempting subtlety. Their boots cut through the leaves, sending rocks and branches tumbling across the path in front of them.

Leyna could make out the familiar uniform of the Namiren commander leading the group coming their way. She'd seen the Namiren people hundreds of times over the past couple of years yet their appearance never ceased to amaze her. The commander's complexion was a deep brown tone, comparing only to the skin of the Carpaens from the hot desert sun. His hair hung like feathers down his back, each strand thick and wide, resembling the tail of a peacock at rest, though the color was shaded in browns and blacks, connecting to his head from the top of his skull down to the base of his neck. A few feathered strands draped over the large bony crest which jutted out from the skin, circling horizontally around his forehead, disappearing under the hairline. The Namirens were a tall race, towering over the Sanarik when standing side by side. Their eyes slanted drastically at an upward angle, the yellow iris giving a predatory glow from under the lids.

Dipping her head lower in the overgrown grass, Leyna slowly reached for her sword, letting her fingers tightly wrap around the leather bands of the hilt. On Feolan's command they would have to be ready to attack. Any delay in their actions would allow the enemy recovery from the surprise, negating their advantage. Any moment now. Feolan and Leyna were to go for the commander. The unit would be more vulnerable without their leader.

Just as the group marched within range of a few feet from Feolan, he gave the call, charging from hiding. Leyna was at his side, her sword drawn before she was even to her feet. The other soldiers leapt from their concealment, moving quickly into the mass of bodies scrambling to unsheathe their weapons.

The idea of killing hadn't gotten any easier on her conscience. Every slice of her blade sent chills down her spine, the sound of metal cutting through flesh making her ill. Still, she kept moving. Between her and Feolan, the commander fell easily; hardly putting up a fight in the time it took them to wound him beyond saving. With their target fallen, they separated to face the other soldiers, cutting them down one after the other.

Lost in the frenzy of battle, Leyna paid no attention to time. It always felt like it flew when the attacks started. Adrenaline pumped through every vein, her focus on nothing but the strikes coming at her and determining the point of weakness of her foe. By the time the enemy finally retreated, her hands were sprinkled with Namiren blood. An occasional smear brushed across her face. She was used to it by now. It was impossible to come out of a battle like this without some stain of her fallen adversaries.

She looked around calmly, taking a count of the faces from her unit that she could still see standing. Their numbers were in good health. It appeared the surprise attack had been successful.

Her least favorite part of the battle was the aftermath, walking around the bodies to take note of who had been lost. It was her job now, verifying who was alive and who was dead. She was just grateful she wasn't the one in charge of notifying the families. That wasn't something she could handle. It was best left in the hands of the Captain.

Slowly making her way around the path, she could see numerous corpses, most of which wore the Namiren uniform. The scene was bloody and violent, the bodies cut up to the point where identifying them would have been an impossible task... even if she'd known them the way she did her own soldiers. From under the masses, she counted twelve bodies. Several wounded. A sad loss, and yet a good outcome for Siscal. All she could do now was worry about the other units scattered about the mountains.

There had been only one commander with the enemy unit they ambushed. The intelligence they received warned of multiple. Thade and Laoter were positioned to the east and west, guarding the other trails the Namirens might use. She wouldn't know the outcome of their battles until they all met back at camp.

"Blood is a good look for you. Kind of sexy."

"Not now, Teagan," she frowned. How typical of him. His comrades lay dead at his feet and all he could think about was women. There were other females in the unit. Why could he not focus his attention on them?

"What? We won. Why are you so sour?" He sounded annoyed by her reaction. She didn't know what else he could have expected. She was busy. The last thing she had time for was avoiding his futile come-ons.

Sheathing her sword, she turned to face him sternly. "Some of our men are dead. I have to determine who. So I suggest you go direct your after-battle lust at someone else."

"Is there a problem, Lieutenant?" Feolan's voice came from behind her, moving to her side quickly. His expression was hardened, his own face and hands covered in spatters of blood from the fight. At the moment his eyes were set squarely on Teagan – and he looked very displeased.

"Not at all, sir. I was just advising this soldier to move on."

Feolan kept his gaze on Teagan, narrowing his eyes after a moment of silence. Teagan continued to stand there, waiting for Feolan to leave. "I believe your lieutenant gave you an order, soldier. Why are you still standing here?"

Teagan made no attempts to conceal his irritation with Feolan, snapping to attention with a half-hearted salute. Despite his lack of common sense, even he knew arguing with his commander would be a fool move. He valued his uniform too much to risk it.

Feolan remained unmoving until Teagan left them, a soft sigh escaping his lips. "I apologize, Leyna. I would have him discharged for his behavior, but regrettably he is one of our better fighters."

"His comments are harmless enough," she shrugged, wiping at a spot of blood on her cheek. "I will only start to care if he ever tries to touch me."

"If he lays even a finger on you, he will be dealt with accordingly. Without pardon." She knew he was serious. It was a well known fact among the men serving under Thade that he didn't take kindly to any form of mistreatment of the female soldiers. To do so meant dishonoring your name and, depending on the severity, could cost you your life. Only once had she seen a situation that serious in the time she'd been with the unit, but Thade had made good on his promise. No one questioned whether he meant what he said after that.

Turning to one of the other soldiers nearby, she gave the order for the bodies of their fallen fighters to be gathered up to take back to camp. There were so many Namiren corpses, she didn't want to think about the possibility of moving them. And Feolan made no mention to indicate for them to.

"Commander, do you think it is possible another wave might come through?"

Feolan shook his head. He looked tired. They'd been in the woods since morning, lying in wait of the attack in case it came sooner than anticipated. They were all hungry and exhausted from battle, anxious to return to the comfort of their camp. "It is possible, yes, but General Matias has his men stationed only a few miles down the mountain. If another wave approaches, his fighters will be fresh and well-prepared to handle it."

Motioning for one of the other soldiers, she gave the order for them to start moving the other bodies. There was no choice in the matter. To leave them behind placed their entire mission in jeopardy.

"You're right, Leyna. I'm not sure what I was thinking."

"You were thinking that we are all tired, and I agree," she sighed, rubbing her temples with her index fingers. "Unfortunately, if you think another wave will come through, then we have to make sure the road is clear. An ambush would be less than surprising if they found an entire unit lying dead in their path."

They both went to work helping the soldiers move the fallen fighters, dragging them off into the thicker grass and trees of the woods. As long as they were out of view, that was the important thing.

It took longer than she expected to get everything cleaned up, counting on the cover of the darkness to hide the blood stains from view on the path. "Well, the good news is that I saw nothing resembling the Ven'shal amongst the corpses," Leyna smiled slightly. She knew she didn't know enough about the Ven'shal to be able to pick one out of a crowd, but she did know the Namiren well — and they were the only faces she'd seen among the blood.

"That is reassuring at the very least." She couldn't tell if Feolan was being truthful in his statement. His words were comforting, while yet his tone led her to believe he was not convinced they were in the clear. "Thade has already sent a messenger to Tanispa to inform the Queen of the incident that happened here in Velorum. Attacks by them are taken very seriously. It is rare one would be skulking about alone. The most likely truth is that there are at least a handful of others somewhere not far from the town."

The thought of that frightened her. She could still feel the painful tug of the man's hand at her chest, drawing the air from her lungs. She had been too afraid to ask Feolan what happened to her. Even more, she'd been afraid to ask him what he'd done to reverse it. Everything had been so confusing. With the unexpectedness of the attack, she had very little time to collect her thoughts and take in what was going on. She reacted by mere reflex — and that reflex would not have been enough to save her if she'd been alone.

There was nothing else to be said on the matter. She averted her gaze from Feolan's as they started to make their way back to their horses left deeper into the woods. It would be a long trip back to camp, requiring them to maneuver the uneven ground without the guidance of the path. They had to stay clear of any possible routes the Namiren might take.

Once back in the safety of their camp, Leyna found her way to her tent, not wanting to risk a conversation with Teagan. She had very little patience for his immaturity. It was a wonder he even managed to gain acceptance to the unit. After their first scout together, she'd been inducted into the ranks of the soldiers almost immediately, having proven her worth as a fighter. Teagan remained a simple scout for several months afterwards. Feolan and Thade had been testing him, trying to get him to behave less rashly. She didn't think such a thing was possible.

Scrubbing at her face with a towel, she removed the last traces of blood from her face and hands. She was exhausted. Her body yearned for sleep, but she didn't want to let herself drift off until she knew their other units were safe. It was only a matter of time before they would return. She and Feolan were stationed as the first wave ambush. General Matias would be in charge of any further attacks beyond that.

The uneven ground was still a relief to her aching body as she allowed herself to sink down to it. There had to be something more to life than fighting. She felt like she was capable of so many greater things, and yet the reality was that fighting was all she could do. While the other girls her age were still learning to sew dresses and knit socks and how to curtsy and smile like a lady, she was covered in dirt and blood in a makeshift tent in the middle of nowhere.

Idly, she positioned her hands together the way Feolan had shown her while they were in the woods. Curiosity made her wonder if she would be capable of recreating the energy he pulled forth from her. She was surprised at how quickly the warmth appeared against her skin, the strange tugging and pulling sensation radiating between her palms. Staring in wonder, she could see the soft blue glow starting to build up around her hands, slowly creeping along to envelope each one of her fingers and all the way down to her wrists. Slowly she increased the space between her hands until the blue light extended across her entire body, tingling like a jolt of electricity shooting between her hands to create a circuit.

Horses approaching in the distance distracted her from the light, her eyes lifting to gaze at the entrance of her tent. Almost instantly the glow dissipated, dimming the tiny space back to the darkness it had been before. The thick material of the tent prevented any light from filtering in from outside. She hadn't realized just how dark it was until the glow was gone.

She strained her ears to hear what the voices were saying outside. Several of them sounded familiar, but the one she cared about was the Captain. He was a brave fighter, yet she found herself constantly worried about his safety. She feared what would happen to her if anything ill were to befall him. The new captain might not be so forgiving of her secret. And even more so, he might not be as understanding as a friend.

At first she could make out nothing but the murmur of multiple voices all speaking at once. The other men were finding their way to their tents, discussing the highlights of their battle. There were enough voices to assure her they'd been victorious. They were much too relaxed and numerous to be returning from a failed attack. Still, she had not heard Thade's familiar tone. She'd yet to even make out the sound of Feolan amongst the racket of celebrating soldiers.

Eventually the noise started to taper off, the men finally settling down for the night. The celebration would continue in full force once they returned to the city of Siscal. For now, all they could do was sleep.

Sliding closer to the side of her tent, she listened intently, aware of soft voices still coming from somewhere just outside. Relief flooded her as she recognized one of them to be Thade, though his words were too muffled to make out. It didn't matter what he was saying — only that he was safe.

Content with knowing everything was well, she moved back into the center of the tent. A single thin blanket offered her a minor respite from the cold. Lying down on the hard ground, she drew the blanket up to her chin, covering herself up tightly; her body curled into a ball. She had survived another battle; but she wondered when they might finally survive the war.

The cool breeze brushed along the skin of Leyna's neck. Even in the height of the daytime the temperature remained frigid, a sign of the coming winter months in the mountains. They anticipated a return to Siscal City before the weather could take a turn for the worst. From outside her tent, she watched the soldiers casually strolling about, enjoying the mild warmth the afternoon sun offered. The night had been even colder than usual, leaving her with a chill all the way through her.

In a mild daze, she worked at doing up the buttons on her jacket, her fingertips frozen to the point where any detailed movement felt clumsy and uncoordinated. The skin was numb, making it difficult to know whether or not she was even successfully getting them done up correctly. She hated not having her uniform perfect. While the men preferred to relax in the more basic pieces of their attire, she tended to remain in full dress, finding it easier to conceal her scrawny figure under the heavy fabrics and layers of clothing.

Behind her, she caught the sound of someone calling her name, her head snapping up attentively in the direction of the voice. Smiling through the cold, she made her way toward Feolan's tent, nodding to him in response to his summons. His tent was larger than many of the others, allowing ample room for himself and Thade to sleep. It acted as more of a portable office, though no one was usually ever allowed inside with them unless there was something wrong. That was the place where they formulated their attack plans. Their dedication to keeping the strategies outside the reach of enemy ears prevented them from most idle chatter while at camp.

Around her she could hear the sounds of the soldiers snickering, heckling her from where they watched her being escorted into the tent. They assumed the same as she did that she was in some kind of trouble. She just didn't know for what.

Inside, she found Thade standing next to a makeshift table, tapping his index finger absently on the surface. He seemed far away in his thoughts. Leyna wasn't even sure he was aware of her entrance to the tent. He appeared mostly unscathed from their battles the day before. A single bruise could be seen on one side of his face, darkening the skin slightly at the top of his high cheekbone. Other than the exhaustion she could see in his eyes, he looked in good health.

"Is something wrong?" she asked, her nervous curiosity getting the better of her. Anticipation caused her heart to flutter. She felt her actions had all been within the rules, but it was hard to tell by the distant expressions on the faces of her superior officers.

"Why would something be wrong?" Feolan chuckled lightly. The tone of his voice helped to ease Leyna's worry, sounding too casual to imply any disappointment in her. "Truthfully, the first lieutenant, under normal circumstances, would share the tent with us to help strategize our defense — so there is no need to worry about being in trouble if we request your presence. We simply gave you your own tent because we felt it wasn't appropriate for a young girl such as yourself to be bunking with two old dogs such as us."

For the first time since her arrival, Leyna could see Thade's shoulders shake with a quiet burst of laughter, his eyes glancing over to them tiredly. "Old? Speak for yourself maybe. I still have plenty of good years left in me."

She'd never pondered his age before. Hearing his comment brought a deeper inquisitiveness out in her mind. He didn't look nearly as old as his stature and mannerisms might suggest, though with the Vor'shai it was too difficult to even contemplate guessing age. Once one of their people had reached adulthood, their features changed very little. It was the signs of life experience that made their age more apparent. A clench to their jaw or creases in their skin from years of worry or thought. The only part of them which held significant truth was their eyes. They were truly the window to their soul in many ways — and for the first time Leyna realized Thade's eyes, though hardened from his years at war, still held a glow of youth deep inside them.

Bashfully, Leyna averted her gaze, embarrassed to find herself staring so directly at him. Regardless of the ages of them all, she understood exactly why it was inappropriate for her to share the tent with them. War or not, there were still social expectations for a young woman to behave virtuously. To disregard that outward appearance, even if she were doing nothing wrong behind closed doors, could still mar her reputation among society. The lifestyle of a soldier was unladylike enough, with their harsh living arrangements and the masculine style of dress.

"Well, I won't argue your decision to keep me tucked away in my own private quarters. The privacy is certainly preferred over the behaviors I saw while sharing camp with the other women."

Feolan checked the entrance to the tent, making sure it was securely closed. Content that they were adequately alone, he motioned for Leyna to step away from the door, gesturing to a stool resting to one side of the table. She'd never been inside the command tent before. A wave of pride washed over her as she accepted Feolan's offer, situating herself confidently on the seat.

She was surprised to find the table empty aside from a single piece of parchment lying near Thade's hand. In her mind, she always pictured the tent to be filled with maps on which they would plot their next course of action. It was hard to think of them creating all the brilliant strategies they had used to maintain the upper hand for so long in the war on nothing but a thin parchment. "So, what is it exactly that you both have been mulling over in here all morning?"

"Always straight to business with you," Feolan nodded. He made his way over to a stool across from Leyna, seating himself and placing his elbows on the table. Clasping his hands together, he gazed at her steadily, seeming to search her face for something she couldn't quite understand before speaking again. "I told you word was sent to Tanispa about the Ven'shal who attacked you when we arrived in town."

Leyna moved her head up and down slowly, unsure of what he was getting at. "Yes, you mentioned it." A brief response felt better than nothing. She wanted to make a good impression. Attentiveness now was crucial in order to solidify her importance in the new position she was in. Hundreds of others had been vying for the first lieutenant promotion, and it had been given to her. She didn't want to make them regret their decision.

"The Prince is coming to Siscal," Thade sighed, his tone sounding almost irritated by the news. Folding his arms across his chest, he turned away from the table, making it difficult for Leyna to see his face to decipher his true attitude on the matter. He seemed to be intentionally avoiding her questioning gaze, his attention directed absently off into the empty back corner of the tent.

"Is this — bad?" Leyna asked hesitantly. She thought it sounded important, but she couldn't tell by the behavior of the others. They were making it impossible for her to know how to react to the thought of seeing the Tanispan Prince. She knew very little about him, but if he was royalty, she could only imagine the honor it would be to meet him.

Unclasping his hands, Feolan straightened his back on the stool. He looked contemplative at first. His brows were furrowed in deep thought, his eyes cast slightly downward at the table. After a moment he looked back up to her, shrugging his shoulders in an oddly nonchalant way. "It depends on your opinion of the Prince. He has a bit of a reputation, but that really doesn't change the fact that he is the current heir to the throne. Some of us are still a bit biased and hold a deep disappointment in his way of conducting business in comparison to his late brother."

"Brother?" she asked, the word slipping from her lips before she had a chance to think over the question. Nibbling her lower lip in embarrassment, she lowered her eyes down to the table, scolding herself for having made her lack of knowledge of the Vor'shai royalty so obvious.

Feolan looked taken aback by her inquiry before quickly regaining his composure, smiling at her with an understanding nod. "I forget sometimes that you were not raised among our people." The comment stung her. She knew it wasn't intended to be as biting as she took it, but she couldn't help her reaction. Any reminder of her poor upbringing for a Vor'shai child hit her harder than any other insult. She wanted so badly to be accepted and yet she was so set apart from her people that it felt out of her reach to accomplish.

At his words she couldn't help but hang her head dejectedly. Her shoulders bowed forward, as if suddenly burdened by some invisible weight. So far she was failing at her attempts to pretend she was knowledgeable of the topics they might present her. It was humiliating.

Noticing her reaction, Feolan quickly tried to retract his statement, his eyes glancing over to Thade for some kind of support. Thade's attention remained distant, oblivious to Feolan's struggle. "There is nothing wrong with that, mind you. I just meant – I tend to talk without thinking that the entire company may not know exactly what I am speaking of…"

"Think nothing of it," Leyna replied dismissively, her eyes still locked on the uneven floor of the tent. "Do not worry about me. I am here to seek the knowledge I don't have so that I can be better prepared for the things you might ask of me."

"Queen Vorsila gave birth to seven children before her husband died," Thade said suddenly, the sound of his voice surprising Leyna with his sudden return to the conversation. "The first daughter died in infancy of an illness which affected her lungs. Her next child, and heir to the throne, Princess Amari, was murdered by the Ven'shal. Her brother, Prince Ehren, became the next tentative heir until a female child became of age. While he was living, the Queen's twin daughters, Kaelin and Kadri, were kidnapped and found dead several weeks later. Although their murderer was never found, the cause of death was assumed to be at the hands of the Ven'shal."

"That is awful," Leyna frowned. She wasn't sure what was worse about the information; whether it was the reality itself, or the detached manner in which Thade addressed it. His voice droned like that of a history teacher giving a lesson to a class rather than a man discussing the fate of his people. "It is as if they were targeting her daughters specifically."

Still facing away toward the back of the tent, Thade continued speaking, his voice steady and emotionless. "That was what the Queen thought as well. With the last of her daughters dead, she thought her sons would be safe. Instead, about twelve years ago or so, Prince Ehren was assassinated while on a trip to Mialan. His assassin was caught and executed. A Ven'shal sorcerer."

"And the current Prince… who is…"

"Prince Enaes," Feolan chuckled, coming to her rescue with the name. She smiled back at him gratefully. There were so many names she'd never heard before; though a vague memory flitted through her head. Something her mother said. Yes. She had spoken the name of Ehren. They had been out shopping one day and passed by – something. The image was too hazy in her mind. She'd asked her mother about it. A memorial of some kind. Erected in Mialan in memory of the Prince.

A wash of excitement flowed through her at the thought. Her mother had spoken of their people on many occasions but so many of her words were lost to the years. She hated the fact that she'd failed to retain her mother's teachings. It was her only knowledge of the life they lived before they moved away from Tanispa. Her mind had just been too young to hold onto it in any conscious form. "Right, Enaes – if so many people feel he is not suitable, why do they not choose another to be the heir. There is still another child, isn't there?"

"The youngest son was pulled from the public eye before he was even old enough to be introduced to society. A precautionary measure for his safety. Enaes is rather fond of his position. To remove him from it would only cause hostility within the family and that would serve little use." Rising from his seat, Feolan moved over to where Thade had been standing, lifting the parchment from the table to look it over carefully.

Sensing Feolan behind him, Thade turned back around to face them both. The distance had left his eyes, leaving behind the familiar calm Leyna had grown so accustomed to seeing there. "This conversation is not appropriate. We should not be speaking so poorly of our Prince. Enaes is a good man and he does well with his position. He will not shirk the responsibilities… unless there is a tempting enough woman to distract him from them."

Thade's lips curled into a curious half-smile. Leyna wasn't sure whether or not she should laugh at his comment, though she found it to be amusing. She waited until Feolan's voice chimed in before she gave in to the giggle building inside her. "I think that is true for most men," Feolan grinned. "Women are the ultimate evil for a man of power."

"Well that hardly seems fair," Leyna smirked, folding her arms across her chest. "Not all women are evil."

"You may not be yet, but some day perhaps it will happen unintentionally for you," Thade smiled, patting Leyna's back on his way over to the stool where Feolan had been seated. "It's the women who do not purposely use their charms that are the most dangerous. They are harder to spot and they hit you before you even realize what is happening. The ones who know how to use their wiles are far too obvious to be successful with a clever man."

"You sound like you are giving me advice on how to seduce powerful men." Leyna couldn't help but laugh at the thought. She lacked in every quality a woman could use to catch the eye of such a man. To even think about attempting to seduce anyone – the thought was too funny to consider as anything more than a joke.

Feolan stepped calmly over to Leyna's side, holding the parchment out for her to see. "Our issue here is not that you will seduce a powerful man, but that a powerful man may try to seduce you."

The words on the parchment blurred together at first, the fancy script delicately showcasing the Vor'shai language. She'd never seen it in writing before – that she could recall. It looked oddly foreign. When spoken, it flowed easily and gracefully off the tongue, but in reading it, she had to sound everything out more slowly in fear of misunderstanding the message.

Prince Enaes was coming to Siscal. He requested the presence of General Matias and Captain Imri, which was to be expected, in her opinion. If he had questions about the situation, the top military men made sense to be in attendance. What she didn't understand was how any of this involved her. "I doubt he will even see me."

"He will," Feolan replied. His serious tone returned, the lightheartedness of their prior conversation no longer visible in his actions. He seemed truly troubled by the situation. As for why, Leyna couldn't even venture a guess. "While he is in Siscal, he will be under the protection of the military here. What this means, is that we will be providing him with a constant guard."

"I would assume that guard to be you, Commander," Leyna cut in politely. Order of command made the most sense when determining who should stand at the side of someone as important as the Prince. There were a great many people in the Siscalian military that ranked much higher than herself.

Feolan paused for a moment, looking over to Thade calmly. A silent exchange passed between them. After a brief silence, they both nodded to one another, with Thade suddenly rising from his seat in a smooth and graceful motion. Setting his eyes on Leyna, he leaned across the table, bracing his upper body with his palms against the surface. "Prince Enaes trusts no one outside the Vor'shai. With this in mind, his guard cannot be anything else. Normally, this would indeed place Feolan at his side for protection, but other details seem to be hindering us."

Leyna started to speak but quickly thought better of it. They were making her nervous. Had something happened that she wasn't aware of? Did the Prince dislike Feolan — or even worse, had he somehow requested her? That was foolish to even think. He didn't know her and Feolan was much too distinguished of a man to have done something to upset their people.

"General Matias suffered a strong loss a few months back during a battle against a band of Sanarik. He lost one of his commanders to their attack. Last evening, during the second wave of Namiren units, his first commander was severely injured. If General Matias leaves to accompany me to Siscal, he would then be leaving the entirety of his men under the watch of a lieutenant — and that is not proper procedure. We have been left with no choice but to place Feolan in charge of his men until General Matias can return from Siscal."

Leyna inhaled a sharp breath at the idea of leaving Feolan behind. He was her support on the battlefield. If anything were to happen in Siscal, it would place a significant burden upon her shoulders. Any men they took with them would be under her direct supervision. She was still in an observational phase of her position as lieutenant. They had not yet approved for her to order a full unit on her own. She wasn't sure she was prepared for such a responsibility. "What about Commander Laoter? Could he not take watch over them, given the circumstances with the Prince?"

"Feolan is the higher ranking officer. Protocol demands that he be the one given the charge. And as Commander Laoter is not Vor'shai, the next in line falls upon you." Thade's eyes gazed back at her evenly, adding a strange discomfort to her already thinning nerves at the thought of what he was saying.

The Prince would be under her care. A child. The fate of the royal heir in the hands of a girl who wasn't even old enough to look upon him in public society. But no one knew. And they couldn't. She would have to find a way to perform the task without second-guessing her abilities. They wouldn't ask her if they didn't believe in her.

Slowly she rose from the stool, masking her racing heart with a solemn expression on her face. It was worse than she imagined. It was more than commanding an entire unit by herself, but guarding the second most important person to her people.

She could do it. She had to tell herself that. In the end, she only hoped she could be convinced. "So you wish for me to stand guard at the Prince's side — and you worry he will take notice that I am female and become distracted?"

"Oh, we're not just worried. We know this for a fact," Feolan sighed, placing the parchment back down on the table lightly. "Not only would he notice, he is very attentive, despite what some may say about him. He will question your age the same way that we do. Now, we know you are within your appropriate rights to serve, but he might challenge that."

Leyna shifted uncomfortably at Feolan's words, her eyes darting over to Thade reflexively to see the look on his face. She didn't know how much Feolan was aware of, but given his statement, she could only assume he was oblivious to the truth. Had Thade lied to him about her? Or had he simply misled him by not disclosing his own concerns. Catching her frantic gaze, Thade met her eyes, keeping them locked with his own while lowering his head forward.

Even he was concerned about the Prince questioning it. It was one thing to dance around the truth with the other officers, but he couldn't avoid a direct confrontation with someone like that. He would be forced to answer truthfully — to a question he didn't know the answer to himself. If she was lucky, it might work to her favor... unless he was to then come to her for the truth. Maybe she could distract him with the fact that she was a woman...

Pressing her lips together tightly, she tried to contain the nervous laughter boiling up inside her at the thought. Her, seducing the Prince. It was so ludicrous that she could barely maintain her composure. She could feel the curious stares of both men, watching her strange display. Finally realizing she was doing a poor job at concealing her amusement, she covered her mouth with her hand, tilting her head away from them and to the ground.

They remained in silence until Leyna managed to repress her childish humor. She cleared her throat in embarrassment, straightening her shoulders proudly. "If I speak little and remain within full armor and uniform, it would prevent him from seeing my face. It is the only thing I can suggest outside of merely trusting me to behave maturely enough to avoid his suspicion of my age to such an extent."

"That there is the conundrum," Thade laughed pathetically. "I know that you are perfectly capable of conducting yourself in a mature and proper manner. In doing so, however, that may lead to the concern we have about him taking a different interest in you."

Leyna wrinkled her nose irritably. It was like they were describing the Prince to be a more powerful version of Teagan. She had handled him for years. She couldn't imagine Enaes being much more difficult to dismiss. "I will keep my helmet on at all times and, as you are my superior officer, I will be sure to remain in your sight so that he has no opportunity to whisk me away. Not that I think you really have anything to worry about."

"All that aside, we need you to understand the danger this task could involve," Feolan frowned. She could hear the concern in his voice. He was worried about her. Like a father sending his daughter out for the first time. "The Prince is fully aware of the threats that might face him in traveling outside of Tanispa. His only quality which might save him is the fact that so many people find him to be superficial and easily distracted. For all we know, the Ven'shal are biding their time for him to take over the throne so they can more easily overthrow it. But we cannot assume. Assassination attempts are always to be prepared for."

She heaved a sigh of frustration, growing tired of the lectures. Their concern was appreciated but, at the same time, she wished everyone would just let go of the fact that she was young. And female. Neither of those things should play any role in how they felt she would perform her duties. "Look. I understand your concerns, I really do. But you should know that I did not join the military under the false expectations that it would be a safe and cozy means of spending my life. Everything we do is dangerous, and I am prepared, at any moment, to die for the cause we fight for. I will do everything within my power to protect the Prince, as is what you are requesting of me, and that should be where the concerns end."

"Very well," Thade nodded, rapping the surface of the table with his knuckles. "If it is decided, Lieutenant, I suggest you start to gather your things. We will be leaving before the sun has a chance to sink much lower in the horizon."

Snapping to attention, Leyna gave a crisp salute, turning away from them both sharply. She dreaded the thought of the long journey back to Siscal, but there was more purpose to their trip than she'd felt before. For the first time, she was being acknowledged as an important member of the Vor'shai. Her eyes stung with unshed tears at the thought of how proud her mother would have been to see her now. Then again, if her mother was still around, she wouldn't be standing where she was.

Another conundrum, she thought. It was funny the way life worked. Doors opening that wouldn't have been available if not for a great tragedy. She had to wonder if the cost was truly worth it. In the end, it was too soon to know. Everything was dependent upon how she performed her duties in protecting the Prince. Perhaps then she would know if she was making the progress that she hoped for.

Chapter Five

Leyna was grateful for the warmer breeze of southern Siscal. Snow had begun to fall on their journey back, slowing their progress due to lack of visibility. They hadn't been expecting inclement weather for another few weeks. She hated the thought of leaving Feolan behind in the freezing temperatures, knowing she and Thade would be back in the comfort of the city. Although the south still experienced snow, the extent was never the same as the northern mountains, the temperature aided by the close proximity of the desert to the southwest.

They feared initially that they would miss Prince Enaes, hoping to meet with him and his associates at the border road of Tanispa and Siscal. Once they cleared the snow, they picked up their pace, pushing the horses to make up the lost time. General Matias parted ways with them at the city, leaving Thade and Leyna with a small unit to continue on toward Tanispa. It was best Enaes be greeted by his own kin.

Now there was little to do but wait. The unit was restless, anxious to get back on the road to the city. It was only on rare occasions they were able to return to the busy streets of Siscal. Their time there was much more pleasant in the comfort of their own homes or local inns than the cold, harsh arrangements of the camp.

"It is too bad Feolan could not have joined us," she said quietly, glancing over her shoulder at the soldiers lost in their own conversations. Since their discussion in Velorum, Leyna had been trying to think of a way to bring up the questions it raised in her mind about Thade. The casual privacy granted them while waiting felt an opportune time to approach it.

"He wanted to come. I felt bad denying him the occasion of seeing our Prince. Even to those who may not agree with his ways, it is still an honor to be in his presence."

"I am sure he will be ecstatic that he is able to head the military there, though. I cannot imagine what it must be like for him, knowing that his superior officer is younger than he is." She stared off down the road ahead of them, trying to appear nonchalant with her remark. Out of the corner of her eye, she could see him watching her, looking her over curiously.

He didn't respond right away. Leyna was nervous at first; afraid she'd struck a nerve with him that would cause him to be upset with her. Avoiding his eye, she continued to watch the road for any sign of the Prince's approach.

"What would make you believe he is older than I am?"

She smiled to herself, pleased that he'd taken the bait she laid out for him. "Oh, I have assumed that to be the case for some time. You really don't look to be that old."

"A bit bold on your part to question my age when you refuse to tell anyone your own," he mused, turning his head to follow her gaze off into the distance. "I think I should leave you to guess."

"You act like you are ashamed of your age," she chuckled. He was playing hard to get with his answer. Given his cleverness, she was beginning to doubt he would give her anything to go by to gather even an approximate number.

Thade laughed quietly, a slight smirk passing over his lips as he slowly turned his eyes back to her. "You amuse me, Leyna. I think you intend to trick me into saying something to imply whether or not your assumptions are correct, but I hope you do not have your heart set on it. I will make a deal with you that I will tell my age when you tell yours."

Cursing under her breath, she avoided his eyes. He appeared to be enjoying his victory over her, the smile on his face growing larger with every moment of silence that passed between them. Accepting her quiet defeat, she lifted her helmet up to her head, aware of the sound of approaching horses in the distance. "I think our Prince has arrived."

"I think you're right," he agreed. "Keep your helmet securely on and try to avoid speaking if at all possible. If all goes well, there will be plenty of opportunities to introduce you to him under better circumstances another time."

She pursed her lips together tightly at Thade before closing the bottom cover of her helmet, shielding her face from view aside from her eyes. The sound of his soft laughter reached her ears briefly until it was drowned out by the horses. Directing her attention forward, she called out a sharp command to the unit behind them, listening to the movement of armor creaking into place as the men hurried into formation.

A single white horse led the pack coming toward them, standing out amongst the dull browns and greys of the rest. From under the saddle was draped a long colorful fabric bearing the crest of the royal family, the intricate details visible in the vibrant threads of embroidery. The man atop the horse was equally as colorful in dress. His clothes were of the finest silks, shimmering in soft hues of gold under the sunlight. A heavy cape attached at both shoulders, hanging down his back in a regal fashion. His posture was stiff and proud, eyes staring straight ahead with a solemn expression until he caught sight of Thade.

"There he is!" the man exclaimed, holding up his right hand in greeting. "I thought you might think yourself too important to greet me personally, what with your minions scattered about the mountains."

"No one is more important than you, aside from your mother. I would never trust anyone else to your safety. Well —" Thade started. His voice trailed off thoughtfully, his arm lifting to motion toward Leyna with his hand. "Except for my lieutenant here, who will be charged with your protection while you are in Siscal. Your Highness, this is Lieutenant Evantine. Lieutenant — this is Prince Enaes."

Enaes looked her over with a scrutinizing gaze. Never once did his posture shift from its perfect poise, his eyes inquisitive. "Evantine? I was not aware the family had anyone outside of Tanispa. Iden keeps such a tight grip over everyone."

Afraid to respond, Leyna nodded her head in greeting, surprised by Enaes's familiarity with her family name. There were so many questions she wanted to ask him, but she knew it would be unwise to start speaking. Now was not the time to inquire about details of her past.

"Possibly a more distant relation," Thade replied absently, directing Enaes's attention back toward him. "It would be impossible to assume that Iden knows every single branch of the family line."

"I will have to ask him next time I am at court." With a single flick of his wrist, Enaes dismissed the men around him. They gave no hesitation to his request. In a clatter of hooves, they turned back on the road, heading in the direction they had come. Situating himself between Thade and Leyna, he began a casual pace forward, allowing them to move partially ahead of him to lead the way. "I should inquire about his daughter anyway. I have not seen her in years. She was always such a pretty little thing."

Thade was silent for a moment, seemingly unsure of how to respond. "His daughter's name escapes me. I cannot recall her face."

"Ah, what was it?" Enaes pondered. He stroked his chin thoughtfully, his bright silver eyes sparkling as the thought came to him. "Sarayi? I lose track of women."

At the sound of the name, Leyna felt her heart skip a beat in her chest. Sarayi. She hadn't heard the name spoken since the night her mother was murdered. To Leyna, the name had died alongside her. Inhaling sharply, she nearly choked on her own saliva, throwing herself into a fit of coughing to clear her throat.

"Lieutenant? Are you alright?"

A question. She didn't dare respond. Not while Enaes was already questioning about her family. If he knew her mother, there was a chance he might recognize her own name – and that would immediately give her away. No, she couldn't say anything. It was best Enaes not press any further about her family.

Waving her hand distractedly, she hoped Thade would accept that as a sign that she was fine. With a final cough, she cleared her throat of the last of the saliva, her breathing returning to normal once again.

"Your lieutenant is strangely silent. Are your men always like this?"

"Speak when spoken to," Thade nodded, his eyes lingering on Leyna with concern. "I like to travel in peace and quiet."

The conversation continued around her, but she was oblivious to everything being said. All she could think about was her mother. Iden. Her grandfather? Had he told no one of what happened to his daughter? She barely remembered herself what led to their departure for Mialan. Something involving her father. No. Not her father.

Another man. The sound of shouting echoed in her head at the memory. A man and woman yelling at one another. Her mother had been desperate for something. But for what?

"Damir, stop it!" Her mother's cries were frantic. Her father was in the bedroom with her, the sound of crashing furniture catching Leyna's ears from the hallway. Something bad had happened. Her father looked so angry when he came home. She had tried to run up to him, her arms out for a hug, but he pushed her away, knocking her down to the floor. She'd been too afraid to go after him. He was always violent when he was angry, and even she knew it was best to stay out of his way when he reached that point.

Slowly, she made her way down the hallway, worried about her mother. Her shouting was filled with fear that Leyna had never heard from her before. As she reached the end of the hall, her mother's figure stumbled out of the bedroom, slamming into the wall under the force of Damir's hands. "You whore! Did you not think I would find out?"

"I can explain. It is not what you might think," her mother cried, flinching at the closeness of Damir's fist against the wall near her head. "I was never unfaithful to you. . ."

"You had a child with another man. No, of course you weren't unfaithful!"

Leyna whimpered pathetically at the sight of her mother cowering at Damir's hands. She had never seen her father strike her mother before. It was frightening to think that he might. His rage was growing with every word he spoke, his eyes flaring brightly as he tried to control himself.

Hearing Leyna's voice, her father turned to face her, releasing his hold on the wall around her mother. The flash in his eyes sent chills down her spine, his gaze locked on hers with a menacing glare. He slowly moved toward her, his arms outstretched to grab at her shoulders.

"Damir, stop! Leave her alone!"

Her mother was shouting again. The words made little sense in her mind as her father gripped her arms tightly, his fingers digging into the skin of her slender limbs. Shaking her roughly, her neck snapped from front to back, tiny speckles of white shooting through Leyna's vision. "I am within my rights to kill her! I should have her head on a pike in my yard!"

An eerie shadow of black began to build up around his hands, his eyes dimming. As the inky dark-ness reached his hands, it started to wash over Leyna's arms, tingling uncomfortably along the skin where it touched. A flash of white light erupted from behind him. The force caused him to stumble forward, losing his grip on Leyna's arms, sending her toppling to the floor. In fear of what he might do if he got a hold of her again, she ran down the hallway, snatching her doll up from the living room floor and clutching it close to her chest by the door.

She wanted out of the house, but she didn't dare leave without her mother. There was nowhere for her to go. Unfaithful. Another word that didn't make sense to her. She didn't understand why her father was so angry. And even more frightening was the way his eyes had looked at her. There was nothing left in them of the man she had grown to know as her father. He looked evil to her. She believed he would have hurt her if she hadn't gotten away.

"Mommy!"

Strange noises were coming from the hallway. She wanted to go to her mother but she was too afraid to move. Her mother would come for her. And when she did, they would leave. Her mother would make sure she was safe.

At the sight of her mother limping around the corner from the hall, her heart jumped in her chest. Tears streamed down her mother's face as she swept Leyna into her arms, giving no pause to look back over her shoulder while pushing her way through the front door. From somewhere deep inside the house, she could still hear the sound of Damir's voice screaming at her to come back. Leyna knew they would never go back, though. The look on her mother's face was all she needed to know that home was not home anymore. With the rush of fear and confusion all coming together in her tiny head, she started to cry. It seemed the only thing left to do as her mother continued running into the night, leaving everything behind them.

"Leyna." Thade's voice cut into her reverie, her body shuddering as she was drawn from the frightening images in her mind. "I need you to be a little more attentive than this before I leave you to watch over the Prince."

Drawing in a sharp breath, she blinked in surprise at Thade, her head finally clear-ing to bring her back to the present. "I am sorry... I was —"

Around her, she could see the sky had darkened. Night had come while she was lost in the depths of her own thoughts, completely unaware of the bustle of soldiers moving around them to set up camp. She expected to see disappointment in Thade's eyes, but all that was visible was a deep concern peering hard into her own. Seeing the uncertainty in her gaze, he held out his hand from where he stood beside her horse, gesturing for her to climb down. "Come. I think we need to talk."

With Thade's help, she lowered herself back down to her feet, glancing hesitantly around the clearing. She recognized where they were, judging it to be another day's journey away from the city. By the lack of ready tents, she determined that she hadn't been lost in her thoughts for too long, the men only having had enough time to start spacing the ground to set up. "There is nowhere for us to speak. Perhaps we can have a meeting after we get to Siscal. I think for now I should focus on helping to get the tents set up."

"Tents are no longer your job. Come with me."

Leyna sighed heavily, knowing it was futile to argue with him. Following him through the clearing, he led her to the line of trees along the other side of the path, guiding her into a small forest. Moving into the cover of the branches and weeds, he leaned up against the trunk of a large tree, looking her over curiously as she opened the cover of her helmet to reveal her face.

"I am sorry. The Prince spoke a name that I recognized and I just – one thought led to another and I somehow lost myself in my own head. It will not happen again."

"The names of the Evantine family? You know of Iden?"

Leyna paused. She wasn't sure how to answer his question. To acknowledge her relation was a sure way to lead her into admitting everything. "I know of him, yes. But I really would rather not talk about him."

"I get the impression you are hiding something from me."

"Impression? Captain, with all due respect, I think we have established quite firmly that I have my secrets. All I can do is assure you that none of them will hinder my ability to perform the duties you assign to me." There was nothing else she could say to him. Now was not the time to disclose the details of her life. It was too great of a risk that someone would overhear them through the trees. She didn't trust the soldiers to mind their own business. She could just imagine the whispers already circulating at having seen Thade lead her off into the woods alone.

"I really wish you would tell me what is troubling you," he whispered, shaking his head dejectedly. She hated to see him like that, knowing it was her fault that he worried so much about her. It was just more stress for him on top of everything else he already had to focus on for the war.

Quietly, she lowered her eyes to the ground, opening her mouth to speak but quickly closing it once again. The sound of footsteps rang clearly to her ears from the path. She could tell by Thade's tensing muscles that he heard them as well, his eyes staring hard into the darkness to see who was approaching. "Identify yourself."

"Well, Captain, I do hate to intrude," Enaes's voice boomed confidently through the shadows. "I thought I heard a woman's voice out here. I did not realize you were entertaining company."

"Your Highness, I thought you would be remaining at the camp with the rest of the unit. It is not safe for you to be wandering about." Thade's voice revealed a hint of discomfort at Enaes's presence. With a purposeful step forward, he moved in front of Leyna, blocking her from view.

In a frantic motion, she closed the face cover of her helmet, concealing her features under the metal. Fidgeting nervously, she tried to arrange herself in a solid stance, not wanting to appear too casual with Thade. Enaes's opinion of her was still very important in order to keep his suspicions at bay.

"I was going to, but I thought it strange that you were sneaking off. Is there anything I should be aware of?"

Thade shook his head, his posture relaxing as Leyna moved back to his side. "We thought we heard something so we felt it best to investigate before we all retired for the night. Everything appears to be in order, however. Lieutenant, you are excused to return to set up camp."

Although her heart was racing, she was thankful for Enaes's intrusion. He conveniently distracted Thade from her. She knew it would only be a matter of time before he approached again, but until then, she was safe.

Giving a sharp salute, she pushed through the trees, making sure not to look Enaes in the eye while passing. All she could think about was getting back to camp and into the privacy of her tent. She could worry about Enaes again after she'd had some sleep.

The rooftops of the city were a welcome sight to Leyna. She couldn't wait to get off her horse and stretch her legs. Throughout the trip, Enaes had controlled the conversations, rambling on and on to Thade about the intricacies of court life. Thade's responses led Leyna to believe he was just as anxious to be back to the city as she was.

Upon approaching the city line, General Matias was awaiting them, his accompanying unit at the ready behind him. "Captain. Prince. I hope your journey was uneventful."

"Too uneventful," Enaes grumbled. "It was dreadfully dull and the unit is lacking in its number of female soldiers, so the scenery left a lot to be desired."

"We brought a minimal group of men back with us. Our female population of the unit was left behind in Velorum," Thade stated calmly, motioning for Leyna to position herself closer to Enaes. She did as she was instructed, keeping her eyes locked straight ahead.

It was frustrating that she was so limited in her actions. Everything she did had to be done just right to avoid appearing too feminine while speaking was completely out of the question. She had barely spoken in over two days and it made her want to scream out the frustrations she was holding inside.

Silently, she continued alongside the men, in awe over the number of citizens gathered on the streets to see the arrival of the Prince. They pushed and prodded through the crowd, craning their necks to see his face. He was enjoying every minute of it. His hand was raised in a graceful wave, giving his most charming smile to every woman that caught his eye. Despite the night they spent on the road, his black hair was perfectly smoothed back, tucked behind his sharply pointed ears. He looked like he had just stepped out of the palace doors rather than arriving after a week of travel on the road.

"Queen Nesperiti regrets that she is unable to attend this meeting, but Lord Dhiren will be present to discuss the views of Siscal," Matias explained, ignoring the growing crowd around them. "Quarters will be arranged for you so that you will be comfortable, however long you plan to remain in our city."

Up ahead, Leyna could see the Siscalian palace coming into view, looking in the distance at the other end of the main street. She had never been inside it before. The thought of even being close to it made her heart race excitedly. She wondered if the others felt the same or if it was merely her childish imagination making the experience bigger than it really was.

As they moved in closer to the palace, she was vaguely aware of Enaes saying something to Matias, but his words were nothing more than noise to her ears. The walls of the Siscalian Queen's home were tall and sturdy, surrounded by a heavy iron gate around the front. Guards were stationed at both sides of the entrance, calling out orders for them to be let through. Two other men from inside rushed to the gate, removing the lock, and opening it for them to pass.

The courtyard was extravagant in design. Every line of flowers around the central point was perfectly spaced and weeded, the soil moist from where the groundskeeper had just been by to water them. At a break in the path, a guard called for them to dismount, ushering their horses over to a post a short distance down the left fork.

Leyna's fidgeting was harder to conceal without the distraction of keeping control of her horse. All the nervous energy inside her filtered throughout her body, senses alert and ready for anything. It seemed unlikely any attacks would be able to get through the palace gates, but it was still an open area. It would be presumptuous to assume they were in the clear of danger.

Taking her place at Enaes's left side, she stood proudly, her chin thrust outward despite the heavy weight of the helmet on her head. Thade had taken up his position to Enaes's right, conversing quietly with Matias while they waited for Lord Dhiren to arrive. She was surprised he was not there already to greet them. It was bad form to make the royalty of an allied people wait.

She tried to block out the sounds of the voices around her. Joining in on the discussions would be detrimental, so she found it best to refrain from even tempting herself to offer her opinion. It allowed her a better position from which to observe the grounds.

It was a beautiful day. The sun was high in the sky, unobstructed by clouds. A gentle breeze wafted through the courtyard, carrying with it a soft warmth that she had missed while in Velorum. Temperatures were sure to drop within the coming weeks, but for now it was absolutely perfect. She only wished she could remove the metal from her head to feel the wind on her face.

The clear sky allowed Leyna to take in the details around her, noting every tiny shadow and color of the landscape. Something moving in the distance caught her attention, a wave of darkness following the object along its path. Quickly, it ducked behind a large stone pillar near the side-yard gate, disappearing from view.

She strained her eyes to see where the figure had gone. There was no trace of it anywhere; leaving her concerned that she'd imagined it. It seemed unlikely anything could have simply vanished into thin air. After several long moments, she saw the shadow again. But it couldn't be. It was coming from the same location where the first had appeared. This one moved in closer before disappearing behind another pillar, setting her nerves on edge even more than they already were.

Sanarik. The figure resembled the body structure of the Sanarik people. The mannerisms were even more fitting, stealthily maneuvering along the palace grounds. From atop the pillar where the first had disappeared, she could make out the vague outline of a bow tilted sideways over the surface, concealing it almost entirely from view. If she hadn't seen the figure take cover there, she wouldn't have noticed it against the dark stone.

Her body stiffened, her hand lowering to the sword at her waist. Enaes continued to talk idly with the others, paying her no attention as she took a step forward, shifting in closer to him. Another bow took shape against the top of the pillar near the second figure. They must have found some means of climbing the gate. She knew their bodies weren't tall enough to reach their current position without some assistance.

Slowly, the bows edged around the top, sliding over along the sides of the stone, still almost perfectly concealed. Time felt like it was crawling while her head raced with the image of what she was witnessing. Tracing the aim of the arrows with her eyes, she found them to be pointed more to her right, bypassing the Prince. Thade. They formed a perfect line to where the Captain stood in plain view of the weapons.

Her sword was drawn before she had a chance to call out a warning to the others. She could hear the snap of the bow string releasing the arrows, covering the short distance between Leyna and the Sanarik with startling speed. Knowing there wasn't enough time to cut off the attack, she shifted her weight, positioning herself between the archers and Thade, subconsciously aware of Enaes's voice shouting something from behind her.

Each arrow struck with a force unlike anything she had experienced before. Two. Three. Four. Where had the others come from? There wasn't time to think about it. The impact sent her toppling backward, her sword slipping from her hand as a searing pain shot through the right side of her chest, radiating all the way down into her fingers. The second struck her left arm, tearing through the leather of her armor to sink into the flesh of her bicep. A third came unexpectedly, piercing into her right side. A loud clang radiated from the fourth, the tip of the arrow smacking into her helmet, deflecting it harmlessly off to the side where she had been standing before.

Through the pain, she experienced a moment of panic at the feeling of her helmet pulling from her head under the force. *My face. Enaes will see me.* The foolishness of the thought would have caused her to laugh if the pain hadn't been so great. They were under attack. The last thing the Prince would be focused on was her face.

Her body never hit the ground. She anticipated the jarring force of the fall, but it never came. The courtyard blurred into a mass of colors in her peripheral vision, making it difficult to see anything that was going on. Swords could be heard scraping the sides of their scabbards from the other soldiers, preparing themselves for battle. Hands groped at her body, preventing her from falling. Someone was shouting her name. More hands were on her now. Her feet no longer touched the ground, the feeling of movement cutting through her confused senses. She was being carried somewhere. Everything hurt too much to care.

It burned. She had never felt a wound burn so much as these. It was like acid pouring over her skin and every movement caused by those carrying her only made it worse. Someone screamed. It didn't register in her head that it was her. She couldn't help the cries which escaped her. The pain intensified with every passing second until she didn't think she could take it any longer. She prayed for unconsciousness to overtake her but it refused, leaving her in agony, unable to escape.

"Help me get her on the table. We need to get these arrows out."

It sounded like Thade. She wanted to argue with them, to beg them to leave the arrows alone. It hurt too much already. If they tried to remove them, it would only exacerbate the wounds. She couldn't take much more.

Feminine hands placed a cool wet cloth over her forehead. Although it did nothing to ease the pain, it brought the room into slight focus, allowing her to make out the walls around her. She was inside the palace. The decorations were much too fine in quality to be anywhere else. Golden vases filled with colorful wildflowers adorned every wall, their fresh scent reaching Leyna's nostrils even through the distraction of the pain.

Thade was leaning over her, his features creased in concentration. He had a hold of the arrow in her chest, gripping it tightly in his hands. His free hand was pressed flat against her sternum, bracing her body to the table she was lying on. With a precise movement, he pulled the arrow from her skin, the sound of her screams echoing off the walls of the room around them.

"Captain, she looks far too young to be in this predicament…"

"Your Highness, I mean no disrespect, but now is not the time to be questioning my soldiers," Thade replied sternly, moving swiftly down to the arrow lodged in her side. The ease with which he had removed the one from her chest was comforting. It hadn't extended too deeply into her, its progress hindered by the heavy leather of her armor.

The agonizing pain shot through her abdomen unexpectedly, her breath catching in her throat before she could scream any more. Enaes continued to argue, his voice rising in an accusatory tone. "Why did you hide her identity from me? Is there some reason I could not know who you were placing at my side to trust my life to?"

In a fluid motion, Thade grabbed onto Enaes's hand, pressing it down against a towel that had been placed over the wound in Leyna's chest. "She just saved your life, so I suggest you focus on returning the favor and leave your questions for another time."

Return the favor. Was she dying? It felt a lot like what she imagined death to be. Absolutely miserable. Even with the arrows removed from her chest and side, the pain wouldn't abate. Her left arm felt completely numb. The arrow had lodged itself deeply into the bone. She didn't have to look at it to know it was broken. Through the pain, she racked her memory to figure out where the other arrows had come from. There had been two figures. Each one would have had to have a partner with them to boost them up to the top of the pillar. While she had been distracted with the ones up top, she had missed the two arming their weapons from below. A horrible oversight on her part. If there had been any more of them, they would all be dead right now.

A nurse was at her side, applying pressure to the wound near her abdomen. All Leyna could think about was getting back out to the others. She had to help them fight. The pain was making her delusional. "My sword. I need my sword."

"Leyna, stay still," Thade argued, pressing her back down onto the table. Struggling against Enaes and the nurse, she tried again to sit up, her eyes focused on the door. Her chest and side burned, coursing through her body. It was excruciatingly painful, her cries filling the room, though she continued to fight to get to her feet. Being careful not to apply too much pressure to her wounds, Thade pressed her firmly down once again, pinning her there securely under the weight of his body. "Stop! You are going to kill yourself if you keep moving."

She didn't want to die. There were too many things she hadn't had a chance to do. Reina. She needed to get back to Reina. She promised her she would come back for her. How could she do that if she was dead? It wasn't supposed to be like this. Nothing was the way it was supposed to be. Everything was all very wrong.

Time passed without her having any knowledge of it. She wasn't sure exactly when Thade released his hold on her shoulders, but she was very aware of him at her left side again, tearing at the sleeve of her jacket to get to the entry site of the arrow. "No — please don't," she begged, feeling the pressure of his hand preparing to pull the tip loose from the wound. It was in deep. The pain was already almost unbearable just from the weight of his hand on the slender piece of wood. If he did anything else with it, the pain was sure to only get worse.

Ignoring her pleading, Thade gave a hard tug, the sound of the arrow dislodging from her bone reaching her ears over the shrill shrieks of pain escaping her lips. There was no masking the agony she felt. For the first time in years, she gave in to the fact that she was still a child, the reality of her injuries frightening her beyond words. It didn't matter anymore who saw her cry. She was tired of pretending to be something she wasn't.

Shock was starting to set in. Through her panic, she recognized the symptoms of it. She'd witnessed many soldiers experience it from wounds they incurred during battle. It had been far easier to deal with when she was the one holding their hand to coax them through. On the other end of it, the feeling was far worse. She was vaguely aware of Thade's hand clasping hers, the wound numbing her left arm. His hand was lightly pressed against the side of her head, the familiar thrum of energy humming in her ears. She'd heard that sound before. After the Ven'shal attacked her, the same noise had been heard coming from Feolan while he fought against the dark magic filling her lungs. She couldn't see Thade's hand though. It hurt too much to move.

Whatever he was doing, she found her fatigue growing rapidly. His voice whispered gently into her ear, almost hypnotic in its tone. "Rest, Leyna. Everything will be alright. I just need you to close your eyes and try to sleep."

Sleep. She'd wanted to do that since before he tortured her with removing the arrows. It had been evading her successfully to that point, though now it felt more within her reach. Her mind was slowly growing blank, the sound of Thade's soft assurances drifting off until they were no longer words. It was like an angel breathing into her ear, silencing the confusion of her thoughts, and replacing them with the impenetrable dark of unconsciousness.

Her mother sat her down on the ground, inhaling a deep breath of the chilly evening air. They had come to a small, cozy looking home on the outskirts of town, the flickering light of candles dancing in the windows. She didn't recognize this place, but her mother seemed to know it very well. For the first time since they left home, there was a look of hope in her eyes.

Gently, she rapped on the door, listening and waiting for some response from inside. Footsteps. Someone was home. They were moving closer to the door, hesitating briefly before opening it just a crack to see who was there. "Who is it?"

It was a woman's voice. Her mother looked startled by the sound, but regained her composure quickly. "Is Lord Diah home?"

"Master Diah is preparing for bed. I suggest that you return in the morning when the hours are more suitable for visitation."

"No, please, you must understand. This is an emergency. If you tell him that Sarayi is here, he will know me," she pleaded, tugging Leyna in closer to her. A flower bush near the porch had caught her attention, her small legs starting to move in to investigate it until the pull of her mother's hand caused her to step back to the door.

The woman narrowed her eyes, staring hard at Sarayi before opening the door to allow them through. "Wait here. I will see what he wishes done with you."

To the mind of a child, the wait seemed forever until a man finally appeared from around the corner of a dark hallway off to the left. He was taller than she expected. His eyes were a deep shade of emerald green that glowed brilliantly in the dim candlelight. His features were sharp and elegant, the high cheek bones and chiseled jawline creating quite a sight in the flickering illumination. His dark hair was tousled, clearly having been pulled back in a rush with a few stray strands hanging down in front of his pointed ears. "Sarayi? My dear, what has happened?"

"It is Damir. He knows — about us. Or at least about Leyna."

"How did he find out?" Their tones were hushed, both of them sounding panicked but being careful not to be overheard by the others who might be inside the house.

"I am not certain. But when he came home today, he knew. I worry my father said something. He has been trying to anger him so that he might do something to prove he is practicing that sorcerous magic. I hate to think he would have intentionally put us at risk just to improve his own position."

"That sounds like your father," the man frowned. "Did he hurt you or Leyna?"

"He tried to kill her, but we got away. I am frightened, Aviden. He will seek to find us and kill us if we stay in Tanispa."

"I would take you in and protect you if I could, you know I would. But I am married now and have a small child of my own. I cannot put them in so much danger."

"What do I do, then? I do not want to die but I have to at least make sure Leyna is safe. She is your daughter as much as mine. Could you not at least take her in until I can find somewhere safe for us to go?" His daughter. What about the other man? None of this was making any sense.

Aviden was quiet for a moment. His emerald eyes were deep in thought, staring down at Leyna sadly. "I cannot take her in without my wife questioning." Silence again. Why was he looking at her like that? Wrinkling up her nose, she stuck her tongue out at him, moving in to lean against her mother's leg. "I have an idea. We need to get you on the road as quickly as possible to Mialan."

"What is there in Mialan?"

"I have a friend there by the name of Rohan. He is a good fighter and would be able to help protect you. His wife recently died in child birth and left him with a newborn and another daughter to raise. He will most likely be happy just to have someone there to help him care for the child. As long as no one is aware of where you are going, you should both be safe there."

"But how do we even get there —"

Grabbing a cloak from off a rack near the door, Aviden laid it over Sarayi's shoulders, pulling it up to cover her face. "Wait out back. I will have one of my men ready a horse for you. You need to be on the road tonight before Damir has a chance to follow your tracks."

He reached his hand out toward Sarayi, sliding it lightly under the fabric of the cloak. Using his thumb, he wiped a tear from her cheek, gazing at her sadly. They both stood in silence, their eyes never leaving the other's. Aviden leaned in toward her, kissing her tenderly before stepping back from her once again. Without a word, he turned away, disappearing into the back of the house as Sarayi gathered Leyna into her arms and carried her through the door into the night.

Her eyelids felt like rocks on her face, weighing down her head. They were swollen. She could tell by the way they impeded her vision, never fully opening. Every inch of her body ached and burned as if fire coursed through her veins. Her left arm was numb; the only sensation to let her know it was still attached was a dull tingle in the tips of her fingers. No matter how hard she tried, she couldn't move them, finding the entire limb useless to her.

The first instinct she had was to panic; but she lacked the energy to follow through. What could she possibly panic about anymore? The damage was done, though she wasn't quite sure of the extent of it. Opening her eyes took every ounce of energy left in her. She had to trust that the rest of her body was still intact without requiring visual confirmation. Just the thought of trying to lift her head made her want to cry from exhaustion.

Her memories were jumbled at first. She couldn't quite remember what had happened to cause her to be trapped on the bed she was lying in. She didn't even remember how she had gotten into the bed. The last thing she could recall was lying on a hard table with Thade lulling her to sleep. She'd been injured badly. There was no way to deny that, given the way her body continued to throb. Arrows. She had been shot. Prince Enaes had seen her face. Once again it struck her as odd that she was still worried about such a trivial detail. It had felt so important to her before, but now – nothing mattered anymore. She would be lucky if she survived her wounds, let alone being concerned about whether or not she would be allowed to continue on in the military.

It had been so long since she'd felt the soft cushion of a bed that it was uncomfortable to her. It molded too perfectly to the shape of her body. She had grown accustomed to the uneven rocky terrain of the mountains under her back. The blankets were painstakingly embroidered, the threads soft and silky against her skin. Smells of wildflowers wafted through the room to meet her nostrils, coming from all directions in the spacious area. The palace. She'd seen the flowers there when her injuries were being tended to. Somehow she was still there, tucked in gently to one of the massive beds in the guest quarters.

"It is best you do not move much." Thade's voice sounded strained, but she couldn't tell if it was genuine or if her ears were having difficulty registering his words. She wanted to see his face, but her inability to turn her head prevented her from doing so. All she could sense was that he was somewhere to her right, seated not far away.

She tried to speak, her voice catching in her throat before she could form any words. She was comforted by the thought that he was safe. A wave of relief passed through her to know the arrows intended for him had missed their mark. "Why does it still hurt so much? It was just a couple of arrows. I should not feel this sick."

A gentle pressure somewhere on her right arm indicated his hand resting against her skin. It felt detached… like it wasn't her body, but that she was watching him comfort her from somewhere outside, looking in on them. "Leyna – the tips of those arrows were laced with a very strong poison. The assassins did not come here with the intent of fighting a battle. Their goal was to kill their intended targets and then flee. I doubt they were anticipating a single person intercepting those blows."

"They were aiming at you –"

"I know." His voice grew quieter. The truth was difficult for him to admit. "It should be me lying here instead of you, Leyna."

"No," she coughed, her throat dry and scratchy from her long sleep. "No... if you were lying here, then I would have failed in my duties and I never would have been able to live with myself if that was so."

"And I am having a hard time living with myself knowing that I put you in a situation with so much risk of this happening. Why the gods are punishing you for my mistake, I am not sure I will ever understand."

"But the Prince... he is safe?"

Thade was quiet for a moment before responding, hanging his head with a soft sigh. "Yes, he is in good health. The arrow that would have struck him was blocked by your arm. The Vor'shai are in your debt more than you could possibly know."

"And the General?"

"He took a single arrow to the leg before the enemy was taken down. Their intentions were to assassinate him and me while we were separated from the unit. A good tactical strategy on their part in order to try and weaken our military. Thanks to you, they were killed before they could succeed."

Through her pain, she was amazed at the clarity with which her thoughts were coming. A sense of calm had settled over her. She was accepting the reality of it all. Her duties were completed and she had been successful. Even if she were to die, she would die honorably instead of merely slaughtered at the hands of the men who had so ruthlessly taken the life of her mother. Her own end would be with dignity, her deeds remembered by her people for years to come.

There was still something nagging at the back of her mind. The Sanarik had intended to take out the commanding officers. Were they directing their attacks only toward those in Siscal, or could Feolan be at risk back in Velorum? He and Laoter were still there... and they would be vulnerable to an attack with the units separated and still recovering from their last battle. "Commander Feolan – has there been any word from him in Velorum?"

"I sent a courier to him as soon as things cleared outside the palace," he assured her. "You have been asleep for several days, but plans have already begun to push into motion. General Matias has returned to Velorum and Commander Feolan and Laoter will be arriving back in Siscal City at any moment. Prince Enaes headed to Tanispa and will return in a day or two with the Tanispan General, Cadell. The royal family took the Sanarik attack quite personally and with their help, we will be pushing forward with a strong offensive plan until Queen Nesperiti is able to convince the Namiren King Galidric to discuss peace."

"General Matias is in good health?"

"His wound was more superficial than anything. A slight fever from the poison, but it did not strike deep enough to cause anything more."

So much had happened while she slept. It felt as though the entire world around her had changed without her knowing. The war would be more dangerous now, with the arrival of the Tanispan military. If the enemy forces were foolish enough to try and make their way into the Siscalian territory, they would be taken down quickly and easily with the addition of the Vor'shai among their arsenal. It would only be a matter of time before they would be forced off the mainland – but what next? Would Siscal's soldiers take chase to Namorea?

"I will be at Feolan's side when he arrives. There is little time to waste in our preparations if Prince Enaes will be here with his troops…"

"Leyna." She didn't like the tone of his voice. It was too somber, the way he said her name. "You will remain in bed, as you are. Prince Enaes is bringing his personal guards with him to Siscal. They have been given orders to see you safely to Tanispa and out of the line of danger that is sure to come upon this country before the month ends."

To Tanispa? She couldn't leave Siscal. Not yet. There was still so much that needed to be done, and Feolan would need her help on the field. She needed to get out of that bed and to her feet in order to prove to Thade that she was strong enough to fight. "There is nowhere for me to go in Tanispa. I refuse to leave the unit here. Please, have someone gather my things so that I can be presentable when Commander Feolan arrives."

"You will not be leaving this bed if it means I have to chain you down to it, Lieutenant. That is an order."

Order. She hated that word, but she knew that even without it, there was no way she was going to be getting out of bed any time soon. Chains wouldn't be necessary to keep her there. Her body still felt detached from her brain, the signals telling her limbs to move cutting short before they could reach the muscles. She was paralyzed and yet still could feel every inch of her veins burning with the fire of the poison in her system.

"Lady Faustine runs a home just outside of Sivaeria. It is a bit like a boarding school for young ladies, but she can only take in a few girls at a time and is widely sought after, especially among the nobility. Prince Enaes has arranged for you to be taken in there while you are recovering," Thade added, his voice softening once again to his usual calmer tone.

The Prince had arranged for her to go to school. She wanted to be upset, but her eerily calm mind wouldn't let her emotions veer toward anger. But did he know her true age? Was that the reason he pulled the strings he did for her, or was there something more to it than what Thade was telling her. "He knows, doesn't he?" she said quietly. No elaboration was needed for her question. He knew exactly what she referred to.

His head shook slowly, the movement barely noticeable in her peripheral vision where she continued to try and turn her eyes to face him. "No. Once the initial shock of the situation passed, he ceased to question your age. However, you are undoubtedly very young, without needing to know the true number of years that you have lived. The arrangement with Lady Faustine is his way of showing his gratitude for your actions. Most young Vor'shai women would die to get accepted into her home."

"Well then, my situation seems a bit cliché," Leyna chuckled, her laughter cutting short from the pain it caused in her chest. Her face contorted into an agonized grimace, gritting her teeth until the sensation subsided, returning to the dull ache which continued to plague her.

With a sympathetic gaze, Thade laughed quietly at the humor in her words, patting her arm gently with his hand. "Perhaps I should have worded that differently."

A click sounded from somewhere in the room, outside of her line of sight. It sounded like a door opening, the soft pressure of Thade's hand on her arm lifting as he rose to his feet. "Ah, Commander. You made it."

"We rode through the night in order to cover more ground. How is she? Has her condition stabilized?"

It felt good to hear Feolan's voice. She'd been worried about him since they left him in Velorum. Though she knew he was perfectly capable of handling himself in battle, she couldn't help but still be concerned. He and Thade had become such close friends that she didn't want to think about what it would be like if she lost them. She felt she was losing them anyway. Just in a different sense. They wouldn't be able to come with her to Tanispa. She would be starting all over again, just like she had done in Carpaen with Reina and in Siscal when she first met Thade. It felt like she would never find a place where she belonged that she wouldn't eventually end up uprooted from.

"The wounds have been treated and are no longer life threatening. We are just keeping an eye on the poison. I have managed to control it slightly, but there is so much. We are not certain if she is out of danger yet with that or not."

"My dear, Leyna – it has been eating me up inside since I heard what happened. It was supposed to be me guarding the Prince…"

"Oh, Feolan, stop," she sighed, smiling up at him. He leaned in to her, kissing her gently on the cheek in greeting. "This mess is no one's fault but my own. I cannot have everyone blaming themselves. You will all make me feel bad."

Noticing the limited movement available to her, Feolan remained standing at her side, his eyes gazing down at her sadly. "You will be impossible to replace, you know that right?"

"Then do not replace me. I will be back on my feet in no time to help you force the Namirens to surrender."

"A brave thought, Leyna, but I think you and I both know that won't be the case," he frowned, squeezing her limp fingers in his hand. It hurt her to admit he was right. When she was lying there, it was easy to convince herself it was nothing and that she would be fine. Hearing it spoken only made the truth that much harder, forcing her to realize she was far from fine. Recovery would be a slow and tedious process.

"If you absolutely must replace me, I only ask that you not promote Teagan. There would be no living with him if you did."

Feolan chuckled to himself, the mournful look remaining in his eyes despite the sound of his laughter. She could tell he still held himself responsible for her condition; and it hurt him even more to know that she would be leaving them. "I will not be replacing you, so you need not worry about Teagan's ego suffocating us all."

"You will both write to me at least. I think the thought of leaving my friends behind hurts more than this silly poison." It wasn't a lie, when she really thought about it. The truth was still sinking in. She refused to cry about it, though. They couldn't see her cry. If she had to leave, she wanted them to remember her as a strong soldier and not a weeping child. Their respect for her mattered more than anything when it came to her acceptance of herself.

"Of course," Feolan nodded. "But the nurse is telling me that it is time for you to rest. You take care of yourself, alright?"

She didn't want them to go. Even more, she didn't want to rest. She was tired of resting. Her body had been asleep for days and the last thing she wanted was to lose any more time to unconsciousness. "Do you have to leave? I am quite fine with having visitors for a bit longer."

Feolan's face disappeared from her vision, replaced a moment later with Thade's solemn eyes staring down at her worriedly. "We have to check on your wounds and perform another procedure to try and fight back the poison. The nurse is going to give you something which will make you drowsy and, if we are lucky, will help you to sleep so that the pain will not be quite so severe."

So that was why they were making him leave. They didn't want to have an audience during her torture. Something was being pressed against her lips, a warm thick liquid pouring into her mouth. The mixture was disgusting. She couldn't place the combination of herbs and other medicinal components that mingled on her tongue, nearly choking her from the lack of cooperation of her throat in swallowing. The muscles weren't functioning normally, taking significantly longer to recognize that the fluid needed to be taken into her body.

If she could have moved to vomit, she would have. The taste was repulsive. Her weighted limbs were the only thing which prevented her from spitting it back in the nurse's face. She lay there miserably, fighting the depression that tried to creep into the depths of her mind. She was tired of pain. All she wanted was to go to sleep and wake up in her tent to find that it had all been just a horrible nightmare.

Chapter Six

The ground was cool and uneven under her bare feet, the soft breeze blowing through the thin white fabric of her simple dress as if it wasn't even there, chilling her skin all over. The sleeves were short, ending just under the shoulder. A scar on her left arm was fully visible; a reminder of the fateful day that brought her to this moment. The moment where she would finally be accepted by her people as a woman.

She was dressed in the traditional gown worn by young girls during their rite of passage into adulthood. It was a plain garment, the threads free of any dyes or impurities, sewn by her own hands. The hem hung down to the ground, brushing lightly over the uncovered tops of her feet. A small satchel was draped over her shoulder, containing the only articles she was allowed to carry with her for the ritual. Lady Faustine had thoroughly gone over every detail of what Leyna would be required to do. It was important she not forget anything. She was already four years late for completing the ritual due to so many factors which had hindered her in her lessons.

Lady Faustine was very strict in that no girl under her care would be able to take the step into womanhood without having fully mastered everything she felt they needed before entering society. Leyna's lack of experience in etiquette and knowledge of the culture had been a large setback, preventing her from moving on with the other girls her age. Lady Faustine had been appalled by the habits she picked up while living on her own and detested even more the fact that she'd served in the military. She had been lacking in almost every social grace expected of a lady.

Leyna was still getting used to the feeling of wearing her hair around her shoulders. At home, Lady Faustine couldn't argue her preference of wearing it up, but for the ritual it was imperative it remain unadorned and natural. After so many years of neglecting it, the thick strands hung down below her waist in gentle waves, standing out against the stark white of her dress.

Her stomach rumbled hungrily. She had been disallowed from eating anything since the night before, the ritual requiring at least two full days of fasting. The first day had been spent finding her way through the Tanispan forests, seeking out the Lake of the Gods. There she would sit in silence until the morning had come.

The lake held an eerie glow under the moonlight, the soft ripples floating lightly across the surface under the gentle breeze. Lowering her satchel onto the soft grass, she slowly knelt at the water line, preparing herself for the long night. It was a test of patience. Once there, she could not move, or make any sound to disturb the scene around her. To do so would risk the ire of the gods.

Throughout the night she wondered how anyone could ever know if the ritual had been performed correctly. Being so far away from the city of Sivaeria, no one would be aware if the girl failed to keep still or uttered even the slightest breath of noise. But the gods would know. And if the girl attempted to continue the ritual after having failed the first task, it was possible that it could end poorly for her. She had heard stories of young girls who never returned from their journey. No one could ever truly say what happened to them. Leyna had to wonder if the stories were nothing but tales thought up to frighten girls into following every direction precisely in fear of falling prey to the dangers of disobeying.

By the time the sun started to rise above the horizon, every inch of her body ached, desperate to move. She held her posture perfectly still until the sun was fully visible in the sky, a sigh of relief escaping her lips to know that the first task was complete.

Reaching down to her side, she lifted the flap of her satchel, drawing out a small ceremonial dagger. Pressing her hair between her left thumb and index finger, she brought the blade across it in a single cut. It was finely sharpened, slicing easily through the delicate strands. Content with the outcome, she placed the dagger on top of the satchel, keeping it ready for when she might need it again.

Carefully, she moved the lock of hair over to the palm of her right hand. Concentrating the internal energy of her body toward it, she envisioned it engulfed in flames over her skin. The fire came easily. Of all the lessons Lady Faustine taught her, it was the utilization of the Vor'shai magic which had come most naturally. For someone who had been so oblivious to its existence for so many years, her mind was surprisingly in tune with it, able to bend and shape it to her will with minimal effort. She watched the hair go up in smoke, the flames bursting from her palm in a bright flash before dissipating, leaving only ashes behind.

Picking up the dagger again, she pressed the tip of it into the flat of her right index finger until a spot of blood appeared over her pale skin. In a short motion, she pulled the blade down along the surface, creating a half-inch cut across her finger. Gathering the blood onto the metal, she wiped it against the ashes in her palm, mingling the remains of the hair with the thick, sticky substance.

She quietly incanted a prayer to the gods, offering up her sacrifice to them. Upon finishing, she traced a circle into the ground with the dagger, placing the blood soaked ashes of her hair in the center. Cupping her hands, she pushed the dirt inside the circle over the mixture, burying it under the moist earth.

As she rose to her feet, particles of grass and soil stuck to her dress, marring the garment in a perfect outline of where her knees had rested upon it. The easy part was done. Only one last task stood in her way of becoming a woman, and it was the most difficult of all. She believed that if any of the stories had been true about the young girls who failed to please the gods, it was the lake which had claimed them.

Holding her head up high, she took a small step into the cool water. Her toes sank into the moist sand of the bottom. The water was clear and clean, allowing her to see down to where her feet disappeared under the ground. She drew in a deep breath, preparing herself for what was to come, moving slowly out to the center of the lake. She was surprised to find the deepest point came up no further than her chest, giving her a brief reassurance that she would be safe before she knelt down, submerging her head completely under the surface.

Lady Faustine had warned that it was the mind which could overpower a young girl during this task. The mind could cause the body to go into a panic before any trust could be shown to the gods. Everything in nature was filled with energy, including the waters of the lake. It was with a peaceful mind that she had to show faith in the gods and trust that they would not allow the water to take her life. This was a holy place. The location where her ancestors had come to perform the same rite over thousands of years. A piece of their spirit was considered to be left within the depths of the water as a gift to the gods, remaining behind to guide her.

She saw how easily panic could destroy everything. Her lungs burned for oxygen, which she purposely deprived herself of. A nagging part of her mind told her that if she just stood up, the pain would go away. But she couldn't. She had to do this; though she wasn't entirely sure what to expect if she were to succeed. It seemed hopeless...

lacking in any direction for her to follow to know if she had properly received the approval of the gods.

Clearing her mind, she choked back on her fear of drowning in the shallow lake. She tried to picture herself above the water, breathing the fresh air into her lungs. Familiar faces flashed before her eyes, gazing back at her with gentle expressions. She could see her mother staring at her solemnly through her deep blue eyes. *Is this what it feels like when you die?* A soft pressure could be felt against her shoulders, like a pair of hands standing behind her, holding her comfortingly. The burning in her lungs started to ease, her mind envisioning the water pushing away from her body. It took several moments before she realized she was breathing again, the cool forest air rushing into her desperate lungs.

Slowly, she opened her eyes, afraid of doing anything that would ruin it all. Gasping quietly, she found the water had parted, held in place by an invisible barrier powered by the peaceful urging of her mind. She could still feel the pressure of the hands upon her shoulders, guiding her back to her feet. It all felt like a dream. She feared she had lost consciousness under the water and that none of what she could see was real.

With cautious steps she made her way back toward the shore. The barrier protecting her from the water followed until she reached dry land, the last of the lake filling in behind her. She had passed — yet she felt little difference aside from the biting cold of the cool air blowing against her wet dress. Had it really been her mother? It all felt so real. Confusion at how it had even come to pass made it hard to believe that she'd ever really seen anything. There was no denying that she'd felt something, though. The thought of it being her mother brought her hope after so many years. Her mother's spirit was still with her, the energy of her life force returned to the earth after death.

In a daze, she reached down to gather up the ceremonial dagger from the ground, wiping the blade in the grass before placing it back into the satchel. She had come a long way over the years. It was hard to believe it had been eleven years since she celebrated her birthday at the tavern in Siscal, surrounded by her friends in a drunken stupor. Although she was grateful for the education that had been given to her, she missed the life she had back then. A life where no one cared if she put her elbows on the table or ate her food with her fingers.

As she set off into the woods toward home, she found herself lost in the memories of the events that brought her to where she was now. It had taken the Eykanua orphanage until only recently to respond to the letters she'd been sending almost religiously in attempts to make contact with Reina. They told her that Reina left them when she turned nineteen, giving no details about where she was heading. It hit Leyna deeply in her heart to think that Reina never wrote her back. The head of the orphanage assured her that every letter had been personally delivered into Reina's hands. So why had she chosen to leave Leyna wondering if her messages were being received? It was such a cruel thing for her to have done. But it was hard to know what Reina was thinking. She probably believed Leyna had abandoned her after so many years.

Occasionally, she still received letters from Feolan and Thade back in Siscal. Lady Faustine would collect them until finally she would break down and allow Leyna to read them. She felt it was inappropriate for men to communicate with a girl of her age. Not yet a woman, and still within the ages where she was not to be seen in society. Every stack of letters had been met with the same lecture about how she should toss them into the fire and disallow Leyna from reading their "ungentlemanly correspondence."

In their writing, they celebrated their victory over the Namirens. The final battles had taken them to Namorea for the better part of a year before King Galidric agreed to discuss peace. Upon returning to Siscal, they remained on watch for stubborn Sanarik soldiers who would still sneak into the city and attempt to gain revenge for the loss of their people. It took over five years before Queen Nesperiti proclaimed the time of war to be over, relieving Thade and Feolan of their duties for the time.

For his exemplary service and performance in the war, Queen Vorsila granted Thade the position of Consul in Siscal, acting as her voice within the borders of their neighboring country. When she last heard from Feolan, he was accepting a position as Thade's assistant, safely removing both of them from the dangers of military life. Leyna rested easier knowing that her friends were safe, even if she couldn't know what fate had befallen Reina.

By the time she reached the carriage waiting for her outside the forest, her feet were sore and aching from the sticks and jagged rocks she stepped on throughout her journey. She felt weak from lack of food and water over the past two days. Food wouldn't be available to her again until morning at the earliest. Lady Faustine would make sure that the fasting period was completed properly.

The trip back home would be long enough to take her through most of the night. She was too excited about having successfully performed the rite to even think about sleeping; not that she was allowed to.

It wasn't until the sun started to lighten the horizon on a new day that her eyes began to feel heavy, reminded of how physically exhausted she was. Sunrise was nearly upon her by the time they reached the path of the quaint little house. A small puff of smoke from the chimney came as a welcoming sight to Leyna's tired and frozen body. Rustling noises could be heard coming from a tiny building in the back where the newly accepted girls to Lady Faustine's care slept. It was around the time they would be getting up, preparing themselves for the morning meal in the main house.

Food no longer sounded appetizing. Her stomach ached from hunger but the desire to sleep overpowered even her need for sustenance. It took too much effort to lift her feet as she walked toward the front door of the house, allowing them to drag behind her loudly over the gravel. Such an unladylike behavior, but she didn't care. She was home. Lady Faustine could lecture her after she had some sleep.

Before she could open the door, it swung inward, revealing the face of a young woman staring back at her excitedly. Her dark emerald green eyes sparkled in the morning light with dark circles hanging heavily underneath them from lack of sleep. Her long black hair was tousled about her head, hanging in a disheveled fashion over one side of her face. "Leyna! You made it!"

"Maeri, you did not wait up for me all night, I hope?" she chuckled, accepting the woman's warm embrace. "I told you to get some sleep and that I would be just fine. Now here I am — just fine — and you look a mess."

"Yes, well, if anything happened to you, I would be left here all alone with these snobby new girls and I wouldn't be able to bear it."

"They will improve over time," Leyna smiled, brushing the hair away from Maeri's face. "You are an absolute wreck. And after all your efforts to be in such perfect shape for the ball this weekend."

At Leyna's words, Maeri gasped in horror, her hands flying up to her face. "Oh, no! I completely forgot! What am I going to do? The Prince is going to be there and I can't have him seeing me like this."

"Relax, Maeri. I was teasing. You still have three days, so unless he is showing up at our doorstep in the next ten minutes, you will look quite alright by the time of the ball. Not that he will see your face anyway. It is a masque. The entire purpose is to hide your features or, in this case, your puffy eyes, from view."

"Speaking of hiding —" Maeri started, her eyes squinting to look Leyna over carefully. "This deliciously sexy man came by yesterday looking for you. Lady Faustine was beside herself. I managed to stop drooling long enough to tell him that you were unavailable but that I would pass along that he stopped in."

Through her laughter, Leyna tried to hide her confusion, unable to think of who would have known to even look for her there. Only three people were aware, all of which were men, but none of which seemed likely to show up at her door. "In order to know who it was, I will need a better descriptive than 'deliciously sexy.' With you, that image leaves far too many options for who it might be."

"Short hair... and the most gorgeous silver eyes. Very noble looking. Oh, and muscles that a woman could only fantasize about. He said he just wanted to wish you a happy birthday but, I tell you, it wasn't even my birthday and he made it a happy day for me." Maeri fanned her face daintily with her hand, giving a quick wink at Leyna as she finally stepped out of the doorway to let her inside. "My question then is... how do you know this man? Have you been keeping something from me?"

Leyna's heart sank in her chest at the thought of who Maeri was describing. Thade. He had remembered her birthday and came all the way to Tanispa to see her. Why could she not have been allowed to perform the rites last year? How miserably perfect that Lady Faustine would choose the one birthday for her to go that Thade was free to make the trip. She hadn't seen him in over a decade. It made her wonder if she would even recognize him if they were to cross paths. It would be hard enough to picture him without his Captain's uniform.

"No, I am not hiding anything. He is just an old friend that I have not seen in years."

"Well, he is welcome to come by and visit again any time," Maeri smiled, her tone growing softer at the sight of the distant look on Leyna's face. "Is something wrong?"

Shaking her head, Leyna pushed the door closed behind her, using it to support the weight of her body against her back. "No, I am just tired. With how I am feeling, if I even attend, I suspect I will be hiding my own red and puffy eyes under my mask."

"There is no 'if you attend' nonsense. You are going," Maeri stated flatly, help-ing Leyna away from the door. Quietly, they made their way through the small foyer, moving down a darkened hallway near the back. The main house only had five bed-rooms aside from Lady Faustine's quarters, reserved for only those girls whom Faustine believed to be worthy of being a part of her home. It was typically her students who had shown the most improvement and had attained the honor of adulthood that were allowed to live under Lady Faustine's roof. Leyna had been an exception from the start, given the circumstances of her arrival. She believed that was the reason why Lady Faus-tine had been so hard on her over the years, pushing her to break the habits of her past.

Finding their way into the room they shared, Leyna sat down on the floor, not wanting to risk getting any stray dirt on her bed. Maeri pulled a blanket from out of the closet, placing it lightly around Leyna's shoulders as she knelt down in front of her with a serious expression passing over her gentle features. "The Queen's masque is the most important social event you will ever be invited to. Even if you are deathly ill, we will find a way to make sure you are standing inside her palace. It is also the biggest test of Lady Faustine's teachings, so you know she will insist you go as well. She has had her eligible students present at every party the Queen has held for more than a hundred years."

None of Maeri's words came as a surprise to Leyna. She was fully aware of the sig-nificance of the event. Every few years Queen Vorsila hosted a masquerade ball which was only open to the highest members of her court and staff. Those within the military that had earned high recognition from Her Majesty would also be allowed within the palace walls and only a select other few were granted invitations.

It had once been open to a larger list of guests without the requirement of masks, but the doors had been closed off to the majority of the city population after Prince Ehren had been killed. Since then it was known to be the only public event where the youngest Prince could be seen with his family, though their faces were concealed in order to grant protection against their enemies learning the appearance of the youngest royal heir. An invitation was highly sought after, especially for any young girl hoping to step into higher society.

"I know, Maeri," she whispered quietly. She was too tired to think about such things right now. There would be plenty of time to get her mind prepared for the ball after she had some sleep and a warm meal. "I will go. When we wake up, though, I ask that you will help me find what I am going to wear. It is, after all, my first social event after being released as a lady into the public eye. I need to make sure I look the part."

Leyna couldn't even recognize herself in the reflection staring back at her from the mirror. In her mind, she was still the same little girl who tried so hard to make herself look like a woman before heading off on her own through the Carpaen desert to Siscal. The difference was that she no longer needed stuffing.

Maeri had dressed her in an elegant gown of deep blue silk. Leyna was too self-conscious about the scars on her body to wear anything revealing, opting for longer sleeves and a high neckline edged in a delicate floral lace. Her corset was uncomfortably tight, but Maeri assured her it fit the way the garment was intended to be worn, accentuating the curves of her hips and slender waist. The thick layers of skirts flowed down and out from under a silver chain wrapped around her hips. Fabric draped gracefully to the floor, hemmed perfectly to rest over her matching slippers.

"The masque is all about accessories," Maeri explained excitedly, bustling about the room from drawer to drawer in search of something. Leyna knew this ball would be Maeri's second time in attendance, so she trusted her advice to make sure that she wouldn't make a fool of herself.

With a breath of relief she pulled a pair of gloves from a small box on the dresser. Leyna eyed them curiously before accepting them from Maeri's outstretched hands, hating the idea of covering herself up any more. By the time she was finished, she feared not a single patch of skin would be visible. The only thing she liked about the thought was how difficult it would be for anyone to recognize who she was if she made any mistakes.

She slowly slid the gloves over her hands, tucking the edge underneath the lace trim of her sleeves. Maeri had insisted that her hair be left long, decorating it with sprigs of brightly colored blue wildflowers to bring out the color of her eyes. "I would tell you to pinch your cheeks a little to get some color to your face, but the mask will make that unnecessary."

"This outfit is impossible to breathe in. How am I supposed to walk around the ball and pretend to be lady-like when I am so focused on trying to get air into my lungs?"

"That is the biggest trick. I think we should place bets on which one of us will last the longest without fainting," Maeri chuckled. The strained look in her own eyes made Leyna wonder if she was really speaking in jest. "The carriage is already out front, so we need to move quickly."

Maeri looked radiant in her deep emerald gown, the sweetheart neckline adorned with tiny golden charms in the shapes of various flowers. Her sleeves were shorter and hung low off her shoulders, revealing her pale flawless skin against the rich color of the fabric. She had chosen to wear her hair up, with a matching flower placed elegantly amongst her long black locks, a single strand curled and hanging gracefully along the side of her face.

She wasn't ready for this. Her heart raced with anxiety over all the things that could happen. Images of her stepping from the carriage and falling on her face played over and over in her head until she thought she might scream, her body twisting to face the feathered mask staring up at her from the bed. *Ah, you are the only savior I have tonight.* Snatching it up, she brought it down over her face, covering all but her jaw line and painted lips. Tall feathers decorated the pieces extending out above the eyes, connecting to several long strands of ribbons which hung down in front of her ears to her shoulders. She would be unidentifiable by simply her eyes and lips. She just had to get through the night without losing the protection of her mask.

Whisking her away down the hall to the foyer, Maeri only came to a pause under the scrutinizing gaze of Lady Faustine who was standing at the doorway. Her dress was far less elaborate than those of Maeri and Leyna, the fabric in a dull maroon, lacking any special decoration. Even with her corset done up, her matronly figure was still prominent, dark brown hair pulled tightly back away from her plump face. "You girls stop right there and let me take a look at you."

With Lady Faustine's eyes giving them a final look over, the girlish excitement inside started to take over above all of her concerns. She was going to a ball. And at the royal palace, no less. When she was younger, such a thought had seemed impossible – and after her injuries in Siscal, it somehow managed to feel even further out of her reach. But here she was. Dressed in the finest gown she'd ever set eyes upon, and one that fit her, unlike the borrowed dress she still was determined to return to Cady in Carpaen.

"I suppose it will do," Faustine nodded, her nose scrunched up disapprovingly. "Not enough time to fix everything. Just remember… Speak only when spoken to, and in soft, quiet tones. Leyna, this is not one of your war parties. Mind your manners."

"Of course, Ma'am," she replied. For some reason she found Lady Faustine's comment more amusing than it should have been. It had been intended as an insult toward her because of her past, but through her fluttering stomach she couldn't be offended by it. All of that was in the past. This was her chance to start anew.

Giving Leyna one last disappointed gaze, Faustine turned toward the door, leading them out into the cool evening air. Her carriage was waiting for them, the coachman standing at the ready to help them inside. Once situated, Leyna tried to hold back her nervous fidgeting, knowing it would only lead to another lecture from Faustine. Somehow she and Maeri managed to keep their lips closed throughout the trip to the palace, too afraid of saying something that would spark further upset with Faustine.

As Leyna stepped from the carriage, the sight of the palace took her breath away. Frozen in place, she gazed up at it, lost in the beauty that she saw there until a prod between her shoulder blades from Faustine signaled her to start moving again. The palace was surrounded on all sides by a forest, the domes of the roof poking out over the trees into the dark evening sky. It looked like something out of a fairy tale, the moss and ivy creeping up the stone walls to the tower windows. Even with the overgrown wildlife that clung to it, somehow it still looked perfectly tended, almost as though the clinging vines had been placed there intentionally for decoration.

It was massive next to the Siscalian palace; and far older as well. There was no comparison between the two. It was no wonder the Tanispan royalty was so well-revered among the other countries. The history of their people spanned back thousands of years, and it could be seen by simply looking upon their home. "Are you going to go inside, girl, or are you going to volunteer as a lawn ornament for the party?"

Tearing her eyes away from the palace, Leyna lowered her gaze to the ground, falling into step beside Faustine. It was best not to respond to her statement. She recognized the lady's rhetorical tone, dripping with her usual disapproval.

Faustine hurried them through the foyer, flashing a shiny embossed piece of parchment at one of the guards. He nodded to them, granting them entrance to a large arched doorway to the left, opening up into an area more spacious than Leyna expected.

The grand ballroom. It was lavishly decorated, the floor already filling with people. She found herself hypnotized by the array of masks staring back at her around the room, hiding the faces of Tanispa's most elite society.

She lagged behind at the entrance to the room. Her hope was to somehow separate herself from Lady Faustine so that she might have a chance at enjoying the party. So long as she was at her side, it would be a rather dull evening of trying to impress her with the lady-like charms that Faustine never failed to stress to the girls. The goal of many young students was to be introduced to society and be married off to a suitable man of position within the city. Leyna failed to see how any woman could catch the eye of such a man with Faustine's stern gaze constantly guarding over them.

A woman tapped Faustine on the arm, her face hidden behind a mass of velvet and feathers. Leyna couldn't hear what was being discussed, but Faustine looked interested, distracting her attention away from the girls. Gently, Leyna tugged on Maeri's arm, hissing a quiet signal for her to turn around. She looked surprised at first before her eyes lit up excitedly, ducking back into the crowd next to Leyna. "You do realize she is going to have our wrists smacked but good for losing her."

"Five minutes without her hawkish eyes will make the pain worth it," Leyna sighed, craning her neck to look around the room. Finding Faustine still engrossed in her conversation, Leyna moved them across the floor, mingling among the crowd to blend in with the horde of people now spilling in from the entranceway.

By the door, she caught sight of a man standing there, his style of dress seeming to announce that he was of some high position above the others surrounding him. His mask was of a simple design, lacking the elaborate featherwork of so many others. It was gold, matching the color of the insignia worn over his right breast. A pair of bright grey eyes gazed through the holes in the mask, coming to rest on Leyna curiously. She ducked her head down by Maeri's shoulder, giggling nervously as she turned away from his watchful gaze.

"We have not been here more than a few minutes and you are already getting us into trouble," Maeri grinned, turning away from the door with Leyna. "Do you know that man or are you simply that good at flirting with your eyes?"

"I was not flirting. I was staring — which I suppose is worse," Leyna blushed. Covering her face with her hand, she tried to avoid making eye contact with anyone else, surprised at how easy it was to be seen in a crowd where no one could see each other's face. She had expected to blend in — to be invisible to everyone there.

A gentle touch on her left shoulder sent her heart into a panicked rush, her head lifting quickly from her huddle with Maeri. *Relax*, she told herself. *You are behind a mask. It should be easier to talk your way out of this when he can't see you.*

Keeping her shoulders back and her body rigid, she slowly turned to see who was behind her. Part of her expected to see Faustine's eyes glaring back at her angrily for having run off. Instead, she found herself staring directly into the grey eyes she'd seen from across the room, his head tilted inquisitively as if trying to picture her face from behind her mask. "Pardon my intrusion, Miss, but you caught my eye when I came in."

"Don't say anything," Maeri whispered into her ear. "Faustine will birth kittens if she sees you speaking to anyone without her here."

"Nonsense, Maeri," she smiled, sinking into a deep curtsy before the man. Her words were soft, aimed for only Maeri to hear, but still loud enough for the man to be aware of their conversation. "If Lady Faustine birthed kittens every time I did something wrong, we would be up to our ears in them by now."

Leyna grabbed onto Maeri's arm, twisting her around to face the grey-eyed man. His lips were curled back in an amused smile, taking in their antics with a lighter attitude than she expected from someone within the court. Barely maintaining her balance from Leyna's pull, Maeri bobbed in an awkward curtsy, her eyes cast nervously to the floor.

His voice sounded familiar. It brought back memories in her mind that had long since been pushed into the depths of her subconscious. Looking him over closely, she envisioned his mask replaced by a thick helmet, his fine garments exchanged for the drab threads of the Siscalian military uniform. It was then that she caught sight of the details in the insignia on his chest. There was no mistaking the man standing there before her. "My goodness, Commander. You clean up better than I do."

"Could it really be my long lost lieutenant?" he smiled, holding his arms out to her shoulders. Stepping back, he took in her appearance, shaking his head in disbelief. "The gown suits you, I say. You are very well disguised. I would have completely overlooked you if my curiosity had not gotten the better of me."

"Well, to be honest, I am hoping my identity goes no further than the two of us. As far as anyone else need be concerned, I am not here."

"Yes, I dare say it would be a wise decision to not let Prince Enaes discover who you are," Feolan nodded. A loud trumpet sounding from the foyer cut him short, his head perking up attentively. In a sharp shift of his weight, he stepped off to Leyna's side, leaving the main walkway into the ballroom open as everyone moved out of the way. "It is too bad Thade was unable to make it. He was disappointed that he missed you on his recent visit."

Her heart sank at his words, though she wasn't entirely sure why it affected her the way it did to know that Thade wasn't present. After so long, she hoped to be reunited with them both. It had seemed a guarantee that they would be in attendance to honor the Queen after their raise in status.

The crowd had grown more hushed since the trumpet was heard. At first, there was no sign of anything changing within the hall that would imply the reason for the fanfare. She slowly became aware of the crowd separating into two lines on either side of the entrance arch, their eyes gazing anxiously toward the door. "What is going on?" she whispered, hoping someone near her would be able to answer her question.

"Someone of the royal family is arriving," Maeri replied quietly, leaning in close to Leyna's ear. "If it is Queen Vorsila, we are to immediately curtsy and remain with our eyes and bodies lowered to the ground until she has passed. If it is one of her sons, it is customary to curtsy, but the available girls tend to offer out their hands in hopes of one taking notice of them."

"What exactly do you mean by take notice of them?"

Maeri grinned deviously from under her mask. "To ask them to dance, silly. If upon entering, the Prince chooses your hand and kisses the back of it, he has picked you to be one of his partners for a dance throughout the evening. Prince Enaes is known to choose several girls. The young Prince, if the last ball was any indication of his normal behavior, he ignored all the ladies and never danced a single song or spoke a word to anyone."

In the archway she could see the figure of a man come into view. His face was completely obscured by a fanciful mask covering all but the lips and chin. It shimmered in shades of oranges and reds with a hint of gold, giving the illusion of a radiant fire molded of leather across his features. The edges splayed outward in carefully designed tendrils, starting back near his ears from where it molded to his cheeks and forehead. The piece which attached it to his head covered his hair from view, leaving nothing to assist the imagination in picturing his true form.

His clothing was plainer than she remembered having seen worn by Prince Enaes, opting for a more simple white shirt with perfectly tailored black trousers. The only design on his garments which gave away their fine make was the shine of the silk used to create it, the buttons keeping the front together made with silver and set in the middle with gemstones to match the fiery shades of his mask.

The only sound that could be heard throughout the ballroom was the rustle of fabric as the guests lowered to their knees, the ladies sinking into deep curtsies with their heads bowed and their hands daintily held out in front of them. Following their lead, Leyna dipped down to her knee, folding her hands lightly over her leg. She had no desire to offer herself like some prize to the royal men. It promised only a single dance to spend twirling about aimlessly on the floor, after which he would never remember her face — and more than likely never learn her name.

"Hold out your hand," Maeri hissed, nudging her sharply with her elbow. "Lady Faustine is watching you and she is nearly ready to leap from her skin."

Leyna ignored her. The whispers became more and more insistent until Maeri finally gave up, her shoulders bowing forward in defeat while offering out her own hand to the center of the aisle. Staring through her eyelashes, Leyna peered up at the man, praying he would not notice her upturned gaze from under her own bowed head. He was moving much more swiftly through the room than she expected of a prince. At his passing, the girls started to retract their hands, his eyes barely taking note of their presence.

Why did it feel like it was taking forever for him to pass by her? For the pace he was using, she thought he would be by them in no time, allowing her to rise back to her feet and resume her idle chatter. As he drew nearer, she let her eyes drop back to the floor, watching his boots move across the tiles in front of her. Upon reaching a few steps beyond Maeri, he came to a stop, the crowd remaining silent in anticipation of whom he would choose.

Go away. She willed him to pick some other girl and leave her be. Maybe he had somehow been enticed by Maeri. She was a lovely young woman and certainly capable of catching the attention of any man in the room... even with her features hidden. It took only a moment before she became keenly aware of the boots stepping in front of her directly, the man's presence looming over her.

Her heart pounded in her chest. She should have just listened to Maeri and held out her hand. The last thing she wanted was to be chastised publicly in front of the most important people in the country. And over something so foolish. So what if she didn't want to dance? They shouldn't take it so personally.

He was kneeling in front of her. The Prince — kneeling in front of her. She thought she was going to be sick. Her stomach fluttered nervously, making it even harder to breathe within the constraints of her corset than she'd already been suffering. She lowered her head down further, keeping Lady Faustine's teachings in mind. Her head must remain at a height below that of anyone in the royal family unless allowed to stand differently. Faustine had said nothing about how to react if they knelt. It seemed impossible to maintain a posture any lower than she already held without lying down on the floor at his feet.

A gloved hand gently clasped hers, lifting it from where she had it resting lightly on her bent knee. With a suave motion, he brought it up to his lips, barely making contact with the back of her hand through the thin cloth covering it. She refused to make eye contact with him as he rose to his feet again, continuing on toward the back of the room to the shocked silence of the crowd.

"Well, that is something I have never seen before," Feolan mused. Leyna could hear him moving to stand where he had been bowed for the Prince's arrival. She was too afraid to move in fear of the reaction the guests would give her. They were more than likely appalled at her behavior toward the Prince... and Lady Faustine would be at the front of the line waiting to make her disapproval known.

Maeri gently urged her back to her feet, leaning into her excitedly. "Oh my, Leyna. You were asked to dance by the Prince."

"Not for lack of trying to avoid it." It made no sense to her. How could it be that she was the only girl in the room not dying to touch him and yet he chose her? Pride, perhaps. Like most men she had come to know during the war and throughout her time in Carpaen at the academy. Men liked to chase what they could not have. Or what was implied to be off limits to them. It was more than likely a simple matter of the young Prince being even more egotistical than Enaes.

Faustine wasted no time in cutting through the crowd to get to where Leyna and Maeri were standing. Pushing past Feolan, she set her hard gaze upon Leyna, gripping her slender wrist roughly in her hand. "You silly girl. Are you trying to make a fool out of me? Have I taught you nothing?"

She winced at the pressure being applied by Faustine. For a woman of such high regard in the art of daintiness and delicacy, she had a grip that would frighten even a Sanarik if she got her hands on them. Leyna didn't dare let the pain show on her face. To make it known would only worsen the punishment she might receive upon returning home, if she was unable to redeem herself in Faustine's eyes before the ball had ended.

"If I may say, Lady Faustine, the young lady is an image of poise and grace. I should have known her to be a student of yours," Feolan smiled, holding his hand out toward Faustine invitingly. Faustine glanced over to him questioningly before noticing the golden insignia on his chest, her face instantly softening into a polite smile.

With a softness that seemed out of character for her, Faustine placed her hand lightly in Feolan's outstretched palm with a graceful curtsy. "You flatter me, sir. Such a compliment from a man so close to Her Majesty's Consul is a great honor to hear."

He smiled charmingly at her, lifting her hand up to kiss the back of it. Faustine's behavior was almost comical to Leyna. A complete transformation, from the bitter old woman who had been scolding her only seconds before, into the semblance of a lady. "Would it be too forward of me to request an introduction to the young misses?"

"Of course not. I feared they had lost their manners and already forced themselves upon your company," Faustine smiled, her pleasant tone sounding more forced than it had during her formal greeting. Her irritation with Leyna and Maeri was difficult for her to conceal, though their recognition by a man of status was too great an accomplishment for her to ignore. "This is Lady Leyna Evantine and the young Lady Maeri Diah. Both are newly introduced into society and are not spoken for at this time…"

She wanted to die. How much more embarrassing could a single night get? To make a spectacle of herself in front of the Prince as well as everyone else in the room, and now to have Faustine attempting to entice Feolan into courtship with her. If her cheeks had been visible, she knew they would be flushed with color, the warmth of her blood filling her face in humiliation.

He took it better than she did, though she realized she gave him little credit at how to deal with a woman like Lady Faustine. In the military such a comment would have been greeted with much more directness in regards to the man's interest in the woman set before him. She forgot that he was a courtier now. Bound by formality to feign interest without giving too much hope to the mother seeking him like a trophy. "I can assure you that with their beauty, they will not remain so available for long."

Another trumpet blast erupted from the foyer, catching Leyna off guard. Before she had a chance to react, Faustine's hands were pushing her firmly to face the aisle which was quickly parting yet again, creating a large opening in front of the entrance. The figure that appeared in the door carried himself in a manner all too familiar to Leyna. His features were more visible than his brother. The mask he wore covered only the area around his eyes, adorned with gold ribbons and gemstones along the edges of the black fabric. His style of dress was drastically more pretentious, displaying yards of golden brocade fabric draping from his shoulders. Rings of various rare stones sparkled from almost every finger, shown off at every chance he had to bend down and kiss the outstretched hands of the excited young girls lining his path.

Reluctantly, Leyna started to hold out her hand, kneeling gracefully at his approach. She was startled by Faustine's sudden burst of movement, grabbing onto her hand and holding it firmly down in front of her. "You are already chosen. I cannot have you appearing overzealous at gaining company with Her Majesty's sons. Who knows what the people would think."

So many rules. Offer your hand, now don't offer your hand; how was a girl supposed to know what behavior was appropriate when the standard changed on a whim? It was too easy to lose favor amongst society if their views were anywhere near as strict as Faustine made them out to be. She missed the simple life of a soldier.

It was a wonder how Prince Enaes could even think of retaining the knowledge of each girl whose hand his lips touched the back of. He barely missed a single eager young woman on either side of the line, bowing with a flourish and accepting several at a time. He gave no question to anything until he approached where Leyna was kneeling, his eyes looking her over closely as he noticed Faustine's hand restraining her.

"I have not seen anyone take such a stance in years. Could it be that my brother actually intends to grace us with a dance this evening?"

Faustine's hand applied pressure at the back of Leyna's neck, forcing her to bow lower. "So it would seem, Your Highness." Leyna couldn't recall the last time she had ever heard Faustine's voice so soft. It wasn't fitting for her at all.

"And he chose to keep the loveliest maiden in the whole place to himself. That hardly seems fair," Enaes chuckled. Leyna lifted her eyes to him in surprise at the sight of him offering out his hand to her, his brow raised questioningly toward Faustine. "There will be more than a single song played. Might I convince you to grant me her hand for one of the many that she will be sitting out of due to my brother's lack of appreciation for the beauty he has found?"

Faustine gave barely a thought to the request. Relinquishing her firm grasp on Leyna's hand, she lifted it into the air, placing it gently into Enaes's palm. He dipped low in a deep bow, flicking the fabric of his cape over his shoulder. His eyes never left hers as he bent in to kiss the back of her hand, holding her gaze steady for a moment before continuing on his way.

She watched him take Maeri's hand out of the corner of her eye, though she couldn't bring herself to observe his ostentatious display any longer. She had been wrong. It would be impossible for the young Prince to be any more egotistical than Enaes. He was the epitome of self absorption. What he wanted, he would be given or he would find a way to utilize his position to take it. It disgusted her, but for this one night she would have to entertain his pompousness. Faustine would never allow it to be any other way.

Unlike when the young Prince had reached the end of the crowd, the guests remained bowed in his wake. Once at the back of the room, Enaes stood in front of a large throne near the wall, his eyes directed toward the archway from which he had just come. The young Prince rose to his feet, standing at attention in the direction of the entrance. No fancy music had accompanied the Queen's arrival. She was already halfway down the aisle before Leyna was even aware that she had entered.

Everything but her vividly glowing silver eyes was covered by her ornate mask, her features molding perfectly to the shape. Rubies lined the lips, their sparkling red color filling in against the pale silver of the mask itself. Dark lines of black paint streaked out around the eyes for a dramatic effect with evenly spaced diamonds pulling out the radiant color of her eyes. They shone brighter than anything Leyna had ever seen before, putting the nighttime stars to shame against her mass of deep ebony hair which framed her face and hung straight down to her waist.

Her frame was smaller than Leyna imagined. In seeing the figures of her sons, Leyna pictured her to be a much more solid woman rather than the almost frail looking girl that floated across the floor so elegantly in front of her. The power within her was so strong that Leyna thought it nearly tangible, energy exuding from every part of her delicate body. She may appear physically weak, but there was no denying the strength that had built within her over her many years on the throne. Her age was imperceptible from under the concealment of her mask.

With elegance and grace she made her way to where her two sons were standing, greeting them both with a formal kiss to each cheek. The room remained in utter silence until she had taken her seat on the glittering throne next to Enaes, her tiny hand rising up to motion for everyone to continue their business at ease.

"Well," Feolan smiled. "Now that the hosts and hostess have arrived, I should be back to my rounds, at least sending the Consul's regrets for missing the party."

"If you seek a partner for any of the dances, sir, my girls would gladly be on your arm – if they are not otherwise occupied by a prince." Faustine sounded more hopeful than Leyna was comfortable with. It was all too much for her. So many things to remember from her lessons while being looked in the eye by so many memories of her past.

She hardly noticed Feolan disappearing into the crowd, leaving her alone with Maeri and Faustine. Faustine's voice droned on in her ear, lecturing her about the proper etiquette when dancing with a partner. It was proper to not speak during the dance with a member of the royal family, but if addressed, it was acceptable. The only detail which stood out in her mind was something she said about names. Even if asked, she was not required to bestow that information while at the masque. They called it courtesy. Leyna called it impossible with some of the men present.

Music started up on the far side of the room to her right. Several couples cleared the main entrance to make their way toward the candlelit dance floor, the soft tones of finely tuned strings wafting through the air. It was the first relaxing sound she'd heard all evening.

Enaes was already on the floor, spinning about with some young woman in his arms. It was hard to miss him among the other dancers with his style of dress. The other men paled in comparison to his golden threads, weaving in and out of the couples swaying gently to the music.

Lost in the depths of her thoughts, she realized Enaes had already passed through multiple partners, each song bringing with it a new tune to Leyna's ears. If she could have stood there all night and just listened to the soft notes of the instruments, it would have been the most comforting thing she'd experienced in years. She couldn't remember the last time that she enjoyed the talents of such distinguished musicians. It would have been long before she and her mother moved to Mialan. Possibly too long ago for her to even connect any image in her mind to the memory of the sounds.

A feather-light touch on her shoulder drew her from her reverie. Her heart crashed into her stomach at the jarring pull back into reality, reminding her of the predicament she was in. She found herself again facing the calm and elegant form of the young Prince, his lips saying nothing to her as he offered her his arm. She accepted it at a single stern look from Faustine, though her knees were trembling so severely that she wondered if she would even make it to the dance floor without fainting.

In the center of the floor, he gently clasped her hand in his, resting his right hand just above her slender waist. It wasn't until they'd begun to move with the music that she truly appreciated his difference in style from his brother's. Too much movement would surely remove the last of the air from her lungs that her corset managed to let through. No matter how she looked at it, the evening boded a poor and embarrassing end to a night that would haunt her forever.

The music played on with them dancing in silence. Leyna was too afraid to speak in fear of breaking some code that would set the Prince off. Faustine had ruined the entire experience. If she had been free of the strict rules laid upon her by her teacher, she could have left the room in awe over her presence on the dance floor. Dancing had been her most favored lesson among the requirements for social gatherings. She just pictured it being far more enjoyable than she was finding it to be at the moment.

"You are a remarkable dancer."

His whisper was nothing more than a soft breath behind her ear, sending a shiver down her spine at the sensation. So he did speak. She'd started to doubt that he was capable given his lack of speech in comparison to his brother's. Even his mother appeared a constant chatter next to him. But he had spoken to her. Did that give her grounds to speak freely herself? Faustine said to respond to questions. She said nothing of reacting to compliments. "You are too kind, though I must inquire as to why you chose me. What if I had two left feet and had fallen all over you on the dance floor?"

"I chose you because you were the only woman I felt would be capable of *not* falling over me on the dance floor. I detest feeling like an object to the female population and you were the one lady in the crowd who did not treat me like one."

Had she heard him correctly? His voice was so quiet. It was a challenge to distinguish his words from the melody of the song. A prince who loathed attention. It was possibly the most peculiar thing she'd heard in quite some time.

"If only I had some witty remark with which to respond, but I must admit that you have surprised me. I was prepared for arrogance —"

The corner of his lips twitched slightly into a restrained smile. The edges of his mask around his cheeks prevented him from showing any more emotion, holding his features solidly in place.

By the end of the song, she found herself wishing it would go on forever, the graceful motion of the dance finally starting to flow comfortably to her feet. Keeping Faustine's words in mind, she dipped into a low curtsy before the Prince, aware of the hundreds of eyes burning into her from around the dance floor. Other girls were jealous of her while many of the men wondered about her identity. She was an unknown to everyone in the room aside from Feolan and those whom she'd come with. There would, without doubt, be whispers about her all throughout the city by tomorrow morning.

She had only just risen back to her feet when she took in a fearful breath at the sight of Enaes standing at his brother's side. "Not bad, brother," he chuckled, stealing her hand away from her partner's. "I think it is time that I showed her how a real dance is done."

Before she could even think to protest, Enaes was pulling her away, his arms locking into position with her dance frame. She cast an apologetic glance toward his brother, unsure if he could even see it through the feathers shielding her face from view.

It was exactly as she feared. Though graceful, Enaes's steps were far more quick than his brother's had been, forcing her into a constant motion around the dance floor. Her breath was coming in short bursts despite her attempts to control it, afraid of passing out mid-turn. "Could we please slow down? I am not as skilled at this as I feel I should be."

To her surprise, he brought their speed down almost immediately, guiding her back toward the center of the floor with a series of small turns. "I am compelled to ask you your name," he said softly, his tone lacking in the gentleness she had heard from his brother.

"I am not compelled to answer." Faustine was sure to have her head now. It was a direct disregard of a question by the Prince, but she couldn't allow the answer to be spoken. Enaes would know her. At least she feared he would. There was always a chance that over the years he had become so wrapped up in himself that he'd forgotten the name of the girl who saved his life.

He was taken aback by her words. For the first time ever, she was witness to the Prince speechless. Silence was fitting for him. If only he wore it more often, his company might have been far more enjoyable. Leaning forward, he brought his mouth near to her ear, never missing a step in their dance. "I can obtain your name easier than you might like to think. It would be more pleasant for us all if you agreed to just tell me."

"You would have me reprimanded for wishing to remain a mystery to you?" she asked curiously, finding his words to have a threatening undertone.

Not responding right away, he twirled her out away from him, putting on a flashy display for the crowd as he drew her back into him tightly. "I am not a fan of mystery."

"That is a shame," she frowned. "I rather enjoy it. It allows the imagination more freedom to add to the suspense of something. In this case, feeding your curiosity so that you might still remember me when you awaken rather than forgetting this dance amongst the blur of so many others you will share this evening."

The final note to the song was like a breath of fresh air to her aching lungs. She wanted to get away from him. She wanted to get away from everyone. Even with her argument, it would be only a matter of minutes before Enaes would have found a means of learning her name. If she allowed that to happen with her there, it would be the end of her hopes for a peaceful night. He would never allow her rest, nor would anyone else in the room who was aware of her deeds. The story of the female soldier that rescued the Tanispan Prince was a popular one among the Vor'shai.

She didn't care that her curtsy was short and lacking in the feminine quality Faustine would have preferred. All she could think about was getting away from Enaes. There was a clear opening to the door; no one would be able to stop her if she made a break for it. Her legs were carrying her toward the large arch even before the thoughts could fully form in her head. Air. She at least needed air. If she somehow became lost in the woods while seeking it, then she would be forever grateful to the gods.

Whispers erupted throughout the room around her as she exited into the foyer. Her escape wouldn't go unnoticed amongst the town gossips waiting for a new piece of drama to add to their arsenal. She could sense the guards tensing at her approach, their bodies preparing to stop her if ordered, waiting for some kind of direction from the royal family. Hurriedly, she moved by them, her heels clicking softly on the hard floor of the foyer. Once she reached the exit, there would be little they could do to stop her. The grounds offered too many places for her to hide.

The temperature outside had dropped noticeably since her arrival, washing over her warm body with a shocking chill. She wasn't entirely sure where she intended to go. Faustine's carriage wouldn't leave without the lady and walking back to her home could be treacherous. The forests weren't the safest place for anyone to be at night, regardless of their combative abilities. Especially for a young woman who was unarmed and hindered by the restrictive lines of her corset.

Footsteps. Someone was behind her. Why couldn't they just leave her alone? And what if it was the Prince? Would he have already acquired her name and come after her to confront her after so many years? *Just don't look behind you. Keep moving and maybe they will go away.*

"Leyna, please stop."

Feolan's voice was a refreshing sound. The tension in her body released to slow her pace, a sigh of relief escaping at the sound of his steps moving in closer to her side. Reaching out, he rested his hands on her shoulders, bringing her to a sudden stop while turning her to face him. "I need to get away from here. You may follow if you so choose, but standing still is not an option."

"Did you tell him your name?"

"I tried to avoid answering. If he knows it now, I assure you he did not hear it from me," she frowned, glancing nervously back toward the palace door. In the entrance she could see someone standing there, gazing out at them without making any move to come nearer. From the distance, the clothing the man was wearing lacked the outward flare of Enaes's, calming her fears of having to face him again. The calm didn't remain for long as her breath caught in her throat, recognizing the fiery hued tendrils of the mask covering the face of their observer.

Feolan followed her uncomfortable gaze, his hands lowering away from her arms. At the sight of the young Prince watching them, he straightened his posture, his actions revealing his own concern over what was going on in the young man's head. "My carriage is near the road on the far side of the yard. I will make my way there. Give a count of ten after I am out of view and then come find me. We will talk then."

Turning away from her, Feolan moved swiftly off between the rows of carriages, the horses and their drivers unaware of the situation happening around them. She fidgeted nervously, knowing the Prince's eyes were still upon her. What did he want? They exchanged only a few brief whispers throughout their dance. None of it seemed enough to merit his concern at her departure, though without the ability to see the expression on his face, there was no way to know if it was concern which held him there at the door.

It had been at least ten seconds since she lost sight of Feolan. Her racing mind distracted her from the count, sending her heart back into a flutter at the realization that she needed to get moving. A commotion was coming from just inside the palace doors, shattering the young Prince's calm stance as he slipped back inside the massive building. *Run.* If they found her, they wouldn't let her leave.

Clutching her skirts in her hands, she ducked into the lines of fancifully decorated horses. The lack of light made the carriages all look alike, blending together in a long blur of shadows across the yard. How was she supposed to know which one was Feolan's? There were too many to choose from under the circumstances. She needed to get out of view as soon as possible, the clatter of the palace doors swinging open and slamming into the side of the stone walls echoing through the night.

A sudden click at her right caught her attention, her head snapping toward the noise just in time to see a carriage door open with a long arm extending outward. It grabbed onto her shoulder, gently yet firmly tugging her inside. Losing her balance, she tumbled ungracefully to the floor, inhaling a sharp breath just as the pressure of another body descended upon her, a slender, cool skinned hand cupping over her mouth.

Her initial reaction was to panic until she recognized the familiar grey glow of the eyes staring down at her through the darkness. Relief flooded her limbs, giving in to his weight to sink into the floor underneath him. She wasn't sure how to feel about anything at the moment. If anyone were to find them in such a position, it would be a worse confrontation than a simple demanding of her name.

Voices echoed through the air outside. They were looking for her. She could hear the commanding tone of a man giving orders to another, directing him to search through the line of horses where they were hidden away. Fear gripped at every part of her, making her too afraid to breathe, though between the corset and the weight of Feolan's body pressed against her chest, she wasn't sure she would have been able to take a breath if she'd wanted.

They were right outside the door now, the carriage rocking gently at their attempts to peer through the windows. Adrenaline pumped through her body. It was a combination of fear and excitement, reminding her of the days she spent in Siscal. The risk of being caught was exhilarating. She had done nothing wrong and yet the guards sought her out like a criminal, hunting her like the cunning Sanarik hiding in the shadows of the mountain woods. Leyna wondered if Feolan could feel the hard pulse of her heart against her chest, beating steadily under his own.

By the time the men finally moved on, Leyna felt as if her heart would burst from her breast. She was aware of Feolan's own heavy breaths, his head tucked down beside hers on the floor. The feeling of his skin against her cheek reminded her of the mask she wore, suddenly becoming aware that she no longer felt it over her face. It was too soon to move, though. Any sudden motion would disturb the stillness of the carriage, alerting the men to their presence.

Without the immediate danger of discovery, her mind began to race over everything at once, overwhelming her senses. Her thoughts leapt from one thing to the next, unable to focus on anything with the rapid thud of her own heartbeat echoing through her head. After what felt like an eternity, she suddenly felt Feolan's hand start to gently slide away from her mouth, his arm bracing his weight against the floor to ease some of the pressure from her chest.

No words passed between the two of them. His eyes opened wide at first, gazing down at her in surprise before softening in recognition. The sight of his face nearly brought tears to her eyes. It had been over a decade since she'd seen him, the mask no longer hiding him from her. He looked the same, but different to her matured mind. She'd never appreciated the fine lines of his features before. He was rather handsome – a word she never thought she would ever have used to describe her old friend. She wasn't sure she even understood what handsome was back then.

"You look – different," he whispered. "I am not sure I would have believed it was you under any other circumstances. The only trace of the girl I used to know is in your eyes, and even they are changed."

Smiling up at him, she hesitated to speak, still afraid of the men overhearing them and tearing open the door to the carriage. "I hope the changes are good, at least."

Every muscle in his body tensed suddenly, stiffening against her where they were lying. He seemed suddenly aware of their position, shifting his weight back in a single fluid motion to rise up onto the seat. "Well, you are very beautiful. Perhaps I am just not used to seeing you dressed in this fashion."

She watched him curiously, his hands straightening his shirt uncomfortably. He looked nervous, for some reason, though she didn't fully understand why. Did he think he had done something wrong? "I might classify myself as many things, but beautiful is not one of them. My body holds far too many scars to ever be viewed in such a way."

"Our people hold a deep respect for those scars which you carry. If they did not, we wouldn't be out here hiding, now would we?"

"Feolan," she started. The truth was embarrassing for her to admit. He still thought her a hero for protecting the Prince, but she and Thade were the ones who knew the truth. "I am not the great person you might believe me to be. When I stepped in front of those arrows, it was not because they were aimed at the Prince..."

Bringing his index finger up to his lips, Feolan hushed her, stretching his free hand out toward where she remained lying on the carriage floor. "The arrows were aimed at both the Captain and the Prince. It is because of you that they are both still alive. Do not try to cheapen the great deeds you have done just because you feel you are being praised for something which may not have been at the forefront of your mind at the time."

She accepted his hand, knowing that what he said was true, but not wanting to believe it. To believe would be recognizing herself as some kind of heroine and she didn't feel anything like one at the moment. Right now she felt like a fugitive trying to escape the guards who would take her captive and bring her in to their great prison. Prince Enaes may have the idea of bestowing thanks and praise upon her for her actions, but she didn't want that. She didn't want to be labeled as a saint in the constant public eye of her people.

The seat was remarkably more comfortable than those in Lady Faustine's carriage. Velvet lined the cushions, the dark fabric having been hidden from view in the dim light filtering in from the moon outside. "This is... nice." Absently she let her hand run over the soft material. It felt smooth against her skin, reminding her that her friends had risen above the horses and rickety tents that had been standard during the war.

"It is Thade's, really. He loaned it to me for the ball as a way of saying thank you for coming in his place. Regrettably, I feel that he would know better what to do in this situation than I do."

"I have to leave," she stated flatly. "Prince Enaes knows where I have been living all this time. He is the reason I am there. If he has learned my name, then he will be reminded of that and he will come looking for me. My preference is to not be found."

It was a ridiculous thought. Never were girls supposed to just leave Faustine's care. Once taken in, a young woman was expected to remain under her tutelage until the time when a suitable husband could be arranged. But she couldn't stay. She didn't want to. Marriage was the furthest thing from her mind and having the Prince's company forced upon her was not a punishment she intended to subject herself to.

Feolan stared back at her steadily, seeming to search her face for any sign that she might not be serious about what she was saying. Convinced she was sincere, he glanced over his shoulder in the direction of the palace, peering intently into the darkness for something. "You are the only woman I know who would run away from the Prince's affections."

"His affections are empty and short-lived, from what I can tell of him. Any woman who would seek such from him is not a lady, in my opinion. I would like to keep my dignity as much intact as I can. All things considered."

"I respect that about you," he nodded, letting his hand rest on the handle to the door. "Because of that, I will take you away from this place, at the very least. We should get you home to gather as many of your personal belongings that you can carry and then we can discuss what you wish to do from there."

Gazing back at Feolan solemnly, she gave a soft sigh, her heart still beating oddly within her chest. "Thank you," she whispered. There were no other words she could say to express her appreciation for what he was doing. He was putting himself at risk by assisting her. If Enaes were to learn that Feolan helped to keep her away from him, the punishment could be severe. He was known for his aggressive means of discipline.

Slipping through the open door, Feolan signaled at a man standing near the end of the yard. With a hurried pace, the man ran toward them, quickly boosting himself up into the driver's seat of the carriage. Feolan mumbled directions to him that were inaudible to Leyna's ears before he climbed back inside with her, securing the door in place behind him. "We will be at Lady Faustine's shortly. Be ready to run. You will have very little time when we get there."

Folding over the clasp of her pack, Leyna gave a final sweeping look across the room to make sure she wasn't forgetting anything of importance to her. For the first time since she'd told Feolan she wanted to leave, she felt a pang of sadness at the thought of never seeing the tiny room again. She would miss Maeri more than anything. It would be a blessing to escape everything else about the house. No more worrying about whether she was sitting just right or speaking softly enough to please Lady Faustine. While she appreciated everything Faustine had taught her, it had been absolute misery to endure.

She hurried down the hallway, knowing that Feolan was waiting outside for her in the carriage. Excitement continued to course through her body, filling her with a thrill unlike anything she'd felt in years. This was the sort of thing she lived for. Danger. Intrigue. She had never noticed how much she missed it until she'd come under Faustine's care. The simple life had proven dull and monotonous after so many years of constant struggle for survival.

Once outside, Feolan pulled open the door, helping her into the safety of the carriage. He signaled the coachman to move without a look back, sliding into the seat across from Leyna. Neither one of them took a breath until the horses stirred into motion, picking up the pace away from the house. "I will take you back to the inn where I am staying and make sure you are safely inside the room before I leave."

"Leave?" she asked in surprise, her nerves flinching at the thought of being left alone at a time like this. "Where do you have to go?"

"Back to the masque in order to put in a final appearance and dissuade anyone from thinking that I am with you."

"Oh."

It made perfect sense. If they had both been discovered absent, the suspicions alone would be enough to merit an accusation by the Prince. She wanted to escape, but she didn't want to leave a bad taste in anyone's mouth about her reputation. There would be enough talk about her behavior come the morning without her doing anything that might add to it.

The coachman continued on at a quickened speed, winding the way down the long country road. Feolan knelt on the floor, his hands reaching blindly for something under the seat. After a moment of feeling around, he managed to find what he was looking for, drawing out a long thin box that had been tucked away in the back. Lifting off the lid, he pulled a piece of heavy dark cloth from inside it, offering it out to Leyna casually. "You should wear this. It will keep your face hidden from anyone who might be around the inn when we get there. They cannot be allowed to see you."

Shaking out the fabric, she recognized it to be an elegantly designed cloak with the insignia of the Consul embroidered onto the left side of the chest. Her knowledge of cloth failed her in determining what it was made out of. It was heavy enough to provide warmth against the cold of the Tanispan winters while yet thin with a gentle shine for a regal outward appearance. Silver thread could be seen along every hem, adding a line of brilliant color to the otherwise rich ebon shade.

She draped it over her shoulders carefully. The fabric was so fine that she hated to think of possibly damaging it in any way. A soft fragrance wafted up from it, pleasant to her senses. Gently clasping a piece of the cloak, she brought it up to her face, inhaling deeply. It was familiar to her, though she couldn't place from where. All she knew was that it was a comforting scent, easing her troubled mind while she sat quietly there in the seat.

Their arrival passed in a blur of motion around her. The carriage hadn't even come to a complete stop before Feolan was opening the door, ushering her through it and into the brightly lit foyer of the inn. In their haste, she had no time to even glimpse the name of the establishment, struggling to keep up with Feolan's long strides.

Only a few other guests were present at the inn, glancing at them briefly for their strange behavior. Leyna could imagine what they must look like. In their concern of getting by without being noticed, they had somehow managed to make themselves stand out even more. Thankfully, despite the watchful eyes, no one could see her face to determine who she was. And even more comforting was the thought that they more than likely hadn't been at the masque to know that anything was going on out of the ordinary.

In the safety of Feolan's room, he closed the door, twisting the latch into place. "I hate to leave you here and run, but I need to get back there as swiftly as the horses will carry me. There is some bread and water in the case near the closet, and the inn provided a bottle of wine, if you so desire. The bed is yours if you are tired. I will hurry back, I promise."

"Do not rush on account of me," she smiled, lowering the hood of the cloak down around her shoulders. "I will be fine here. Concentrate on you. If you leave the palace in too great a haste, they might still suspect. I would recommend that you linger until it is nearly ended and then find your way out gracefully. It will appear less conspicuous."

He forced a smile as he turned back toward the door, slipping through it quietly. With slow steps she made her way over to it, watching the lock twist under the direction of Feolan's key from the other side.

She was alone. The relief was overwhelming. Alone and free. No more tedious lessons in etiquette and lectures on all the things she was doing incorrectly. No more caring about what everyone would think of her, in fear that she would blunder and disgrace someone else. Her mistakes from here on out would be only on herself. There was no longer any need to worry about anyone else's opinions on her manners.

Nonchalantly moving around the room, she looked over the items that had been set out. It probably was rude of her to be going over Feolan's personal belongings, but her curiosity was stronger than her concern about being invasive of someone's privacy. He trusted her, and she knew that she wouldn't do anything to break that. She desired to get to know more about the man he was. Although they had been such close friends, there was no denying that they were both different people now. Their relationship as commander and lieutenant was over a decade behind them. It was like starting all over again.

She was impressed by the finery he had collected. Several medals were situated on the desk, strewn about aimlessly. Carefully lifting each one up to inspect it, she could see the tiny inscriptions on them, denoting various honors for military service. She had already been long gone from Siscal when the war ended. If any medals had been intended for her, they were unable to reach her. It was sad, in a way. After dedicating every aspect of her life to the defense of the country for such a time, and to have received nothing in return.

Rewards were not her intention when she came to Siscal. That was the most important thing for her to remember. The reasons for her participation in the war had been fulfilled, though she had nothing to show for it. She finally had the means of providing a good home for Reina but Reina was nowhere to be found. It had taken her too long to achieve her goals... and her injuries had set her back even further. If she was lucky, Reina would understand. Unfortunately, she doubted that would be the case.

A tall chair was placed against the wall by the bed, the velveteen cushion matching the deep plum colors of the sheets. He had given her permission to use the bed to sleep, but she felt it would be inappropriate of her to do so. It was his, for the time. As a lady, she shouldn't be accepting invitations into anyone's bed, regardless of whether they were in it or not.

Sitting down in the chair, she tried to find a comfortable position with which to attempt resting. The gentle aroma from the cloak she wore continued to soothe her. It reminded her of Siscal. Everything always seemed to remind her of Siscal. It had been the one place that she truly felt like she belonged.

That was it. The realization dawned on her suddenly, bringing a sense of peace over her troubled mind. Siscal would be the perfect place for her to escape to. With the help of Feolan and Thade, there was a chance for her to become someone. Not only that, but it was where she had told Reina she would be. If ever Reina sought to find her, it would be there that she would go. For now, it was the only option that made any sense. She would just have to convince Feolan to allow her to accompany him home.

Chapter Seven

The trip was longer than she remembered. Endless trees had been the only sight for miles until they finally reached the mountainous regions of the Siscalian border. Feolan had been more amenable to the idea of Leyna returning with him than she expected. She'd spent her entire night thinking of ways to persuade him up until her eyes gave in to sleep. Maybe it had to do with his exhaustion from the evening, having only returned to the inn a few hours before Leyna awoke to the sun rising, lighting the entire room through the windows.

He'd been quiet since his arrival. Even throughout the days of travel through the countryside, Feolan barely uttered more than a few sentences. His eyes looked troubled. Something plagued his mind, but he constantly denied it when she asked on his silence. She feared the worst about what occurred at the masque in her absence. It was the only thing she could think that might cause his behavior to shift so drastically.

Sleep proved the best way of passing the time on their journey, giving in to it at every opportunity. It eased the racing thoughts in her own mind while at the same time made the trip seem shorter and more bearable. The landscape had only just begun to strike her as familiar when she drifted off again, praying they would reach their destination by the time her eyes opened.

"Leyna." Feolan's voice drifted softly over her ears. "Leyna, we are nearly to the city."

At last. Through her groggy mind, she felt relief at the words, slowly starting to stir from her slumber. Still clumsy from fatigue, she brushed at the soft fabric of her dress, making sure it was clear of any wrinkles. She wanted to look her best upon her return. The dress she'd chosen was a pale blue, the empire waist wrapped by a strand of silver cording. It allowed her the freedom of loosening the tight laces of her corset, while yet not fully granting her the option of removing it altogether. Since becoming a woman, she'd learned that fashion was never intended for comfort.

Clutching nervously at the clasp of the cloak, she made sure it still concealed the skin of her chest from view, not wanting anyone to see her scars. It was simple enough to cover the ones on her back and abdomen. Her left arm occasionally posed a problem, though it was the mark on her chest which was the most difficult to keep out of sight. So many dresses were designed to reveal the collarbone of the wearer, showing off the round patch of scar tissue just off-center over her right breast.

"You look fine," Feolan smiled, squeezing her hand gently to pull it away from the clasp. Giving a faint smile, she inhaled at the abrupt stop of the carriage wheels, listening to the coachman calling out for the horses to stay still.

The door opened to reveal the familiar streets of Siscal. She recognized the old wooden sign above the door to a small building, advertising the business within. It had been the location of almost every celebration of their unit, including her own promotion to lieutenant. Malic's Tavern. Still bustling with people coming in and out of the weathered doors, their eyes peering with interest at the sight of the carriage stopped just outside.

Lightly taking her hand, the coachman helped her down the steps to the ground, her legs aching from the long journey. It felt good to straighten them and move around, circulating the blood through her veins. "Are you sure this is the most appropriate place for a young lady to be? I am not exactly a military girl anymore."

"Malic's has cleaned up a bit over the years," Feolan chuckled, extending his arm out to Leyna. "During the day it is a more casual atmosphere for the people of Siscal. I just would recommend trying to avoid it once the sun goes down."

It was cleaner inside than she remembered. The air smelled fresh, with only a mild lingering scent of alcohol as they moved closer to the bar. There at the end, Leyna recognized a Mialan man seated on a stool, pushing a mug of ale back and forth between his hands. "Teagan?" she asked, squinting her eyes to get a better look. "Dear me, is that you?"

His light brown hair was neatly trimmed, hanging loose down to his shoulders. He was dressed in a fancy golden shirt which matched the color of his eyes, the fabric much nicer than what she would have expected of a retired soldier. He peered back at her for a moment, unsure of her identity. When he finally made the connection, she could see it in his eyes, his face brightening in surprise. "Leyna? My god, you look so..." He paused at first, seeming to consider what he was about to say before the words tumbled from his mouth in his usual fashion. "Womanly."

"Thank you, I think," she laughed uncomfortably, thankful for Feolan's presence at her side. It would have been asking too much for Teagan to have matured over the years. He appeared just as uncouth as ever, only dressed in finer garments while doing so.

Rising from his stool, he took Leyna's hand in his, kissing it gently. Without letting it go, he stared deeply into her eyes, still in awe at the sight of her. "Your beauty is without compare, Milady. You can feel free to order me about in any way you see fit."

He was standing closer than she was comfortable with. The hungry look in his eyes sent chills down her spine, looking so deeply into her that she feared he was seeing more than she wanted to expose. Desperate for anything which would force him to step away, she patted Feolan's arm gently, hoping he would play along with her.

"Feolan and I only just returned to the city. He is such a good man to me. He treated me to a vacation in the Tanispan valley. It was the most beautiful week I have ever had the pleasure of experiencing."

Shifting his gaze over to her, Leyna could see the brief moment of confusion in Feolan's eyes before he realized what she was doing. His mouth hung open, speechless, until he managed to regain control of his senses, stammering out a hesitant response. "I – yes. It was absolutely stunning there for the time of year..."

"Really?" Teagan mused. "I had no idea you were courting the young lieutenant."

It seemed to be working. Teagan slowly released his hold on her hand, ceasing to touch her while yet remaining close. She was aware of his eyes wandering down to look over her body, making her even more grateful that she had chosen to keep Thade's cloak on despite the warmer temperatures in the city. "Neither did I," Feolan whispered, leaning down by Leyna's ear awkwardly.

She laughed, the sound coming a bit louder than she thought was necessary. Placing her palm gently against Feolan's chest, she smiled up at him, hoping Teagan hadn't heard what was whispered to her. "It is still rather new. We have not been telling very many people, just in case. I do not want to have the whole city talking. I am sure you can understand. You will not tell anyone, I hope?"

"No, of course not. Your secret is safe with me." He looked annoyed. His eyes continued to burn into hers, revealing his uncertainty at their act. A smile curved up one corner of his mouth suddenly, his attention turning toward Feolan's silent form. "No one in here would care if you gave your beautiful lady a kiss. I, for one, would love to see it."

"Feolan is not a fan of public displays of affection," Leyna argued. She could already feel her plan backfiring on her. Teagan was a fool, but he could read people better than she liked to give him credit for. Especially when it came to women.

Patting Feolan on the shoulder, Teagan smirked, leaning in closer to speak. "Why would you not want to be seen kissing such a stunning beauty? If you do not, then I will assume she is in fact still available for the taking and will kiss her myself."

"You would not dare behave in such a manner to the lady..."

"Oh, yes I would," Teagan chuckled. Cutting his laughter short, he held Feolan's gaze steadily, unflinching at the growing anger building in Feolan's eyes. "I am curious if her lips taste as sweet as they look — and don't think to chastise me for my actions. You have no authority over me anymore."

Leyna could feel the panic rushing through her. She'd lied to him in order to avoid such behavior and yet he'd somehow become better at being a scoundrel than he had been when she saw him last. She didn't want to kiss anyone. She didn't have the slightest clue how to even do it. It was just a word to her. One that she never anticipated ever doing. "Teagan, stop. You are going to make a scene. The last thing I want is to draw attention to us."

"You don't think I'm serious?" Leyna flinched at Teagan's hand grabbing onto her slender arm, tugging her in closer to him, away from Feolan's grasp. "I'll tell you what. I will let this little lie of yours go if you will agree to have dinner with me. We are no longer separated by rank like we used to be. It doesn't seem like much to ask of you."

"What makes you think I am lying?"

Another tug at her body caused her to stumble backward, finding herself in Feolan's arms again. Leaning in, his eyes flickered at her apologetically. The gentle pressure of his lips against hers sent a rush through her body, filling her with an uncomfortable warmth. His hand lightly cupped her cheek, stroking the skin delicately before he pulled away, never taking his eyes off her. "Teagan, you will accept this as a warning to keep your hands off her. If I ever see or hear of you dishonoring her like this again, I will remove your head from your shoulders the way I should have long ago."

"You wouldn't dare strike at me, Feolan. I am an influential man now, and you know there would be consequences for laying a hand on me."

"Do not presume to tell me what I dare to do or not do," Feolan replied coldly, the tone of his voice causing Leyna to shiver. "You forget who you are dealing with. I am being merciful by letting you live right now. You should leave here before I change my mind."

Throwing his head back, Teagan burst into raucous laughter, the noise catching the attention of everyone in the room. In a single gulp, he swallowed the last of his ale, slamming the mug down on the bar. With a wink, he pursed his lips at Leyna. Blowing her a kiss, he pushed by Feolan toward the door, hitting their shoulders together roughly on his way past.

Leyna could see Feolan struggling to maintain his anger, his chest rising and falling with his deep, controlled breaths. It was all he could do to keep from chasing after Teagan. His dignity wouldn't allow it. She knew that to be true. In his position, he couldn't be seen involving himself in petty bar-room brawls. He could easily take Teagan in a fight. Teagan had to be aware of that. But he knew just what buttons to press with Feolan to get under his skin without putting himself at risk of an actual confrontation.

Her lips still tingled from his kiss, a part of her worried about whether she had done it right. She knew it didn't matter and that Feolan wouldn't think twice about it in regards to performance. He'd only done it to keep Teagan from doing worse. "Feolan, it is alright," she said calmly, rubbing his arms gently with her hands. "I had no idea it was possible for him to become an even bigger piece of scum. Had I known, I never would have spoken to him. I guess some part of me thought that he was actually a friend."

"With him, he cares only about one thing when it comes to women. I would recommend that you let go of any thought of him being a friend to you and just be wary of him. He is a snake and deserves to be stripped of all that he possesses which classifies him as a man."

Leyna's jaw fell open in disbelief at Feolan's harsh words. She felt there was something deeper between the two men that she wasn't aware of, though now hardly seemed the time to ask.

"Feolan, sir, I was not aware that you were seeing anyone."

Feolan drew in a sharp breath at the sound of the voice, his muscles tensing before gradually beginning to relax. "I am not," he stated firmly, turning to face the source. "This is simply a very dear friend of mine and the Consul's..."

"Leyna, yes," the strange man smiled, bowing his head toward her politely. "I have heard much about her, but no one told me she was a goddess in the flesh."

"I assure you that I am not," Leyna sighed. Was this really all men could think about? Since emerging back into society, all she'd heard from the male species was about beauty and how she looked. What happened to the days where she was respected for her ability to fight and strategize and not for the way she filled out her bodice?

The man was of distinct Vor'shai heritage, his eyes a light shade of blue that reminded Leyna of tiny circles of ice shining out from his fair skin. His angular features were surrounded by long jet-black hair tied neatly behind his shoulders. The suit he wore showed off his lean figure, the various shades of grey in the material blending together in the shirt, brought out by the dark black of his trousers.

"Leyna, this is Zander. He does some – work – for the Consul." Feolan's eyes darted around the area suspiciously. "But that is all on that which can be said."

Zander patted down his pockets, furrowing his brow. "I would offer to buy the young lady a drink, but alas, I find myself out of money."

"Well, if we find a table which will allow me to order some food, I will treat the men to drinks," Leyna smiled, motioning toward a booth at the opposite end of the bar. She could still sense the tension in the air. It was whether or not the tension exuding from Feolan was between him and her that made the situation more awkward.

He said nothing as he followed her over to the booth. For the sake of putting distance between them, she slid into the seat across from him, positioning herself at Zander's side to allow Feolan his seat to himself. If Zander was aware of the discomfort, he showed no signs of it in his behavior. "The wine here is quite good, if you were thinking to try one of their drinks. It is my beverage of choice when I visit."

"I will take your word for it," she replied quietly, smiling up at the waitress that came over to the table. "From the sounds of things we will be needing a glass of your wine and a couple cups of tea… and for now, two bowls of whatever soup you have on special."

"Not daring enough to try the wine?"

"Too early in the day for drinking. I only just arrived. It would be best not to lose my senses so soon."

An awkward silence settled over the table. She could tell by Feolan's eyes that he was far away in his head, the creases in his forehead giving away the strain his thoughts were exerting upon him. There was no denying her own confusion over the situation which had occurred between them and Teagan. The malice she sensed from Teagan was almost frightening. As if he intentionally was trying to get something from the confrontation.

He had seen through her lie. She knew it was a poor idea to attempt feigning any form of courtship between her and Feolan, but she needed to make him think she was unavailable in order to avoid his advances. It was unexpected for Teagan to call her bluff in such a way. It put Feolan in a position which was unfair to him and forced him into a scandal he didn't have to endure, had it not been for her. Whatever troubled him now, she felt it to be her fault, in some way. She would have to be more cautious about her actions in the future.

"Since we are more than likely all thinking about the same thing, I'm going to just come out and say it," Zander stated calmly, nodding politely to the waitress as she sat the drinks down on the table in front of them. "Feolan, you do realize that in kissing her, you let him win?"

Feolan tilted his head curiously at Zander, the expression on his face never changing. "Only to an extent."

Now the conversation had taken a turn for the worst, in her mind. It had been easy enough to avoid the awkwardness surrounding the kiss while it was not the focus of the discussion. She wasn't comfortable detailing it out. Her own feelings were too confused to be able to think about it clearly. "You know, we could just discuss it later..."

"Do you really think he would have forced his own lips upon hers in front of everyone here? It wouldn't have looked good, on his part."

"I fully believe he would have. He has no issues about what people think of him and women in this city. To him, his position grants him the power to do whatever he wants with them. The people have come to expect it as normal for him."

Position? Teagan had made mention of something himself before he left. *I am an influential man now.* What did that mean? Had he been given some kind of honor after the war? If so, she couldn't think of what he could have been honored for, knowing his reputation and behavior, even of that time. "What exactly does he do?" she asked quietly. She hated to cut into their conversation with her lack of understanding, but she needed to know the severity of the situation they had just encountered.

"Teagan had a string of good luck in one of the final battles of the war and held the blade that took down the Namiren Captain," Feolan frowned. "Because of that, Queen Nesperiti granted him high honors and placed him within her court. Since then, he has wasted no opportunity at flaunting his position among the nobles and abusing the power that such grants him."

"I took the display to be his way of coercing you into acting outside your usual honor by kissing her, especially if he truly didn't believe there to be any courtship between the two of you." Zander took a long sip of his wine, savoring the taste before continuing to speak. "Therefore, in doing so, he claims victory over you."

Feolan shook his head dejectedly, closing his eyes to avoid Leyna's sympathetic gaze. "There is no doubt in my mind that he would have taken advantage of the situation to justify kissing her himself if I had not – though I will admit there were other reasons behind why I gave in to it that I am in no way proud of, and I owe Leyna my deepest apologies for treating her in such a manner."

"If I may say, if my lips were to be pressed against either of you two, I certainly prefer you over him," Leyna smiled hesitantly. It had been far from unpleasant for her, at the very least. Her heart fluttered at the memory. His lips had been the only thing she could think about while they were in contact with hers, preventing any feelings of humiliation that he might believe he caused her in his actions. If anything, he'd protected her from the black spot a public display between her and Teagan might have caused to her reputation.

"What exactly makes you so certain he would have acted upon his threats?"

Leyna could see Feolan's face tighten at Zander's question. He was holding back a flood of emotions that neither she nor Zander could possibly understand. When they finally burst forth, Leyna couldn't believe what she was hearing. "He would have acted upon it because it would have directly insulted me, the same way he did when he seduced my wife just because he thought it would be fun."

"Wife?" Leyna breathed, nearly choking on her tea. "Feolan, I wasn't aware you were married."

"That is because I no longer am. Teagan saw to that before he left my wife dishonored and pregnant with his child."

His words came like a punch in the stomach for Leyna. What could she possibly say in response to such a revelation which would make anything feel right again? It sickened her to think of the pain Feolan was experiencing, forced to relive the horrible memories of his past because of her foolish idea to get Teagan to keep his distance. "Feolan, I am so sorry…"

"No, please, don't apologize," Feolan argued. The insistence in his tone caused Leyna's voice to trail off, unsure of why he wouldn't accept her request for forgiveness. "If anything, this granted me a brief moment of victory over him, though I am loathe to say it. I could just as easily have broken his nose in defense of your honor, but instead, to avoid violence, I took a more silent strike by taking advantage of you."

"I don't understand how this hurt him in any way."

"Leyna," Feolan replied softly, clasping her hand gently in his own from across the table. She stared down at it in surprise, glancing back up to see his grey eyes gazing deeply into hers. "Teagan has wanted you since the day he met you. Everyone in the unit knew that, which is why Thade and I intentionally did our best to keep a constant eye on you so he would leave you in peace. With that, I knew it would sting him to see my lips upon yours, even if he doubted there to be anything between us. I took the only shot I had, at your expense, when I should have struck him for his insolence."

"You chose to react nonviolently, which I am more favorable to," Leyna sighed. She wished there was something she could say which would wipe the melancholy expression from his face. How could she explain to him that she didn't mind his actions and had even taken her own pleasure in seeing Teagan's face at the sight of them? "I have so little experience — was my kiss so horrible that you cannot bear the thought of having endured it for the greater good?"

She could hear Zander chuckling to himself from behind his wine glass. Feolan looked confused at first, his eyes squinting at her. Giving him a warm smile, she squeezed his hand tightly, hoping to reassure him that she held no negative feelings toward him for his actions. After a moment, his features softened, his hand returning the pressure against hers with a grateful smile. "I was trying not to admit to myself that it was enjoyable. Your lips are rather soft."

"Well, then. So long as the experience didn't scar you for eternity, I see no reason for us to dwell on it any longer." Warmth flooded up to her cheeks at his compliment despite her efforts to fight it off. He had enjoyed it. She must have done something right, however unintentional it may have been.

She appreciated Zander's presence, helping to keep the flow of conversation going throughout their meal. He seemed a rational man. Very intelligent. It made her wonder what sort of work it was that he did for Thade. He didn't come across like any usual worker to her, his manner of speech not resembling that of a simple servant. He and Feolan avoided any in-depth conversation regarding business, piquing Leyna's interest even more regarding their arrangements.

The crowd started to thin, the dishes from their meal long cleared away by the waitress who was growing more and more irritated by their continued occupancy. It was too relaxing for Leyna to care if they were being a bother. She'd spent so many years within the walls of Lady Faustine's; the experience of being back out on her own felt incredible. Finally, life was beginning to feel as if it were hers again; like she had some kind of control over the path she would take. She only wished Maeri could have come to experience it with her.

Maeri had always been a free spirit, barely contained under Faustine's strict rules. As long as she remained there in Tanispa with Faustine, she would never escape the monotony of that life. It felt unfair to Leyna that she'd left there without bringing her friend.

Leyna was pulled from her thoughts by a sudden curse muttered from Zander's direction. His body stiffened at the sight of a young woman coming through the door, her eyes sweeping over the tavern casually. Pressing himself against the wall, he blocked himself from her view, his eyes opening wide toward Feolan uncomfortably. "I think now would be a good time to part ways."

"Pull up your hood, Leyna," Feolan whispered, peering around the corner of the booth to see if the woman was watching. Content that her attention was focused elsewhere, he rose swiftly, trying not to draw attention to himself as he started to slink along the wall toward the door. "Meet me outside when you are able. Try to make it quick."

Doing as she was told, she lifted the heavy fabric of Thade's cloak up over her head. Feolan was out of sight before she had a chance to question their strange behavior, leaving her alone with Zander in the privacy of the booth. "What is going on?"

"They think I deal in slave trading. It is imperative they not be aware of any affiliation between myself and the Consul's men... or women."

Her heart skipped at the realization of whose cloak she was wearing, the golden insignia embroidered into the material. Quickly, she lowered the hood back down, unclasping it at the neck to let the fabric fall to the seat around her, obscuring the design from view.

The woman caught sight of Zander, her wide brown eyes gazing at him curiously. Her blonde hair was cropped short, a style uncharacteristic for most women of any status. A strange glow surrounded her slanted eyes, resembling the familiar trait of the Vor'shai though her ears lacked the sharp, pointed tip Leyna expected to see from under her short locks. Her skin held a mild tan, reminding Leyna of the humans she'd seen in Carpaen, their hair sun-bleached in contrast to the deep bronze of their complexion.

"Zander, so funny seeing you here," she laughed, her voice high and light. The folds of her sunny yellow gown swished with her quickened steps toward their booth, coming to a stop at the table beside Leyna. "Oh dear, do I want to know who this piece of work is?"

"My latest conquest. She will take a bit of work to break in, but even the strongest of spirits can be shattered."

She didn't want to be there. The woman's eyes were like fire, burning her with their steady gaze. "She looks like used goods to me," the woman mused, poking a slender finger at the scar on Leyna's chest. Reflexively, she batted the woman's hand away, staring up at her in disbelief at the sound of her giggling. "When did you start treating your property to drinks?"

"What fun would my job be if I couldn't enjoy my own spoils from time to time?" The wink Zander gave to the woman caused Leyna to shiver. She may be naïve to many things in the world, but she could determine at least the base implications for his words.

"I suppose," the woman shrugged absently. "Much like horses, I assume. The trainer has to ride them in order to break them in for their owner. What's its name?"

The woman ran her hand along Leyna's hair, petting her like she would a small animal. It was all Leyna could do to keep from slapping her, the only thing holding her back was knowing that this was all somehow important to her friends. "I heard her people screaming something like Eleni while I was carrying her away. Whether that is it or not matters little. It is suitable."

"You know, Mikel has been in the market for a new slave girl. You will have to let me know when you are finished breaking this one in."

"A new slave for the Master, hmm?" Zander peered quizzically up at the woman. "That would be a pricey charge. But for you, I would be willing to cut him a deal."

Batting her eyes at Zander, the woman gave him a seductive smile, running her hands daintily along the low neckline of her dress. "That would be wonderful. And I would make it worth your time, of course."

"Excellent," he smirked, grabbing Leyna somewhat forcefully by her arm. "All this talk, however, is making me anxious to get started with her training. If you will excuse me."

"By all means. Do enjoy yourself. Oh, and Eleni..." the woman started, placing her hand on Leyna's arm as Zander began pushing her to her feet. "He likes his women to struggle at least a little – and make lots of noise. The louder, the better."

Leyna's jaw fell open, aghast at the woman's words. She was speechless. This woman dressed like a lady yet had the mouth of an uncouth barmaid. Clutching up the cloak from the seat, she felt Zander's hand tugging her harshly toward the front of the room, nearly causing her to fall flat on her face while she struggled to regain her balance. He herded her to the door quickly, dragging her along behind him.

Once outside, he pulled her out of view of the door, releasing his grip on her immediately to look her over for any sign of injury. "I am so sorry. I didn't hurt you, I hope?"

"No — what in the name of the gods just happened in there?" She couldn't restrain her frustration any longer. That woman now believed her to be the property of this man, whom she'd only just met that morning. Such an image would make things a bit more complicated for her if she intended to live a normal life among these people.

She could hear footsteps approaching from behind them, followed by Feolan's concerned voice. "Leyna, what happened? Why are you not covered?"

"Feolan, I cannot stay here… and neither can she. Can I meet you at the Consul's after dark?" Zander's tone revealed a hint of nervousness which Leyna hadn't noticed before. Whatever just happened, he was worried about it. Possibly even more than Leyna was.

The men stood still, staring at one another silently for a moment before Feolan nodded his head, taking the cloak from Leyna's hands and draping it around her shoulders. "Very well. Be discreet."

Leyna was completely and utterly lost. Nothing made sense to her anymore. They'd spent such a calm and normal afternoon, and now everything felt wrong. There was one very important detail being kept from her; and that one detail now put her in the middle of something she wasn't sure she wanted to be in the center of.

Pulling the hood of the cloak over Leyna's head, Feolan guided her over to the carriage, hurrying her inside. He seemed nervous about anyone seeing them. Somehow this situation made her presence with him dangerous. His eyes remained locked on the windows while the carriage shifted into motion, searching for any signs which might indicate they were being watched or followed. What were her friends involved in that was so bad they couldn't be seen together?

Just outside of town, they came to a stop at a small village, nestled on the outskirts of the city. A large stone house filled the view from the carriage windows. It appeared to be their destination, the coachman jumping down from his seat to open the door. Feolan wasted no time in getting Leyna from the carriage into the house, closing the heavy wooden door behind them.

"I fear we may have a problem," he announced, seemingly to no one in particular. In a fluid motion, he turned the lock on the door, moving quickly around the room to draw the curtains closed.

The room was larger than it appeared from outside. Bookshelves lined the walls to the right and left, each one filled, edge to edge, with the old bindings of various published literature. A sitting area was arranged in a little nook toward the back, out of view from the door and windows at the front of the house. There, in a stately high-backed chair sat the familiar figure of Thade, his face hidden behind the cover of a book held in his hands. At the sound of Feolan's voice, he started to lower it, his words cut short at the sight of Leyna standing there at the door. "You know how much I despise hearing those words, especially – Leyna?"

Time had treated him well. He was much like she remembered, his perfectly chis-eled face looking more like a sculptural masterpiece than that of a living man. His hair remained cut short, though held in place with a more aristocratic style rather than the windblown look he'd always worn during the war. Maeri's words floated back into her mind while she stared at him. *Deliciously sexy.* She hadn't been sure what that meant exactly until now. His muscular physique was hidden beneath the fine silk of his buttoned shirt, but while his skin couldn't be seen, the presence of his fit body was undeniable.

Nervously, she sank into a more formal curtsy, taking advantage of the brief moment with her head lowered to hide her face from view. She couldn't think about him like that. It was inappropriate. "Captain… it is good to see you again."

"Captain? I have not been called that in years," Thade chuckled, moving gracefully across the floor to stand before her. "My my – you have changed. What say you, Feo-lan? I believe my cloak wears better on her than it does me."

Leyna gasped at the realization that she was still wearing it. Reaching up for the clasp, she started to unhook it, pausing only at the gentle pressure of Thade's hand over hers, preventing her from removing it. "I hope you don't mind that I borrowed it…"

"Mind? Why would I mind? You may remove it if you like, but do not do it simply on account of my mention of you wearing it."

Securing the last of the curtains into place, Feolan moved over to where Thade and Leyna were standing, his expression solemn as he caught Thade's eye. "We need to talk. It is of the utmost importance."

"Then let us talk. Did something happen at the masque?"

"No. Well… yes," Feolan stammered, glancing uncomfortably over to Leyna. "That trouble was bypassed in Leyna coming back with me. The current trouble involves something more sensitive."

"We are among friends. There is nothing that I find necessary to hide from young Leyna, here."

"It has to do with Zander and Gislan —"

"Yes, except maybe that…" Thade said suddenly, the soft expression on his face hardening with concern. "We can step into my study for a moment, Feolan. Leyna, if you do not mind, you may wait here. Make yourself comfortable."

"With all due respect, Captain — Consul… I was just manhandled like a lowly slave in front of everyone at Malic's Tavern. I understand that you clearly have your secrets these days, but after that humiliation, I will follow you into whatever private room you attempt to retreat to in order to discuss this matter, so I recommend you spare that uncomfortable scene by simply discussing it here in this room, in front of me."

Thade stared hard at Leyna, his brow furrowed in concentration. "Is this true?" he asked, turning to face Feolan sternly. "Did someone touch her?"

"Honestly, I don't know," Feolan sighed. "When Gislan entered the tavern, I left in order to avoid suspicion. Leyna remained behind with Zander, but what occurred after I stepped away, I am not privy to. When they came out of the tavern, Zander had a hold of her and requested an emergency meeting with us tonight."

Both men shifted their gaze to Leyna. It was all on her now. She was the only one who knew what had happened, and yet she didn't know at all. None of it made enough sense for her to begin an explanation. "Zander said the woman couldn't be allowed to know of any connection between him and... you both. I realized that the cloak I was wearing bore the insignia of the Consul. That left me with little choice but to remove it or risk her seeing it."

A whispered curse slipped from Feolan's lips, his face twisting into a frustrated grimace. "How could I have been so foolish? I did not even think about that, or I never would have left you there."

"Our leaving together would have only drawn more attention. Why can't you just tell me what this is all about? I am involved now, whether you like it or not. I have a right to know."

"I am not comfortable with the thought of involving you in this, Leyna," Thade frowned. The joy that had been in his eyes at the sight of her was now diminished. She wasn't going to give up, though. She had to know what was going on.

"How about you explain to me what I stumbled into, and then *I* will decide how comfortable *I* am with being involved."

Thade heaved a sigh of defeat, knowing there would be no persuading her otherwise. Motioning absently toward the little nook, he made his way back toward his chair, discarding his book unceremoniously onto a small end table nearby. "I know better than to argue with you. Come have a seat."

She followed Thade over to the neatly arranged chairs, sitting stiffly down on a small settee across from him. Their reunion had been far from what she'd hoped it would be. Her whole trip back, she imagined it filled with joy and excitement. This was more like a funeral than the reuniting of friends.

"A few years back, Queen Vorsila became aware of a small group of people thought to be working in conjunction with the Ven'shal on some unknown conspiracy. I was put in charge of arranging a network which would bring information from the inside of this group in order to determine its motivation and intent." Thade paused for a moment, looking Leyna over carefully before continuing. "I have two men currently ingratiated within the group. From them, we have learned that there are three people involved in the leadership of this traitorous lot. Gislan Deboriac is one of those three."

"And Zander is one of these… spies – for lack of a better word?" Leyna asked. It certainly made sense, given his behavior. He was too intelligent to have been a mere servant.

Drumming his fingers on the arm of his chair, Thade nodded. "They prefer the more shady sorts, which is why he masquerades as a slave dealer. To my knowledge, however, he has never had to actually provide proof of it. Gislan is too fond of him at this point. Our other agent is still working on getting closer to Gislan's sister, Oksuva. That task is made more difficult because of her husband, Mikel. He does not let very many people near his wife."

"Mikel?" Leyna pondered. It rang a bell in her mind. The woman, Gislan, had mentioned it to Zander. "That is the name of the man Gislan said she wanted Zander to sell me to."

Feolan's head shot up from where it hung miserably, his eyes glancing at Leyna curiously. "Sell you to him? That could certainly be fortunate for us."

"You are not seriously considering allowing that to take place, are you, Feolan?" Thade raised an eyebrow in his direction. The tone of his voice was all it took for Leyna to know he disapproved of the thought. "It is far too dangerous to get her involved. These people are ruthless and they would do anything they could to corrupt her. Do you really want to expose her to that?"

"No. I was just thinking that she would have a better chance at gaining the information we needed than Kael…"

"I think the bottom line here is that I am already exposed to this," Leyna sighed, rubbing her temples with her fingertips. "If I do not play along, there is a chance it could ruin Zander's cover. Sure, he could claim I got away, but then I would never be able to show my face in Siscal without them wondering why he does not take me again."

Thade rose from his chair, pacing along the floor between the seats. In one afternoon they had managed to jeopardize a mission which had been in the works for years. The only way they could avoid possible disaster was to bring her into it. Strangest of all was that she didn't mind. A part of her was excited by the idea of being involved with such espionage. It would be a drastic change of pace from the monotony of the life she'd endured for the last decade.

"Thade," she said quietly, the sound of his name forming on her lips feeling foreign after knowing him by his title for so long. "If it will assist our people, and serve our Queen, then I am willing to do it. Whatever you ask of me."

"I could never ask this of you."

"Then do not," she said flatly. "Simply tell me what needs done and I will do it, if that will ease your conscience."

At her words, he paused in his pacing, lowering himself slowly down onto the settee beside her. The look in his eyes was painful for her to see. "Leyna, you do not understand. These people are evil, and they associate with people who are even more so. If they were to discover your position, they would kill you. There would be no saving you from it."

Death held little meaning to her after her time in the war. She had looked death in the face with three arrows lodged into her body and came through it. Her time ever since then felt borrowed. Like the gods never intended her to still be alive. But she was. She just had to figure out what they were keeping her around for. "Trust me, I understand. Just tell me what I would be looking for. If it starts to feel over my head, I will find a way to back out. They do not even know my real name."

"Zander told them a false name?" Feolan peered at her, his eyes reflecting more interest now than at the start of the conversation.

"Yes," she nodded. "Gislan thinks my name is Eleni."

Feolan smirked to himself, leaning back in his seat. "Clever boy. That could very possibly work to our benefit. My concern was that they would recognize your name from stories of the war. If they don't know it — they can't put two and two together."

"Trouble does tend to follow you, doesn't it?" Thade frowned, standing back up to leave Leyna alone on the settee once again. Resuming his thoughtful pacing, his shoulders drooped forward in defeat. "If you really truly desire to do this, I will not try to stop you... but I want it to be very clear to you that I disapprove. It is not willingly that I concede."

"You want what is best for me, I know. But this is what I want. You and I both know there is little in the way of other options at this point. The gods seem to have thrust this upon me for a reason. They spared my life once before. I owe them at least to try."

Returning to his seat, Thade leaned forward, resting his chin in his hands in contemplation. She felt bad putting him in this position again. Before, she had asked him to allow her to fight, knowing she was ten years too young to even be considered to do such. Now she was asking him to place her in the line of danger yet again. She couldn't blame him for being hesitant after seeing how her last request ended.

"Very well," he said calmly, successfully hiding the concern from his voice that she could still see in his eyes. "So far, the intelligence we have gathered suggests that Oksuva has ties to the Ven'shal. She claims to know of one who is capable of utilizing magic similar to that used by Arcastus before he was killed centuries ago. Their intentions appear to be leaning toward finding where the ancient Ven'shal buried Arcastus's body so that they can use this power to revive his corpse and wage a new war on the Vor'shai people like that in the past, only stronger. I am sure you can see why this cannot be allowed to happen."

"But your other spy... Kael, you said? He has yet to be able to get close enough to Oksuva to learn the name of this Ven'shal or any other details regarding their plans?"

"That sums it up quite right, yes," Thade nodded, straightening his back against the cushion of his chair. "You should also know that Kael is not aware Zander is working for me. It is important things remain this way. I am trying to avoid any possible connections between the two of them which might draw suspicion."

A sudden knock at the door caused them all to jump, caught off guard by the sound. They were on their feet instantly. Realizing what the sound had been, Leyna lowered herself back down on the settee, pressing her hand against her chest to try and ease the pounding of her heart. Could it be the sun had already set? It hadn't seemed so late when they left from Malic's.

Feolan cracked the door open just enough to see who was standing outside. With a nod of his head, he pulled the door open further, allowing Zander to step in out of view of any watchful eyes that might be on them. "Consul," he greeted with a deep bow. "We have some matters which need to be discussed..."

"I suspect that these matters have already been discussed and decided upon. You are late, if that is the case," Thade replied. Leyna couldn't help but admire the way he carried himself, filled with an air of dignity despite the doleful look in his eyes. She wondered if Zander or Feolan could even see it there.

Zander's mouth opened to speak again, his words barely having a chance to form on his lips at Thade's response. "Already discussed? How is that – ah. Leyna. I did not see you there."

Inhaling a deep breath, Leyna rose from the settee, turning around to curtsy gracefully to him. "I believe that is Eleni to you. Master." The word was harder to speak than she expected. She'd never done well with submission. It would make things much more difficult on her part to get used to taking orders from others. If she did not learn to do it, then she would be wasting her time trying to convince them that she was a slave.

"You are going to allow her to continue the charade?" Zander asked, making no attempt to hide the disbelief in his expression. "You do realize just how dangerous –"

"I realize exactly what this is," Thade cut in, spinning away to face his back to the room. "I will toil forever in the deepest pit of the Underworld for allowing this to transpire. But, as it would seem, I am outnumbered and my duty will not allow me to exercise my full authority in giving up an opportunity. Especially knowing that, if I give it up, we risk losing twice as much, if not everything."

"Well, well. Leyna, you seem to be the lucky piece of the equation for everyone to take advantage of today. First against Teagan and now this?"

If she had been closer, she would have found a way to cover his mouth to keep Zander from speaking. Now was not the time to mention Teagan. She knew this – but there was no way for Zander to know. He lacked the social graces to recognize that the mention of it was inappropriate, given the circumstances.

At the mention of Teagan's name, she could feel the tension flare in the room, Feolan's breath coming to a stop while Thade's body grew taut, fists clenched at his sides. "In reference to a woman, the words 'take advantage of' and 'Teagan' never bode well in a sentence together."

He was losing control of the situation. Nothing anyone could say now would change that. There was already enough going against his desires that to hear of the incident with Teagan would be the icing on the cake for him. Leyna wished there was some way she could ease his mind, to assure him that she would be safe, but even she knew it to be an impossible reassurance to make. "It is nothing. At least for now. We should all get some rest and take time to think on things…"

"Zander, I very rarely give direct orders, but as you are the one who brought it up, I am going to give you one more chance to enlighten me on the details of your comment before I am left with no choice but to sink to forcing my hand."

"I assumed, Consul, that Feolan had already told you about it, given that you seemed aware of everything else which happened at the tavern," Zander shrugged. Leyna could see Feolan's head lower from where he stood at the door. The tension between them was suffocating. He knew as well as she did that the topic should not be brought up; though he looked to be more nervous about it than she was.

Turning back around to face them, Leyna could see the strain in Thade's features. "No, the mention of that name was conveniently left out."

"Consul, I believe that would be better discussed between you and me after Zander and Leyna have safely gone for the evening," Feolan said quietly, casting a disapproving glare in Zander's direction. "For everyone's sake."

Zander peered in turn at Feolan and Leyna, then shifting his gaze back to Thade in confusion. The minute his lips parted, Leyna knew it was pointless to fight him about it anymore. He was going to say it whether they were prepared or not. "You both act like it was something grander than it was. Teagan was being his usual charming self. He gave the ultimatum that either he would kiss the lass or Feolan would. Feolan did, Teagan was pissed that his brilliant plan to take advantage of the lady backfired, and everyone went their separate ways."

"I see." Thade drew in a deep breath, situating himself back down on his chair. He was silent, thinking over his words carefully before speaking again. "Well, you are both adults – now." He looked at Leyna calmly. "If that was the extent of the incident, then it is your own business. Knowing Teagan, I feared it would be far worse."

"You know I would never let him touch her," Feolan started. A simple wave of Thade's hand brought him to silence.

"We will discuss that later, Feolan."

She had expected things to go worse, fearing how Thade would react to hearing about Teagan's behavior. It bothered her to know Thade was aware of the fact that Feolan had kissed her, but it didn't make sense to her why she should care. Like he'd said, she was an adult... now. He knew she wasn't before. It was his subtle way of reminding her that he was at least somewhat knowledgeable of her past secret. She wondered if Feolan had ever known, or if he allowed himself to be misled by Thade in regards to her age. He never gave any indication one way or another.

Everyone was waiting for someone else to speak. It made for a long, awkward silence between them, no one's eyes making contact with anyone else's. They were lost in their own thoughts. Leyna would have given anything to know what they were thinking. "I guess that settles it, then. I will go with Zander and see what I can find out."

She started to move toward the door when the sound of Thade's voice stopped her. It was softer than she was used to, filled with a gentle urgency for her to listen. "Leyna. I wish to speak with you before you go."

"Of course," she nodded, moving to sit down on the settee. He rose from his chair, shaking his head at her.

"No. Not here. If you would follow me."

Something was wrong. Private conversations between the two of them were rare occurrences during the war. To them, there was nothing that couldn't be said in front of Feolan – perhaps it was the presence of Zander which made it necessary.

They moved down a long hallway with Feolan and Zander staring after them. Leyna could tell Feolan shared in her confusion over Thade's request to speak with her alone.

At the end of the hall, Thade entered a wide wooden door, stepping off to one side to allow Leyna entrance, without removing his hand from the knob. He waited for her to pass, carefully closing the door behind them. A soft click echoed through the room as it shut, leaving them cut off from the others in the front of the house.

It was a study of some sort. A large desk took up most of the room with a hard-backed chair pushed up against it. Quills and parchment paper were strewn about the surface, a half-written letter left in the center. The ink looked to be dry, having been neglected there for some time.

"I always thought your return would be under more pleasant circumstances."

"You knew I would return?" It struck her as odd that he would have expected to find her back in Siscal when it was common knowledge throughout Tanispa that Lady Faustine's students tended to remain under her care until marriage.

He never moved, his hand still wrapped around the handle of the door. "I hoped that you might. I even came by not long ago with the foolish notion of trying to convince you to leave Tanispa. I knew how much you were against going there in the first place."

"Maeri did tell me someone came by to wish me a happy birthday. I thought it might have been you."

Nodding his head, he slowly turned away from the door, covering the distance between them in only a few long strides. "I found it unusual that you were absent from Lady Faustine's watch on your birthday. As you can imagine, it brought a few possibilities to mind."

"A few which I will not confirm or deny for you," Leyna frowned. "There was much going on that week in preparation for Queen Vorsila's masque."

"Yes, had I known you would be in attendance, I would have gone myself instead of sending Feolan."

"Well, he brought me back, so it would seem he succeeded in doing what you intended."

"My intentions were to bring you back, yes — but to join me in business of the court… not like this." She could hear the strain in his voice. His hands moved suddenly, reaching up to her neck. With a precise movement of his fingers, he undid the clasp of the cloak, the heavy fabric sliding from her shoulders down to the ground.

She flinched reflexively at this hand, breathing in a deep intake of air. Her entire body tensed as the cloak slipped away. The absence of the voluminous material left her feeling vulnerable and exposed in front of him. "Thade —"

Her voice trailed off at the feeling of his hand lightly brushing over the bare skin of her left arm. The scar tissue was still sensitive to the touch, causing her to shiver.

She'd never let anyone near enough to it other than Lady Faustine while it was still heal-ing. His eyes lingered over the scar on her chest, grimacing painfully at the sight of it. "You saved my life, Leyna. And now I feel as though I am repaying you by throwing you in front of the arrows again."

"I would gladly take the arrows again if it will save our people." It was true. Though she could tell it hurt Thade to hear her say it, she couldn't deny it to be how she felt. Serving her country and Queen gave a purpose to her life which she longed for. It made everything feel like it was for something rather than the idle life of a simple girl whose only goal was to play wife, cooking and cleaning. She felt she was capable of greater things, and she wasn't content to settle for less.

"If anything happens to you, I will hold myself accountable."

"Don't," she whispered. "I will not let anything happen to me. Just promise me you will trust that. I may be dressed like a lady, but I can still fight like a soldier... and I learned how to plot and plan from the best. You taught me well. This is just another opportunity to put my training to good use."

Gently, he rested his hands over Leyna's slender arms, gazing deeply into her eyes. "Promise me that you will be careful. These people are harder to protect you from than Teagan ever was. Many of them are assassins and thieves lacking any scruples. They care only about power. As for the Ven'shal – they will make even the most cunning Sanarik look weak and helpless."

"I promise –"

"No, you do not understand," he cut in, a hint of desperation echoing in his tone. "You cannot allow them to drag you into their magic or rituals. Even if your refusal to do so results in the fall of the entire mission, do not let them convince you to dabble in their sorcery. It slowly destroys the user from the inside out until there is nothing left of them but a shell of who they once were. You might think one time is harmless, but even that can be seen in the soul of a Vor'shai. It reflects in their eyes, dulling the purity of the light inside them. I could never live with myself if I ever saw that happen to you... knowing that it was because I am being careless enough to allow you to do this."

She couldn't blame him for his concern. Her lack of experience with the Ven'shal left many questions unanswered in regards to their magic, but from what she had seen, she knew that she would feel the same if the tables were turned. Even worse was knowing they would be unable to speak to each other the way they had during the war. This was a different mission than her role of lieutenant. She would take orders from him as her superior officer, but no one could know from where her directives came. No one could be allowed to know that she had directives at all.

Lack of communication between them would be the hardest part for him to bear, never knowing where she was or what was happening until she found some means of contacting him. Yes, she understood his concern, at least to an extent. All she could do was promise him that she would be careful, and that she would keep in touch as much as she could. "Do not worry about me, Thade. I will heed all of your warnings and I will be more insidious than the Sanarik could ever dream of being. They will never know who I am, or what I do, until we have uncovered the secrets we need to bring them down."

"You never cease to amaze me." His eyes remained on hers with a look of respect, giving in to her assurances with a decisive nod. "How could I say no to you when you look at me with such determination in your eyes? It is an admirable quality. One that I have seen in very few throughout my entire life. But why does that trait have to put such an innocent woman in the path of danger so often?"

"Because I enjoy it," she smiled, kneeling down to collect the cloak from the floor. "You may think me crazy, but I love the excitement. The thrill of never knowing what might happen. It certainly beats out the tedium I have endured for every day of my life since you saw me carried off to Tanispa. A girl needs to feel her heart race once in a while to remind her that she's still alive."

"There are other ways to make your heart race than throwing yourself to the wolves…"

"Then I will discover those when I grow tired of the wolves." She paused, feeling the weight of the cloak in her hand. Rising back to her feet, she offered it to Thade, wishing she could take it with her, if only for the comfort it had provided her throughout her journey back to Siscal. There was no time for comfort anymore.

Reluctantly he accepted it from her. What more could he possibly say? Her mind was made up and she had no intention of changing it. The gods brought her back to Siscal for a reason. Her people needed her. "Tell Zander I will speak with him more when next he has a chance to visit. I have some writing to finish before it gets too late."

Acknowledging his request with a graceful curtsy, she turned to make her way to the door, preparing herself for the life that she had just accepted. Faced with the curious stares of Feolan and Zander in the front room, she gave the most believable smile she could manage. She hated to leave Thade the way that she did, but there was nothing else she could do. This was what she wanted with her life, and until something happened to sway her otherwise, nothing was going to stop her.

"Is everything alright?" Feolan still looked concerned; the spark in his eye telling her that he feared she was in some kind of trouble.

Patting him lightly on the arm, she tried to remain casual, not wanting to give away the fact that she was growing more and more uneasy about her decision. Her mind was still made up, but she was suddenly aware of the severity of what was being asked of her. Was she up for the challenge? It didn't matter. There was no longer any choice. "Everything is fine. The Consul has some work to finish and will not be rejoining us. I think it best Zander and I be on our way to prepare for tomorrow."

"Sounds like a good idea," Zander nodded, glancing cautiously toward the door. "My horse is in the bushes off the main road to the village. Keep close, and stay to the shadows. Welcome aboard."

Chapter Eight

"Okay, we need to go over a few things," Zander announced, pushing the curtains open to let in the light from the morning sun. Leyna brought her hand up to shield her eyes, peering at him quizzically. "Gislan is supposed to come over for lunch today. That leaves us very little time to get you up to speed before you will be put on the spot to show off your acting skills."

"Today?" she gasped, sitting up straight in the bed. It was too soon. She needed more time to prepare herself; to get into the mindset her role would require. How could she possibly gather information when she didn't fully understand what she was looking for?

Tossing a piece of tattered cloth onto her lap, Zander motioned for her to stand up, pacing back and forth like a trapped animal. "Put that on. It's the best I could find on such short notice. I wasn't expecting to be harboring a slave for this meeting…"

"The best you could find?" Holding up the dingy material, she could see that at one time it had been a simple dress, the fabric now worn and frayed in several places. "You expect me to wear this?"

Zander paused in his pacing to look at her, his brow furrowed in frustration. "Do not turn into a princess on me all of a sudden," he grumbled. "A slave isn't going to be dressed in the finest fashions. You will have to get used to wearing rags for a while. At least until we can get you situated in a better position amongst these people. If I can sell you to Mikel, maybe he prefers his slaves in silk."

The sarcasm was evident in his tone. She wasn't in the mood to deal with his attitude. "I am a slave to you only in this charade, not in real life. I suggest when we are alone, you treat me with a little bit of respect as a partner in this or we are going to have some issues. Are we understood?"

"Plain as day. Now put the dress on."

"Get out of my room."

Raising his eyebrow in her direction, he started to argue, thinking better of it at the last second. "This is my room. I could have made you sleep on the floor last night, if I had known you would be like this."

"What? You think I am going to just strip down and dress in front of you? I may be playing your slave, but allow me a bit of dignity."

A look of realization crossed over Zander's features at her words. For an instant, his face softened, a hint of the lighthearted man she'd met at the tavern flashing back to the surface. "I'm used to working with men. You will have to excuse me."

"I will think about it. You can speak to me through the door. I can listen while I dress." She hesitated to uncover herself in front of him. Her situation was likely to force her into positions which would be uncomfortable enough without having to add to it when it wasn't necessary. It wouldn't be proper for him to see her in her bed clothes.

He never gave a second look as he walked through the door, leaving it open a crack to allow him to continue talking without being muffled by the thickness of the wood. Leyna watched the opening before she slipped out from under the blankets, making sure he wasn't looking. Satisfied that he wasn't, she tugged at the laces of her night-gown, letting it fall to the floor around her feet.

The dress was nothing more than a rag, but it was clean. She had to at least appreciate that. She didn't dare ask him where he had found it. "Tell me about Gislan," she called out, pulling the scratchy material over her head. "What is she? At first glance I thought her to be Vor'shai but she lacks other qualities to back that up."

"She is a mixed breed, as is her sister," Zander explained through the door, his voice sounding closer than Leyna was comfortable with. "We call them Esai. In this case, their mother was Vor'shai and their father was a human. Most half-breeds don't merit paying attention to, but an Esai is a child of mixed heritage who managed to somehow inherit the magic of the Vor'shai, to some extent. They are rarely as potent as a true Vor'shai, but they can utilize the energy, nevertheless."

Though loose, the dress fit her, looking more like a sack with holes cut into it than a garment intended for actual wear. If it had been any thicker in texture, she might have believed Zander to have stolen a fruit bag from the market and was passing it off as clothing. "And Mikel? What is he? Another Esai?"

"Yes, but his heritage is a little shadier. His parents are known among the Ven'shal. His mother is pureblood. I suspect his father to be mixed, but I have never been able to convince Gislan to discuss much else about him."

Clutching uncomfortably at the bottom of the dress, Leyna tried to pull it down further, uncomfortable with the short length. It stopped just above her knees with a small tear creating a slit up the right side, nearly to her hip. When she was younger, it might have fit her more appropriately. As a woman, it felt more like an undergarment than anything else.

She inhaled a deep breath on her way to the door. The thought of Zander seeing her in such a state of undress was embarrassing, but it was required if she wanted Gislan to believe she was a slave under Zander's hand. It would be the first of many humiliations she would have to endure. She operated under no false ideas that she would be treated in any respectable manner.

"His wife, Oksuva, she has ties to the Ven'shal, but she tends to —"

Zander's voice trailed off at the sight of her, his eyes blinking in surprise. "Well," he stammered. "I didn't expect you to make that look so good."

"This is degrading enough just having to put it on. Let us try not to keep pointing it out to me that I look so... cheap."

Folding his arms across his chest, he leaned up against the wall, gazing back at her casually. "You know, I should warn you that in order to effectively convince Gislan that you are my slave, I will have to say things, and occasionally touch or strike you. I hope you will accept my advanced apologies for this."

"I would hope you could avoid touching or striking me whenever possible." That was one detail she'd failed to consider when agreeing to this task. She had never owned a slave, but she'd watched others and the way they treated them. It was vulgar at times. The slave was nothing more than an animal to their master. Thinking about the things that would be expected of Zander to do to her was almost enough to make her call the whole thing off. More and more she was gaining a better understanding of why Thade had been so against it.

"Of course," he shrugged, the look in his eyes growing more serious. "But keep in mind that Gislan thinks I am taking advantage of you in every possible way. Flinch when I raise my hand to you, and it will help to avoid the need to actually strike you. Look uncomfortable in general when I touch you. A slave doesn't have to enjoy being an object to their master. You need to look frightened, and speak very little. Slaves typically aren't allowed to talk. It can be grounds for punishment."

It made sense. Frail was never a quality she'd exhibited before, but it seemed simple enough to mimic. She had seen the other girls at Lady Faustine's. They cringed at the sight of snakes and spiders and cried at the drop of a hat. It was irritating to watch, but easy enough to portray. She just had to imagine Zander's touch to be like a slithering snake dropping out of a tree onto her — but with less theatrics in screaming than the other girls she'd seen.

Pushing himself out away from the wall, Zander headed toward the stairs of his house, leaving Leyna there to stare after him in the hallway. "Get to cleaning, woman. She'll be here any time now."

Oh, she wanted to slap him. It had been a long time since she'd wanted to strike anyone as badly as she wanted to strike him. She couldn't tell if it was an act, or if he really was the scoundrel he appeared to be. Completely different from the man they sat with at Malic's. Her only hope was that he was a good man deep down, and that it was his time spent around such villainous people which made him so insensitive. He had to know that any mistreatment of her by him would be reported to Thade. If he was smart, he would do his best to keep his hands to himself.

She was no stranger to house work. Maeri and Leyna had been in charge of keeping Lady Faustine's home clean and tidy in case of visitors. It was obvious to Leyna that Zander's house was neglected in the way of cleanliness, the dust and cobwebs covering the furniture and floors in a thick layer. Fetching water and a rag, she went to work scrubbing the floor of the dining area, grateful for the distraction from the task they would be facing.

Dust filled her nostrils, tickling her senses to a point where she thought she would dissolve into a fit of sneezing for a week. Zander sat with his feet propped up on the table, watching her every move while she cleaned. "You are surprisingly convincing as a slave girl."

"You may want to be careful. I will be the one making your food." Tossing the water soaked rag down onto the floor, she wiped the sweat from her forehead. The sound of Zander's self-amused laughter was cut short by a rap at the door. Panic rushed over Leyna at the noise. She wasn't ready for this. What had she been thinking? Acting was never something she practiced in her spare time.

Grabbing onto the rag, she lowered her head down to the floor, continuing to scrub at a more vigorous speed. Keep her nose down. That was all she had to do to get through this. If she could just avoid having to make any contact with Gislan...

Zander was already at the door, pulling it open to greet his guests. "Gislan... I didn't realize you were bringing a friend."

From the corner of her vision, Leyna could see the blonde woman from the tavern brushing by Zander into the home, followed close behind by another man that she had never seen before. In knowing the common heritage among Gislan's people, she questioned whether the man was truly a full Vor'shai, as he appeared. His ears rose up from his neatly combed black hair, coming to a sharp point at the tip. His skin was pale, the features on his face more wide-set than most others of her people. The glow of his soft green eyes told her he was at least gifted with the Vor'shai magic. His appearance looked pure enough to pass as a full blood.

"Zander, I think you have met Kael before?" Gislan waved dismissively, ignoring the disappointment on Zander's face. "I asked him to come and help me get a good look at this girl of yours. I want his opinion before I put in the money."

Closing the door behind them, Zander stood with his back to the room briefly, muttering a silent curse to himself. Regaining his wide grin, he spun around to face Gislan and Kael, motioning over to where Leyna was knelt down, scrubbing meticulously at the floor. "You are buying her? I thought you were thinking I should sell her to Mikel? I've been training her accordingly."

"Well, yes. Mikel's birthday is in a few days. I thought it would be a lovely gift for him. His very own Vor'shai slave girl – and I figured you would maybe give me a bit of a discount." Slinking over to Zander, Gislan traced her fingertip along his chest, batting her eyes at him flirtatiously. "If you did, I would compensate the price in other ways."

Perfect. If she could convince Gislan she was a worthy slave, she would be exactly where she wanted to be. It was just a matter of pulling off the difficult task to get there.

Pressing the rag hard into the floor, Leyna slid it forward across the surface, flinching in surprise as her hand struck the thick black boot of someone's foot. Fearfully, she shifted her face upward to see who was standing there, finding herself staring into the green eyes of the man that had been brought in with Gislan. Kael. How convenient that her guest would be the other man mentioned by Thade and Feolan as an ally. If only he knew about their plan, it would be easier to convince Gislan that she was worth the price for Mikel.

She inhaled a hesitant breath at the sight of him, retracting the rag away from his foot with a wide-eyed gaze. Afraid. She had to make him think she feared his hand striking her for dampening his boot. A pained expression passed over his face, the sight of her there hitting him harder than Leyna anticipated. "You make a habit of enslaving your own people, Zander?"

"That one was already a slave. I figured I was doing her a favor by taking her away."

"Doing her a favor would have been setting her free." They hadn't even been there for more than a couple of minutes and Leyna was already at a loss for how to react to Kael's behavior. He was offended by her position. That could pose a problem if he argued against allowing Gislan to purchase her. Their plan would be foiled by their own ally.

Gislan stepped away from Zander, glancing over to Kael with an irritated glare. "Kael, relax. The only reason I brought you here was to tell me whether or not she is pretty... not to argue her predicament. Mikel would never accept an ugly slave and in my opinion, all women are less than adequate in comparison to me and my sister."

It was made easier to feign her discomfort by her honest uncertainty about this man who was presumably on their side. For someone who was supposed to be undercover, he made no attempts to hide his favoritism toward the Vor'shai. She reflexively jerked away from his hand reaching out to her chin. His speed was admirable, catching her in his grasp despite her efforts to avoid him. Gently, he raised her to her feet, twisting her head from one side to the other to examine her intently. "She is Vor'shai, so I will say she is already superior in beauty than Mikel's wife. If that is what you are looking for, then she would be the perfect choice. If not, then I would say to kill this dog keeping her and release the poor girl."

"Look at her, Kael," Zander prodded. Leyna couldn't see his face, but she could feel his hand lightly stroking the skin of her cheek, trailing down her neck to her collar bone. "You can't tell me you wouldn't want her doing your bidding, if you could have her."

Kael's hand released its hold on her chin, clenching into a fist angrily. He thought better of it, lowering his arm to his side, furrowing his brow in frustration. "Have you had her, or are you just making an observation?"

"It is the best way to tame them —"

With incredible speed, Kael pushed his hands against Zander's chest, sending him stumbling backward across the floor. Anger flared in Zander's eyes at the insult, balling up his fists at his sides. This was exactly why it was a bad idea for them to not be aware of the other's true intentions. Leyna hoped in the end it would prove more beneficial that Kael was left in the dark.

Zander's body twitched sharply. He wanted to take a swing at Kael but something in the back of his mind wouldn't let him. It was either knowledge of Kael's allegiance with Thade, or the fact that a fight between them might jeopardize their plans. "Eleni. Why is lunch not ready yet?"

Anxious to get away from them all, Leyna hurried off toward the kitchen. She was used to men throwing their weight around to look more masculine, but the animosity between Zander and Kael appeared to be deeper than a simple show of strength. As long as Leyna was present, there would be no chance at Zander being able to conduct business talks with Gislan for her sale to Mikel.

The kitchen was a cleverly disguised mess. On the surface, everything looked to be orderly until she opened the cupboards, finding dishes tossed about haphazardly wherever they would fit. She was happy for the peace and quiet. The time it took her to dig out the pots needed to cook the meal gave her a chance to think about everything in more detail. There were still some aspects of the plan which were gradually becoming clearer to her that she wasn't comfortable with.

Cooking was easy enough for her to manage, however it was the least of her concerns. If Mikel was a breed of Ven'shal heritage, she was almost certain her work wouldn't be nearly so simple and pleasant as cleaning and preparing meals. For him, it would be like having his greatest enemy at his service whenever he snapped his fingers. She would be a trophy for him, above all else. Any disgusting task he had that needed to be done, it would fall on her to do, and he would bask in every minute of it.

She avoided going out into the dining area other than to serve the food to Zander and his guests. Her eyes remained low to the floor, not wanting to make contact with any of their watchful stares. Kael never once took his gaze from her, following every movement she made. It was uncomfortable for her to know that he was so attentive to her. She couldn't be sure if he watched her because he felt sorry for her, or if he was looking for signs that would belie her ruse.

From the doorway of the kitchen, Leyna watched and waited for everyone to finish eating. Their voices were too hushed for her to be able to make out most of their conversation. Kael's eyes drifted over to where she was standing, causing her to duck out of sight, not wanting to draw attention to herself. She hated the idea of lying to him about her situation, but there was no other choice at this time. Truth would have to wait until she was securely in place within Mikel and Oksuva's home.

When the plates were empty of food, she slipped quietly from her hiding place, collecting the dishes from the table. Leaning over to gather Zander's utensils, she jumped in surprise at the impact of his hand, slapping boorishly against her rear. Unsure of how to react, she cast an uncomfortable glance at Gislan and Kael, hurrying quickly back to the kitchen with the dishes she managed to fit in her arms.

This was ridiculous. Throughout the war, she'd knocked men off their feet for less than what she was allowing Zander to do. Even Teagan had been more respectable – back then. There was no saying what he would be like now. If their meeting at Malic's was any indication, she could only assume he would treat her similarly to Zander. An abuse of power.

Calm yourself. It was all an act. He warned her that he would have to do it. There was no doubt he was enjoying it, however. A cheap thrill at her expense with the excuse that it was for the good of their mission. How much longer would she have to expose herself to it?

One of the plates fell through her fingers, shattering into pieces on the floor. *Idiot.* She was letting everything get to her. This was what she had wanted. The excitement and adventure of working undercover. She couldn't keep letting every little thing bother her. If she couldn't play along with her role without becoming offended, she would have little chance at convincing anyone that she was what she claimed.

That was quite possibly the most frightening thing of all. Once she was under the employ of Mikel, it would no longer be just an act. She would be his slave in reality. This meant she would no longer have her freedom when out of the eyes of her enemies.

If Mikel told her to do something, she would have to do it or risk a punishment like that which Thade had feared. Her role required more of her than she'd considered before jumping to accept it.

"Eleni?"

She almost let another dish crash to the floor at the sound of Kael's voice coming from the doorway. *Don't speak. Slaves don't speak.* The words repeated themselves over and over in her head, her eyes looking up to him from where she was crouched down on the floor, gathering up the broken pieces of the plate into her hands. Everything else was scattered about the counter, placed there in a rush to get them out of her grasp in fear of dropping it all.

His eyes were hypnotizing, the way they peered down at her with such emotion, the sight of her there stinging him to his very core. He made no effort to conceal his discontent for her position. It was charming, in a way. She was a complete stranger to him and yet he cared so deeply about the trouble she appeared to be in. Forced to do the bidding of her kin while being taken advantage of in every way imaginable. *If only he knew it wasn't true...*

"Let me help you with that —"

"No..." Her voice was nothing more than a whisper. Quickly, she snatched up several pieces of the broken plate, trying to gather them all before Kael could get a hold of them. He grabbed her hand lightly, preventing her from collecting any more.

Their eyes met, her arm pulling away from his nervously in fear of someone walking in and seeing them there together. "You will get me beaten. This work is for my hands, not yours."

"He would not dare to strike you in my presence," he replied calmly, picking up the last of the pieces from the floor. "If he knows what is good for him, he will never lay another finger on you."

She found herself watching his lips. There was something about the way they moved with every word he uttered in their native tongue. Every syllable was perfectly pronounced, laced with an air of confidence similar to that which she had grown accustomed to hearing from the nobility in Tanispa, though his features were almost too rugged to be of noble birth. Aristocrats tended to have sharper and more elegant shapes.

Finding herself staring at him, she averted her gaze, looking down to the floor bashfully. He was good looking, she couldn't deny it, but this was hardly the time and place for her to be admiring him. There was still much work to be done in order to guarantee her a place among Mikel's people and Kael's chivalry risked destroying it all if he felt compelled to force her to escape captivity. How could she explain to him that she wanted to stay if he opened the door for her to leave?

She remained on the floor as he rose to his feet, disposing of the broken plate fragments in a container near the far counter. Gislan and Zander had to be aware that he was no longer in the dining area with them. It felt strange that they had allowed him to wander off without questioning his intentions – especially knowing his disapproval of her treatment. To leave him alone with her seemed foolish. "You should not be here."

"Me?" He peered back at her quizzically. "I am here as a free man. If anyone should not be here, it is you." With long strides, he made his way back over to her, taking a knee. Gazing deeply in her eyes, he brushed a stray piece of hair from Leyna's face, tucking it lightly behind her ear with a delicate motion. The gentleness of his touch surprised her, sending a shiver down her spine. "You deserve better than this. Your beauty should be showcased in finery instead of these rags he places upon you."

Silently she scolded herself for letting him so close to her. She should have flinched from his hand. A slave would never have trusted someone of higher station to touch them without fear of being struck. Something about his presence was scrambling her thoughts, making it difficult to focus on her task. "You should not say such things. I am but a slave. I deserve none of these things you speak of."

The sound of approaching footsteps brought them both to their feet instantly. Her eyes gazed nervously toward the door while Kael stood tall and proud, his fists clenched in preparation for a confrontation. Gislan's lithe figure stepped through to the kitchen, leaning casually against the door frame. "Find anything interesting, Kael?"

"I was coming to check on what the noise had been. Zander will be short a plate for his next luncheon."

Gislan laughed an airy, almost haughty laugh, tossing her head back in amusement. "You went through the trouble of coming in here just to check on the status of Zander's dishes? Do you take me for a fool?"

"Of course not," he frowned. Gislan had backed him into a corner with her words. He hadn't shown enough care for anything of Zander's for him to convince her that the shattered plate was the only reason for him coming to the kitchen. "She is rather enticing. I think she would do much better under Mikel's employ than this wretch's."

Her laughter stopped abruptly, the sound of it echoing throughout the silence of the room. She looked him over carefully, ascertaining whether or not he was speaking truthfully before choosing her words. "I am glad you think so, because the deal is already done. She will be returning with us when we take our leave for Dalonshire."

"We will be taking her with us today then?"

"No," Gislan giggled, stepping backward through the door with a motion for Kael to follow. "You would like that too much, I think. She will stay here until we are ready to leave. That will give Zander time to have her better prepared."

At Gislan's retreat back to the outer room, Kael turned to Leyna, leaning his face down close to her ear. "I will make sure that you find your freedom, somehow. It may not be possible right away, but eventually —"

"Kael, stop fondling Zander's wares and get out here!" Gislan's voice rang loudly through the doorway. Letting his words trail off, he straightened his back, sharply twisting on his heel toward the door.

Curiosity pulled Leyna forward after him, taking hesitant steps from the kitchen into the room with the others. She remained cowered against the wall, hoping that if she stayed still enough, they might not notice her presence. Zander's eyes lingered on her for only a moment before he moved to Gislan's side, wrapping his arms around her in an affectionate embrace. "I do love when you visit. You should try to come by more often."

"We shall see," she mused, glancing over to Leyna disapprovingly. "Make sure you clean her up a bit. She looks like a pathetic ragamuffin. That will never do for Mikel."

"Ah, he and I have different tastes then," Zander winked. Lightly, Gislan pressed her lips against both his cheeks, smiling up at him in adoration.

Her movements were fluid and graceful, more than would be expected of a common woman. She carried herself with a strong confidence that would intimidate a normal man. Without saying anything in response, she stepped through the front door, leaving Kael to linger behind near where Zander was standing.

The men locked eyes, staring each other down sternly. Neither of them budged, their muscles tensed in a show of strength and power, be it to appear threatening to the other, or a display for Leyna's benefit. With barely a twitch to signal the motion, Kael lifted his right arm, winding back to bring his fist in to strike hard at Zander's face.

Zander stumbled backward from the force, knocked to the ground while his hands reached up to his nose in surprise. Kael took a step forward, looming over Zander briefly before retreating again. "You are a disgrace to our people," he spat, the anger behind his words evident in the burning glow of his green eyes. The sound of his boots crossing the floor filled the air, followed by the loud slam of the front door behind him.

Rushing over to Zander's side, she knelt down, cradling his head worriedly in her arms. "Zander, are you alright?"

"Well, I don't think it's broken," he groaned, relaxing his head onto Leyna's lap. His voice was muffled by the nasal sound from his hand covering his nostrils, a small trickle of blood escaping down to his lip from under his fingers. "But I would let him punch me any time if I knew it would result in you holding me like this."

Leyna stared down at him, her expression flat and emotionless. She couldn't tell if he was joking at first. He managed to keep a straight face until he saw the discontent on hers, his lips curling up into a pained smile. "You're such a dog." Standing up, she let his head fall with a thud to the floor, unamused by his humor. "Try not to stain your floor with your blood. I will not be scrubbing it up."

"My luck, you probably spit in my food also." With a grunt, Zander sat up on the floor, moving his hands away from his face to inspect the blood covering his skin. The amount of it made the injury look worse than it was, the bleeding already having started to ease.

Folding her arms across her chest, Leyna watched him irritably, trying not to laugh at the ridiculousness of what had just occurred. "Only once. But there are still a few more meals left to cook before I get taken away."

The pain from his nose caused Zander's eyes to water slightly, their glassy stare peering back at her curiously. "You know what," he chuckled. "I'm not entirely sure I can believe that you speak in jest."

"I will let you stew about it, then," she smiled sweetly, turning away to leave him sitting on the floor, his face starting to swell from Kael's strike. Leaving him there to stare after her, she made her way back into the kitchen, enjoying the satisfaction of knowing that, in the end, they had been successful. Now all she had to do was prepare herself for whatever life might have in store in the days to come.

The cool afternoon air felt refreshing to Leyna's senses. Morning had come and gone quickly while she finished scrubbing the floors of Zander's house. She knew it wasn't required of her, but the dust accumulation was too atrocious to ignore. Everything in the house was covered in layers that had been gathering for years, ignored by his lack of interest in upkeep. He felt that as long as the roof and walls kept out the elements, the rest mattered very little.

Giving a strong heave, she tossed the soiled water from her bucket to the ground, frowning at the feeling of the last few drops splattering against the fabric of her dress. It was the only one she had, aside from the sack that Zander called clothing. He had agreed to provide her with an outfit slightly more presentable to wear until Gislan came to take her away. There wasn't much to the dress but a simple white material edged in a delicate lace around the neckline and hem. She cared only that the skirt covered her legs down to her feet, the bottom edge now dampened from the water.

The sun was warm upon her face, reminding her of springtime in Tanispa. She and Maeri used to pick wildflowers to brighten up the dreary décor of Lady Faustine's house at this time of year. Looking up to the sky, she gave a wistful sigh, surprised by the sadness she felt at the thought of leaving that life behind. Homesick. It didn't make sense. She'd wanted out of that place for years – and yet she longed for Maeri's company. Their long talks had been the only thing which kept her sane throughout her time there.

"Leyna? Is that you?"

She must be hearing things. Her head perked up, listening intently for the sound to come again. The voice echoed on the breeze, resembling Maeri's melodic tone, but for it to be her would be impossible. She was still under Faustine's care until a suitable husband had been arranged. It must be some cruel trick of her mind.

Lowering her eyes back to her work, she heard the noise again, more insistent than before. It was coming from somewhere around the side of the house. Quiet. Almost hesitant to draw attention. Curious at the oddity of it, Leyna stepped down from the porch, scanning the area with a watchful gaze while moving in the direction of the voice. Her heart nearly leapt out of her chest as she rounded the building, nearly running directly into the familiar face of Maeri pressed up against the wooden exterior.

An initial feeling of excitement rushed through her to see her friend. It was as if the gods saw fit to grant her wish for Maeri's company, and yet something in the back of her mind prevented her from catching her friend up in the joyous embrace she so desired. A wave of fear coursed over Leyna unexpectedly. If anyone were watching Zander's house, her cover would be lost instantly if they heard her real name... or saw her consorting with a woman of obvious status such as Maeri. Even more frightening were the possibilities which passed through her head as to why Maeri was there. Had something happened in Tanispa?

Unsure of how to react to the sudden visit, Leyna ducked around to the back of the house, speaking nothing out loud, but motioning for Maeri to follow. They couldn't risk being seen outside together. Any questions she had for her friend could wait until they were safely in the cover of Zander's home.

Maeri gave no hesitation to Leyna's strange beckoning, following her inside to the sparsely decorated foyer near the front. Instinctively, Leyna shifted the lock into place on the door, her eyes glancing toward the windows to make sure the curtains were securely closed. "Maeri? What happened? What are you doing here?"

"I convinced Faustine to let me take a leave in hopes of finding where you disappeared to. You know you aren't supposed to go away without her permission. It looks bad for her business."

"And she just — let you go?" It didn't make any sense. Faustine wasn't the type to give in so easily when it came to her girls. Regardless of Leyna's mysterious disappearance, there would have to be good reason for her to release one of her charges, even temporarily. Especially one such as Maeri.

"Not exactly," Maeri glanced hesitantly around the room. Slowly, she removed the hood of her cloak, her long black hair hanging in waves around the pale skin of her face. Her emerald eyes were locked on Leyna's with a piercing gaze, filled with concern. "You left so abruptly from the ball. The whole city was in an uproar for days. I suspected you to have returned to Siscal with the gentleman from the party, knowing the stories you always told me about the city, but I didn't dare say anything to Faustine. But then Prince Enaes came to the house looking for you."

Reminded of that night, she couldn't help but feel an initial panic at what was being said about her. The whole city was in an uproar? Had anyone noticed Feolan's sudden disappearance at the same time as hers? What would they think, having seen both of Queen Vorsila's sons passing her between them on the dance floor — and with Prince Enaes so desperate to learn of her identity while she fled from the ballroom? If he'd shown himself at Faustine's door, he'd certainly discovered who she was. But how many others knew?

"What made you think I left with the gentleman from the party?"

"Lord Feolan?" Maeri asked. "You appeared to be close friends and I remembered the name vaguely from your stories about Siscal. I lost sight of him after you left which made me think he had taken you away, but we crossed paths later in the evening, so I wasn't quite so sure."

Ah, their plan had worked. The relief she felt was astonishing, knowing they'd managed to at least partially conceal their tracks behind them. "What were people saying? Not that I should care about such rumors, but my curiosity is getting the better of me."

"You are like a fairy tale in Sivaeria. The Prince's savior shows up out of nowhere, steals a dance with him, and then disappears into the night, never to be found again? It's almost romantic, in a way."

"Prince Enaes doesn't know the meaning of the word romantic," Leyna muttered, rolling her eyes heavenward. "Quite frankly, I am amazed he even remembered who I was. But, that aside, what did he want? Did you hear what was said between him and Lady Faustine?"

Maeri shifted uncomfortably on her feet. "He wanted to know where you had gone. It isn't like Faustine to let her girls loose like that. I am sure you can imagine how disappointed he was to learn that you'd slipped through her fingers."

"The last thing I wanted was for Faustine to get in trouble. I never considered the possibility of my actions coming back on her."

"Well, I managed to distract him from being too hard on her," Maeri smiled briefly, the expression fading away with another awkward glance around the room. "He recognized me as having been there with you at the masque. I managed to convince him that I might be able to find you and talk you into returning to Tanispa. The idea must have piqued his interest, because he gave Faustine no say in the matter of my leaving to seek you out. Though, she informed me I was to return immediately upon discovering your whereabouts, and I was to drag you back by your ears if I had to."

"I am not letting you anywhere near my ears," Leyna frowned at the thought of going back to Faustine's. It was strange to think that only moments ago she'd almost convinced herself that she missed being there.

"Trust me; I don't want to have to drag you anywhere by anything. You look to be doing well for yourself here, however. Is this place yours?" Maeri peered about the room, wrinkling her nose up at the lack of furniture. It was a bachelor's nest through and through, decorated only with the bare necessities needed to entertain an occasional guest. Little else occupied the small sitting room to give it any style for the eye of a fashionable woman.

Leyna weaved her fingers through her tangled hair, wishing desperately that she'd been able to find some kind of brush to tame it had she known to expect company. She was grateful at least that the worst of the dust had been cleared away before Maeri's arrival. "Oh, this? No – no, this... this is a long story, is what it is. How did you find me?"

Maeri looked her over closely, clearly conscious of her evasiveness. "Well, I expected it to be more difficult than it was, really. Faustine never would have willingly given me any personal information about you. You know how she is about sharing the last names of her students amongst the others in the house. She is always so afraid one of her noble ladies will discover herself to be sharing a room with a common girl and create a fuss. Thankfully, I remembered her saying your name when she introduced us to Lord Feolan, so I had that to go by. But no one around here knew of you, or those who did had not seen you in years."

"Well, I refuse to believe that you came upon me here by chance," Leyna smiled slightly, the humor of her words falling short of amusing herself. "You must have come across someone, but I am only aware of one or two who know where I am."

"Then I must have happened upon both of them."

Leading Maeri over to the dining area, she pulled out a chair for her to sit in. "Both?" she pondered quietly. "Who exactly did you find?"

"I could never forget the face of that man who came by Faustine's to visit you for your birthday. With a body like his, I figured, if you were anything like me, he would have been one of the first people you would want to see," Maeri winked. "And Lord Feolan — I know I could only see his lips when I met him at the masque, but I have dreamt about them every night since. It was without a doubt him who was next to your mystery man."

"That mystery man is the Consul to our Queen. I try not to think about his body when I am around him," Leyna blushed, dropping down uncomfortably into her own seat. "He is much too good for the likes of me to be drooling over. I accepted that long ago."

Leaning forward, Maeri placed her elbows on the table, smiling deviously at Leyna. "There is nothing wrong with looking at even those whom we cannot touch. Such features are meant to be admired. I only wonder if he looks as good with his shirt off as he does with it on."

Warmth flooded into Leyna's face at Maeri's words. Such a forward comment for a young lady to make, yet it brought back memories in her own mind which had been long forgotten over the years. Her eighteenth birthday, though clouded by the alcohol she'd consumed at Teagan's insistence, remained a constant play of images in the back of her mind. She'd thought over her conversation with Thade in the ladies' room many times after that night, unsure of how she should feel regarding it. Even to her young mind, the sight of him there, unbuttoning his shirt, had not gone unappreciated in any way. It didn't take a fully matured woman to know that he was, in Maeri's words, deliciously sexy, but way out of her league. She blamed her thoughts back then on the alcohol, but she couldn't deny it now in her sobriety.

"I didn't think it possible for your face to turn such a shade of red. Is there something you are not telling me?" Maeri's voice pulled her from her reverie, only adding to the embarrassment she was already feeling. The last thing she wanted to admit was that she'd been in any situation with a man where his shirt was removed. What would that make her look like?

She was fidgeting. That would do nothing to divert Maeri's inquisitive gaze. Leyna's hand rubbed uncomfortably at her neck, averting her eyes from Maeri. "It is nothing. I was just thinking about something, is all."

"I think you were picturing him with his shirt off," Maeri laughed. "The question then would have to be whether you have personal experience to base that image on, or if you are just left with your imagination, like I am."

"You are so out of line for one who claims to be a lady," Leyna shook her head, laughing quietly to herself. Her nerves had given way to an uncomfortable fit of giggling, a feeling she hadn't experienced since she left Maeri behind at Lady Faustine's. "I saw it once. Years ago. But there is nothing to the story at all, so don't start thinking anything of it."

"Was it as nice as I like to think it would be?"

"Better," Leyna laughed. She couldn't believe she was saying such a thing. If anyone else were to overhear her, she would crawl under the table and die. It was wrong of her. He was a dear friend and it wasn't right for her to be discussing him like he was a mere trophy to be gawked at by women.

Cutting her laughter short, she leaned back in her chair, clearing her throat uncomfortably. Where had their conversation been before Maeri managed to distract them with her uncouth thoughts? If she didn't know any better, she would have considered Maeri to be far more experienced in matters of men than she let on. "Anyway," Leyna coughed. "You recognized Lord Feolan?"

"His lips, yes," Maeri chuckled, her voice trailing off at the sound of someone entering the room from the kitchen.

"She knows all about his lips, don't you, Leyna?"

Zander. Oh, how long had he been listening? Covering her face with her hands, she ignored his question, not wanting anyone to see her flushed skin. "Go away." she grumbled, muffled from under the pressure of her palms.

He was unfazed by her tone, moving casually over to lean against the table beside her. "I knew about your locking lips with Feolan, but I had no idea about you and the

Consul. Now you have me curious. Dare I ask how you convinced him to allow you to participate in our mission while you two were alone in his study?"

"Zander," she replied calmly, slowly lowering her hands away from her face. "If you do not hold your tongue, I will strike you... and unlike Kael, I will make sure that your nose breaks."

Clearing his throat, Zander lightly brushed his fingers over his swollen nose, wincing at the sensitivity of the skin at his own touch. It had turned a deep shade of mixed blacks and blues, extending out to the right and along his cheek, an eyesore to the rest of his handsome features. "I will not ask about it then," he frowned. "However, I will ask who this lovely woman is whom you've brought into my home."

Leyna stood from her chair, the discomfort she felt throughout her body making it impossible to remain seated. How much could she expose Maeri to before it became dangerous for her? It was already a risk having invited her into the house. And she still wasn't certain exactly how she'd found her in the first place. "This – is my dear friend Maeri..." her mouth hung open, as if somehow a last name would come to her. She couldn't recall it. Lady Faustine had only uttered it once, and that single occasion was not enough to commit it to her memory. Too many other things had distracted her from retaining it at the time.

"Diah," Maeri smiled, rising up to give a polite curtsy. Of course. Leyna could hear Faustine's voice clearly in her mind now. The name had struck her with its familiarity at the time, though the nervous excitement of the evening had prevented her from thinking on it.

Images of the past flooded Leyna's thoughts while she watched Zander moving over to gently kiss the back of Maeri's hand. That name. Her mother had spoken it the night they fled from Tanispa. The flickering candlelight in the otherwise darkened windows of that unfamiliar house.

"Master Diah is preparing for bed. I suggest that you return in the morning when the hours are more suitable for visitation..."

What had been his name? She could remember him being tall – but to a child of her age, that meant little. His eyes. They had been a deep shade of emerald, glowing brighter than any other source of light within the home. *"I am frightened, Aviden. He will seek to find us and kill us if we stay in Tanispa."*

"Leyna, I had no idea you were important enough to be invited to the Queen's masque. It's an honor to have you as my slave," Zander laughed, turning away from Maeri's shocked expression to take a seat across from her at the table. "That explains Feolan's interest."

Shaking her head to clear her thoughts, she tried to take in what Zander was saying, only somewhat grasping his meaning. "You mention many things which you lack an understanding of. Perhaps you should think before you speak implications to which you have no backing."

"No backing? Leyna, I may speak in jest currently, but I watched the way he kissed you. There had to be at least some enjoyment in it on his end for the tenderness I sensed." The lighthearted tone had disappeared from Zander's voice, his eyes staring back at her steadily. "Regardless of what either of you say, he wanted it and you certainly did not seem opposed. You stood there and let it happen; and even you cannot deny that you returned the kiss."

Had she? It was hard to believe, but everything had happened so fast. One minute she was being pulled into Teagan's gruff embrace while the next she was being held close in Feolan's arms, his lips pressing gently against her own. She hadn't moved to prevent it or to stop it. There had been no time to. By the time she'd realized what was happening, Feolan was already drawing away from her. "You linger on an act which does not matter at all, nor is it any of your business."

She was very aware of Maeri's questioning gaze. Her confusion was justified, given the heated banter between her and Zander. Maeri was learning much just from their bickering. No doubt the mention of her being Zander's slave had been the first thing to catch her attention. The discussion about kissing Feolan would likely have been the second, considering her obsession with his lips. She would want to know all about them, once the initial shock wore off from the rest of the information being tossed about. "Leyna," she said hesitantly. "I nearly forgot the reason I sought you out, but I am reminded now."

"Oh?" Leyna peered over to Maeri quizzically. Somehow their conversation had veered off course drastically. "I was curious myself as to how you learned of my whereabouts. You say you spoke with the Consul and Lord Feolan, but I find it hard to believe they would have told you where I was."

"You are correct," Maeri nodded, making no attempt to argue the truth in Leyna's statement. "Honestly, it took far more work to pull anything from them than I would have liked. The Consul is like a rock. I had to wait until he left the room before I could try and whittle away Lord Feolan."

"I was under the impression, based on what you said before, that you merely bumped into them on the street – "

"Of course not." Noticing Zander's questioning gaze upon her, Maeri fidgeted in her seat. "I might seem ignorant at times, but I'm smarter than you think. I recalled Lord Feolan to be associated with the Consul. When I arrived, the first thing I did was seek out the Consul's home in hopes of either finding you there or, at the very least, someone who could tell me whether or not you were in the city."

Rolling her eyes heavenward, Leyna exhaled an exasperated breath. So she'd manipulated the information from Feolan. It explained a great deal, though how Maeri pulled off such a feat, she wasn't entirely sure she wanted to know. "So that is why you approached the way you did. I thought it curious for you to be so discreet. What all did you extract from him?"

"Only bits and pieces, but enough to know that I needed to find you and convince you not to do this. Have you lost your mind, Leyna? Because I made sure to tell the Consul that he clearly lost his in putting you in such a position."

"If you came here to convince me not to do this, then you are wasting your time. Does Feolan know you were coming to find me? They were okay with the idea?" It was foolish, in her opinion. Maeri's arrival to Zander's home could ruin everything. Thade was an intelligent man. He never would have allowed it, nor would he have trusted a woman he barely knew to cross such a dangerous line.

Maeri pursed her lips irritably. "They were going to try and keep me away from you. Once the Consul discovered Lord Feolan divulged your location to me, he insisted I remain there with them. He was convinced that my association with you could be detrimental – but I fail to see why. No one in this city knows who I am."

"So you directly disobeyed the Consul's orders?" Zander's mouth hung agape at the thought. "Do you have any idea of the repercussions that could bring?"

"Well, I could not just stand around there knowing my best friend was being used as some kind of bait. Leyna, you could be killed!" Caught up in her emotions, Maeri's hand slammed down on the table, the impact causing her to flinch in surprise at her own action. "I had to get away from there. For all I know, they are still out looking for me. What exactly is it that you intend to do? And why does this man call you his slave?"

"Because, in a sense, I am," Leyna sighed, sitting stiffly back down in her chair. There was no point in lying to her. Zander had opened up the questions with his absent-minded rambling, not to mention whatever Feolan unwittingly let slip under Maeri's prying. It would all come out eventually – it would just cause less frustration if she was honest about it now.

"In a sense? In exactly what sense is that?"

"The one where she is serving our people and the Queen," Zander cut in. "I would never actually enslave her. It would be traitorous to do so to my own kin."

Reaching her hand across the table, Leyna lightly rested it on Maeri's arm, hoping she would understand what she was about to say. "What I am about to tell you can never leave this room. If anyone were to find out, I could be killed for it… and possibly you as well for being an accomplice. Do you understand?"

"Yes. Of course, I understand, Leyna. I understood that much before I even came here, which is why I disagree wholeheartedly with your participation in this."

"But do you swear not to speak of it?"

"I will tell no one. Just tell me what is going on so I can better understand why our Queen's men would do this to you."

"I am working secretly for the Consul in order to infiltrate a group of possible traitors to our people. In order to do that, I have had to disguise myself to arrange for my sale as a slave to one of their more powerful leaders. This will allow me access to their home, and if we are lucky, to whatever information they might have which will help to prevent – whatever it is that they are planning to do."

"You are spying on them but don't know what they are planning to do?" It was a logical question for Maeri to ask. Possibly one of the most difficult ones for Leyna to accept as well. They had speculation, but no facts.

"We have ideas," she frowned. "We know one of them has ties to the Ven'shal and that they might be planning to find a means of bringing Arcastus back to life — but we have nothing else to support that. We need someone to get in close enough to find out more… and that person right now is me."

Maeri leaned back in her chair, taking in the details presented to her. Leyna couldn't blame her for the disapproval she read there on her friend's face, barely contained by her gentle features. Maeri was no fool. She knew the history of their people very well, thanks to Faustine's teachings, and while she couldn't possibly know the full extent of the danger, she clearly knew enough to drive her to argue. "And once you are 'sold' to these people, then what? How do you anticipate getting this so-called information to the Consul? Slaves are not exactly allowed to roam about freely to sneak around and visit whoever they please. They will be watching you like a hawk… imagine if a man was attempting to court you and Lady Faustine was leaning over your shoulder every step of the way."

She couldn't help but laugh at the mental image of Faustine tagging along with one of them while out with a prospective suitor. Her point was valid, however. Nothing would get past Faustine's eyes much the same way nothing would get by the watchful eyes of those in charge of the slaves.

How could that detail have slipped by her? It was difficult enough for Zander and Kael to keep the communication between themselves and Thade as free men within Gislan's circle. That task would be made ten times more difficult for her as a mere slave under Mikel's employ. She wouldn't have the freedom like the others. They would have to find a stealthier means of extracting the information and slipping it through the cracks.

"I was still working on that detail," Zander grumbled, flopping back in his chair in frustration. Leyna didn't know what else she could say. Their mission would be pointless if she was trapped inside it with no way of getting information out. "I guess I hoped the Consul would have told us how to accomplish that."

Propping her head up with her hand on the table, she heaved a sigh, shrugging her shoulders in defeat. "I am sure he expected us to think of it, since this whole thing was our idea. You know how much he disapproved of it in the first place."

"He did? Given how easily he folded on the matter, I assumed he did not mind too much."

Leyna peered quizzically at him from under her long lashes. How could he possibly not know? He had been there... "Ah, yes. You showed up after I had already argued him into submission. I suppose that makes this my fault, then. All I was thinking about was getting him to let me help. The smaller details really weren't at the forefront of my mind at the time."

"Well..." Maeri nibbled her lip thoughtfully. "Since clearly I have no chance in changing your mind — is there anyone else involved who would be closer to you?"

Shaking her head, Leyna tried to picture how angry Kael would be if he were to learn the truth about her. To be kept in the dark by his own people. Thade and Feolan must have had their reasons for hiding such details from him. But why, then, had they revealed so much to her? They had no choice other than to tell her about Zander, but Kael — his involvement could have remained a mystery.

"There is no one."

It wasn't really a lie. There would be no one close enough to her that could know about her intentions. Regardless of his status as an ally, Kael had to remain a stranger to the truth. She couldn't rely on him to pass word to Thade for her. There was no saying he would even be allowed near her once under the ownership of Mikel.

"What if I could help?"

"No." She couldn't allow Maeri to get involved. It was too dangerous to even consider. If she was caught as an accomplice, they would both be killed. Much the same way that Maeri knew could happen to Leyna. Why would she fight with her to convince her not to do this only to willingly throw herself into the middle of it as well? "Maeri, I know you mean well, but I cannot allow you to even think about putting yourself in that position."

Maeri raised her eyebrow at Leyna, her gentle features transforming into an uncharacteristic frown. "So I came here fearing you to be in danger, only to find that you are, in fact, in deeper than I thought and too stubborn to listen to my pleas of stepping down from the idea — and now you refuse to let me help you?"

"Within the next day or so, they will be coming to take me away to Dalonshire. I have no way of knowing where I will be once there or anything else about what my predicament will escalate to."

"Dalonshire? I could travel there ahead of you and keep watch for your arrival –"

"Maeri!" The thought alone was scaring her. It frightened her to think that Maeri's idea could have merit while knowing it was such a risk to take. If anything happened to her friend because of her, she would never be able to forgive herself. "I cannot, in good conscience, allow you to do anything."

Anger was slowly starting to build in Maeri's eyes once again. Leyna could see it there, the deep green glow flaring brighter. Her hand dropped hard down to the table, her back stiffening against the chair where she sat. "From the sounds of things, however, you cared little about the consciences of others in regards to your own involvement. I could see it in the Consul's eyes when I questioned him. Neither he nor Feolan wanted to let you do this. Do you have any idea what they must be feeling right now? Or if they discover you are ill-treated in any way, how much do you think that will hurt them, knowing it was their fault because you convinced them to allow it? You will force others to experience that pain but yet you will save yourself from it? Even though you know you need help and I might be capable of providing that?"

Her words were like daggers to Leyna's heart. The truth behind them was startling. She'd been unable to get the thought out of her mind about how Thade would feel if he knew anything about the treatment she was already receiving simply for the sake of their act, let alone the pain it would cause him if anything happened to her in Dalonshire. The tortured look in his eyes that night in the study when she insisted he allow it. Yet she'd fought with him. She had worn him down with her own twisted logic, convincing him that he would be doing her a greater injustice by preventing her from doing what she wanted. It was selfish of her then much the same way it was selfish of her now to deny Maeri her request.

Leyna hung her head shamefully. She couldn't believe what she was about to agree to. It went against everything she believed. "What do you have in mind?"

The anger on Maeri's face dissipated instantly, her entire body relaxing with relief. "What I was thinking is… I could head to Dalonshire and try to keep watch for you. Now, obviously, with how little I know, there is no saying that any of this would work but, I could try to follow where they take you and keep an eye on you. If they ever allow you outside where you could hide a letter for me to retrieve, then I could bring it back to the Consul. That sounds safe enough. I could simply check back at that location every so often to see if you have left any further notes. They would never even have to know I exist."

"There are a lot of variables in that plan which could easily fall through," Leyna frowned, her features creased in contemplation. Was it worth risking Maeri's safety for something with so little guarantee?

"Leyna, frankly anything we try to arrange at this point is going to have variables and holes all over," Zander shrugged. "Any plan is better than no plan, and if it doesn't work, then essentially you get what you wanted in the first place. If there are no letters to collect, then Maeri doesn't get involved, and you have nothing to worry about except how to get yourself out of there. That's my biggest concern. No one can protect you once you are inside. They could kill you, and none of us would even know it."

"Fine." They were both against her now. There was no chance at convincing two people who were just as stubborn as she was that it wouldn't work. "If you see me in Dalonshire, do not approach me and never call me by my name. They know me as something else. But promise me – if you cannot find me there, please come back to Siscal City."

Rising from her chair, Maeri gazed solemnly at Leyna. "I can't promise you that," she sighed. With hesitant steps, she moved over to Leyna, leaning forward to wrap her arms around her tightly. "If I cannot find you, I will do everything in my power to change that without putting you in any more danger than you already are. Don't worry about me."

Leyna gave in to her friend's embrace. Something about knowing Maeri would be close eased her spirits at the thought of being sent away to Dalonshire. The future for her would be grim, but to have her friend supporting her gave at least a soft light to the situation. "Thank you," she whispered. "I will do what I can to make sure I am visible when we cross into the city. It's been years since I was there last, but if they still have the gates near the border; that would be the best place to wait for me. Any carriage even just passing through has to cross through it. I will find a way to show my face from the windows."

"Thankfully, I have a carriage ready for me. I should be heading for Dalonshire as soon as possible, I think," Maeri smiled, straightening her back up proudly. "If I linger here, the Consul might find me and prevent me from going." There in the dim light of the room, Leyna couldn't help but think that her friend looked more like a woman now than she had before.

"Be careful, Maeri." What else was there to be said? Lowering into a curtsy before Zander, Maeri was already heading toward the door. Her mind was set. She would find Leyna, whatever the cost. Of that, Leyna was certain. Her friend had proven to be crafty as a young girl when they'd gotten into trouble around the house. She had a silver tongue that could persuade almost anyone of anything she wanted. Leyna just hoped it would work as well on these people as it had on Feolan.

Chapter Nine

The trip to Dalonshire felt different from inside a carriage than it had on horseback during the war. More comfortable, but longer. She lacked the control to speed up the pace of the animals.

Kael had accompanied Gislan to retrieve her from Zander's possession. Gislan disliked getting her hands dirty. The job of loading Leyna into the carriage had been left to Kael. The sight of him at the door sent her into a panic, afraid he would strike at Zander again the way he'd done before. Her biggest fear was that Kael would argue against Gislan's purchase of her, ruining the only chance at getting close to Mikel. Instead, he seemed to endorse it, though making sure to never let her out of his sight.

Throughout the trip, he was at her side. She was constantly aware of his presence, watching her with his sympathetic eyes. It was unnerving to Leyna while at the same time she didn't mind the feeling. His face had occupied her dreams since the day they met. Nothing more than an infatuation. He'd stood up for her, trying to comfort her in her time of strife. Those deeds couldn't be ignored, even if they were unnecessary at the time. To him it was real and he had acted for her honor.

His position at her side in the carriage kept her heart rate steadily above normal. At Faustine's, they were rarely in the company of men. It was forbidden under any circumstance unless the man was the driver of Faustine's carriage. Because of that, she found her body's reaction to Kael confusing. Her hands trembled at the thought of him next to her. The sound of his voice made her stomach flutter uncontrollably. She didn't like the feeling one bit. During the war, she always had control of her senses around the men, which made it easy for her to dismiss their affections. Now there was some part of her that both craved and feared Kael's attention. It made no sense to her rational mind.

"How much further do we have to go? If I have to stare at these dreary walls another minute, I am going to go mad," Gislan complained.

"It will not be long," Kael replied calmly, his eyes glancing casually out the window. "We will be passing through the gates in another ten minutes or so."

Ten minutes. Her heart raced again, wondering if Maeri had made it to the city safely. She had a full day's head start on them. More than enough time to settle herself at an inn and seek out a hiding place near the border.

It was impossible to keep her head clear. So many thoughts and emotions ran wild in her mind at everything around her. From this moment on, it was no longer a game that she played. The danger was more real now than it ever was before. It was one thing to think about how life would be as a slave – it was a completely different feeling to realize that she was one. She was the property of Gislan... and Zander had profited well at the cost of her freedom.

She was bothered that Zander accepted the money from Gislan, though she knew very well he had no choice but to do it. If he'd given her away at no charge, Gislan might have become suspicious. Zander was supposed to be a businessman, after all. And businessmen didn't get anywhere by giving away their wares for free. It just hurt to think that her life had been attached to a price tag. *You did this to yourself when you forced Thade to let you help.*

Thade. She couldn't think about him. The mere mention of his name caused her heart to ache. He must be miserable, knowing that the trade had gone off successfully. Zander told her he would be heading to see him as soon as their carriage was out of sight. By now Thade and Feolan would both be aware that she was gone and there was no longer any hope of her backing out.

The terrain outside was starting to look familiar. They would be approaching the gates soon enough, the landscape already breaking up with a spattering of houses in the distance. This was her time to start moving around. She'd kept completely still and silent to this point, not wanting to draw any attention to herself. It might have come across as suspicious if she appeared anything but frightened and timid of her new owners.

Leaning forward, she stretched her neck to see outside the carriage from over Kael's lap. As she pressed against him, she heard him draw in a sharp breath, his upper body stiffening at her touch. It was strange to her. His body language suggested that he was nervous, but she couldn't place if it was a hesitation at what Gislan would say about her actions, or if it was simply at her being close to him. He was harder to read than any of the other men she'd ever encountered… not counting the Consul. She had determined that he was absolutely impossible to decipher. There was no comparison to him.

Up ahead, she could see the gate approaching. She worried about the subtlety of Maeri, afraid that her presence might be noticeable from inside the carriage. Well-groomed trees and flowers lined the gates, creating ample places for one to hide from view of the road if they had need to. Finding no sign of her, Leyna felt only a brief moment of relief at the thought of Maeri having utilized such cover – the feeling quickly replaced by a gnawing fear that she wasn't there at all. "Is this your first time to Dalonshire? You look intrigued by it."

His voice rang loudly next to her ear, reminding her of how close she was to his mouth. Watching the town gates pass them by through the window, she hesitantly leaned back in the seat, lowering her eyes down to the floor of the carriage. She couldn't respond. It was important that she not come across too comfortable with her situation. There would be plenty of time to speak with Kael later, if his position amongst Mikel and Oksuva allowed him regular access to her. It was hard to judge with him. Without knowledge of how their house worked, she could only assume it would be similar to Gislan and Zander. Frequent visits, but otherwise private housing for their family alone.

"Answer the man, girl. He asked you a question." Gislan's voice was sharp, cracking like a whip to Leyna's confused senses. How should she respond? She couldn't tell the truth. They suspected her to have been a slave for years, even prior to being taken captive by Zander.

Nervously, she cast her eyes up to Kael's for a moment before quickly averting them once again. She couldn't look at him. The look in his eyes burned through her in a way that she couldn't bear to endure. "Yes, sir," she lied, her voice barely above a whisper. "I have never been to Siscal at all before my master brought me here."

"He is not your master anymore," Kael cut in sharply. It granted her the opportunity to take up her silence again, not wanting to continue speaking in Gislan's presence. Her story had too many holes in it which she had yet to fill in. Discussion of her past right now could pose serious issues to her cover.

His statement ended any chance at conversation, his jaw clenched tightly with restrained anger. No, he could never know the truth. She tortured him with her lies. To let him know it was all for naught would surely cause him to hate her… and she couldn't bear the thought of him hating her. Quite the contrary, she longed for him to keep his affection for her that she believed he carried, for she was certain that she had somehow fallen prey to him with her own.

The carriage continued on through the city at a steady pace, the wheels grinding along the gravel of the main road. The shops were filled with streams of people moving about, in and out of the doors, hurrying along the streets to do their shopping. Though not as large as the city of Siscal itself, it looked to be almost as populated, the people merely condensed into a smaller area.

In the distance loomed an impressive estate set back away from the hustle and bustle of the city. A well-constructed fence of stone and mortar surrounded the perimeter to the front, though it couldn't hide the massive building behind its meager height, more for decoration than any practical use. Aside from the homes of nobility, it was the largest Leyna had ever seen, growing bigger with every step closer the horses brought them, the roof climbing higher in the sky until it blocked the clouds from view where the carriage came to a stop in front of it.

Before the horses finished their final steps, Gislan was already on her feet, preparing to step through the door. "I need out of this blasted cage," she grumbled, wasting no time in clambering outside. In the freedom of the late afternoon breeze, she turned back around, blocking Kael's exit through the door. "You know your way around here better than I do. Take her down to the cellar and see that she is properly shackled. We must keep her out of the way until Mikel's party tomorrow night."

"Shackled? Gislan, I doubt that will be necessary —"

"Kael, you will do what I say." Gislan's voice was firm and unyielding. Leyna knew there would be no changing her mind. The evening would come to pass for Leyna in the darkest corner of this house, no matter the protests Kael might try. He lacked the obvious sway over her that Zander had exhibited. It was clear which of the two she favored.

He thought to argue with her more. Drawing in a deep breath, he prepared to launch into a heated debate, his mouth twitching irritably at the realization that he was wasting his time. He pursed his lips together tightly, bobbing his head up and down in a short nod of acceptance.

The stern look on Gislan's face faded away, replaced by a false air of sweetness about her entire person. She patted Kael's cheek lightly with her hand as if he were a small child. From where she was sitting, Leyna could feel every muscle in his body tense at the gesture, barely holding himself back from slapping her hand away. Gislan missed nothing. Sensing his tension, she erupted into high-pitched laughter. She was taking a grotesque pleasure in forcing him to act against his wishes. He didn't dare say nor do anything to Gislan in return.

How it must hurt his pride to have to stand there and take such treatment from this woman. An Esai. If he held the same contempt for her kind that Zander had displayed, it would have to be eating away at him inside. On the surface, he hid it extremely well. It wasn't until Gislan had taken her leave of him and he had returned his attention to Leyna that she could see the frustration in his eyes. "This is only temporary, I promise you," he frowned, taking her hand gently in his own, leading her out of the carriage onto the street. "Once Gislan has transferred possession of you over to Mikel, I will try to bargain with him for your freedom. Or at least a more pleasant living arrangement than that of his slaves."

A more pleasant living arrangement than his other slaves? Oh, that did not bode well in her mind. How bad could those arrangements be? Shackles in a damp and darkened cellar? Or could he imply that the conditions were even worse?

Now wasn't the time for questions. He was leading her through the carved wooden door of the grand house, slipping quietly down a back hallway off to one side of the foyer. They moved too quickly for her to see anything within the house, noting only that the entryway was spacious and well-tended, the tiles on the floor gleaming brightly from the afternoon sunlight pouring in from a glass setting in the domed ceiling.

Further down the darkened hallway, Kael came to a stop in front of an arched wooden door with a heavy steel reinforcement running along the top and bottom of the boards. Leaving her off to one side, it took both of his hands to remove the sturdy latch from its resting place, allowing him to pull the door open on its grinding hinges. Fear gripped Leyna's heart at the feeling of his hand clasping hers once again, tugging her closer to the thick black hole that extended beyond the door. It was completely dark. There was no sign of light to lead the way or warn her of what lay hidden in the depths of that place.

It reminded her of the suffocating darkness of the chest her mother had hidden her away inside the day she was killed. The scar from the chest latch burned on her back. She'd hoped to take whatever her mission threw at her with dignity, but the suppressed emotions from her childhood held her back, her feet stiffening, locking her legs in place at Kael's efforts to pull her forward.

"Eleni, please," he urged gently. She didn't care how softly he spoke to her. The last place she wanted to go was through that door.

Her breath caught in her throat at the feeling of Kael's arms wrapping around her legs, sweeping her up off her feet. No. She didn't want to go. Panic overpowered every other conscious thought in her mind, her hands pressing hard against his chest in her attempts to free herself from his grasp. She didn't know exactly where she would go if she managed to break loose and regain her footing. All she knew was that if they were going to force her to go there, she refused to go without a fight.

Foolishness. She hated the fact that she maintained such a ridiculous weakness after all these years. After so many battles and everything she'd seen, her mind couldn't overcome the simple fear of that box she'd been captive in for those long hours, listening to the sounds of her mother being slaughtered while she hid away. That absolute darkness she couldn't escape to offer aid to those she loved. And here she was allowing herself to be put into it again. What if her friends were in danger and she was again trapped, unable to get to them?

She wasn't sure exactly when her struggling ceased, her frantic squirming changing to a desperate hold around Kael's neck, clinging to him in the impenetrable darkness around them. He held her against him tightly, hushing her quietly to ease her trembling body. Somewhere in the distance she could see a soft flicker illuminating the end of the hallway. The glow of the sconce against the wall sent a wave of relief throughout her entire being, her head slumping against Kael's shoulder. Light. The darkness wouldn't be claiming her quite yet.

Upon reaching the corner where the sconce lit the thick stones of the walls, Kael lowered Leyna back down to the ground, holding tightly to her hand in case she tried to run. There was no need for that anymore. The gentle flames helped to restore her senses, reminded of how imperative her mission was. She couldn't put it all at risk because of her silly phobias. Their goals were too important for that.

A set of steep stairs wound its way deeper down, the smell of soil telling her that they were making their way below the surface of the yard outside. The faint scent of mold clung to the stone walls, mingling with other fragrances that she couldn't quite separate. It wasn't entirely pleasant, while not the most unpleasant she'd ever experienced. It would take a bit of getting used to, if she were to be kept away in this miserable place.

The opening for the stairs was only wide enough for a single person to fit. Guiding her in front of him, Kael lightly pushed her along, blocking her path back to the entrance. There was something foreboding about this place. It was like a dungeon from the fairy tales she was told as a young girl when Nasha would read to her and Reina before bed. Only there would be no prince to rescue her from this prison. Her prince was most likely distracted by some other young female, frolicking about the streets of Tanispa. Her well-being would be the furthest thing from his mind.

At the base of the stairs, she felt her legs lock up once again. Not expecting her sudden halt, Kael continued forward, nearly knocking her off her feet with his momentum. Reflexively, he reached out for her, wrapping his arms around her waist to keep her from falling. She was only vaguely aware of his hands against her. The sight before her was too shocking for her to focus on anything else.

Along the walls, the stone broke open into several rooms, separated by heavy steel bars crossing from the floor to the ceiling, intersected by another set running side to side. It was more than just similar to the stories she'd been told as a child. This was the closest thing to those horrible dungeons she'd ever seen. Submerged underground, there was no natural light to break the shadows within each cell, the walls dingy and covered with specks of mold near the corners. "What is this place?"

She didn't care about the rules of speaking anymore. There was no one close enough to hear her whisper other than Kael. "This is the cellar. Mikel likes to keep most of his slaves here. Only a select few stay on the upper levels." He was so close to her. She hadn't realized just how much until his soft voice breezed by her ear, his breath warming her skin. Her heart didn't race the way she expected it to. Instead it beat with a steady, almost hollow rhythm within her chest. Each pulse hard and jarring, making it difficult to breathe.

"Am I to remain here forever?"

"No. No, I would never allow that to happen," Kael shook his head, spinning her body around to face him. "I just need you to be strong for me. Only for a night at least, until Mikel decides what he wants to do with you. After that, I will do everything in my power to convince him to let you move to the slaves' quarters upstairs until I negotiate the terms of your freedom."

Hanging her head, Leyna stepped away from Kael. One night at least. Worded in that fashion implied the possibility of a lengthier stay. Even a single evening sounded like an eternity when faced with this dismal place. And what if he couldn't negotiate her freedom the way he hoped? The thought alone sent shivers down her spine. None of this was working according to their plan. It would be impossible to sneak any form of written correspondence to the Consul if she were locked in this dungeon. Even worse, the chance of her determining any intelligence to benefit their cause was unlikely through the thickness of the stone walls and ceiling. It was too easy to fall to the daunting thoughts that she had given her life up for nothing.

Kael guided her forward, leading her up to one of the cells at the far end of the hall. She tried to ignore the sickly looking figures of slaves lying on the floors of other cells, curled up for warmth in the corners. The depression was overwhelming, filling her with anxiety at the thought of ending up like them. Tears moistened her long lashes. All she wanted to do was sit down and cry – to let out all of the emotions which had been slowly accumulating inside her up to this point. None of her earlier fears could even compare to the reality she was faced with now. But she couldn't allow herself to show that kind of weakness. She had to be strong, for the sake of her people. For the sake of Thade. She'd given him her assurances that she would be fine. What would he think of her if she were to collapse into a heap of tears in the cage of her enemy?

The creaking of the hinges pulled her back from her thoughts. She was better than this. She just had to keep reminding herself. It was hard to believe that only a few weeks ago she had been welcomed as an adult among her people by the gods. They couldn't abandon her now. And she couldn't abandon them with premature defeat.

With her chin held high, she stepped through the open bars into the cell. Gracefully, she made her way to the center of the tiny space, kneeling down on the floor without regard of what might contaminate its surface. *Think back to the night by the sacred lake.* Clearing her thoughts, she imagined the fresh air of the Tanispan forests surrounding her; the rustle of the leaves in the trees fluttering on a cool evening breeze. There had been no fear that night. No negative feelings of defeat. Only a pure devotion to her people, her ancestors, and to the gods, placing her life and soul in their hands for guidance. This night would be no different from the test she had completed then.

In her meditative state, she never heard the bars of the cell closing behind her, sealing her in without any chance of escape. They would not have the satisfaction of seeing her broken on their dirty floors. She may be their slave in body, but her spirit was that of the Vor'shai. Her enemy would not wear her down so easily.

Her legs were numb by the time the sound of footsteps could be heard echoing through the narrow passage of the stairs. The gait sounded masculine. A part of her prayed silently for it to be Kael's face on the other side of the bars when they opened. She refused to turn around until she was summoned, holding her posture erect and unmoving from where she remained kneeling in the center of the floor.

"Have you not moved at all since I left you last night?"

The gods had heard her prayers. She thought to rise up to greet Kael, but the lack of blood flow through her legs would have made it impossible. It would make her look dedicated to her meditation at the very least. He need not be aware that her stillness at this point was owed to her physical inability to move rather than her iron will.

She was thankful for the feeling of his hands lightly grabbing onto her arm, lifting her carefully to her feet. The uncomfortable tingling sensation pulsed through her legs at the blood slowly easing back into circulation. *Please don't let him make me walk. Just one more minute. . .*

"I regret to inform you that I have yet to have an opportunity to speak with Mikel. He still is unaware of your presence here in the house. I expect to find time to approach the matter this evening, however." It was as she expected. But had a whole day really passed since he led her down to this dreary place? It felt like only a few hours, though the stiffness of her limbs told her she'd lost more time than that. She must have fallen asleep while sitting up.

Easing her toward the open cell door, he acted as a support for her unsteady legs, helping to keep her upright while she regained her strength. Apprehension set in at the thought of walking through that darkened hallway again. The only comfort she could offer herself was knowing that it was nothing more than a corridor leading to the light of the upper levels. It would prove nothing for her to lose her senses through it the way she had the night before. To do so again would only be a greater humiliation than she'd already exposed herself to.

Kael paused inside the cellar door, hesitating to open it and relieve the heavy darkness surrounding them. Leyna fought internally to steady her mind. Her hands trembled, fidgeting at her sides to keep from reaching out and opening it herself. The familiar panic coursed through her, making her want to scream at the uncomfortable rush of adrenaline through her veins. It was thick, filling her lungs with tension until she could hardly breathe.

The creak of the hinges was like a breath of fresh air to her senses. She was free. The smell of food filled her nostrils, overpowering the stench of mold and dirt which had settled over her senses throughout the night. It brought with it the sharp, stabbing pangs of hunger in her stomach, reminding her that she had consumed nothing since the evening before Gislan and Kael arrived to take her away. There hadn't been enough time to worry about food that morning when they came... and nothing was provided to any of the slaves held captive in the cellar.

Her body felt weak from the lack of nutrients in her system, but it was something which she could use to her advantage. The trembling in her hands would give the appearance of frailty and hesitance that was necessary to keep up her act in front of Mikel. She didn't know what to expect from him, but from what she'd heard, he was not a man to be trifled with. He would be able to see through her ruse if she did not veil it properly.

"If I could have your attention please!"

There was no denying the sound of Gislan's voice rising above the din of conversation reaching Leyna's ears from near the foyer. They were drawing closer to the sound. With every step, the words being spoken through the idle chatter started to come more clearly, forming sentences that made sense in language, but not in the subjects of which were spoken. At the announcement, they fell to a hushed tone, trailing off into silence as Leyna and Kael reached the end of the hall.

The foyer was immaculately decorated for the affair with candles and flowers arranged all throughout the spacious area. The room was filled with unfamiliar faces dressed in their best suits and gowns, holding goblets of what might be wine in their hands, their necks craning and their eyes focused on Gislan's confident figure, creating a space around her in the middle of the floor. "I think now would be the perfect time for me to present my gift to my dear brother-in-law. I have hardly been able to contain myself from telling the secret, but I somehow managed to keep it in."

Laughter erupted around the room at her lighthearted remarks, rippling like a wave throughout the crowd and then gradually falling silent once again. A man at the front of the room caught Leyna's attention from among the others. He was sitting at the center of a large table, his long black hair lying perfectly straight over his shoulders, the sharp point of his ears protruding from either side. His clothing was of a fine make, the crimson cloth of his tunic edged in golden cord, the high lacy collar concealing almost all of his neck but a single line which could be seen through the opening at his throat. His lips were curled up in a jovial smile, his eyes so dark that she couldn't decipher their color from where she was standing.

A woman was seated at the man's side. Her resemblance to Gislan was uncanny, though her hair was significantly longer and more stylish for that of a lady. It was currently pulled back away from her face to reveal her rounded ears, tiny strands dangling in elegant blonde curls along the sides of her painted cheeks. Her eyes shared the familiar glow, radiating forth with the inner magic of the Vor'shai. Oksuva. That had been the name given to Gislan's sister. If this woman was in fact the other Esai of the family, then it left the male to be none other than Mikel himself, watching Gislan's performance with unveiled amusement.

"Kael? Will you bring it forward, please? I cannot wait any longer."

Leyna's heart leapt into her throat with its sudden pounding beat. That was her cue. The crowd was already separating to create a path for Kael, his eyes sweeping over the people calmly as he led her through to where Gislan was standing. Hushed murmurs passed through the onlookers, questioning who she was, and why she was there. Mikel was on his feet in a single fluid motion, nearly sending his chair toppling backward from the momentum of his body.

The soft expression on Oksuva's face vanished at the sight of Leyna standing there. Her gaze was like fire, narrowing her eyes disapprovingly toward her sister, making no effort to hide her irritation. Leyna thought she would speak out in protest of the gift, but instead she remained seated, her dainty mouth pursed tightly into a thin line across her petite face.

"My wonderful sister, could this be what I think it is?" His voice was deep, carrying easily across the room from where he made his way around the table to reach where they were standing. Up close, Leyna could see the dark color of his eyes filled more than the thin iris surrounding the pupil. The deep shade of black extended outward, fading into thinner bands of grey that grew gradually fainter out to the corners of his eyes. She had never seen anything like it before. They radiated with an energy different from that of any Vor'shai she'd ever met, the eerie feeling of his gaze reminding her of the Ven'shal that had attacked her outside the tavern in Velorum.

With a hard grip, he pulled Leyna away from Kael's hands, spinning her around to look her over appraisingly. The whispers through the guests were growing more distinct, a few revealing a hint of distaste at the display while others reacted with approval at a Vor'shai being brought to the hands of this man. "What an interesting specimen you have uncovered with this one. I must say I would never have expected the market to provide one quite so…"

"Pleasing to the eye?" Kael cut in, finishing the sentence for him. His tone lacked the pleasure that was so obvious in every rise and fall of Mikel's voice.

"Mm, yes, that would be one way of putting it." Mikel's eyes were the most disconcerting thing for Leyna to see. They slid over her body with a hungry gaze, peering at her in a manner that made her think he was seeing through the thin fabric of her dress. Lifting her arms uncomfortably, she wrapped them around her chest, averting her eyes modestly to the floor. Her fear of this man only added to the uneasiness she already felt. She could no longer hide her trembling hands, fidgeting nervously with the fabric of her dress.

Grabbing Leyna harshly by the shoulders, Mikel turned her around to face the crowd, holding her in place in case she tried to run. "My friends and guests! Tonight my sister has brought me the best gift I could have asked for." A sharp impact of his foot connecting with the backs of her legs caused them to buckle, dropping her instantly to her knees in front of him, grimacing painfully. "Behold my proud enemy, kneeling before me, and before all of you!"

Cheers could be heard from all over the room. They were nothing but a distant echo in the back of Leyna's mind as Mikel clenched his fist tightly around her hair, yanking her head back with a hard snap to reveal her exposed neck to the crowd. "Such a pity, really," he whispered into her ear, tracing his free hand along the line of her throat. "But this, my friends, will be the gift that keeps on giving."

Humiliation burned through her veins in a way she never knew it could. She was at the mercy of this man. Whatever he wanted to do, she was powerless to stop him, stripped of any weapon other than her hands, which even she knew would be no match for him in her weakened state. Before she could register what was happening, she felt Mikel's hand press forward, the sight of the floor rising swiftly up to meet her face sending a jolt through her body before it made contact. The pain was excruciating. Warm liquid poured over her lips from the strike, the coppery taste mingling with the gritty feeling of dirt in her mouth.

It all happened so quickly, she had no time to think about the pain until after it was already there. The discomfort came at her from all over her head, making it impossible to focus on any one injury. Her nose throbbed from where it collided with the floor, and yet the constant sting of Mikel's hand still entwined with her hair pulled her attention away. Through her pain, she could hear Kael's voice speaking softly to Mikel, the words making no sense to her incoherent thoughts.

"No scream? I'm almost impressed," Mikel scoffed, releasing his grip on her head. "Either way, that brought me great satisfaction. Kael, you will take her down to the cellar so she will stop bleeding on my floor. We still have much to celebrate and I cannot have my guests getting their feet dirtied."

"Perhaps we should have a doctor see to her injuries…"

"Why would we do that exactly, Kael?" Silence fell between the two men. Kael held Mikel's gaze for only a moment before his eyes lowered to the ground in defeat, his arm wrapping around Leyna's gently. "Take her to the cellar and then you are to return immediately. You will be at my side before dessert is served or I will have you thrown in your own cell."

The room around her was spinning, the faces in the crowd blurring into a mass of colors against their brightly decorated clothing. Blood still ran from her nose. She could feel it, soaking into the thin fabric of her white dress. Her legs wobbled with every step she took, trusting Kael to lead her, the pain too great for her to think clearly about how to respond. There was no way for her to react other than how she already had. As a slave, she couldn't retaliate. She would have to swallow her pride and simply accept the beating. It hurt her to the core to think she would be subjecting herself to such treatment on a regular basis. She didn't know how much of it she would be able to stand before her instincts got the better of her, pushing her into action against him, and ruining everything.

In the whirl of motion, she somehow lost track of the time it took for them to pass through the crowd, hurrying down the hallway toward the heavy door leading to the horrible darkness of the cellar corridor. Her head was too distracted to focus on the fear. She felt her unsteadiness, knowing she would have fallen to her death at the foot of the stone steps had Kael not been there to hold her up, supporting the weight of her body in his arms. His strength was impressive, even through her unfocused thoughts.

"I will be back to check on you."

They were in her cell. Had she blacked out before reaching the bottom of the stairs? She had no recollection of the final distance between them and her cage. The cellar floor was cold against her skin, the chill seeping through her dress easily. There wasn't enough fabric to protect her from it. Not that she cared. Nothing mattered right now. All she could think about was the throbbing which pulsed through her entire face, her nose already swelling from the impact of the floor. It was hard to breathe. She suspected the bones had been broken somewhere along her face, but without a means of examining the wound, it was too difficult to determine exactly where the worst of the injury was.

He was gone before his words registered in her mind with enough clarity for her to think of responding. For the best, she believed. She wasn't up to entertaining him with her misery. Her despondency outweighed her desire to be near Kael, wanting only to be left alone in the cold cellar to think over what had become of her life. How had she gone from the arms of the Prince only a few short weeks ago – to the damp stone of a Ven'shal's personal prison, starved and dehydrated, covered in her own blood?

What was that sound coming from the stairs? Footsteps, light on their toes in an obvious attempt to mask their presence. Kael would have no reason for stealth in these halls. It had been made very clear to Leyna that he was closer to Mikel than she'd been led to believe through her conversation with Feolan and Thade. Could they possibly be unaware of Kael's true position amongst these people? There was no way to know how frequently he provided his correspondence, or to what degree he divulged his information.

The steps grew closer, pausing occasionally. Stopping in front of the cells? Someone was looking for something. *Oh, gods, please let it be anyone but me.* A hushed voice broke through the cell, whispering what sounded to be her true name before catching the mistake. "Eleni... I'm getting you out of here."

Zander? Great. She was hallucinating. Had the trauma to her head been that severe?

"Can you move? The stairs aren't wide enough for me to carry you, but if you are unable to —"

"I am not leaving." She didn't care if he was real or not. To think of leaving now would be foolish, making her suffering worth nothing if she returned to Siscal empty-handed. No, she would be remaining there, whatever the cost. "Besides, no one would let us out the door, even if we did manage to find a way up those stairs."

"Please, Leyna."

"That is not my name." Holding her head in her hands, she groaned under the effort it took to lift herself off the floor, sitting up to gaze around the cell with her unfocused eyes. The swelling was hindering her vision. It had begun to extend out across her cheeks and up to her lower lashes. The blow reached far along the bridge of her nose. She could only imagine how it must look.

Through the liquid in her eyes, she could see a figure kneeling outside the bars of her cell. She wasn't convinced that her mind was not playing tricks on her. In her pained and weakened state, it was possible for her subconscious to be creating these images for the sake of her own comfort. But the figure's arm was reaching out to her, pleading for her to come closer. "When I agreed to bring you into this, I knew it would be dangerous, but I never would have allowed it if I knew you would be treated this harshly. I expected maybe a dirty room and a slap on the face here or there, but this? No, I won't allow it to continue. And the Consul —"

"Hush!" The effort it took to silence him caused a wave of dizziness to wash over her. Standing wouldn't be an option, if she wished to move closer to the Zander figure. Her legs wouldn't be able to support her own weight, and even if they could, the vertigo would have her on her back faster than she could think to steady herself against the bars.

The pressure in her head was unbearable. It obscured her thoughts worse than the pain of the arrows during the war. Location of the injury had much to do with it. While the pain of the arrowheads and the burn of the poison had been distracting, it was nothing compared to a direct blow to the head, disorienting her from everything around.

She pulled herself along the floor, feeling her fingers slip occasionally on her own blood which still covered her skin. Drips had fallen from her when Kael carried her in, creating small puddles on the stone. The figure's hand was able to touch her shoulder. It felt real. It had to be real. How had Zander managed to find his way down to her without being noticed? The joy she felt at the realization that his presence wasn't a figment of her imagination made none of it important. What mattered was that he was here. A friend among her enemies, for even the short time he might be able to stay with her.

"Oh, gods, Leyna."

His breathy voice revealed the shock he experienced at the sight of her. She couldn't focus her eyes on his features to know what his expression was, but the pain in his words was all it took to know it must be bad. Something was wiping against her chin and her mouth. A piece of smooth fabric. A handkerchief. Within moments it was drenched in her blood. She was amazed it was still running so freely. If it didn't stop soon, she was likely to lose consciousness in her state of health.

Finding his attempts futile, Zander gave up on the handkerchief, tucking it back into the pocket of his jacket. A rustle of fabric filled the air as he removed the jacket from his arms, reaching in to pull her gently against him through the bars. She was bleeding on him. He didn't seem to mind. Her body flinched painfully at her nose bumping against his chest, sending a violent pain shooting through her head. Inhaling a sharp breath, she felt her body reflexively start to jerk away from him, his hands holding her gently in place. "Shh, it's going to be alright. I am going to get you out of here. These locks won't be that difficult to pick through."

"I will not allow you to do that," she whispered, resisting the urge to shake her head for emphasis of her protest. "I am not going anywhere."

"The Consul ordered me to come here tonight to make sure that you were alright. I cannot, in good conscience, return and give him my assurances you are safe after what I just witnessed. Not only will I have to face the Consul's questions for why I didn't get you out of here, but I would have to face myself, and I couldn't if I sat idly by."

"I am fine. And that is exactly what you will tell the Consul." Oh, Thade would be frantic if he was allowed to know anything about what transpired during the short minutes at that party. She couldn't let him find out. For his own sake. She couldn't bear to think of causing him any more worry than she already had. "It was most likely a mere show for the sake of his guests. Once they leave and he has had time to think on things, I will be released from this cell. I trust that at least. He cannot flaunt me as his slave if I am hidden away like this."

Zander was quiet. She could sense his uncertainty at how to react to her request. "Under any other circumstances, I would fight with you, but these aren't the best conditions for me to even think of winning, so I will back down... but that doesn't mean I won't continue to work tirelessly at finding a way to get you free of this ridiculous slavery."

"You are going to get yourself caught if you stay here much longer."

The thought hit her with a frightening truth. Kael assured her that he would return. She trusted he would do everything in his power to step away from Mikel's attention at the first opportunity to present itself. If he were to find Zander here with her...

"Maeri will distract anyone at the door as long as she can." Maeri. Oh, for the love of all that was holy, Maeri had seen it all? The humiliation grew by the minute with every familiar face she became aware of having witnessed the terrible scene. "Before we entered the party, we were inspecting the stone fence out front. There are a few places where the mortar has broken and chipped away which would be large enough to fit a piece of parchment while yet small enough to prevent notice. If you are able to write, find a way to fit the letters in one of those. Maeri will be checking every so often in hopes of some word from you."

"I will do what I can."

There was nothing more she could promise him. They had learned all too well that no plans could be laid out with any hope of keeping them. Everything was out of their control and completely in the hands of their enemies at this point. They would have to work under Mikel's rules and simply pray that they were able to complete the task required of them.

"Leyna, I am almost positive your nose is broken. You need a doctor –"

"What I need is for you to stop calling me that name and to get yourself safely back to the party before anyone finds you here and exposes us both," she sighed, lifting her head away from Zander's chest slowly. It took too much effort to move. All she wanted to do was lie down on the cold floor and sleep in hopes of waking the next morning to find none of it to have happened. "I will find a way to write. I cannot promise exactly when, but have Maeri be on watch for my letters."

"I'm not leaving here until you at least let me take a look at your nose. If it doesn't get set, there will be a very unsightly notch there for the rest of your life.

Zander was right. She couldn't rely on Kael to convince them to send anyone to tend her injury. Mikel called the shots, and in the short time she'd been in his presence, it was obvious he wasn't the type to show pity on a mere slave. If Zander was going to let her stay without further argument, the least she could do was humor him. "Fine. But make it quick, please. I don't want you to get caught down here with me."

As if afraid she might change her mind, Zander wasted no time in reaching through the bars to pinch his fingertips against the sides of her nose. The pressure of his touch was insufferable. A soft moan escaped her lips, struggling to hold back her agonized cries. She couldn't risk drawing more attention to them than they already had. The other slaves were likely already aware of Zander's intrusion, their curious eyes peering through the dim light to see what was creating the stir.

With a sickening crunch Zander adjusted the bone, Leyna's face jerking away from Zander's hands, her head dizzy from the new wave of pain washing over her. Some of the discomfort seemed to be alleviated, though the injury itself continued to throb. Through her tear-filled eyes she could hear Zander speaking, blinking to try and focus on the image of him once again.

"Please, let me take you out of here —"

"No!" It came out more forceful than she intended, but there was no way to take it back. She needed to be forceful with him or he wouldn't back down. Her eyes lingered on him, her adamant response hanging heavily on the air between them in the silence.

Nodding his head, Zander rose back to his feet, gripping his jacket tightly in his hands. He held out his arms to inspect the blood soaked through his shirt where her head had been, staining the white fabric all the way down to his belt. Closing his eyes, it was obvious he was struggling against his conscience, wanting to tell her she had no choice but to let him take her away. She wouldn't give in to it, no matter how much he insisted.

He must have come to the same conclusion. His eyes opened once again, giving another slight nod as if to reaffirm his decision. Sliding his arms into his jacket, he carefully did up the buttons to conceal the blood-soaked shirt underneath. "If you ever decide that you want out, we will find a way to make it happen. The Consul has made it very clear that this mission will be cast aside at the first sign of your safety being jeopardized. There will always be other means of gathering information if this option is lost, but your life cannot be replaced if they take it from you. That can't be allowed to happen."

"It will not," Leyna replied quietly. Her strength was leaving her quickly. She lacked the will to fight with him about her safety. It was best to just acknowledge what he was saying without argument for the sake of his comfort — as well as the Consul's — in believing she would call for help if she were in trouble. Deep down, she knew if it came down to a choice between losing the mission, or losing her life, she would die for the cause. What else was there for her in this world? To die for her people and for her Queen was the most honorable end she could ever ask for. It only pained her to think of what her death would do to the Consul.

Unable to stand the sight of her any longer, Zander turned away, the sound of his cautious steps echoing lightly through the narrow hall until it disappeared around the stairs. She'd done everything she could to convince him that she would be fine. It was hard enough to do while looking the way she did. Inside, she was surprised that she'd managed to succeed.

Crawling back to the center of the floor, she laid the side of her face against the cold stone, exhaling in both relief and pain at the sensation which filled her head. The chill was refreshing against the wound, while the pressure of the hard surface sent waves of discomfort through her senses. The bleeding was finally starting to ease. It was hard to imagine there to be much more blood for her body to spill out.

The lightheadedness was uncomfortable, adding to the pounding headache that had already begun to throb in her temples. Her body longed for sleep, her muscles aching from exhaustion, among everything else. There would be time to think about food and water after she'd slept. Until her head was able to clear of its fog, she wouldn't be able to focus on anything, preventing her from keeping her mind perceptive to any details which might benefit their cause. Sleep was already taking over. She felt detached from everything around her, the pain seeming distant as she released the last remaining ties to consciousness she clung to, giving in to the darkness that surrounded her.

Her wrists hurt. The shackles restraining her had been tightened to a painful degree, pressing hard against her slender bones. She didn't know how much time had passed for her down in that dark cellar. After she lost consciousness, the only memory she had was opening her eyes to find a strange man placing the shackles over her arms, only to leave her again almost immediately. She'd been too tired to care at the time. Sleep had taken her back instantly.

Water was brought once every so often. The length of time between each mug set through the bars for those in the cells felt long enough to be a day, but without any windows to reveal the light from the sun, it was impossible to tell for sure. Food came less frequently. Sometimes with every other cup of water, and others longer than that. It was served whenever someone remembered them down there, hidden away from view of everyone and everything that went on in the house.

What a waste she was to her people if she did not change her situation soon. How could it be that Mikel would be given his enemy as a slave and not want to utilize her in a more gloating fashion? To show her off to his friends when they visited while she cleaned his floors or shined his shoes. There had to be some reason that prevented him from doing so. The display he'd given at his party was enough to tell her that he desired to treat her like a trophy. In his own way.

Kael had yet to return to her, unless he visited while she was asleep, which she couldn't discount as being possible. It felt as though she did nothing but sleep these days. Sleep and stare off into the distance, lost in her own thoughts.

She'd come to terms with the current path her life had taken. Acceptance was the only thing she could really do, at risk of going insane from the fear and anxiety of what might become of her. If she spent all her time dreading the pain and torture they might force her to endure, she would lose her mind in the silence of her prison. It was better to remind herself that she was above it all, and that she would have to face it with the courage of a soldier, the way she had when she was still a child, facing her enemies on the battlefield. There was always a chance, even then, of being taken captive by the Sanarik, or the Namiren. Back then she'd already accepted that possibility. This was no different, in the grand scheme of things.

Someone was approaching. Was it time for water already? Perhaps they felt generous and thought to bring an extra glass for her dried up mouth. The steps made no stops along the hall at the other cells. No water, then. Another prisoner? They were getting closer.

Lifting her head, she could see Kael staring at her through the bars. He carried some kind of torch in his hand, illuminating his face eerily in the flickering light. Her eyes flinched at the brightness, having grown so accustomed to the dim cellar, the only light there provided by two lonely sconces placed along the hall.

He turned a key in the lock. He was coming inside. The thought caused her heart to jump nervously. She still was uncertain of why his presence made her feel that way. It was an awkward sensation, but pleasant, most times. It distracted her from the pangs of hunger in her stomach with the fluttering feeling which filled her.

She watched him closely. He had something else in his hands that she hadn't noticed before. A small bucket of some kind. It must have been at his feet when he was unlocking the door. He carried it inside now, placing it on the hard stone next to Leyna's trembling form. She sat there, completely still, as he hung the torch against the wall, finding the remains of an old sconce to hold it in place and light the entire cell with its soft glow.

"I am sorry it took me so long," he spoke gently. His hands lightly touched her face, turning her head from side to side to examine her nose. They were warm in comparison to the chill of that place. She welcomed the feeling, only wishing that he would hold her against him to take the cold away from the rest of her body. Carefully, he removed the shackles from around her wrists, letting them fall to the floor with a heavy thud. "Things have been confusing around here lately, but I managed to speak with Mikel about you. He is going to allow you to move into the servants' quarters in the back of the house. That will be a step up from this place, at the very least, until I can continue to negotiate your freedom."

Could it be? She was to be released from this horrible place? She wanted to hug him. But that wouldn't be appropriate. Not that she had the energy to move in such a way, anyway. "How long have I been down here?" Her voice was scratchy. She had no reason to use it while sitting by herself. She couldn't remember the last time she had spoken to someone. Zander, whenever he had been to visit. It felt so long ago.

"Almost two weeks." The sadness was evident in his tone at the length of time he'd been forced to leave her there. Two weeks. She had to wonder if Maeri was still in Dalonshire, waiting for her letters that had yet to come. If she were able to write now, would her words still reach the Consul to tell him that she was safe? That he need not worry about her?

Reaching his hand into the bucket, Kael pulled out a soft rag, wringing out the water that dripped from it. Carefully he wiped it along her face, cleaning the dried blood off her skin. She'd forgotten it was even there. The pain had subsided after a few days, dulling to a minor throb in her head until it disappeared altogether.

He started with the cloth around her chin, taking great care in making sure he cleaned it thoroughly before moving on to her mouth. His hands lingered there. They dabbed gently, the cool water feeling good against her dried lips. He stared at her with an expression she had very rarely seen a man use when looking at her. It reminded her of the way Thade had gazed at her the night in his study, after removing her cloak, as if she'd been somehow exposed to him in a way that she didn't fully understand. As if he was seeing her for the first time.

"You have very elegant lips."

She wasn't sure she'd heard him correctly at first. Elegant lips? Was he really saying that to her, or was she imagining things? "I... what?"

Shaking his head, Kael moved the cloth away from her mouth, rinsing it off in the bucket before lightly brushing against her cheeks, the sensitive skin there causing her to flinch from his touch. "The bruising is still pretty bad, but the swelling has gone down, it looks like."

"It is healing well. I suspected the bruising had begun to lessen also."

"Lessen, yes. But I can still see it. Perhaps it is just the lighting," he replied. Gently, he tried to brush the cloth across her cheek again, moving in closer to her nose. Her body tensed at the discomfort, but she managed to hold herself still. It wouldn't do her any good to keep pulling away from him while he was trying to help her. She would have to just deal with the pain for now.

Gritting her teeth, she tried not to make any sound to let her pain be known to Kael. He was being as cautious as he could. She could tell by the way he hesitated with every brush of the cloth against her skin. "There is a bath set specifically for use by the servants. I had it filled so you could wash before we get you into something clean to wear. After that, I will find what chore Mikel wishes you to begin with."

A bath. Oh, it sounded wonderful. Even if the water was freezing, it would remove the filth from her that had built up while trapped in that moldy basement. She felt disgusting, hating the fact that Kael was seeing her in such a state. It was amazing he could bear sitting so close to her. Dirt was caked on every part of her skin, the natural oils from her hair matting it down against her head, along with the mixture of blood from where she'd been lying on the floor. Combing it would be next to impossible without tearing much of it out to rid the strands of the accumulated tangles.

Tossing the rag back in the bucket, Kael helped her to her feet, supporting the weight of her body against his own. She couldn't remember having ever felt so weak. Her dress hung from her body, looser than it had been when she first arrived there. The lack of any kind of a diet had already begun to show, her arms like those of a skeleton's wrapped around Kael's back to hold her up. She'd always been a slender girl, but the definition of her muscles had dwindled away, leaving her looking starved and frail.

Kael left the torch behind where it hung on the wall, focusing his attention on helping her through the door. Her head was spinning from the exertion. She lacked the energy required to make this trip, and the stairs would be the most difficult thing of all. She would have to find a way up them herself, or else Kael would have no choice but to drag her along behind him down the narrow corridor.

The task was easier than she anticipated. Holding her out in front of him, Kael wrapped his arms around her thin waist, lifting her feet up from off the ground. It was effortless for him to do. He was a strong man, and she was even lighter now than she'd been the day he carried her through the cellar door against her will.

Once at the top of the stairs, the corridor widened, allowing him to pick her up into his arms. Closing her eyes, she ignored the thick darkness of the hall, forcing the thought out of her mind until she heard the cellar door open in front of them, light spilling in from the outer halls.

His footsteps could be heard echoing through the empty passage. Leyna couldn't detect any sign that would suggest someone else to be near them. All the way through the house, he carried her in silence, the plain walls of the kitchen rooms blurring together in Leyna's vision.

Light. There was light. That was all that mattered to her. There was no scent of mold or stale air gagging her senses. Homemade bread was cooking somewhere, filling her nostrils with the smell. She was hungry. The pains in her stomach were returning, stronger than before, aching for a taste of the bread.

A young girl stood outside an open door, her head lowered respectfully at Kael's approach. Her long brown hair was pulled back away from her face into a tight braid which hung down to her waist. The slant of her eyes was unlike anything Leyna had ever seen before. They angled downward, giving her a constant expression of melancholy, their light golden color standing out against her dark skin. A crest of tiny bone-like lumps around the top of her forehead resembled that of the Namiren soldiers Leyna had fought against during the war. She appeared to be a mixed breed of some kind, though outside the Namiren blood she so clearly carried, it was impossible to decipher her heritage.

"Oriane, is the bath prepared?"

"Yes, sir," the girl replied quickly, bobbing into a short curtsy. "I have a dress set out for her as well…"

"Good, good." Lowering Leyna back down to the ground, Kael transferred her weight from his own arms into those of the strange girl. "You will need to help her. I will have some food and water brought in for her from the kitchen. Once she is cleaned and fed, bring her to my quarters and I will have her orders then."

His quarters. So he did live there. Or at least had rooms in which to stay for extended periods of time. How odd that it had never been mentioned. There would be time to think about it later. If he had his own rooms, then that meant he would have access to parchment and ink. When she was well again, she would have to find a way to convince him to provide her with at least a single piece for a letter.

The girl hurried Leyna into the room behind her, closing the door to separate them from Kael's lingering gaze. Oriane. An interesting name for such an odd girl. Her features made it difficult to determine her age. Leyna hadn't taken much time to learn any details about the Namirens and how they matured. While Oriane looked young,

Leyna believed it was possible for her to be a fully matured adult among her people, her thin figure caused by her limited nutrition and lack of physical conditioning.

Undoing the laces of Leyna's dress, Oriane helped to pull it up over her head, tossing it in a heap on the ground. She guided Leyna into the large bath, the steps cut into the tiled floor to create a large opening, filled with clear water. It was warm. An unexpected surprise. She'd been prepared for the cold, her muscles relaxing at the gentle warmth of the water against her skin.

She sank down into the bath, submerging her head under the water. Perfect. The first comforting thing she had experienced since her arrival to Siscal. It felt so long ago now, the two weeks in the cellar feeling more like two months in her mind. Lifting her head back up for air, she opened her eyes wide, refreshed by the water and sweet smell of bread surrounding her.

If only she had food, it would make everything feel right, for once. Cleaning the floors, and whatever other chores might be asked of her, would be simple tasks if she had access to food and water. She didn't even require a bed to sleep on. Just anything but that cold stone floor.

"You must be the one I have heard everyone talking about."

Of course the girl would talk. Peace and quiet would be too much to ask so that she could enjoy this moment of bliss. "Talking about? I am far from noteworthy."

"The Lady Oksuva has been in fits since her sister brought you. She and Master Mikel have been fighting nearly every day about what to do with you."

Focus. This was an opportunity for her to find out information which might be helpful to her. She couldn't just pass it up because she was tired and hungry. "What to do with me?" she asked. "Why would that be something which causes them such distress?"

The girl spoke as though she was desperate for someone to talk to. Leyna had to wonder if the other slaves were allowed to socialize, or if it was a rare occasion for them to be in the same room, conversing about the personal lives of their masters. Oriane knelt down on the tiles beside the bath, keeping near to Leyna's ear so as to not have to speak very loudly. "The master has had a Vor'shai slave woman in the past. Before he and his wife were married. She discovered he was using the slave in ways she didn't approve of, accusing him of infidelity."

"He was sleeping with the slave? But that is not exactly uncommon amongst men, however disgusting it may be."

"She almost called off the whole marriage," Oriane continued. "Lady Oksuva is a very jealous woman. She felt the intimacies between the slave and her husband went beyond that of a mere show of power, and that he had feelings for the Vor'shai woman. In the end, Oksuva had the slave killed as part of an agreement with Mikel to maintain their marriage contract. But it was specifically agreed upon that he would never utilize his physical rights to his slaves ever again on threat of divorce."

"And she thinks he will do the same with me as he did with the other?" The thought made her shudder. She'd always taken pride in the fact that she had remained pure, despite the difficulties her life had thrown in her path. It was a quality any respected lady was supposed to possess until they were married in the Tanispan custom. Her insides cringed at the fear of being taken advantage of in such a way by Mikel. The last thing she wanted was to be dishonored at his hands, or anyone else's. Whether or not it was in the service of the Queen would make no difference to any man who might take her as his wife in the future. It would ruin her forever, leaving her to live out her life as an old maid, outcast from society.

Being a slave would be a black mark on her reputation enough as it was. She could only hope it would be overlooked due to the reasons – or bypassed altogether because of the false name by which she was known.

"That is what the arguing has been about. She does not trust him with you."

It was all too much for her to take in at once. Satisfied with her cleanliness, she made her way toward the steps, the weight of the water dripping from her body causing her to strain just to remain upright. Oriane was at her side instantly, wrapping her in the warmth of a large towel, drying the water from Leyna's skin. For the first time, she took notice of the scars on Leyna's back, her eyes shifting up to look at her hesitantly. "Did your last master whip you? These marks look bad..."

"Does your master not whip you?"

"Never me personally, no. He very rarely has used the whip on any of his slaves, unless he feels the need to make an example of them." What a relief it was to hear that. She just had to hope Mikel didn't feel the need to make an example of her just out of some show for his wife.

She wished her strength was more abundant, wanting to take the towel from Oriane's hand to cover herself with it. The girl was taking too much of an interest in the marks that marred her skin. Leyna dreaded any questions Oriane might ask in regards to the scars on the side of her abdomen and chest. Those would be much more difficult to explain, as they resembled no weapon of punishment commonly used by any slave owner.

Stepping away from Leyna, Oriane retrieved a simple white dress from off a nearby table, similar to the garment Leyna had been wearing when she first arrived there in Dalonshire. It lacked in any decoration, the fabric thin and delicate. The neckline was lower than hers had been, but at a more dramatic angle, dipping down in the front through the center, while still covering the sides almost completely. It would hide majority of her scars from view, though the sleeves she couldn't be sure about until it was on.

"This should fit you well enough, for now, until we know where in the house the master will have you working. He likes to keep his slaves a bit more segregated than some other masters do."

The fabric of the dress was soft against her skin. Lighter than the dress she'd been wearing before. It would make the coming summer months more tolerable if she were to be working in the heat of the sun. Even during the warmest months, it would be nothing in comparison to the scorching temperatures of the Carpaen desert. This garment was more of a luxury than anything else she could have asked for.

Tugging at the sleeves, Leyna tried to make them stretch low enough to cover the mark on her arm. There was no way she would be able to make it work without exposing the scar on her chest. Her arm seemed the lesser concern of the two. Arm it would be. If she was lucky, no one would notice it. After all, they did believe her to have been a slave before. She could simply deny comment if another servant questioned her. If Mikel or his wife confronted her — she would have to think of something else, and quickly.

A knock at the door caught her attention. Could it be food? Kael had said something about having something brought over from the kitchen. She had never before been so excited at the thought of eating. It was amazing to think how much she'd taken food for granted prior to coming here.

Oriane opened the door, accepting a small tray from someone in the hallway. With barely a nod to acknowledge them, she closed the door again, carrying the tray over to where Leyna was standing.

It smelled absolutely divine. Fresh bread was set off to one side of the plate, separated from the rest of the food there. Some kind of meat had been prepared and sliced into thin, even pieces, covered in a dark gravy. Manners were the furthest thing from her mind as she picked up the utensils, quickly lifting large pieces of the meat into her mouth. It was like heaven after the scarce and tasteless meals served to her in the cellar.

Within mere minutes she cleared every last bite from the plate, soaking up the leftover gravy with the warm bread. The water was equally as delightful. She guzzled it down until there was nothing left of it in the cup. She wanted more. Her throat was still dry from dehydration, her body craving the refreshing liquid.

There was no chance at getting more now, but she kept her hopes that if she did everything asked of her, she may yet see another meal before the sun went down.

"Master Kael will be angry if we keep him waiting much longer," Oriane frowned, turning away to set the empty tray off to one side. Ah yes, Kael. She had forgotten about him in her rush to fill the aching pit in her stomach. The pain of hunger had subsided for now. All that remained was the uncomfortable dryness in her mouth.

But she was free. No shackles bound her hands and the doors were nothing like the horrible bars of that cellar. She never wanted to see them again. It had done nothing to ease her fear of being trapped inside dark, enclosed spaces. That cell had been no different from the chest her mother hid her away in, aside from the fact that with enough effort she had been able to free herself from the box. Still the same, in a way. It would simply take a different type of effort to keep herself out of it.

Nodding her head, she looked herself over. For some reason it was important to her that she look presentable for Kael. What did it really matter, in the end? But it did. She couldn't explain why. If only she could make the unsightly bruise in the middle of her face disappear before she reached his quarters.

Her feet remained bare. They dragged along the hard floors of the house where Oriane led her through the halls, her body lacking the energy to lift them up. That would get better. With more meals like that which she had just eaten, her energy would slowly start to return. Soon enough, she would be back to her old self, and the nightmare of the last two weeks would be nothing more than a memory in the back of her mind.

The house was larger than she thought at first, the halls twisting and turning deeper into a maze of rooms and corridors. A flight of stairs brought them to the second floor, sunlight pouring in through the windows lining the long hallway. They came to a stop outside of a large door set at the end of the hall. With a sharp rap of her knuckles against it, Oriane stepped back, waiting for a response from inside.

Kael's face appeared in the doorway, the hinges silent and smooth as it opened. His eyes fell on Leyna expectantly. Oh, how she wished she had a mirror. She knew her hair was still a tangled mass atop her head. It had been an unimportant detail next to food. The thought of asking for a brush had never crossed her mind.

"She has been fed?"

"Yes, sir."

"You may go now." At his request, Oriane turned away, hurrying back down the hall the way they had come. Leyna remained there, stiffly. The unusual flutter started again in her chest and stomach. What was it about him that made her body react in such a way?

Leading her inside the room, Kael closed the door behind them, twisting the lock into place. Her whole body was trembling. Why would he lock the door? There was no reason for secrecy if his only intent was to provide her with her orders.

He positioned her in the center of the spacious room. Making sure she was steady enough on her own, he moved away to bring her a chair, placing it firmly on the floor in front of her. "Have a seat."

She did as she was told. Her legs wouldn't have been able to hold her up much longer even if she'd wanted them to.

Everything in the room was neatly in its own place, absent of any dust at a glance. A large desk was situated in the middle of the back wall. There on top of it she could see a stack of parchment. And quills. Ink bottles rested on a shelf behind it. All that she needed to send word to her friends was right there in front of her. But she couldn't get to it. Not yet. Kael still couldn't be allowed to know the truth.

He disappeared through another door to the far right, leading deeper into his grand quarters. He was more respected among the family than she would have thought, given what she'd been led to believe from everyone. She couldn't get past the idea that Kael had somehow neglected to share this information. Or could it be that it was a recent development since she'd spoken with Thade and Feolan on the matter? The items in the room looked too settled to be a recent occupation. These things had been here for some time.

Tensing her muscles, she contemplated going to the desk, wondering if she could get to the ink and parchment before he returned. There wouldn't be enough time to pen a letter to the Consul. She would have to wait. But it was tempting to try.

Who was she kidding? Her legs would never hold her to make that trip, however short it may be. The desk was only a mere four or five steps away from her, but that was like a mile in her current condition. What was there to write anyway, other than some word to assure them she was alive and well? If she could be considered well. Alive. Alive was well. That would make the words feel more truthful.

She settled back into the chair as Kael entered the room again. Something was in his hand that hadn't been there before. A brush of some kind. She smiled in spite of herself at the sight of it. How thoughtful. It was either because he wanted to help her, or because she looked awful and he couldn't bear to see it.

"You are being tasked with the gardens and yards for now. This will include the stables and anything else on the property that is outside the walls of this house. Mikel's wife prefers you remain out of sight from her indoors until she comes to terms with your presence here." The brush hurt. Every stroke pulled painfully at the roots of her hair, ripping several strands from her head. Her eyes watered, but she refused to make any sound to give away her discomfort. "Your room has been prepared in the servants' quarters. Is there anything I could provide for you so as to make you more comfortable? More at home?"

Yes. There was. But how could she ask for it? "Might I have some paper and ink?" Too direct. He was sure to question her now. What was wrong with her? If she continued in the manner she was going, her cover wouldn't last very long. At least not with Kael.

"That is a minor request. I expected you to require something more. Extra pillows, or a thicker blanket — why do you desire to write?"

There it was. Just as she feared. How difficult could it be to concoct a lie about why she would want to put words on paper? Women were known for writing journals and songs. It was a sentimental thing for her gender. He couldn't argue with her if she claimed to be so. "I like to write poetry. If I have time to do so, that is. But just knowing I would have the materials necessary… it would ease my spirits greatly."

"Simple enough, then. I will deliver it to your room before dinner."

Perfect. And to be charged with the keeping of the grounds? She couldn't have asked for anything more convenient. She would just have to make sure no one else was near enough to her to see her by the fence at the front of the house. Oh, how she hoped Maeri was still in Dalonshire. If she was no longer there, then the letter would go unnoticed, and undelivered, leaving her trapped there with no means of getting her information to the Consul.

But Maeri had promised her. Maeri had assured her that she would remain, no matter what, and wait for some sign from her that she was safe. How often had she already been by the massive estate, anxiously awaiting to find a letter pressed into the hole of the missing mortar between the stones? Soon. She would find one there very soon.

He continued brushing her hair, running the thick bristles through her long black strands. The tangles had eased significantly, the number of times his strokes caught, jerking her head back, were fewer and less frequent. She felt almost normal again. Clean. Refreshed. Her confidence in her mission was growing. It would only be a matter of time before she was able to sneak in closer to Mikel and Oksuva to eavesdrop on their private affairs and plans. She would have to get Oksuva to accept her back into the house first. There would be nothing to overhear in the gardens unless another talkative slave like Oriane happened to be at her side, with nothing better to do while pulling weeds than pass along the whispered gossip. Even that wouldn't be so bad.

"For today, I will have Oriane show you around outside, to where everything you will need can be found. She worked in the gardens before Mikel had her moved indoors as a maid," he explained. "After you have become acquainted with the property, you will return to your room, where dinner will be served to you, and you will rest. Your work will begin tomorrow. It is my hope that you will be in better health by then."

Fresh air. It sounded too good to be true. "You are most kind, sir," she whispered, bowing her head forward. "I will forever be in your debt."

The feeling of the brush against her scalp came to a halt. From the corner of her eye, she could see Kael moving around to stand in front of her, kneeling down at her feet. Gently he took her hands in his, squeezing them comfortingly. "You have no debt to me. Never feel that you do."

It felt unnatural to smile at him. Her lips hadn't found occasion to express such an emotion in so long. The muscles felt strained at the attempt, but it didn't change the sincerity of the gesture. There was no doubt that she was here because of Kael. He was the reason she had been accepted by Gislan, and he had worked to see her released from the cellar. If her mission was successful, it would be because of him.

"Wait here. I will find Oriane to have her help you. I would take you down the stairs myself, but it would look poorly on my part if Mikel or Oksuva were to witness it." He was leaving the room again. Leyna's eyes shifted quickly toward the desk before settling back on Kael, hoping he hadn't noticed her distraction. If she was careful, she could reach it. It would take him several minutes at the very least to reach the rooms where Oriane would have returned to, as well as accompanying her back to his quarters. There would be time for her to try and pen at least something, anything, to leave outside today that could let Maeri and the others know that she was safe.

As he rose back to his feet, she watched his steps. He had a quick pace. That would surely lessen the time she had. Her heart raced with excitement. The thrill of being caught. It was the same she felt that night in Tanispa when Feolan hid her away in his carriage from the guards. Maybe the adrenaline would give her the strength she needed to reach the ink and parchment.

She waited until the door clicked shut behind him, cutting her off from view of the rest of the house. Speed would be her only downfall. She would have to make every motion slow and precise. It was only a few steps and then she could use the desk as a support to make her way around it.

Slowly, she climbed to her feet. The height of the chair made the action easier. Less distance to cover. Her heart beat hard against her chest, adding to the trembling of her limbs. Shuffling forward, she held her outstretched hands to the desk, her weight falling against it to hold her body up. She was there. The hardest part of her task was over, though returning to the chair would be difficult. And how would she hide the letter?

Why did she always jump into things without thinking over all of the details? She would have to work on that in the future. Luck had helped her through to this point, but she couldn't count on it to always be there to save her. She was already at the desk, though. There was no sense in turning back now. Her legs were sliding carefully across the floor, her hands shifting to keep her body supported. Almost to the other side. Just a few more steps to go.

There. On the surface of the desk was an open bottle of ink, a blackened-tipped quill resting alongside it. That would make things easier. Hiding a freshly opened bottle would have been much more difficult.

Her eyes glanced up to the door, listening intently for any hint of someone's approach. Silence. Good. She still had time.

Sliding a piece of blank parchment to the center of the desk, she lifted the quill into her right hand, dipping it anxiously into the ink. The words scrawled messily under her unsteady hands. She had to wonder if Thade would even be able to read the mess of ink and garbled letters she was putting to the paper. Something simple.

Your Grace,

I apologize for not having written you sooner. All will come in time. Please be assured that I am safe and all is well for now. When I am able, you will hear from me again.

Sincerely,

Your loyal servant

Someone was coming. In the distance, the echo of their footsteps could be heard through the empty halls. Frantically, she laid the quill back down on the desk next to the ink bottle where she'd found it. She'd used as little ink as possible, keeping it faint and light against the thick parchment to allow it to soak in quickly. There was no time to worry about it smearing. She needed to get back to her chair and somehow conceal the letter.

Folding it into a tiny square, she pressed it down into the bodice of her dress, thankful for the extra fabric of this one from her last. The parchment was uncomfortable, but other than a tiny lump, was unnoticeable without looking closely. And she hoped that Kael wouldn't be looking that closely at her chest.

With hastened steps, she slid along the side of the desk, making her way back to the front. The footsteps were getting closer. Almost to the door now. In one last frenetic motion, she threw herself toward the chair, the sound of it scratching across the hard floor loudly filling the room around her. Her body collapsed to the ground. The force jarred her face, sending a wave of pain through her nose up to her forehead.

As the door opened, she laid there helplessly. Her breath came in short spurts of air, her chest heaving with the strain she had put on herself in her haste. "Eleni!" Kael sounded concerned. She could hear his footsteps along with someone else's, rushing to her side to check on her. Oriane. The strange complexion of her skin was unmistakable.

"I... I must have fainted," Leyna lied, playing up the role dramatically. If they gave out awards for such performances, she would have taken one, without doubt. Increasing the frequency of her breaths, she let her eyes roll back in her head, relaxing her muscles to lie heavily on the floor. She was deadweight in Kael's arms as he tried to lift her to her feet. Oriane stood by in confusion, fanning her hands at Leyna's face to create a soft breeze.

"The fresh air will do her good, but I insist that you keep the tour short," Kael instructed. Gently, he stepped over closer to Oriane, gesturing toward her to help hold Leyna up. "Try to have her back inside to her room before the sun gets much higher in the sky. The heat will harm her like this. Do you think you can support her down the stairs?"

For the sake of Oriane's weak arms, Leyna regained control over most of her movements, supporting her own weight with the help of Oriane to keep her upright. "I will be fine. I just was dizzy. It is getting better."

"I will not keep her long, sir," Oriane nodded obediently. Kael released his hold, the look in his eyes revealing the concern for her that he felt. He didn't want to let her go. He looked almost afraid, in a way. Afraid that Oriane would drop her, or otherwise be unable to prevent her from injury.

Noticing Leyna watching him, he turned away, hiding his face from view. Without a word, he walked away from them, disappearing into the deeper rooms of his chambers.

He hadn't noticed the letter. For now, it had slipped by him. If only she could do the same with Oriane, then it would be a success.

An unusual longing sensation came over her at the sight of the empty doorway where Kael had gone. It hurt her to know that she was lying to him. But it had to be so. She had no choice for now. All she could do was focus on getting her letter to the Consul to let him know she was still there — and prove that the hurt she was causing him would be well worth it, in the end.

Chapter Ten

The cool morning air felt good to Leyna's aching senses. After only a week out of the cellar, she could already feel her strength returning, invigorating her with a new determination for her task.

It had taken little time for her letter to the Consul to disappear from its hiding place in the fence. While enduring Oriane's tour, she had found a moment of privacy in which to conceal it, locating a portion of mortar to have cracked and chipped through, allowing her to deliver it without having to exit the perimeter of the property. To hide the parchment from view, she had collected a handful of soil from the flower bed below, pressing it into the hole behind it. By the next morning, she found the letter to be gone, though who had taken it remained unknown.

Days had passed since then. It seemed that if it had been discovered by some-one from the house, word of a suspected traitor would have spread. Things, however, couldn't have been more calm and quiet. Not a word had been heard from Mikel or Oksuva, their presence scarce, or at least to her. They perhaps didn't frequent the gar-dens where Leyna spent the daylight hours.

Wrapping the ribbons of her wide sun hat around her chin, she prepared herself for the work ahead of her. A week had passed since she last rid the front flower beds of their weeds. The area went overlooked since her first day when she checked for the progress of her letter. It was imperative that she not show any favor to one particular area for fear of drawing any unwanted attention. Someone might grow suspicious if she was always lingering about the dilapidated section of the fence.

Enough time had passed now for her to return to it. She had no letter to send out, to her own dismay. The work around the yards was in her hands, for most of the day. There were few others to whom she spoke or even passed by from the time she woke to the time she returned to her room at night. Information was not yet abundant, and it would be too great a risk to send unnecessary correspondence.

She knelt down in the damp, dew covered grass, feeling the moisture soaking into the fibers of her dress. It was a comforting feeling. A connection between her and the earth, refreshing the natural energy within her body.

Leaning forward, she began to pluck at the tiny weeds that had begun to poke up through the rich soil, something catching her attention out of the corner of her eye. The hole in the fence was darker. Light was blocked from shining through, but why? She had removed the dirt she'd placed there. It was necessary in order to verify her letter had been collected. In finding it gone, she had left the hole as it was, filtering a sliver of light through from the other side of the fence. But that light was no longer visible. Something was blocking it.

Sitting up straight, she looked around the yard, trying to appear nonchalant. It was too early for there to be many people awake, and the other servants tended to remain in the house until after breakfast had been served.

Satisfied there was no one watching, she moved in closer to the hole, sticking her fingers inside hesitantly. There. The feeling of something pressing against her fingertips. It was difficult to grasp in the enclosed space. She had to press it against the cool stone with her index finger, slowly edging it closer to the opening. Her eyes never ceased to look around the area, afraid someone might see what she was doing. How suspicious she must look! Her constant watchfulness was sure to draw the attention of anyone who might have been there. But there was no one. And her hand was conveniently concealed behind a well-pruned shrubbery decorating the fence line. If anyone were to see her, they would have to reveal themselves in order to get close enough to determine what she was doing.

Finally freeing the item from the tiny space, she stared down at it silently. A piece of parchment. Meticulously folded. Every edge was perfectly aligned, showing the care that had gone into each crease. More precise than the frantic wrinkled mess which she placed in there herself. She was curious if the words had been legible at all by the time it reached the hands of its courier.

Despite everything she suffered in her time there, the novelty of her mission still remained with her. In her heart, she was still like a child, her excitement rising at the thought of receiving some secret message intended for only her eyes to see. By now, it felt as though the wonder of it would have faded, replaced by the harsh truth. That wasn't the case. Although reality had certainly sunk in, it didn't curb her racing heart at the sight of the letter she held in her hands. Who could it be from? Zander? Maeri would have had nothing to write worth endangering the mission. She wouldn't have been so careless.

There was no time to read it now. It would be too hard to conceal it once she opened it, making it too obvious to any passerby that she was doing more than merely pulling the unsightly weeds from around the flowers. Carefully, she tucked it into the neckline of her dress, pressing it down around her breast. It would have to stay there until her work was finished for the day. Once in the privacy of her own room, she would then have an opportunity to investigate it further.

"Eleni, is it?"

Leyna thought her heart ceased to beat in her chest. She froze, afraid to move. The woman's voice was too confident to be one of the other servants. An air of intelligence rang through the words, each syllable pronounced perfectly and precisely, the way Faustine had stressed a lady should speak. "It is, yes. Milady..."

"Hush yourself. I will make it very clear to you when you are to speak and when to stop." Her tone was biting. "Stand up and face me. I want to see you for myself."

How much had she seen? Leyna had not heard the sound of anyone approaching. She shuddered at the thought of this woman having witnessed everything.

Slowly she rose to her feet, not wanting to make any sudden movements. Her eyes remained lowered to the ground respectfully. She waited fearfully for the woman's hand to reach out to her dress and snatch the parchment from where she had hidden it beneath her breast. Instead, the woman remained perfectly still, eyeing her coldly with detestation. "So scrawny. Pathetic, really."

Catching Leyna's chin in her hand, the woman forced her gaze up from the ground, staring her in the eye, unflinching, allowing Leyna a glimpse of her face. The blonde woman from the table at the party. Oksuva. Her hair was down, hanging in long waves over her shoulders. It covered her ears from sight, but the glow of her eyes was unmistakable. Not as bright as a full Vor'shai. She was curious why a man of Ven'shal heritage would have sought a woman like her. The mixture of the Vor'shai blood seemed an unlikely candidate for him to take interest in as a lover rather than just another enemy. It didn't make any sense to Leyna, but now was hardly the time to ponder over it.

"You cause me a great dilemma," Oksuva stated, releasing her hold on Leyna's chin roughly. "My insolent sister gave you to my husband as a gift, knowing how I would disapprove of the idea. As you come from her, however, I would be thought rude to have you sent away. I want you as far from my husband's grasp as possible, but I cannot do that without selling you off, or having you killed. On the other hand, Kael pleads with me to spare your life, and I value his loyalty too much to risk him turning on me. So what to do with you, I ask?"

Leyna didn't dare to speak. The comment sounded more rhetorical than an actual request for a response. She didn't want to anger this woman again by talking out of turn.

"It was suggested that I find a way to keep you close to me, in order to assure my husband has little opportunity to find you alone." She walked from one side of Leyna to the other, looking her over appraisingly, clearly disapproving of what she saw before her. "Sadly, my ladies have requirements which I doubt you possess."

Letting out a quiet breath of relief, Leyna felt her muscles relaxing. Oksuva couldn't have seen her retrieve the letter from the fence. She was certainly not the type who would have let such a thing remain unspoken. But how should she react to the statements being made? This woman was offering her exactly what she wanted, but she was in no position to argue her qualifications for the job. From the sounds of things, Kael had already done a good bit of talking on her behalf.

"Any woman who tends to me must know how to fight. I deal with business ventures that are not the most savory and at times are known to turn dangerous. My attendants are charged with my safety in these situations. Tell me, you wretched excuse for a woman, can you fight?

She wanted to laugh. Could she fight? Of course she could – but would that be the most appropriate response? Slaves were not usually skilled at the finer points of combat. To give such a strong assurance of her abilities would look out of place for someone of her supposed low status. "A little, Milady. But I am a fast learner –"

"Hold your tongue."

Leyna closed her mouth, cutting off the rest of her sentence awkwardly. Oksuva seemed to have already made up her mind before approaching her, making anything Leyna said meaningless.

"You will finish up your chores in the gardens today. Tomorrow, after breakfast, you are to meet Kael at the training ring in the courtyard. I will leave it to him to determine if you are, as you claim, a fast learner," she scoffed. "If in a month's time you are able to hold your own in a contest, overseen by me and my husband, then I will consider raising you from your current position."

Shifting her gaze back down to the ground, Leyna bobbed in a quick curtsy, unsure of how else to respond without speaking. Oksuva gave no indication that she required a reply, not even a thank you. She wasn't doing this for thanks. She was doing this to keep Mikel away from Leyna. She hated Leyna, simply for being what she was. A Vor'shai owned by her unfaithful spouse. She was miserable. Leyna could see it in the depths of her glowing Esai eyes.

With a flick of her long blonde hair over her shoulders, she turned away from Leyna. What more could she say? One month. Leyna would have one month to get her strength up enough to prove to Oksuva that she was capable of physical combat. Capable of being one of Oksuva's ladies. Then she would be at Oksuva's side, to hear what dark plots she might weave, and who her accomplices were who helped her plan the demise of the Vor'shai people. The people of whose blood she shared in her own veins. A traitor to her own half-blood family.

That explained Mikel's interest in her. He had a strange obsession with the Vor'shai, in that he physically desired them while, at the same time, longed to cause them pain and suffering. Was that why he did the things he did to his wife? Or did he truly love her, if only for the fact that she hated her own people and was an outcast among them? He must have said or done something to rekindle the fear Leyna saw written in the depths of Oksuva's features. She was convinced Mikel wanted her for more than just weeding the garden or cleaning the floors.

The worst part about it all was that Leyna couldn't disagree with the concern. She herself feared it. The way he had looked at her when Gislan and Kael presented her at his party. Lustful, at first, seizing then the opportunity to force his hand upon her with violence. Putting her in her place. Showing her that she was his slave and he was her master. Making her fear him so that he could coerce her into whatever disgusting thoughts he might have been concocting in his evil head.

Her heart was racing. It pounded hard against her chest at the sight of Oksuva's slender figure walking away, moving gracefully back toward the front door of the house, giving no pause to look over her shoulder. Leyna was a slave, after all. No reason to care whether or not she was watching. She meant nothing to Oksuva other than as competition with her own husband. How utterly sad the thought was.

The quickened pulse of her blood through her body was uncomfortable, causing Leyna to tingle awkwardly, anxiously, afraid to move in case anyone else was watching. Placing her hand over her chest, she could feel the thud of her heart, the folded corners of the tiny parchment pressing against her skin through the dress, held tightly in place between her hand and her breast. More than ever she wanted to read it, but she'd nearly been caught once already. Now was not the time. Kael had managed to open an opportunity for her that she couldn't have planned herself. Unwittingly, he placed her exactly where she needed to be. She just had to do her part to make sure it worked.

The day couldn't have gone by any slower, the folded parchment against her chest constantly reminding her of how long she still would have to wait until it could be opened. It kept her attention throughout the day, even during dinner despite Oriane's attempts to distract her. Leyna had complained of a headache being the reason why she was so quiet, knowing that she wasn't able to hide her frustration and impatience from the girl's watchful eyes. She was almost worse than Faustine when it came to reading others. Leyna had not needed to speak a word for her to pick up that she was far away in her head.

A part of her hoped to find the words within it to be from the Consul. She wasn't sure why she wanted to hear from him so badly, but thinking on the way she'd left him that night in his study still pained her, the look on his face and the dejected tone of his voice. She had hurt him, but she didn't fully understand how or why. After she'd done so much to save him, it bothered her to think that she, now, was the cause of his pain.

Slipping quietly into her room, she closed the door, sliding the mangled lock into place. It would do nothing to keep someone out if they were adamant about getting in. The bolts holding it were loose, one of them having fallen completely from its grounding to dangle uselessly. Either way, she felt safer with it latched.

Her room was bare, save for a single bed with a marred wooden stand beside it. Focusing her internal energy into the palm of her right hand, Leyna created a soft glow of light to guide her into the darkened space, locating the candle resting at the back of the night stand. She pressed the wick between her thumb and index finger, redirecting the energy to her fingertips. With a puff of smoke, a bright light flashed as a tiny flame burst forth under her skin, igniting the candle.

Excitedly, she drew the folded parchment out from her dress. It was smooth to the touch, her fingers fumbling in her attempts to open it in a rush. Kneeling down on the floor next to the stand, she pushed aside the blank parchment left there for her by Kael, unable to think about anything but the letter she held in her hands.

There at the bottom were the familiar initials she had seen inked on so many letters over the years while she was in Tanispa. The fine calligraphy, detailing two letters. "TI." Thade Imri. It was from the Consul. Her heart fluttered nervously, happy to hear word from him, while yet afraid of what he might have to say. She had no way of knowing what Zander said to him about her. She remembered pleading with him to tell the Consul that she was fine and to not let him know of the scene which occurred at Mikel's party, but she doubted he would listen to her, his own concerns outweighing her desire to keep Thade from worrying about her.

She could hear his voice speaking the words she read there, his elegant speech patterns ingrained in her mind, the sound melodic and strangely comforting. He made no mention of her name, real or false. A precautionary step in case someone was to find the letter other than her. And so well spoken. His words flowed gracefully, like the diplomat that he was, seeking to convince her of his views with every stroke of his quill. A single sentence stood out amongst the rest.

"I beseech you; allow us to extract you from this mission."

He besought her. No command? Clearly, he was aware of her stubbornness and had taken it into consideration while putting these words to ink. If he commanded her, and she refused, it would place her in a very delicate situation. Instead, he had resorted to begging. His desperation was evident. Perhaps he hoped that would be enough to win her over, to convince her to return to Siscal. He even spoke of coming to Dalonshire personally to retrieve her.

She couldn't allow that to come to pass. Not with the new opportunity laid out before her. If he came for her, not only would it place him in great danger, as well as herself, it would ruin their chances at having someone involved with Oksuva's direct dealings. It was exactly what she'd come here to do. Kael certainly wouldn't be able to do it without her. Mikel would never let another man that close to his wife. No, she would not be leaving. Not now.

But the sorrow she felt in his words ate away at her inside. He was genuinely concerned. Fearful of her safety. And with good reason. If Zander had gone against her wishes and told him of her treatment and where she was being kept, then she couldn't blame Thade for his insistence in getting her out of there. How could she possibly assure him, convincingly, to ease his troubled mind, that she was safe? That from what she could see, the worst was over? If she could pass the test to become one of Oksuva's ladies, it seemed doubtful she would ever see the despicable cellar again, or the violent hand of Mikel's punishment.

Clutching the letter to her chest, she closed her eyes, grimacing at the thought of Thade awaiting her response, prepared to leave Siscal and ride in on a white horse to rescue her from this place. It was almost romantic. But that was silly. She was exaggerating the emotion behind his requests. He was the Consul of Her Majesty the Queen, Vorsila of the Vor'shai — she, on the other hand, was a mere servant; a nobody. A homeless whelp who had ridden into his path by accident, lying about her age, and pretending to be worth his notice. His concern couldn't be anything more than his self-determined obligation to protect her after she had saved him during the war. And her feelings for him should never be anything other than a deep loyalty to his cause, and to the Queen, whom he served, and she through him.

With a heavy heart, she dangled the letter over the flickering flame of the candle, letting the fire catch along the edge. She couldn't keep it around. If anyone were to discover it, she would certainly be extracted from the mission, but not in the way the Consul was requesting.

She watched it burn. The heat rose up, closer to her hand as it spread across the dry parchment and ink, crackling softly. Ashes trickled down to the nightstand. Remnants of a letter no one else would ever know existed. But now she had to think of a way to send her reply.

If she planned to have it delivered, she would need to find a means of getting back to the fence without causing suspicion. Come breakfast the next morning, she wouldn't be in the yards to place it in the fence. She would have to think of some excuse to go to the garden there — or slip out before the sun had risen, out of the eye of anyone in the house.

Hurriedly, she began to gather her quill and ink, laying out a blank piece of parchment to write. Her penmanship was vastly improved from her last letter. That would make it more convincing for her argument of her being in better health. Her hand was steadier, her head more collected, so as to give more detailed arguments for why she should remain there, against his wishes. She only hoped he would understand.

Expressing her gratitude for his concern, she assured him all was well, explaining to him the importance of her continued service there under Mikel and Oksuva's ownership. She comforted with the fact that she had someone there to help her, though making sure not to mention Kael's name, for the sake of his own safety were her letter to be found before Maeri's hands could reach it. Signed "Your loyal servant." It was what she was, and therefore the only name which she would place there.

All she had to do now was wait. Once the sun had set and the sky darkened, the others within the house would be slowly finding their way to their rooms, leaving the back corridor through the kitchen wing unattended, a perfect route for her to take to the yards. A single door was situated at the back of the house, leading outside to the main garden. The cooks used it when bringing in fresh vegetables from the crops. If she could make it to the garden, it would be a simple task to sneak around the front of the house, so long as she kept to the shadows and out of view from the windows in the lower levels of the building.

Convinced that the house was quiet for the night, she slid the lock free on her door. The letter was folded neatly, having had plenty of time to dry and preserve the ink, hidden away in the folds of her dress. She could feel the familiar rush of excitement coursing through her as she made her way down the hallway, lightly tiptoeing along the wall, finding her way easily to the door at the back of the house.

Out in the garden, the cool evening breeze whipped through her hair, tossing it about wildly atop her head. She could tell the change in seasons would be coming soon. The chill in the air reminded her of the time she'd spent in Velorum, the cold winds bringing with them the first snow of winter. It would take longer for the inclement weather to reach Dalonshire to the south, but it was coming, soon enough.

Why did the yard have to be so big? And open. Few trees dotted the landscape, leaving her completely exposed. There would be nowhere to hide if someone were to come along. She didn't want to think about how she would explain herself.

The sight of the stone fence was a welcome relief to her overactive senses. Every noise around her was amplified to her ears, causing her to jump nervously, fearing it was some-one coming. From over the fence she could still see the occasional citizen hurrying along the streets to get home, most of which were weaving drunkenly away from the local tavern. At this time of night, there was no reason for any sensible person to still be out. It was prime time for thieves in the streets, awaiting some unsuspecting traveler to pass them by.

Across the road, Leyna caught sight of a figure standing there, concealed under the heavy fabric of a hooded cloak, blowing gently in the soft breeze. The deep green glow of its eyes illuminated the shadows, though not enough to reveal the details of the face. It was watching the house. By now it was already aware of her presence, having spotted the movement out of the corner of its eye.

Drawing in a deep breath, she ducked down behind the low fence, pressing her back against the cold stone, a chill going through her from the thin material of her dress. Had it seen who she was? Oh gods, it would surely find her there and expose her to everyone. A spy perhaps? A night guard that she hadn't been aware of? People like Mikel and Oksuva would be wise to have constant surveillance over their home. Especially given those whom they were rumored to have dealings.

Footsteps echoed across the gravel. It was coming closer. She didn't care about stain-ing her dress, sliding through the soft soil of the flower bed, the tiny edges of the shrubbery poking into her skin. It wouldn't be enough to shield her from sight if the person looked over the fence. She would be caught red-handed. Assumed to be escaping. What other reason would there be for a slave to sneak out to the property line in the dead of night?

"Leyna?"

She pushed herself closer against the wall, bumping her head painfully on the edge of one of the protruding stones. Leyna? This person knew her name? Her true name, no less. "Who is it?" she hissed. She wasn't sure she'd be able to hear them over the deafening pounding of her heart, pulsing through her head loudly.

"It is me. Have you escaped? Will you be returning to Siscal like the Consul requests?"

The voice was being whispered through the hole in the fence, reaching Leyna's ears quietly like a breath of wind through a tunnel. Maeri. Those eyes had looked famil-iar... "You scared me to death, Maeri. I nearly had a heart attack."

"Leyna, I will take you with me back to Siscal tonight if you will let me.

"I am not leaving. I hope you will all understand the reasons why I cannot." They wouldn't. At least not Maeri. And more than likely Zander would never understand as well. Thankfully, they weren't the ones who mattered. The only person whose opinion counted was Thade's. "I was bringing another letter to explain the situation. You shouldn't be out so late alone. It is dangerous."

"I am not alone. We have been eager for a response from you, and unable to act until we knew. Lord Feolan brought his carriage here when he asked me to deliver the letter from the Consul. His other man inside the house has not written him in over a week. They fear for both of you."

Turning over onto her knees, Leyna removed the parchment from her dress, pressing it through the tiny hole where Maeri's voice was coming from. "His other man is fine. More so than the Consul may even realize. Things are moving smoothly and according to plan at this point. To leave now would be disastrous to the mission when I have so many opportunities being presented to me. I will be staying here."

Maeri was silent. All Leyna could hear was the scrape of the parchment sliding through to the other side of the fence under Maeri's hands. After a moment she could hear another set of footsteps treading lightly across the gravel, moving quickly over to Maeri's side. Whispers passed between whoever it was, their words too hushed for Leyna to make out. Friendly, at least. Deeper. A male, perhaps?

"Leyna, I must beg you to rethink your decision."

Feolan? Ah, Maeri mentioned he had come to Dalonshire with the letter. The one lying now in ashes on the surface of her night stand. "Feolan, I cannot. You could get yourself killed for even coming here. They would recognize your face instantly."

"*You* could get yourself killed by being here, and your presence within this place is on my conscience, as well as the Consul's. If it had not been for me, he never would have agreed to allow this, and after what Zander told us —"

"And what did Zander tell you, exactly?"

"He came to the Consul's home covered in your blood the morning after the party, having ridden through the night to reach the city. We did not even need to see the handkerchief he threw at our feet to decide that you needed to be taken away from here, but Zander said you refused him in his attempts to get you out that evening."

"Odd. I could have sworn I asked him specifically to do the opposite... Yes, I refused his help. And it was nothing. You know as well as I that some wounds bleed more than seems necessary. It was not nearly so bad as he must have made it out to be."

It was only a partial lie. She had recovered quite well, which meant that it hadn't been on a scale as grand as it might have appeared at the time. Broken noses mended themselves, and hers had done exactly that. Even the bruise was no longer visible on her face. Only a mild tenderness around the location where the damaged bone itself had been.

"Both Zander and Kael verified that your nose was broken and that you were being kept behind bars in a cellar. Neither the Consul, nor I, will believe that to be nothing."

"You will have to, for my sake," Leyna frowned. "Give me just a little longer to prove to you that this will work. Oksuva is looking to have me placed as one of her ladies. That will put me in a perfect position to gather the information I came here to get. If I leave now, then the suffering I endured those first two weeks would have been for nothing, and I cannot accept that."

A long exhale of breath could be heard from the other side of the fence. "In the end, the decision is not mine to make."

"Then you must convince the Consul to let me stay."

"Do you really think he could tell you no?"

His words cut through her with their familiarity. She could still hear Thade's voice in her head that night in his study while she tried to convince him then that everything would be alright. *How could I say no to you when you look at me with such determination in your eyes?* "He could, and he has the power to do so," she sighed, sinking back against the cold stones. "My hope is that he will not know how to."

"You play off his weaknesses. What exactly is Faustine teaching you young girls?"

"It was you, I believe, who said women were the ultimate evil. We have to learn it somewhere."

The quiet sound of a laugh came from Feolan at her words. "Yes, I suppose I did say that."

"Go, please," she begged him. "Tell the Consul I am sorry I cannot return with you, but I promise it will be alright."

Being careful of the flowers already dug up by her careless actions, Leyna slid herself back out from behind the shrubbery, climbing slowly to her feet. The fence wasn't quite tall enough to conceal her. She peered over the top, seeing Maeri's concerned eyes glowing brightly from under the hood of her cloak. "Leyna, please..."

"Shh." Why did they have to keep saying that name? "Keep watch for my letters. You will see soon that everything is alright."

Feolan's familiar face lifted from where he'd been knelt at the fence, his height bringing him to look down upon her sadly. It had been easier to argue with him when she couldn't see his eyes. When she wasn't faced with the worry, it was nothing to dismiss it.

Gently offering his hand out to her, he clasped hers tightly in his own, staring down at it in dismay. "You are skin and bones."

"I am fine," she stated plainly, her voice rising barely above the quiet of a whisper. They were just going to have to trust her. The only thing which would make her not fine now would be if she was caught standing there with them. "I have to get back inside before someone notices me gone. I beg you send my best to the Consul. Tell him I will see him again soon."

With a swift brush of her bare foot, Leyna wiped away the prints left in the soil of the flower bed, erasing any obvious signs that anyone had been there. A couple of the flowers were pressed down, but they would eventually rise up enough to not be a concern. Quickly, she snatched up the one which had been completely uprooted, gazing down at it in the light of the moon. The petals were a deep plum color, spread open wide in a beautiful fan around the center. Smaller petals curved upward from the middle, their dark hue gradually lightening to a soft lavender near the tips. Handing it over the fence, she placed it in Feolan's still outstretched hand, closing his fingers around it. "Give this to him. It will brighten his spirits, at the very least."

She couldn't bear to look at their faces any longer. Turning away from them, she ran quietly across the yard. Tears burned in her eyes, threatening to fall, but quickly wiped away by her trembling hands. They couldn't see her like this. And they wouldn't. No one would, because she wouldn't allow it. There was nothing for her to cry about. Everything was going exactly the way she wanted it... and even if it wasn't — she had to believe it was, or she would crumble.

The courtyard was set deep into the center of the large house, surrounded on all sides by well-trimmed hedges and trees which shielded it from most of the windows. Sections were set apart for different types of relaxation, chairs for resting in the shade or sun, a grassy clearing for picnics, and in the middle a grand arrangement of packed sand with stones outlining a private arena ring. Archery targets were arranged at the furthest end, still displaying several weathered arrows protruding from various positions around the bullseye.

Racks lined the edge of the ring opposite the targets, though mostly empty now in preparation of the coming winter. Only a few scattered swords could be seen there, already showing rust along their blades from age and past neglect.

It had a familiar feel to her from her days at the academy. Though they never practiced archery, at least with her, the targets had been accessible to the more advanced students. She and Blaise had chosen to focus on melee combat, never discussing the details of a ranged attack. During the war, there had been special units specifically trained with bows and arrows, even the newer models of crossbows. As a lieutenant, she'd been placed behind these units, never requiring her to learn their art.

Her heart sank in her chest at the sight of Kael standing between the two targets, holding a longbow securely in his hands, casual, leaning against a backboard positioned behind him. Of all things to start with! Why this? It did nothing to boost her confidence, though was a minor relief to her tired legs. Her nighttime excursion had kept her from her bed until shortly before dawn, and even then she'd been distracted beyond any hope of reaching sleep.

"I thought we would start easy today," Kael smiled. She hoped he couldn't see the dread in her eyes as he handed her the bow. It was lighter than she anticipated. Still heavier than her arms were prepared for, drooping under the weight of the weapon.

Kael chuckled quietly. "That is the lightest one I can find. Yew, so it's sturdy. Little else matters at this point in your training. As long as you know the difference between the grip, limb, and string, I can teach you the basics."

This was going to be embarrassing. And she'd had such high hopes at impressing Kael with her skill. "If I was unable to tell the difference between a string and a piece of wood, then we would have more issues than simply whether or not I could hold this thing."

"True enough," he nodded. Reaching behind him, he lifted up another bow, thicker in structure than her own. With confident strides, he positioned himself in front of the empty target, motioning for Leyna to follow, putting more distance between him and the mark. "The basic concept of the bow is rather simple. Perfecting the art is the most difficult. It will take time, so I do not expect you to master it in a single day. Truth be told, I don't even expect you to stick an arrow into the target at all today."

So much faith in her ability he had. What did it matter? She felt the same way. Though she doubted she would manage to lodge an arrow into the target within the month, let alone a week, or a day.

Pulling an arrow from the leather quiver wrapped around his thigh, Kael positioned it on his bow, holding it out for her to see. "The arrow will load here, by the grip. You will place the other end here, against the string, but without squeezing it. If you squeeze it, you will never get it to go anywhere."

She could hear the tension in the bow as he drew the string back, the muscles in his arms and chest tightening under the fabric of his pristinely white shirt. When he released the tension, Leyna felt her muscles flinch instinctively, the bow falling from her hands to clutch at her chest. Painful images flashed through her mind at the sound the arrow made while cutting through the air, seeing herself back in the manicured yards of the Siscalian palace, Sanarik archers creeping behind the pillars, each one of their strikes slamming into her flesh with frighteningly accurate precision and speed. It was all she could do to keep from crying out at the memory, the scars on her body almost burning at the thought.

With a distinct thud, Kael's arrow lodged perfectly in the center of the target, his eyes turning away from the shot to glance curiously at Leyna, confused by her sudden reaction to his demonstration. "You are white as a ghost, Eleni. What is wrong?"

What an awkward moment this was. Since that day at the palace, she'd never come across anyone with a bow, nor anyone who had need to fire one. It was surprising that the sound affected her the way it did. She hadn't even realized her mind retained the details so clearly from that tragic moment. If she'd known, she would have been better prepared to brace herself, allowing her to not make such a scene in front of him, sparking the inevitable question he had already asked. "Nothing, sir," she said quietly, inhaling a deep breath to slow her racing heart. "I was caught off guard. I have never seen one of these fired before."

"That is odd," he mused, bending over to retrieve her bow from the ground. His eyes stared deeply into hers as he handed it back to her, searching her expression for something. "That mark I saw on your chest looks like the entry wound of an arrow head. From my experience, at least. Same with the one on your left arm that is visible even now."

Damn. How could she have not expected him to know? An untrained eye might think them to be mere superficial wounds from a beating of some kind, but Kael, no — he was not a simpleton, and was far from untrained. He was a spy. Was it not his job to be able to spot such details?

She covered her arm with her right hand, averting her eyes nervously to the ground. Did she dare admit to the lie? Or let him pry further? If she allowed him to continue pressing, she might be able to lure out whatever suspicions he'd drawn in his head without giving him any reason to think on what the actual truth was.

The bow felt heavier in her left arm as she retrieved it. She didn't want to move it. To take it in her right hand would again reveal the scar to him, and she didn't want to risk that. It was best to keep it from his view until the matter had been spoken on. How much did he know about the fabled heroine of the Vor'shai? He would have been old enough to hear about it. But would he have enough information to pin the identity to her? She couldn't imagine he would. The false name would be her savior — and the fact that he couldn't verify anything about her origin other than that she had supposedly been a slave for years prior to coming here. A couple of scars couldn't possibly be enough to undo all the lies already woven.

"Your silence concerns me. Do not think you have any need to lie to me about what has happened to you," he said comfortingly. "I will not think any less of you if you cringe at the memory of some injustice done to you."

Gently, he pried her fingers away from her arm, exposing the scar there once again. She didn't know what to say to him. The kindness in his voice only served to rekindle the guilt inside her for having lied about everything. He was genuine, his concern for her evident in his tone, and the soft glow of his green eyes. His line of work made him mysterious, suspicious almost, but he had been so good to her. "I should try to see if I can even lift this thing," she whispered, tapping the bow against the ground.

He continued to hold her hand, gazing thoughtfully into her eyes. The look on his face caused a shiver to course through her. In a pleasant way. He was so close, she wondered if he intended to kiss her. It was such a casual thought in her mind in comparison to that day at Malic's when she was presented with the idea of kissing Feolan.

The initial uncertainty about her first kiss was gone. And she was glad for it. No more fearful, childish worries, about whether or not she would do it right. There had been so little to do, and yet even in her confusion, Feolan appeared to have found her lips satisfactory. But would Kael? He seemed a more seasoned type with women. Rugged. Confident in his own good looks. What if she was less than adequate in his experience?

The awkward fear was creeping back over her the way it had before. Part of her hoped he would look away. She wasn't ready. He couldn't kiss her now. Not yet. But that said nothing of her desire for him to. There would be no argument if he did.

"Well, first you must learn the proper technique to wielding it, like so," he replied suddenly, pulling another arrow from the quiver at his thigh. Ah, she was safe for now. He had decided against whatever thoughts were going through that head of his.

Stepping behind her, he assisted her left arm in raising the bow, positioning the arrow over the grip the way he'd shown her before, his own hand holding the arrow in place. Her stomach was fluttering. Did he have to stand so close? She liked it. But she knew she shouldn't. It wasn't proper. Then again, what exactly was proper about anything she was doing? Her most proper time in life had been under the hawkish eyes of Faustine, who never failed to give up an opportunity at pointing out how unladylike she was. This was no different.

He kept hold on the arrow near the grip with his left hand, placing her fingers around the string of the bow. Her fingers looked so fragile next to his. They were nearly double the size, and certainly stronger than hers. She could feel the rough texture of his skin where it had callused under the string. It was clearly not a mere pastime for him to use this weapon. "Now, remember what I said about the hand on the string. Never squeeze the arrow. It has to be able to go without anything hindering it."

Most of the effort in drawing back the string was done by Kael. Her arm simply pulled under his guidance, having nowhere else to go but where he led it. She could feel the muscles in his chest tensing, flexing at her back under the strain of the taut string. He made it look so easy, and so good. Her frail arms would have difficulty managing the strength required for this weapon. She didn't care if he stayed behind her demonstrating, however. *You are starting to think like Maeri.* She wanted to giggle. *Keep your face straight. This is hardly the time to lapse into a fit of laughter like a silly girl.*

When he released the string, the arrow snapped forward under his well-trained aim, striking solidly into one of the circles surrounding the bullseye. Not quite perfect, but then again, she was there to hinder him.

"Your turn," he announced. Clearing his throat, he moved away from her slightly, offering her another arrow from his quiver. "See if you can do it on your own."

Place the arrow over the grip. Good. She had that much right. The other end by the string, resting between her index and middle fingers. How had he made the draw look so fluid? The string was taut enough without her applying any pressure to pull it back. It gave her a newfound appreciation for Kael's well-conditioned muscles. No wonder he was able to carry her so easily up and down the cellar stairs. She was nothing in comparison to this.

Awkwardly, she released the string, her eyes gazing ahead toward the target in wait of where it would land. To her dismay, it never reached her vision, having fallen harmlessly to the ground at her feet. He was laughing at her. Sure, it was funny enough for him. He hadn't been locked up with hardly any food or water for two weeks. A single week back on a somewhat regular diet hadn't been enough to recondition her muscles. Especially not after over a decade of playing a lady at Faustine's.

"You are squeezing the arrow too much. I told you, it will never go anywhere if you do not let it."

He was handing her another one. This was too entertaining for him. The sound of his laughter continued to ring through the courtyard, though he did his best to keep it muffled. She would show him. She wasn't sure exactly how or when, but she would get it — and they would see who was laughing then.

With a determined look on her face, she repositioned the arrow on the bow, straining to pull back on the string. Aim. That might be a good start. She hadn't even considered the target before she let go of the last one. How could she have? All she could focus on was the pain in her shoulder from the tension of the draw. She was afraid the bow would break under the pressure, hearing the wood creaking with every tiny bit she managed to move.

She'd watched the archers in the battles do this hundreds of times. How hard could it really be? The close range archers had been impressive to her then, but she doubted she ever truly appreciated the art behind their skill. It was harder than it looked, but she was a practiced soldier. If she could swing a sword and aim for an opening that was only visible for a brief moment on her opponent, then she should be able to easily lay a single strike to a target that wasn't moving at all. Envision it. The imagination was a powerful thing, and the gods knew she had plenty of it.

Ease up on the arrow — thankfully she caught herself. Another fumble like the first and she wasn't sure she would be able to recover from the humiliation. She'd always been one of the top performers. Being set back as a beginner was more frustrating than she liked to admit.

It was now or never. Her eyes were locked on the target, her thoughts praying silently for the arrow to at least move in the right direction this time. Even if it fell short of her aim, anything beyond her own feet would be an improvement. She couldn't bear to hear him laughing at her again. This was hard. Did he not remember how difficult it had been for him when he first picked up the bow? There was no way he'd been so perfect from the start.

Giving one last heave with her arm on the string, she set the arrow into flight, closing her eyes the instant it left her fingers on the string. She couldn't bear to watch. A solid impact came like a dull thud to her ears. But what had she hit? The backboard? There was no laughter coming from Kael's mouth. Through the silence she heard a mumbled curse word, sounding more like an utterance of amazement rather than dismay.

Slowly, she lifted a single eyelid, peering through her lashes in the direction of the target. Her own breath released from her lungs in a shocked gasp at the sight of the arrow stuck into the target. Nowhere near the bullseye but, there within the confines of the circles, and embedded solidly.

Her fingers stung painfully, causing her to grimace. Holding up her right hand, she could see what looked to be a tiny spot of blood staining the skin where she'd been drawing the bowstring. On the release, the string had torn the skin clean from the surface, reminding her of the lack of conditioning her body had for this type of weapon. Her skin was not hardened to it the way Kael's was. It would take some time for it to toughen up.

One month. She had one month to toughen up. Her skin was just going to have to fall in line, or she would have to learn to ignore the pain.

"I am speechless," Kael murmured, stepping casually over to the target to inspect her arrow. "A clean shot. Straight through. Impressive, Eleni. Some take weeks to reach that point."

"They have weeks. I have one month. I can only hope that this is one of many miracles I might be able to pull off in such a short time."

"And that is why we are not going to get overconfident with a single success," he nodded. In a fluid motion, he drew another arrow from his quiver, handing it to her expectantly. "The next several days are going to be very tedious and repetitive. I will not move onto melee techniques until I feel you are proficient enough with the bow to handle yourself if necessary."

Again? The stinging from the torn skin between her fingers was aggravating enough as it was without tearing off another chunk. Just the thought of drawing back on the string again was like rubbing salt in the wound. "Is it too much to request that I be allowed a pair of gloves? This weapon is not the most obliging to my feminine skin."

Kael settled his gaze on her, straight-faced, serious. He stood there silently, making no move to respond until a hint of a smile curled up around the corners of his mouth, his right eye winking at her playfully. "Gloves? I suppose, but a real archer shouldn't require such a thing."

"When I am a real archer, then, I shall remove them," she quipped, relaxing her hold on the bow. Her left arm burned from the weight of it. And she still had the rest of the morning and afternoon left to go.

Chuckling to himself, Kael pulled a pair of dark leather gloves from the pocket of his trousers. "Fair enough, then," he smirked, offering them over to her. "But if you miss the next shot, I am taking them away."

"You are not funny, sir," she chortled, snatching the gloves out of his hands. She'd succeeded in her goal too early in her practice. After seeing her ability to properly fire the weapon and lodge it in the target, it would be expected of her every time, her own confidence in that being possible dwindling in her mind. The only thing she was sure of was that, with Kael as her teacher, it would be all about perfection of her technique, and improvement of her accuracy – and with her chest already sore and her fingers raw beneath the protection of the gloves – it was guaranteed to be a very long week.

Just the sight of the practice yard made Leyna's body ache. She'd spent almost every waking moment there for the better part of a week, stuck in a constant loop of loading and firing her bow. Her arms burned; fingers still raw despite the use of the gloves. It was beginning to feel more like torture than training. And Kael was loving every minute of it.

She dragged her feet along the sand in the arena, her arms dangling heavily at her sides. The thought of lifting them was painful enough without actually doing it. If she had to shoot one more arrow, she thought for certain she was going to scream. To her delight, he wasn't standing next to the targets the way he normally had come to be when she arrived to the courtyard every morning.

"I think I have seen enough of your skill with the bow. It could still use some work, but there will be time for that later," Kael pulled a wooden practice sword from a rack off to the right of the training area, offering it to Leyna hesitantly. "Melee combat is more difficult to learn. There are many different ways an opponent can strike at you; the combinations of maneuvers really are seemingly endless. It might be overwhelming at first, but after seeing how quickly you picked up the bow, I have faith that you will be able to master the sword in no time."

Finally. They had reached something she understood. It felt strange to hold the practice sword in her hands, the wood lighter than any of the blades she utilized during the war. Even her own weapon, designed for her weaker arms, had weighed a significant amount more than this. Securing her grip on the sword, she held it up in front of her, taking on a traditional stance in preparation for a duel. The motion strained her aching muscles, but she didn't care. This was what she had been looking forward to since their first session.

Kael looked her over curiously, unable to hide his surprise at her ease with the weapon. "You have remarkably good technique for someone who has never wielded a blade before."

"Just because I was a novice with a bow does not mean I have never touched another form of weapon," Leyna smiled, holding her stance firm. After all the time they'd spent together as of late, she felt comfortable enough around Kael to act in a more relaxed manner than she would around the others in the house. "I may be a bit out of practice, however. Try to go easy on me."

Taking up his own makeshift sword, Kael stepped up to Leyna in the sand, readying himself to strike. Leyna could tell he was hesitant. He wasn't sure of the degree of knowledge which she held for the blade, making it difficult for him to determine just how hard he could go. Hoping to ease his mind, Leyna lunged in for the first attack, catching him off guard with the precision of her strike. With a simple maneuver, she twisted his weapon from his hand, sending it falling to the sand, the tip of her blade pressing into his chest.

He looked a bit put-off at first, surprised by the accuracy of her technique. There was a moment of uncomfortable silence before he quickly regained his composure.

"Impressive," Kael smirked. His hands lifted up defensively until Leyna relaxed her sword, lowering it back down to her side. Retrieving his from the ground, he repositioned himself in front of her, preparing for another match. "You certainly are more proficient than I expected. I will keep that in mind this time."

Confidently, she resumed her stance. She knew he wouldn't allow her to succeed again so easily. His pride was at stake in losing to a mere slave. The first win, he would consider to have been merciful, and claim to have let it happen, to be generous. She would have to fight for a second victory.

They circled around one another, each watching the other closely for any sign of movement to strike. An occasional feint sent them into a flurry of motion, only to return to their stance a moment later. He would not give her the opening she needed.

He was too skilled for that. She would have to create a weak point if she had any hope at breaking through his guard.

Shifting her weight to one side, she moved forward, aiming high with her weapon to draw his arms up away from his body. It was met by the dull thud of their wooden blades clashing. They traded blows back and forth in a swift rhythm, blocking and countering with ease. Through her battle-clouded thoughts she couldn't help but admire the way he moved. The finesse of a nobleman. It was far different than the techniques she had grown accustomed to in the soldiers on the field. Every movement was precise and well-timed, keeping her on her toes for what he would do next.

The strikes continued in perfect time, neither one managing to break through to dominate the duel. Leyna knew it would start to fall apart soon enough. She was out of practice. Endurance was not something a young woman needed and therefore Faustine preferred to keep her girls still. It was considered grotesque for a lady to break into such a sweat. The stickiness was unappealing to a man of good standing. She could already feel her lungs starting to burn from the exertion, aching for a breath of air.

She thrust her hips backward to avoid Kael's blade slicing at her midsection. A lucky strike, perhaps, but she was starting to make mistakes. Her tired mind was losing its focus. The well-aimed counters and blocks became a frantic attempt at keeping him at bay, no longer able to pay attention to continue offensively. Defense was always a trickier game to play. She was at his mercy for whatever he threw at her, forced to proceed on his timing and speed.

Air. She needed air. The burning in her lungs and muscles was becoming a searing pain coursing through every inch of her. She was amazed that she had lasted the length of time she already had against him. If he won, it wouldn't mean he was more skilled, only that he was able to outlast her stamina. With any luck, she would be able to improve upon that in time. For now, she just had to keep his blade away from her as long as possible.

With a sudden burst of speed, Kael broke through her guard, easily disarming her sword from her hand. Unwilling to give in and accept defeat, she ducked under his outstretched arm, delivering a quick strike with her fingertips to a pressure point near his wrist. Rendered immobile for only a second, it was enough to release Kael's grip on his weapon. The match was a draw. They had both been disarmed, leaving them with nothing but their hands if Kael thought to continue.

In a fluid, sweeping motion, Kael lunged toward her legs, grabbing onto them tightly with his hands. She felt her body falling backward. There was nothing to be done to stop it. Pulling her legs out from under her, he took her down to the ground, controlling the impact of her fall with his own body.

The racing of her heart grew almost unbearable. Part of it was caused by the adrenaline pumping through her while another was frighteningly aware of Kael's sudden closeness. His soft green eyes stared deeply into her own from his position on top of her, his arms still holding her legs to either side of his body. Their chests heaved from the rush of the fight, the air from their breaths coming in short bursts as they struggled to regain their composure. He was so close to her. She could feel him, the weight of his body, pressing against her. Nothing else could be seen aside from his face – his lips hovering just above hers.

A warm rush coursed through her veins at the feeling of his mouth against hers. She knew she should push him away, but her body wouldn't listen to her mind. It felt right, somehow, despite the number of reasons why it was wrong for them to be as they were. More than just the thought of her being a slave and him a follower of her master. She didn't understand any of the emotions which filled her thoughts... and her lack of understanding was the most frightening thing of all. It was as if her body was acting on its own without any heed to the rational thoughts going through her mind. *Stop him. Push him away.* Yet she didn't. Instead, she felt her own arms wrapping around him, embracing him, pulling him in closer to her.

"Find something of mine you like, Kael?"

Her blood ran cold in her veins. Mikel. How long had he been standing there? How much had he seen?

Kael slowly pulled his lips away from hers, his eyes staring down at her with concern. He knew the same as she that he had overstepped his bounds. What had they been thinking? Although she knew the answer to that. She hadn't been thinking at all. Not any thoughts which would have prevented their actions. In the heat of the moment, they had allowed their bodies to act on their own whim. Only now, they would have to face the consequences.

"Sir. I did not know you would be stopping by." There was no hesitance in his voice. Inhaling a deep breath, Kael shifted back onto his knees, making sure Leyna's dress was covering her legs before he rose to his feet. "I was teaching her the art of the sword – "

"And what type of sword exactly would that be? When I requested you to teach her, I was referring to actual weapons… not whatever it was you were attempting to thrust at her."

Mikel moved in closer to them, his pace slow and steady, his eyes locked firmly on Kael with a challenging gaze. Nervously, Leyna scrambled to her feet, adjusting her dress back into place. She knew she was blushing. The warmth of the blood rushing into her face and ears burned noticeably to her senses. *Stupid. You may have just gotten us both killed over such a silly attraction.* If she had to ask herself if it was worth it, she wasn't sure she could give an answer so quickly.

"It was just a kiss, sir. I swear it," Kael stated, his voice trembling slightly as Mikel drew nearer. "I had no intentions of going any further than that. Truthfully, I am not entirely sure why I even did… what I did."

The expression on Mikel's face was unnerving. His eyes barely blinked while staring into Kael's with a harsh authority. "Do not lie to me, Kael. I know exactly why you did it. As do you." Turning away from Kael, he directed his piercing gaze upon Leyna, his features softening at the sight of her. "We are men, after all. And men share the same needs and desires. There is no need to deny that. Just look at her. She is fetching, is she not?"

Kael hesitated in his response, the silence hanging uncomfortably in the air between them. His mouth opened to speak, but no words came out, the confidence in his demeanor quickly fading away. Prodding him for an answer, Mikel asked again, his tone louder and more insistent than the first. "Is she not?"

"She is, sir. Yes," Kael stammered. "I don't think there is a man alive who would deny that."

"Except maybe a blind one." Gruffly, Mikel lifted Leyna's chin up with his hand, catching it between his thumb and index finger. It didn't require any acting for her to appear frightened by his touch. She tried to flinch away from him, but he held her firm, the pressure of his grip squeezing painfully against her jaw. "You know… when Gislan presented me with this gift on my birthday, my first thought was 'oh, how I wish

I weren't married.' An unmarried slave owner is a lucky man. But me – I have a very loving, though very jealous wife."

With a thoughtful expression, Mikel wrapped his free hand around Leyna's waist. Giving a sharp pull, he brought her in close to him, releasing his hold on her chin while continuing to speak. "Were that not the case, I'm sure you can imagine how much more I would be getting out of this present. My own enemy under my thumb. Doing my every bidding. Any fantasy, no matter how twisted, I could have her do. Anything to disgrace your pathetic people. I should have known to expect this of you, Kael. Your people are always trying to take from mine what they want."

"That was not my intention – "

"Yes it was, fool," Mikel snapped, casting an icy glare in Kael's direction before focusing his attention back on Leyna. "You've had your eye on her since she came here. I am not stupid. I could see the way you looked at her. The way you argued for her freedom. You wanted her for yourself... and as a slave, do you really think she would have told you no, if you had tried anything? She might as well be a whore. Slaves are trained to do exactly what their masters tell them to do. So don't start thinking you can have her all to yourself just because I have a wife."

He was so close to her that Leyna could feel the warmth of his breath upon her face. He was disgusting. In appearance he was an attractive man, but his mannerisms made the elegant curves of his features worthless. He reeked of the Ven'shal taint. It reached her nostrils as if by some sixth sense sparked in her Vor'shai mind. "Tell me, Kael. Do you care about her?"

"I beg your pardon, sir?"

"It is a simple question, now answer me. Do you care about her?"

Kael's jaw clenched at the thought of his response. Leyna could tell he was thinking over his words carefully before speaking them. Whatever he chose to say would carry more weight in Mikel's decision of what to do with them than Leyna was comfortable with. "I do, sir. I admit I know very little of her, but I carry a deep affection for her."

"Then let me make one thing very clear to you." Holding her tightly against him, Mikel let his other hand slide up the side of Leyna's body to her chest. She turned her head away from him at his touch. She felt like she would be sick. The thought of being nothing more than an object to him, a prize to show off to his followers, made her cringe inside. After so many years becoming a lady, she had willingly placed herself into the arms of her enemy, allowing him to use her in ways a lady should never allow.

She could feel his lips on the skin of her neck. Her body shuddered, stiffening with her desire to push him away. It was possible, if she was willing to risk everything for the sake of escaping his touch. There was no doubt in her mind that she was capable of overpowering him at least enough to break free. Beyond that, it was hard to say if she would be any match for the power of the magic he was rumored to wield. No. She couldn't risk it. Thade tried to warn of the reality involved in her request for this mission and she had adamantly refused to listen to him. There was nothing else to be done now but accept what came her way for the sake of her people and their Queen.

"I forgot what it was like to feel a woman trembling in my arms," Mikel whispered, his breath gently brushing over Leyna's ear with his words. "You are afraid of me, as you should be. Your life is in my hands to do with as I please. Do you understand me, slave?"

Kael's entire body tensed visibly at the sight of Mikel holding Leyna against him, unable to hear what was being said between them. Angrily, he took a step forward, stopping himself abruptly at the realization of what he was doing. "Sir…"

"Do you wish to strike me, Kael? Does seeing me with her fill you with enough hatred to betray me after you swore your loyalty?"

"I would not betray you, sir." His voice was strained. It took all of his willpower to force the words out of his mouth, knowing he had no choice but to say it if he wanted Mikel to release her.

The hand at Leyna's waist slipped away, grabbing onto her slender wrist. Gradually increasing the pressure, Mikel lifted it up, watching her face twist into a painful grimace. Opening her mouth in a silent scream, she tried to hold back her tears, not wanting to give him the pleasure of seeing her cry. "If you choose to pursue her, that is your own business. But my commands will come first and foremost. You may continue to train her to be my wife's servant, but to make sure it is only the art of combat you teach her, I will have one of my men observe every training session. It would also do you good to remember that no matter how close you may become with her, she is still mine. I will do with her what I want, if I so choose, and you will remain loyal to me. If you fail to do so, then I will take pleasure in making sure you regret ever laying eyes on her."

"Yes, sir," Kael replied quietly, lowering his head respectfully.

"I feel the two of you have seen quite enough of each other for one day," Mikel frowned. His grip remained firm on Leyna's wrist, her eyes watering despite her best efforts to hold back the tears. It felt as if the bones would shatter if he pressed any tighter, his arm moving to drag her behind him toward the house. "You are relieved of your duties for the day and will be returned to your shackles in the cellar," he said through gritted teeth, pulling her harshly. "Maybe that will give you the time you need to think about your predicament."

Chapter Eleven

The cellar was surprisingly more accommodating than before, though it helped knowing she would be allowed to roam the house freely again when the sun rose. It was a punishment for her to have to spend her nights there, but who was really the one being punished? All things considered, she believed it was intended as a reminder to Kael exactly where he stood with Mikel. A display of superiority and power. He had the control to take her away from him. What bothered her were the reasons why Mikel might have felt the need to exercise his authority.

He had been angry at the sight of Kael with her. His tone had remained calm, his actions well-controlled and calculated, but it was obvious that he was furious at Kael's behavior. Mikel had struck back at him in every non-violent way which would wound him more deeply than anything physical. Putting his hands on her, locking her away in the cellar that Kael worked so hard at getting her free of. This punishment was a display for Kael's sake, not hers.

Another of Mikel's men had been charged with keeping a close watch on her, monitoring her interaction with Kael and making sure they didn't see each other outside of their practice in the courtyard. They called him Yasar. She was never out of his sight, his muscular Namiren frame hulking even now in one of the dark corners of the cellar hall. His height alone was intimidating, standing at least a foot taller than Leyna. Likely more. Even Kael had to look up to meet his eyes when they spoke.

It was strange to her, constantly being in the company of a man against whose entire race she'd fought years before, killing their armies, leaving them broken and defeated. Now he guarded the keys to the cell which confined her, controlling the tightness of her shackles, and when she would be allowed any freedom. To see him brought back waves of memories to her tortured mind. Nightmares of her younger days haunting her in her sleep.

Lying on her back in the cell, she could feel the cold metal of the shackles weighing heavily across her abdomen where she rested her hands. By her count, it had been well over a month since the first day of her training with Kael. Nothing had been said in regards to the challenge Oksuva spoke of. She was beginning to wonder if they had forgotten about her.

The creak of her cell door opening jarred her from her thoughts, her body sitting up straight to see who was coming. She expected to see Yasar's long, feathered, brown hair and yellow eyes staring back at her from the hall. Instead, she gasped in surprise to find herself face-to-face with Mikel's steady gaze, his jaw clenched tightly as he looked down at her. "You look out of place in this wretched room. If I thought you could behave, I would let you return to your old quarters."

After their last meeting, she wasn't comfortable with the thought of being alone with Mikel, and especially not in an area of the house where they were so cut off from everything. Yasar could still be seen leaning against the cell across from hers. His eyes seemed to almost look through her, focusing on the wall behind. He wouldn't make any move to stop Mikel if he thought to go on another power trip with her. Mikel's men had no scruples. Yasar would more prefer to stand by and watch than step in to her aid.

Slowly, she pulled herself to her feet. The movement was more strained due to the shackles binding her wrists, the chain clattering noisily through the small stone-walled area. There was nothing to say in response to Mikel's comments. Fighting with him would be worthless, leading only to more trouble than she was already in. She stared back at him silently, hoping he would bypass the small-talk, moving on to the business which had brought him to her cell.

"Unexpected business forced me to allow you more than the allotted month for your training," he stated. "Lucky for you, though, the day is finally here."

Today? She didn't have time to panic. He was already grabbing onto the chains of her shackles, dragging her through the door of her cell.

Yasar was on her heels, pushing roughly at her back to keep her moving forward. In the end, she preferred the possibility of physical torture over what she feared Mikel had come to her for. Broken bones could be mended in time, but there were some things which could never be taken back. If the worst that happened to her were more scars to add to those already marring her body, then she was content to endure the pain.

They were leading her to the courtyard. Lines of people had gathered around the sandy arena, cheering their entrance. Her eyes searched the crowd, curious if Kael had come, or if he'd been allowed to. She already knew she would forgive him if he was unable to bring himself to watch the spectacle. Were the tables turned, she would find it impossible to see the things being done to him without feeling an uncontrollable need to help. Such actions would end poorly for them both.

The onlookers wore heavy cloaks to warm them from the autumn chill filling the air of the open courtyard. Through her racing thoughts, she was still able to recognize the familiar dull light of many of the eyes gazing back at her, heavily tainted by the dark magics of the Ven'shal. It was all a show to Mikel. He cared little about whether she could fire a bow or parry a sword. To him, it was another chance to show off his trophy to his friends. Public humiliation for a member of their rival race. She could feel the expectant eyes upon her, wanting to see her maimed, possibly killed, for the sake of their own entertainment.

Oksuva was like a vision of peace among the roaring crowd, sitting calmly on a high-backed chair at the side of the arena. Her hands were folded neatly in her lap, the thick green fabric of her dress fluttering in the breeze around her slippered feet. She was solemn, her posture perfectly erect. And there at her side, opposite the matching throne-like seat on her left, sat an anguished Kael, his forehead creased with concern as Mikel led her onto the sandy ground. They both remained silent while the rest of the audience cheered her shackled state, shouting heckles and other derogatory statements toward her.

From behind, she felt Yasar's meaty hands push her forward, knocking her down to her knees in the sand. The crowd went wild, whooping anxiously. "My friends," Mikel announced. "I guarantee you a show this day!"

To the roaring crowd, he gestured down at Leyna's kneeling form. The scrape of metal against leather could be heard from somewhere. With a dull thud, a sword was tossed to the ground in front of Leyna, sending a puff of dust into her eyes and mouth. She gagged, spitting in disgust to clear it from her tongue.

Metal. The blade was designed of well-constructed steel, sharpened to a fine point which glistened with the light of the sun overhead. It wasn't the light, innocent wood of the practice swords with which she and Kael had trained for the last month. This weapon was capable of removing limbs if utilized properly. *What have you gotten yourself into?*

The question echoed in her mind, realizing that Mikel and Yasar were already exiting the arena ground, taking their positions next to Oksuva and Kael. No. They couldn't be. Her wrists were still weighted down by the heavy chains of her shackles, binding her securely. How was she supposed to fight anything if she couldn't have full use of her arms?

Kael's voice could be heard from his seat. Something about her bindings. He had noticed as well. But Mikel was unyielding. The protests fell on deaf ears, met only by the hearty laughter of Mikel and Yasar.

So much for her promises to Thade and Feolan that everything would be safe. She couldn't bear to think of what Thade would say if he knew what was happening. Not that it mattered. If he knew what was happening, he would have found a way to prevent it — or stop it now before it could escalate any further. Her heart was pounding. Did Mikel truly expect her to wield this weapon in combat under her current circumstances? It was like a cruel joke that had gone on far too long. So long, in fact, that she was beginning to think it wasn't in jest at all. The odds were stacked against her.

But that had been his plan all along. She'd been foolish to think he would have willingly allowed this fight to be fair when it risked him losing full control of his personal Vor'shai slave. It had sounded simple; the way Oksuva's bell-like voice had described the bargain. In truth, she was stuck in the middle of a battle between a husband and wife whose intentions couldn't be more drastically opposite. Oksuva desired to see her win out of spite for her husband; while Mikel arranged everything he could to see her fail.

Proudly, she rose to her feet, catching up the hilt of the sword in her right hand. The weight was impressive. It reminded her of the weapons used by the other soldiers during the war. On occasion she had found need to use them, though she'd opted most times for the lighter design of her own blade.

She stood on guard, her eyes shifting sharply from one side of the ring to the other. The attack could come from anywhere. Mikel wouldn't have made it quite so easy as to grant her a fair start. Her opponent would have the advantage of surprise, setting her in a defensive stance in preparation for whatever might come.

When the man finally showed himself, she was ready for him, her muscles instantly twitching into motion, the movements instinctive to her well-trained mind. He was taller than she was, but not by much. His head was shaved on the sides, leaving only a thin line of close-cut brown hair curving around just above his ears from front to back. The whites of his eyes were almost nonexistent. A dull black film covered over where it should be, bleeding into the iris to conceal whatever color it once held. A trait of the Ven'shal. This man could be of any combination of Vor'shai or Ven'shal in heritage, but the magic which he studied was obvious. The taint of his darkening spirit sent shivers over Leyna's skin.

Her restrained wrists forced her blocks to be more sluggish than preferred, her left arm flopping uselessly about from the short chain between the shackles, pulling her off balance. The only thing which eased her troubled thoughts was that the man she was fighting appeared sluggish himself, lacking the refined quality to his strikes that she had come to expect from Kael. It slowed him down. An unplanned disadvantage for Mikel's fighter.

The blocks and counters came in a flurry of intense concentration, flowing reflexively from Leyna's muscles. The techniques came back to her quickly through her training. All that mattered at this early stage of the fight was to disarm the man of his weapon. As long as they were both wielding blades, the danger of severe injury was too great a risk. She wanted to impress Oksuva with her abilities, but the last thing she wanted to do was kill some stranger for no reason.

This wasn't war. Unnecessary deaths should be avoided at any cost, unless it became apparent that death was the only means of defending her own life. She wasn't willing to die for the sake of sparing anyone who seemed to willingly serve the perverted rituals and magics of the Ven'shal.

It was hard to tell whether he was picking up speed, or if she was slowing down. His precision was improving rapidly, pushing her back, their swords clanging together loudly, echoing in her ears over the cheers of the crowd. They wanted blood. She didn't. There would be no avoiding it, however. Aim for non vital-targets. She tried to keep focused on the match, finding it harder to accomplish with every swing of the man's sword. Growing frustrated, her concentration began to fail.

She had to disarm him. Steeling her resolve, she gripped the hilt with both hands, steadying the awkward sway of her body caused by her restraints. This allowed her a stronger hold, lightening the load of the heavy blade. With a newfound strength, she pressed forward, bearing down on her opponent with a combination of strikes, forcing him to the defensive.

Openings were revealing themselves to her at every turn, his arms overextending on the blocks, rising up a little higher than they should, leaving his midsection vulnerable. She hesitated to strike at such a dangerous target. The sword was too sharp to think that she could properly judge the depth of any wound she thought to inflict. There had to be something else. His arms. On the overextension, the length of his arm would be exposed. A strike there would be easier to control.

He moved perfectly into her plans, his motions growing more frantic to block her strikes. No more effort was being made to attempt counter attacks, placing her in a dominating position to overwhelm his guard and relieve him of his weapon. Drawing his arms out for another parry, she directed the feint off to his left, shifting her stance to drag her blade painfully along his bicep.

The distraction of the wound was all she needed. His attention was diverted, his grip weakened. Twisting her own blade downward in a circular motion, she sent his weapon flying from his hands, safely out of reach to prevent him from retrieving it.

Leyna was surprised to hear scattered cheers throughout the crowd at her success. She wanted to see Kael, to know if he was on his feet, his own voice adding to her praise, but she couldn't allow her focus to break. The wound inflicted on her opponent was superficial at best, leaving him fully capable of retaliation.

His counter came unexpectedly, his body dropping down, extending his right leg and gathering momentum in a hard spin to sweep her legs out from underneath her, slamming her back onto the ground. Air escaped her lungs, exhaled in a single sharp breath. The sensation left her stunned for only an instant, her body rolling out of the way to evade the stomping foot that followed.

As she rolled, the pressure of some resistance weighed down her sword, preventing her from pulling it back to her. If she let it go, she would be disarming herself and leaving her own weapon in the hands of her opponent. The man's heavy boot pressed against her right wrist. It dug the edges of the shackles deep into her skin, crushing the bone with a grotesque crack while her left hand was powerless to fight back, her reach hindered by the short chain connecting her wrists.

The pain was too great for her to overcome. Tendons strained in her wrist, the muscles failing in her hand, causing the hilt of the sword to release from her grasp. Desperately, she tried to maneuver her left hand over his foot to it, hoping to snatch it back into her possession. He couldn't be allowed to get it. Her position was too poor.

If he gained back a blade, the fight would be over. Unless she was willing to sacrifice a few broken bones. Such an expense seemed an adequate price to save her life.

Leyna drew back her left fist as far as the chains would allow, striking the man hard in the shin, unable to reach a more effective target. His body doubled forward, painfully mashing his foot harder down onto her wrist. She repeated the motion. Over and over, hoping the area would grow tender enough to force him to a mild retreat. Stumbling back, his foot moved just enough to grant her freedom again, her hand retracting to her chest protectively.

It hurt. Every inch of her fingers to the tips tingled, lacking circulation, among whatever injuries might have been incurred. She could hardly move it. Gripping her weapon would be out of the question. At least until she'd regained some of the feeling in her hand.

Her body moved as if it functioned on its own. Like a marionette on a string, her left hand pushed the sword away, wasting no time in getting back to her feet. For a hand to hand brawl, her back was the last place she wanted to be. The only position she could think of to be any worse was her stomach. Neither one of those could be given to him.

There was no chance for an attack of conscience at the thought of assaulting this man with her bare hands. Not only was he already upon her, fists pummeling her repeatedly, but she took comfort in knowing that the blows dealt by her hands would create wounds less lethal than a blade.

Each strike that connected with her face and head sent her vision into a blur of flashing white spots. *Block. Lift your arms to block!* Why were her arms not listening? They felt as though they were disconnected from her brain, hanging worthlessly at her sides.

A final blow knocked her back on the ground. His elbow struck across her left temple, her eyes darkening in a flash of unconsciousness. This was all a nightmare. She was a far more skilled fighter than this man and yet he was finding ways to defeat her mental focus and drop her guard. If she wasn't careful, she would be beaten. This match had too much riding on it for defeat to be an option.

It was then that it hit her. This man was not the one defeating her. It was herself. Her own mind was distracted by the little details of her situation which meant absolutely nothing in the end. When she was at war, there was no concern for who was watching, or how much pain the incoming blows caused. Nothing mattered but the person in front of her, the openings he left, the weaknesses he showed. Why did she care what this crowd of Ven'shal thought? So what if they wanted to see her die, crushed under the foot of this sluggish fighter. He was stronger than her, without doubt, but physical strength wasn't enough to defeat her. It never had been in the past, and she had no intention of letting it start now.

She was on her feet again. The noise from the onlookers fell to a dull tone in her head. Their voices no longer formed words, their chants and shouts meaningless murmurs. Her fists were clenched. Pain was trivial to her, the tingling in her right hand ignored with every punch she delivered to the man's face and body. Something in her head told her she was injuring herself worse by continuing, but that wasn't important. Not at this moment. She could worry about that when the fight was over.

The man's hand slipped by her guard, his knuckles slamming against the bones in her face. It was excruciating. A cracking sound emitted from under it, encircling her right eye. She'd never noticed just how large his hands were, until that moment. Her vision swam under the force. But she kept moving. Her arms never ceased their determined strikes.

Her right eye was beginning to swell. It already was starting to interfere with her line of sight, closing off her ability to see her opponent from that angle if he moved in just the right way. Oh, if only she could rid herself of those blasted shackles! She would be able to utilize her body to its full potential, pressure points, joint locks, take downs – so much was limited with her restraints.

He was taking advantage of her visual impairment, moving just outside her available line of sight. If she was going to close in on him at all, she would need to stop him from moving, to hold him in place somehow. Then it came to her. The thing which hindered her the most could be used to her benefit. While her fingers were weakened from their injuries and easily pried away from him, the chains on the shackles would be stronger. More difficult for him to escape.

How to do it was the question. The man was in a constant state of movement, making him impossible to keep within her line of sight. But then again, why did she need her eyes? How many times had Blaise tested her combat prowess by wrapping that piece of cloth over her face to force her to use her other senses? That first scout in the mountains with Thade and Feolan – she'd utilized it then to defeat a far more skilled fighter in that Sanarik warrior – there was no reason for it not to work against this man.

Closing her eyes, she ceased to follow the man in his endeavors to keep her off balance. No more would she play into his hands. This fight would be under her conditions. And if it meant sinking to a more brutal method, she would have to do it. Mikel would never consider the fight over until one of them was unconscious... or dead.

Sand shuffled about under his feet, and she could sense his confusion at her sudden stillness. Yet he continued moving. Foolish on his part. She could tell exactly where he was, listening to the sound of his naïve attempts at forcing her to follow him. He lacked the experience of a real fight. If he knew anything, he would have stopped moving to leave the sand still and silent. He wasn't even smart enough to try and distract her with a tossed handful of stones to divert her attention away from his actual position.

Patience. She had to wait for him to come back around. It was unlikely he would be expecting her to strike, which would offer her the upper hand. But only if he made his way back within her grasp. If she made any movement to turn toward him, he would start moving again, warned of her intentions by the signal given off from the gesture. No, he would have to come to her. And he would. She didn't doubt that. He wasn't intelligent enough to understand what she was planning.

When she heard his footsteps coming in closer, the muscles in her body tensed in preparation for the strike, waiting, listening, until he was within a close enough range that she felt able to wrap the chain around the back of his neck to pull him in to her. Sensing the opening she sought, she sprang into motion, maneuvering her arms over his head until the chain pressed firmly into the man's throat with every ounce of strength she could conjure. His surprise mingled with rage at having fallen into her hands. Pressing in close to his body, she pulled the chain down hard, keeping her arms in close to her chest. From his position, nothing he could throw at her would cause much harm. His face was buried into her shoulder. Her midsection was protected by his own body being too close to her own, his arms flailing wildly at her head.

Weak slaps. His pathetic strikes made her want to laugh. Sure, he could still deliver blows to her lower back, leaving a few targets open to him, if he had been clear-headed enough to think of them. He was in a panic. All his body was attempting to do was break free of her grasp, which would never happen under the circumstances. She had no intention of letting him go until he was no longer capable of movement.

Holding the position of her upper body, Leyna allowed her hips to shift backward, creating an opening between the two of them. It was enough to grant her a perfect target for her knee, winding it back, and slamming it hard into the stiff muscles of the man's abdomen. Again and again, she struck. Slowly moving up from the stomach to the solar plexus, taking the wind away from her opponent.

While he was distracted by the lack of air in his lungs, she moved her shoulders back, pressing the man's head down into her knee with a solid impact to his nose. He cried out painfully, his limbs becoming more languid than they'd been before. No longer was he even thinking about breaking free of her grasp. His thoughts were overcome by the need to breathe.

Content with her dominance in the match, she opened her eyes, still unfocused on anything specific. Lifting her arms, she released her hold on the man's neck, reinforcing her right arm by clasping her left hand over her right fist, bringing her elbow up to strike again at his face.

His body fell to the ground with a dull thud in the sand. Blood flowed from his nose. It brought back painful memories of her own blood pouring forth onto her hands, soaking the little handkerchief that Zander tried to use to help her, staining the fabric of his shirt – but this was different. She had to remind herself. And as long as he was still conscious enough to groan and writhe about on the ground, the match was not over.

Finishing it would be a simple task, lacking in any need for further violence. Easily, she slipped around behind him, wrapping the chain over his head to allow her right arm to squeeze his neck. *Sleep. Just go to sleep and this will all be over.* She willed him to hear her thoughts, his fingers prying uselessly at her arm. Within moments, his body grew limp against hers, his arms flopping to his sides, head dangling heavily from his neck. Releasing her hold, she straightened her posture, rising back to her feet.

The man was out cold, lying still and almost lifeless there in the sand at her feet. She'd won. And the crowd was speechless. An occasional applause would start, only to fade out again after a few short claps. No one knew what to do. This was not the way the match was expected to go, and surely not the way it had been intended. Mikel made it very clear that his bets were placed on the man now unconscious, his blood staining the light colored sand of the ring.

"Well, that is deserving of an encore!"

Leyna could hear Mikel's voice, closer than she expected, having left the chair at Oksuva's side to make his way over to where she now stood. "I cannot prove myself at the archery challenge with my hands bound, sir," she whispered, presenting her shackled wrists to him hesitantly. He glanced down at them, sneering before spitting disgustedly at her feet.

"What good is an archery contest to me?" he asked. "So what if you can shoot a target on the other side of the courtyard. No one here wants to see it. They wanted to see a Vor'shai mangled in battle, but you made sure to ruin that for them all, didn't you?"

She was confused. He was angry with her, yet she'd only done what was said to be expected of her by Oksuva. If her eye was not so swollen, she would have tried to catch sight of Oksuva from over Mikel's shoulder, curious to see the expression on her face at the result of the match. Leyna had won. Wasn't that what she wanted? What other choice would there have been? That man had no qualms with killing her there in front of everyone. He would never have shown the same mercy which she bestowed by sparing him.

In a quick motion, Mikel grabbed onto the chain connecting the shackles of her wrists, jerking her harshly to him. Fear gripped her at the look she saw there in his eyes. She'd never gotten used to the darkness that resided there, a deep void of blackness from end to end. If his eyes were any indication of his soul, then there was no hope of redemption for him from the tainted magic. It also meant that he lacked the capability of feeling guilt for anything which he might choose to do to her in his rage. An enemy like that was the most frightening. Unpredictable.

A shadowy aura began to envelope his hand, causing Leyna to shiver at the sight of it. She'd seen it before, back in Velorum, when her assailant utilized it to crush her lungs. Since then, she counted her blessings that such power had never been used again by any of their opponents in the war. It was impossible to know what a man like Mikel was capable of doing with it. He was much more powerful than that stranger outside the tavern.

Her one good eye was locked on the inky blackness creeping from Mikel's hand over the sturdy chain. An icy chill covered the metal, freezing the skin of her wrists where it was in contact with her body. She could feel a pressure against her bones, as if the shackles were somehow shrinking, tightening painfully around her wrists. *Don't cry out. Don't give him the pleasure.* It was easier to think it than to hold back the agonizing scream building inside. He was crushing her.

The pain in her right wrist was beyond excruciating, pressing against her already injured bones from where her opponent had dug the shackles down into it. She couldn't keep on her feet. Her legs wobbled, knees giving out under the strain. The only thing holding her up was Mikel's strong hand still clutching the chain, his laughter ringing through the courtyard at the sight of her dangling there from his grasp.

Sharply, he brought the back of his hand across her right cheek, snapping her head to the side under the force. She wasn't sure how much she would be able to take before the pain would send her into a faint.

His fingers gradually opened to release their hold on her, letting her fall in a heap to the ground. "Fight me, slave!" he shouted, playing to the cheers of the crowd erupting around them. "If the magic of your people is so superior, then show me. If you can somehow best me at it, then I will consider you worthy of serving my wife."

"Mikel, stop this at once!"

Oksuva's voice was drowned out in Leyna's head by the sudden force of some unseen hand pressing her backward, knocking her to the ground. Her thoughts raced in her head. How was she supposed to fight this man? This evil creature whose strength she couldn't even fathom. Faustine had trained her well in the art of the light magic, how to heal in the way of the Vor'shai physicians, and how to gain the favor of the living earth around her. But she knew nothing of what the black arts could do. Everything she was capable of and more, but with a twisted way of it.

She was being lifted back to her feet by the same invisible force which had taken her off them, holding her up in the air, her toes hovering over the sand. Mikel's hand was extended toward her, still enveloped in that ominous aura. This was his doing. He was the puppeteer and she his puppet. How could she break free of a grip when she couldn't even see what was holding her?

Think back on the lake in Tanispa. You were able to maintain control of the magic while faced with the fear of drowning. This is no different. She begged silently for the help of the gods, and her ancestors. Were they still with her? Or had they forsaken her in this damnable mission?

Nothing. She could conjure up no energy with which to fight back. The pain that racked her body was too great a distraction. She wasn't skilled enough with the magic to manipulate it under such duress. She'd been wrong. This was nothing like the lake at all. When submerged under the water, she'd been comforted by the thought of knowing the spirits would guide her, that the gods would be with her, and if nothing else, she could have stood up, escaping the suffocating liquid. There was no comfort to be had here in this miserable courtyard, so many enemies with their eyes upon her, cheering at her pain, wanting to see her defeated — while her only ally was powerless to stop it without destroying them both, her other friends too far away to help her. They didn't even know what was happening. She was alone.

In an instant, a bright flash of light surrounded her, breaking her free of whatever hold Mikel had on her. She dropped back to the ground, trying to break her fall with her hands. Grimacing in pain, she retracted her arms to her chest, clutching them there as she curled up into a ball on the sand. "I said that is enough, Mikel. I have seen all I need to know that she is capable of the job offered to her, and I will not sit here and watch you torment one of my ladies."

Kael was beside her. She couldn't see his face, but she recognized his scent, his arms wrapping around her gingerly. "It is over, Eleni. You won."

His whispered words brought no joy the way she thought they would. She felt broken. Vulnerable. There was no happiness to be had in the feeling of her spirit being crushed. Yes, she had won. But what exactly did that mean? She was still a slave. Mikel was still free to torture her in any way he saw fit. Her promises to Thade and Feolan were empty, and she hated it. She couldn't guarantee the beatings would end. Everything felt utterly hopeless, and to this point she hadn't learned anything worthwhile to her people in order for it to feel like it had been for a reason.

There was nothing for her to say. It hurt too much to cling to Kael's comforting arms, leaving her there stiffly for him to embrace, unable to return the gesture. She wanted to leave. To send word to Thade to come take her away from this place and end her suffering. Her conscience would never allow it. She knew that much. Sleep, then. Even if it was in the darkened cage of the cellar, it might offer her some sort of refresh to her will. A defeatist attitude was unlike her. It had to be caused by the pain and frustration, which would pass in time. *You won.* Bittersweet were those words.

Mikel and Oksuva were still arguing loudly, their voices rising over the sound of the crowd. People were starting to slip out, dwindling the numbers to only a few who remained out of curiosity. It was only then that the true oddness of what happened sank in to her troubled thoughts. White light. Who had broken Mikel's hold on her? Kael? He wouldn't have dared. But then it left only Oksuva, whose mere association with Mikel had convinced Leyna of her dabbling in the darker magic. If that were true, then her own energy would have been tainted with the same darkness as her husband's.

She felt her desire for answers somewhat renewed at the realization. There was more to that woman than met the eye. Could that have been the reason for the Vor'shai's interest in her and her business? Everything about her was a mystery. Why had she married this man who hated those of her mixed heritage, and who dabbled in magic darker than her own? He was unfaithful, yet she still tolerated him. He was almost detached from her completely. Even now, while they fought one another, Leyna could hear no tenderness in her voice. No love. Only hatred. She spoke like a woman who despised the creature standing in front of her.

"Kael?" Oksuva said suddenly, turning away from Mikel's reddening face at his growing anger. "Undo her bindings and take her back to her quarters by the kitchen. I will not have one of my ladies sleeping in the cellar. Tomorrow, you will take her to Siscal City. Buy her a couple of dresses so that she will not look like a peasant at my side. I give you leave for no more than three days. I have a meeting coming up, and she will be properly attired and present for it."

Siscal? Her heart jumped in her chest. To have her friends so close again. And if she was able, she could try to slip away to visit them. Kael would have to sleep at some point. But then, it was hard to say whether or not Mikel would insist on sending Yasar with them to oversee things. Sending her away alone with Kael would only serve to heighten his rage. All she could do was hope Oksuva would be able to overrule him on his desire to have them supervised.

A vacation was what she needed. A few days away from this place, and away from the constant fear of what would happen to her. And with Kael by her side. The familiar flutter in her stomach returned at the thought, distracting her from the feeling of defeat threatening to send her into a deep depression. She would come back from this. And in the end, she would get the information necessary to confirm any suspicions about these people. She wouldn't let them break her. She was a Vor'shai, and nothing could ever take that away from her.

Leyna was amazed at the number of different clothing shops scattered throughout the city of Siscal. Never before had she found herself with any reason to seek them out. During the war, the standard issue uniform was the only clothing option she had, and upon her return, she'd been swept away by the mission before she could even think about shopping. Many of the stores were in areas of the city she had never set foot in, unaware they even existed.

Despite the coming winter, Siscal remained remarkably warm in the midday sun. Due to the severity of her visible injuries, she was forced to conceal herself under the cover of a thick cloak, the hood pulled down over her face protectively. Her right eye was swollen almost completely shut by now, though an improvement from when she'd first woken up the previous morning to begin the trip.

The marks from her opponent's strikes left bruises over much of her skin on the right side of her face, the cheek and temple area turning shades of deep purple and blue, while the eye had deepened to black. Over the brow, distinct bruising revealed each individual knuckle from the fist which struck her, dotting the puffy skin. Scratches from the rough sand ran at all angles on both sides of her face and neck, her lower lip split open to the left.

She was a wretched sight. And her head felt about as her face looked. Pains of a migraine settled into her temples and all through the front of her forehead, trailing back down the length of her neck. Light strained her one uninjured eye, making it difficult to see where she was going. If it hadn't been for Kael at her side, she knew she wouldn't have been able to complete the task given to her by Oksuva.

Find a few nice dresses. Nothing too nice, though. She couldn't outshine her mistress when standing next to her. Not that she would have been able to anyway, looking the way she did. Attention might be drawn to her, but not because she was any more attractive. People would be more curious about the horrible marks on her face. No one would care what she was wearing, so long as she was clothed. Their eyes would be elsewhere.

They had successfully picked out three dresses which seemed suitable for Oksuva's taste. Leyna was impressed by Kael's knowledge of women's clothing, handling most of the transactions himself. He was a regular expert with sizes and measurements, keeping up the conversation with the sales clerks in order to divert their attention away from Leyna's concealed features. Anyone who saw her would believe her wounds to have been caused by him. She didn't want to risk those accusations.

Much of the day was still ahead of them. Kael had decided to take up the full extent of the time allotted for the trip, planning their departure for the later hours of the morning the following day, wanting to take advantage of every moment they would have without Yasar's company. There was no need to rush back to Dalonshire when the weather here in Siscal was so lovely. She only wished she didn't have to hide under the heavy material of the cloak, leaving her a bit warmer than she was comfortable with.

"Have you ever seen the Siscal palace? We are not very far from it."

How could she forget the sight of that place? It was ingrained in her memory forever on that fateful day. A day which Kael couldn't be allowed to know about quite yet. "No, I have not. But I hear many wonderful things about it."

"It is one of the grandest palaces in the world, next to the Tanispan palace, of course. Very little could ever top Queen Vorsila's home," Kael chuckled. "It is a sight to see, nonetheless. Let us walk there. The weather is far too perfect to spend the afternoon inside our rooms at the inn."

The idea would have sounded enticing had it not been for her fear of someone recognizing her. So many of her friends had become important figures within the Siscalian government. Queen Nesperiti may not have ever seen her face, but she had granted Teagan a place among her court. How many others from her old unit had been given the same honor? Not to mention the Consul and his assistant. The main street of Siscal was a risk for her to traverse. "Surely, there are other sights more interesting than the home of royalty? It is nothing but a building which reminds us how unimportant we really are in the grand scheme of things."

"Nonsense," he argued. "The palaces are works of art. You seem like the type of woman who would appreciate fine art." His eyes gazed at her fondly. It was hard to tell him no when he looked at her like that. She feared he could convince her to do anything with those soft green eyes, staring into her own as if seeing the very depths of her soul.

If he could see into her soul, he wouldn't look upon her quite so fondly. He would see that she was lying to him about everything, playing off his ignorance, using it to her own advantage within the house. "It is not my decision to make," she replied guiltily, lowering her eyes to avoid his gaze. "If you desire to see it, then we shall, but I would prefer not to linger there for very long. The heat is making me feel a bit tired."

His face lit up at her submission. A sinking feeling built up in her stomach and even the smile on Kael's face wasn't enough to calm it. "A few years back, I actually had the pleasure of meeting the Lord Dhiren. There is rumor that Queen Nesperiti might accept him in marriage. As he is a Duke, his status is acceptable enough, and Siscal has been without a king for nearly two decades now. Nesperiti is desperate for an heir to the Lenrisa dynasty."

"I do not know how the royal families deal with it all," Leyna sighed. "The constant socializing, entertaining the court, maintaining relationships with the other countries and their governments — the never ending worry about who will take over the throne when they die, and who their children should marry in order to better solidify their position, wealth, and alliances. It is a miracle any of their marriages last. If my parents had ever told me they had picked a husband for me, I would have run away."

Kael looked her over carefully, peering into the shadows of her cloaked face. "Arranged marriages are not as bad as people might think. They are business arrangements, and therefore they are upheld under that understanding. Children are made solely for the purpose of providing an heir. When that is all that is required of the relationship, they can spend as much time away from each other as they want, so tolerance is all they need."

"But what about love? Can the royal family never be allowed that luxury?"

"What does royalty care about love? Love is for the peasants. Once you step up to a position of nobility, everything is business. How to better raise your status amongst society."

"It is unfair, is what it is." Leyna frowned, not intending to speak the words out loud. She'd never taken the time to consider any of it before. The bedtime stories read to her by her mother when she was younger had always made royalty sound like a glorious fairy tale, filled with love and riches. Never in the stories did the princess marry the prince simply because her father told her she had no choice. The prince always rescued her from the clutches of some evil witch — how ironic it would have been in those stories if the princess had been rescued by some peasant boy. In reality, such a circumstance would never have the happy ending the writers liked to lead everyone to believe royalty had. In fiction, they always married for love. What horrible lies those books fed the naïve minds of children.

"What is unfair? The fact that they are born to such privilege and therefore must make sacrifices for their responsibilities?"

Not wanting to continue the conversation, she found herself backed into a corner, Kael's expectant gaze upon her, anxious to hear her answer. Averting her eyes, she gave a long sigh. It wasn't common for slaves to be so outspoken about what was fair and what wasn't. The better choice would have been to keep her mouth shut in the first place. "They did not ask to be born into that position. It is more like punishment for a crime they did not commit." As she spoke, she pictured the suave grin of Prince Enaes, his eyes sparkling from under his velvety mask at the ball.

Perhaps she was wrong. Maybe not all royalty felt the responsibility such a burden to carry. Enaes always appeared to revel in it, using his position to seduce any woman he felt he wanted. It seemed more likely that a royal upbringing left them unaware of what love even was, having never experienced it, or witnessed it between their parents. And if they knew nothing of it, then how could they know what they were being deprived of?

And who was she to even think to argue for the sake of love? She was not yet thirty years old. Barely beyond the age to be considered an adult, and having never known the emotion for herself. All she had to go by were the stories her mother had told her. And look at how things turned out for her mother? Maybe love really was nothing but a fable, used to make children believe the world to be a better place than it really was. In her little experience with life, she'd already learned that it was nothing like those fairy tales. It was filled with murder and corruption... torture – and those who were not faced with it lived a life of tedious monotony like she endured under Faustine's care.

"You are right," she said suddenly, shaking her head at her earlier argument. "In the end, love is nothing more than a word we all speak and yet never truly understand. With that in mind, royalty is no different from any of the rest of us."

"No – I would never say that. About love," Kael shook his head. He paused in his forward pace, turning to face Leyna with a look in his eyes that she had never seen before. "Love is not nothing. It is something that is merely out of our control. It has no boundaries and cares not for rank or riches. A king could fall in love with a maid and the feeling would be no different than if two servants were to experience it. We do not plan for it, but we understand it enough to know the feeling when it comes over us. Many simply choose to ignore it, out of fear, or in the case of the royals, out of necessity."

"Have you ever felt love before?"

It seemed such a harmless question, rolling off her tongue before she could even stop to think about whether it was appropriate for her to ask. Kael looked taken aback for a moment, unsure of how to respond. Something was troubling him behind those green eyes, his voice softer than usual when he spoke. "I believe I am experiencing it right now."

She choked on her breath. It was awkward, the way his words made her feel, setting her on edge in ways she'd never felt before, denial creeping into her head, telling her that she was misunderstanding his implications. He couldn't possibly be referring to her. They barely knew one another, and in their time together, they had seen so little of each other, and shared even fewer opportunities to talk and get to know anything about their pasts, or opinions. How could he, then, claim to feel such an emotion for her? No, it was not so. And she couldn't say what she felt was remotely close to what she imagined the feeling would be like. Butterflies in her stomach when near him certainly didn't guarantee love.

"You do not mean that," she whispered. She didn't know what else she could say. In her mind, she felt he'd been swept away by the pity he possessed for her, believing her to be in distress, and drawn to her for no other reason than the strong sympathy he held at her predicament. Their time together had been filled with drama. It would be impossible to compare the strong emotions which such turmoil brought upon them, distinguishing any of them to be that deep.

He looked almost hurt by her words, his head lowering dejectedly. Honesty was the best course for them at this point in their relationship. They would never get anywhere if he was convinced he was in love with her when she couldn't be so sure that she felt the same. It would only lead to heartbreak, in the end.

"I know what I feel for you," he replied calmly, moving to take her hands in his. The flicker of pain in her eyes at his touch forced him to stop, pulling away with a grimace. "You may not feel it yet yourself, and I understand. You have a great deal on your mind that I could never possibly understand. I have no intentions of rushing you into anything you do not desire. I've never been a slave before, therefore I can't understand what you've gone through in life."

She was relieved to hear him say it. Things were uncomfortable enough without having to feel the guilt of knowing that she was leading him on in any way. Then again, she had to wonder over her actions in the past. Had she done anything which might

have led him to believe she shared that strong emotion for him? She enjoyed his company, yes, and she thought of him as the closest thing to a friend, given her situation.

The kiss. Of course. She couldn't deny the electricity which pulsed between them
in that brief moment before Mikel made his presence known. But a kiss did not indicate love. It indicated passion – a physical lust that she had felt for him. The loss of
control was frightening, really. When their lips touched, it was like nothing else in her
mind mattered. Her body reacted instinctively... and not in a way with which she was
comfortable.

Before she could respond, she felt a noticeable tension build over him, his breath
drawing in sharply. His eyes, though directed at her, were now staring at something
beyond, just over her shoulder to the side of the road. "Eleni, there is someone I think
you should meet – but you can never mention it in front of Mikel or Oksuva. Do you
understand?"

The pit in her stomach returned, churning worse than before. Oh, who was he
referring to? She was in no condition to entertain anyone, and his warning narrowed
down the possibilities in her mind. "I understand. But I really am not in any shape..."

Gently, Kael placed his hand against her arm, turning her around to face the
opposite side of the street, cutting off her protests. She felt as though she would be
sick. There, outside a small group of courtiers, stood the all too familiar figure of
Thade, the jovial smile on his face quickly fading away at the sight of Kael, their eyes
meeting with a somber expression of silent understanding. "That man there is the
Consul to our Queen. He is the next thing to royalty among our people, serving as
her voice here in Siscal. You should consider yourself very lucky to have the honor
of meeting him."

"You speak as though you are absolutely certain he will converse with us," she
argued. Hesitantly, she ducked her head closer to Kael's shoulder, praying Thade would
not come near them for the sake of their mission. After all, it was a simple conversation
between Zander and Feolan which had led to her current state. A meeting, however
brief, could prove disastrous if witnessed by the wrong eyes.

Pressure was already being placed upon her back, guiding her across the street.
"Your Grace! What a pleasant surprise to see you."

Thade's eyes bypassed Kael's, staring directly at the shadows of Leyna's cloaked face. He suspected her identity, but gave no indication on his features which would incriminate his knowledge of her. "Kael Hadaren. I have not seen you around in quite some time. Might I inquire of your companion?"

"Ah, you will have to forgive her. She is rather ill, and the light causes pain to her sensitive eyes," Kael lied, his voice never faltering. "Might I present to you the lovely Eleni."

Keeping her arms flat to her sides, she bowed her head, sinking into a deep curtsy before him. The injuries to her wrists and hands prevented her from performing the motion the way Faustine had instructed. She dreaded Thade's reaction. He was a gentleman, and without knowledge of her condition, would be inclined to reach for her hand. To refuse him would be rude, though allowing it would cause immense pain, which would draw more attention to her discomfort than she liked.

There was no getting around it. She watched his movements as if in slow motion, his hand extending out to hers. Pain shot through her fingers, down into her wrist, a sharp gasp escaping her at the sensation. Instantly, Thade flattened his hand, leaving them palm to palm, easing the discomfort that she felt, while exposing the hideous bruises and swelling along her fingers, extending up her hand and wrist to where the soft lace of her sleeves covered her skin.

"My goodness, Kael. What sort of illness causes a reaction such as this?"

For the first time, Leyna could sense Kael's confidence slipping away, bumbling over his own tongue in desperation for some excuse. There was none. Kael was aware that no lie would be logical enough to fool the mind of one as intelligent as the Consul. "I am afraid that would be too difficult to explain under the current conditions," he mumbled.

Careful of her wounds, Thade lowered Leyna's arm back down to her side. She could sense his concern, mingled with guilt which was unmistakable in the depths of his silver eyes, their glow dimming somewhat under his restrained emotions. "Then I must insist that you join me for dinner this evening at my home, in order to enlighten me with the story. Then, perhaps, my assistant and I could have the pleasure of seeing the lovely face of Miss Eleni, here."

"As you wish, Your Grace."

Thade granted them no opportunity to back down from the offer. Giving a distinct and sharp nod of his head, he turned away, moving swiftly toward his carriage waiting for him several feet away on the street. Leyna was in a panic at the thought of meeting with Thade and Feolan at their home. What would they say if they were to see her face? It was bad enough that Thade had caught a glimpse of her hand. He was sure to pull her from the mission now, recognizing that the promises of her safety were empty and unable to be kept.

"I cannot attend that dinner with you, Kael," she frowned. It was useless to argue with him. Everyone was against her. Kael would insist upon her going, while her presence then would lead to Thade's removal of her from Kael's company in returning to Dalonshire, neither of which were options she wanted to accept. She couldn't face Thade the way she was, but she couldn't give up, not after her painful victory. She had been successful. Oksuva now was within her grasp.

Shaking his head, Kael pressed her forward, ushering her quickly along the crowded streets. "In this matter, I cannot give you a choice. You will be there at my side, and afterward you will speak nothing of it. To anyone. Our lives depend on your silence."

Nothing had been able to ease the pounding of her heart, her insides trembling nervously at the mere thought of setting foot in Thade's home. It had been almost two months since she'd been there last; her first and only visit to him. Meeting on pleasant terms had not been something she'd managed as of yet. She was beginning to wonder if it was possible.

Kael had insisted she dress in one of the new gowns they had purchased. He wanted to display her as a lady, rather than the slave she was, hoping to leave a better impression with Thade than they had on the street that afternoon. Guilt bubbled up inside her at his ignorance to the truth, working so hard to make her presentable to the Consul. If he only knew his efforts were in vain. She was well beyond first impressions at this point.

They had chosen a dress with longer sleeves, keeping in mind the impending winter, as well as a means to conceal the wounds already present, and in the event of any further injuries to her arms. Higher necks concealed any skin which might draw attention away from Oksuva during their meetings. Leyna took added comfort in knowing that these features would also keep her old scars safely out of view. The fabric was a soft grey, decorated with silver cording and embroidery over the lines in the bodice. The skirt was full, falling elegantly to the floor from her slender waist. Though it hid her skin from view, the design clung to her figure, accenting her curves despite the heavy material it was created from.

Unlike her previous visit, Kael made no effort to stash their horses and carriage out of view from Thade's home. He drove it himself, directing it up to the front of the house, in plain sight of anyone who might happen through the tiny neighborhood. It felt unsafe to her. Though it was unlikely anyone would recognize their carriage, or pay it any special attention, it still seemed reckless, a foolish decision on his part. "Kael, do you not think that we should leave the horses down the road a ways? To avoid suspicion?"

"Let me do the worrying about all that. I need you to focus on yourself. This is a very delicate situation, and the Consul is not a man who will easily believe any nonsense. Make sure you are able to convince him that you are in perfect health and safety."

Outside the door, it felt like they stood there for hours, knocking, waiting for someone to open it and usher them inside to the warmth, leaving the cool night breeze locked away from them in the dark. A wave of nausea swept over her at the sight of Feolan's calm face in the flickering candlelight of the entrance, motioning for them to come in. She was sick. Really sick. But not from any physical illness. Nerves sent her into a tremble, her breath shaky, sporadic.

Her ears didn't register anything being spoken around her. Someone was offering to take her cloak. Come in and stay awhile. Dinner would be served shortly. She argued politely, declining to remove the protective covering she wore. She was cold. They would have to forgive her.

The room was spinning, much the way she had watched the mountains whirl about her that day when she first met Thade, woozy from the trauma of slamming her head against the rock under the force of the monstrous ghereac. She had no concussion this time. The cause of the dizziness was unknown. The only thing she knew was that she needed to make it stop.

Kael had his arms around her, steadying her on her feet. Or trying to. She felt herself stumbling to the left, her hand reaching up painfully to her head. What a horrible feminine feeling this was! A fainting spell. She'd witnessed the other girls at Faustine's claim to experience it, but she had always laughed at them, believing it to all be in their head. And it was. Much the way this was all in hers. *Calm yourself.*

"Do you have a washroom? I need a moment to freshen up before dinner."

One of the spinning faces resembling Feolan was speaking to her. Something about the hallway. A door on the right. She nodded to one of the dizzying images, assuring it that she would be fine.

She recognized the hallway. Down the way to the right was the heavy door leading to Thade's study where she first convinced him to let her into this all. If she'd known then what she knew now, it may have all been different. She may have had her own desk within that room, with her own quills and parchment, settled into the life of a courtier in her own right. Not this sickening, spinning world that she saw around her now.

Fumbling with her left hand along the wall, she strained her one eye in the darkness, searching for the door Feolan directed her to. It was on the right. But which one? Not that it mattered. Anything out of sight of those men would be sufficient. She needed to get control of herself, and she couldn't do so with their watchful eyes.

Several doors lined the hall to the right. Many of them were closed, some locked, preventing unwanted guests from happening through them to the rooms on the other side. Further down, a flickering light drew her attention from an open door, beckoning her toward it. She quickened her pace, stepping on her own feet in her rush to get to it.

The light drew her in, invitingly, tempting her with the privacy it offered. Once through the frame, she pressed it shut with her back, leaning against it for support, unable to stop the blur of the furniture in her head. Candles decorated the room, their dancing flames bouncing every which way from their positions atop the dresser and nightstands beside a massive canopy bed. The curtains were drawn back, the heavy dark blue fabric draping elegantly over a thin, sheer, gauzy white lining. A matching royal blue comforter was laid neatly across the bed, pulled away from the white, feathery pillows. Golden thread cinched it together in an abstract design. It looked so warm after being in the cold of the night. She could just curl up in it, hiding away from everything.

A soothing ambiance filled the room, the dancing orange flames hypnotic to her limited vision. Slowly, the spinning walls came to a halt. The spacious room was quiet, aside from the heavy thudding of her heart against her chest. It was peaceful. And utterly inappropriate for her to be there.

"Of all the rooms I had to stumble into," she muttered, straightening her back up away from the door. Her rational thoughts were to turn around and leave. It was an invasion of privacy for her to be there, among other things, knowing the room to belong to one of the two men who resided there. Any servants under their employ would never be surrounded by such lavish comforts as these, regardless of the generosity their employers might show them.

With her focus mostly restored, she could see now the exquisite paintings hanging from the walls, depicting the beautiful landscapes of the Tanispan forests. Lakes filled with blossoming lotus flowers. And there, beside the detailed brush strokes of the lotus petals, sat a crystal vase, displaying a single dried flower with its deep plum petals splaying out around the center to reveal another rounded layer folding up in a delicate spiral in subtly lightening hues of lavender.

A Tanispan lily. The same shade as the ones planted in the flower bed lining the fence of the house back in Dalonshire.

"Be careful with it. They are significantly more frail when preserved in such a manner I found most effective for that one."

Leyna retracted her left hand away from the flower, unaware that she had come to stand in front of it. Her head was in a daze, her brain functioning to move her limbs without conscious control of her thoughts. "I am sorry," she whispered. "I should not have come in here, but in my defense, I was unable to find the door I was looking for."

The soft click of the door closing sent a nervous shiver down her spine. Silence followed. She was aware of Thade's presence in the room, lingering at the door, watching her. How had he managed to slip away from the other men? Kael must be pacing the floor impatiently, anxiously awaiting her to return and dine with them. No one would have questioned Thade if he said he was going anywhere within his own house.

It was unnerving, the quiet of the room, neither of them speaking for several long moments. Words didn't feel enough to explain the thoughts crashing inside her head. She could fall into a tangent of all the reasons why he couldn't ask her to give up the mission, and how she was sorry for everything — but none of it came out. She didn't have it in her to beg. Not right now. Something about the silence made it feel unnecessary and out of place for her to plead with him, having received no hint of what was going on in Thade's mind in regards to their meeting in the street that afternoon.

"You are ill. Perhaps you should have a seat and lessen the strain on your body." His voice was calm and quiet, soothing to her tortured and exhausted soul. "You can rest here, if you like. I have much to discuss with Kael and it may be less awkward to do so without everyone sitting there together, so you need not feel guilty for bowing out."

"Separating myself may be a good idea, but I do not think it would be appropriate for me to rest in this room."

"I rarely utilize it myself, if that does anything to ease your concern on behalf of modesty."

She wanted to see his face. He was always such a perfect image of calm, the elegantly chiseled lines of his features like that of a regal statue in the Queen's courtyard, while his voice could soothe the fury of the mightiest storm. He was like a rock there to rescue her from drowning, but she knew she couldn't allow herself to hold onto him. She had to appear strong. Any sign of weakness might spark the underlying protests she knew he was suppressing under his stoic exterior.

Turning around slowly, she took comfort in the fact that her cloak was still drawn low over her face, shielding the worst of her injuries from his eyes. "It really changes nothing, on mere principle. It is still your private quarters, whether you use them regularly or not. I should not even be in here now — much the same as we certainly should not be in here alone together."

"Context, Milady," he chuckled. "You act as though I have come here with some great and ungentlemanly intention in mind. I assure you, that is not the case. Your honor is not tainted in any way by my presence, or the simple fact that there just happens to be an unused bed in this particular room. Though, if I make you uncomfortable, I will respect your wishes and return to the men in the sitting room."

"No — that is not necessary. I have merely been on edge lately and in the end, a woman can never be too cautious."

Tentatively, she took a step forward, frustrated by the lack of depth perception caused by her injured eye. She could feel Thade's gaze settle on her. He drew in a shallow breath as if preparing to speak, holding it in quietly before allowing the words to escape his lips. "Your hood may shadow your skin, but it does not dull the fire of the energy in your eyes. Tell me, Leyna — why do I only see one of them staring back at me?"

"Oh, why must you torment me so?" she replied sadly. "Nothing escapes your notice and yet you had me convinced that I…"

"Had fooled me into believing that you were fine?"

"I could never fool you. I would never think I was capable of such a thing, nor would I ever try."

For the first time since entering the room, she could see Thade step away from the door, motioning for her to come closer. "Please, sit." He gestured toward the bed. "Allow me to look at you, so that I might determine for myself whether or not you truly are as fine as I know you will attempt to argue."

There was no point in fighting with him. Not that it would be right for her to. He was her superior officer and could just as easily order her to remove her hood. It was out of respect for her that he gave the opportunity to act of her own free will.

Admitting her defeat, she begrudgingly made her way over to the bed, settling herself on the soft mattress, sinking down under her weight. The candlelight was brighter there, illuminating her with its orange glow. She brought her hands up, intending to pull back her hood, but finding the task daunting, dreading the pain the motion would cause in her right hand. Sensing her apprehension, Thade stood in front of her, gently slipping the fabric away from her face.

She couldn't bear to look at him. To see the pain in his eyes at the sight of her. He said nothing, staring at her in quiet disbelief, his body lowering absently on the bed beside her. "Do not tell me you are fine. Please."

"Would you rather I tell you that I am miserable? That my head has ached unbearably for the past two days and the thought of touching anything with my hands right now makes me want to scream in agony? What would you have me do? Weep on your shoulder and beg you to end my suffering?"

"If that would be the truth, then yes. Whatever that may be, I prefer honesty over the lies, even if those lies are spoken with the best of intentions in humoring my guilty conscience."

"Then it is so — though I have no intentions of weeping and begging. I feared it might come to that when I came here tonight. That you would insist on removing me from the mission and thus forcing me to plead with you to let me stay there."

"In shackles?" he sighed, clasping her left hand gently to look over the bruises along her wrist. "I did not need to see your face to know you were in pain when I touched your hand today."

Leyna laughed miserably to herself, the pain in her head increasing under the tension. "The shackles are harmless. It is what was done with them that caused these injuries. And it is my own fault. Had I been strong enough with my magic to fight against that sorcery, it may not have been so severe."

"No sorcery left those marks upon your face. I could trace the outline of the hand which struck you by the imprint."

"My face is the least of my concerns!" She inhaled deeply, glancing toward the door uncomfortably. She hadn't intended to speak quite so loud. Hopefully they were deep enough into the house that her exclamation would go unnoticed by the others. "I cannot move my right hand. I fear the wrist is broken, and I cannot even begin to think of what damage has been caused to the rest of it."

Gingerly, Thade lifted Leyna's right hand, grimacing at the pained intake of breath he could hear from her at his touch. Through the dim light, he examined it carefully, the fingers of his free hand brushing softly over the skin. "If it is broken, then it is at least set properly and will heal in time. Your index finger, however, is dislocated. I could realign it for you, but I will not falsely assure you that it will not hurt."

Dislocated? How could she have missed that? It was not an uncommon injury during the war, and on many occasions she'd been the one playing the doctor to reset the bones. Never had she tried to do such a technique on herself.

"Are you certain it is out of place? I know it is swollen, but I did not think —"

"It is," Thade nodded. "The swelling is bad, but I have seen enough of this kind of thing to know."

Oh, she didn't want him to do it. While at the same time, she did. She couldn't leave it like that, and they would never grant her a physician in Dalonshire. "Fine. Do it, but do not tell me when... I do not think I could bear it."

"A finger is not quite so bad as a shoulder. If you recall, I experienced that during one of our battles at the Carpaen border."

She did remember. Though it did nothing to comfort her. All she could think of was the sound of grinding bones while Feolan had set it back in place. But this was nothing more than a finger. It couldn't possibly be the same. Still, she had no desire to endure it. "If you think that will be enough to distract me from what you are about to do, then, with all due respect, sir, you are wrong."

It came out as a laugh, feeling the pressure of Thade's hand, securing her index finger in order to prevent any extra strain on her injured wrist. Laughter somehow felt more appropriate than tears. It was odd to her, but even with such a justifiable reason to cry in front of him, she refused to do it. He could never see her in a state of weakness like all the other girls who would weep at the drop of a hat.

"Well, there was another matter I hoped to bring up to you. Perhaps that would be more sufficient." Why was he looking at her like that? He scooted in closer, getting a better grip on her hand. "Prince Enaes came by about a week ago to speak with me. It seems he has been desperately seeking information on you and thought I might be able to shed some light on a few things. Unfortunately, his questions only added more to those which I already have been desiring to know the answers to."

Prince Enaes, of all people. Here in Siscal? And for her, no less. Two months, and he had not moved on from her yet. How very uncharacteristic of him. "Information about me? What exactly did he want to know?"

He was so close to her. The flickering light of the candle danced across his pale skin, almost eerily, reflecting off the bright silver glow of his eyes. They were the only color that remained constant in the orange light. Her heart raced. But was it his closeness, or the fear of what Enaes had asked of him?

"You might recall our discussion when you first met the Prince, and he spoke of a man at the Tanispan court by the name of Iden," Thade said. She nodded to him, remaining silent in wait of what else he would say. "Iden is the current head of the Evantine family, and therefore is the most informed as far as records of descendants. Iden claimed to have no knowledge of anyone by the name of Leyna. He said the only child of his was a woman by the name of Sarayi and that she had no children while she lived in Tanispa. He said she moved to Mialan with a man there, but if she had any children, they would not have been full blood Vor'shai."

His words struck her more painfully than anything he could have done to her physically at that moment. Denied by her own grandfather. Surely there had to be papers somewhere. Records which would prove her birth. "Did the Prince tell him why he was inquiring? I am certain if he had, this man would have changed his story."

Confusion filled Thade's eyes. Of course he wouldn't understand. She shouldn't have said what she did, at risk of incriminating her age. But what did it matter at this point? Why did she still feel the need to hide any of her trivial secrets from him? She was an adult now, and well within the appropriate age to be in public, and in service to the Queen. And yet she couldn't bring herself to speak of it. There were too many unanswered questions of her own in regards to her past that she wasn't prepared to face.

Thade looked her over curiously, searchingly, trying to find the answer in her eyes. "What do you mean? Are you saying he should have known you?"

"Nothing. I meant nothing by it," she sighed. Why didn't he just set the bone and be done with it? The anticipation of the pain was driving her mad. "I imagine the Queen has documentation of births among her people. The Evantine family is of noble heritage. Certainly they would have kept some kind of record for the sake of positions at court."

"The Prince found nothing. The last born child in the royal records linked to the Evantine family was the daughter Sarayi, and she is shown to have died at least twenty years ago."

A sudden pull on her hand sent a jolt of pain shooting up her arm, breath catching in her throat, choking her with surprise and agony. She stiffened at the initial sensation, her body then slumping forward against Thade's shoulder, her mouth open in a silent scream buried in the soft fabric of his shirt, fighting back the tears already moistening her lashes.

He sat there, staring down at her with his usual expression of calm, arms held out as if to hug her, but unsure of how to react. She hadn't meant to throw herself on him in such a way. But it was comforting to her. And when his arms finally came to rest gently around her, it only added to the security she longed for.

She didn't exist. There was no record of her birth — but that was impossible. She had lived within the borders of Tanispa for almost five years before her mother took her away. Two men laid claims to being her father in that time. And with her mother being the direct descendant and heir to the family title and property, it made no sense for her own child to have not been documented. Unless Iden found a means to dispose of the records out of fear that the scandal would ruin them.

"Leyna," he whispered. "I must ask you again if you are willing to tell me the truth about you, after all this time."

"I no longer know the truth. Therefore, there is nothing to tell you."

"Your age no longer matters. You are not a member of the military anymore, nor am I, and will have no one to answer to for any deception you felt forced into those years ago."

"It is much more than simply fearing any repercussions of my age. Do you not see? I do not exist. For all anyone knows now, I am not Leyna, but Eleni, a slave in the house of a Ven'shal sorcerer. I need to find answers for myself before I can start to explain to anyone else."

Pulling away, Thade held her out in front of him, gently grasping her just below the shoulders. "And I suppose it would be a waste of my breath to try and convince you to remain here in Siscal when Kael leaves?"

Your breath is never a waste. . . "I cannot give up what I have worked so hard to achieve."

At that moment, she felt an overwhelming desire to kiss him. They were face-to-face. And that mouth. The elegant curves of his perfect lips. It was nothing like the lustful experience which had taken her over that day in the courtyard with Kael. She wanted to hold him. To brush her lips against his and forget everything and everyone else who would try to hurt them. She tried to push the thought away.

"Just be careful," he urged quietly. "Enaes uncovered documentation which Queen Vorsila was able to verify. Sarayi Evantine was married to a man by the name of Damir Rohld. She exposed him as a traitor and conspirator with the Ven'shal, leading to his banishment from Tanispa, and his fall from the Queen's good graces. It is rumored that he had a hand in the death of Iden's daughter, and that he still holds a deeply rooted hatred for the Evantine family. If you are what you say you are, and a descendent of Evantine blood, be wary if you hear that name spoken amongst those in Mikel's company. The association, be it true or false, if discovered by him, could be dangerous for you."

"I will be vigilant. I promise." When his hands slipped away from hers, she was overcome with a wash of relief and disappointment.

He looked troubled. No doubt caused by her lack of cooperation in divulging information. It pained her to think he was questioning so much about her, hesitant to believe she was who she claimed to be. He doubted even her name, which he had known to be hers for over a decade. He knew the name which she told him, and had believed it, but she'd been surrounded in mystery from the day they met. She could only imagine the struggle he was feeling internally over this new information from Enaes.

Rising to his feet, he made his way toward the door, his hand lingering on the knob before twisting it. "I owe you too much to question your loyalty, by whatever name, but I ask that you will never forget your promise to share your secrets with me in time. Do I still have your word on this?"

"A thousand times, yes, sir. I beg you to believe me when I say that I would never deceive you."

"Only keep things from me."

"Thade, that is not fair —"

He turned sharply away from the door, the knob snapping back into position. Leyna drew in a breath at his hasty approach. Keeping in mind her injury, he reached out for her left hand, clasping it in his own while kneeling at the bedside in front of her. "Leyna," he breathed. "Forgive me. It is selfish of me to wallow in my own self-pity over my confusions and guilt. Do not think I value you any less because of whatever Enaes believes he has discovered. Who your parents are does not change the fact that I am here before you now only because you were willing to give your own life for mine.

It does not change the fact that I see you, wounded and tortured in the name of our Queen."

Gently, he lifted his hand up to her face, brushing his fingertips over the swollen purple skin of her eye. She flinched, expecting the pain she so often experienced when anything came into contact with her injuries. To her surprise, his touch was like nothing more than the tip of a feather, his hand pulling away again, clenching into a fist before returning to rest on his knee.

She couldn't know how long they sat there, staring into one another's eyes, saying nothing and requiring no words of the other. They would have remained there longer had it not been for a soft rapping against the door, breaking through the silence. "Consul? Dinner is served, if you are ready to speak with Kael."

"Ah, Feolan," he nodded, fluidly rising from the floor. She watched his every move, the way his body carried him with such grace and poise and confidence. Opening the door, he revealed Feolan's hesitant gaze, his hand still raised to knock again.

Feolan caught Leyna's eye from over Thade's shoulder, blinking in shock at the sight of her. "Good heavens! What happened to —"

"She is going to rest here. I will have some food brought to her but I think it best that she not try to stay on her feet," Thade replied loudly, glancing over his shoulder one last time at Leyna. Leaning forward, he brought his face in closer to Feolan's, his tone falling hushed and secretive. "We will discuss it later, Feolan. For now, we need to get back to Kael and hear what he has to say."

After a moment, Feolan nodded, hesitant to walk away, but recognizing there was nothing else he could do. Leyna watched them both disappear out into the hallway, the door closing quietly behind them. She felt giddy. Food was the furthest thing from her mind, and she felt convinced that if she were to eat, she wouldn't be able to keep it down.

The blanket was comforting to the touch, fabric soft and inviting to her tired and aching muscles. She didn't have it in her to fight it any longer. What did it matter whether Faustine would approve of her actions? It was just a bed, offered to her out of generosity by a member of the Queen's court. As Thade had said. Context. There was nothing wrong with lying in a man's bed if the man was not in it, and if the intent was to be out of it before the man even thought to rest himself. It was innocent enough.

Sliding along the mattress, she let her head fall back on the line of pillows, caught up in the sensation of warmth and comfort beyond any which she had ever experienced before. *I could get used to life at court if I came home to this every night.* But she couldn't. She had made her decision, opting for the promise of excitement in the field of battle, though in a much different way than during the war. This would likely be the only chance she would have to bask in such luxury. And with sleep taking over her thoughts, she let her mind wander, letting go of the lectures of Faustine and the pain in her body, giving herself completely to the peaceful dreams.

"The Consul took a strange interest in you this evening, Eleni." Kael was suspicious. As well he should be, given the disappearance of her and Thade before dinner. Time had felt quick to her while faced with Thade's pleading eyes and sculpted lips, but it had been slow. And Kael was painfully aware of just how long they were alone together. "Tell me – did he say anything to you? Did he ask of your position within Mikel's employ?"

Leyna followed him into the room, groggy, unfocused from her slumber. Dinner had come and gone without her touching it. She wasn't hungry. She wasn't anything, at the moment. "What? No … well, he questioned me about my injuries, but that was to be expected. It was nothing out of the ordinary."

"And what did you tell him?"

What had she told him? All she wanted to do was sleep. Why was he asking her so many questions? She couldn't think of the words which had passed between her and Thade. He mentioned shackles – and the imprint of a fist being no form of sorcery, but she had no recollection of confirming anything. "I – told him nothing. Nothing at all. I was tired, Kael. We said very little before I fell asleep."

"You slept in his presence?"

"No."

"Then you expect me to believe you told him 'nothing' while in that room for the better part of an hour?"

"Kael." An hour. Had it really been so long? "What is wrong with you? What kind of girl do you take me for? And even more, what kind of man do you think the Consul is?"

He looked her over, a stern expression on his face. "I love you dearly, Eleni, but you are a slave, and have been in the clutches of men for so long that I fear you may not be able to tell them no if they requested anything of you."

"You think the Consul would have forced himself upon me? Are you insane?" The fog was lifting from her thoughts. He believed her a whore. Well, that certainly explained a great deal. "Ah, but no. You are trying to determine whether he forced me, or I gave in willingly? Would you even believe me if I insisted nothing happened?"

"No. That is not it at all. If you give me your word that nothing happened, then I will trust it. I merely get... nervous... when I feel I may have competition from a man more influential than myself."

Competition. What an odd way to describe their situation. It was as though he were convinced the Consul had any interest in her romantically. And while she was becoming increasingly aware that she harbored some complicated emotions toward him, she was certain that those feelings were not reciprocated beyond friendship. Yet Kael felt threatened by him.

"It is no competition, Kael. I only just met that man, and will more than likely never see him again. You are the one who will be traveling home with me. That should ease your mind."

She heard the lock clicking into place from under Kael's hands, a thoughtful expression crossing his masculine features. Fatigue still lingered over her senses. Her room at the inn was across the hall, beckoning to her, tempting her with the thought of the bed, made up, and waiting for her to crawl under the soft blankets.

But Kael was blocking the door. Her bed would have to wait a bit longer.

"Stay with me tonight, Eleni."

His words sent panic through Leyna's heart, the way his eyes lingered over her. "I cannot. I should not even be here now. It is not appropriate."

With only a few long strides, Kael was to her, his arms wrapping around her slender waist. Heat rose up in her cheeks. Lost in his eyes, she felt him guiding her backward, pressing her up against the wall gently, planting soft kisses over the surface of her neck. She hated that it felt good. Chills ran up and down the length of her spine with every touch, her head tilting to the side, taken in by it all.

Closing her eyes, she sank against the coolness of the wall, supported by Kael's strong arms holding her tightly. In her mind, she was transported back to the flickering orange light of the candles in Thade's room. She could feel the silky fabric of the luscious comforter, sinking under her weight on the bed. And there above her, she could see Thade, tenderly caressing her face, his exquisite lips brushing over the skin on her neck.

Slowly, his lips made their way to hers, drawing her in closer. It thrilled her. Blood pulsed quickly through her body by her wildly beating heart, his hands lightly touching her hair, over the sharp point of her ear, and down her neck.

Swept away by the images and the unusual sensations filling her mind and body, it wasn't until she felt a hand sliding up the bare skin of her leg under her skirt that she was brought back to reality, her uninjured eye snapping open. She wasn't met with the gentle gaze of Thade she saw in her mind's eye. Her heart sank to find herself in Kael's passionate embrace, pressed up against the wall with his groping hand working its way over her thigh.

Gasping for air, she pulled her lips away from his, struggling to break free of where she was pinned under his weight. "Stop. Kael, please, stop."

He wasn't listening. She was near hysterics before he suddenly became aware of her protests, releasing his hold on her immediately.

She was at an utter loss for words, her breathing ragged. Her hands were shaking. Every part of her body was shaking. Trembling fearfully at what she'd almost allowed to happen. It was all she could do to keep from screaming, covering her face shamefully with her hands.

"Eleni, what is the matter? You act as though you have never done this before. I will not hurt you." He started to move toward her again. She cried out desperately, holding her left hand between them as a barrier. What a sight she must be to him! Battered and bruised, her face flushed, hair disheveled. The pain in her right wrist was too much for it to be of any use, flopping pathetically down in front of her. And she was crying. Hot tears flooded from her left eye. Through the swollen lump of her right eye, the salt burned over the wounds, adding to her pain and frustration

Without a word, she rushed past him to the door, fumbling awkwardly with the lock through her tears. She could hear him calling out her name after her. The name he believed to be hers. And it was all a lie! He loved a woman who didn't exist. Eleni wasn't real. But then, neither was Leyna Evantine. No documentation of her birth. Nothing to verify her mother or father – nothing. A ghost in a world that she once thought to have figured out.

Once in the privacy of her own room, she secured the lock, sliding down the door into a heap on the ground. None of it made any sense. In Kael's arms, she had felt the presence of Thade in her mind. But why him? Why the one man with whom she could never be? And she had enjoyed it! Every inch of her wanted to give in to him, completely and without hesitation. He would be appalled if he knew.

And Kael. He would be furious if he ever discovered the thoughts which went through her mind. After her assurances that she held no feelings for the Consul to then replace Kael with Thade.

Even worse, she didn't understand why. Thade had never given her any reason to think of him in that way. But the way he looked at her tonight. It sparked something inside of her that she'd never been faced with when she knew him during the war. Her adult body was playing tricks on her.

Pull yourself together! She was an absolute mess. How could she ever think to succeed in her mission like this? From day one she'd been plagued by the fear of what Feolan would say or how the Consul would react if he knew of the things that occurred while she was away. She needed to focus. Kael would be the perfect means of distraction from them for her, if only he would understand her need to move slow. In time, she believed her feelings for him could grow into those which he claimed to already possess for her, but it would never happen if things continued as they were.

Everything had become suddenly more personal for her in a single evening. Damir Rohld. Finally, she had the name of that wretched man. Associated with the Ven'shal. Rumored to have killed Iden's daughter. Her mother. The name had never been spoken by Mikel or Oksuva, but there was no saying that she couldn't drag it from their lips. If there was any proof he was involved in the slaughter of her mother, she would do whatever it might take to find him and avenge her death. To avenge Reina's father and sister. It all had a new meaning to her now.

She couldn't deny the feelings she so clearly held for Thade, but they would have to be forgotten. Locked away, never to be allowed into her mind again. Her relationship with him was nothing more than friendship and business. It would be best if she went out of her way to fill that void in her heart with someone else until it no longer could hurt her. As for the mission, she would continue to gather the information requested by Thade, but she would also be seeking the truth she needed for her own peace of mind. Someone out there had to know who killed her mother. She wouldn't rest until that person had been brought to justice.

"Eleni?" Kael's voice was quiet and muffled through the heavy wood of the door. "Please, will you open the door so we can talk? I cannot sleep knowing I may have hurt you in some way."

A distraction. That was exactly what she needed to get the image of the Consul out of her head.

Inhaling a deep breath, she tried to regain her composure, smoothing the wrinkles out of her dress with her left hand as she climbed back to her feet. She gathered her courage, opening the door to see Kael's worry-filled eyes gazing back at her from the hall.

"Can I come in?"

Quietly, she stepped out of the way to allow him entry, her eyes cast down to the floor until he passed, closing the door behind him.

"I am sorry —" They spoke simultaneously.

"Kael," she whispered. "You have nothing to apologize for. It was me. I do not know what came over me."

"You looked frightened."

"I was. This is all new to me." She scrambled in her mind to think of a good reason without exposing the truth about her relationship with Zander. "I have never before been with someone who I truly cared about. It is far more emotional than I was expecting, and I do not think I am ready for... quite so much. I need more time."

He looked skeptical at first. It must have sounded strange to him, but she was not going to change her mind. Even slaves could have feelings. If he wanted to be close to her, he would have to understand that she was more than that. Or at least treat her as if she were.

"I think I understand." His voice was quiet. "I got carried away at the occasion of being alone with you, without the constant fear that someone would see us. Oksuva told me that she wanted us to have this time. To strengthen our relationship, since it will be so difficult to do so back home."

Of course. It was the first thing that actually made sense to her. Their whole journey here together was arranged with the hope of her being with Kael so intimately. After all, a woman whose heart belongs to a man is less likely to allow herself to be taken by another. It was all a means for Oksuva to further keep Mikel away from her.

"Then she will need to grant us a little more. I know nothing about you, and you even less about me."

"I know enough about you to know that I love you."

"You know that you think you feel that way, but do you really know who it is that you love? Do you know where I came from, what my opinions are, my dreams, my likes, dislikes – anything?"

His shoulders drooped dejectedly. She had won. There was nothing he could say to deny it. "If you desire more time, then we shall do what we can to acquire it. I want to be close to you, and I am willing to do whatever you ask of me."

It was a cruel joke, leading him on in this way. No amount of time in the world would tell him the truth about her and who she was. He would be learning about Eleni, the slave, whose entire history was nothing more than fiction. She would have to think of something to tell him, at the very least. More lies to stack on top of lies.

Guilt was the worst part about it all. She felt she owed him something, however little it may be, to make up for her deception. But she had nothing of which she could give or offer him.

She made her way over to the small single bed, tucked against the wall at the back of the room. It was harder than the luxurious mattress she'd slept on at the Consul's.

But it was soft enough. And far superior to the cold and damp floor of the cellar. "Come," she said softly, patting the blanket on the bed beside her. "You may hold me until I fall asleep."

The smile on Kael's face eased her troubled conscience. He was at her side, embracing her, taking in the scent of her hair. She knew it probably smelled like the pillows of the Consul, soothing in their gentle floral fragrance. Lavender sprinkled on the bed to help the mind relax and drift off to sleep.

Stop thinking about him. It sounded so simple, but yet he haunted her. Everything reminded her of Thade, the familiar sights and smells, sparking images and memories in her mind.

Lying back on the bed, she situated herself on the pillows, feeling Kael's muscular arm sliding underneath her head. This was nice. An experience that she couldn't link with anyone else. Only Kael. With a content sigh, she curled up beside him, gently resting her right hand on his chest. It hurt at first to apply pressure to the injured wrist, but it quickly ebbed away to a dull throb.

Silently, she repeated his name to herself. Kael. Kael. No thoughts of Thade. In time it would be easier, but for now she had to keep Kael at the forefront of her mind in everything. Come tomorrow evening, they would be back in Dalonshire – and everything would change. She could only hope it would be for the best.

Chapter Twelve

Musicians played a gentle waltz that flowed lightly over the room. It was calming. A welcome relief from the usual fast pace of day to day life. The foyer was filled with bodies, several faces Leyna had never seen before, while others held a vague familiarity in her mind.

Many had been guests at other gatherings held in the house. Over the years, she felt like she should know more of these people but Oksuva rarely gave her an opportunity for socializing. Leyna was to remain out of sight unless Oksuva specifically requested her presence. She only did so on rare occasions. It came as a surprise to Leyna when Oksuva informed her that she would be attending the party tonight.

It was Mikel and Oksuva's anniversary. The less-than-happy couple were seated at each other's side, their expressions forced, their smiles strained. Mikel's eyes drifted over the young women in the crowd while Oksuva kept her attention on her sister, making every effort to avoid conversation with her husband.

What a miserable existence they led. Despite her time in Oksuva's service, Leyna had never been able to unearth the reasons behind why they ever agreed to matrimony. Possibly a premature romance. It was the only thing which made sense. Mikel was the type of man to feel strongly toward a woman for a brief period of time, claiming it to be something grand, and then losing interest. It was Oksuva who puzzled her. She had never given any indication that she loved her husband. She watched over him jealously for the sake of her own pride, showing no sign that she really cared one way or the other if he lusted at the other women he kept in his sights, as long as he kept his hands off them.

Leyna always enjoyed seeing Gislan's carriage arrive at the front walk, knowing she would never visit without her beloved Zander at her side. It was humorous, to see Zander toying with Gislan, stringing her along in the belief that he cared for her. He'd made it clear to Leyna during their brief moments of privacy that he held no feelings for the Esai wench. She was nothing more than a method of gathering information, and he intended to use her to the fullest extent, regardless of what it might require him to do.

From her position at the end of the host table, she could smell the mingling scents of the various entrees and side dishes prepared for the banquet. Her mouth salivated hungrily while her stomach ached from having consumed too much during dinner. The presence of someone at her side caught her attention, drawing her eye over to the dessert table to her left.

"They may have their faults, but they certainly do know how to feed people."

Leyna chortled quietly, watching Zander lift a ripened cherry from a tray. With Gislan's gaze settled on him fondly, he raised it slowly up to his mouth, winking deviously. "She is not tired of your bedroom antics yet?" Leyna laughed, trying hard to mask the smile on her face.

"No woman could ever tire of my bedroom antics," Zander smirked. "And what of you? Have you bedded your persistent suitor yet?"

"Now, now, Zander. Underneath this façade, you must remember that I am a lady. I would never do such a thing."

"What's it been? Five years? Six? You must be doing something to keep his interest."

"Almost six," she rolled her eyes. "And maybe it is the fact that I am not doing anything that keeps his thoughts on me. He respects me."

"Or he has other women to occupy him until you are suitably swayed from your virtuous ways." Leyna jabbed her elbow roughly into his side, offended by his comment. She dared not speak out angrily in response, as similar fears had crossed her own mind over the years. She tried not to focus on them.

It was shocking to think it had been so long. Six years. Or would be within the next few months. No one really seemed to be counting anymore, these days.

Her letters to the Consul had grown fewer and farther between, the information less and less pertinent. Initially, she had documented every name she overheard spoken by Oksuva and her other ladies. In time, the names became repetitive, falling into a routine of common business associates with no real power in the scheme of things. Then again, Oksuva still preferred to leave Leyna out of her meetings, bringing her in only on occasion when the topic was less sensitive for her ears. Her job was to take up space when necessary, and when she wasn't needed, she was to tend to Oksuva's quarters, dusting, sweeping, and whatever else Oksuva felt would occupy her time productively.

"He is a perfect gentleman when we are together, and if you must know, he is far too busy of a man to be seeking any other women. His only free time is spent in my company."

"So Oksuva still allows you both to meet in private? If so, I am more amazed by your claims at purity." Reaching out for another cherry, Zander bit into it, faster this time, his posture relaxing at Gislan's diverted attention. "I didn't think she was ever going to look away. She disgusts me. Really."

"Nearly an hour every day, yes. And I do not need you to believe me in order for my claims to be true. Think what you will. I am not the one whoring myself for an invitation to these parties in order to hoard their leftovers," she chuckled.

From across the room, she could see Kael's soft green eyes watching her carefully. He was leery of Zander. As he had been from the day they first quarreled over her. Kael harbored a deeply seated hatred over what he believed Zander had done to her. Ruining her. It would make her laugh if it wasn't for the guilt she still held inside over all the lies.

"You wound me, Madam," Zander replied mockingly. His head leaned in closer to her ear, following her gaze to where Kael was standing. "You may want to keep an eye on that man. His eyes used to glow brighter when he tried to strike me down with his stare from across the room. Either he is slowly starting to come around to my charming ways, or the light is dimming in there."

"What do you mean?" she asked, peering into the crowd to get a better look at Kael.

He was set apart from the rest of the guests in his finely tailored suit, hair slicked back away from his face. The ends curled up around the collar of his shirt, blending in with the shimmering grey and silver threads of his jacket and accented by his pale skin. Though she so often gazed into his eyes, she had missed it before, the dullness to the usual brilliance there, hardening the green hue.

But what could it mean? The Vor'shai tended to mask their inner energy when it was appropriate to do so, blending in with the crowds of the locals in countries outside of their own. Never before had she seen it masked in such a way.

"I've seen it before – but I would not want to worry you. I am sure it is not the case..." Baiting her, Zander turned his eyes on Leyna curiously. He could see the questioning expression on her face. Her thoughts were too confused to hide it.

"You believe he is dabbling in their sorcery."

Zander was surprised by her candor. She could tell by the way his head shifted away from hers and the length of time in which he pondered over his own words before responding. "Well, that is one way of putting it, yes."

"And what might be another way of putting it?" she asked. "It seems pretty straight forward to me. But I would have to rely on your previous experience to urge me into believing it, for I have never witnessed a Vor'shai's descent into darkness before. Tell me – is it really so subtle that the person closest to him would never notice it?"

"Those closest to the dabbler are more likely to notice, but then deny it. Make claims that it isn't true. Convince themselves of it so wholeheartedly that it is completely overlooked until it is too late."

It was a frightening thought. Kael would never use such blasphemous magic. He couldn't. To do so went against everything she believed – and what she'd been convinced he believed in also. "I will ask him about it," she said quietly. "I am confident it will be nothing but a misunderstanding. A trick of the light in this room, perhaps."

She could feel Zander's hand on her shoulder, comforting her. An innocent gesture. Seeing him touch her, Kael's eyes flashed angrily in their direction, storming across the floor with long strides to confront them.

"Ah, the demon cometh. I do hope he avoids my nose this time..."

"Is this man troubling you?" Kael demanded. His hand shot with incredible speed out toward Zander's arm, forcing it away from Leyna harshly. "He seems to forget that he no longer has any right to lay a finger on you."

Leyna sighed heavily. Her gaze traveled over to Oksuva and Gislan, aware that Kael's hasty approach had drawn their interest, their eyes settled on the trio, watching intently. "Kael, you know Zander and I are friends now. This is not worth creating a scene over."

"Creating a scene?" Kael laughed. Almost sinister in the sound. "After what he did to you, how can you possibly call him friend? He treated you like an object. A whore! And you still think him to be good to you?"

The room was quieter than it had been before. Guests were edging away, creating a space around them at the end of the table, displaying them in front of the entire room like a dramatic act in a play. Zander stood with admirable confidence. His left brow rose, amused by the claims Kael made against him. Only he and Leyna knew the truth; and neither one of them could say anything to set things straight.

"Think what you will, I never caused any harm to the lovely Eleni —"

"Save it for the gods. It is up to them to decide the fate of your soul for your heinous acts against your people, not me." Kael's hand tightened around her wrist, squeezing painfully, his eyes focused on Zander, unaware of his own strength. "Come, Eleni," he scoffed. "You will honor me with a dance while this creature finds his way elsewhere."

"But I do not —" he pulled her forward, leaving her with no opportunity to finish the protest until they were already standing in the middle of the foyer floor, "— know the dances here…" Everyone continued to stare at them, clearly curious. Whispers already were circulating around the room. Rumors. Gossip. More scandals in the home of Mikel and Oksuva. There were so many as it was, without needing help in creating more.

She knew it was a lie she told him about the dance, allowing him to lead her through the motions as the music started up again with a lively tune. It was a traditional dance of the court, though the Siscalian style varied from that which she had learned in Tanispa under Faustine's tutelage, it was simple enough to grasp the pattern.

A slave would never have any knowledge of the steps, of course. After all the years that passed, it remained the one constant in her mind which reminded her daily that she would never fit in with these people. That Kael would never fully understand her, or know her. She spent much of her time concentrating on forgetting the steps, unable to focus her attention on Kael's lingering stare. The expression she saw on his strong features sent shivers through her. He had never before looked at her with such heated anger.

"I beg you to never grant him your private company ever again. Do you promise me?" he asked, his voice stern. His rage was gradually subsiding while watching her twirl under his arm, stumbling over her feet to face him again.

"You are unfair to him, really. But for your sake, I will try to maintain a greater distance when there is no one there to chaperone."

"I am not unfair to him. If anything, I am too merciful for letting him live after what he has done. He deserves to die the most painful of deaths that Queen Vorsila could ever bestow upon a traitor as detestable as him."

With another spin out away from his body, Leyna let her eyes trail over to the table where Zander had been standing, his face now lost in the crowd of people gathering at the dessert trays. Nervously, she searched for him. Fearful of the thought that he might have left without any farewell to her.

Gislan. It only made sense that he would have returned to her side at the host table, flirting with her unabashedly, the way he always did. Distracted from the dance, she let Kael continue to lead her through the motions blindly, scanning the line of people at the table for Zander. She was surprised to find him absent, though something else stood out to her that she hadn't noticed before. An unfamiliar pair of blackened eyes were fixed on her from behind Oksuva and Gislan. Cold and hard in their abyssal darkness from one side to the other. Two endless holes positioned on either side of his nose. There was no color which would indicate where the pupil faced, but there was no denying their focus.

"Kael, do you know who that man is?" If Kael had spoken anything further on their previous topic, it had fallen on deaf ears. And she didn't care if her random inquiry revealed her lack of interest in his stubborn grudge against Zander. All that mattered now was this strange man, his gaze ever present on her skin even when she looked away, hoping to escape the uncomfortable sensation.

Following her eyes, Kael shrugged nonchalantly, seemingly unfazed by the odd presence this man was emanating. He exuded power unlike any of the Ven'shal associates who had visited these walls. "That is Oran Bedrick. Mikel's gift to Oksuva for their anniversary. Did you not hear anything I said?"

"I heard you," she said, distracted. "What do you mean by gift? He is giving her another man? Why would he do that?"

"He is not giving her the man in the sense you might think," Kael grumbled. He was annoyed with her. She'd ignored his ranting about Zander and it was obvious to him that she wasn't going to allow the conversation to veer back to it. "Since the day Oksuva met Mikel, she has been trying to gain an audience with a particular Ven'shal man, but his name has never reached my ears. All I know is that Mikel had no means of contacting the one she wanted, this man being well outside his realm of knowledge and the social circle he kept. From what I gather, Oran is an associate for someone who knows her desired subject personally. Through him, it could grant her a means of finally meeting her target."

"How did he come to know Oran then, if these people are so elusive?"

"Why do you ask so many questions?" Kael ceased his movement on the dance floor, drawing Leyna off to the side against the wall. "I recommend that you not take any interest in it. These men are not anyone you should go anywhere near, and certainly shouldn't let your curiosity pull you in."

She stared hard into his eyes. It was difficult to look beyond the dimness there that she'd overlooked before, now irrefutable. But when had the change happened? How could she have missed it? Or could it be something new. Something that had come to pass between the time she last saw him and the present.

"You tell me not to let my curiosity pull me in, and demand I not go anywhere near these men — and yet what of the things which you should not be curious about? The things which you should not dabble in?"

"Eleni, you aren't making any sense. What are you talking about?"

Firmly grasping the sides of his face in her hands, she held him still. "Do you think it is not noticeable? Did you think I would not see it?"

Realization. It was obvious in his eyes. He knew suddenly, with absolute clarity, what she was referring to. A glimmer of shame flittered over his features. The anger she'd seen there only moments before dissipated into nothingness, returning the gentleness to his gaze that she was used to seeing there. "I could not help it. Mikel insisted on it. He is too powerful of a man to deny. Not to mention he knows how to tug on someone's strings just right until they do exactly what he wants."

"What could he have possibly said or done which would possess you to manipulate that sorcery?"

"He questioned my loyalty… and threatened to harm you if I did not comply." He cast his eyes downward, avoiding her steady gaze. "It is no secret around this house that his marriage with Oksuva is hanging by a thread. If I had not done as he commanded, he wouldn't have thought twice about taking you, the way he threatened the first time he saw you and me together. I couldn't bear to see him do that to you."

"But why did he command it?"

"A test."

A test? To Leyna, it sounded more surreptitious on Mikel's part. A hidden reason for his requests. But what? What would Mikel stand to gain from Kael sinking into the Ven'shal magic? "Did something happen which would have caused him to think you disloyal?"

"Now is not the place to discuss it."

It was a yes without having to speak the word. Her heart sank in her chest, wishing everyone in the room would disappear. She pulled her hands away from his face, slowly, unable to look at him. She couldn't remember ever having wanted a glass of wine as badly as she did at that moment.

Rubbing her head, she started to walk away from him, her body pulled back roughly at Kael's strong grasp on her wrist. "Where are you going?"

"Away," she snapped. With a hard twist of her wrist, she broke free of him, storming off into the crowd. The heavy golden fabric of her skirt swished at her quick pace, nearly tripping her with its length. In her haste, she'd failed to gather it up in her hands to prevent stepping on the hem, grabbing it irritably as she managed to maintain her balance, hoping no one witnessed her stumble.

Her skin crawled, alerting her to the eyes of Oran following her through the mass of guests clogging the room. Dancers had taken up the center of the floor, pushing the rest of the crowd along the outer edges, and into Leyna's path, preventing her from making the progress away from Kael that she'd hoped for.

For the sake of the mission, she needed to get back to Oksuva. She couldn't do what Kael asked of her, avoiding this mystery man who held such rank amongst the Ven'shal. Her job was to find out as much as she could about them. What use would she be to her people if she knew there was something of possible interest and she passed it up because a man told her to? Since when had she ever listened to what anyone told her to do, anyway?

Finally, the table was within her sight, the crowd thinning to allow her passage along the back wall to where Oksuva and Gislan were seated, talking excitedly to the mysterious man. From her closer view, she could see him now, clad in heavy damask, the black threads matching the color of his hair and eyes. A tiny upturn on his nose gave an appearance of constant disapproval. His lips curled in a sly smile, noticing Leyna's approach.

"Ah, she is even more fair than I thought from a distance," he greeted, bowing low, while gallantly taking her hand to kiss the back of it. "I beg you, Miss Oksuva. Will you introduce me to this stunning creature?"

"That? That is merely one of my attendants. Eleni. One of my husband's slave girls." Leyna could hear the detestation in Oksuva's voice at Oran's interest, ignoring his previous company with her and Gislan. "While you are here, Eleni, make yourself useful and tell Oran that it would be worth his master's time to come visit us here in Dalonshire. He does not seem to believe me, or my sister. I am running out of ways to convince him."

Yes. He had to bring his master there. She needed to know who it was, and what Oksuva's intentions were in meeting them. But it would do her little good if Oksuva refused to allow her to be present for the meeting. "What would it require to convince you to bring your master here for my lady to speak with?"

She didn't like the way his eyes slowly moved over her body, taking in every detail, appraising, and apparently pleased with what he saw there. "For you? I tell you what, Oksuva. We may be able to work something out after all."

Sitting up straight in her chair, Oksuva's eyes opened wide, glancing over to Leyna in confusion. "Really?" she asked. "And what exactly would you ask of me to make it so? You know I would be willing to give you almost anything you desire."

"Do you think your husband would mind if I took you away for a bit? To discuss this matter privately?"

"I really couldn't care less if he minded or not," Oksuva frowned. Fluidly, she rose to her feet, offering her arm out to Oran. "He might have more fun in my absence, anyway."

Curious, Leyna turned to watch Oran and Oksuva, their tall, wiry bodies weaving easily through the crowd, disappearing down a dark hallway. Gislan looked miserable, deprived of her sister's company, left without even Zander to occupy her need for constant attention. "Well, you clean up nicely, at least," she waved dismissively, shifting in her seat to face back to the plate of food on the table in front of her. "I don't see, however, what any of these men find so attractive about you."

"Perhaps it is my endeavors to not make it appear as though my body is easily accessible, the way some people do."

It felt good to take a passive jab at Gislan. So many times, Leyna had been the focus of Gislan's ridicule, assumed to be due to jealousy at the thought of Leyna having been with Zander, whom she now claimed to be hers; and hers alone. She could feel the anger rising up in Gislan as she brushed by her, making her way to her station at the end of the table.

"You are a slave, Eleni," Gislan said suddenly. "Everyone knows that your body is easily accessible to any man here that wanted it. Do not forget your place."

Again, the crowd near the table fell into silence, watching, waiting to see how Leyna would react to Gislan's harsh insult. It hurt. After her efforts to maintain the image of a lady rather than a slave, Gislan never failed to throw it in her face, reminding her of her lowly status. Speaking out against her in retaliation would only worsen the situation. Biting her lip, she kept silent, screaming inside with all the things she wished she could say to that wretched woman.

For now, it was best she maintain her composure. Gislan would be leaving come morning to return to Siscal City, and Leyna would be free of her for a while before she would venture to Dalonshire to visit again. She just had to get through the rest of this despicable party without losing her mind.

It felt good to be out of the scrutinizing eyes at the party, alone in the privacy and quiet of her own room to relax and gather her thoughts. Her feet ached from standing for hours upon hours of endless, mindless chatter of the guests, the drone of their voices still humming noisily in her ears. How anyone was able to hear themselves think in that room was beyond her, let alone those who felt compelled to attempt conversation, yelling over the din of the others, struggling to be heard. Her temples throbbed at the mere thought of it.

Little had been discussed after Oksuva returned from her meeting with Oran. She looked pleased, to say the least. Her eyes sparkled in a way that was uncharacteristic for her, and even more so when in the company of her husband. Leyna found herself questioning the appropriateness of what was discussed between her and this man whom she knew nothing of, other than that he had something Oksuva wanted, and she was willing to give anything for it.

But Mikel surely would never have allowed that. He had to hold some sway amongst his people. The half-breed. He was so tainted with the sorcery that she found herself forgetting time and again that he only carried a portion of Ven'shal blood in his veins. That placed him in a position of being considered an outcast the way many Esai were to the Vor'shai. Weakened magic. Thin blood. Their loyalties were always in question, in regards to the Queen, and her subjects. Knowing the cruel ways of the Ven'shal, it seemed likely worse to try and be considered an equal when your heritage was less than pure.

Unless he had managed to find some form of respect with them. Something to force them to take notice. After all, she'd heard stories of pure-blooded Vor'shai who had fallen to the darker energies and been accepted into the most prominent ranks of the Ven'shal. That could be different in many ways, though. A pure Vor'shai would still be closest to a pure Ven'shal when they fell. In the end, they were the same species. Just a variation on the gifts granted to them by the gods. Mikel had proven to have many friends within their people. It was just a matter of how powerful those friends were, and how high they could raise him up.

Tugging on the laces of her bodice, Leyna exhaled in relief at the pressure being lifted from her midsection, air flowing with greater ease through her lungs. The golden threads of her dress were stunning, adorned around the waist by a fine chain fitted with golden beryl gems, glittering even in the dim light of her lone candle flickering on the nightstand. It was borrowed. Oksuva would never allow her to purchase a garment of such quality and style, but she took pity on Leyna's lack of options for the party, break-ing down to let her search through the back of her own closet for one of her old – and outdated in design – dresses.

The cool, cottony fabric of her nightgown brushed gently against her skin as she slid it over her head, adjusting it on her body, enjoying the airy comfort of the material, free from the restricting designs of her everyday clothing. The sleeves were long, the wrist line ruffled with matching white floral lace. The hem draped just over her feet on the floor. Simple and delicate. For a dress intended for nothing more than sleeping, it served its purpose.

A soft brush against the wood of the door from the other side sent her heart into a flutter, the blood pulsing, throbbing harder in her temples. The lock. She'd failed to latch it, the tiny chain dangling, almost laughing at her from its base on the door.

She hurried, light footed, over to the bed, reaching for the sword given to her by Oksuva from behind the frame. The motion remained instinctive to her. Gripping the sheath, she slid it easily from inside, the dancing light of the flame glinting off the sharp, polished steel of the blade. At the ready, she watched the door slowly opening, the hinges making only a faint creaking noise under the strain.

Instantly, she recognized the familiar shape of Kael slipping quietly into the room. Relaxing her stance, Leyna sheathed her sword, tossing it breathlessly onto the bed. "I could have killed you!" she hissed. "What are you doing here?"

"I had to see you," he said, his voice sounding desperate, strained. "I have been doing a great deal of thinking, and the decision I have come to could not wait until when next we would be granted time alone together."

"If they find you here, we will never be granted time alone together. I would be thrown back in the cellar and only the gods know what would be done to you."

"It is worth the risk. Anything for you is worth the risk." Gliding effortlessly across the room to stand in front of her, Kael caught her hands up in his, clasping them tightly to his chest. "For nearly six years we have been hiding our relationship, keeping secrets from everyone within the house. Only Oksuva has been aware of it, and if not for her kindness in allowing us to be together, I would have gone mad from my love for you. Having to admire you from a distance, and only ever being able to be near you for brief periods in a day, unable to touch you, or hold you."

She swallowed hard. If only she could have broken her hands away from his. The direction of his thoughts had her nervous, trembling uncomfortably, wishing he would go away. Naïve she may be to many things in the world, but she was not blind, nor was she ignorant of the way relationships functioned. Her fear was how she would respond if he continued the way she expected he would. "It is all we can do for now," she said quietly. "In time, things may change, but this is how it must be."

"No," he argued, clutching her hands tighter. "It does not need to be this way." He drew her in closer to him, his eyes staring deeply into hers, focused and insistent in his gaze. "Marry me, Eleni. My heart will not be at ease of this pain until you are my wife."

So that was it? He had come all the way here, risking everything, to ask her that? Just as she suspected. But how could she possibly say yes? He loved a woman that didn't exist. Guilt would eat away at her, ripping her apart inside, if she were to say yes to his offer. None of it was real. But did she feel the same for him? Did she love him? Possibly. How could she really know, in the end?

All the arguments flooded her mind, her eyes searching his fearfully, aware of his anxiousness to hear her answer. She cared about him. If anything were to happen to him, she would be devastated, crushed, and broken-hearted over the loss. She would give up many things if he asked her to, but not everything. Would she throw herself in front of a volley of arrows for him? Maybe. But she had obligations to her people, and to her Queen. Obligations that only she could fulfill. Throwing her life away for something as trivial as love felt wrong. Selfish, really.

No. She wasn't ready for something like that. Not yet. And not for some time. Her head was not in the right place for that kind of commitment. "Kael," she whispered. A grimace passed over her features, unsure of how to tell him her decision, dreading the pain it would cause him. "You do not know me. We may have been in each other's company for years, but how much could you really learn of who I am when we speak for less than an hour and on only a random basis? There is so much that you still have no idea —"

"I know enough, Eleni."

The sound of that name stung her, rubbing the lies harder into her face. "No, you do not. Do you know anything about me other than that we share similar views in regards to the Ven'shal and their sorcery? The same loyalty to our people... but do you know anything about *me*? Who I am? My past, my dreams, my aspirations – or the more superficial details – my favorite foods? Tell me, Kael," she said flatly. "What is my favorite color?"

Kael stared back at her, confused. "What does that matter?" he asked. "Your preferred color will not change the way I feel about you."

"There is just a great deal that I would need to tell you before I could ever agree to this – but I cannot discuss it here. The walls in this house have ears."

"Eleni, answer me truthfully. If all of these things were discussed and in the open, would you then accept my hand? If nothing else stood in the way of your heart, would you say yes?"

His words were like a punch in the stomach, knocking the wind from her chest. She didn't know. She couldn't answer a question that she herself didn't know the answer to. If he knew the truth about her and he still desired marriage, would she do it? Did she really have any other options? Men would never be beating down the door of a slave. An orphan whose name, her real name, no longer existed. She had nothing that any good man of status would ever desire.

"Yes," she sighed. And why not? There were far worse men out there that she could attach herself to. "If everything was spoken, and you still wished to have me as your wife, then I would accept you. But I must insist on following the marital traditions of our people." It was the only loop-hole she could think of which would force Kael into holding off on an impromptu marriage. Among their people, engagement alone required a ceremony to create the bond. A promise of marriage. Once performed, it was like a legal contract, binding the couple to one another until the day of the actual marriage. It was a tradition originally utilized by the nobles when arranging marriages between their children not yet old enough to enter into matrimony. Over time it had become more widely practiced by people of all ranks and status. A religious and essentially legally binding promise. It could only be broken by petitioning the priests for an annulment of the contract entered into by the couple.

"Of course," he replied, seemingly having expected her request. "An actual marriage would require witnesses, which we do not have. Not here in Dalonshire. Once we reach Siscal, I can arrange for that better. And just think, Eleni – once we are married, you will no longer be considered a slave. It will remove you from that wretched title."

Her stomach clenched at the thought of what he was suggesting. No longer a slave. But how would that affect her position with Oksuva and Mikel? The traditional engagement alone acted so similarly to marriage. It was nothing but an added step in accomplishing the same thing, in the end. An exchange of rings and a contractual promise to devote their lives to one another. Her only comfort was in that the engagement was significantly less binding. It would allow them more time to discuss the details causing her guilt before they took the final step.

"Very well. I suppose I cannot argue."

"Then it is decided," he smiled excitedly. "Meet me near the flower gardens when the sun rises tomorrow morning. Oksuva agreed to give us the morning to seek the priest at the church to perform the engagement rites. After that, you will have plenty of time to tell me everything you feel I should know, but I will not hear a word of it before then. There is no time, and this will be our only chance."

"Kael – that is exactly the opposite of what I agreed to. We need to talk before we see the priest."

"I said there is no time," he breathed, kissing her gently on the lips. "The day after next, we will be leaving with Oksuva for Siscal City. That fellow from the party agreed to take her to his man, by the name of Kyros. He is in town only briefly, so we will be making great haste to reach the city. If everything goes as she hopes, then Kyros will arrange for her to meet the Ven'shal sorcerer she's been trying to find for years. All of that would prevent us from doing anything due to the circumstances, but there will be plenty of time for us to discuss any matters your heart requires. Whatever you have to say, I assure you I will not hold it against you. I will remember that you wished to tell me, and tried to tell me, and that will be enough to forgive it, though I doubt forgiveness will be necessary."

We will be leaving with Oksuva? How strange it was to hear those words. He couldn't possibly be referring to her. A matter that sensitive, Oksuva was sure to take along only her most trusted ladies. "By 'we', I assume you were referring to a more generic 'we' in the sense of — you and several others — as opposed to you and me?"

"I meant exactly what it sounded like. Oran specifically requested you to be present. All the more reason for me to request you to be my wife so that he will not feel compelled to take advantage of you, if that is his interest."

"You assume far too often that men only take interest in me because of my body."

"I assume it often, because I know it to be true. You are an attractive woman, and a slave. Those two things tend to lean a man's mind toward the many ways they can take advantage of you physically. You give them too much credit," he frowned.

There was nothing she could say which would change his mind. That much was obvious. He was hard-headed and stubborn. But it was such a large step for her. And though she hated to let the thought slip through her mind, she wondered what Thade and Feolan would say.

After all these years of having not spoken with them face-to-face, what did it matter their thoughts on it? They knew nothing of the relationship, by her letters at least, and with everything Kael had done for her, she would be ungrateful not to accept his proposal. He was the reason she'd been accepted by Oksuva. It was because of Kael that she had been released from the cellar and allowed the opportunities to gain all of the information that she had been able to share with the Consul. She owed him too much to deny him.

"Alright," she nodded, pressing her lips softly against Kael's cheek, having to lift herself up on her tiptoes to reach him. "I will meet you in the morning. Before noon we will see the priest. All I ask is that we find time to speak as soon as possible afterwards so that I can console my weary conscience."

The morning came and went in a blur for Leyna, her head never having a chance to think clearly until everything was said and done. She vaguely recalled the details of the tiny church where Kael led her. The priest had been all too willing to perform the ceremony, and she thought that maybe she even smiled once throughout.

It had been a short and hasty event. Unlike a traditional Vor'shai engagement, but circumstance didn't allow for extensive ritual. It was done. There would be no going back, and she was surprised at how little remorse she felt over it all. She didn't feel any different now while cleaning the dust in Oksuva's room than she had when she'd woken up that morning. The only change was the thin simple golden engagement band encircling the finger of her left hand. A traditional symbol of betrothal amongst the Vor'shai.

She'd hoped to feel happier than she did. After all, such a day was supposed to be one of the happiest days of her life, next to the actual wedding. This was no different from any other day, cleaning, scrubbing, and whatever else Oksuva demanded. Only now, she would have to work harder in deterring Kael if he came to her bed in the middle of the night. Arguments of modesty and virtue had saved her up to now, but as her betrothed, he could easily disregard her protests, if he chose. Many men tended to view the engagement to be the same as the wedding itself, granting them more privileges with their wife-to-be. All she could do was pray the trip would serve as a distraction and keep them both too busy to find time alone together. Engagement was one thing, but until she was convinced that she felt deeply enough for him, and until he had been informed of the truth about her, it still didn't feel right. If she was lucky, that argument might buy her more time.

"Have you seen my wife?"

The sound of Mikel's voice cutting through the silence caused her to jump, nearly knocking the jewelry box from atop the dresser. "No, sir," she replied, still trying to slow her racing heart. "She said something about going shopping in town with her sister."

"I thought that wench was leaving today."

"They decided to postpone her departure until tomorrow so they could travel to Siscal together." Awkwardly, she placed her arms behind her back, leaning against the dresser to conceal her left hand from view. He appeared distracted enough to overlook the tiny circle of gold, but she didn't want to chance it. There was no saying what he would do if he noticed.

He walked quietly around the room, slowly taking in the details of every article that came in his line of sight, running his fingertip along the surfaces of the dressers and chairs. His eyes remained averted from her, forehead creased in thoughtful contemplation. "I hear you will be accompanying my wife when she leaves."

"I am, sir."

"Then maybe you could help me out with a little something." He was coming closer. Each sound of his foot connecting with the floor came as if in slow motion. He was an intimidating man, the way he carried himself, and the effect only intensified when he was standing right in front of her, looking down at her in his towering height, his eyes staring through her. "You may or may not know, but my wife and I have come to an agreement. Our marriage no longer serves either of us the way it once did, and quite frankly, I cannot stand her company. She graciously agreed, if I could arrange a means for her to be granted a meeting she has longed for since the day we met, she would grant me my freedom with a divorce. I fear, however, that she may believe this agreement allows her to behave in ways that a wife should not."

"I am not sure I know what you mean," Leyna replied, hesitant, unsure of how to react to his strange behavior. What he was saying came as a shock to her. Though it explained their cold demeanor toward one another at the anniversary party. No need to feign love and devotion when both have long since given up on it.

"You know exactly what I mean. You may be a slave, but I know you are no fool. Then again –" Suddenly he reached out for her arms, easily pulling them from behind her back. There on her finger, the golden ring shimmered in the light, his lips curling in a sinister smirk. "I see I was not misinformed. Guilt must have propelled him into it. I can think of no other reason for the rush."

Guilt? What was there for Kael to feel guilty for? Any deception in their relationship rested solely on her shoulders. "How does my relationship with him have anything to do with your wife?"

"It has everything to do with my wife!" he shouted. "I made the mistake of trusting him. Never have I allowed any man in my service to get close to my wife but he – he swore his loyalty to me and assured me he would never touch her – and then I catch them both together the night before our anniversary celebration. Here, in this very room, on that very bed!"

Her jaw fell open in disbelief. It had to be lies. All of it. Kael would never have done something like that. On several occasions he had voiced a specific dislike for her, detesting her mixed blood. Why, then, would she have any reason to believe he would involve himself intimately with her?

"It cannot be so. There must be some mistake."

"Are you calling me a liar, slave?" he hissed, shaking her roughly in his grasp. "Do you think my eyes deceived me? In his blatant disrespect and disregard of that supposed loyalty he swore to me?"

Images flashed through her head. Strings of conversation from the party that had been harmless, yet confusing to her at the time. It made sense, despite her unwillingness to believe any of it could be true. *He questioned my loyalty… and threatened to harm you if I did not comply.* Had he ever explained why his loyalty was in question? His responses were vague. Never did he tell why anything had happened or why Mikel would have felt compelled to force the magic on him. *It is no secret around this house that his marriage with Oksuva is hanging by a thread. If I had not done as he commanded, he wouldn't have thought twice about taking you.*

"You made him use your magic," she whispered, pushing the thoughts from her head, not wanting to believe it. It fit too perfectly, but there were so many other possibilities that to settle on the first thing which fell into place would be foolish, and unfair of her. She couldn't let her emotions get out of control over something she had yet to give him an opportunity to deny or explain.

"I had to punish him. To make him do something to mark him as the slime he is. Do you think he would be accepted with open arms if his people saw the taint in his traitorous eyes? It would let the world know that he cannot be trusted."

It was true. Zander had noticed it immediately, and it was very probable that any other Vor'shai would take note of the dimming light in his eyes. But what did he want her for if Kael had already been punished for his actions? He'd cast the magic, which meant if what Kael said was true, Mikel would have no reason to come after her. "What is it you desire my help with, then? If this matter has already been dealt with accordingly."

Mikel laughed. The venomous sound sent chills coursing up and down her spine, shuddering visibly under his hold. "Until the deal is completed, she is still my wife, and therefore she is held to the requirements that such a title dictates. She made a fool of me!" He shook her again, his rising anger causing her head to snap back under the force. "That bastard of a man knows I could destroy him. I could take you away, and I told him I would. But think on it! I am not the only one he has betrayed here. He has made a fool of you the way my wife did of me."

"You are hurting me —"

"You will help me to get my revenge on both of them. If you do not, then my deci-sion will be quite simple," he snarled. Digging his fingers into her arms, he slammed her up against the dresser, ignoring her painful gasp. "If you will not comply, then he will be sent away from here. I will not allow him to set foot back in this house once he leaves for Siscal on threat of death if he returns. Do you understand me?"

She understood perfectly. Not that she could tell him the reasons why she wanted to beg him not to make it so. If Kael was sent away, it would hurt the mission. She would lose her partner, the one person close enough to Mikel to gather the information for their people that she couldn't get. But was it worth what was being asked of her? She couldn't think of enough reason to justify it.

Mikel had proven long ago to be a minor pawn in Oksuva's schemes. It was her and the people she was seeking who would provide the information the Consul desired. That was the reason why Feolan had argued for Leyna to join the mission in the first place. They needed someone close to Oksuva, and Kael couldn't do it. Perhaps it was his attempts to get closer to her which led him into her bed. Foolish of him. On many levels that she couldn't even begin to think about in her mind, her thoughts scattered with the fear of this man who posed a more prominent threat to her at the present.

"I cannot," she breathed, struggling against his grasp. She wanted away from him. Away from this room. There was no saying when Oksuva might return. Or perhaps that was his intention. To have Oksuva come in and find them there together the way he claimed to have found her and Kael. She couldn't let that happen. If Oksuva saw it, she would cast Leyna out and they would both have failed at their mission.

"Impudent wretch!" he shouted. In a display of strength and speed, he threw her down to the floor, her flailing arms taking everything atop the dresser down with her in a loud crash.

Her head was reeling, making it impossible to think. Her body moved reflexively to escape. Mikel's legs straddled her on either side, pinning her arms down to the ground over her head. Lifting her knee, she brought it up repeatedly against his tail bone, jar-ring him forward, preventing him from situating his balance on top of her.

Releasing his hold on her left wrist, his right hand connected hard across her face, her head jerking to the side. She was too frightened to register the pain. To her mind, all she could see was an opening. A chance to strike back at him while she had a free hand. With the heel of her palm, she struck upward at Mikel's nose, feeling the bone cracking, blood trickling from his nostrils.

The pain seemed to strengthen him. He came at her again with a newfound vigor, letting her hands free to rain a flurry of punches at her head. Protecting her face, she continued her attempts at disrupting his balance, driving another blow with her knee. It was less effective from where he was positioned now, her strike uselessly meeting only the flat of his back.

By now, she took comfort in knowing his thoughts were distracted from his initial intentions, fueled by his fury at the pain shooting through his nose and face. If she could just get a hold of something to hit him with that would cause more damage than her fist. In strength, he would always overpower her. She would have to rely on other means of getting free of him.

"Stop it!" she screamed, squirming under him to try and work her way free, her arms still shielding her face from his hands. They came at her with more power than before, his agitation building at his inability to break through her guard. Eventually she knew he would grow tired of it, but what he moved on to then, she didn't want to risk finding out. He could easily render her unconscious and leave her incapable of defending herself.

Oksuva's shrill scream echoed through the room around them. The blows ceased, Mikel's face twisting into a scowl, his plan failed. "What in the name of the gods are you doing?" she shrieked. "Get off my lady this instant!"

"You know what I'm doing, dear Oksuva. My beloved whore!"

"I know what you are attempting to do, but it looks to me that you are failing. Do you really think I care anymore what you do or with whom? The only thing I care about is that you are going to mark up that poor girl and I need her to look presentable."

Seeing her break, Leyna grabbed for the broken jewelry box lying on the floor where it had fallen from the dresser. With all her strength, she brought it up to Mikel's head, the wood shattering against his skull with a loud crack. Caught off guard by the strike, Mikel's eyes rolled back into his head, his body toppling over to the side. She scrambled to her feet. Her whole body was trembling, her knees barely able to carry her weight.

"My Lady," she stammered. She could hardly bring herself to look Oksuva in the face. Shame filled her over what Mikel had planned to do, while at the same time she felt an overwhelming need to know the truth. To know if what Mikel said had any claim to accuracy. "Is it true? You and Kael?"

Oksuva steadied her gaze on Leyna. Calm. Unfazed by the question being presented to her. She made no move to deny it. Not even a flicker of surprise affected the glow of her stare. "Go clean yourself up. I have changed my mind. We will leave for Siscal tonight. I need to get away from this place before I lose my sanity."

Oh god. It was true? Then again, it was possible she'd felt the claim too ridiculous to merit answering. Who was she fooling? Some part of her was desperate to hear the words spoken out loud, and yet her subconscious knew already. It was just a matter of how bad it was. How far had they gone? And why? Surely Kael must have some kind of explanation. If he truly loved her, he would never have done something like that. But then, what did she really know about men and love? Maybe all men were like Prince Enaes and merely made less of a show of it than he did.

Hanging her head, Leyna knew it was pointless to object. Yes. They needed to leave for Siscal as soon as possible. She wanted away from that house and everything inside it. And she had no desire to ever return, if she could help it.

In the hallway, she caught sight of another figure standing just outside the door, having been there the whole time, hidden behind Oksuva's slender form. Oran Bedrick. Perhaps he was the key to her escape from Mikel's employ. She let her eyes lift ever so slightly to his face as she passed, demurely gazing at him through her long lashes. He was watching her. The dark abyssal holes that were his eyes stared forward, curious, intrigued. He was worth more to her and her mission than this house ever had been. It was time to move on from the frivolous games they had been playing with Mikel and Oksuva. If only she could convince him to help her. Something told her she'd already piqued his interest. She just needed a chance to speak with him. Alone.

Chapter Thirteen

"Well, you were uncharacteristically quiet on the ride here," Zander mused, tugging the curtains closed in the tiny room. A small bed was situated in the center of the left wall, serving as the only piece of furniture. Leyna recognized the room to have once been nothing but storage space, no doubt transformed into a guest room specifically at Gislan's request in case of her sister coming to visit. "Normally I would think nothing of it, but the tension between you and Kael was smothering me. Care to tell me what is going on?"

"I would rather not," Leyna frowned. Had it been that obvious? She'd been on the move from the minute she woke that morning. Her body was exhausted, mentally drained. Emotionally, she felt there was nothing left in her at that moment. As long as no one was aware of what happened, she could at least maintain some shred of her dignity.

She should have known Zander wouldn't let up quite so easily. "I am going to insist that you do, given that I heard you knocked Mikel out this afternoon. Would you like to explain to me why you did it, or was it just for giggles to see how badly it would hurt the mission? Experimenting?"

"Hush," she whispered loudly. Carefully, she pushed the door closed, turning the knob to press it quietly into place, not wanting to draw attention to their location, or the fact that they were alone together. "It is a lot more complicated than that, I assure you."

Folding his arms across his chest, Zander stood there, waiting, his foot tapping impatiently. Under any other circumstances, she would have been irritated by his attitude, but she knew their time was limited. It would only be a matter of minutes before Kael finished helping Oksuva and Gislan unload the carriages and came looking for her. He would lose his head if he found them there.

"I do not intend to return to the house in Dalonshire."

"I'm sorry, what?" he blinked. "Have you discussed this with the Consul? What exactly are you going to do?"

"Zander, everything there is falling apart. Oksuva and Mikel have arrangements made which will inevitably end in their divorce. Because of that, there is nothing but constant fighting and manipulation. Not to mention, Mikel has already caught Oksuva seeing another man."

She wasn't comfortable delving into the details with Zander. He was trustworthy. She didn't doubt that. She trusted him more than she did Kael, which was a depressing thought. And she had bound herself to marry him? How could she have been so stupid? *Calm yourself. There is no sense in getting worked up over it until you have given him a chance to explain.*

Zander was eyeing her curiously. He was reading her like a book, picking out the uncertainty in her expression. "I am getting the impression that there are a lot more details to this than you are letting on."

"There is not enough time to explain. If Kael comes inside and finds us —"

"He'll what? I'll show you how little I care about what he has to say about it." Moving swiftly across the room, Zander stepped around Leyna, securing the latch in place on the door. "You and I are partners in this, remember? If something is going on, I want to know about it."

A brief wave of panic washed over her at the sight of the locked door. Kael would be furious. If Zander continued in this manner, there was going to be another fight between the two of them. And she wasn't sure who would come out on top if Zander chose to fight back. "Zander, I am betrothed to him," she said breathlessly, throwing her arms up in the air in defeat. "He has every right to be angry at some other man locking me away in a room. We cannot risk any more fighting between the two of you. You are on the same side, he just doesn't know it."

Slapping his forehead with his palm, Zander lifted his head to gaze up at the ceiling, his mouth open to speak but no words coming out. With a quick shake of his head, he focused his eyes back on Leyna, barely containing his voice to a whisper. "Leyna, what the hell did you do? Are you insane? Do you even love him?"

"I do not know. I think so," she said hesitantly.

"You think so? You are engaged to him, and you do not even know if you love him?"

"How am I supposed to know? All I know is that I care about him. A lot. If anything were to happen to him, I would be heartbroken. But how can anyone know for sure, so soon, if it is love? I do not even know what that feels like."

"If you love someone, you know," he sighed. He began a slow pace back and forth across the room. "Besides, you have had years together. That is not exactly a short span of time. I assumed you were both simply using each other to gather more information. He could get in close to Mikel and you to Oksuva. It was the perfect set up. I never once believed you two to actually be serious."

"Zander, he has been courting me for almost six years. I owed it to him, at the very least. It is not like anyone else would ever have me. What man in his right mind would find it in his heart to love a slave?"

"Any man who knows you, Leyna. Have you really been there for so long that they have you convinced you are a slave? Have you forgotten who you are?"

She looked at him, surprised by his comment. She hadn't forgotten who she was. The world had chosen to forget her. "Kael has been there for me through everything. I care about him, and he loves me. I cannot expect anything more than that."

"Leyna," Zander started, exhaling to regain his composure once again. "You are not a slave. You are a hero among our people. You were first lieutenant in the Siscalian military. A student of Lady Faustine, the most prestigious teacher for feminine etiquette in all of the Queen's lands. You are still one of the most loyal servants of Her Majesty. How could you have let all of this make you forget that? You claim you could not expect anything more than Kael – do you realize that the Crown Prince of Tanispa would have you in an instant if he could find you?"

"Have me?" she laughed miserably. "Define 'have me,' and we shall see if that is something of which I should be proud."

"And you say you do not intend to return to Dalonshire... Have you thought about how that will affect Kael's position in the mission? Besides – if you insist on marrying him, you would be emancipated. Freed of your position as a slave. You wouldn't have to worry about Mikel."

There was no sense in hiding anything from him at this point. He was going to find out one way or another, be it through her, or through the Consul. "It will change nothing. Kael has been instructed not to return to Dalonshire by Mikel. He is out."

The expression on Zander's face was absent. She couldn't tell what was going on behind his icy blue eyes. "Dare I ask why Mikel has removed him?"

"He was the man said to have been caught with Oksuva." It hurt her worse to speak the words than she thought it would. For the first time, it was as if she were accepting it as reality. A reality that she didn't want to think about. "But I have not had a chance to speak with Kael on it. For all I know, it was just a story Mikel was making up in hopes of convincing me to sleep with him."

"Oh gods, Leyna," Zander grimaced. "Let me guess then. The swelling on the side of your face was caused by Mikel's hand when you then denied him and he tried to force it anyway? Am I right? Is that why you knocked him unconscious? Because it makes perfect sense to me, although I am praying you will prove me wrong."

"I would prove you wrong if I could, but your suspicions are accurate. And that is exactly why I cannot return to Dalonshire. With Kael gone and Mikel's marriage in shambles, he will only get worse. I refuse to leave myself in a situation where there is no benefit to remaining and would only serve to place me in greater danger."

Zander was quiet. He made his way slowly over to the bed, lowering himself down on it thoughtfully. Gently patting the mattress, he beckoned Leyna to come closer, gazing up at her with a sympathetic gaze.

Sitting down at his side, Leyna folded her hands in her lap, her eyes cast down at the floor. It was humiliating. Men never had to deal with this kind of treatment. If Zander or Kael were ever approached by the women they were spying on, they were in control of what happened. They never had to deal with the shame of being bullied and muscled into submission the way Mikel did to her. In the end, it all came down to the title bestowed upon her those years ago when Gislan first handed her over to Mikel. She had to wonder if she'd been introduced as something other than a slave, if things would have progressed differently. But there had been no other option at the time. There was no sense in thinking over what could have been.

"Does Kael know about you? About what you are? Does he know your real name?"

"No." She hated how terrible it made her sound. "I tried to tell him that I didn't want to go through with anything until we had an opportunity to discuss some details about me, but he insisted the betrothal ceremony happen first. My hope was that he and I would have a chance to talk while we were visiting in Siscal, away from the prying eyes and ears of the other servants in the house."

"You cannot," Zander stated. "He cannot be allowed to know. It could be detrimental to your mission. And to mine. He can't be trusted."

"Why can he not be trusted? He has been our ally since the day this all started —"

"He has dabbled in their sorcery. That alone makes him a huge risk. It has power, Leyna. Once someone experiences the strength of it, the weaker minded will find themselves wanting more. He is at a precarious stage where we have to watch him closely to see if he starts giving in to it. Practicing it on his own, even when away from Mikel. And tell me; when did he ask you to marry him?"

"Last night. After the party..."

"Did he know then that he was going to be removed from the house? Did he suspect?"

Leyna thought over it carefully. Kael had never said one way or another, though he had appeared desperate. His strange behavior at the party could have been an indication that he was fearful of the worst. He'd avoided contact with almost everyone there but her, and he was not himself. Above all, he had already been exposed to his punishment for his actions. The actions he conveniently chose not to mention when she questioned him about his use of the magic. He had to have known something. And a mistake on that level would have undoubtedly led to concerns of being removed, if not worse.

"I believe he may have, but as I said, I have not had a chance to speak with him yet."

"Leyna, you are far too kind-hearted for this line of work. Don't you get it?" Zander asked. "He has been using you for information all along. He might feel an attachment to you, but from the start, you were his means of getting close to Oksuva when he couldn't. Pulling you from the cellar and arranging you to be one of Oksuva's ladies?

It was the perfect means for him to find out what was going on with her, through you. And with him being removed from his position, if you were his wife, it would allow for the two of you to still talk, without creating suspicion. You would be his means of staying abreast of what happens inside that house once he's gone."

It was frighteningly fitting, she had to admit. But there were so many times when Kael had shown her his devotion with such sincerity that she couldn't doubt his feelings for her. Sadly, she also couldn't doubt the convenience of their relationship for him. She should have known something was out of place when he was so desperate to move forward with the engagement, without regard of the secrets she insisted he must know first. And she had fallen for it.

"I had convinced myself, if any of it was true, that Kael's actions with Oksuva were done in an attempt to get closer to her to gather more information, since I was unable to gain her trust in a timely fashion. Do you think that may yet be true?"

Wrapping his arms around her comfortingly, Zander rubbed her back, rocking back and forth. "It may be, yes. It is hard to know for sure, especially knowing him. If that was the case, then he was a fool. A fool for taking such a risk, and a fool for doing something that would hurt a woman like you. He has no idea how lucky he is – but that might have something to do with the fact that he doesn't know who you are. But either way, he should know he has something great, and he should have been more careful."

"You are going to make me blush," she laughed quietly, trying to hold back the tears that flooded to the surface. Something about having someone there to confide in made her feel an overwhelming need to weep uncontrollably and ramble about all of the things she'd been bottling up for so many years. Now hardly seemed the time for it. Not to mention, she couldn't do that to Zander. She'd worked far too hard at maintaining her image of strength. The last thing she wanted to do now was break down in front of him.

"I will change the subject, then," Zander chuckled. Gently, he pulled her back, looking over her face closely. "You are not a rash person, in my experience. Have you thought of a plan which would extract you from Mikel's service?"

"I have an idea, but it will need some work, and quickly," she nodded, rising up from the bed to wander aimlessly about the room. "I think I can take advantage of the strange interest that Ven'shal man, Oran, has taken in me. But I need to be careful I do not end up in the same situation with him that I did with Mikel. Any agreement I make with him must have me as an equal, not a slave. I would be a fool if I walked from Mikel's grasp into the hands of someone even worse. I have thought to negotiate some kind of business relationship with him, but the issue I have is that... I have nothing to offer him in return which he might be interested in."

Zander stroked his chin in contemplation, his eyes following her idly in her movements. "You might," he mused. "There is one thing a Ven'shal of any standing would never turn down." Noticing Leyna's curious gaze, he grinned slowly, giving a devious wink. "You could offer him information on the Vor'shai. Agree to try and ingratiate yourself with the Consul and Feolan in order to gather intelligence for him. I am sure we could all make up some rumors to keep his interest without actually giving him anything worthwhile."

"That is genius!" she exclaimed, covering her mouth hesitantly with her hand at the sound of her voice echoing off the bare walls.

"Of course it is," he smiled. "I thought of it."

She couldn't help but laugh at him. The hope that flooded her at the thought of having an honest chance at her plan working was overwhelming. It was all she could do to keep from breaking into a fit of excited giggling. "This is fantastic! And if it is important enough to Oran, or better yet, the man he works for – Kyros? – they might be convinced to stand up to Mikel if he will not willingly release me."

"You will, of course, need to talk it over with the Consul before you move forward. I made sure to give you a room on the ground floor in case you ever felt the need to sneak out in the middle of the night." He gestured toward the window. "Just make sure you lock the door before you leave, or certain people might ask questions if they find you gone."

In a fluid motion, Zander rose from the bed, his eye twitching irritably at the sound of Kael's voice coming from somewhere in the house. Quickly, he made his way over to the door, unlatching the lock in a hurry.

"I will try to go to him tomorrow evening after everyone has retired," Leyna replied quietly, rushing over to Zander, her arms enfolding him in a warm embrace. "Thank you so much for everything."

"Just be wary of Kael," he whispered, squeezing her tightly. "And if you see the Consul, tell him I send my wishes for him to get well soon. I ran into your friend Maeri in Dalonshire before we left and she told me he was quite ill. I am not sure when I will have a chance to visit him myself."

Ill? It was hard for her to imagine a man like Thade falling to any sickness. In all the years she had known him, he was always the perfect image of health. "Do you know if he is alright?" she asked, unable to hide her growing concern. A feeling of guilt crept into the back of her mind. After she'd spent so long purposely ignoring her thoughts of him, only now to discover that he was ill. As a friend, she felt he deserved more than that from her. She would need to make sure she got to him, no matter what happened.

"I know very little. Maeri appeared concerned, but I told her that you and I were both returning to Siscal and that she could come back here to help look after him. We didn't have a chance to discuss it any further."

Nodding her head, Leyna stepped away from Zander, helping him to pull the door open quietly to avoid detection by Kael. With a half-hearted smile, she watched him slip out into the hallway, disappearing around the corner, leaving her there, alone, with nothing but the company of her own troubled thoughts.

The distance between Zander's home and Thade's felt longer to Leyna, traveling the roads by foot while keeping to the shadows of the trees, not wanting to be seen. Everyone else had retired to their rooms for the evening, many of the flickering lights from the candles in the house having already been extinguished before she slipped through her window into the bushes outside. This was her only chance to get to Thade and Feolan before her meeting with Kyros the next day. It was imperative she get their approval on her change in plans for the mission before she could move ahead.

Her legs were exhausted by the time she reached the familiar porch of Thade's house. The windows were dark all the way around, giving the appearance that no one was home, or that they had already gone to bed for the night themselves. She'd lost track of the time while waiting in her room for everyone to settle in. Judging by the darkened windows of the other houses surrounding her, it was well beyond a reasonable hour for visitors. But this wasn't just a simple visit. She hoped they would forgive her intrusion, all things considered. And after years of losing contact with her outside of an occasional letter every few months, she prayed they would still be happy to see her. Especially after she told them the news she was bringing.

A brief twinge of fear entered her thoughts at the quiet click of her shoes against the steps. What if no one answered? She couldn't leave there without talking to at least Feolan. There was always the option of knocking on windows, but she didn't dare wake Thade if he was ill, and she realized she had no idea where Feolan's chamber was within the house. If she was lucky, that knowledge wouldn't be necessary.

Lightly, she rapped her knuckles against the sturdy wood, cringing at the echo it created down the deserted street. It was an eerie sound. The way it almost vibrated off the other houses, seeming to alert the whole neighborhood of her presence. It had to be her mind playing games, exaggerating the noise.

She waited, anxious, afraid to knock again. When the door opened, she nearly fell backward off the porch, her heart pounding with surprise. An equally shocked Feolan stood on the other side. Reflexively, he reached out, steadying Leyna to keep her from falling. "Leyna? My god, what are you doing out at this time of night? What are you doing out at all? It is not safe."

"A bit of an emergency… May I come in?" she asked, motioning toward the house. In a daze, Feolan stepped back, creating enough space for her to slip by him, his eyes giving one last glance up and down the street to make sure no one was watching before closing the door behind her.

He absently made his way over to the sitting area near the back of the room, a single candle flame dancing over a nearly burnt up wick. In the light, she could see that he looked wretched. His hair was mussed, the shirt he was wearing wrinkled, only partially buttoned. He wore no jacket over the white fabric; giving him an unkempt appearance that was out of place against his elegant features, which currently were drawn from worry and fatigue.

"Forgive me. I am tired and not thinking straight. It is good to see you, Leyna. It has been — years." The thought seemed to strike him suddenly, dawning on him when he had seen her last. She'd been in Kael's company, battered from her victory over Mikel's man. They'd had no chance to speak to one another then. "You look better, at least. They treat you well enough, I hope?"

"Truthfully, that is why I came here," Leyna started. She hesitated. There was no good way to explain her situation, given how detached from it all Feolan was. Zander had been easy. He knew the inner workings of those people and had seen her on a more frequent basis throughout Gislan's socializing. It had been months since she'd written last, leaving Feolan and Thade far behind in the way of things.

She didn't know where to begin. Feolan's expression was filled with interest and concern, while at the same time he looked as though he would fall asleep sitting up in the chair beside the candle. "If you are seeking a means to get out of that place, you know Thade and I will do everything we can to help you. Honestly, it would comfort that poor man more than anything to know you are safe, in the event that things do not improve. For him to leave this world with that on his conscience —"

Leave this world? Her throat choked up at Feolan's words, her voice catching as she tried to speak. "You speak as if he is dying."

Feolan closed his eyes. In that moment, he looked serene, peaceful. She wondered whether he was still awake until he slowly re-opened them, gazing solemnly at her through the dim light. "Things do not look good at the moment. I fear the fever will take him before the physicians can arrive from Tanispa. We waited too long to send for them, I am afraid."

"I heard he was ill, but no one told me just how precarious the situation was. They made it sound like a mere cold or chill. What is it that ails him?"

"It is hard to say," Feolan sighed. "The symptoms resemble that of an illness which he suffered as a child, or so I am told by his mother. He nearly died from it then, but the physicians were convinced he had beaten it, and that whatever caused it was gone. In truth, it would appear it simply went dormant; though what has triggered its return remains a mystery. No one really knows what causes it."

"So this is something the physicians are familiar with? Something they might be able to treat?" She was desperate. The trivial drama of her personal life felt so minor next to this. Thade couldn't die. She needed him.

Oh, how selfish of her to think in such a way, but she couldn't help it! He had been her support for so long. If he was gone, she would be utterly lost in this world. And there was still so much she wanted to tell him! Things she had promised him. The secrets of her past in the military. She'd given him her word that she would share them with him. When the time was right. But what if that time never came?

No. He couldn't die. She wouldn't allow it – if there was anything she could do to prevent it. Which was unlikely. Faustine had only taught the most basic of healing magic. Just enough for a Vor'shai woman to be able to care for her children when she had her own family, in the event one fell ill with a minor infection. Nothing on a scale quite so large as this... whatever this was.

"Something they have seen before, yes, but I would not go so far as to say that they are familiar with it. There have only been a few rare documented incidents with it, if it is the same thing. It was virtually unknown until the King suffered from it shortly after his marriage to Queen Vorsila."

"And the King survived it? He had to... it was not an illness which caused his death in the end."

"He survived, true," Feolan nodded, his eyes drooping forward sleepily. His voice trailed off for a moment, his train of thought leaving him. He looked confused. Pathetic. Leyna realized he must be operating on little to no sleep at all, constantly worrying over the health of the Consul. It was his duty, after all. "I forget where I was going with that," he mumbled. Rubbing his forehead, he shrugged, heaving a sigh as he gravely looked up to Leyna's somber face. "Instances of survival are even rarer than the number of people who have contracted the illness. The King lived because he was given immediate and constant care by the best physicians in Tanispa – and the Consul also. When he was a child. His family... they had him cared for around the clock. This time, however, he has already been seriously ill for three days and it will be another two before the physicians arrive. And that is the very earliest we can expect them."

"Can the physicians in Siscal not help him? Surely they must know something." Leyna paced across the floor, unaware she was doing so until she caught Feolan's eyes following her, hypnotized by the repetitive motion like someone staring idly at a swinging pendulum. Trying to calm herself, she forced her legs to stop, her hands clasping tightly in front of her. "Even the humans here are quite advanced with their knowledge of herbs and medicine. They could give him something to ease the symptoms until the Vor'shai shamans can get here."

Shaking his head, Feolan rose to his feet, swaying unsteadily. "Their herbs did nothing. We sent word to the Queen the instant they washed their hands of it and told us he was as good as dead. Now, not to change the subject, but I doubt you came here to discuss the incompetence of the local medics. What did you have to say about the mission? Are you seeking to be released from the charge?"

The mission. She'd already forgotten. Now seemed a terrible time to spring her idea upon Feolan, seeing how drained he already was from everything. To inform him she was moving from one dangerous place to something even worse. But it was a better chance for them to find the information they needed. Though she found it hard to see how it would be beneficial if Thade was not there to see it come to fruition.

Feolan would take over. It was what he was trained to do, after all. An assistant went hand in hand with the idea of an apprentice. Everything would continue on without Thade. The only difference would be that Thade would no longer be there to greet her when she came by to share her news, or if she needed someone to talk to her, to offer guidance when things felt overwhelming.

She covered her mouth with her hand, feeling her fingers trembling. Was she going to cry? For so many years she had trained herself to hold in her emotions. The sensation she felt now was foreign to her. Uncomfortable. Her eyes stung, her lashes moistened. She closed them, fighting back the feeling. She would not cry. She couldn't allow it.

"Some circumstances, which are far too complicated to explain under the current duress of the Consul's situation, have led me to the conclusion that I will not be returning to the house in Dalonshire," she breathed, her voice shaking under the strain of her emotions. Taking a moment, she paused, gathering her composure before continuing. "Mikel presented a man to Oksuva, a Ven'shal, by the name of Oran Bedrick. He is said to be well-known amongst his kin, and works for an even more prestigious man by the name of Kyros, who we will be meeting here in Siscal tomorrow evening. I know not who Kyros works for, but Oksuva is convinced it is someone of significance. I intend to ingratiate myself with these men in order to gain their trust, and whatever else I can learn from them."

"Whatever you do, please do not tell any of that to the Consul," Feolan frowned. His shoulders slumped forward, dejected by Leyna's words. "I need to go check on him, if you wish to accompany me. If he, by some strange chance, is awake, say nothing beyond the thought of leaving the home in Dalonshire. You know he and I will support whatever you choose to do, just be careful. I do not want to risk losing you as well."

The thought of seeing Thade frightened her. It was one thing to hear that he was so close to death, but to have to witness it? She wasn't sure she would be able to keep control of herself.

Guilt filled her mind over all the things she'd neglected to do over the years. She had intentionally stayed away from this place, though there had been little chance for her to visit. If she had desired to, she was convinced it wouldn't have been impossible. She was cunning enough to have managed it. Instead she'd chosen to ignore them both. What if it was too late to make it up to them now? And for what? Her silly infatuation all those years ago?

Against her will, her legs carried her forward, following Feolan down the darkened hallway, turning into the familiar door of Thade's bedroom. It still looked the same to her. She remembered every detail, right down to the paintings decorating the walls. Her heart sank to see the dried lily, perfectly preserved in the vibrant lavender hues, untarnished from age, adorning the vase amidst the paintings, the same as it had when she first found it there.

Moving to the bedside, Feolan extended his thumb and index finger to the candle situated on the nightstand, the flame bursting to life at his touch. There on the bed Leyna could see a man's face, his complexion paled by a deathly pallor against the deep blue fabric of the pillow case. Sweat beaded on his skin, soaking his dark hair, already matted against his head. He twitched occasionally. Feverish dreams. Nightmares. He looked like death against the luxurious blankets, tucked away in the grim drapes of the canopy bed.

A small bowl of water rested on the nightstand next to the candle, a white cloth floating gently on the surface. Taking advantage of Feolan's sleep-hindered reflexes, Leyna quickly grabbed it up, moving over to the other side of the bed, away from him. "Just rest, Feolan. I can keep an eye on him if you need to sleep. Even for an hour, it would be good for you. In the nicest way possible, you look awful."

Feolan slumped down in the chair beside the bed. A soft chuckle escaped him, trailing off absently. She watched him, the way his head rolled back against the cushioned chair. For the first time since she arrived, his body relaxed, sinking into the comfortable seat. Within moments, he was asleep. She followed the steady rise and fall of his chest. Smiling to herself, she turned her attention back to Thade's weakened form lying there, unaware of her presence while lost in his fever-induced slumber.

She looked around the room idly, frowning at the realization that there was no other chair for her to use. Being careful not to disturb Thade, she lowered herself slowly onto the mattress, setting the bowl on the nightstand closest to her.

Dipping her hand into the cool water, she wrapped her fingers around the cloth, wringing it out. When the last droplets had fallen, she placed the cloth lightly over Thade's forehead, dabbing it along the skin to clear away the sweat in hopes of easing his rising temperature. It was scary to think it was him lying there. The man who was always so strong. Reduced to this, unresponsive to her touch and unable to care for himself.

In the back of her mind she felt compelled to do something to help him. Anything. It seemed to her that something from her lessons with Faustine could be utilized in this situation. Even if only to ease the fever. But it could be dangerous to one or both of them if she made even the slightest error. Cleansing and healing uses of her internal energy were very sensitive. Intricate. It required control that she knew she had yet to achieve. That was why the Vor'shai physicians were so well-respected. It was an art that they had worked and studied to perfect for decades upon decades. A silly girl like herself would have no comparison to their knowledge.

Wetting the cloth again, she dabbed it over his skin, tilting her head to one side curiously at the sight of him sleeping. Lost in dreams that only he could see. They were far from pleasant. She didn't need to see what was happening in his mind to know it was terrible. But what things haunted the feverish mind? Hallucinations – or possibly the inescapable horrors of the images ingrained in his subconscious from years at war. She wasn't sure which would be worse.

The coolness of the cloth didn't last long against the heat rising from Thade's skin. It was a losing battle, wetting and rewetting the cloth, trying to keep the fever at bay. She could hear his breathing becoming more ragged. For a split second, she thought she saw his eyes open, but she couldn't be sure. It was so quick; it was hard to know if she was imagining it from her own desires, the bright silver glow of his handsome gaze settling on her, miraculously healed of this sickness. Wishful thinking. Reality didn't work that way and she was well beyond the age where she believed in fairy tale endings.

Hearing the increasing wheeze of his labored breaths, she sat the cloth on the nightstand next to the bowl, pressing her cool hands against the skin of Thade's cheeks. He was practically scalding, the heat burning her own skin. The drastic difference in their body temperatures caused Thade to twitch suddenly, jerking awkwardly under her gentle hold.

All at once, he fell still. The whistling air seeping into his lungs ceased, leaving the room in complete silence. Her insides lurched. Despite the urge to vomit from the overflow of emotions choking her, she was amazed to find her hands remaining steady, her fingers sliding along Thade's skin to his neck. A pulse. It was so faint she could barely feel it, unsure if it was even there at all.

"Oh gods, please... don't do this," she whispered desperately. Pressing her ear to his chest, she sat there, her body racked by the heavy beats of her own heart. There was no rise and fall to indicate any breath entering into him. In a moment of utter panic she pressed her lips against his, pinching his nose between her fingers while she exhaled her own breath into his lungs. "Wake up, Thade." She exhaled again, harder, watching his chest closely for any sign of movement. "Come on. I did not risk death at the hands of those arrows just to watch you die like this."

A strained whistle sounded from his mouth. A breath? Was she hearing things? Through the silence she heard another one. Fainter than before, but unmistakable. He was back — but for how long?

Silently, she cursed the distance between them and Tanispa. Why did the road have to be so long? If the shamans were here, they would be able to save him. But they weren't. And it would still be days before they arrived.

He didn't have days. If no one could help him, he didn't appear to have the rest of the night.

Faustine's teachings came back to her. More insistent than before. *What could it hurt?* It was such a harmless question with so many very dangerous possibilities. He could die. And how was that any different than what would happen if she did nothing? The possibility of her own death was less worrisome to her. If she wasn't careful, there was a chance the illness could shift from him into her. Her hands were already fumbling over the blankets, pulling them down away from Thade's chest. Those risks were all ones she was willing to take, if there was any chance it would save him.

Under other circumstances, she would have blushed at the thought of undoing the buttons to Thade's shirt, revealing his chest. Her fear and the rush of adrenaline made it feel normal, taking no notice of his body. All that mattered was locating a point where she could access the flow of his internal energy to meld it with her own. A location to form a conduit.

There were several points over the body where the flow was more potent. Faustine had stressed the knowledge of them when it came to the healing magic, most specifically a point just below the naval. If she could get a clean circuit of energy between her and Thade at that point, she could attempt a cleansing. It was said to work on minor infections or viruses, to help rid the body of the impurities, but there was no guarantee it would function the same for this illness. There was no way to even know what the root of the illness was, let alone how to combat it.

Gently, she pressed the palm of her right hand over the skin of Thade's lower abdomen, his body heat instantly warming the surface. She needed to focus – but how could she focus at a time like this? So much was riding on her and she knew next to nothing about what she was doing. Every inch of her wanted to panic. To start screaming for Feolan to wake up and do something. Anything.

But she knew Feolan was not trained in how to manipulate energy in such a way. Military training was drastically different, focusing on flushing poison or controlling blood flow to help staunch serious injuries at most. None of that would be of any use to her in this.

A steady thrum started to build under her palm, sending a wave of excitement through her at the realization that something was working. Or rather, that something was happening, though whether or not it was working was yet to be determined.

Breathing in deeply, she centered her thoughts on the unnatural warmth connecting her palm with Thade. A soft blue glow lit up the area around her slender fingers. To strengthen the conduit, she placed her left hand beside her right, shifting onto her knees beside Thade's still form on the bed. *Envision the impurities being cleansed from the body.* The blue glow traveled from her hands, down into the depths of Thade's skin. She could see it coursing through him, traveling along the paths of the veins, illuminating him from the inside. It maneuvered, unhindered, down to his feet and swiftly back up to his midsection, coming to a halt in the center of his chest. The heart. Lungs. None of the organs there could be reached.

Dismayed, Leyna slid her knees up further on the bed, positioning herself next to his chest. It was more dangerous for her to attempt anything from such a sensitive point, but there was another location there from which she could attempt the link. However, it was less likely she would be able to perform any type of cleansing. The sickness and impurities were too deeply embedded. One wrong move and she could send them directly into his vital organs, seizing his system and killing him instantly. Her only chance would be to attempt a transference of the negative energies into her own body; she just wasn't entirely sure she was capable of the task.

If she could just take enough of it into her to allow the energy to flow more freely. That was all she needed. It would be enough to stabilize him until the physicians could reach him, at the very least.

Focus. Any distraction could be the death of them both. She rested her palms over the center of Thade's chest, feeling the dull thud of his weakening heart. Only once had she ever directed the energy inward. It was a completely different sensation, the blue glow slowly enveloping her hands in their entirety, creeping up her arms and into her neck, spreading out over her body.

Instantly, she began to feel her insides tremble. Fatigue coursed over, weakening her, a sudden chill sending shivers down her spine.

Her point of contact with Thade was like a magnet, holding her in place. She needed to let go. If she transferred too much, it was sure to kill her, already building heavily around her lungs. *What was I thinking? I am going to get myself killed!* She just needed one firm pull to separate her energy from Thade's. He was stronger than she anticipated. The magic inside him was superior to her own, overpowering her.

Steeling herself for one last tug, Leyna yanked her entire body backward, tumbling head over heels from the bed onto the floor in a mass of fabric and hair, shaking the room with the impact. Her heart was still racing. The blue glow remained around her hands and arms and torso. She lay there, gazing up at the ceiling, watching from the corner of her eye as the light gradually faded, lingering longest over her chest before winking out of sight.

From somewhere nearby, she was suddenly aware of Feolan's hushed voice whispering her name. He was standing over her. The outline of his face was fuzzy in her vision, blurring the edges, making him appear disjointed. Was she hallucinating? Had she hit her head when she fell and lost consciousness?

Someone was pulling her to her feet. Feolan's voice continued to repeat her name, over and over, growing more insistent until her eyes settled on him, following the wobbly figure drunkenly. "Feolan? Is that you? I think I fell..."

"Leyna? What in the name of all that is holy were you doing?"

She felt intoxicated. Fits of giggles broke up her thoughts, her hand covering her mouth to keep them quiet. Consciously, she found nothing humorous about what had happened. Inside, she feared the outcome of her dabbling. She wanted to see Thade, to check his pulse, listen to his breathing, feel his temperature. But her movements were clumsy, her body resting heavily against Feolan as he guided her back to the edge of the bed where she'd been sitting.

The blankets were still pulled away from Thade, his unbuttoned shirt lying open. Groggily, she extended her hand out, thinking to feel his chest, to see if it was still moving with his breathing, thinking better of it at the last second, retracting her hand. There was no saying that the transfer would not begin again. The break between them had been sloppy. Lacking in closure. It was the only excuse for the strange behavior of her physical self while her mind remained coherent, mostly. She had disrupted her own balance.

"Leyna? Can you hear me?"

"Hmm?" Who was talking to her? She was tired. Oh, so tired. Her body wanted to curl up on the soft mattress and drift away into sleep, but that wasn't possible. This bed was already taken by someone. There wasn't enough room for her.

Absently, she extended out her hand, feeling the cool sensation of Feolan's skin under her fingers. He was real. She hadn't been imagining his presence. Her fall had woken him, and alerted him to what she was doing. Her mind registered the sound of his voice, speaking to her questioningly, shaking her. Was he angry with her? What was he saying...?

Squinting her eyes, she peered through the dim light of the room, straining to make out the details of Feolan's worried face. The touch of her hand on his cheek helped her to steady the image, bringing him into focus. All at once everything came back to her, painfully clear in her desperation. She was still in Thade's room. He was still sick. Had she helped at all?

She turned away from Feolan. There weren't any words to explain to him what she had done. How could she possibly explain the reasons which made such perfect sense to her? He'd been asleep. He hadn't witnessed the brief moment where the life drifted away from the sweat-soaked body of the man lying on the bed.

Instinctively, she reached for the cloth, now practically dry, resting on the nightstand. Dipping it down into the cool water in the bowl, she squeezed the excess droplets from it, basking in the glorious chill against the skin of her own hand. She couldn't be sure if there was any conscious thought drifting through her mind as she dabbed it over Thade's face.

Odd. He felt cool to her touch, his breath quietly moving in and out through his nostrils. Feolan was trying to take the cloth from her. He was speaking again. How could she have missed the sound of his voice. "You are burning up, Leyna."

Burning up. Yes. It was warm in there. Dreadfully warm. Chills ran up and down the length of her spine, causing her to shudder visibly. Bringing the moist cloth up to her own face, she wiped it along her skin, exhaling blissfully at the cool sensation. "I need air. It is suffocating in here. No wonder he is having such difficulty breathing."

"The air in here is fine," Feolan frowned. "You need to sleep. Whatever you did has caused a dangerous imbalance of the energy in your body. The more you try to do is only going to disrupt it worse."

Sleep? She couldn't sleep. Kael would be furious if she — Kael. Of course. That was why she couldn't sleep. She needed to get back to Zander's. The gods only knew what the hour was. Morning would be fast approaching, and when the sun started to brighten the horizon, her concealment in the darkness along the road would be gone. Anyone could see her sneaking back into the little window of her room. No, there would be no sleeping. She needed to leave. Now.

"I have to go," she breathed, rising quickly to her feet. The sudden motion caused her to sway unsteadily, nearly falling back onto the bed, saved once again by Feolan's strong arms. "If they find me gone —"

"I will take you back..."

"No," she gasped. It was too dangerous to even consider. It would be one thing if she was spotted along the road. Quite another if she was spotted with him.

"You will not make it back by yourself. We can take a horse most of the way, and then I can walk you back when we get closer. Where are you staying while here in Siscal?"

"Zander's." Why was she telling him? She couldn't possibly be considering accepting his offer. "But that does not change the fact that they cannot see me with you. They cannot know I left. I have to go alone."

Dipping the cloth back into the water, Leyna brought it up to her face, failing to wring the moisture out of it. Her body was on fire. She didn't care about the water soaking into the bodice of her dress, dripping all the way to the waistline of her skirt. It felt good. But only for a moment. Almost as quickly as it had fallen, it dried up against her skin, leaving nothing but the dull damp stain on the front of her dress.

The nap, however brief it was, had done wonders for Feolan. His eyes once again had their usual flare, their soft grey burning into hers defiantly at her continued protests. Leaning forward, he pressed his fingers against Thade's neck, counting softly to himself for the pulse before stubbornly taking up a position in front of Leyna. "His pulse is normal and his breathing is regular. He will be safe for the short time it will take me to see you back to Zander's. By horseback, we should be there within the hour."

Her eyes drifted over her shoulder to gaze at Thade. In her mind, she could still hear that dreadful wheezing noise that had been his breathing. The sudden lifeless pause of his chest. To hear Feolan's assurances now. *His pulse is normal and his breathing is regular.* If only he knew! And what if that changed while they were gone? There would be no one to revive him. Why did she have to leave? If only she could stay there, for just a few more hours. A day. Anything at all to make sure he was safe.

"I will find a way to come back and visit in the next few days." Calmly, she slid her hand around Thade's. It was cold and clammy to her touch. Heavy. "There is still so much I need to discuss with you both in regards to the changes that will be happening. It will be easier to plan the details when you have had some sleep and when the Consul is healthy again." Turning to face the bed, she moved her head down lower to Thade's ear, her balance faltering from the weight of her upper body. "You hear me, Thade? You will get better. You and I both know there is still much I have to tell you before you can go anywhere, and you me. We promised, and I refuse to let either of us out of that agreement."

As she struggled to straighten her back, she paused, staring down at her and Thade's clasped hands. For a moment, she thought she felt something. A gentle return of the pressure between them. It was so subtle that it seemed she had imagined it. She must have. With her own eyes she could see he remained motionless on the bed. Sleeping. Unresponsive, the way he had been since she arrived, unaware of her presence there beside him. And yet she was certain she'd felt it. At the very least, it comforted her to believe it. Squeezing his hand a final time, she let her fingers slip away, giving one last somber look over him, pulling the blankets back up.

"Leyna, did you hear me?"

"What?" she asked. Confused. Had he spoken? "I must not have. My head feels a little funny."

"You look sick. I am worried about leaving you with those people. They will not get you the care you need – especially since I fear the illness was contracted by whatever you did," Feolan said, his voice filled with concern. "For the first time in hours, his breathing is even; his fever clearly lower than before… and oddly you have acquired those symptoms, quite suddenly."

"I need air," she whispered. Feolan knew. She saw no reason to explain anything to him when he had witnessed the light of her energy melded with Thade's, seeping into her chest while she had laid there on the floor, gasping for breath. He was no stranger to the magic. "Do you have something with a hood I can wear to conceal my face while we ride?"

Feolan waved his hand at the candle, extinguishing the flame with a simple trick. The darkness only added to the cloudiness of her thoughts. Had Feolan not taken her hand in his to guide her from the room, she would have never made it to the door.

Something heavy was placed over her shoulders. A cloak. Her fingers fumbled over it, searching for a hood to pull up over her head. Noticing her trouble, Feolan helped to situate it over her hair, his grey eyes staring deeply into hers. "If I have not heard word from you to tell me of your condition by the time the doctors have arrived in Siscal, I will come find you. Do you understand me?"

"Come find me? Why would you do that?" In the back of her mind, it felt as though it should make more sense than it did at the moment.

"So they can see to your illness as well. I will accept no objections from you, and you will find that I am equally stubborn as you are, when I choose to be."

She smiled. The room was spinning. If they didn't get outside soon, she was at risk of losing consciousness, and if that happened – there would be no chance of convincing Feolan to take her back to Zander's house. "Come," she replied quietly, stumbling awkwardly toward the door. "Let us get on the road before it gets any later."

Chapter Fourteen

By the time Feolan helped her through the small window of her room at Zander's house, the sun was starting to lighten the horizon, heralding the coming of the dawn. All she could think about was the bed and how wonderful it felt to lie down. The sheets were cold against her burning skin, soothing her until her body heat transferred to the fabric.

Feolan had seen to it that she was covered and drifting off to sleep before finding his own way back out the window, closing it behind him. She wished there was some way for her to know if he made it back to Thade safely but her feverish mind was too scattered to focus on those concerns. Occasionally she was aware of someone knocking at her door. Calling out her name. She didn't recognize them, the sound muffled and hollow in her head. When they received no response from her, they eventually would wander off, returning a short time later. Again, she lacked the energy to reply.

The sun had been high in the sky for hours before she became suddenly aware of the lock on her door moving. The metal scraped against the track as if pulled by some invisible hand, slowly, precisely, falling with a click against the wooden door. She wanted to move, to climb up from the bed, ready to attack if the person intended her harm. But physically, she wasn't capable. Her limbs were like deadweights, holding her down under the thin blankets, at the mercy of whatever came through that door.

She was both relieved and frustrated to see Kael's face peek through the crack of the door before letting himself in. Her heart and her mind were not strong enough to handle a confrontation with him right now. Whatever he had to say, she wasn't interested, not caring about any explanations for the terrible things she'd heard. There would be plenty of time when she was healthy and clear-headed to discuss those matters.

"Eleni? Everyone is asking about you. Are you alright?"

Words built up in her mouth to give assurances that she was fine, their form never taking shape on her lips. It took too much effort to speak. Her voice came as a mumbled unintelligible noise from under the blankets.

The mattress sank under the weight of Kael's body where he sat down next to her. He seemed to not notice the misery on her face. Her skin was paler than normal with dark, sickly circles drooping under her eyes. She could feel the sweat from her fever soaked into the long strands of her hair matted against the side of her face and neck, drenching the pillow under her head. "I came to you last night, to be with you. Can you imagine my surprise when you did not answer the door and upon entering, I discovered you were not even here? Where did you go?"

She couldn't bring herself to feel bad for him. He had come to her? That was just great for him, but she had not been interested in being with him last night. To her, their engagement was the furthest thing from her mind. It all felt like a mistake anyway. "I was not feeling well," she coughed, her voice strained. "Quite frankly, I still feel as though I am dying. In a matter of speaking."

He seemed to take notice of her, for the first time since entering. His eyes blinked in shock, his hand reaching out to rest over her forehead, checking her temperature. "My god, Eleni. You are burning." Rising swiftly to his feet, Kael took long strides toward the door, pausing slightly to speak before heading out into the hallway. "I will fetch someone to call for a doctor."

Great. A worthless Siscalian physician. They wouldn't be able to do anything for her. If what she suffered was remotely similar to that of the Consul's, only the Vor'shai shamans would be of any use. Being seen by them was out of the question. Too much effort to contact them, and even more time wasted in waiting for them to arrive in town to see her. For all she knew, she would be cured by then. It couldn't possibly have advanced to the severity of the Consul's illness. She just needed to drink plenty of water and get lots of bed rest.

There was no time for bed rest! They were set to meet with Kyros that evening. She needed to be back on her feet by then. It was imperative that she be present for that meeting, attentive to everything the man had to say so she could properly manipulate him into accepting her business proposition. She couldn't count on Kael to unknowingly help her the way he had with Oksuva. It was more likely that he would be attempting to gain Kyros's trust in a similar fashion, knowing his position was precarious in the mission. If he couldn't gain the trust of Kyros, he would be out of the way completely, useless to their people until another opening presented itself. Given his previous involvement, however, a second chance at weaseling his way into anything would be next to impossible.

It was Zander who reappeared in the doorway, his breathing heavy from running. "What happened?" he asked, reaching her bedside in only a few fluid steps. "Do you think you are having a reaction to something you ate yesterday? What hurts? Your stomach – head – what is it?"

"Zander," she chuckled. The effort it required to laugh caused her chest to tighten, making it difficult to maintain her breath long enough to continue. "It is my own fault. I do not need a doctor, if you will just help me out of this bed so that I may get dressed. I can tell by the sun's position in the sky through the window that it is nearly time to meet with Oran's man."

"You look like death warmed over. I think it would be unwise to let you go any-where tonight."

"I did not ask you what you thought. Now, please – help me up?" Begrudgingly, he did as he was told.

Sleep had done wonders for her, in and of itself. The energy inside her still felt scattered and misaligned, but not to the extreme she'd suffered while at Thade's home. It had settled throughout her body in strange places, adding to the heaviness her arms and legs experienced. The sickness was more a constant discomfort than the pain and confusion it had been that morning. An improvement. By far.

"What do you think you are doing?" Kael's voice boomed loudly from the doorway. "I told you to get a doctor. She needs to stay lying down."

"She insisted I help her to her feet. That is what I am doing. Save your lectures for someone who cares," Zander grumbled, holding Leyna steady before slowly stepping away, testing to see if she was able to stand on her own. Satisfied that she was managing well with her balance, he made his way over to the tiny closet near the window, retriev-ing a garment bag from inside it. "I would help to dress her as well, but something tells me that would not be approved of by you. Or have you already made plans to help Oksuva out of her clothes – Oh, into them. I meant into them."

Kael moved with such speed and ferocity that Leyna wasn't sure exactly how he covered the distance to Zander, only that he was on him, clutching the front of his shirt angrily. "What are you implying, you imbecile?" he hissed. Zander's casual, nonchalant expression seemed to add to Kael's irritation, his grip tightening as he shook him roughly. "Tell me! If your intentions are to insult me, then speak plainly, coward!"

"Only someone with reason to be insulted by my words would be angered by them. I see no reason to justify anything I have said."

Silently, Leyna hoped for Zander to press the issue. She wanted to hear the way Kael would explain himself to someone other than her, without the need of sugarcoating it in hopes of lessening the pain that the truth brought.

His eyes flashed in his fury, their strange coloration sending a shiver through Leyna's veins. Dull. Shadowed. The gentle green was warped with tones of grey that she'd never noticed there before. "Kael," she whispered. "Let him go. We have other things we need to do before this meeting. Fighting will only waste what little time we have."

"Get out!" Kael shouted, pushing Zander toward the door. "We will discuss this later. Don't think I will forget it."

Zander smirked, idly straightening his shirt where Kael's hands had been. "I look forward to it."

When the door clicked shut behind Zander, Leyna feared she would faint. The change in Kael was disturbing. For years he had been there for her, always thinking of her, never caring about himself. How could a person suddenly become somebody else? Once in a while she would see traces of the old Kael, hidden away inside the mind of this new creature living in his skin. He was in there, somewhere, but she didn't know how to reach him. The tainted energy was more powerful than she'd given it credit for.

"What kind of lies has he been feeding you?"

"He has said nothing," she replied. Her legs carried her unsteadily over to where Zander had been standing, the garment bag from his hands having fallen to the floor while Kael had been pushing him around. She came to a stop over it, debating whether or not she should attempt to bend forward to lift it up. The strength the motion required felt somewhat beyond her limits. "Why are you so defensive about a random comment? Do I have need to be concerned about your involvement with Oksuva?"

"I was not the one who was out all night. If anyone should be answering questions right now, it is you," Kael huffed. "Where were you? And I already know the truth so if I were you, I would think very carefully about how you answer."

The truth? There was no way he could possibly know where she had gone. "I just went for a walk. Did you follow me?"

"A walk? A walk!" he shouted. "And that walk just happened to lead you to the house of the Consul? Until morning? So which one of them was it? Did you wear him out, causing his assistant to give you a ride back home, or is the Consul not aware of the little fling you have going on with his partner?"

The last of any remaining color in her face drained away. All she could do was stare at him, dumbfounded by his accusations. He accused her of an affair? And with the Consul and Feolan, no less! He, who had himself been unfaithful to her prior to their engagement and kept it hidden from her, was now pointing the finger at her for such adulterous actions.

Unable to maintain her balance, she dropped to her knees next to the garment bag, gazing blankly off into the distance. She didn't know what to say. No words could describe the feelings boiling up inside her. They increased her heart rate, her blood pressure rising, adding to the fever she already suffered. "You are out of line," she said through gritted teeth. The room was spinning, but she no longer cared to look at him. The creature standing there with her was not the Kael she had grown to care for over the years. This was nothing but a monster in his flesh. "You make these claims and yet you ignore my questions about Oksuva? Do you honestly believe I do not know about the two of you? That Mikel found you with her? And no, it was not Zander who spoke of it. I heard it from Mikel himself while he was attempting to take advantage of me in order to exact revenge for what you did."

"He did what?" Grabbing onto Leyna's arms, Kael lifted her into the air, looking into her eyes as if to determine whether or not she was lying. Speaking of the topic idly in hopes of calling his bluff.

She had to admit it was partially so. There was enough evidence to tell her that it was very possibly the truth, but a part of her hoped he would immediately deny it, assuring her that it was not what had happened and explaining to her, in detail, exactly why Mikel would have said something so outrageous. Instead, there was no immediate denial. Only more anger. "You heard what I said," she replied quietly, closing her eyes to avoid the blur of the moving room across her vision. "Did you ever plan to tell me about it? Or is that why you refused to hear the things I wished to speak with you on before I was bound to you? Did you think that if I told my secrets, that you then might tell me about what you did, and that I would deny your proposal? Or did it simply slip your mind?"

"I was drunk! Alright?" He shouted, throwing her back down to the ground at his feet. "We were talking and she offered me some wine and we just kept drinking and the next thing I knew, she was on top of me. I don't even know what happened before Mikel walked in. In my alcohol warped memory, I have no recollection that we ever did anything beyond kissing."

"But the fact you were drunk means that you are not required to tell me about it? Does alcohol give you forgiveness if you behave inappropriately behind my back?" Leyna snapped. "If I were to get drunk and kiss another man, would it be overlooked because I had imbibed that wretched liquor?"

"You were not mine yet when it happened! And if I ever find that your lips have been on another man's mouth, drunk or not, I will kill them. Do you understand me? I don't care if that man is the Prince himself, I will strike him down!" He was scream-ing. His breath reeked of some cheap wine, most likely taken from Zander's cabinet in the kitchen. It explained some of his actions, but in no way did it justify them, or forgive them.

She slapped him, hard, bringing the flat of her right palm against his left cheek. The crisp smack echoed through the tiny unfurnished room. She'd never before lifted a finger against him but she refused to just sit there and take such ridiculousness from him. There was little else she could do in her condition, but it was enough to let him know he had crossed a line.

Wasn't his when it happened. How dare he! For nearly six years he had courted her so desperately. Had none of it meant anything to him? Was it so easy to throw it all away in a single evening over a few glasses of wine? And with an Esai! Of all people, to have touched a half blood. A woman whom he, on many occasions, insulted specifically for her heritage and insisted he would never have considered her romantically.

And the standard was different with her. Sure, he could get drunk and sleep around with other women, but if she did it, it was intolerable. But she was just supposed to forgive him? To pretend it never happened? Whether it was just a kiss or not, it didn't change the fact that he had so easily forgotten about her in his wine-induced stupor –

and then chose to keep it from her! Then that afternoon when he came to wake her, to tell her he had tried to come to her that night, to be with her. As if she would have given herself to him! Betrothed or not, he was not showing her the respect a man should show a woman.

Fury continued to build in his eyes, his mouth sputtering in disbelief. She feared he would strike her back. The real Kael never would have considered it, but there was no saying what this man would do. He'd proven many times now that he was unpredictable. Downright cruel. Her fear was that a single blow from him would render her unconscious in her weakened condition, causing her to miss the meeting with Kyros.

"Kael," she said softly, hoping to get through to him in his enraged state to calm him. "Nothing happened last night. I went for a walk and I began to feel ill. I was nearby the Consul's home and thought it the safest place to stop. The Consul is sick as well, and Lord Feolan was already awake caring for him. He allowed me to rest and some water to drink and then saw me back home. I would never have done anything else, even if it had been suggested, which neither of those men would do."

"You don't know that," he spat. In a blur of motion, he grabbed up the garment bag from the floor, throwing it down on top of her. "I have known them far longer than you have, and I know that they are just like all the other men in this world. If given the chance, they would both try to take you away from me. I will not let that happen. Don't let their fancy titles among our people fool you, Eleni. They can't be trusted."

"But you never answered me, Kael. How did you know that I was there?" She hated to bring it up again. His anger was only just starting to taper off.

Tapping his index finger under his eye, Kael smirked. "You would be amazed the things we are capable of. The things our people never told us about."

"You used sorcery?" she breathed. Her chest tightened at the thought, aggravating her infected lungs. It hurt, a searing pain radiating throughout her upper body, speeding up her heart while choking off her air supply. Lost in a fit of coughing, she clutched at her chest. Kael did nothing. His eyes stared down at her in confusion, as if not registering what was wrong with her.

"I am not going to listen to a lecture right now, Eleni," he frowned, moving over to the door, leaving her there in her misery. "Get yourself dressed and be downstairs within the hour. I will not hold the carriage for you."

Sprawling out on the floor, she gasped for air, tugging at the laces on her bodice that she'd been wearing since leaving Dalonshire. An outline down the front of the silken grey fabric showed the stain caused from the water she spilled while at Thade's. She needed to get it off. Anything which might help to open her airway.

Part of her wanted to regret her decision to attempt the transference. She knew all of her pain and misery was linked to that moment. But she didn't care. She couldn't regret what she had done, unless it turned out to have been in vain. If her suffering did not spare the Consul, then it would have been for nothing. Everything would have been for nothing. Guilt would plague her for having not done more to help him, not that it already hadn't crossed her mind. She couldn't help but think there was more she could have done. Her lack of experience with actual healing magic was the only thing which prevented her from doing so.

Desperately, she removed the bodice, tossing it haphazardly onto the floor beside her. The cool wood felt good against her burning skin. If she could just lie there forever! But that wasn't an option. She needed to get herself dressed and focused on the task at hand. Now more than ever she wanted to find a means of interesting Kyros in her proposition. Kael might be desiring to do the same, but he couldn't be trusted. The magic was warping his judgment. Though why he was continuing to use it while away from Mikel was baffling.

Zander had spoken of it having an unnatural draw to those who had a taste of it. But Kael was so strong-willed. It didn't make any sense that he would so easily succumb to the darkness. There had to be something more to it.

Holding her hands palm to palm over her lower abdomen, Leyna tried to draw her internal energy to them, clearing her mind of everything else. A similar exercise to that which Feolan had shown her when she first utilized the magic. A balance in the flow of the energy was necessary. It was clear to her that whatever she had done to Thade had broken that flow, leaving her feeling incomplete, heavy, exhausted. Unable to function. It was preventing her from being able to fight off the illness.

The familiar tug between her palms came as a relief. There was still a mild flow of energy through parts of her, which was better than she had feared it would be. She could still feel the stagnant pools of it in various points throughout her body. Once she felt it had sufficiently gathered to the surface, she slowly began to raise her arms out to the sides and over her head, directing the energy through her body, pausing at the top of her scalp, her palms aimed downward. With precise movements, she then brought her hands down, stopping again, palms facing her forehead between her eyes and just over her nose. Continuing the motion, she completed the circuit, hovering over the center of her chest by her heart before returning to her lower abdomen.

Her entire body was beginning to pulse from the change inside her. She repeated the motion, calmly, holding each position until she could feel the energy radiating forth between her hands and her body. It invigorated her. Gradually, she acquired the strength to rise to her feet, starting the pattern again. She felt alive. Energized. Her physical form still suffered from the fever, but the pathways through her lungs and her internal organs felt clearer, unobstructed.

The thin linen of her chemise was soaked through with sweat, clinging to her skin uncomfortably. With the fog lifted from her mind, she realized how little time she had to prepare herself for the meeting. Less than an hour stood between her and their departure.

Frantic, she bustled around the room, desperately seeking the pieces to the dress she had intended to wear for her introduction to Kyros. The bulk of the garment remained securely in its bag, lying in a heap on the floor where Kael had thrown it at her. Arranging everything neatly on the bed, she inhaled a deep breath, quickly setting herself into motion to prepare for the evening.

The cold bath water had done wonders for her, cleansing her skin of the sticky sweat that had covered her body, easing the fever heat somewhat until it was more bearable than before. Dressed in a clean linen chemise under the heavy crimson damask fabric of her gown, it was only a matter of time before the temperature would rise again.

Her bodice was cinched tightly at her back. It held her posture straight. Oksuva insisted she dress in a way which would catch Kyros's eye, given Oran's fondness of her. They had spent an extra twenty minutes at the house while Oksuva tightened the laces, squeezing her securely into the garment, accentuating her womanly features to the best of their advantage.

It had been almost comical for her to watch the reactions of the men by the time Oksuva accepted Leyna's appearance to be 'tolerable.' The sleeves of her gown were long and flowing, dipping elegantly off the shoulders, revealing her slender neckline while still covering the scar on her arm. Her bodice was enticingly low-cut, though it had not been quite as scandalous when she initially slid it on. Oksuva had insulted her sense of style with fashionable gowns, which Leyna couldn't argue. She had very little experience with them. The nicest dress she had ever worn had been the one she donned for Queen Vorsila's masque. Since that night, she had found herself in rags, aside from the past few years of simple dresses so as to not outshine her mistress.

She felt like royalty. The gown she wore had been one of Oksuva's personal wardrobe, complete with the matching jewels designed specifically to accent the rich color of the fabric, right down to the golden embroidery along the sleeve and down the center of the skirt from the tightly laced waistline. The choker she wore sparkled with brilliant red rubies set in gold around her neck. It sat high over her throat, the labyrinthine design of the chains hanging down low, splaying out widely over her chest. The sparkle of the gems detracted from the imperfection on her skin, hiding it under the glamorous array of precious metals and stones.

Kael had instantly argued that she needed to be covered up, offering her his cloak to conceal her body from view. Oksuva of course declined, demanding she be the first thing Kyros notice when they entered the room. Leyna got the impression she was not the only one hoping to strike a bargain with this man. And with good reason. If Leyna was what this man wanted, Oksuva would never argue, especially in seeing an opportunity to rid herself of the woman that her husband clearly held some deeply repressed desire for.

It was Zander who surprised her the most. For the first time ever, she found him to be speechless, his jaw agape at the sight of her. Had Kael noticed his reaction, there might have been another confrontation between them right there in Zander's front room. Even now, while seated in the carriage, he remained silent, Leyna's eyes occasionally catching his gaze straying over to her, shifting away again when he realized she'd noticed.

She felt out of place going into Malic's dressed in such finery. On top of it all, it was a huge risk. There were enough people who might recognize her for who she really was. She had come too far to have it ruined now.

When they arrived, Oran was there to greet them, his pale hands helping Leyna down the carriage steps. "Ah, my goddess! You look stunning," he smiled. His eyes lingered over her until Oksuva's voice interrupted his thoughts, her femininely gloved hand reaching out for Oran to assist her down. "Lady Oksuva. It is a pleasure to see you as well."

"I have never ceased to think of you since we parted ways last," she replied, batting her eyelashes demurely at him. "The others are right behind us. I believe then we shall be ready to head in to meet your man."

"He is quite anxious to meet you both. I have told him much about you. Especially the sweet Eleni, here." Staring up at Leyna, he gently lifted her hand to his lips, pressing them against her skin. She could see a flicker of confusion pass over his eyes. There was no doubt in her mind that he could sense the heat of her fever. He might have spoken on it, had the noise of the approaching horses from the other carriage not distracted him.

Yasar was the first to exit the carriage, his towering frame looking awkward in his finely tailored suit. The brawny Namiren figure seemed more fitting to fighting gear. His broad shoulders filled out the seams to their limits, looking as though they would split at any moment if he flexed his muscles even the slightest. Mikel had insisted Yasar join them for the meeting, not trusting Oksuva away from his company. "Sorry to keep you waiting, Master Oran. The ladies take forever to get ready, as I am sure you can imagine by looking at them."

"It is the way of women, and you will find no man who could ever complain after seeing the finished product of their work," Oran chuckled.

Upon exiting the carriage, Kael's eyes were instantly drawn to Oran's hand clasping Leyna's. Without a word, he made his way over to Leyna's side, wrapping his arm possessively around her waist. Oran's brow rose, curiously looking Kael over.

Zander was the last to join them. He had been seated beside Gislan in the carriage with Oksuva and Leyna, though why it took them so long to find their way outside had Leyna confused. But not enough to merit asking. When it came to those two, she found it better to just leave their reasons unspoken. Gislan was far from proper in her actions and Zander did anything she commanded him. She tried not to imagine what might have passed between them while left in the privacy of the carriage, for even the brief period of time they had. Zander appeared his usual calm and debonair self while Gislan looked irritated, exhaling in a huff as she came to Oksuva's side. "I need a drink," she grumbled, running her fingers through her blonde hair. "A strong one."

"Come," Oran announced, offering his arms out to Leyna and Oksuva on either side. "We should not keep my master waiting."

Stepping away from Kael's arm, Leyna hooked her elbow around Oran's, falling into step beside him as they made their way into the tavern. The place was alive with people and chatter, the clinking of glasses and plates filling the air. Sconces along the walls and hanging chandeliers illuminated the room with the dancing orange light of the flames. It was bright as daytime in most areas near the door, the light dimming the closer they moved toward the bar.

A shadowy figure was situated in one of the larger booths, the heavy black velvet of his tunic blending in with the shiny strands of his long, perfectly trimmed ebon hair. At their approach, he rose from his seat, greeting them with a cold, calculating stare, eyeing them with disapproval.

"Kyros, if I may have the pleasure of introducing you to the Lady Oksuva and her attendant, Eleni," Oran announced. Gently, he pressed them forward, releasing his hold on their arms. Leyna lowered herself down in a graceful curtsy, averting her eyes from Kyros. "And this young lady here is Oksuva's sister, Gislan — and these are their men, Kael, Zander, and the bulky one is Yasar."

"Why did they require to bring so many people? The ladies would have been quite enough," Kyros grumbled. Unlike Oran, he lacked the refined manners of a gentleman, ignoring Oksuva's outstretched hand in greeting, lingering in front of him in wait of a kiss. Embarrassed by the rejection, she hesitantly drew it back in, fidgeting uncomfortably.

"I can request the men to leave, sir —"

"Yes, but..." Kyros started, his eyes falling on Kael curiously. Looking him over with a scrutinizing gaze, he nodded his head approvingly, motioning for him to have a seat in the booth. "That one can stay. The rest, I apologize, but there simply is not enough room for us all at this table. You will have to find the bar suitable until I have finished my business with Lady Oksuva."

Yasar gave no protest to his orders. His long legs carried him over to the bar stools in only a few strides, leaving Zander behind to stare blankly at Kyros's stern expression. "Gislan—"

"You heard him, Zander," Gislan replied curtly, motioning dismissively at him with her hand. "Go sit by Yasar. I have nothing to say to you at the moment anyway."

Shrugging his shoulders, Zander walked away. His frustration was evident, but he knew better than to fight with them. To make a scene now would lead to more trouble than they were willing to risk.

They stood around, all waiting for the others to move. It was Kael who broke the stillness, following the direction to slide into the booth across from where Kyros had been seated when they approached. Oran followed, slipping in across from Kael.

Leyna took a step to sit next to Kael, finding her motion stopped by Kyros's hand on her arm. She looked down at it in shock, quickly shifting her gaze back up to him, questioningly. When their eyes met, she felt a shiver course through her, chilling her to the marrow of her bones despite the heat of her fever. His eyes shared the same distinct quality of every Ven'shal she'd ever crossed paths with. Black. Seemingly endless pools of darkness situated on either side of his nose, staring through to her soul. A painful looking scar slanted over his right eye. It cut through his brow, reaching up far into his scalp on the side. His nose was slender, his jaw wide, thin lips pressed together tightly into a slim line over his chin. Every part of his face looked somewhat disproportionate to the rest.

She inhaled sharply. There was a familiarity in his features she had never expected to see again. His face was unmistakable. Burned into the furthest depths of her mind. It had filled her sleep with nightmares for years while living in Carpaen as a child. Images flashed through her vision.

She could see this man, with his awkward features, coming toward her where she knelt beside her mother's corpse, sword drawn, charging. She could feel the panic again. The screaming fear. Her body moving to run from him without ever really knowing who he was or what was happening. Through the door of Reina's father's study to crawl under the table next to the desk. The scars on her back tingled. And then all at once, it came to an end, the sickening crunch as Nasha had come to her rescue, knocking him unconscious with the bottom of her sword hilt.

"Are you quite alright?" Kyros asked. His eyes were looking at her just a little too closely for comfort. Searching her face. Had he noticed the fear there? Was it possible he recognized her the way that she recalled his image in her mind? It was impossible to forget that face. It was the only one she had to blame for that day. The only one she had seen, that she had loathed every waking moment of her childhood after that night. And the marks on her back were all she needed to remind herself that he was someone she should fear.

"I – yes. I beg you forgive me, sir. I have been a bit under the weather today. At times I find it rather difficult to breathe, but I will be fine." She forced a smile. There wasn't anything else she could do.

Oh, how she wanted to strike him down right then and there. To exact her revenge for the misery and torment he had caused her. But no. She couldn't let herself do it. Not yet. Although she knew he had been one of those men present, those who ruthlessly slaughtered her and Reina's family, he was not the only one who had been involved. There were others who remained nameless. Faceless. Someone had hired them to do the job, and it was their leader whom she intended to strike at first. She would just have to be careful how she played her cards. One wrong move and she could lose her only chance to discover who had given the order. Or worse, he could finish the job he started that night. She was putting herself right in front of him.

Impatient, Oksuva brushed by Leyna and Kyros, sliding into the booth next to Kael. "Come now. We have much to discuss and we should not keep this man waiting, Eleni."

His piercing gaze remained settled on Leyna. He didn't seem to notice Oksuva's voice, coming again from the booth, her arms gesturing at Leyna to come sit down. "What is your name, Milady?" he asked, his tone hushed.

"Eleni, sir," she replied. His question didn't make any sense. Oran had introduced her. She could still hear his voice speaking her name, ringing in her head. Not to mention the fact that Oksuva had only just called for her. She hated that his expression was so impossible to decipher.

"I meant your surname," he growled. "What family do you claim heritage to?"

Another wave of panic came over her. In all her years under Mikel's employ, no one had ever requested that information from her. She was a slave. The family name was unimportant to a person of such low social standing. "I have no family name, sir," she lied, glancing nervously over to Oksuva. "I have been a slave since I was a little girl. Eleni is the only name I know."

"A slave?" Releasing his grip on her arm, Kyros turned away from Leyna, settling himself in the booth beside Gislan and Oran. Leyna stood there next to the table in a daze, unaware Kyros had moved until she felt the tug of Oksuva's hand on the back of her skirt, urging her to sit. "Tell me, Lady Oksuva. Where did your husband purchase this slave from? I have never known a family to dress their trash in such finery."

"Eleni may be a slave in our house, but she has been one of my ladies for a few years now. She was originally a birthday gift from my dear sister to my husband. Is that not correct, Gislan?"

Gislan leaned forward, resting her elbows casually on the table. "Biggest mistake I ever made," she sneered. "Zander sold her to me. Said he stole her from some rich family on the trade routes of Tanispa. Used goods, so worthless if you ask me. I fail to see what he saw in her."

Blinking her eyes in surprise, Leyna gazed at Gislan. Her hostility was unexpected. They had always shared a mostly friendly relationship, finding it entertaining to pass jokes between one another at Zander's expense. Why she would suddenly speak with such harshness struck a chord in the back of Leyna's mind. More than before, she was curious what had happened between Gislan and Zander in the carriage. Her behavior wasn't making any sense.

"Ah, the biting jealousy of women. I had almost forgotten what that was like," Oran smirked. "Worry not, my dear Eleni. She is only bitter that you are more fair and youthful than she is. The Esai do not carry their age quite as well. No offense, Lady Oksuva."

"I think Oksuva, on the contrary, carries her age quite well. She does not look a day over twenty-five for a human," Kael smiled.

Leyna had to do a double take, caught off guard by Kael's words. A compliment? Toward Oksuva, the half blood? Countless times he had ranted about her aging skin, pointing out the wrinkles which had begun to form around her mouth, the dark circles under her eyes. She was well over fifty, and while she looked younger in comparison to other humans of her age, she could not hide her climbing number of years.

And Oksuva was positively glowing at his flattery. A pressure built up inside Leyna's stomach, twisting and turning, like a boot striking her full on. She had to divert her eyes from the sight of the two of them. Kael's arm was propped absently over the back of the seat, resting just behind Oksuva's shoulders. She giggled flirtatiously. Leyna had never seen her behave in such a manner.

It pained her to watch the two of them together. Images in her mind taunted her, picturing them together in Oksuva's room. The man she was bound to. Of all the foolish things she'd done, their engagement was the worst. But how could she have known? She couldn't. But she still could have insisted they wait. If he truly loved her, he would have honored her request.

Lost in her thoughts, she couldn't focus on what was being said around her. Oran was giving an explanation for their meeting. Small talk. Mikel's name was brought up occasionally, someone's arm reaching in front of her vision to point at Yasar where he was seated, apart from the group, laughter erupting around the table. Unaware of the joke, Leyna let a quiet chuckle mingle with the rest of them, not wanting to make it obvious that she wasn't paying attention. Chills continued to plague her from the fever. It was a miracle no one said anything in regards to her constant shivering, beads of sweat occasionally forming around her brow, quickly wiped away by her trembling hands.

From a distance, she heard the sound of a young woman's voice. She was calling out something. A name. Leyna's name. Her true name, not the false one she had been using for more than six years. It was so faint; she didn't believe it to be real. A fever-induced hallucination. In the back of her mind, she knew it would be a mistake to seek out the source, on the chance that it wasn't her imagination. The chances of someone knowing her at Malic's were too great. If she responded, it would only draw suspicion. It came again, louder this time. Lifting her head, she stared across the table, suddenly aware of Kyros's eyes watching her.

Out of the corner of her eye, she strained her vision to see where the voice was coming from. To her surprise, she could make out the familiar figure of Zander crossing the floor to a young Mialan woman, her blonde hair swept up away from her face, tiny ringlets framing her high cheekbones. Her green eyes were filled with confusion at Zander's approach, preventing her from getting any closer to Leyna's table. A pit in her stomach added to the discomfort she was already feeling. It wasn't possible. The girl looked like her little Reina, trapped in a woman's body. But she would be a woman now. Nearly thirty years old.

She followed the two with her eyes until Zander guided the girl into a crowd of people near the front of the tavern, disappearing from view. Her gaze lingered for a moment, waiting to see if they would return, disappointed by the absence of their faces amongst the jovial group of drinkers.

Shifting her eyes back to the table, she flinched at Kyros's gaze still upon her. There was something in the way he was looking at her which made her uneasy, beyond the usual discomfort she felt whenever a Ven'shal was so close to her. The corner of his mouth twitched, a secretive smirk only she could see. Breaking his gaze, she lowered her head, staring down at the table in front of her. Had he heard the name spoken? He would recognize it. She didn't doubt that. If he drew the connection between the name and her appearance, everything she'd worked for would be undone instantly.

"Eleni? Are you going to answer the man, or not?" Oksuva's voice cut through Leyna's thoughts, a wave of fear bubbling up inside her. They were talking to her? A lot of good she was doing gathering information by ignoring everyone around her.

"I am sorry. My mind must have wandered," she replied quietly, wiping away the sweat from her brow. "I did not hear the question."

Gislan sat up in her seat, motioning dismissively toward Leyna. "She's just a slave. I wouldn't worry about what she has to say. Couldn't we just get back to business?"

"Back to?" Kyros snorted. "We have yet to have a chance to begin. This night has been one distraction after another. I am starting to wonder if we should not reschedule for another time and place."

Sitting up straight in her seat, Oksuva's eyes opened wide, frantic at the thought of missing out on her meeting. "That will not be necessary. We are already here, after all. Once we get a few glasses of wine around this table, our business will be impossible to distract us from any further. I have prepared an offer that would be worthwhile to both parties involved, if you will just hear me out."

How was she supposed to focus on this meeting, knowing that Reina might be there? Every inch of her body was tense, anxious to get out of that place so that she could have a free moment to think of what to do.

"I am already to the understanding that you have had Oran arrange this meeting in hopes of my granting you an audience with my man. Is this accurate?" Snapping his fingers, Kyros motioned toward a waitress at the bar, signaling for her to bring them a bottle of wine without ever speaking a word out loud.

"It could be. That all depends on if your man is who he is rumored to be. I cannot be going around making bargains with just anyone. I need to know up front who and what I am working with."

Kyros chuckled to himself. "Then perhaps you could tell me what you believe, and we can go from there."

"I am told the man I need to speak with goes by the name of Rohld," Oksuva replied calmly. "He has proven very difficult to track down, but his name comes linked with yours."

Leyna could feel herself starting to hyperventilate. What had she been thinking, believing she could handle all of this while in her condition? The fever was worsening. She could feel the sweat starting to bead up around her forehead. Rohld. She recognized that name. It had been spoken to her the night she learned of her identity having been erased from existence. *Sarayi Evantine was married to a man by the name of Damir Rohld.*

It couldn't possibly be the same one. If Damir had been known to have ties with the Ven'shal, it was likely that other people in his family could have as well. There was more than one man in the world that bore the last name. Jumping to conclusions would be foolish of her, though she could still hear Thade's warning in her head. *Be wary if you hear that name spoken amongst those in Mikel's company.* Well, they weren't in Mikel's company, but she had given Thade her word that she would be careful. She needed to try and keep her wits about her long enough to determine what Oksuva possibly could want from this man, Rohld.

"And what exactly do you feel you have to offer that would be worth his time? If you know anything about him, then you know he doesn't just give his presence to any old wench that comes along."

Leyna felt an overwhelming desire to laugh, coming out of the blue at Kyros's comment. Covering her mouth, she tried to hold it in, still fighting to catch her breath.

"I think he holds a similar interest as my own to a man by the name of Arcastus," Oksuva said quietly, her eyes searching the nearby area to make sure no one had overheard. "I assume this name requires no explanation to a man of your obvious intelligence."

"Flattery will get you everywhere, Milady," Kyros smiled, ignoring the waitress bustling about the table, pouring the wine absently into the glasses situated in front of everyone present. "You have my interest, but I make no guarantees how long that will last. I suggest you speak quickly and state your point."

Taking a sip of the wine, Oksuva smiled sweetly at Kyros, her eyelashes fluttering demurely. "I have come into possession of an artifact of sorts that once belonged to the one and only Arcastus. His ancient energies are difficult to manipulate or examine myself, given my less than adequate control, but from what my researchers have determined, this artifact contains remnants of his magic."

"And what good will this supposed artifact do my master?"

"Look," Oksuva stated flatly, all her playfulness draining from her demeanor. "Those at this table aside, I have a severe hatred for the Vor'shai. I feel you can sympathize with me on that, at the very least. The last thing the Vor'shai want is for the memory of Arcastus to be reborn amongst the Ven'shal. Over the years, their number has been gradually increasing. By now, after the Queen stepped in to raise her military hand against the Namiren and the Sanarik during the last war, it is my belief that the Ven'shal could rally more support than before."

Kyros remained quiet, leaning his elbows on the table to prop his chin on his hands, listening intently to Oksuva's words.

"This artifact that I have found is believed to hold enough magic, when wielded by one of significant strength and knowledge, to activate the ritual Arcastus devised to restore life to the dead. Rohld is said to have uncovered clues which could lead to where Arcastus's corpse has been sealed. Can you just imagine the strength our army could have if we had the legendary Arcastus among us? The older magic of the Vor'shai has been all but lost to the younger generations out of fear that another would fall and warp it the way Mescavis did when trying to revive his family. This would severely weaken them in a battle in which they would already be outnumbered and overpowered."

Leyna snatched up her glass, the scent of the wine reaching her nostrils as she lifted it to her lips. Tilting her head back, she let the thick liquid pour into her mouth, guzzling it down without heed to the bitterness of the taste. She disliked wine. But in this case, it was something to do, to drink, to distract her body from its failure at maintaining a steady breath. Her chest heaved wildly. She struggled to keep her quickened breaths quiet despite their rapidness, but she feared she wouldn't be able to keep it under control for much longer.

A war. So that was what Oksuva was plotting. But for how long? Had it been her plan from the start when she first involved herself with Mikel? What better way to secretly plot such a plan than using someone else to do your dirty work, searching for the people you need, arranging the meetings, putting himself in danger so that you remained squeaky clean if anyone were to catch wind of it. And if this Rohld was the man she'd been seeking all these years, it explained why she would have agreed to give Mikel his divorce. When she already had what she wanted, what good were his connections anymore?

"You have convinced me that Rohld would be intrigued by your proposal, but what is in this for me?" Kyros asked. "What do you have to offer for my service of arranging this meeting for you? You know as well as I that I am under no obligation to do so."

"You can have anything of mine that you desire," Oksuva smiled, the seductive sparkle returning to her eyes. "Simply name it, and it shall be yours without question."

As Leyna sat her empty wine glass back down on the table in front of her, she became suddenly aware of Kyros's eyes on her, looking into her own appraisingly. Placing her hand over her chest, she forced a charming smile, hoping he didn't notice the strain in her eyes.

"That is a tempting offer. But I will need to think on it. One cannot rush into choosing a prize of this proportion," he smirked. His eyes remained on Leyna. She shuddered to think what could be going on inside his mind.

If he had recognized her... No. She wouldn't think about that. Fear would only cloud her mind. She needed to keep focused on her goals; which would be easier if she could just get a single breath to ease her racing heart. Her hands grabbed at her bodice, failing to pull it away from her enough to grant her any reprieve. It was only made worse at the sight of Kael gently easing Oksuva in closer, her head leaning casually against his shoulder.

"If you all will excuse me, I need to go to the ladies' room," she said, her voice more of an exhale than anything else. The corner of the table dug into her leg as she tried to stand up, fumbling awkwardly, finding the dizziness returning to her vision the way it had before they left that afternoon.

Nerves. She was letting everything get under her skin. If she wasn't careful, she would ruin her cover over an inability to get her thoughts straight.

She could hear the others at her table whispering about her. They found her behavior strange. Blaming it on the fever. Good. That was exactly what she wanted them to think. It wasn't entirely false. Rubbing her hand lightly over her forehead, she could feel the sweat on her fingers, sticky and wet. Excusing herself would, at the very least, grant her a chance to determine how to get Kyros alone. By now, he must be convinced she was insane, given her actions.

Pushing through the door of the restroom, she immediately moved to the washbowl. The room was cleaner than she remembered it being when she'd been there last. Not that she would risk touching anything any more now than she would have back then. The clientele the tavern brought in wasn't very promising in the way of cleanliness, regardless of the lack of visible grease and grime on the floor.

Her mind was a mess, the thoughts dancing around without cohesion, her attempts to find her way through them met only by dead-ends. Fear gripped her at the possibility of Kyros having heard the name spoken by the girl in the tavern. But if he had, she expected him to react differently. More harshly. He'd been instructed to kill her all those years ago, so why would he now discover her identity and let her live without saying a word? Maybe she was reading into his expression too deeply. She was acting strangely. It was possible he was simply amused by her behavior.

With big gulps, she tried to fill her lungs with air. It was useless, as long as her body was on edge. She needed to calm herself. Force her lungs to breathe evenly. She was exaggerating everything because of her illness. The world wasn't going to end just because of one tiny mistake. Even if Kyros had heard the name, there were many possible resolutions. She was a clever girl. She would think of something.

Closing her eyes, she tried to control her breathing, inhaling deeply through her nose, exhaling through her mouth. It was working. Her heart was slowing, the burning in her lungs that had lingered since she left the table finally fading away. Fumbling for the washbowl in front of her, she dipped her hand into the water, pressing her moistened fingers to her forehead to wipe away the sweat lining the edges of her hair. Not wanting to use the towel hanging from the wall, she lifted up the skirt of her dress, using her slip to dab away the moisture, examining her reflection in the mirror.

It was still difficult to breathe. A pressure had built up around her lungs, pressing on them uncomfortably. But there was no time to think on the discomfort. She needed to get back to the table before anyone became suspicious. Or came looking for her.

Shakily, she moved through the door, grateful to find no one to be watching her. The closer she came to their table, she realized that Kyros was gone, his wine glass having been cleared away. Oksuva raised her brow curiously, a hint of irritation showing in her expression. "It is about time you came back. I am tired of this place. I want to go somewhere else to celebrate my success."

Several empty wine glasses were scattered about in front of Oksuva and Kael, their drunken laughter ringing through Leyna's ears. They wanted to go out and celebrate? But Kyros had not agreed to arrange her meeting. A celebration seemed a bit premature.

"I think Eleni should go home and rest," Zander's voice came quietly from behind her, his hand resting lightly on her shoulder. "If her fever does not improve by tomorrow, we will need to call for a doctor."

Leyna jumped at the sound of Zander's voice. He had returned, but where was the girl? Was she gone? Or worse, what if he had chased her away in fear of jeopardizing the mission? She would never have a chance to determine if it was really Reina or simply a woman who looked remarkably like her.

"You take her home then, Zander. We will enjoy the celebration more without you anyway," Gislan drawled. "I am going to find myself a real man tonight, so don't wait up."

Kael sat up in his seat, narrowing his eyes at Zander. "No, that man is not going to take Eleni anywhere alone. I will not allow it."

"This is not something you have a say in," Oksuva smiled, tapping his nose playfully with the tip of her index finger. "You have to come with my sister and I to protect us from the big, dangerous men out there."

At the display, Leyna could feel Zander squeezing her shoulder, his thumb gently rubbing the back of it comfortingly. There was too much going through her mind for her to focus on what Kael was doing. In her heart, she knew it was hurting her to witness it, but another part of her wanted him to go away with Oksuva and Gislan. She didn't have the strength to deal with him that night and if he came home with her, there was sure to be a fight. He was too drunk to reason with.

"Come on," Zander whispered, guiding her away from the table toward the door. "Let us get you out of here. There is somewhere else we need to go. All of this can be dealt with in the morning when you are feeling better."

When the carriage pulled up to Zander's house, they waited inside, his eyes watching Leyna, curious. Her breathing remained labored, a quiet wheeze having begun with every intake of air she attempted. After a moment, the driver came around to the door, opening it to let them out. Climbing down, Zander offered his hand to Leyna, helping her out of the carriage. Sensing her unsteadiness, his arm remained close to keep her on her feet.

Leyna listened to the sound of the wheels over the gravel as the carriage moved away, leaving them there in silence outside the door. Zander waited until it was out of view before guiding her away from the front of the house, slipping through the bushes toward the stable in the back.

"Zander, what are you doing?" she gasped, her feet stumbling over the uneven ground as she tried to keep up with him. He didn't answer. Instead, he left her standing against the stable door, moving inside to gather a horse, his hands expertly arranging the saddle over its back.

Content with his work, Zander swung his leg over the animal, mounting it with ease. Maneuvering over to where Leyna was standing, he reached down to her, his strong arms lifting her up and into the saddle behind him. "The mission was almost ruined tonight," he stated. "I had to promise a visit in order to keep things quiet."

"The girl from Malic's," Leyna nodded. The effort it took to stay atop the animal was only adding to her discomfort, her breath coming in shorter spurts.

Digging his heel into the horse's side, Zander snapped the reins, signaling it to move. With every step, a wheeze sounded from Leyna's lungs, her arms wrapping around Zander's waist to keep from falling off.

"You know her, then?"

"I don't know," Leyna grimaced, finding it difficult to get enough air to speak. "Until now, I wasn't sure she was even real. I thought I was hallucinating."

"Well, she certainly knows who you are. Do you know any Mialan girls by the name of Reina?"

Unable to keep her head held up, she buried her face into the back of Zander's jacket. So it was true. It was Reina. But why was she at Malic's? After all this time, she chose now to show herself. It was the worst possible timing. She only hoped Reina would understand. "Reina?" she breathed. "I haven't seen her since I was a child."

They were moving at a quick pace along the road before Zander steered them down a trail cut through the trees off to one side. The main streets of Siscal weren't far. It seemed dangerous for them to continue. Oksuva and the others were still in the city. They couldn't risk being seen by them. Not when the others expected her to be home. What would Kael think if he saw her and Zander out together, alone? *It couldn't be any worse than what he already thinks about Feolan and I...*

After a few moments they came to a stop in a small clearing, surrounded on all sides by trees, concealing them from view of the road. Off to the right, Leyna caught sight of another figure standing next to a tree, the sound of fabric brushing over the grass giving away the approach of the young woman, her skirts muddied from the damp soil of the woods.

"Leyna?"

She wanted to run to her. To wrap her arms around her in a warm embrace. But her limbs were no longer cooperating. As she tried to lift her leg over the horse to jump down, her foot caught on the side of the saddle, nearly sending her falling face first into the ground. Zander's hand shot out with incredible speed, managing to hold onto her by nothing but the sturdy backing of her corset. The added pressure sent her into a fit of coughing, her lungs burning from the lack of air. Seeing her struggle, Reina rushed over to the horse, her arms reaching up to help Leyna to her feet.

"She's very sick," Zander frowned. "I'm not going to let her stay out for long. I suggest you keep this conversation short."

"Thank you for bringing her. I promise I won't take up much time."

With a nod of his head, Zander turned the horse away, moving over to the tree line once again. He remained there, guarding the clearing in case anyone happened down the trail they'd taken from the road.

There was so much Leyna wanted to say, but no words would come out. Her emotions were everywhere between joy and regret. After so long she finally had Reina back; the girl who had been like a sister to her so many years ago. Nothing else seemed important at that moment other than seeing the little girl she once knew, now grown into a beautiful woman.

"I thought I might find you at that place," Reina said quietly, breaking the silence between them. "You wrote about it all the time in your letters. It took me several tries, but they finally gave in and hired me. I kind of thought I'd see you sooner, though. It's been almost two years and you've never come."

"I wasn't in Siscal for quite some time. I wrote about it in my letters, but I don't know if you ever received them." It hit Leyna like a kick to her stomach to think of Reina working at a place like Malic's. The waitresses there were nothing but objects to the drunkards in town. To think of the men pawing at her like a prostitute sparked anger in her heart. She'd have voiced her displeasure if it wasn't so hard to get up the energy to speak.

Reina wiped away a drop of sweat from Leyna's brow, a look of concern on her face. "I read them, but I didn't believe them for some reason. I guess I thought you were just hiding out here. Avoiding me. Making up the story about being sent to Tanispa in order to give an excuse for not coming back for me. I figured you'd forget about me after a while."

"Forget about you?" Leyna said, her disbelief evident in her airy tone. "Reina, I could never forget about you. It took longer than I expected to get up enough money and then I nearly died. I wanted to come back for you then, but they sent me away."

"Well, I couldn't wait forever in that miserable desert." A hint of bitterness could be heard in her words, her hand slipping away from Leyna's face, dejected. "You always sounded so happy here. When you were with me, you were always sad. I thought I would be nothing but a burden to you, so I left the orphanage. At first I didn't want to be found. I didn't want to see you again. In a way, I blamed you."

Leaning into Reina's slender frame, she wrapped her arms around her, pulling her into a tight hug. "You were never a burden to me. I thought about you every day when I was in Siscal. You were the only reason I had to keep going. To keep fighting. But you never answered my letters. And then the teachers at the orphanage told me you'd left. I thought I'd lost you."

Reina pulled away from her suddenly, her petite features twisted into a look of disdain. She stared back at Leyna, quiet for a moment before speaking again. "You've had such great experiences in your life. I envy you, Leyna. Every letter I got spoke of your friends and how happy you were. You were making something of yourself. Lieutenant of the Siscalian military! At times I wanted nothing more than to send your Captain some kind of letter to tell him the truth about you, just so that you would be miserable, the way I was."

"I wrote of the happy things because I didn't want you to know the truth of my suffering," Leyna grimaced. Her shoulders slumped forward under the strain it took to keep her posture straight.

"Suffering?" Reina laughed pathetically. "Other than being sick, you don't look like you're suffering. You're beautiful, Leyna. You have friends, fancy clothes — and I see that ring on your finger. You have a man that loves you. I only hope you remember me when you're planning the wedding."

It took all her strength to hold back the tears threatening to fall. So that was how Reina felt. Underneath it all, she blamed Leyna. She doubted the truth to everything she had been told. If only she knew! But how could Leyna make her understand? How could she make Reina believe that she was always in the back of Leyna's mind, worrying about where she was and whether she was safe?

"They're not my friends," Leyna shook her head sadly. "Those people are nothing to me. For the past six years, I've been seeking out the men responsible for the death of my mother and your family. And tonight, I've discovered that I am closer to finding them than I thought. The people you saw me with, they are just the tools I need to get that revenge. You of all people must understand that. Or at least know how important it is."

"I'm not sure I do," Reina sighed. "I don't know what it's like, Leyna. I was too young, and then you left me. I wanted to experience the things in your letters. I wanted to have friends. To be loved. Instead, I found myself with child and abandoned again by someone else I foolishly believed loved me."

Her words stung like salt in Leyna's already festering wounds. She wanted to think that she'd made the right decision in leaving Reina at the orphanage in Carpaen, but to hear her speak of it, she was no longer so sure. Reina needed someone there to help her. To talk to her. To teach her. The other children at the orphanage weren't enough. And while Reina had no idea the torment Leyna had experienced since the day she left Carpaen, it only showed that Leyna also lacked understanding of what Reina was feeling. To be so utterly alone. And without the knowledge of the truth that Leyna at least was granted to help her get through her days.

"You had a child?" Leyna whispered. There were so many other details she wanted to ask about, but nothing felt appropriate anymore.

"Why else do you think I left the orphanage? If they'd discovered my condition, they would've hidden me away. I ran from them in order to protect myself and the child from that kind of reputation."

"And you came here to work at a tavern?" Leyna asked in awe. "Where is your child? This hardly seems the place for you to raise it."

"She's at the orphanage now. I'll go back for her someday, but I can't right now. Not if I want to make something of myself so that I can provide for her the way she deserves."

"Then you know exactly how I felt the day I left you there."

Reina's eyes glistened with tears at the thought of what Leyna was saying. For the first time since they'd started speaking, a hint of regret and understanding was visible there. Reaching out for Leyna, she brought her into a hug once again, the embrace so strong that Leyna feared it would force the last of her remaining breath out of her body. "I'm sorry," Reina whispered.

"You don't have to apologize, Reina. But I need you to be careful," Leyna struggled to get up the energy to return Reina's embrace. "If any of those people at that table with me heard you say my name, they might come for you. It is imperative that you not tell them anything. They don't know who I really am and they can't ever be allowed to. Please, promise me that you'll be on your guard."

"I will," Reina nodded, pulling away to stare into Leyna's eyes. "I don't know what you're doing with them, but I won't mess things up."

A rustle came from the trees, reminding Leyna suddenly of Zander's presence. She jumped in surprise to see him approaching them, the icy blue of his eyes revealing his uncertainty at lingering there much longer. "Leyna, we really need to get you back to the house."

"I know," she replied, a hesitant smile passing over her lips. "You take care of yourself, Reina. I'll find a way to get some money to you. So you can get your child. My promise hasn't changed. One of these days, we'll be like a family again. You're the closest thing I have to one."

Reina released her hold on Leyna reluctantly, helping to guide her back behind Zander on the horse. "Good luck," she said quietly. "I hope you find the men responsible. If I thought I'd be of any use, I'd offer to help, but I would only be in the way. Just keep in touch. I'll write back this time. I promise."

With a smile, Leyna nodded, giving a final wave as Zander set the horse into motion. It was a weight off her shoulders to know that Reina was safe. She'd grown into a beautiful woman, and one of these days, all of the pain of their past would be behind them. Right now, they just had to get through the present. "I'm sorry to interrupt, but I thought we should get going before it gets much later," Zander mumbled, his words barely audible through the wind as they rode. "I assumed you might want to meet with someone else tonight as well."

"You assumed correctly," she chuckled, her words choked off by a fit of coughing. Regaining a bit of her composure, she tightened her hold on Zander's waist, not wanting to risk falling. "I learned a bit of information that needs to be passed on to the Consul immediately. If there is time, I can brief you on it before I leave, but I should not wait long."

"Just concentrate on yourself," he stated plainly. "I'll find out eventually, one way or another. Let's just get you home in one piece and worry about the rest later."

Chapter Fifteen

Leyna gave little thought to her bed when she stepped through the door to her room that night, sliding the lock into place. She didn't want to be disturbed. Although her body screamed under the strain, she pushed the small bed across the floor, positioning it in front of the door to keep anyone out who might try to come in. It was suspicious, sure, but that mattered little to her now. If anyone asked her about it, she would willingly admit that she snuck out the window for fresh air. She just wouldn't tell them where she went to breathe it.

Zander had been nice enough to leave a horse for her. The trip to the Consul's house would be more tolerable for her that way than walking in her condition. Every downward thud of the horse's steps knocked the breath away from her, leaving her gasping for air by the time she reached the country road leading into the upper-class neighborhood.

When she came to the edge of the street, she climbed down from the horse, securing it amongst the trees and bushes the way she'd seen Zander do the first night they were there together. The cloak covering her skin was adding to the temperature of her fever. If it hadn't been essential for her to leave it on, she never would have brought it. She wanted to feel the cool breeze blowing against her face.

She couldn't get the fabric of it off fast enough while she made her way hastily along the gravel road to the front door of the house. If she could breathe, it might have made things easier, but her lungs were tightening more with every intake of air.

As she drew closer, she became aware of a small carriage stopped in front of the house, the horses calmly grazing on the grass over the hitching post. Her pace slowed, hesitant to knock. It had only been one full day since she'd visited last. Could it be possible the doctors had arrived from Tanispa? If so, she didn't want to interrupt them from their work.

Lights flickered from inside the windows. Beyond the door, she could hear voices, pressing her ear against the wood to see if she could make out what was being said. There was a woman's voice coming from somewhere very near, growing louder, until suddenly the front door swung open, revealing a startled looking Maeri on the other side.

"Leyna! My goodness, how long have you been standing out there?"

"Only a few minutes now," she breathed. Her heart was still racing from her unexpected entrance. "I came by to see how the Consul was feeling. I did not realize you were back in town."

Ushering Leyna inside, Maeri closed the door behind her, twisting the lock into place. "Well, with you and Kael not being in Dalonshire, and knowing that Feolan was here all by himself caring for the Consul, I thought it would be best if I came back to help out."

"That was sweet of you." Her voice trailed off, seeing Feolan rising from a chair in the sitting area. He looked more composed than he had that morning. More vibrant. Either the sleep had done him a great deal of good, or he was enjoying having Maeri's company there with him. "Feolan, you look well."

"I wish I could say the same for you," he said, his eyes quickly blinking in realization of what he'd said. "I mean – you look lovely. I was just saying that you look... sick."

Leyna started to laugh, quickly shifting into a fit of coughing. Her lungs still burned. Just the thought of taking a breath was painful. Maeri was at her side instantly, rubbing her back, trying to ease her breathing. "I am fine. Or, I will be. I saw a carriage out front. Have the physicians arrived, or are those the horses that brought Maeri?"

"By the grace of the gods, the physicians rode through the night to get here. They are over a day ahead of schedule and have already managed to coax the Consul back to consciousness," Feolan smiled. The glimmer of worry was still evident in his eyes when he looked at her, coming over to help Maeri guide her to the settee. "While you are here, I insist you have one of them take a look at you."

"They need to focus on the Consul. I regretfully came with bad news which I must share with you. I admit it is much of the reason why I have come, although deep down I was more concerned about his health."

Sitting down on the settee, Maeri positioned herself beside Leyna on the cushion, continuing to rub her gently. Feolan opted to situate himself on the arm of the settee next to Leyna.

Their behavior was odd. It appeared to Leyna they were making great effort to keep distance between each other, using her as a distraction. Or possibly trying to distract her? An occasional hesitant glance at one another could be seen, their speech patterns quickened. Almost nervous. The flirtatious sparkle in Maeri's eye was all Leyna needed to know what was going on. "Did I come at a bad time? I suddenly feel as though I am intruding."

"Nonsense," Maeri laughed awkwardly. "We were only just talking about the upcoming masque when I discovered you outside. Queen Vorsila has already sent out a wave of invitations. You know you would be welcomed there with open arms if you chose to attend."

"When I tell you of the bad news which I bring, if it is passed on to Her Majesty, I suspect she may be postponing the party." Placing her left hand over her chest, she struggled to inhale a breath, giving pause before continuing again. From the arm of the chair, she felt Feolan's body stiffen, drawing in air as if to speak before falling silent again, motioning for Leyna to continue. "Oksuva had her meeting with that Ven'shal man, Kyros. Zander helped me to escape from there only a short while ago, which is why I still look like a bit of a clown.

Absently, she rubbed at the make up around her eyes, sighing at the heavy charcoal color staining her fingertips. She waited for any interjections that Maeri or Feolan might have before continuing, finding them silent, anxiously anticipating the news.

"As it turns out, Kyros works for a man known as Rohld. Oksuva is arranging to meet with him to discuss some kind of artifact she has found. Apparently years ago now. She has had people researching. She claims it belonged to the Ven'shal Arcastus and that her researchers have ascertained it to contain some kind of magic stored there by him personally. But she doesn't have enough control over the energies to wield it, given that she is not pure Vor'shai or of any Ven'shal blood."

"How is it that we have never heard anything about this supposed artifact before now?" Feolan asked, idly taking Leyna's left hand in his, patting it comfortingly. "Did Kael know about any of this or was this only just revealed to you both this evening?"

"Truth be told, I am at a loss as to what Kael knows and does not know. But my concerns about him will have to wait until some other time when there is less pressing business," Leyna said quietly. Now hardly seemed the time to break into a tangent about Kael using the sorcerous magic when there was still a chance she could talk some sense into him about it when he was sober. "Rumor has it that Rohld has some information regarding the location of Arcastus's body. I was not even aware that his corpse was still around."

"Yes, the legends say it was hidden away in some secret tomb, but no one knows where and there has never been any indication to make us believe it to be true," Feolan nodded.

"Well, Oksuva is trying to meet with Rohld. They intend to use the magic inside this artifact to raise Arcastus from the dead and wage a war against our people. With that, they are also planning to recruit the Sanarik and Namiren, playing off their possible bitterness toward Queen Vorsila at her involvement in their defeat at the end of the Siscalian war with Namorea."

Maeri's face contorted in horror at the thought of what Leyna suggested. "A war? Resurrecting Arcastus? This can't be allowed to happen. We can stop them, right?"

"If I can gather more information and allow us to plan an interception, then yes. It is possible. But it will be a very sensitive task —" Leyna became suddenly uncomfortably aware of Feolan's hand twisting the golden band around her finger. The expression on his face made it impossible to decipher what was going through his head. At Leyna's unexpected pause, Maeri followed their eyes, a sharp gasp escaping her at the sight of the ring.

"Leyna."

"Maeri, we are not discussing that right now," she exhaled, pulling her hand away from Feolan. "Do you not understand what I am saying? This is dangerous! This is the sort of thing we feared we would find but always secretly hoped would never come to be. All this time we thought it was Mikel who would be plotting, and it turns out that it has been his wife. She was using him for his affiliations with the Ven'shal to try and track down this Rohld and set this all into motion."

"I will need to send a letter to Her Majesty," Feolan frowned, rising stiffly from the arm of the settee. "The Consul is not well enough yet to hear this kind of news, but it needs to be passed on immediately. You were right to come to us when you did. For now, however, you will come with me, Leyna."

Come with him? It sounded almost ominous. The way the words rolled off his lips, absent of any emotion. Was he angry about the ring? Did he know who had given it to her? She found herself curious if Kael had ever mentioned their relationship in his letters to the Consul. Or if Kael was even still sending his correspondence.

She was wheezing considerably more than when she first left that afternoon. She'd thought it was improving with the stabilization of the energy flow throughout her body. No longer did she feel quite so confident in her assumption. It took Maeri's help to lift her off the settee so she could follow Feolan, motioning for Maeri to come with her. She didn't know what Feolan wanted, but what she did know was that she wanted Maeri to be there, regardless.

He led them down the dimly lit hallway to Thade's room. Pillows were propped up on the bed, elevating Thade's shoulders and head where he lay. His eyes were closed. His chest could be seen moving up and down with a steady rise and fall, slowed to the even, deep rhythm of someone lost in a peaceful sleep. A slight color had returned to his face in comparison to when she'd seen him last. It was a good sign that he was improving. And the physicians appeared calm in their periodic checks of his pulse and temperature.

"Good evening, gentlemen," Feolan announced quietly, alerting the men to their arrival without speaking too loud, not wanting to wake Thade from his slumber. "If I could trouble one or both of you for a minute to take a look at this young lady here? She is the one who kept the Consul stable enough for you to treat when you arrived today, though I fear she may have taken a bit more of his illness than I at first thought."

She would have released a sigh of relief in discovering why Feolan had requested her to come there, if not for the pain in her chest. Any strenuous use of the lungs created a massive discomfort. Too much air inhaled sent her into a fit of coughing and wheezing while exhaling too strongly left her breathless for several frightening moments where it felt as if she would suffocate.

One of the physicians looked up at Leyna from where he was bowed over Thade, squinting at her through his glasses. He didn't resemble anything like what Leyna expected of a Tanispan shaman. In her mind she retained the childish notion that they would be like the wizards in the fairy tales she'd grown up on, with long white beards and pointy hats to match their flowing robes. Instead, they looked unremarkably normal.

The man who took notice of their presence was an older Vor'shai. Possibly one of the oldest of her people Leyna had ever seen before. His hair was greying, though peppered with remnants of the deep black that had once lent color to the strands. He was dressed similarly to a priest of the temples. A simple cotton smock draped over his torso, giving him a sterile appearance. His thin-rimmed spectacles rested low on the bridge of his nose, his head tilted back to stare through the bottom of the lenses at Leyna.

He walked around her like a vulture circling its prey, observing every detail about Leyna, occasionally muttering and nodding his head as if in communication with some invisible consultant. Facing her, he placed his cool hands against the sides of her neck, his lips pursed in thoughtful contemplation. Leyna was unfamiliar with the methods of the physicians among her people. He used no implements like the doctors she'd visited in Mialan when she was a child. It was hard to imagine how they could possibly retrieve any accurate readings in using nothing but their own senses.

Stroking his chin, he moved around behind her, placing his hands against her upper back. "Take a deep breath?"

She cringed at the thought. A deep breath? Shallow ones were painful enough without willingly subjecting her body to that kind of torture. "It – hurts to breathe. Do I have to?"

"Try. I need to listen to your lungs."

It was hard not to laugh at his statement. Listen to her lungs. With what, exactly? His hands? Even to a race of people skilled in incredible feats of magic, it sounded preposterous.

Bracing herself for the impending pain, she tried to draw in a deep gulp of air, grimacing and stopping before she could fill her lungs. The pressure of the doctor's hands moved away from her back, his aging face reappearing in front of her, somber and quiet. "As I feared, the lungs are being crushed. When she created the circuit between them, she must have gone through the meridian at his chest, transferring a good portion of the pressure from his lungs into her own. While this relieved the strain on him, it only served to pass it on to her. We will need to extract the fluid before it builds up any worse than it already has."

"Extract it?" Leyna blinked, stepping away from the doctor nervously. "I am not entirely comfortable with the thought. How does that even work?"

"I watched him do the same procedure on the Consul a few hours ago, Leyna. I am not sure you want to know," Feolan smiled half-heartedly. The attempt at humor was lost on Leyna in her uncertainty, her eyes looking over to him fearfully.

"You knew they would have to do this to me?" she asked, dumbfounded by the entire situation. "How could you have known? I am absolutely fine. You should be able to see for yourself that I have improved since you saw me last."

The doctor was deep in a hushed conversation with the other shaman, oblivious to anything being spoken between the others in the room. Leyna wished she could hear what they were saying, to prepare herself for what they intended to do. The sound of the procedure alone was enough to make her shudder.

"You look more stable, but every breath you took while trying to tell us what you discovered tonight was strained and shallow. Every time you opened your mouth, it was obvious that your symptoms were identical to those of the Consul's. To be honest, I was finding it difficult to focus on everything you were telling me. You may have to go over it again once you are better."

Better? How was she supposed to get better? It had been well over a decade since she'd been visited by a doctor and even longer still since she had been ill to the point of requiring any form of treatment outside of disinfecting and bandaging a wound. Medical science was beyond her scope of understanding, and therefore well beyond the point of comfort for her. "On second thought, I think it might be best if I just left and came back another time when you are all more relaxed..."

They were drawing the canopy closed around the bed like a thin privacy curtain between Thade and where Leyna stood on the far side of the room. Her mind was racing, calculating the distance between her and the door. If Maeri moved out of the way, she felt she would be able to make it before any of the men could reach her and hold her back. The doctor was old. He couldn't possibly out run her. The other man with him might pose a bit more of a challenge. He was significantly younger. Less dignified in appearance. Almost hesitant in his mannerisms. She got the impression he was nothing more than an apprentice. An aspiring shaman. If she was lucky, he would be too confused by her sudden movement and might not react quickly enough to take chase after her.

Seeing the panic in her eyes, Feolan lightly placed his hand over her forearm, acting as a gesture of comfort while doubling as a means of stopping her if she tried to run. "Leyna, judging by the severity of your condition, if I allow you out that door, you may not survive long enough to make it back to Zander's home. I cannot have that on my head, nor could I bear to witness the guilt it would cause the Consul."

"I will be just fine," she snapped, the sensation of hyperventilating coming over her again the way it had back at Malic's. Her mind was too scattered to break free of Feolan's cautious grip, his fingers tightened to keep her from getting loose, while being careful not to press hard enough to risk injury. At that moment she caught sight of the doctor coming around from the other side of the drawn canopy. There in his hand he was carrying something long and sharp, resembling a thin metal shaft of an arrow only without the feather flights.

A needle. She thought her heart would stop dead in her chest. Turning sharply, her instinct was to run away, her escape foiled by the sturdy muscles of Feolan's chest blocking her path. There was nowhere for her to go beyond him anyway. Over his shoulder she could see nothing but the brilliant colors of the artwork decorating the wall, surrounding the single preserved Tanispan lily in the elegantly crafted vase. *Think about the flower. Calm. Take deep breaths. . .*

Who was she kidding? While the flower was pretty, it did nothing to ease the pain in her chest, preventing her from utilizing any deep breathing exercises. They would just have to see her panic. She'd suffered through many things, but she was not prepared to willingly subject herself to something of this nature. The needle was more menacing to her than a drawn arrow on a Sanarik bow. The Sanarik she at least had a chance at overpowering physically and escaping the strike.

The smell of Maeri's floral perfume invaded Leyna's nostrils as Feolan stepped away to allow Maeri to take his place, holding Leyna gently in her arms. "It is going to be okay, Leyna. I will sit with you through it. It will be over before you know it."

They were guiding her over to a small stool near the back of the room. Defeat hung heavy over her. It would be useless to try and get away from them. Even more disheartening was the thought of what the other men from her unit in the war would have said if they'd witnessed her reaction to the needle. Their lieutenant, always willing to run full on into battle against the enemy blades, quivering like a lost child in front of such a small, frivolous object.

Positioning her on the stool, Feolan slid the nightstand away from the bed, placing it in front of Leyna to act as a support. The actions of everyone around her meant little at this point. She had resigned herself to whatever it was the doctor intended to do to her. She'd brought it on herself, after all. In the end, it would be worth it, knowing she had helped Thade. She would just have to find a way to keep reminding herself of that until this was all over.

Maeri knelt down on the other side of the nightstand. Her deep emerald eyes gazed sympathetically at Leyna over the finely polished wood. The room felt brighter than normal, the array of flickering candle flames dancing from every corner to create strange, waving shadows on the walls. They were hypnotic in a sense. The way they twisted and bent before disappearing, only to reappear again to take on a new shape.

Through the veil of her thoughts, she heard the doctor's voice coming from closer behind her than he'd been before. He was giving directives to everyone, explaining the procedure in vague details which Leyna couldn't quite grasp. His assistant would be remaining with Thade to maintain a constant vigil of his condition in case anything was to happen. This would require more from Feolan and Maeri to make sure the procedure went successfully.

At least she knew Feolan and Maeri could be trusted. Many times Leyna had watched Feolan tend to the wounds of the injured soldiers in battle. His hands were steady. She trusted him with her life.

Her anxiety had begun to slowly ebb away when she suddenly felt a tug at her bodice laces, loosening them until it was supported by nothing but the pressure of the nightstand, holding it precariously in place. If there had been any shred of energy left in her, she would have been embarrassed by it.

It wasn't until she heard the doctor give orders to remove the top of her chemise that she started to feel uneasy. Despite the melancholy mind state that had taken over her, she was constantly aware of the scars which covered the skin on her back. They would raise questions in the minds of her friends. Possibly even the doctor. It was not common for a woman of any standing to bear such marks. Her only comfort was in the fact that Feolan would be more likely to assume them to be remnants of some old punishment enacted upon her by Mikel. Although it was inaccurate, it might at least buy her some time to distract them from it without having to explain the truth.

Closing her eyes, she waited for the reaction she knew would come. With Maeri holding the bodice against Leyna's front, the cool hands of the doctor and Feolan gently slid the fabric of her chemise down away from her shoulders and arms to expose her back. The silence was all Leyna needed to know they had spotted the scars. Part of her was grateful she couldn't see the expressions on their faces. The questioning looks in their eyes.

Murmurs could be heard from somewhere behind her back. Feolan and the doctor had stepped away, leaving Maeri staring off over Leyna's shoulder in concern. She couldn't see what it was the men had witnessed. The curiosity in her gaze was obvious; driving her mad with her desire to know what was going on. "Is something wrong? Is there something which would hinder the procedure?"

"No, we were just discussing something. Leyna, if you are ready, we are going to begin." Feolan's voice sounded forced. He was frustrated by something. Leyna could only assume it had something to do with her.

"I am not ready, nor will I ever be, so if this procedure is one that you insist must occur, then I suggest it be done now before I change my mind," Leyna sighed.

"I will explain what I am going to do while I get things started," the doctor mumbled, bustling about behind Leyna to gather the things he needed. An ice-cold splash of something could be felt against her skin on the left of her back. She shivered reflexively from it. "I am applying an anesthetic salve over the area where the needle will be inserted. You might feel a little bit of a pressure, but what I need for you to do is remain perfectly still once the needle is in place. Too much movement could cause a lung to be punctured, and we want to avoid that."

Nothing like stating the obvious. Doubt was creeping back over her at the thought of allowing this ridiculousness to continue. "Feolan, if you are not needed for anything specific back there, could you please come around and stand or sit by Maeri? We can continue our discussion. If you think you will be able to pay attention this time. The only way I am going to be able to bear this is — if I can distract my mind with something else."

"You can go ahead," the doctor said. "I only needed help getting things prepared. Just make sure there is a bowl here for me to set the line into." Leaning forward, he directed the rest of his statement to Leyna, hoping to help in easing her mind about what he was about to do. "After I get the needle in, I will be drawing the fluid through it. If you start to feel sick, let me know immediately. It could be dangerous if you pass out during the procedure."

"I am not exactly prone to fainting spells, but stranger things have happened. I will keep you informed if I sense one coming on," Leyna grumbled. "Please, Feolan. Come join Maeri so we can start talking before he comes near me with that thing."

She couldn't remember the last time she'd been so relieved to see Feolan's face. Doing as she asked, he knelt down on the floor beside Maeri, placing his hand lightly over Leyna's clasped fingers. "I did hear what you were telling us earlier. A part of me was hoping I was not hearing you correctly, but I realize now that my mind was not playing tricks on me. If what you are saying is true though, then we need to rethink our strategy a bit."

"My intentions are to break away from the original targets and find a way to get in closer to the new ones," Leyna explained. It struck her that they couldn't discuss the matter openly in front of the physicians. It was a sensitive topic, and although she doubted either of them were enemy spies, it was still safer to keep them as oblivious as possible. "If I am able to do that, then I will focus my efforts on finding the clues to where the body is. We need to either find it first, or the artifact, or somehow intercept one or the other after they have retrieved it. Waiting until they have their hands on anything though seems dangerous to me."

"Your involvement at all with those people seems dangerous to me. What if they catch you snooping around?" Maeri asked, squeezing Leyna's hand tightly in her own.

Leyna's face contorted in a grimace. She tried to hold it in, but the feeling of the needle piercing through her skin was almost unbearable. The anesthetic did little to ease the pain. If it eased it at all, then she dreaded what any of this would feel like naturally. It was like a constant tugging and pulling sensation in the middle of her body, focusing around her left lung, overwhelming her with the need to cough.

"They will not catch me," she wheezed. Desperate to mask the discomfort, she struggled to keep the conversation flowing, finding it hard to find the breath to form the words. "There is too much at stake... If Rohld is what I fear... it could be difficult... But I am the only person who can do this."

"Kael could befriend them," Feolan said, wincing at the sight of Leyna's discomfort. He squeezed her hand tighter, hoping to ease her suffering. "That would keep you out of danger if you think this man might pose a threat to you and the mission."

Focusing on the conversation was no longer possible. Her features were twisted in pain. She was afraid to move in fear of puncturing her lung with the needle, still aware of it pierced through her back. The sensation was more uncomfortable than her breathing had been throughout the day.

A desire to cough came over her, but she was afraid to give in to it. Her friends were staring at her, watching her every move, listening to every sound she made. They sympathized for her, and yet it was because of them that she was in this position. If they would've listened to her when she said she was fine. But even she knew her assurances had been lies. There was no denying the misery she'd been in from the illness slowly taking over her lungs. In another few hours, it would have rendered her unable to function in her mission. A few moments of discomfort were worth it in the end if she would be able to return to her work.

She felt the tug of the energy drawing the liquid from around her lungs. A morbid curiosity made her want to sneak a glance over to the bowl where the doctor had arranged the needle to flow, but the sickness in the pit of her stomach prevented her. There was no saying what it would look like, or how her mind would react to seeing it. If they feared a simple cough, something told her that vomiting was out of the question.

"How are you doing?" Maeri asked, peering sadly into Leyna's stricken eyes. "Don't hold your breath. It will make you need to cough more, and we don't want that."

At Maeri's directive, Leyna realized with surprise that she'd stopped breathing. Her fear of the needle was too great. Subconsciously, she found it hard to trust this shaman and his strange medical practices. Skilled or not, it seemed too easy for him to slip up. To move just right, or lose his focus, causing the needle to plunge deeper into her body. She shuddered to think on it, the sudden twitch of her muscles causing the needle to shift, her heart jumping in panic before she noticed the motion having been directed by the doctor. He was keeping a close eye on her. It was reassuring, even if only minimally.

Answering Maeri's question wasn't possible. There was no more air in her lungs to utilize for speech. It was a miserable sensation. And it was only getting worse. The need to cough was growing, intensifying with every second that passed. But she couldn't. She needed to hold it in. To fight it.

The pity in the eyes of her friends was the worst. They had no idea the torture she was experiencing. It was like someone had driven their fist into her chest and was clenching her lungs, tightening their grasp slowly. Time crawled by, tears of pain moistening her lashes. She didn't care anymore. What difference did it make if they saw her cry? It was impossible to think of anyone who wouldn't shed a tear when there was a metal object pierced through their internal organs.

With the increased pain, she tightened her grip over Maeri's hands, afraid she would crush them if she squeezed any more. Her knuckles were whitened from the strain, her lips pursed to hold back the urge to cough. From behind her she could hear the doctor shifting the bowl around. The needle wobbled slightly, her muscles tensed in preparation of the worst.

Racked with a fit of coughing, Leyna clung desperately to Maeri's hands. She couldn't hold it in any longer. The build-up in her chest was too much. She could feel the doctor's hands moving over her back. They were cold to her bare skin, reminding her of her state of undress in front of so many people. The tugging increased momentarily, fueling her coughing, before finally starting to fade away.

She could hear the faint clink of the metal needle against the ceramic bowl Feolan had provided the doctor. It was out. She'd survived the procedure. Her head started to turn reflexively toward the sound, wanting to see with her own eyes that the needle was no longer near her, but she managed to divert her gaze back to her friends. She didn't really want to know what was in the bowl, having been drained from her body. It was a disgusting thought which made her stomach turn.

Her back ached. The muscles felt as though she'd just run from Siscal to Dalonshire, her lungs drawing in air with more comfort than before. It was a miracle. A small one, but a miracle no less. She could feel the familiar texture of a bandage being placed over her back, covering the entry wound to prevent infection. "Is it over? Please tell me it is over. May I cover myself properly?"

Feolan and Maeri glanced at one another uneasily. The silence was awkward, similar to the tension Leyna had sensed between the two when she first arrived. After several long moments, Maeri finally gave a soft smirk, releasing Leyna's hand, stepping around behind her to assist with readjusting her chemise, diligently working to correct the disheveled mass of ribbons and laces that had originally held the bodice together. "Men. You would think you would be more skilled with women's clothing," she murmured.

"It is hard to keep up on the latest fashions and you do so like to leave us guessing," Feolan chortled, averting his eyes while Maeri pulled at the bodice, squeezing Leyna back into it the way she'd been when she arrived. "Frankly, I am at a loss as to how you women can tolerate wearing such restrictive clothing. And so much of it. A shirt and a tunic is all that is necessary for me. Why do you insist on covering yourself with layers upon layers of fabric and undergarments?"

"We are like a present that is very well wrapped," Maeri flirted. The tone of her voice was unmistakable. Playful. The way she talked to any boy while they were younger whom she'd found attractive, in hopes of winning their affection.

Leyna turned her head, gazing curiously at her friend. It was as if she were trying to make Feolan think about unwrapping her. She found it humorous, despite the moroseness of the situation. "I suddenly feel as though I am interrupting something," she laughed quietly, rising from the stool. It hurt to move about, causing her to hunch forward uncomfortably, the pressure of the tight bodice adding to the pain. "Now that you have succeeded in sufficiently torturing me medically, perhaps I should be on my way..."

"Leyna, wait. There is still much we need to discuss. We were not finished," Feolan coughed, clearing his throat. "You never answered with your opinion about having Kael step in for this part of the mission. It would keep you out of any direct risk."

"Tell me Feolan," Leyna replied quietly. The burning in her lungs had eased, allowing her to inhale deeply as she made her way around the room, coming to stand by the bed next to the physician's assistant. Nodding to the man, she motioned for him to step away, taking his place at Thade's side. "When did you last receive any form of correspondence from Kael? Does he remain in contact with you on a regular basis?"

"Truthfully? It has been nearly a year since he wrote. With your letters being more infrequent as well, we were of the assumption things were... uneventful."

"On the contrary, things have been quite eventful. At least recently."

"Do these events have anything to do with the ring you are wearing on your hand?"

Leyna pursed her lips together thoughtfully. She didn't want to discuss that. But how could she explain anything without touching on it? It didn't seem entirely necessary. Kael's behavior had been extreme enough to distract them from almost anything. The question was in how much she was willing to reveal without first having confronted Kael. Going to Feolan with the information could be detrimental to him and his reputation, and if her fears were misplaced or premature, it would be very difficult to undo the damage she might cause.

"The ring is unimportant," she said dismissively. "What you should be made aware of is that Kael is also being removed from Mikel's home. His position is rather precarious at the moment and I really am at a loss as to how he intends to come back from it."

"Removed? I was not even aware he was having any issues which could have caused that."

"It is somewhat recent, honestly. He found himself in a bit of a strange position with Mikel's wife."

Distractedly, Leyna pressed her fingers against Thade's wrist, feeling for his pulse. Stable. It was reassuring, at the very least, while everything else had long ago spiraled out of her control and comfort.

"Position? What do you mean? What kind of position?"

"From what I hear, it involved her being on top."

From under the finely curled ebon locks of Maeri's hair, Leyna could see her pale complexion brightening to a soft pink around her cheeks. "Leyna, I am not used to hearing you speak that way."

"No matter," she said. "Mikel was the one to discover this. It created quite an uproar throughout the house, and made the lives of a few… miserable. To say the least. No one knows how long it has been going on, or if it extended beyond the one incident, but you can imagine the question alone would be enough to drive a man like Mikel over the edge. Kael will never fully recover from the consequences, but," she exhaled slowly. "I intend to help him try."

"That only heightens my curiosity," Feolan stated. His gaze settled on Leyna, staring deeply into her eyes until she couldn't hold it any longer, averting her gaze down to look sadly at Thade's sleeping form. "It may have been presumptuous of me, but I suppose I had assumed Kael to be the one who wore the matching ring to that of yours. Is it not so?"

There was no good way to respond to his question. And ignoring it wouldn't make it go away. She was backed into a corner now, unable to retreat. The truth would leave a sour taste in their mouths regarding the relationship she had with Kael, but it was the only thing he had done which could never be undone. With her help he might be able to redeem his soul, in part, from the taint of the magic, but his unfaithfulness to her could never be taken back. Of all the things she could tell them, it was the least damaging to Kael.

Slowly, she lifted her eyes back to Feolan's, nodding solemnly. "It is so. I will not deny it, but I beg you not to judge him for it yet. Since the incident, he and I have not had an opportunity to discuss it. So that I can hear his side of the story." It wasn't entirely true. But what could she say? That they should pardon his behavior because he said he was drunk and that made everything better? "I have faith there is good reason behind his actions. I merely...have to discover what it is."

She couldn't stand the pity in their eyes. She didn't want to be pitied. What she wanted was to know the answers for herself. Her head was not clear enough to allow her to respond with the calm and control she wanted to maintain in their presence. An emotional breakdown could wait until she was again in the privacy of her own room.

"Leyna?"

The fragile sound of Thade's voice demanded the attention of everyone in the room, Feolan and Maeri rushing over to stand beside Leyna at the bed. "Consul! By the gods, you are awake," she smiled in relief, her voice quiet still from the discomfort. "That alone shows a miraculous improvement in your condition, I would say."

"I thought I had been hearing your voice, but I believed myself to be dreaming."

"If I have started appearing in your dreams, then surely you must still be sick," Leyna chuckled, patting Thade's hand lightly. "What terrible nightmares those must have been!" The usual vibrance of his silver eyes had dulled, the lids barely cracking open to let in the light of the room.

"Some of what I heard has me hoping it *was* a bad dream. I fear that is not so, however."

"Then do not think on it," Leyna smiled. Gently, she wrung out the damp cloth on the nightstand next to where the doctors had been working, rubbing it over the clammy skin of Thade's face. "There will be time to dwell on reality once you are healthy again. Until then, you need to save your strength and not waste it on trivial drama."

At hearing Thade's voice, the doctor hurried back over to the bed, pressing Maeri and Feolan off to the side to get in closer. Leyna maintained her soft hold on Thade's hand, moving the cloth away with the other to set it down as the other young man came up from behind her, motioning for her to move. "If you would not mind, Milady. We have much still to do."

Not giving her a chance to respond, the two men pushed their way in front of her, forcing her out of the chair. Stepping back, she could feel a faint pressure around her hand where she still held on to Thade, his fingers grasping for hers, but too weak to maintain their grip. "There is no need for them to leave. Can you not work around them?" he asked, his voice so quiet Leyna could barely hear it over the sound of the doctors' curious back-and-forth mumblings.

"Lord Feolan can remain in case we need his assistance," the doctor stated plainly. "I think it would be a good idea if the ladies retired for the evening."

It took Leyna a few moments to realize her left hand was still slightly extended in front of her where it had been pulled away from Thade's. Of course they would ask the ladies to leave. There was no telling what sort of things the doctors would need to do. What tests or procedures they would need to perform. If they were anything like the one she had experienced, it would not be something for a lady to witness. Especially if it required the removal of clothing the way they'd done to her.

Turning her eyes away, she felt her cheeks flushing with warmth, immediately overcome with guilt for the thoughts which passed through her mind. He was still so ill and all she could think of was removing his shirt. *You are a promised woman!* Not that it meant anything to her betrothed.

Bitterness was like poison to her mind. She didn't remember ever having been that way before. Never had she allowed self-pity to reign over her thoughts, despite the number of good reasons she had, for all the terrible things the world had put her through. To let it in now felt unnatural. But how did one combat their own mind? A mind that had been betrayed in ways far more severe than anything she ever thought she would experience in her life.

It was the reason she had avoided relationships for so long. They were distracting. Worrying about other people only took her eyes off the goal. When she had no one to think about but herself, it was easy to throw herself into her work with the dedication she'd shown during the war, not caring what became of her or what anyone thought, so long as they showed respect. Now it was all about the way she presented her body. Whether she was attractive enough to hold the attention of the men she was forced to work with — or if she was attractive enough to hold the attention of her own husband-to-be. Had she known the truth before Kael asked her to marry him, things would have been different. She cared about him. Possibly even loved him. But she never would have opened her heart simply to be stabbed and torn into pieces, to bleed over the hands of the one holding the knife.

She was already through the door and half way down the hallway before she realized she'd even moved away from the bedside. Maeri was on her heels, whispering her name worriedly, begging her to slow her pace. "Leyna, what it is? What is wrong?"

Maeri's fingers grabbed at Leyna's skirts, trying to pull her back, shortening the length of her strides. The confusion was too much for Leyna to bear. For so many years she'd been the perfect image of calm and grace while her head was a constantly raging sea of confusion. She doubted she even knew who she was anymore. And why should she know? No one else did.

A novel could be written of the mistakes she'd made. Thirty-four years. Such a superficial amount of time among her people! And yet she'd experienced more in those years than many experienced in their entire lifetime. She'd made more mistakes than many of her kinsmen would make throughout centuries. How could she even pretend that she had everything together, perfectly planned out, watching it unfold before her exactly as she intended it to be?

No. Nothing was what she wanted it to be. Her intentions would have brought her and Reina together years ago. Almost *decades* ago. Nearly twenty years since she'd stuffed fabric into that borrowed gown of Cady's, thinking she would be able to convince anyone that she was a woman. The only reason anyone believed it was because Thade had told them it was so and they listened. They trusted him. And he kept the wool pulled over their eyes for a girl he didn't even know himself.

That man now was suffering. She was suffering. Her friends were all suffering. Intentions aside, there was no changing the dark path life was hurtling her down. Still pretending to be older and wiser than she really was. Would there ever be a time when she could stop all the lies and pretending and just be herself? This time the lies had bound her to a man she no longer knew. How utterly fitting it was! She'd lied to him for the better part of six years. He knew nothing of her either. What a perfect couple they made. A marriage of lies and deception.

There was no way out of it. Not now. Not yet. The lies would have to continue if they wanted to have any chance at saving their people. She would have to keep up the façade in order to get closer to the people who would either help her to achieve her goal, or end her suffering with death.

But revenge! If she let herself die, her mother's life and death would have been in vain. Her mother did everything for her. All of the sacrifices her mother made had been for her, so that she could be free. So that she could live a normal life. This was just another sacrifice Leyna would have to make in honor of her mother. In honor of Reina's father and sister who died trying to protect them. Even if Reina couldn't see the love she held for her, she would see that their murderers were brought to justice.

But it was frightening. The one emotion she'd most tried to deny feeling. She was afraid. Not only of the mission, and of death, but of life itself. The web she was weaving would eventually become too tangled and there was no saying what would happen then. Happiness would be impossible. But there were more important things in life than happiness. Weren't there?

"Leyna, stop!"

Suddenly obeying Maeri's commands, Leyna ceased her long strides, coming to a halt in front of the door of the house. Clumsily Maeri collided into Leyna's back, stumbling awkwardly as she tried to regain her balance. Inhaling sharply, Leyna tried to hold in a cry of pain at the pressure of Maeri's body against the bandage covering the wound left by the needle.

"I cannot answer your question, Maeri. I have no way to know what is wrong. All I know is that I have become something terrible and in the end I fear I will only hurt those closest to me. I think it would be best if I left now before I do anything else which will only worsen the pain I have already caused."

"Why would you think you have hurt anyone? If anything, you are the one who is suffering. Not us."

Leyna's shoulders sank forward, the aching in her back exacerbated by the motion. "When everything is revealed, I fear I will be left alone in the wake of everything I have done." She turned toward Maeri, grimacing, desperately trying to hold back the tears stinging in her eyes. "How horrible it feels to realize that I do not even know all I have done. Every day I find something else that has been caused by me and I did not even know until it was too late."

"You aren't making much sense, Leyna. You should come and sit down. You must have so much built up that you need to talk about. It might help you to get it out."

Maeri's emerald eyes were so genuine. A part of Leyna's heart was warmed at the honesty she saw there, the concern. And Leyna had no way of knowing what her friend had experienced over the last six years, dedicating her life to watching Leyna, to be there for her if anything went awry. Such a selfless existence. Yet here Leyna found herself drowning in her own depression. She felt so selfish!

She couldn't let the conversation revolve around her. After all that Maeri had given up to be with her, walking away from Faustine's and a chance at a happy and prosperous marriage to a wealthy man of position. Leyna owed her more than what she was giving now. "Actually, I would rather talk about you," she smiled, a little oddly. "You have been simply glowing all evening in the presence of Lord Feolan. I want to hear all about you both. Has he been courting you?"

"What?" Her face was crimson. Leyna had managed to strike a chord somewhere, instantly relaxing the strained lines of Maeri's face, replacing them with the excited smile Leyna had seen so many times while they were in Tanispa. "No. No, he is not courting me. But I think he might want to," she whispered, her tone hushed to avoid being overheard by the men in the bedroom. "I want him to, at least. He is absolutely perfect in every way. When I think about him, my heart flutters and I feel like wings of butterflies are waving about in my stomach. I loathe the time when I must leave him again to return to Dalonshire, but I know he will come visit me. He likes to surprise me on occasion by showing up at my door."

Something about the innocent excitement in Maeri's eyes warmed Leyna's heart, dousing the intolerable self-pity which had been threatening to drive her insane. "He comes to visit you? That alone sounds to be a good sign of his intentions. Has he said anything to imply his feelings?"

"I think he almost kissed me this evening. We were sitting there on the settee, discussing our concerns in regards to the future. Somehow we got on the topic of what would happen to the two of us, and he said he hoped that no matter what happened, that I would still stay in Siscal. With him. He leaned in close to me, but I panicked," she breathed. "I leapt up from the settee, claiming I had heard something outside the door and the gods saw fit to enforce my lie by bringing you here."

"Why did you panic?" Leyna laughed. "You were always the one so anxious to experience such things. I never would have expected you to choke at such a moment."

"Lord Feolan is not just any man. He is like an image from my dreams. I fear that if I let myself give in so completely that I will wake up and find none of it to be real and my heart will break. Have you ever felt that way about anyone before? Kael, perhaps? Tell me about the engagement? I cannot believe you kept it a secret."

Guilt quickly swam back up inside her. She knew it was inevitable that the topic would turn to her again. Maeri loved gossip, and it was easier to do when the conversation was not aimed at her own personal life. It required her to coax others into talking about themselves. "I think I may have felt something like that before with him, yes." She gazed absently into the distance. A vague memory in the back of her mind told her there had been sparks between her and Kael at one time. Though those sparks had long since been doused after the truth was revealed. "When he and I first met, I feared it was more lust than love. When we were together, all I could think about were his lips, his arms, the curve of the muscles on his body —"

"Are they anything like the way you described the Consul's?" Maeri grinned. It was intended as a lighthearted joke to bring back the laughter of their younger days, but something in it hit hard inside Leyna's heart. She wished she understood what it was.

"I have made it a point over the years to not think about the Consul in that way. It is not appropriate of me to, and especially now while he is sick — and I am betrothed. My thoughts should not be on the muscles of another man."

Linking her elbow around Leyna's, Maeri guided them toward the sitting area, lowering down casually on the settee, gazing excitedly into Leyna's eyes. "One only has to see the way you look at the Consul to know you care deeply for him. When Feolan told me what you had done to save him, I couldn't believe it. That is true devotion and loyalty there. You were willing to risk your own life to save his."

"I would do the same for any of my friends," Leyna waved her hand distractedly. "I would take an arrow for you, even." She couldn't help but laugh at the thought. It was true. There was no denying it. And her friends couldn't argue her courage to back up those words.

"The way you did for the Prince?" Maeri smiled. "You are so brave, Leyna. I could never do the things you do. I hope you know how much we all respect you and appreciate everything you have done for us, and our people. If we are able to stop this war, you will be a legend."

"I do not want to be a legend." The tears were coming back. A wave of panic came over her, not wanting to let Maeri see her like this. "All I want is for our people to be safe. I do not do this for glory or self-gain."

Maeri craned her neck, looking around Leyna toward the hallway. The house was silent. Not even the sound of the doctors bustling about Thade's bedside could be heard out here, blocked by the thick walls. Satisfied no one was coming, Maeri took Leyna's hand in hers, the playfulness leaving her eyes, replaced by a look of concern. "We never had a chance to speak in any depth with one another after I came here from Tanispa and found you at Zander's home. Some things were discussed that day which I have not forgotten and I feel now it would be only right for me to ask you about them."

"Yes, life has been a bit of a long and twisted road since the night of the masque. I miss being able to sit with you and just talk about nothing in particular – though you clearly seem to have something specific in mind which troubles you."

"Zander spoke that day about you and Feolan. Something about a kiss, or an interest of some kind," Maeri said quietly. "I should have asked you about it long ago, before I let my heart settle on him. Was there something between the two of you before? Am I somehow coming between you both in my hopes of winning his heart?"

Leyna smiled, relieved by the innocence of the questions. She'd feared it would be something more drastic. This was a matter of little importance in her mind. She was happy for Maeri to have found Feolan. They deserved to be together. After everything

Feolan had been through, Maeri would be perfect for him to ease the pain his last relationship had caused.

"Goodness no," she shook her head. "Feolan and I are close friends, yes, but we have never been anything more than that, nor would we ever be. The situation Zander alluded to was pure happenstance. We kissed, but it was under duress, and not because either one of us necessarily harbored any deeper feelings for the other. You have no need to worry about it. I would be happy for you both and fully support his courting you. And you know Lady Faustine would be proud."

Maeri chuckled, looking almost giddy at Leyna's words. "I am so glad to hear that. I have been so worried! Tell me, then," she said suddenly, curling her legs up under her on the settee, her eyes brightening with excitement. "Is he a good kisser?"

Mouth agape, Leyna stared in disbelief at Maeri, completely thrown by her question. Inappropriate in so many ways, and yet inside she wanted to sit there and laugh with her. To discuss it the way they'd whispered about boys when they were younger and too inexperienced to actually know what they were talking about. "Maeri!" she exclaimed. "I cannot answer that question. Especially not here, and preferably not anywhere."

"Of course you can answer it!" Maeri pleaded. "You are the only one I know who can, and I think I have a right to know what I am getting myself into."

"You amaze me," Leyna chortled, rolling her eyes heavenward. She couldn't believe she was actually going to answer her. "If you must know, I would say that he is. I have little to compare it to, but if I had to rate him against Kael, he would be the victor. He was more tender. It was somehow passionate without feeling as though he would swallow you whole."

Maeri giggled. "Are you saying your man is not a good kisser?"

Contemplating her words, Leyna furrowed her brow, overcome with a burst of laughter. She was nervous. The entire conversation felt completely wrong but for some reason she couldn't help but indulge herself in it. Making light of the situation helped to ease the pain and heaviness which had come over her heart. "I believe I am, now that I think on it. But Kael has other redeeming qualities. For instance, he has on many occasions risked himself to protect me. And if anyone says anything even remotely insulting about me, he would fight them without hesitation, to defend my honor. Those things always seemed to matter more than whether he knew how to use his lips."

"Over the years, I have seen the ladies the Consul and Lord Feolan have courted. I am always worried I will not be good enough," Maeri confided, leaning in close to Leyna's ear to avoid being overheard. "I was not exactly Faustine's most prized pupil. We both know that," she grinned. "Feolan needs a woman who is skilled in the ways of the court and able to carry herself like a lady. I fear I may be a bit too free-spirited for him."

A feeling like a dagger pierced through her chest. The Consul had courted a lady? Of course he had! What did she expect? He was a man, a very handsome one, of great power, position, and rank. The women of the court would likely be weeping in their rooms, praying for him to look their way.

To her, she couldn't imagine him being with anyone. None of the women could possibly be good enough for him. Superficial and only caring about how to better serve their family and raise their social standing. He deserved someone more genuine. Someone who loved him for who he really was, and not what title the Queen had bestowed upon him. But she couldn't expect him to remain single forever. It was the way life worked. He would marry some undeserving woman who would then bear his children to carry on the family line. He would eventually have to forget about Leyna. To move on from the shady business he dealt in now. His life would go on without Leyna in it, and she would be left, cold and alone, in the arms of a husband she no longer knew if she loved.

"Leyna?"

"Hmm?"

Blinking her eyes, Leyna realized that she had fallen silent. Warmth radiated in her cheeks. What a strange line of thought to have about her friend! But it was all true. She would never approve of any woman Thade might choose. Lucky for him, her opinion didn't matter.

"Your eyes got a little starry on me. What are you thinking about? Did I say something wrong?"

"Oh, no," Leyna laughed, her nervousness adding a noticeable tremor to her voice. "I was just trying to picture the women the Consul might choose to court. They must be stunning to look at. Noblewomen have always been a target of my envy. I wish I could conduct myself with the same grace and poise as they do. The ease in which they carry themselves in these ridiculous gowns which make breathing nearly impossible, let alone movement. I suppose I felt a little bit of jealousy."

"Jealousy? At their ability to move about and breathe easily in their clothing, or in the fact that they have sought the arm of the Consul?"

"Why would I be jealous of them for seeking the Consul's arm?"

"Because you are a woman. And he is a man. A very sexy man, if I do say so myself," Maeri winked. "Any girl would be jealous of the one he chose, and it must be worse for one who has known him for so long."

"Maeri, I am engaged," Leyna argued. "That simple fact should tell you that I hold no jealousy for any woman with whom the Consul finds happiness."

Maeri inhaled sharply. It was as if Leyna's words had been like the crack of a whip, the lighthearted sparkle in her eyes disappearing in a flash. "Leyna, you are a wonderful woman, and an even greater friend, but you have always been absolutely horrible when it comes to sharing your feelings. You lie to everyone about them, and I know you do not do it intentionally. I am convinced you do it because you also lie to yourself. You force yourself to think you don't feel anything, and it's not healthy for you. In the end, it will only make you unhappy. Why can you not – just once – admit that you might actually feel something?"

"Because I no longer know what to feel!" The words burst forth from her, filled with an emotion she hadn't intended to release, echoing loudly through the quiet room.

She knew Maeri was right. She did hide her feelings from everyone, but it was what she had to do! To open up to anyone would leave her vulnerable, and she couldn't risk that. She would start to let down her walls, and all of her secrets would pour forth, and she would be ruined. They would hate her for the lies. And she would no longer be good enough for them. In a society that cared so much about position and money, no one would be able to accept her for what she was. It had been the cold hard truth she'd come to realize when she was still a child and now, even more than ever, she knew it was the way things would always be.

"I think you know how you feel, but you are afraid of it." Maeri's voice was eerily calm. Her words cut through Leyna, deep into her core, with the accuracy of the statement. She couldn't be more right. But Leyna couldn't admit that to her. If she admitted it, Maeri would only want to know more about what was going on inside her mind, and she couldn't discuss it. It was too painful to think about, and speaking of it out loud was out of the question.

"Maeri," she whispered. "You are a beautiful woman. You come from a respectable family and were raised and trained to be accepted among the nobility. Your heart is kind and your free spirit is a trait that only adds to your beauty. You are honest, which is something many women of any position cannot claim, and these traits make you better than all of them, and Feolan would be a fool not to marry you. I would tell him that to his face if I had to, in order to make him see it. On the other hand, I have none of those things. I fall short in more places than you could ever know because I have kept them hidden, and I am sorry but it must remain that way. My path has led me to Kael, and while he may not have been the first choice in my heart, he is soon to be my husband and I love him, and I owe him my loyalty and respect, which requires me to not think on any other feelings I might have thought I felt a long time ago."

Maeri sighed at Leyna. "If a man loves you – and I mean really loves you – he wouldn't care about money or position, or the lack thereof. He would want you exactly how you are; and you are a wonderful person, Leyna. Any man who knows you would be able to attest to it. There is something about you that no other woman has. I mean, just think about it. Faustine will brag for the rest of her life on how you were asked to dance by both of our Queen's sons in the same night, one of which is known to never to do that. He saw something in you, and that should mean something."

For the first time, Leyna found herself feeling completely exposed. Maeri had a way with words which touched her deeply. It was enough to make her question all of the decisions she'd made in her life. She had been foolish. In her mind it made sense to accept Kael's proposal that night because she convinced herself he was the best that she could have. And while it remained a nagging truth in the back of her mind, she knew it should not have been something she took so lightly.

She should have talked to someone. But who? Zander would have laughed at her. And with good reason. Kael was a joke to him, but he didn't know him the way she did. No one knew the things he had done to help her and all the times he stood by her side. She cared about him dearly and yet it had taken only one night back in Thade's presence for her to fall again to her childish infatuation, causing her to second-guess everything. It wasn't fair to Kael. And it wasn't fair to her.

"Maeri, I love Kael," she sighed. "I know he has made some mistakes, but I have to stand beside him. I have to help him through them. He needs me now, more than ever. Regardless of what anyone says, he is a good man, and he will make me happy. He did before, and I have faith he will do so again. Please try to trust me on that."

"I hope you are right." Standing up from the settee, Maeri opened her arms to Leyna. With a smile, Leyna went to her, wrapping her in a warm embrace. She wasn't entirely convinced, but it didn't change the fact that her argument was true. If things were going to work out, she would have to put forth the effort.

There was just so much working against her. And Zander's concerns about Kael's current loyalty were justified by Kael's actions, and telling him the truth about her now was out of the question. It would take a great deal of work to get things back to where they had been before everything blew up in her face.

"I really should be getting back," she whispered. "As much as I would prefer to stay here with you and Feolan to make sure the Consul is getting better, if Kael comes to my room and finds me missing again, I am not sure I will be able to explain my way out of it. He is already suspicious of me."

"Just be careful, Leyna. I have a really bad feeling about things. About all of this, with the Ven'shal, and the war you spoke of. Something does not feel right."

"We will know more soon enough. I hope to know by morning when we will learn if our meeting with Rohld has been approved. If possible, I will try to send a letter to you here to inform you of what I find out." Casting one last glance toward the hallway, Leyna bowed her head, moving quickly in the direction of the door. "If anything happens, please try to find a way to contact me. We should be at Zander's home for a few days. And take care of Feolan. No more panicking if he gets close to you."

At the sound of Maeri's soft laughter, Leyna slipped through the door. The color of the sky told her the sun was already well on its way to rising. The others were sure to have been home for hours. It might already be too late to get around Kael's suspicions again, but she needed to move fast. With a final nod, she accepted her cloak from Maeri's hands, sliding it over her arms and head to conceal her from view, running off into what was left of the night.

Chapter Sixteen

Leyna was surprised to discover Oksuva's carriage still missing when she arrived at Zander's house. Part of her was grateful. It allowed her a safe return through the window of her room, pushing her bed back into position against the wall, without fear of being overheard by the others. It called out to her, the comfort of the warm blankets. Relief from the aching of her back where the doctor had inserted the needle.

She shuddered at the thought. Everything about her evening confused her, not making any sense how so much could have happened in such a short amount of time. Throughout a single night she had endured a heartbreaking reunion with her long lost Reina after coming so close to those responsible for her mother's death. She had witnessed Kael being too cozy with Oksuva for comfort, while at the same time she had gone against his wishes in returning to the Consul's home. She was thankful that she'd chosen not to inquire of the doctor about the procedure he had performed on her. Her stomach had been so twisted all night that she might have lost the little bit of wine she'd consumed while at Malic's.

Sleep came and went, restlessly, bringing no dreams with it through her tossing and turning, waking to every noise that invaded her ears. The window was brightened by a sun well-risen into the sky by the time she caught the sound of the front door opening and closing. Could it be they were only just returning home? *Close your eyes*, she urged herself. There would be time to ask questions after they had slept off the alcohol.

The house remained quiet with the stillness of its sleeping occupants when she pulled herself out of the bed. Outside the sky had already begun to darken into the deeper shades of blue and grey, bringing the night upon them once again. Leyna sat in the small, confining room, unable to bring herself to leave it. What was there for her out there but more pretending, playing the role she'd grown so tired of?

Footsteps outside her door caught her attention, her eyes lifting to stare toward the sound with uncertainty. It was hard to say who it might be. There were reasons for many of the others to come to her. Zander was aware she'd gone to the Consul's and was likely anxious to hear word of his condition, and above all, his reaction to the news they had learned. Oksuva, on the other hand, was probably angry with her for her behavior at the meeting. She could be coming to chide her for it — or to give her new instructions based on whatever word Kyros left before he took his leave of Malic's.

Deep inside, she knew it would be Kael. She could almost sense him through the wooden door. There was no anger in what she felt, which was reassuring. It meant she had possibly made her trip to the Consul's unnoticed. That was one fight she might be able to avoid, if so.

"Eleni?"

She nodded to herself. Kael had come, as expected. He sounded calm. Sober. Perhaps in a state of mind which would allow her to speak with him of her concerns. Her heart fluttered at the thought.

Rising from where she was seated on the bed, she rushed over to the door, sliding the lock from its position to open it. A faint smile passed over her lips at the sight of him.

For the first time in a long time she saw him the way she did the day they met. The gentleness in his eyes had returned, though tinged with the red of the vessels, blood-shot from lack of sleep and too much wine the night before. Although the anger was not there in his expression, nothing could bring back the bright glow that had diminished from his eyes. They were dull, covered by the thin film of grey over white, resembling those of the Ven'shal. Her smile faded away at the thought. Could it be that it worsened since she saw him last?

"Kael," she whispered, opening the door wider to allow him entrance to the room. "Come in, please. There is much we need to discuss."

Moving quietly, he made his way past her, following her motions with his gaze while she closed the door behind him. "I have been thinking," he stated. "It pains me when I realize all of the mistakes I have made over the last few weeks. Many of which have directly affected you. Us. I wish I had an explanation which would make it all forgivable, but I do not. There is nothing I can say other than that I have been a fool, and I am sorry."

Leyna leaned back against the door, unsure of how to respond. There were no words to describe the things she wanted to say. Her desire to hear his side of the story was too great to interrupt him in fear of distracting his line of thought.

"I can assure you that prior to the incident of which you have become aware, I have never been unfaithful to you. The night before Oksuva's anniversary party, I had been drinking. I admit I was depressed over some details which have plagued my mind since I met you. Things I have wanted to tell you, and should have before asking you to marry me. But I wanted you to be my wife. So when Oksuva came to me that night and asked me what was troubling me, I was too drunk to know better than to reveal everything to her about my love for you, and my intentions of marrying you. She sympathized for me, knowing Mikel would never allow it. I was thinking about you and then the next thing I remember is being in her room when the door flew open and Mikel came in. I suppose fear was enough to create that sober moment to realize what I had done, but by then it was too late."

Sitting down on the bed, Kael leaned his upper body forward, supporting his elbows on his knees, propping his chin on his hands. "Mikel is crueler than I ever realized. He knew it would cause me more punishment to dabble in his magic than it would to simply kill me for the dishonor I caused him. There is so much riding on my position with his family that I couldn't simply deny him. I had to swear to him my continued loyalty and do everything he demanded to prove it. It makes me sick to think of what I have done, but I did it for our people. For our Queen. But the part which frightened me was that deep down inside, I wanted to do it. I wanted to know what it felt like. And that caused me more distress than anything you could imagine. It led me to continue seeking the wine to escape the confusion and self-hatred I felt over these feelings, and in my drunkenness I continued to fall to the draw of the magic even after I decided to never practice it again."

"If you will let me, I could help you to cleanse yourself of the unnecessary taint to your soul this has created," Leyna replied quietly, lowering herself down beside Kael on the bed. Resting her hand gently on his shoulder she leaned in, kissing him softly on the cheek. "I know it cannot be erased, but you can still be redeemed. If you want to be. But you have to really want it in your heart, or you could keep falling, and lose yourself. I could never bear to see that happen. I still love you, regardless of what you have done. Do not ever think any differently."

"Eleni, I have to be honest with you," Kael sighed heavily. "I am not what you think I am. I lied to you about my involvement with the Consul the day I introduced you to him. I work for him, collecting information for Queen Vorsila about Mikel and Oksuva and those they work with. I have told him about you. He knew a great deal about you already when he met you. The interest he has shown in you over the years when discussing you has had me concerned. I worry he will try to take you away from me. Or that Zander will try to take you back. I am a very jealous man, Eleni. If I caused you any distress yesterday, I did not intend to, but the wine was hindering my ability to control myself, and knowing you had gone to the Consul's home, alone, has still been eating away at me."

"I already told you, Kael. Nothing happened. Nor will it," Leyna assured him. "Feolan is a gentleman and is interested in another woman, and at the same time the Consul was extremely ill and is bedridden. I can forgive your jealousy if you will trust me on this. And as for your involvement with them in your work, I have suspected it since I met you. You are not evil like the rest of the people in that house in Dalonshire. I knew there had to be some other reason you were there."

"I just ask that you not go there without me. It is not proper for a woman to be paying visits to men alone anyway, without adding the fact that you are engaged. If you want to go there, you need only tell me, and we will arrange to go together. Especially now that you know the truth."

Her guilt was like a knife in her gut at his request. Here he was, baring his soul to her, and she still held her secrets, offering him nothing in return. She couldn't. And certainly not until she'd seen his progress in fighting against the magic taking him over. The Consul couldn't be allowed to see him like that. It would ruin Kael, and although she hated to keep secrets from Thade, for now she believed it was for the best. Once Kael had regained control of himself, it would be easier to explain the situation to Thade and Feolan. If Kael failed — well, she would have to cross that bridge if she came to it. She refused to think on it until then.

"We have a few days, I am sure, during which we can try to rectify everything that has come between us," she said. "You can stay here with me in the evenings instead of going out to the taverns with the others and we can start working on cleansing your body and mind."

Kael dejectedly shook his head. "No," he frowned. "We have no time at all. Kyros and Oksuva have come to an agreement. He found her this morning to explain the conditions he was requiring and she didn't even try to bargain him down, merely accepted the terms without question. I don't know what the details were exactly, but I know he has already sent Oran ahead with word to Damir that Oksuva is coming."

"Damir?"

"Damir Rohld," Kael replied, oblivious to the sudden stricken expression on her face. "You have been specifically requested to accompany them by Kyros — and I have been requested to remain here in Siscal."

It was true. Rohld was the same man Thade had warned her about. The man who once called himself her father. She was frightened by the thrill that went through her entire body at the thought. Finally, she would be face-to-face with the man who had chased them from their home. The man who betrayed their people and their Queen to consort with the Ven'shal. Now, to see where he had ended up, banished from Tanispa and working to organize a war of grand proportions against them all, and she had a chance to stop him. It seemed so easy in her mind to go to the meeting and strike him dead, caring nothing for the hatred and punishment Oksuva would threaten for it.

Oh, but how foolish that would be! If she raised a hand to Damir, she would find herself lost to the wrath of Kyros and Oran, and whatever other men Damir had in his service now. They would know who she was, and Oksuva and Mikel would send their own people after her for the deception.

Why did things have to be so complicated? It would have to be done with caution in order to avoid suspicion from the others. She needed to get Damir alone. Unarmed, if possible. But then, if he was skilled in the art of combat, his hands and feet would be weapons enough to defend against her. She lacked the training she needed to take on a battle of that degree. And if he suspected her at all to be the child of his ex-wife, the woman he was rumored to have had murdered, he would never allow her close enough for a chance at retaliation. He would have her killed with a wave of his hand. She would die, nameless and alone.

"You look as though you have been run through with a blade. What troubles you, my darling?"

"Nothing," she lied. Forcing a smile, she rubbed his back, not wanting to let him know the new fears racing through her mind. "Who has requested you to remain here in Siscal? I would much prefer you to be there with me when Oksuva meets this man. I do not feel safe going there alone."

"Though I am loath to consent to it, Kyros has asked me to stay behind. He has something he needs my assistance with, but has not given any details beyond that. You will be going with Oksuva and the others to the town of Kaipoi, which is just over the border in Carpaen from Tanispa. It is a week's ride from here, if the journey is made without stop. Oksuva intends to leave as soon as she awakens from her drunken stupor."

"Kaipoi?" Leyna asked, still bewildered by everything. "That is further away than Sivaeria. Why do they have to travel so far?"

"Because Damir doesn't dare step into the borders of Tanispa. Not until he has raised the army that Oksuva intends to help him build, and if that happens, there is no telling what will become of our people."

Always moving so quickly! Never had there been plans to go anywhere with Oksuva that she did not insist they leave immediately. It left no time for Leyna to get word to Feolan and Maeri, the way she had promised, so that they could know where she was going and what was happening. She needed to let Feolan know the name of the mysterious Rohld. He would pass it along to Thade when he was feeling healthier, and Thade would understand her concerns. Then again, she also feared he would try to find a way to prevent her from making the meeting.

Thade wouldn't do it. If she wrote in the letter and expressly told him she wanted to go, he would let her. Though he argued with her constantly over the things she got herself into, he had never once told her no. It was like he didn't know how to, and yet she had witnessed him say that word to so many others over the years. A miserable laugh built up inside her. How could it be that a man of his position would be so easily swayed by a lowly girl such as herself?

Catching sight of the closet, Leyna felt her mind spark with an idea, remembering vaguely two mornings past, the cloak Feolan had provided her for cover when he saw her back to the house. There were pockets inside it. Deep enough to hold a letter without being noticed. And if she folded the fabric, it would conceal it even more from the prying eyes of whoever played courier. She could pen a note to Feolan. But who could she have take it? Kael would be remaining behind, but she couldn't let anyone in that house see his eyes.

"Well, if I am to be leaving so soon, I should make sure my belongings are packed and ready for travel," she nodded, standing up from the bed. "It will not take me long, if you wish to come back and see me one last time before we go. You can help load my bag into the carriage."

"As you wish," Kael smiled, hesitantly. He looked uncomfortable with the situation, and how could she blame him? He would be left behind in Siscal for weeks without her, never knowing where she was or what was happening at any given moment.

Another wave of fear passed through her. He had made it clear that the sorcery allowed him to see her when she was away. What if his worry led him to utilize the magic again, out of fear for her safety?

No. She wouldn't let that happen. She would make sure to express her disapproval of it before they parted ways. For him to continue to use it in her absence would go against everything they discussed in hopes of helping to save him. "Meet me back here in an hour, then," she said, walking with him anxiously toward the door. "There is still much we need to speak on before I leave, so do not be late. I will be waiting."

The next two weeks passed in a blur of landscapes through the carriage window. Conversations were dominated by Oksuva and Gislan, chattering excitedly about Kyros and Damir. Gislan had acquired something of an obsession with Kyros. She couldn't talk about him enough, rambling about his body and his lips, and how she intended to seduce him, to have him for her own. While she spoke, she kept her eyes on Zander, watching for him to become jealous at the thought, only to grow more agitated at Zander's lack of interest.

They bypassed much of the desert by following the border along Carpaen and Siscal, moving through the lusciously green forests of Tanispa. Leyna was amazed by the fertile lands of Kaipoi, given its close proximity to the harsh heat and sands, managing to maintain its climate from where it lay to the furthest northern reaches of the country.

When they reached their rooms at the inn in Kaipoi, Oran was waiting for them, providing directions to a location where Damir agreed to meet. He required them to wait another week before he would accept them for a visit. Another week with her trapped in the company of these people she couldn't stand.

"So what exactly did you do to anger Gislan," Leyna asked Zander curiously, gazing at her reflection in the tiny vanity mirror of her room. "She has been doing everything she can to get under your skin and you could not be less affected by it. You are going to drive the woman insane."

"She is already insane," he laughed. "I have been enjoying the freedom from her constant need for attention. Do you have any idea how hard it is to pretend to enjoy her company? It is even worse when we are alone. I would much rather kiss a ghereac than touch her."

"What a horrible thought." Twisting her hair around her index finger, Leyna toyed with the spiral curls she'd chosen to wear for their meeting with Damir, hoping to make her appearance look less similar to that of her mother's. She knew she bore a remarkable resemblance, which would only make matters worse when faced with Damir. She couldn't expect him to have forgotten the woman he once called his wife. Inevitably, she would bring back the memory in his mind. She just had to make sure it wasn't quite so obvious.

"If you must know, she caught me looking at you while we were in the carriage, on our way to meet with Kyros in Siscal," Zander explained. "You have to know that you looked stunning that night. I couldn't keep my eyes off you, and since she still believes that you and I were intimate, she took offense to it, viewing you as a challenge and doing everything in her power to make me jealous. But I really don't care. She is worthless to me. She has not been able to provide any pertinent information for the mission in years. The only benefit my relationship with her has had is that I was able to still see you every once in a while to make sure you were being treated well."

Rising from the vanity stool, Leyna smoothed out the linen fabric of her chemise. "It must be killing her to know you came up here to visit with me, rather than her." Absently, she pulled the gown she intended to wear from the closet, laying it across the bed to inspect it. "Under normal circumstances, I never would have allowed you in here while I need to get dressed, but you are the only person here I can stand and I cannot tie up my own corset."

"You women are all crazy for wearing those. But I like it."

With practiced fingers, she wrapped the corset around her midsection, fastening up the clasps in the front. The stays forced her back straight, improving her posture as she motioned for Zander to come closer, pointing over her shoulder to the laces. "I typically do not wear one, but this dress requires it and Oksuva insists this be the one I wear."

Her eyes trailed over the deep forest-green shade of the dress laid out over the white sheets. The neckline formed a diamond shape over the chest, creating an opening to reveal the skin before connecting again at the top of the breastbone to elegantly cover the throat. Tight at the upper arms, the sleeves came down to the elbow where they flared out, draping down with a bell-shaped design, accenting the green with a pure white floral lace around the edges.

She coughed at the tugging of Zander's hands over the laces, drawing the corset tighter over her ribs. He was surprisingly skilled with it. Leyna wondered how many corsets he would have had to lace and unlace to become so accustomed to the design. "You are more familiar with women's garments than I gave you credit for."

"I have been around a fair share of them," he chuckled, leading Leyna over to the high posts on the bed to hold onto, the pull becoming more severe. She circled her arms around the wood, nearly falling over from the force of Zander's hands. "I know, you must think me terrible. It is nothing like it sounds, however."

"I am sure it isn't. Those poor girls." Her breath left her again with the final jerk of the corset laces. "Though perhaps you were doing them a favor in helping them to breathe by taking off their clothes."

Snickering to himself, Zander moved around Leyna to the bed, lifting the dress over her head. "While the conversation amuses me, I find it hard to believe you asked me here to talk about my excursions with women's clothing. You looked a bit troubled. Was there something on your mind?"

Well, that was an understatement. Everything was on her mind. It had been so easy to convince herself the meeting would be to her advantage, but now that the day was upon her, she was not so sure. "I need to tell you something, and it cannot ever go beyond these walls," she sighed. Awkwardly, she shifted the dress down over the rest of her body, her movement limited by the stiff stays of the corset. "Not even the Consul is aware of this, and it must remain that way until I have an opportunity to explain it to him."

"You have my attention and concern, Leyna. I will speak of it to no one."

"I have a bit of a history with this man. Damir Rohld." Hearing the words come from her lips, she regretted speaking of it. Why did she feel so compelled to share this information with Zander? Maybe because he was the only person there who would be able to help her if things went awry? "While I cannot and will not elaborate on the details, it is important that you know this situation could be very dangerous for me. When I was a child, he wanted me dead. I doubt his opinion has changed much over the years. If he recognizes me, it could ruin everything."

"What kind of history could you possibly have with this man?"

"I said I would not elaborate. I was not speaking in jest," Leyna stated flatly. "In time, I am sure all will be revealed, whether I desire it or not, but for now, while I still have some say in the matter, it will remain unspoken. I ask that you respect that, and simply promise me you will try to help me if anything happens."

"Of course," he nodded. His hands moved up the buttons on the back of Leyna's dress, fastening them securely into place. "Stay by me when we get there. Keep your head down, eyes to the ground. Oksuva may want to have you stand out to him, but you need to do everything you can to blend in. There is only so much I can do, however. If he demands to see you, we have to obey. We can't risk the whole mission unless we know for a fact there is no other choice."

Before Leyna could respond, Yasar's voice sounded through the door, raspier than she was accustomed to. "Bedrick has arrived. Lady Oksuva has asked that you come down as you are. There is no more time to waste."

Hurrying to the door, Leyna pulled it open, breathless, but wanting to make sure Yasar was witness to her being fully clothed and ready to go. She suspected the order from Oksuva was indicative of a suspicion regarding her being alone with Zander. Leyna didn't want to risk any false rumors getting back to Kael after they had only just managed to work through their troubles. "We will follow you down, then," she huffed, placing her hand over her stomach. The corset was so tight she could hardly breathe. The exertion of her movement to answer the door only made it worse.

They moved quickly down the stairs to the lobby of the inn, finding Oksuva and Gislan waiting for them. Leyna's chest was burning. It was reminiscent of her illness when the fluid had been crushing her lungs, only this time it was her clothing to blame, and she for some reason was doing so willingly. Why anyone would want to feel so miserable was beyond her grasp.

"I hope we interrupted," Gislan sneered, laughing irritably to herself.

"That requires us to have been doing something which could have been interrupted," Zander smirked. "Unlike you, Eleni knows how to keep her skirts down."

If Leyna could have gotten the breath to laugh, she would have. The expression on Gislan's face was priceless. At first the insult failed to register in Gislan's mind, realization slowly dawning, the finely arched brows over her eyes furrowing in rapidly growing anger. "Or maybe she just knows that you are incapable of satisfying a woman."

"You would be easier to satisfy if you had not bedded every man within the borders of Siscal."

"Oh, stop it!" Oksuva shouted. "I do not have time to deal with your petty lover's quarrel right now. If you cannot act mature for one evening, then I suggest you both just go back to your rooms, because I will not tolerate it." She started to move toward the lobby door, pausing briefly to glance over her shoulder at Gislan. "However, he does have a point, sister. You really should work on a technique called playing hard to get – if you ever come across a man who does not already know that you are easy."

"I am not easy. I am very particular about the men I choose."

"Is that why you were in the presence of Kyros for less than five minutes and had already decided you wanted to crawl into his bed?" Oksuva rolled her eyes. Waving dismissively, she stepped through the door, not giving Gislan a chance to speak.

Leyna followed her out with Zander at her heels. Oran greeted them somberly at the carriage door, his eyes opening wider at Leyna's approach. She hated not being able to read what was in his eyes through the darkness there. It was impossible to know what he was thinking or feeling, those black holes seemingly looking at everything and nothing at the same time, never changing to reveal any emotion.

He helped them into the carriage, taking his seat on one side of Leyna, placing her in the middle between him and Zander. Yasar and Oksuva positioned themselves across the coach. Gislan entered a few moments later, sitting down next to Yasar, staring daggers at Leyna through her narrowed eyes and painted lashes. She relied more on the make-up these days than she had when Leyna first met her. The years were not being kind to her features; making her appear older than her sister, despite Oksuva's climbing age in comparison.

During their ride, Leyna couldn't help but admire Oksuva's regal countenance, show-ing no sign of concern or worry for what would come to pass at the meeting. She was confident. The item she possessed was of great importance and she knew it, counting on it to be enough to gain Damir's favor, as well as his aid in her dark plans. Her dress was golden, accented by jewels everywhere she could find a place for them. Gold-set pearls dangled elegantly from her rounded ears, matching the elaborate necklace and brooch decorating her dainty collarbone. Rings sparkled from nearly every finger on her hands. She could have passed for a woman of rank easily had she chosen to try.

Their silent journey dragged on for nearly three hours with nothing but the sound of the horses' hooves. Leyna was anxious to get out of the cramped carriage. While it was large enough to hold all of them, it was clear to her that the capacity was beyond what was intended, squeezing them in at an uncomfortable proximity to the others.

Stepping down to the moist earth, she felt her slippers sink into the soil. A chill ran through her at the sight of their destination. An open field, surrounded on all sides by trees spreading into the distance, the only method of reaching it being the thin gravel road they had traveled on. From the unkempt grass in the field rose numerous headstones of granite and sandstone, cluttered in some places while others were scat-tered further out, separated by sections of untouched ground.

A cemetery. But why would Damir have requested them to meet there? She had to admit it lent a foreboding feeling to the business. The stories she'd heard of the Ven'shal were enough to make her leery of what Damir's intentions would be. Arcastus was known to be able to raise the dead, though the requirements to do so were beyond Leyna's knowledge. After all, it was his refusal to attempt raising Mescavis's wife which had sparked an entire war. But did anyone really know what Mescavis had done to the corpse? And was it that Arcastus drew the line at reviving it, or was he incapable of doing so?

Off in the distance she could make out a shadowy figure propped up against a large grave marker at the back of the cemetery. It was cloaked, concealing the face from view, the posture resembling that of a man. Broad shoulders, tall, even while leaning.

She didn't want to see him. Her courage was slipping away in his presence, remem-bering the way Damir had looked at her the last night she saw his face. The flashing rage in his eyes. They had not yet been taken over by the inky blackness then, but it had been there, slowly building, growing darker while he summoned the sorcery in his attempts to kill her. *I should have her head on a pike in my yard!* She recalled his words vividly.

Fearfully she turned around. In her panic, she couldn't think clearly enough to maintain her composure, walking straight into the solid form of Oran standing directly behind her. "What is the matter, my dear?" he asked calmly. She shivered at the touch of his skin against her arms, holding her still to look into her eyes. "You look frightened."

"Not at all," she stammered. Silently, she scolded herself for her behavior, hoping it wouldn't draw any unwanted attention to her. "I just wanted to make sure everyone was still coming. I think Lady Oksuva should lead us, since she is the one who has requested the meeting. I would not want to look like I was attempting to over step my bounds."

"You looked as though you were attempting to flee."

"I have no reason to flee. It is an honor to meet Master Rohld," she lied, her eyes shifting pleadingly over to Zander as he stepped from the carriage. Catching her gaze, he crossed the grass to where Oran held her, smiling charmingly.

"I will escort Eleni. I suspect Lady Oksuva would rather you be on her arm during the introductions to your man there."

Oran looked Zander over appraisingly, his head tilting to one side in curiosity. "You do not want to escort the Lady Gislan?"

"I would rather pluck out my own eyes," Zander smirked. "You may want to watch out for her yourself, and send a warning to your man Kyros. She is on the prowl for a new toy to chew up and spit out."

A twitch of a smile passed over a single corner of Oran's mouth. It was quick, but served as the only reaction in his face to reveal a hint of amusement at Zander's words. Giving in to his request, Oran released his hold on Leyna's arms, motioning for her to go to Zander. "Very well. But keep to the front. Damir has expressed an interest in meeting Miss Eleni."

Another wave of panic washed through her. How did he know about her? There was no telling what Kyros and Oran had told him. She feared that Kyros had recognized her. But to have continued the meeting so nonchalantly, making no move to show that he knew. She felt as though they were toying with her like a cat with a mouse, batting her around before they sank their teeth in. It wasn't safe for her to be there.

For the first time since she'd gotten into the business of undercover work, she genuinely wanted out. She was in over her head.

It was a miserable feeling, the truth. Inadequacy. She wasn't sagacious enough to handle this by herself. Things were becoming too personal for her to focus on the mission, and the danger was far greater with these men than it ever was with Mikel, even more so with her past involving them. And no one knew! That was the worst part about it all. If Thade had been aware of the details of her past, he never would have allowed her to come to this meeting, regardless of how difficult it might have been for him to tell her no. And if he'd stood firm on his decision to prevent her from coming, she wasn't sure she would have been able to say no to him either.

Zander was already leading her forward. Oran guided Oksuva through the unevenly spaced headstones, bringing them closer to the casual figure, watching them, scrutinizing, taking in details of their mannerisms before any of them could even say a word. She couldn't see his face, but she could feel his eyes on her. He'd taken note of her so soon. There would be no hiding from him the way she'd hoped to, losing any chance she had of blending in at Zander's side.

Oran stopped them before reaching the man, motioning to remain still while he continued forward, whispering something inaudible to him. Taking advantage of the pause, Oksuva stepped backward, leaning in to speak quietly to their group. "Leave all the talking to me. If he asks you questions, keep your responses short and sweet. I am the one he needs to be dealing with, and I have enough information about his past that I can use against him if necessary."

"What things of his past?" Leyna asked. The question fell from her lips before she had time to second-guess whether it was appropriate.

Oksuva looked her over irritably. "Regarding his ex-wife. Nothing that is any of your business."

"It may not be any of my business, but it would be my suggestion that you not bring any of that up. He could react poorly."

She could feel the eyes of everyone staring at her. They were confused by her, and in awe that she would speak against Oksuva. Not that she cared anymore. If Damir recognized her, she would die there in that cemetery anyway. And if Oksuva were to be so bold as to speak of his past, it was likely everyone else would die along with her.

"Damir will see you now."

Oksuva cast Leyna one last icy glare before turning back around, her lips curling up into a pleasant smile at Oran's approach. Nodding her head, she moved forward again, the others following behind her hesitantly.

As they drew nearer, Damir carefully lowered his hood away from his face, causing Leyna to twitch reflexively with a start. Zander's eyes never moved away from him, but his hand tightened over hers, holding her in place at his side. Her breath came in short, ragged bursts of air, her chest rising and falling rapidly. The corset she was wearing felt suddenly too tight. Constricting.

Oksuva's voice was soft and melodic, but her words were lost to Leyna's frantic ears. The cemetery was spinning around her dizzyingly. She felt ready to faint until Zander's arm slid up around her back, resting gently against the opposite side of her neck. "Stay calm," he whispered. No more than a wispy breeze to her senses. "I will not let anything happen to you, but if you do not regain your senses, you will draw attention to yourself in a manner which I will not be able to talk our way out of."

He was right. And she knew he was, but it was easier said than done, staring into the blackened eyes of the man she once called her father. There had been a time when she'd been excited to see his face, racing to meet him at the door, wrapping her arms lovingly around his shoulders, and he had done the same to her, smiling at her warmly. They had been a happy family. Or it seemed to her at the time. She was so young then! Her mother had been living in torment every day of her life, married to this man, and loving another; the true father of her child.

"You talk too much, woman," Damir's voice cut through Leyna like a knife. It was the voice she remembered from her childhood. Deep and frightening. There was a touch of constant disdain in his tone. "We will discuss the items you are interested in once we have addressed those which I require. Tell me, who is the silent girl standing there behind you?"

"Her?" Oksuva asked, agitated by Damir's distraction. "That is Eleni. She is one of my husband's slaves and no one of importance, though all of your men seem enamored by her for some unknown reason."

For the first time since their arrival, Damir stepped away from the grave he'd been using as a support, moving swiftly past Oksuva to stand in front of Leyna. She shivered.

Shrinking back against Zander, she gazed up at him, amazed at his towering height. She always believed him to be tall, but in her mind it had been because she was a mere child when she saw him last. His expression was stern, brows slanted into what almost looked to be a glare, grabbing her chin in his hand to inspect her face more thoroughly.

His skin was cold. Like ice in the warm country breeze.

Turning to Oran, a silent communication seemed to pass between them as Damir made his way back to Oksuva, folding his arms across his chest impatiently. "They have their reasons, as I have mine. Now, tell me of this artifact."

Mild relief flooded Leyna's mind. She'd escaped his wrath for now, but there was yet time for him to reveal his true intentions. They were still in the middle of nowhere, far away from help if she were to scream for it, and standing in a place where their bodies could be easily disposed of. Silently she prayed her letter had reached Feolan's hands so that he would know to become suspicious if they did not return.

"Years ago I was conducting research regarding the war between the Ven'shal and the Vor'shai. While on a dig at one of the historical sites, we uncovered an amulet resembling that which was said to be worn by Arcastus, documented in the journals of several of his men, fitting every detail. We performed extensive testing and examinations, and it has been proven authentic."

"And what do you know of this amulet?"

"I know it has some link to Arcastus's spirit, even now, after his death. It contains energy that is more powerful than any of my fellow researchers dared to attempt utilizing. They wanted to destroy it," Oksuva laughed. "They feared that in the wrong hands it would cause another war to break out. So I stole it to continue my own research. Unfortunately, my abilities with the energy are weakened by the impurity of my heritage. I thought my husband would be able to help, but he showed little interest in it. I am of the opinion he did not believe it to be the real thing."

Damir thoughtfully stroked his chin, his pale fingers long and slender, like the bones of a skeleton. "So you know essentially nothing?"

"I know that you have been seeking this amulet for decades," she scoffed. "I know it was your search for it which led to your banishment from Tanispa."

"Hold your tongue!"

Leyna flinched at the anger in his tone. It brought back the flood of memories in her mind, hearing her mother's screams. She sensed the treacherous ground Oksuva was treading on bringing up his past. In dealing with Mikel's worthless lackeys of Ven'shal contacts for so many years, she had no experience in how to handle one like Damir. One who knew the intricacies of the sorcery to the extent of those in legend, who had been forced into hiding on threat of immediate death by the Vor'shai. He was dangerous. And sparking his ire was not something anyone should risk.

"Tell me," Damir exhaled, his tone calming. "What exactly are you hoping to get out of this – arrangement – for lack of a better term. If I did wish to barter with you for this amulet, what would you ask in return?"

"I intend to be a part of it all. I want to see Arcastus's body revived from death. And when his army wipes out the Queen and her kingdom in Tanispa, I want to reign at your side. You will need a Queen, and together we could conquer even more than the Vor'shai. We would be like gods."

Oran barely contained a laugh, turning his face away to regain his composure. Damir smirked in amusement, stepping back over to the grave where he'd stood at their approach and leaning his shoulder against it once again. "That sort of bargain would require a good bit more on your end. I would require more than just the amulet of you in order for that to pique my interest. The negotiation table is open. Feel free to lay out what you are willing to offer."

"I would offer you my own men to help with the arrangements of reviving the corpse," Oksuva replied coolly. "It may be necessary that you have good help at your side, given that I have heard your men have proven incompetent in the past."

"My men? Incompetent?"

Oksuva chortled knowingly, narrowing her eyes at Damir. "It is no secret they failed you in the past. Had it been my men, they would not have let that bastard child of your wife's live."

In a flurry of motion Damir was away from the headstone, a dark wave of light shooting from his hands to where Yasar was standing behind Leyna. Instinctively she cried out, cringing away from it, nearly knocking Zander off his feet in her attempt to put distance between it. Yasar's body fell to the ground with a heavy thud at her feet.

"You speak of matters you know nothing of, nor are they any of your business," Damir spat. "Your man is now dead. Tell me how his dying so easily is supposed to make me consider him to be more competent than my own?"

Kneeling beside Yasar, Leyna placed her fingers against his neck, checking for a pulse. There was nothing. His skin remained warm to the touch, but the heart no longer beat in his chest. "He is dead," she whispered, glancing up to Oksuva and Zander hesitantly.

Damir threw his head back, laughing maniacally. "Of course he is dead!" he shouted. "That is how useless you are to me." Raising his arms to the sky, a dark aura built over his hands, swirling and thrashing about between his palms. Slowly drawing his hands apart, he let the shadowy substance shift outward, lowering to the ground.

It spread like a wildfire over the grass. Crawling along the headstones, it crept over the granite slabs, sinking down into the earth again before rolling forward, covering everything in its path. Leyna took a step backward to avoid it, barely missing the toes of her slippered feet.

She could sense the unease of everyone in their group. No one knew what to expect. Such power had never been demonstrated to them before, having only witnessed the mere parlor tricks of Mikel and his friends. And they had been considered so powerful! They were capable of nothing more than cheap illusions.

As the darkness passed, a soft, silver light began to lift out of the ground around the headstones, taking on the shapes and forms of what appeared to be people, their features twisted and disproportioned to their bodies. The green of the grass pulled away, dying rapidly, turning deep brown and then brittle black as though burnt. Nourishment from the decaying plants seemed to feed the smoky, lifelike figures, growing and writhing about on the wind.

Each ghostlike form whirled through the air, the faces slowly taking on greater detail while the legs remained tendrils of wispy clouds floating along the ground.

Leyna was too afraid to move. She'd faced many enemies in her lifetime, but never had she been confronted by a creature that no longer belonged to the realm of the living. They lacked in substance, passing eerily through her body as if she wasn't there, their wide-mouthed expressions locked in silent screams of agony. When they filtered through her skin, she could hear the faint echo of their wailing spirits tugging on her insides. With every pass they grew stronger, striking her with greater force until she could feel the impact, slamming against her chest like a frozen hand.

The figures had them surrounded, jumping from body to body, gathering speed and strength with every round. Fearful, Leyna gathered her energy in a desperate act, pulling it inward and focusing it down to her center, feeling it build between the palms of her hands. Drawing on her internal strength, her shoulders and upper body curved, directing the energy outward in a wave, sending one of the approaching apparitions reeling backward.

With a hiss it regained control, baring its hideously disfigured teeth at Leyna. It was a menacing sight. Ghostly tendrils fluttered out from its skeletal fingers, reaching toward her, taunting her. A whistle passed through it as it inhaled. She stared, unsure of what it was attempting. Spirits had little need for air to breathe, making its actions unnecessary and strained.

A sudden lurching sensation shot through her. Every meridian in her body came to life, the energy flowing outward, away from her center, coursing through her with a speed she'd never experienced, her heart pounding with an unnatural rhythm. Racked by the unseen force, her head snapped backward. Lines of energy began to drift from her body toward the wraithish creature, seeping into its mouth with every breath it drew in. It was like her soul was being sucked from her body. Rendered motionless, she was helpless to the sensation, watching in horror while the others continued to be pushed around by the aimless flight of the spirits.

In a flash, the apparition dissipated before her, leaving behind the hardened features of Damir standing in its place. "Enough," he murmured, directing the remnants of the spirit toward the ground with a flick of his wrist. "There is something about you which makes me less inclined to see you die just yet. Your friends should consider themselves lucky."

Released from the invisible hold of the specter, Leyna collapsed to her knees before Damir, panting for breath, her hands clutching at her chest. Her mind reeled from the confusion at what had happened. None of this felt real. It was like something out of a feverish nightmare, haunting her subconscious mind with the unspeakable horrors that could only happen in dreams.

Easily he cast the remaining spirits away, their smoky tendrils floating back down to sink into the earth around the graves. Seeing her on the ground Zander rushed to Leyna's side, clearly shaken from his own experience. "Are you alright? Are you hurt?"

"She is fine," Damir said dismissively. "But let that be a warning to you, Oksuva. I don't take kindly to fools. And you – I think you very well could be one. You try to goad me into giving you what you want by tossing about things from rumors you have heard through questionable sources. I assure you my men are fully competent, and while things may not have gone to my liking in the past, it would not be the case presently. If my men had known then what they do now, they would have laid the entire island of Mialan to ruins. I recommend you not tempt me to prove that."

"That still leaves the question of what you would give me in return for the amulet," Oksuva said. Her voice was trembling. "I still desire to have some involvement with the ritual. To at least be witness to Arcastus being restored. I do not think that is too much to ask, but now you have killed one of my husband's men. How am I to explain that to him? Or do you have the means of returning life to his body as well?"

Looking Yasar's corpse over derisively, Damir scoffed, prodding it with the tip of his finely polished leather boot. "This creature is not worth the time or effort it would require of me to restore. If your husband demands compensation, have him speak with Kyros. He will work out some manner of payment. As far as the amulet, if all you seek is participation, I see no reason why that cannot be done."

Oksuva's smile faltered, the muscles in her face twitching uncomfortably with her attempts to conceal her obvious unease. Leyna wasn't used to seeing her tiptoe around her words. She was always so free with her voice, now reduced to a shaking, hesitant, mouse of a woman. "I am glad we could come to an agreement then. I suppose all that is left now is to arrange a time and place to carry out the terms."

"You do not have the amulet with you?"

"I might be a bit rash on occasion, but I am not a complete fool," she smirked. "One should never bring the goods to the bargaining table. I will provide it to you at the site of Arcastus's tomb. You are said to be the only one aware of its location and therefore I require that knowledge before I hand it over. It is not that I do not trust you, it is merely that – it is best to never trust anyone when bargaining over life, death, and unimaginable power."

"She's not as stupid as she looks," Damir chuckled, casting a glance over his shoulder to where Oran still stood, unfazed by any of the sights played out before him. "I guess I have no choice but to agree. I must warn you, though. The tomb is not easy to access. I recommend you leave your feminine fashions in the closet and don more suitable attire for traversing a very unforgiving terrain. Word will be sent to you when I am ready to reveal it. Until then, I suggest you return to your homes. There is nothing else in this desert of any use to us."

So he had found the tomb. Oksuva spoke of him having clues which would lead them to it, but nothing had been said to imply he was already aware of its location. The pieces of the puzzle were falling together too perfectly for Oksuva. Leyna had been counting on the need to search the tomb out. It would have made it easier to collect the clues and pass them along to the Consul in order to prepare an interception of the body. Without that, it would be too late to stop them once they were standing before it. Damir would be preparing the ritual while they approached. There would be nothing she could do to stop it once the corpse and the amulet were at Damir's disposal.

"I will anxiously await your invitation," Oksuva smiled. The irritation was plain on her face, though she hid it well in her voice. Damir no doubt had noticed it. She wanted everything to be faster. Waiting was not something she was accustomed to and patience was not a virtue which she possessed in abundance.

Pulling the hood of his cloak up to cover his face, Damir nodded, motioning toward Oran. They conversed quietly, their backs turned to the others. Leyna strained her ears to hear what was being said, her eyes sweeping over the area in awe and disbelief, mechanically following Zander's urges to stand her back on her feet.

The grass around the group of headstones remained blackened by the extinguished flow of energy and life through the roots. Dead. The essence of life sucked from it by the blasphemous sorcery. It went against everything the Vor'shai believed. She'd never witnessed it used to such an extreme, but the strength of it had been terrifying. How had the Vor'shai ever combated it all those years ago? Feolan had spoken of the land still being marked with scars of the battle. In her mind she could see the horrible images of lush, green forests transformed into a brown and lifeless wasteland, destroying everything in the path of the magic, without care to the havoc and repercussions it would cause.

She was still lost in her thoughts when she realized Zander was guiding her back through the maze of grave markers toward the carriage, leaving Yasar's lifeless form lying amongst the deadened earth. "Come on. We need to get somewhere that will give us some privacy to figure out what we are going to do about all of this," he whispered, his eyes darting sideways to make sure no one had overheard his words. "This is even worse than any of us anticipated. A war will be unavoidable unless we can somehow stop this exchange from taking place. Our Queen needs to be made aware so the troops can be rallied and ready. I foresee this could be a very long and bloody battle."

Chapter Seventeen

The journey home was devoid of conversation. Leyna struggled to grasp the truth of what she had witnessed and experienced at Damir's hands, never having seen anything like it before. And to think Arcastus was stronger! Leyna shuddered to imagine what he would be capable of if restored to life.

It seemed like it shouldn't be possible to revive him, even with Damir's strange magic. Time would have deteriorated the corpse beyond recognition or repair. His soul should have been collected by the Goddess Sytlea and taken to her home in the Underworld, leaving him nothing but an empty shell of the man he once was in life. To force breath back into the rotted flesh and bone would be simply animating a mindless skeleton.

Oksuva insisted on privacy upon reaching Siscal. Her belongings were moved into a room at one of the more expensive inns in the city, where she shut herself behind her door, refusing the company of even her sister.

Not far from Malic's Tavern, a weathered building housed an inn that served the middle class. Directing the carriage to stop at the entrance, Zander gazed solemnly at Leyna, the uncertainty showing plain on his face. "This is where Kael was said to be staying while we were out of town. The clerk should be able to direct you to his room and provide you with a key. That is, if he is still here. Do you want me to come in with you in case there is any trouble?"

"I will be fine," she smiled, the expression faint and unconvincing. "The worst they can do is deny me a key. He will open the door if I knock."

"Then I will wait outside to make sure this is the right place."

"That will not be necessary. If he is not here, I will enjoy the fresh air and exercise in searching him out."

Zander hesitated. "And if he is not at any of the inns? What would you do?"

"He will be at one of them. Where else do you think he would go?" Leyna chortled. Patting him reassuringly on the shoulder, she stepped through the carriage door, grateful for the feeling of her feet on solid ground, her legs aching from the long ride.

They had left immediately from their meeting with Damir. She felt sticky and uncomfortable in the same dress she'd worn to the cemetery, having no chance to change during the journey. The corset was digging into her skin, pressing painfully against her lower ribs. It would take days to recuperate from the discomfort it was causing.

"We will talk tomorrow, then," he replied quietly. Leyna gave a short nod before turning away to face the inn. The familiar churning in her stomach had returned, adding to the pressure already afflicting her from the stays of the corset. It had been over three weeks since she'd seen Kael. She hoped that in her absence he had begun the cleansing process, ridding himself of the taint of sorcery and returning the man she'd fallen for so long ago.

It was obvious by the bustling crowds that the day was drawing to a close. People hurried in and out of surrounding stores, the sound of loud conversations and raucous laughter reaching her ears from Malic's Tavern. A dull ache built in her heart at the thought of the crowd inside. Sharing drinks and passing stories of the day, reminiscing of times past. She missed the days when she'd been a part of it all. Even with the ongoing war, they had been carefree, enjoying the company of their friends, thankful to just be alive.

With a wistful sigh she made her way through the entrance of the inn, the muddy hem of her dress dragging along the wooden floor behind her. Smiling, the Siscalian clerk greeted her, his hazel eyes friendly and welcoming. "What can I do for you this evening?"

"I believe a man by the name of Kael Hadaren has a room here. I am to meet him this evening. I am his... wife."

Rummaging through a journal on the desk, the man peered over the top of his spectacles, lips pursed in concentration. "I do show him here." His chair scraped across the hard floor as he reached for a key on a nail poking from the wall behind him, handing it to her with a smile. "Second floor. Third room on the right just up the stairs."

"Thank you, sir," Leyna breathed in relief. While fresh air sounded pleasant to her when first exiting the carriage, her desire to lie down and sleep overpowered it. She was exhausted. The strain of the long trip and the stress of the situation were draining her. It would be easier to think of a plan after a full night of rest in a bed, rather than the rocking carriage she'd been confined to for the last week.

She found it difficult to lift her legs to carry herself up the stairs. They were steep, making her progress slow and tiresome. Third room on the right. Her eyes fell on it, shoulders relaxing, sinking down at the sight. She couldn't get to it fast enough. Oh, glorious sleep awaited her! Freedom from the restricting garments she had been trapped in for days.

Anxiously, she turned the key in the lock. In her mind, she could envision Kael's face, lighting up to see her, the soft green of his eyes restored to their old vigor and shine, his arms wrapping around her lovingly. A smile crossed her lips as she stepped through the door, opening her mouth to speak excitedly. But no words came.

Her voice was silenced instantly at what she saw there in the room, the smile fading in a single, paralyzing moment. Her body froze, numbed of all the pain and discomfort that had plagued her up until then. On the bed she saw the horrified expression on Kael's face, matching that which covered the familiar, petite features of Reina, clutching desperately at the blankets to cover her exposed body from view.

"Eleni," Kael gasped, pushing Reina off of him abruptly. "I didn't know you were on your way back."

Grasping at her stomach, she tried to pull the corset out away from her body. She couldn't breathe. The feeling was miserable, the restraining clothing only adding to it, causing her to become dizzy, wobbling on her feet. She wanted to walk over to the bed and strike him. To pull Reina from under the covers by her hair and drag her across the floor.

Reina! To think she would do something like this. The little girl that she had cared for all those years in Carpaen. Had she taught her nothing of being a lady? And the teachers at the orphanage, it had been their duty as well. But no, she should have known

Reina was not the innocent girl she'd been back then. That had been made clear the night they first spoke in Siscal.

"What do you think you are doing, Reina?" she exclaimed, finally finding the breath to speak. "Have you no dignity? No decency or respect for your own body? Your reputation?"

"I serve drinks in a tavern. My job is to entertain men and give them something to look at while they lose themselves in their ale. What do you think my reputation is, exactly?" Reina scoffed. Her slender hands tugged the blankets up further, pressing them tightly against her neck.

Kael was already on his feet, fastening his trousers around his waist. "Eleni," he started, becoming suddenly aware of the conversation passing between the two girls. Glancing from one to the other, Leyna could see the confusion in his eyes, but she didn't care to explain anything to him. "How do you two know each other?"

"You are not in any position to be asking questions," Leyna snapped through gritted teeth. Her head was spinning. Placing her hand on her forehead, she tried to steady herself, to make sense of what was happening. But there was no sense to be made of it. "What the hell is this Kael? I thought we worked through whatever had been wrong before I left. We were going to make things work. Have you changed your mind?"

Making his way over to Leyna, Kael wrapped his arms around her. "Eleni, you don't understand. It isn't what it looks like. I can explain everything." She could smell the wine on his breath. Suffocating her with its stench.

"Explain?" she shouted. She tried to push him away with all the strength she could manage. The thought of his touch disgusted her. "What else could it be other than what it looks like? I am not a fool, Kael."

Heat shot through her body, radiating up into the tips of her ears, her skin turning red, flushed with rage and humiliation. How could he have done this to her? How could he claim to love her and then continue to drive them further apart? Winding back her arm, she brought her hand across his face, stinging her own skin with the impact.

A brief moment of silence fell on the room while Kael's drunken mind registered what she'd done. His face contorted in a look of pure, menacing rage, grabbing her shoulders tightly in his hands, his fingers digging into her skin painfully. She cried out, choking on her own scream as she felt her back slammed against the wall near the door. "How dare you raise a hand to your husband!" he yelled, thick spittle shooting from his mouth with the words.

She couldn't escape the darkness in his eyes, staring through her. It wasn't him. This was not the man she had spoken to that afternoon before she left for Kaipoi. Not a hint of the gentle green remained, replaced by a dull grey which completely enveloped the iris, like a hazy shadow.

Through the fog of her thoughts she could hear the sound of footsteps pounding over the floorboards of the room. Frantically, Reina collected her clothing, dressing herself, unable to tear her eyes from Kael holding Leyna securely against the wall. Leyna could see the fear in her expression. Her naivety had prevented her from seeing exactly what this man was. It was too late now. Reina's fingers reached for the door beside them, pulling it open, only to have it slammed shut by Kael's hand, moving at lightning speed before she could get through it.

"Where do you think you're going?" he hissed.

Reina's scream resounded across the room, piercing through Leyna's head. Her hand was free. In his attempts to prevent Reina from leaving, he released his grip on her, his focus directed toward Reina's trembling form, shaking uncontrollably in front of the door.

In that moment, Leyna was taken back to the days she and Reina had spent in Carpaen, relying on each other to get through the misery their lives had been thrust into. Reina had been so young. The reality of life hadn't truly hit her. All she understood was that they couldn't go home and that her father and sister would never again be seen. The confusion and anger she'd harbored all of these years had made her the woman she was now, scared and alone, trying to make her way in a world that had never made sense to her. Leyna couldn't hate her for the choices she made.

While Kael was distracted, Leyna let her free hand slide over to the door, tentatively wrapping her fingers around the knob. Reina caught her eye, trying not to draw attention to what was going on.

Kael was reaching out to Reina. Panic rushed through Leyna, watching the inky black aura building up over his hand. It pained her to see him like that. But it wasn't him. Somewhere in the depths of the alcohol and the shadow, she prayed the man she cared for was still there, fighting to get his body back from this creature that had possessed it.

Steeling her resolve, she drove her knee hard into his groin, the reaction to the pain somewhat delayed before he doubled forward, his dark eyes flashing angrily at her. Reina lunged forward, pushing him off balance, a grunt escaping him as he tumbled to the ground.

"Go!" Leyna shouted, twisting the knob on the door. They burst through into the hallway, racing down the stairs to the lobby and out into the street, afraid to look back, in fear of seeing Kael's face behind them. Reina clasped Leyna's hand in hers, pulling her toward Malic's. "We will be safe in the tavern. He wouldn't dare attack us in front of all those people."

As they pushed through the tavern door, the familiar outline of Zander's carriage stood out to Leyna, stopped near the side of the building on a small side street leading deeper into the city. Silently she prayed he would see them.

Every head in the room turned to look at them as they entered, frantic and out of breath. Pausing just inside the door, Reina straightened her dress, running her fingers through her hair in attempts to appear casual, a charming smile on her face. The regulars of the tavern recognized her, lifting their glasses to her jovially in greeting.

Leyna couldn't get the room to stop spinning. It was becoming worse, building rapidly. Unable to fight the dizziness, her vision faded to black, the feeling of the floor rapidly coming up to meet her face as her mind gave in to the pull of unconsciousness.

A strong stench roused Leyna to consciousness, her eyes opening to find her lying on the bed in her room at Zander's house. Reina was standing at her side, clasping her hand tightly while Zander held a small vial under Leyna's nose, pulling it back at the sight of her eyes snapping open.

Everything flooded back into her mind. She could still see the darkness in Kael's eyes, the shadowy aura building around his hand while he held her there against the wall. He was a monster. His behavior was no better than what she had witnessed from Mikel. It was obvious they'd been working closely for many years for Mikel's habits to have rubbed off on him so completely.

"Zander, we cannot let Gislan see Reina here," she gasped, trying to sit up on the bed. Zander hushed her softly, his hands pressing her back down.

"Gislan is out in search of some new man to entertain her for the evening. I don't expect her home for some time, and if she surprises us, we know we can fit this young lady through the window," he said. "Now, would either of you like to explain to me what is going on? Without hysterics, preferably."

"I'm sorry. I didn't know what to do," Reina grumbled.

"Where is Kael? Was he not in his room?" Zander closed the vial in his hand with a small cork, setting it down on the floor next to the bed where he was kneeling. "You're lucky I decided to stick around even though you told me to leave."

Leyna laughed pathetically, leaning her head back down against the pillow, her eyes gazing up at the solid white ceiling overhead. "My arrival interrupted him. It would seem he was not expecting me. However, I still have some questions of my own in regards to that."

"I had no idea he was your husband," Reina said defensively, glancing nervously over to Zander. "If I had known, I never would have become involved with him. But he has been following me for weeks now. Asking about you. I remembered seeing him at the table with you that night at Malic's, when you told me that those people didn't know who you really were. So when he started questioning me about the woman I mistook you for, I was hesitant to answer him."

"Oh, gods," Leyna whispered. Her heart sank in her chest, twisting the invisible knife that had already begun to stab through it. Was that what Kyros had asked of him? To investigate her? "He is not my husband. But that is not important. What did you say? Did you tell him who I am?"

Reina shook her head. "No. I assumed he was just another one of the men you spoke of. I didn't want to risk them coming after you, but when he still pursued me,

I thought I could try and get some information out of him as well. It seemed more easily accomplished by getting closer to him. I don't understand. I thought he said he was your husband..."

"He was more than likely doing the same thing to you. But that doesn't tell me anything about what happened," Zander frowned. "I've picked up that you are the woman who was sleeping with Kael. I recommend not asking questions about marital status right now. We have bigger things to worry about."

Climbing back to his feet, Zander began a slow pace across the floor. His eyes darted nervously toward the door with every turn. Leyna could sense his unease with the situation. And who could blame him? He was stuck in the middle of something he knew nothing about, but potentially could destroy everything they had worked toward all these years. "So why would Kael be interested in Leyna?"

With a sharp intake of air, Leyna sat up, her eyes following Zander's movement back and forth from the door to the window. "Because Kyros is interested in me," she shrugged. "I cannot say for sure, but Kael mentioned before I left that Kyros had requested him to do something for him. He wouldn't elaborate on it."

"But I thought you said it was Damir who knew you..."

"They both do," she sighed. "Kyros was with the assassins who killed my mother and Reina's family." Her throat contracted, tensing with the emotion which filled her at the memories. The scars on her back tingled, sending a shiver down her spine, her head shaking to get rid of the image of Kyros's face. "Kyros was supposed to kill me, and failed. Reina's sister knocked him unconscious before he could finish the job. I was nine at the time. From the moment I recognized him, I have feared he would see the resemblance between me and the child he chased through the house that day. If he didn't draw the connection right away, then hearing the name might have done it for him. It is only a matter of time now before they figure out who I am."

"We need to remove you from the mission then. It's too dangerous." Zander paused in the center of the room. His eyes were focused on Leyna. Solemn. An expression she wasn't used to seeing cross his features. "The only option for you is to either return to Dalonshire, or go into hiding. Anything that will get you out of their sight. My suggestion would be whatever gets you free without having to go back to Mikel. Honestly, he doesn't exactly seem much better than these people."

Leyna stared at him. Making no movement at all, she held his gaze, her anger rising at the thought of having to give everything up and run away. She couldn't hide in a trunk the way she did as a child. She had to face these men or they would just keep killing, the same way they killed her mother. Only this time it would be her entire race they slaughtered, while she sat in the darkness of that little box.

She refused to run and hide. Not while there was still a chance she could help take them down. "I can't just walk away from this. You have to understand how important this is to me —"

"It's important to all of us! But you will do little good to your people if you are dead. Don't you see that? If these men want you dead, then we need to keep you away from them so that you can continue to help us fight them."

"And how do I fight them if I am hiding?" she demanded, her eyes narrowed angrily. "Do I just lie down somewhere under a bed and pray things work out? My mother had that same idea for me. Hide away so they can't find me. You see how well that worked out. She's dead because I couldn't face them."

"You were nine!" Zander shouted. Throwing his arms up in the air in frustration, he ran his fingers through his hair, turning to face the window. "Things are different now. You had to hide then because you weren't capable of fighting them."

"You're right. Things are different now," Leyna stated firmly, squeezing Reina's hand tightly in hers. "I am capable of fighting. And that is exactly why I cannot keep running and hiding. I have to stand up to them. They need to be stopped, punished for what they have done. For what they intend to do."

Zander's head turned slowly. Understanding flashed in his eyes, staring back at her with concern. "You want revenge." The words were simple. But they were true. These men had to pay for what they did to her mother. If she succeeded, it would be so much more than simple revenge, but it would be revenge all the same. In the process it would save thousands of lives. It was all justified in her mind. There was nothing that could convince her otherwise.

"Wouldn't you?"

She knew him too well to expect an argument. He stood there, staring deeply into her eyes, making no attempt to disagree with her. After a long silence, he nodded his head.

"Very well," he said. "I suggest then that you go to the Consul and tell him about what we witnessed in Kaipoi. I would go, but I have no way of knowing when Gislan will be home. She expects me to be here, but not you." He turned to face Reina calmly. "You should lie low for a while. If they believe you to have the information they need, they will come after you also. Take some time off – go on a vacation – anything. Just don't let yourself be seen."

"I suppose using the front door is out of the question then," Leyna chuckled. Her legs still ached from the trip, the muscles trembling as she rose to her feet. Part of her was excited at the thought of seeing the Consul, while deep down she realized she was afraid. Afraid of what she would have to tell him, about Kael, and about everything. She wasn't ready to bare her secrets to him. Not that night, and certainly not like this. She always imagined the truth would come out between them in a way that showed she trusted him, and wanted to share it, rather than feeling as if she was only doing it because she was being forced to.

He had to know about Kael. As much as she hated the thought of telling Thade what she had witnessed him doing, she couldn't keep it from him. Not anymore. Kael couldn't be trusted. He needed their help, but until they were able to get him back under control, they couldn't allow him to gain knowledge of their plans to counter Damir and Oksuva. She didn't want to betray him like that, but he had chosen his path. And while she didn't believe he should be cast away for his mistake, she knew it wasn't something that could be easily changed.

"Neither one of you should use the front door," Zander agreed. "We can't risk anyone seeing you both leave the house, or what direction you go. If Reina is seen, they could follow her, and Leyna, if they catch you heading toward the Consul's…"

"I know, Zander. Trust me," she smiled, patting his cheek gently with her hand as she moved over to the window. Her fingers glided over the latch, expertly twisting it, lifting it upward without a sound. "We need to try and get as much in order tonight as possible, because come tomorrow morning, when all of this comes out in the open between everyone about what Kael did, and it will; things will become an even bigger mess."

"Which is exactly why I'm worried," he frowned, helping to hold her skirt while she slid her feet over the ledge. "Now go quickly. The sooner you get moving, the sooner Reina can get herself to safety, and I can start trying to think about how to get us out of this."

Leyna raised her hand to knock at the familiar door, glancing up and down the street cautiously. She was afraid to think about what she must look like. Her hair was windblown and flat, the curls having lost their hold, lying now in soft waves hanging in a mass of tangles over her head. The dark green of her dress was marred with stains, damp soil from the cemetery darkening the hem, the front marked from where her knees had sunk into the dirt at Damir's feet. She felt disgusting. Never before had she ever wanted to bathe as badly as at that moment.

But there was no time. Taking a deep breath, she let her knuckles rap against the wood, listening intently for any sounds coming from inside the house. It had been weeks since she was last there. Her pulse quickened with the fear that something had happened while she was away, a heightening of the Consul's illness, or worse. Everything had been so out of control that she was beginning to believe anything was possible. And with her luck, it would be the absolute worst.

A soft click came from the door. She followed the knob with her gaze, lifting up to find Thade's silver eyes glowing brightly at her from inside the darkened house. They opened wide, surprised to see her there on his porch. He looked unsure whether or not to smile, opening the door wider for her to enter. "Leyna – you look…"

"Awful, I know. I apologize," she sighed. Her gaze trailed over the room, taking in the strange shadows which covered everything in the darkness, devoid of any light at all from even a single candle. "Did I wake you?"

"Not at all," he replied, closing the door behind her, fastening the lock securely into place. "I have been enjoying the peace and quiet. Feolan and Lady Diah left this afternoon to go on a bit of a picnic in the country. They are due back – eventually – but I am not entirely sure when. Can I get you something to drink? Water? Tea?"

Leyna shook her head uncomfortably. She didn't understand why her heart was pounding the way it was. An urge to burst into a giggling fit came over her, lost there in the dark, unable to see anything but the brilliant light of Thade's eyes. They were like two glowing lanterns, faintly illuminating the features of his face. "No, actually, it may be best if you stayed a bit of a distance away from me. I must look and smell wretched. Oksuva insisted the carriage not stop at all during our trip back from Kaipoi, which allowed no one the opportunity to freshen up."

"Then you only just arrived back into town?"

"A few hours ago," she stated, realizing suddenly that she had lost all track of the time. The sky still retained some light from the sun when she and Reina burst through the door of Malic's Tavern. She was beginning to question just how long she'd been unconscious before they managed to wake her, the clouds overhead now completely devoid of any light but the moon. "It has been an eventful homecoming, to say the least."

Thade maneuvered his way around the furniture by memory, a flicker of flame erupting from under his fingertips on a candle situated near the sitting area of the main room. It was barely enough light to chase away the darkness, but it was sufficient to guide Leyna across the floor to where Thade was standing, motioning for her to have a seat on the settee. "Please, sit. I regretted my inability to speak with you when last you visited."

"Oh, I could not possibly risk getting dirt on the cushions. Besides, this dress is not the most accommodating."

"Yes, you do look a bit… cramped." Thade blinked as if in surprise at his own words, averting his eyes with a dismissive wave of his hand. "I am not worried about the cushions. If it would not be too uncomfortable, I would love for you to have a seat and relax. You appear distressed, despite your calm countenance. Your eyes say much."

Hesitantly, Leyna gave in to Thade's request, settling herself on the settee. "Well, you did not seem surprised to hear I was in Kaipoi, so I will assume then that Feolan received my last letter."

"He did," Thade nodded. "It was an interesting method. We are not entirely certain who delivered it, but there was a knock at the door and Feolan's cloak was the only thing visible upon answering it. The unusual arrival piqued enough interest that we were compelled to look it over in search of some possible hidden reason for its appearance on our doorstep."

"It was the only way I could think of to get word to you both. The decision to leave Siscal was rather sudden and unexpected."

She found herself fidgeting. Her fingers clasped and unclasped in her lap. There was so much she wanted to say. To know about what happened while she was gone. Thade looked much healthier now than he had when she saw him last. The color had returned to his face. Or so it appeared. It was hard to tell in the dim light if his complexion had returned, or if it was just the discoloration of the dancing orange flame on his skin.

It struck her as odd to think they had never before been alone in this way. Even in their most private of conversations in the past, there had always been someone nearby, just outside the door or standing on the opposite end of the room. She found herself intimidated by it. All the guilt from the thoughts she'd had about him made it hard for her to find her voice.

What was wrong with her? She had come there for the sake of business, and the safety of her people. It didn't make any sense why she would be so lost in her own trivial thoughts, feeling bad for things which held no bearing on the situation at hand. So what if she had imagined what it would be like to kiss him. Those soft, perfectly sculpted lips. She coughed, clearing her throat nervously. Her subconscious was being impossible. She needed to get control of herself, to gather her thoughts and lay out the news she'd come there to bring.

"Unfortunately, I have come here with two pieces of very disheartening information," she frowned. "I just cannot decide which I should give first. Both are quite disturbing, but one is more so than the other."

"Let us start small and work our way up, then. I am still getting back into the swing of all this. You are the first to visit me in quite a while. At times I worry everyone has given up on the mission."

"I fear that one of us has," she said. Her eyes drifted away from Thade's face at his raised eyebrow, peering at her quizzically. How much did he know? So much had been shared with Feolan and Maeri when she was there last, but Thade had been so ill. How could she know what he was aware of already? She dreaded having to explain the engagement to him. She didn't understand why it pained her to speak of it, but for some reason she felt guilty. "While I believe that his intentions were true and he was loyal to the Queen throughout his mission, there have come to be some – complications – with Kael."

Sitting down on the chair across from Leyna, Thade drummed his fingers idly on the arm, staring off into the distance over Leyna's shoulder. "Your betrothed?" His voice was quiet. Leyna let her eyes trail back up to his, searching his expression. He sounded almost saddened to say the words.

"Yes. I suppose Feolan told you."

"I overheard of the news while drifting in and out of consciousness. Feolan merely confirmed it for me. While I have my questions and doubts regarding why you did it, and whether or not it should remain so, I recognize that you are a woman and free to make your own choices."

"That is exactly why I am here," she said calmly. It had to be said. There would be no getting around it. Sitting there in Thade's presence reminded her of how much more important her friendship with Thade was than her loyalty to her people and Queen. It outweighed even the devotion she felt obligated to give to Kael. "I did not tell you before, and I know I should have. I just was not certain then, and a part of me thought, perhaps foolishly, that I could help him. But I see now that I will need help, if it is even possible at all."

His eyes focused, shifting to look Leyna over curiously. Almost hopeful. "What is it you wish to tell me?"

Leyna stared back at him. She could see the spark in his eye, anxious to hear what she would say. Thinking over her words, she tried to place what might have caught his attention in such a way, nothing standing out in her mind. With a shake of her head, she gave a sigh. "He has been using the sorcery. Only a little at first, and I thought he could be swayed from it. But I have seen it, gradually taking him over. I no longer can find any trace of the man I once knew in his eyes."

"How deeply has he fallen?" Thade grimaced. His hopefulness twisted into a strange sympathetic gaze, looking unsure on how he should react toward her regarding the admission.

"Oh, sir, I fear he may be beyond redemption," she said quietly. To hear the words out loud, spoken from her own lips. It drove the blade of reality deeper into her back. The betrayal that Kael had laid upon her. He claimed to have dabbled in it for her own sake, to keep her safe from Mikel. But she would have preferred Mikel come for her. At least then she would not have found herself bound to a creature of evil like Kael had become. It hurt to think it all sparked from an original betrayal that was in no way linked to the sorcery at all. Nothing had altered Kael's decisions the night he climbed into that bed with Oksuva. Only the alcohol. And it seemed a pathetic excuse.

Thade was watching her. She wondered how much pain he was reading in her eyes, the way he stared so deeply into them, as if seeing into her soul. If only he knew everything she'd been hiding there! Tucked neatly away from anyone who had ever been close to her.

"I returned from Kaipoi tonight and went to see him at the inn where he was staying. I found him there with another woman. I may have reacted a bit dramatically, but he lost himself in a rage. His eyes have lost all color, even that little which was still there when I left. We had talked about trying to help him. He wanted assistance. I do not know what happened while I was away, but tonight I saw him use it. I saw that evil magic come from inside him."

There. She'd said it. The hardest part of her visit was over. Though it was difficult to say how he would react to the news of Oksuva's plans. The evil that Leyna had witnessed in the cemetery in Kaipoi was far more dangerous than anything Kael could do to them. At least for now. If he continued to become stronger with the magic, there was no saying what damage he was capable of. Kael was aware that the Consul was gathering information. What if he found a way to come after him?

Stop being foolish, she scolded. He wouldn't dare come after Thade. Would he? "He cannot be trusted anymore," she added, breaking through her own frantic thoughts. "I ask that you exercise caution if you come into contact with him. He is currently doing work for Kyros. I cannot verify exactly what it is, but I have my suspicions, and if I am correct, it could prove detrimental to my place in the mission as well." It could kill her. Why could she not bring herself to speak of the true danger? Because it would require her to expose more of herself. Her secrets. She hated feeling vulnerable in front of Thade.

Silently, Thade rose from his chair, moving over to sit beside Leyna. She tried to remain composed. Something about his sudden closeness sent a tremor through her body, her heart rate increasing uncomfortably, pounding loudly through her head. "You amaze me, Leyna," he whispered, calmly shaking his head. "He has treated you so terribly and yet you still speak nothing of your own pain, and instead worry about the safety of everyone else. This must be eating away at you inside."

"There are far worse things for me to be concerned about right now than whether or not my future husband is being faithful." A pathetic laugh escaped her lips before she could stop. It was the truth. How could she wallow in self-pity over her own misery when Damir and Oksuva were plotting to raise an army against them? She might be confused, but she could still prioritize which dangers required more attention than others. There would be time to mourn over her personal downfalls when Damir had been stopped. "You do remember that I spoke of there being worse news?"

"A part of me hoped that you decided to tell me the worst news first," he frowned, leaning back against the arm of the settee, his eyes closely following every move Leyna made. "I think I am prepared."

Again, she was at a loss at how to tell him. It had all been so easy to say in her head! Why was it so much more difficult to form the words when he was looking at her like that? Sympathizing with her. And the questions she saw in his eyes. They haunted her, with their bright silver hue, so friendly and understanding, while she kept her secrets from him. Information he should be made aware of, but she was too frightened to share. Too afraid of how he would react. Or the repercussions of admitting all of the things she had hidden for so long.

She needed to just go for it. To let the words fall from her lips without thinking about him, or his eyes. Looking straight ahead, she tried to ignore his presence, speaking to the empty air in front of her. "Oksuva has made an arrangement with the man known as Damir Rohld. You have spoken of him in the past, I believe. She has an artifact. An amulet, said to be the one worn by Arcastus. Damir in turn will divulge the location where Arcastus's corpse has been hidden away all these years. They intend to use the amulet, and the magic still contained within it, to bring Arcastus back to life. They want to raise an army against the Vor'shai. Had I not witnessed the things that I did, I might not be so concerned over their ability to do what they wish, but I have reason to believe that Damir is entirely capable."

"You have met Damir?"

Leyna shuddered. "I have, yes."

"I can see the pain on your face whenever you hear or speak his name. Has he done something to you?"

Hanging her head, Leyna let out her breath, growing weary of constantly hiding, pretending everything was fine when inside she was screaming. She still felt like the lost little child that had limped away from her house in Mialan that night. Her mother murdered. Her life left in shambles. And because of that man! The man who now stood in the way of completing this mission. She wanted him dead. She wanted to be the one to plunge the blade into his heart. "No," she lied, swallowing hard to choke back the emotions welling up in the back of her throat. "He has not done anything specifically to me. But he killed one of Mikel's men. He used his magic to raise the spirits of the dead from their graves, to threaten us. I am convinced one attempted to pull the soul from my body. I was powerless to stop it. It would have succeeded had Damir not stepped in."

"You are choosing your words very carefully in regards to him. I hope you do not think I would not notice."

Leyna glanced over to him, surprised by his statement. "I am not lying to you. I assure you."

"Not lying, no. But in the same way that you have since the day I met you, I still see you avoiding details. Conveniently bypassing the truth without having to directly mislead me. Are you aware that Prince Enaes continues to search for information in regards to who you are? He has come to me a few times. Once recently, after the doctors returned to Tanispa and mentioned that it was you who helped to stabilize me until their arrival. Hearing that, he assumed I still had contact with you, and came to speak with me. He wants answers that I still am not capable of giving him."

"What news has he found now which makes you question me? I am not certain things could get much worse than his claims that I do not exist. That the Evantine family holds no knowledge of my life. Do lay it all on me now while I am too emotionally drained to care about the accusations."

"Leyna, no, that is not it," Thade frowned, leaning forward to rest his hand gently on her shoulder. She stared down at it, unsure of how to react. "I am not accusing you of anything. I mention it in hopes of figuring out what you are hiding. It is hurting you. I can see it in your eyes."

"You see a great deal in my eyes, sir," she breathed, exasperated by his actions. Confusion settled on her even thicker than before. She wanted to tell him everything. For him to take her in his arms and tell her that it all would be fine. While yet another part of her was angry. Not with him, but at the thought of having to defend herself. At his constant claims of seeing the truth in her eyes and yet still asking her for more. "Please tell me what he has told you. I am hoping to learn something about myself that you have heard, or plucked from my eyes."

She was amazed at the steadiness of his gaze, never flinching at her outburst. Hurt was evident in his expression, but she couldn't tell if it was pain caused by the way she spoke to him, or if it was at the thought of what he had learned of her. His voice was soft, soothing. "It is not important right now, but if it will ease your mind at all to know, he has traced you back to the academy in Carpaen. When he questioned me about you, I told him you were said to have been an assistant to one of the teachers there. It seems that while there was no record of a Leyna Evantine as a student, a human male there recognized the name and confirmed that she had helped him teach for a few years. Sadly, he knew nothing of her parents, or where she came from before she arrived there. All he said was that she cared for a young child, but no one had seen either of them in years."

"Blaise," she whispered. A smile passed over her lips. She was grateful to him. Finally, someone had been able to confirm her existence. But what more did they want? They required records. Birth documentation. Proof of her parents and heritage. None of that was accessible to her. If Enaes had been unable to locate them in Tanispa's books, then she was at a loss as for an alternative. Unless her mother had held a copy of it — but no. How would she possibly be able to know? Her mother had been dead for so long, anything belonging to her had most likely been destroyed or sold.

"You know this human?" Thade asked, hearing her speak the name under her breath.

"Of course I do, sir," she sighed, leaning back against the settee cushions in defeat. "I taught at his side for years. I know this to be true, regardless of what anyone else has to say. But none of this matters right now. Who I am does not change the fact that we are facing a possible war. They want to join forces with the Namiren and Sanarik, using Arcastus to rebuild the Ven'shal army. Oksuva is awaiting word from Damir and then she will be headed to meet with him. To perform the ritual to revive Arcastus's corpse. There will be no notice beforehand to allow us a chance to intervene."

"And what of you? What are your plans for the mission at this point? Do you still insist on remaining among the enemy, or will you now accept my offer to have you work alongside Feolan and myself to arrange a defense against them?"

"What help could I possibly be to you if I am not gathering information from the enemy?"

His face brightened somewhat at her words. It was the closest to bending she had ever exhibited in regards to the matter. "Queen Nesperiti has granted you a position on her court for your exemplary service during the war. With that status, you could accompany us to speak with the governments of possible allies to build up our own military strength. We know the intentions of our enemies. That will allow us a head start, at the very least, in preparing our defense."

It was tempting. She wanted out, away from Mikel and Oksuva. After her last meeting with Kael, it seemed almost necessary for her to leave. But to accept his offer now would take her away from her chance to get her revenge on Damir. How worth it was the risk, though? If she stayed with them, it was more likely that she would meet her own demise at Damir's hands before she ever found an opportunity to strike. She was outnumbered. If it came to war, she could always seek him on the battlefield.

"You have my attention. But I cannot simply just leave. Nothing is that easy."

"Do you know anyone who might be able to bargain for your release from Mikel's employ?" Thade asked. "Although Kael may not be trustworthy to us on the mission, he might be a valuable tool in getting you out of there. I vaguely recall hearing something about his removal from Mikel's home. Perhaps he could argue for the release of his betrothed."

She couldn't believe she was actually considering the offer. For years she had fought against leaving the mission, but now it meant so little to her. There was nothing there for her. Mikel was useless. He had been nothing but a pawn to Oksuva. Leyna's continued involvement with Damir and Kyros would possibly be more of a threat to the mission than a benefit. Not to mention the draw of finally being able to make her own choices, rather than having to follow the orders of someone else, down to the way she dressed and did her hair.

Once Kael was sober, it was possible he could be reasoned with. It was doubtful he would be able to argue Mikel out of ownership. But he had powerful friends. If she could convince him it was to their benefit that she be removed, then perhaps he would willingly seek a means of assistance. "I will see what I can do. Kael will be impossible to speak with until he is sober. And even then, it could take some work."

"Leyna."

In her excitement, she almost missed the sound of his voice speaking her name. It was so quiet. Hesitant. "Yes?"

"It is not any of my business, but I feel compelled to inquire," he said softly, once again catching her eye, staring deeply into them. "Have you given any thought to ending your engagement if Kael continues down the path he has started?"

It was an innocent question. But one she had not considered. Never once had it even crossed her mind through this all. It was logical, at the very least. Release from an engagement, however, was not something easily attained. It lay in the hands of the priests to decide if there was just cause, and history had proven it difficult to convince them it was appropriate. "I am not certain the priests would see fit to grant me that request," she said quietly. "They would view his choices as a hardship that I should stand by him through and try to help him. My only chance would be to find a way to convince them that the engagement should not be valid at all."

Thade nodded his head, rising slowly from the settee. "We will have to look into that matter once we have you safely out of harm's reach. If you desire to do so, that is."

"We will see how things go. For now, I need to figure out what I am going to do. The morning will be upon us soon. I need to get back into town before anyone finds a reason to start looking for me."

Moving across the floor, Thade peered through one of the curtains, his face revealing a hint of concern. "Feolan and Lady Diah should have been back by now. I feel I should go searching for them, but I would not want to intrude if they are alright and merely – staying out."

"I am sure they are fine," Leyna smiled. She wasn't sure how to respond to his concern, or what would be appropriate to say. It was strange to think that she would be working by his side again. She only hoped that her misplaced feelings for him would not cause any awkwardness. For now her behavior remained appropriate. Or at least Thade had not given any sign to indicate he had noticed a difference.

He let the curtain fall back into place over the window, leaving them there again in the silence of the dimly lit room. Shifting uncomfortably, Leyna took a step toward the door. She didn't know what else to say. The quiet was unbearable. She feared he would hear the loud thudding of her heart pounding inside her chest.

At the door she stopped, turning to face him again. He was watching her. It made her shiver slightly to think that his eyes had followed her across the room. She stared back at him, wishing and praying he would say something to break the silence.

"You know you can come here if you ever need," he said quietly. She nodded to him, smiling nervously. He was acting odd. His posture had stiffened, as if suddenly more aware of his surroundings. Stepping closer, every motion slow and precise, gauging his distance based on her reaction to his approach, he spoke. "I wish there was more I could do to help. You have done so much for me…"

"Thade, please," she whispered, holding her hand out to stop him. "You owe me nothing. You have done more than you could realize and it is I who am in your debt. Someday I promise I will make everything right between us."

"I did not realize there was anything wrong between us."

She gazed at him, enamored by the way he looked in the dancing light of the distant candle. There could never be anything wrong with him. All the faults lay within her. The childish infatuation which she couldn't seem to escape, even after all these years. She could hide from it when not near him, but in his presence it came rushing back, haunting her. "I should go," she breathed, her hand already on the door, twisting the handle, letting in the cool air of the night.

Flustered by the unwanted emotions, she emerged onto the street, ignoring the confused look which spread across Thade's face. A gasp escaped her at the feeling of his hand reaching out to hers. She stopped, prevented from stepping down off the porch, her body turning to face him in surprise. "Why must you leave so suddenly? Have I said or done something to offend you?" he asked, his eyes burning into hers.

"No," she breathed, her awareness of the open street distracting her from the emotion she would otherwise have felt at his desire for her to stay. Anyone could see them there on the porch. How would that scene look to an uninformed observer? It was scandalous for her to even be there with him. Especially without the presence of Feolan. "People will see us," she pushed his hand away, gazing up at him in desperation. "Kael has already accused me of having some sort of affair with you or Feolan. I cannot risk him hearing that I was here —"

"He accused you of what with me?" Thade was taken aback by the thought.

Leyna wanted to answer him. To share the ridiculous claims Kael had made. But something was stopping her. A feeling of being watched, appraised from the darkness, somewhere along the street.

Shuddering, she turned away from Thade's questioning stare. Someone was there. But who? No one knew where she headed other than Zander — and he would have no reason to skulk in the shadows.

Thade sensed it also. Leyna could tell by the way he stiffened at her side, the way she'd seen him do so many times during the war when preparing for an attack. Reaching back inside the house, he retrieved a sword from somewhere near the door, gripping it tightly in his hand and guiding her behind him, shielding her from view. "Show your-self," he demanded. "Only a coward would spy on a member of the Queen's court and refuse to show their face when discovered."

"And give up the best seat for the show? Where is the fun in that?" The sound of Kael's voice was like ice, brimming with an undertone of pure unabashed rage. "At least I know now which one of you it is. To think, all this time, I was convinced it was your little man servant. I actually thought you were better than this."

"Speak plainly, fool. If you wish to make an accusation, do not waste my time with veiled innuendo."

He appeared as if from nowhere, the sound of his sword echoing through the street with the draw of his blade against its sheath. The darkness in his eyes glittered eerily in the light of the moon. Menacing. His hand held the blade out, directing the tip threateningly toward Thade. "You want it plainly?" he scoffed. "Take your hands off my woman."

"I have not laid a hand on her."

"You lie! I watched you. My eyes do not play tricks on me. Did you really think you could keep her to yourself and I would never find out?"

"I suggest you think very carefully about whom you are pointing your weapon at, and the severity of the accusations you are making," Thade replied calmly. He showed no sign of faltering at Kael's demeanor, his guard remaining steady while his voice was confident. "Lower your blade, or I shall be forced to relieve you of it."

Lunging forward, Kael jabbed his sword at Thade, the clashing metal echoing through the street as Thade easily knocked it aside. Leyna's mind shut down at the sound of Kael's strike, no longer thinking clearly. She had to stop this. It was all a misunderstanding and someone was going to end up dead because of it. "Stop this," she demanded, stepping boldly in front of Thade, positioning herself between him and Kael protectively. "I have already told you there is nothing between the Consul and I."

"I do not trust him!" Kael shouted. Sharply, he lifted his sword back up, pressing the flat of the blade underneath her chin, forcing it upward. "Now get out of the way so I can defend what is left of your honor, and my own, after your actions."

It had been some time since she'd found herself on this end of a sword. Her heart fluttered wildly in her chest. So exhilarating, but not in the way she remembered it. Back then it was for a reason. A good cause she could get behind and feel justified in dying for. This was nothing but Kael's desire to make himself appear more powerful to the Consul. To try and show him he was someone to be feared.

"My honor is perfectly intact. I give you my word there is no need for defending anything here."

"Intact?" Kael laughed. "The only man your honor is intact with is me, darling. You seem to give it away freely to everyone but your own husband." Slowly he lowered his blade, aiming it at her chest, hovering just above her heart. "I should have known you would come here. I mistakenly believed you would run back to Zander's bed like the good little slave that you are."

"I was never Zander's slave," she stated firmly. That truth was harmless to her now. Not that he would believe it.

Eyes flashing furiously, Kael moved in closer, pressing the blade against her skin. "So you were his willing whore? Is that it?"

"Kael, I never slept with Zander – or Thade or Feolan – or anyone for that matter," Leyna replied, her voice steadier than she expected to hear come from her own lips.

Shifting backward, she pushed down on the blade of Kael's sword with her palm, side stepping quickly to reach his hands, her fingers groping to pry the weapon away from him.

"You expect me to believe that?" Kael shouted. With precision, he lifted his elbow up, catching Leyna's jaw painfully with the strike, sending her stumbling back under the impact. Pain shot through the right side of her face. It blinded her momentarily, white flashing before her eyes. "Do you realize the fool I look? Everyone knows that my wife sleeps with anybody but me. You have humiliated me!"

"You humiliate yourself." Thade's blade thrust neatly at Kael's hands, their swords clashing together, distracting Kael from Leyna's disoriented form. "It is my honor you attempt to tarnish now. Your betrothed and I are friends. We have never been more than that, nor will we ever be. If you intend to continue your mistaken claims, then I will be forced to prove my honor by my sword against yours."

Something knocked Leyna breathless with a force more devastating than Kael's elbow. Deep in her chest it was like a knife twisting, piercing through the very heart that felt to have stopped beating inside her. She didn't need to see to know where the blow had come from. No hand dealt it; the lingering echo of Thade's words reverberating inside her head.

Nor will we ever be.

Why did it matter to her? She had, even just that night while in his presence, forced down the feelings which welled up inside, chiding herself, telling her heart it was nothing more than childish infatuation. The pain in her chest indicated it was more than that. It was beyond any mindless crush she'd seen the girls at Faustine's experience at the thought of the young boys they happened to pass in town.

The truth stung her. Wounded her. She couldn't focus on the words passing between the two men, the clanging metal of their blades drowning out everything. It hit her like a revelation that had come too late to save her from her own naivety.

She loved him. Zander had lectured her about the feeling, her own heart having never fully understood what he meant until that moment. That moment when it became clear that she could never have what she wanted. All those years she'd been too afraid to admit the way she felt, worried that it would ruin everything. Worried that she wasn't good enough.

But she wasn't good enough. Just watching Thade, fluidly parrying and redirecting Kael's strikes, the movement of his body a work of art in motion before her very eyes. The Consul for Queen Vorsila. A man could not gain a higher rank among their people unless he was a prince – or the General. Who was she to think that she could ever be good enough for him? That she could ever be worth the effort he put forth now to defend against the dishonor her very presence had brought to his name under Kael's jealous allegations.

Through the haze of her thoughts, she became suddenly aware of a third blade entering into the fray. Another voice shouting sternly through the night air. "Kael, have you gone completely mad? Drop your weapon now or you will be taken into custody for treason."

"Leyna, what happened?" Maeri's voice was quiet, cautious not to speak the name loudly enough for Kael to hear.

Clutching to her, Leyna held Maeri tightly, her head reeling. She couldn't tell her the truth of what she had learned of her own heart. No one would understand. Even worse, no one would disagree with the simple fact that it could never be. How could she have let this happen? How could she have let herself fall for the one man who had always been so far out of reach?

Over Maeri's shoulder she could see Feolan and Kael fighting. The alcohol hindered Kael's reflexes just enough to place the advantage with Feolan. With little effort he bypassed Kael's guard, slamming the pommel of his sword hilt against Kael's head, laying him out cold on the ground at Feolan's feet.

"Consul, what happened?" Feolan asked, turning to face Thade with concern. "You know you are not well enough to be exerting yourself in this way. You could have been killed."

"He left me with very little choice. For now, if you please, save your lectures for another time."

Long strides carried Thade over to where Leyna and Maeri were standing, still wrapped in their desperate embrace. She didn't know how to act. She feared looking at him, horrified at the thought of him reading the feelings in her eyes. It had been easy to hide from him before. When she didn't know it for herself, she didn't have to worry about shielding it from anyone else. How would she talk to him? What was appropriate for her to say or do without making herself a fool in front of him?

She pulled away from Maeri, stomach churning at the ache in her chest, affecting her more greatly than the stinging of her jaw where Kael's elbow made contact. Eyes to the ground, she straightened her dress, tugging the corset back into place. "I am sorry." There was so much more behind her words than he could know. Her entire heart was behind them. And yet she couldn't bring herself to look into his eyes. He'd always been able to read her so easily. She couldn't risk opening up like the pages of a book for him now.

"Are you hurt?" His hand was on her face, searching through the darkness for any sign of injury where she'd been struck.

Fighting against his gentle pull, she kept her gaze lowered. "Sir, you have fought beside me in many battles. You know I have sustained far worse – where physical injury is concerned."

At her resistance, Thade knelt down on the ground, placing himself in the center of her vision. She averted her eyes. She couldn't bear to see him, looking up at her so sincerely, oblivious to the thoughts racing through her mind. "Leyna," he said, his voice soft and consoling. "I know that this is well beyond the realm of what is appropriate for me to ask or speak of to you, but as Consul, with my duty being to see to the safety of our people, and as your friend, with the desire to see that you are safe, I must request you answer one question for me."

"As your friend and loyal servant, I will answer anything you ask of me."

He looked almost hurt, his forehead creasing with strain at the sound of the word servant. Consternation filled his gaze. Despite her permission, he knelt there silently, seemingly contemplating whether or not to continue with the question he thought to ask, suddenly uncomfortable. "I must know. Is it true what Kael says? Have you never lain with him?"

Just when she thought the awkwardness could not get any worse! The last thing she wanted to discuss with him, of all people, was the intricacy of her private life. It was inappropriate. "I fail to see why that matters," she stammered.

"Because, if it is so, you may find the priests more amenable to your request for an annulment of your engagement; if you still are considering the option. And I must implore you to think on it quite seriously, given what you have told me, and what I have witnessed now with my own eyes."

"Is it not enough for the priests if the bond was documented under a false name?" Maeri inquired. Curiosity evident in her tone.

"It will help the case, but it would not be enough alone," Thade explained. "They would find ways to argue it, if the traditional rites of marriage had been exercised prematurely."

"But how would they prove I was telling the truth?" Leyna asked, the wheels in her mind turning at the possibilities being presented. They were both right. "I shudder to think of how they would judge my innocence, while at the same time; you and I both know proving my true name would be an impossible feat when Prince Enaes has been attempting to do so for years and remains at a loss."

"You are both Vor'shai. The decision would be in the hands of the Tanispan priests. I believe I could sway them to lean in your favor, but I would need you to give me your word, not as a servant the way you say, but as a friend," Thade replied quietly, clasping Leyna's hand in his. "If you swear to me that you are Leyna Evantine, and that everything you have told me is true and accurate, then I will vouch for you to the priests."

A single question nagged at the back of her mind. "Why do you do so much for me?"

"Why have you done so much for me?"

It was a simple question. One she couldn't answer. His eyes were steady, gazing into hers against her desire to look away. She couldn't say everything had been done out of love. During the war, she'd been too young to have fully understood a concept as complicated as that. Then, she had only known that she cared about him. But as a friend. A colleague. Her superior officer. It had been duty mingled with the personal emotions that already were out of her grasp of understanding even then.

"The night will not be with us much longer. Kael cannot be allowed to go free. His behavior is out of control and a threat to us and the mission. It can no longer be overlooked," Feolan interrupted. "I will take him to Queen Nesperiti and request him kept in her prison until transport can be arranged to carry Kael to Tanispa for a proper trial. My recommendation would be for Leyna not to return. The situation is far too dangerous. Zander will be fine on his own."

"Zander." Her heart pounded hard in her chest at the sound of his name. Kael's words echoed through her mind, chilling her to the bone. *For some reason I mistakenly believed you would run back to Zander's bed like the good little slave that you are.* "We need to get back to Zander's home. If Kael thought I would be there, he more than likely paid a visit to him before he came here. And all things considered, I fear what he might have done."

Rising to his feet, Thade nodded, his brow furrowed. "As much as I dislike the idea of you returning, Leyna — I will see you back, for Zander's sake," he stated, turning to face Feolan, cutting off his protests before the words could fully form. "You can take Kael into the city. Find a way to get him there out of sight. We cannot risk any of his friends seeing him or they will fight. Lady Diah, you are welcome to accompany Leyna and me, or you may remain here. I leave my home open to you if you prefer to wait for Feolan inside."

"Consul, I cannot let you risk being seen with Leyna or Zander. To do so would be putting you in direct danger –"

"Feolan, it is not up for discussion," Thade cut in. "I have been stuck here in this house for months. For all the danger Leyna exposes herself to on a daily basis, I feel a single trip to see her home safely is the least I can do."

They stared at each other silently. Leyna could read the displeasure on Feolan's face at the idea of letting Thade go. It was dangerous. For everyone involved. If Gislan was there, it could draw attention to them. They would have to be extremely cautious to avoid being seen by anyone on the road – or by any unexpected guests who might be inside Zander's home.

In the end, it was Thade who won the unspoken argument. Feolan's eyes shifted away from Thade's face, down to the limp body of Kael at his feet, a trickle of blood rolling down his skin from where Feolan's sword struck him. There was no way to know how long he would be rendered unconscious from the blow. Leyna feared he would wake up before Feolan could get him somewhere and escape.

"I will go with Leyna as well," Maeri chimed in. She avoided Feolan's devastated look. It was a losing battle for him to try and convince them all to change their minds.

"I am in no position to order any of you not to go, but I will express to you all my severe discomfort at the thought of you leaving here," he frowned. "I could simply take

Kael to the palace and go check on Zander myself, and the ladies could stay here with you, sir. It would be safest for everyone."

Thade moved past Feolan, through the front door of the house, emerging a moment later with a heavy cloak draped over his shoulders, the hood pulled down to conceal his face. "A single horse would be the easiest to keep out of sight, but with three of us, we will need to take a second one. I will leave it up to the ladies to decide which one of you will ride with me and which one will take the other horse."

"As embarrassed as I am to admit it, I do not know how to ride a horse without a saddle. Preferably one designed for a woman," Maeri blushed. "Faustine didn't exactly let us experiment with any other form of riding."

Leyna chuckled to herself. A bit of her old spark came over her the way it had during the war. She'd always been proud of her self-sufficiency. It mattered little that it wasn't considered to be lady-like to do the things she was able to do, but it was assuring to know that she was not so dependent upon men to help her through life. "I will take the other horse then. Saddles are rather overrated anyway," she chuckled.

In a way it was a relief that she would be riding separately from Thade. She was still too confused by her own emotions to know how she would handle being so close to him if she had to share his horse. It excited her in a way to think about it. But it was best she keep her distance. If she had any hope of maintaining their friendship despite her foolishness, she would need to do everything in her power to keep from putting herself in situations where they would be alone together. Or too close. Time would surely help to ease the feelings she had and allow her to again view him as the friend she did before.

He flashed her an approving smile, nodding to Maeri in understanding. "I will bring them around from the stables," he stated, patting Feolan on the shoulder comfortingly. "While I do that, you will find an extra cloak for Leyna on the hooks in the front closet of the house. See that she is properly covered. Once we are all ready we will have to move quickly toward town. We have very little time."

Chapter Eighteen

Wind whipped through Leyna's hair, tossing it about her face wildly with every clatter of the horse's hooves along the gravel road. She felt free. In the back of her mind she could picture herself just running, never stopping, until she reached the furthest coast of the land, leaving everything behind her. To start a new life. But she couldn't do that to her friends. They meant too much for her to leave them behind in exchange for her own selfish desires.

The closer they came to Zander's house, their pace slowed to ease the sound of the horses' approach. When they were within several houses of their destination, Leyna signaled for her horse to stop, kicking up stones behind her. "We will have to avoid the road from here. The woods to our right lines the properties between here and there. They will grant us cover all the way up to the window of the room where I have been staying. If everything is as it was when I left, the window should still be unlocked."

Their pace was hindered by the dense foliage. No path could be found to lead through it, only an occasional patch of ground where old hoof prints could be seen, breaking up clusters of wildflowers with the upturned soil. Leyna's heart raced frantically with every step they took. Grotesque images were conjured up by her subconscious, of Zander's body lying mangled and broken in a pool of blood on the floor of her room.

Kael was unpredictable. It was hard to say how far his anger would have taken him. Convinced there was some affair. Even considering what Kael believed to have been between them in the past, his accusations were unwarranted. She hadn't done anything to lead him to a conclusion involving infidelity. The only one to blame was Kael for his own behavior, luring out his jealous nature to a level beyond what Leyna would have imagined.

Easily she maneuvered her horse through the woods, her leg swinging over its back and down to the ground upon catching sight of Zander's house through the tree line. There was no time to bother with tying the horse in place. She needed to get inside.

The skeletal fingerlike branches on the ground tore at her skirt as she ran. She could hear the crackling of the ripped fabric. None of it mattered. It was just a dress. One that she was anxious to be out of for many reasons anyway.

Through the dim light of the coming dawn, she found her way up to the window of her room, her fingers sliding along the edges, lifting it up enough to grasp the bottom, pushing it open. She listened intently. Fear remained in the back of her mind; fear that someone other than Zander would be inside, waiting for her when she crawled through, calling out her deception. No sound came from the house. It was a relief, while also chilling her with the possibilities of why Zander was not there to greet her.

She wasn't sure when Thade had reached her side. In silent communication, he offered her his hand to step on, boosting her up through the window into the darkened room. Bracing herself for the worst, she pulled her body over the sill.

Within, everything looked exactly how she had left it, aside from a small red stain pooling on the floor in the middle of the room. Blood. Fresh, but soaking into the wood. She was startled by the sight of Zander sitting on the bed, clutching his left arm to his chest painfully. "Zander? My goodness, are you alright?"

"Leyna," he breathed. The relief was evident in his eyes to see her there. Uninjured. "I was afraid Kael found you."

"He did." A thud at the window caused them both to jump, glancing over to see Maeri working her way inside, finding it difficult to hoist herself up the final few inches. Rushing over to help, Leyna grabbed onto her arms, pulling her the rest of the way in.

Seeing Maeri, Zander rose quickly to his feet, wincing at the movement. "Lady Diah. This is an unexpected surprise."

"For you and me both," she huffed, catching her breath from the exertion of the climb. "Had I known I would be testing my physical prowess on this trip, I might have dressed more appropriately."

Leyna leaned her head back out the window, extending her hand down to Thade. With her help he ascended the side of the house, sliding into the room with ease. She felt awkward. He was still seemingly unaware of her feelings for him, unfazed by the contact of his hand with hers, paying no attention to the closeness of his body while pushing himself higher over the sill. Once he was nearly through, Leyna released her hold, stepping nervously away, her gaze shifting over to where Zander now stood.

"Consul," he gasped, his body bending at the waist in a courteous bow. "I feel a bit guilty for having left you to sneak into my home rather than greeting you appropriately."

"The climb was far more exhilarating," Thade chuckled quietly. His hands smoothed over the folds of his cloak. "This whole trip has made me miss the old days. Every day was like a new adventure. Politics have left me a bit out of shape, though, it would seem."

He looked out of place there in the tiny room. The fine cloth of his cloak shimmered in the light, his short hair tousled from the wind, yet still somehow looking perfect in Leyna's eyes. Even when disheveled, he carried an air of nobility unlike anyone else she'd ever known. It radiated from him, exuded from every inch of his body. There wasn't a single bone in him which didn't belie his attempts at appearing like a common man.

Tearing her eyes away from him again, Leyna tried to focus on Zander. He was injured, though the extent of his wounds couldn't be seen from where she stood. She made her way across the floor, lightly touching his favored arm with her hand. "What happened? Did Kael do this?"

"A better question is if there are any other people in this house with us right now," Thade asked. Zander had barely shaken his head before Thade continued, his hands reaching up to remove the cloak from around his shoulders, laying it along the floor by the window. "Lady Diah can see to Leyna. If you would not mind. Help her to get cleaned up and make sure she has suffered no injuries. Zander, I will inspect your wound and get it dressed before it becomes infected."

He didn't give Zander a chance to protest. Not that any of them would have. He was the Consul for their Queen. Whatever direction he gave, it was an order, and they would be expected to follow it. Never did he give an impression of pompousness, but it was obvious he was used to giving directions. His time as Captain had played a large role in that. Or so she could only assume.

Ushering Zander out the door, they left Maeri and Leyna alone, staring at one another through the dim light of the room. For the first time Leyna took note of the candles which were lit, placed around the floor to illuminate it. The low level of their flames caused shadows to play about their faces and darken the ceiling.

"Leyna, you never did answer me about what happened."

No, she hadn't. She didn't know how to. It didn't make enough sense to explain to anyone else. And she hated the thought of being a burden to her friend. Maeri had been out with Feolan. She was happy. Things were going well for her. Leyna didn't want to be the cause of strife for her after the many years Maeri had sacrificed to help. "It was nothing, really," she lied. "I am tired, Maeri. Nothing in my head is coherent right now. It might be best if we discussed things later."

Maeri's elegant features scrunched together in frustration. It was an interesting look for her. Leyna had never seen her make such a face before. Grabbing Leyna by the shoulders, she twisted her around, pulling off her soiled dress, working to loosen the laces of her corset. By the time she finished, Leyna already felt refreshed, her sides aching but free of the restraining stays. She breathed in deeply, enjoying the large gulps of air filling her lungs.

In nothing but her chemise, she let herself be escorted from the room, shuffling down the hallway toward the bath. The water in it had been sitting there for a while, cold, but tolerable. Capable of cleaning the unwanted dirt from her hair and skin. She tugged the chemise up over her head, letting it fall to the ground. All she could think about was the water.

It was like an escape. A moment of peace in the middle of all the torment life constantly threw at her. She was only partially aware of Maeri's eyes watching her, surprised by something she'd seen, but hesitant to speak. Sulking, Leyna lowered herself down, immersing herself completely into the water, her head submerged to hide from the questioning gaze of her friend. Her scars. Maeri had not seen them the night the doctor removed the fluid from her lungs. Could it be that she never asked Feolan what they saw which startled them so much? Or had Feolan avoided the question?

"Leyna?"

The voice was muffled from under the water. Begrudgingly she lifted her head up, wiping the water away from her face, gazing at Maeri solemnly. "Please don't ask. It is not something which I am comfortable explaining."

"Those marks look old. Too well-healed to have been caused by anything recent. Have you had them all while I have known you, and I simply never noticed?"

"Yes. But I said, I do not wish to speak of them," she sighed, leaning back against the cool tiles of the bath. Why did she hesitate to speak to Maeri? There were questions Leyna wanted to ask her as well. It was a perfect opportunity, but how could she possibly bring them up without also having to share information about her own life that she preferred not to offer. Much like her curiosity about Thade, she couldn't expect details from her friends without providing some of her own in return.

"Are they from the war?"

Why would she not leave it alone? Leyna straightened, holding Maeri's gaze steady. She refused to answer the questions. But she would see how willing Maeri was to speak on her own past. "Who was your father, Maeri?"

She looked shocked by the question; her eyes blinking rapidly. Her jaw hung open in silent confusion. "My father? That is a strange question. How does that have anything to do with the marks on your back?"

"Tell me your father's name, and we will see."

"Aviden Diah," she replied proudly, her chin jutting outward. "The Duke of Escovul. Given his title by Queen Vorsila herself. Is that satisfactory enough for you to now answer my question?"

Aviden. Deep down, she'd known. Her suspicions had run rampant since the first time she heard Maeri's family name. Really heard it. It sparked curiosity at the masque that night but it was when she had introduced herself to Zander that the reality had sunk in. Aviden Diah. Her mother's voice rang clearly in her head. They'd gone to Aviden the night they left Tanispa. *It is Damir. He knows — about us. Or at least about Leyna.*

She is your daughter as much as mine.

"Where is your father now?" she asked, ignoring Maeri's prodding to get her own answers from Leyna. This was far more important than the marks on her back. If only Maeri knew! This changed everything.

"He is dead," Maeri frowned. "He was killed when I was seven. No one ever really explained to me what happened, so I hope that reminding me of his death is enough to satisfy your curiosity."

"How old are you now?"

"Thirty-three."

"And you were seven when he died?"

"When he was murdered, yes. Leyna, please," Maeri begged, her expression contorting to near tears at the memories Leyna's questions recalled in her. "Why does any of this matter? I have spent years trying to get past it."

Thirty-three. Leyna wasn't hearing the quiet protests of her friend. There were two years between them. A smaller gap than she'd thought before. She had been nine when her own mother was killed at the hand of Damir and his assassins. Which would have made Maeri seven at the time. She gasped in horror, looking up to Maeri desperately. "Oh, gods, Maeri."

"What is it?" The misery instantly left Maeri's voice at the sight of Leyna's face. Kneeling down at the side of the bath, she reached out to Leyna. "What is wrong? Are you in pain?"

Rising from the water, Leyna hurriedly climbed up the steps from the bath, snatching a towel off a shelf near the door. She wrapped it around her body, concealing the scars on her back from view, her eyes still burning into Maeri's. *He knows — about us.* Damir knew. Aviden was her rightful father and Damir had found out. "I think I know who killed your father..."

Maeri froze, aghast at what Leyna was suggesting. "How could you know?" she stammered, shaking her head in disbelief. "No one could tell me anything. I asked my mother for years and she refused to answer me."

"She refused because she likely did not want to admit to you the truth," Leyna exhaled, pacing the floor excitedly at the realization. Sarayi and Aviden had been lovers. It all made sense to her now. The details had been hazy to her as a child because she didn't understand what was being said, but now — It all fit. *Father, you are the one that married me to that Ven'shal scum. You know Aviden had already asked for my hand in marriage before you decided to get in the way.* "Your father had been involved with another woman prior to marrying her. He had another child. A daughter."

"I have a sister? That isn't possible," Maeri argued. "Besides, you still haven't told me how you know of all this. How can you be so certain it is true?"

"Because I was the daughter."

The room fell deathly silent. She had said it. For the first time since her mother's death, she had spoken the truth of her past. And it was frightening. The timing of everything was too perfect. Damir must have discovered the identity of her mother's previous lover. He was the vengeful type. Never would he have allowed that man to live.

"But I have heard Feolan and the Consul talking about Prince Enaes's attempts to find you. They have not been able to verify your identity. How can you be so sure of who your father was? Surely if a Duke had fathered a child, the Queen would have documentation of the birth. There is nothing. The Prince has looked everywhere."

That was the most frustrating thing of all! How could she prove anything to anyone when her missing identity constantly thwarted her? And how? Who had been so thorough as to erase all records of her and influential enough to have accessed the Queen's records?

A member of the Queen's court, perhaps. One who had good reason to fear the scandal being discovered. Iden? Her own grandfather? He had screamed at her mother about what a disgrace she was. How the truth would ruin their family. And more recently, he lied to Enaes. He claimed to have no grandchild. Only a fool would blatantly lie to their prince about something if they knew there was proof against their lie. But it would be easier to fabricate the story if he knew such proof was gone.

In a rush, Leyna ran out of the room, moving swiftly back to the cover of her own chambers. Digging through her bags, she retrieved her nightgown, pulling it over herself desperately, afraid Zander and Thade would come walking in to find her there in nothing but her bathing towel. The nightgown covered her completely, the simple white fabric lined with lace around the high neck. Reaching to her wrists, the sleeves were loose, elegantly billowing out from the shoulders. A single cornflower blue ribbon wrapped around the empire waist. It draped lightly down the front of the garment, fluttering in the air almost to the ground at the hem, brushing over her bare feet.

Maeri's soft footsteps on the hard floor alerted Leyna to her presence in the room once again. Unasked questions could be seen in Maeri's eyes, but Leyna didn't want to talk about the past anymore. There were too many questions she couldn't answer which would only create more confusion. She hoped that in accepting Thade's offer to join Queen Nesperiti's court, it might open up possibilities for her to uncover the truth. She needed to know it if she had any hope of righting the wrongs that had been done to her and her family. She needed to know who had destroyed her. Who had led her mother down the road to her death.

"Kael is convinced that I am having an affair with the Consul," she said quietly, avoiding acknowledging anything they had discussed before. In changing the subject, she prayed Maeri would be distracted from prolonging the uncomfortable topic. "He showed up there tonight and found us together. Talking. In truth, I was already leaving. But he accused the Consul of dishonoring him, and attacked."

"You would be better off with the Consul, in my opinion," Maeri shrugged.

Leyna grimaced at her words. The painful pressure in her chest returned, reminding her of the miserable reality that she could never have him. "That may be so, but the Consul is a good bit above me in rank, if I do say."

"What does rank matter? If you love someone, there should not be specifications of title standing in the way."

"Rank matters more than anything when it comes to someone of his status," Leyna gasped, turning to face Maeri in surprise. "He is next to royalty. Do you not think his family would step in to prevent him becoming involved with a nobody? He could never love someone like me, so therefore I must never allow myself to think it possible."

"You love him."

The smile on Maeri's face made Leyna blush. "I did not say that," she breathed. "I said I cannot pretend he could ever think that highly of me. We are separated by his rank. I am lucky he even associates with me as a friend."

"Your eyes tell the truth while you try to cover it up," Maeri laughed softly, moving over to stand beside Leyna in the center of the room. "No one would ever blame you for feeling that way, Leyna. You shouldn't be so ashamed of it. And rank or not, how could he deny you? You have saved him from death at least twice. That has to count for something."

"Maeri, he cannot know that I think of him as anything more than a friend. Too many things are against us. I am sure it is a feeling which will go away with time."

"If my father is in fact yours, then rank is not one of those things coming between you. The Evantine family is of noble blood. Iden Evantine holds firm to his position as the Count of Voiene while the Diah family remains linked to the Dukedom."

"And I have nothing which proves my heritage to either line, so therefore I am nothing but a nameless orphan who just happened to save his life."

"That act alone could earn you a position of nobility and rank, regardless of your heritage. But you refuse to let anyone commend you for it. You run away from the Prince and avoid all praise from anyone else for your deeds. There are many things which could be in your favor if you desired him. You just need to let down your walls."

"Maeri," Leyna cut in. She feared that if she allowed her friend to continue speaking, she might actually start to believe it was possible. That was a heartache she didn't care to endure. "I am engaged. Plain and simple. My betrothed has now accused me of having an affair with the Consul. In the event of my engagement being dissolved, I still could not be with the Consul, even if I wanted to. Even if he wanted me. Can you imagine how it would look if I denied accusations of intimacy between myself and Thade and then, upon separating with Kael, suddenly was seen to be close with him?"

Understanding flashed over Maeri's face at Leyna's explanation. How could she think to deny the truth in it? Such a scandal would ruin them both. And she couldn't bear to think of causing that much dishonor to Thade. He didn't deserve the accusations already being tossed at him so wildly by Kael. She couldn't risk unintentionally giving the empty allegations any appearance of truth to those around them.

Before Maeri could say anything, the sound of approaching footsteps echoed through the hall, silencing their conversation. Leyna felt the heat building in her face at the sight of Thade entering the room. She was afraid the men might have overheard their discussion. She'd never be able to look Thade in the eye again if he knew the way she felt about him.

He paused in the doorway, his eyes glancing over her. For a moment he looked almost surprised. She realized how she must look to him, standing there in her night-gown, her hair damp and tangled about her head and face. It was embarrassing. In her distraction she had failed to think about her appearance. Regardless of whether or not she could ever be with him, she didn't want him to see her looking so bedraggled.

There was a brush in the closet, resting atop her bags. Reaching out for it, she began to run it through her hair, wincing at the tangles catching in the bristles. "How is Zander? The wound is not too severe, I hope?"

"It is deep," Thade nodded. As if only just realizing he had stopped moving, he stepped further into the room, allowing Zander an opening to stand beside him. "But we managed to get it cleaned and stitched. It will hurt for a while, but it will not cause any permanent damage."

"The Consul is faster with a needle than any doctor I've ever seen," Zander chuck-led. He was still favoring his left arm. The fabric of his shirt was pulled up, tinged with red over the laceration. It had fallen down just enough to hide most of the cut from view, only revealing a few small stitches on the bicep, an inch or two above the elbow.

Leyna smiled in spite of her discomfort. "He has used them on many people over the years. Myself included. A handy one to have around if you accidentally block a blade with your body instead of your weapon."

"I think I tend to forget that, unlike most people who frequent the court, the Consul actually knows what it is like to serve on the battlefield. Makes him more respectable," Zander mused, fumbling over his sleeve to pull it back down, hiding his injury completely from sight. "Leyna, you look to be alright, save for the swelling I see starting on your cheek. Does it hurt at all?"

Mid-stroke, she paused her efforts to tame her knotted hair. She'd forgotten about her own injury. It was mild in comparison to any others she had sustained over the years. It was hard for her to even consider it more than just a simple bump. Shifting her jaw around, she tested the function of the joints, feeling a slight pressure and tightness over the right side, not enough to cause her any alarm. "I have endured worse. Swelling only lasts for a few days and then it will be good as new."

"I cannot believe he hit you," Maeri scowled. "Has the man lost his mind?

"Possibly," Leyna frowned, idly continuing her careful work on her hair. "It is hard to say what was affecting him more tonight. The magic or the alcohol. If it was the alcohol, then it may be possible to speak rationally with him at the prison when he wakes up. If it was the magic, I fear he could be lost to us for good."

"Either way, we are increasing our risk of being caught by remaining here into the daylight hours," Thade announced calmly. "Maeri, you will either have to attempt to learn how to ride the other horse without the feminine tack, or we will have to quickly find a way to tow it behind us."

Maeri's face fell at the thought of riding the horse on her own. "I do not know the first thing about riding without the proper equipment," she stammered. "It just seems so horribly uncomfortable and hard."

The sound of Zander's snickering only added to the pink in her cheeks, rising up to the tips of her ears. Giving in to the humor of Maeri's embarrassment, Thade joined in with Zander's laughter, patting her on the back while making his way over to the window. "I will not torture the poor woman this time, though I make no promises, if we are ever forced to ride like this again, that I will not make you try to ride." He turned a solemn gaze on Leyna. "It is my hope that you will still consider leaving the mission as we discussed this evening. I would feel more comfortable knowing you were safely working with me rather than like this."

"I will make my decision based on how things go tomorrow. With Kael no longer here, there will be questions. If things get too dangerous, I will find a way to leave and seek you out."

"That is exactly what I am afraid of. If the others discover you to have been in any way involved with his arrest —"

"Consul," Leyna replied softly. Formally. It felt less personal to say what she needed to say if she addressed him by his title rather than his name. "Words cannot express how sorry I am for all of this. Things got out of control and it is not fair that your name has been dragged into this mess."

Shaking his head, Thade held up his hand to silence her. "Please, do not apologize. This is in no way your fault, and I do not want you to worry yourself by thinking it is. Kael's accusations are misplaced and hollow. His words should not cause either of us a single moment of unrest." Motioning toward Maeri to follow him, he pulled the window up, his legs swinging over the ledge. "Just remember what I said about helping you. You need only say the word, and I will go to the priests."

The priests. Yes, they had discussed it, but the conversation had been interrupted before she could say to him what she had wanted to say. He asked her to swear to him that she was being truthful. She only hoped he would accept her word on her honor.

She let the brush in her hand clatter to the floor, moving quickly over to the window, grabbing Thade's arm before he could lower himself all the way down to the ground. He looked up at her, surprised by her sudden desperation. Their eyes gazed back at one another. It was as if he already knew what she intended to say before the words even touched her lips, anxiously waiting to hear the sound of her voice speaking them.

Leaning forward, she brought her face down close to his, her lips hovering near his ear. A flutter ran through her heart at being so near to him. It took her a moment to regain her composure, nearly forgetting what she wanted to say. "I swear to you that I have never lied to you," she whispered. The sound of her own voice was so quiet; she feared it would be carried away on the morning breeze, never reaching Thade's ears. "One day I will find a way to prove it all, but until then, I can only give you my word that I would never lead you astray."

"You do not have to prove anything to me, Leyna." His response was soft, barely even a whisper. The sound was familiar to Leyna, though she couldn't place from where, seeming unimportant at the time. All that mattered was that he believed her. The sound of his voice whispering her name made it all feel worth it.

Without another sound, he dropped down from the window, making no more than a gentle, barely audible thud where his feet touched the grass. Leyna stared after him. She didn't want to let him go. She wanted to leave with him. To go back to his house and forget about this stupid mission and the dangers they were facing. It didn't seem fair that everything always had to be in constant turmoil. The gods had a funny way about them, teasing the world with a brief time of peace, only to toss them back into the bloody throes of war.

Gathering up her skirt in her hand, Maeri stepped over to the window. She peered down hesitantly. It wasn't a long drop, but for a woman with the upbringing that Maeri had been given, it looked like a drop off the highest mountain in Velorum.

Thade remained just under the window, offering his hand out to help Maeri to the ground, beckoning her to come quickly. She started to move toward the opening. At the last second, she turned back to Leyna, whispering something only to be heard between the two of them. "You should tell him how you feel about him."

"Goodness, Maeri," Leyna breathed, blushing in spite of herself, though she knew Zander couldn't have possibly heard what Maeri said. "No, I will not. Nor can I; and neither will you. Promise me that you will not say a word to him. Or Feolan. Confiding in him would only lead to it getting back to the Consul and his friendship means far too much to risk it over something so foolish."

"It is not foolish. The only thing that is foolish is denying yourself happiness because it is easier to convince yourself that you don't deserve it." Dangling her legs over the window sill, she prepared to jump, squeezing Leyna's hand tightly in her own. "Forget about what other people will think. If the opportunity presents itself, do not give it up. You may not get a second chance."

"Maeri, go!" Leyna huffed. She didn't want to hear more advice. No one could know what was going on inside her heart or head. It was frustrating the way everyone wanted to tell her how she should act, and how she should think. They all believed they knew what it required for her to find happiness in life. In her mind, there were too many other things which were more important than her own happiness. She would worry about regrets and missed opportunities after her people were safe.

Maeri disappeared over the edge with nothing more than a muffled cry from the bottom. They managed to escape the house before Gislan had returned. As long as they kept to the cover of the trees, they would be safe.

"I think I should try to get some sleep," she said quietly, averting her eyes from Zander's questioning gaze. "I will discuss this all in more detail later, but for now I need to rest. I need to be prepared to handle whatever might come of this tomorrow."

Chapter Nineteen

Sleep evaded Leyna throughout the day, leaving her tossing and turning in bed. There was so much to think on. So many things she wanted to do. It frustrated her to know that she couldn't possibly accomplish them all.

Her plans would have to change. It had been convenient, at first, to think that she could infiltrate the Ven'shal. Had those involved been any other men, she might have been successful. But her past haunted her, leaving no choice but to retreat, questions still floating in her mind which now might never be answered.

Giving up, Leyna climbed out of bed, staring absently toward the little window which was still standing open, grey light filtering in from the cloudy skies. In her chest she could feel an excited flutter from her heart. Deep down she hoped to find Thade there, staring at her while climbing up to the window to be with her though she also knew it was too dangerous for him to risk coming back. It was foolish to think he would want to see her so desperately anyway. Why did her emotions have to make her think like a child lost in a fairy tale where the prince climbs up the tower to rescue his love? Reality never worked that way. She knew well enough about that.

With the dimming light of the sun fading away into night, she was surprised no one had yet sought her out. It was possible they were searching for her. No one other than Zander knew where she was. Everyone expected her to be at the inn with Kael. A tightness in her stomach accompanied the fear that Kael might have escaped and returned to Thade's to confront him again.

Quickly, she put on her clothes, opting for a more traditional dress with no need for the dreaded corset she had been pained to wear for the last week. Threading the laces through the heavy bodice before she slid it on, she struggled to pull them tight, fumbling with the ribbons behind her back. The fabric was a thick burgundy and gold damask. Another from Oksuva's personal collection. The skirt was simple with folds of matching cloth flowing out and down to the floor, concealing her feet from view.

Slipping her feet into her shoes, she hurried over to the door. In her rush, she pulled on the latch, letting it fall down from the locking mechanism with a scrape of metal against wood, opening the door up to the hallway. Her breath caught in her throat at the sight of Kyros's blackened eyes gazing at her from just outside.

"Eleni," he smiled, stepping forward, pressing Leyna back into the room, almost forcefully, without need of laying a hand on her. She stumbled backward, her heel catching on the fabric of her dress, causing her balance to falter before she could regain her composure.

"Sir. I did not know you were here —"

In a fluid motion he closed the door, passing it between his hands behind his back, his eyes locked on her, burning into her with his abyssal gaze. "I wanted it to be a surprise," he smirked. "I hear interesting things about you, Eleni. Things which I must admit pique my interest beyond the norm."

"Depending on the source, it is difficult to say whether or not those things are true," Leyna stammered. Clutching her skirt in her hand, she tried to step away from Kyros, his body moving with hers, preventing her from putting distance between them.

"I have taken a large risk on my part, under the assumption that these things I have heard are true. For many reasons, I am convinced they are accurate, but those reasons are not for you to know. Yet."

Something in his face told her she should be afraid of him. Of his intentions. Not because he had any desire to take advantage of her physically, but because he was capable of overpowering her in ways that she had no knowledge of. Military training in Siscal didn't require any means of defense against magic because the enemy they faced used only tangible weapons. If Kyros wielded energy even half as well as Damir, she had no chance at getting away.

She had to stay calm. The trembling in her body made it too obvious that she feared him. She couldn't allow him to be aware of her discomfort, or it would give him the upper hand, letting him know he could push her around by brute force. "Tell me, then," she replied, her voice strained but steady. "What are these rumors you have heard, so that I might tell you if they hold any validity?"

A smile passed over Kyros's lips. "Your husband tells me you have some kind of connection with the Tanispan Consul. One that might grant you some favor with him?"

"What?" She was appalled to think Kael had said anything to Kyros about the Consul. Especially anything regarding her personal friendship with him or Feolan. To think that he had even spoken of them with Kyros sent chills through her body. "I hold no favor with the Consul..."

"Don't lie to me!" Kyros snapped, grabbing her right wrist painfully in his hand. She stared down at it, horrified, her eyes glancing back up to him in fear and confusion. "Kael told me he discovered you at the Consul's home prior to leaving for Kaipoi. That alone was enough to make me curious, but now – now he tells me he found you there again last night. What would a woman like you – a slave – have that the Tanispan Consul would have interest in? Your body?"

"I... I –" Leyna stammered. Her anger and frustration were growing, making it easier to hide her fear, while harder to maintain her composure from yelling back at him. "Why would Kael even be discussing these matters with you? None of this is even remotely your business. It is between me and my betrothed."

Tightening his grip on her wrist, Kyros pulled her in closer to him, their faces nearly touching as he spoke. "Your *betrothed* made it my business when he asked me to free you from Mikel's enslavement. I had a deal with him that I would do something for him in exchange for him doing a bit of work for me. Now I see this as an opportunity for both of us. You and I."

"Then we will talk about it after I am freed from Mikel."

"You are already free," Kyros hissed. "I tried to talk to Mikel about it like businessmen, but he was unwilling to reach an agreement. It was simple enough to see the life choked from his body. Once he ceased to breathe, you were free. And you have been for at least a week, so I suggest you listen to what I have to say or you will join him in death, and your soul will serve as a slave for all eternity under my command."

Leyna inhaled sharply, the stench of the tainted energy filling her nostrils. The Ven'shal were all the same. He was no better than that man who attacked her in Velorum when she'd first laid eyes on one of their kind. She was trapped. If what he said was true, then she was his. A toy to use however he wanted. He had granted her freedom only to use it against her for his own gain. "Does Kael know you are here?" She knew it to be impossible. By now Kael would be in Queen Nesperiti's prison...

"Kael would never agree to what I am going to ask of you, which is why I had no choice but to make sure he wouldn't get in my way," he chuckled, releasing his hold on Leyna's wrist. "You see – he told me he has had suspicions of the Consul having a spy amongst Oksuva's people for years. The worthless fool didn't know who it was, but he has reason to suspect that information has been leaked. Now, I am quite displeased to hear of this. I am inclined to believe that you are not involved in the dissemination of sensitive details regarding our business since Kael has told me all about his prior work for the Consul and that he is the one who introduced you to him. But I want to know who the other spy is. I want to know what the Consul knows."

Her blood ran cold in her veins at his words. Kael had told him everything. Betrayed them. Even worse than she could have imagined. For the first time since she met Kael, she felt the guilt of having kept her secrets from him dissipate. How could she feel remorse when in the end it was the only thing which would offer protection to her and Zander? His lack of knowledge prevented him from destroying the entire mission.

"What do you expect me to do?"

Kyros leered at her, seemingly annoyed by her question. "What do you think I want you to do?" he sneered. "I want you to get closer to him. If you aren't already in his bed, seduce him. Get him to talk. Find out who he associates with and what he knows of our plans. You are an attractive woman. I have no doubt that you could wrap him around your little finger with minimal effort. If not him, then his little man servant, but I prefer the bigger fish."

"And if I refuse?"

"You have no choice in the matter." Gritting his teeth, he pressed forward, forcing her to step back. "I did not bargain for your freedom because I wanted to help. You are in my debt and your options are to either do as I say, or die. Which would you prefer, Leyna?"

Leyna's eyes opened wide at the sound of her name coming from his lips. Frantically, she tried to hide her recognition, narrowing her eyes to stare back at him, confused. "You are the second person to call me by that name. It is not mine."

"No, of course not," Kyros looked her over carefully, scrutinizing every detail of her face to read her reaction. "You were young. It wouldn't surprise me if you'd forgotten. Regardless, my order stands. You will find the information I want. I trust you're more than capable of pulling it from the lips of those men."

"How am I to do this? Oksuva would never allow —"

"Oksuva? What does she matter?" Kyros scoffed. "You're mine now. What you do will be determined by me. If being around these imbeciles will hinder your work, then I will see you removed from his house. Away from your beloved Kael. He would only get in my way. That was made obvious when he came to me last night. Can you imagine? The man is livid over your involvement with the Tanispan Consul. If you are going to bed him, we can't have your betrothed getting in the way."

Leyna gasped, exasperated by what Kyros was suggesting. Her cheeks flushed with color, embarrassed. Bed the Consul? Had Kael polluted everyone's head with his insane notions? "I am not going to bed anyone. You are out of line to even think it."

"Out of line?" Kyros asked derisively, jerking her roughly in his grasp. The blackened holes of his eyes were settled on her, sending waves of shivers through Leyna's spine at the anger she felt radiating from him. "You belong to me, girl. You've been a slave long enough to know that when your master tells you to do something, it isn't optional. Kael has let you get away with too much. It's as if you think you're in a position to make your own decisions. Well, you listen to me, now. I will be back here tomorrow morning. When I arrive, you will be packed and ready to leave."

"Leave? Why do I have to leave?"

"Because I can't trust you to do your job if you stay here. The others will be nothing but a distraction for you. I will arrange a room for you at one of the inns in town. Your location isn't to be disclosed to anyone, do you understand? These people in this house are nothing to you anymore. Forget about them. I am the only one you are to speak with, under any circumstances. You have one night to say your goodbyes and gather your things. There will be no more discussion on the matter." Raising his hand, a plume of black energy erupted from Kyros's palm, hurtling into Leyna's chest with incredible force. Unable to maintain her balance, she stumbled backward. Screaming, she felt as her legs bumped against the window sill, the pressure of the darkness sending her toppling through the opening.

It all passed in a blur. She felt her body flip over the ledge, connecting hard with the ground, branches and rocks cutting into her skin. She lay there, trying to catch her breath, her face buried in the soil.

Overhead, she could hear Kyros's voice from the window. Shakily she lifted herself with her arms, gazing up at him pathetically from the ground. "You are insignificant to me," he stated plainly. "Your death would be nothing more than a mild amusement to pass my time. I suggest you keep that in mind."

As Kyros's face disappeared, she let her body flop back down to the ground. This was an absolute mess. Things had finally started to go in a direction which made some semblance of sense and this only added complications to it all. Kael had betrayed them in more ways than she could have known before.

Kyros's words floated through her mind, sending shivers down her spine. He knew who she was. There was no doubt anymore. He didn't need to say it in so many words for her to understand his implications. *You were young. It wouldn't surprise me if you'd forgotten.* So what was stopping him from killing her? After all these years he had her in his grasp and he let her go. He was using her. Convinced that she was unaware of who he was and what he intended to do. She would be useful in gathering the information he needed from the Consul. Once her task was completed, he would kill her.

Something else tugged at the corner of her mind, adding to her discomfort. Kyros mentioned Kael having told him about the events of the previous night. But how was that possible? Kael was taken to Queen Nesperiti by Feolan. There wouldn't have been any chance for Kael to speak with Kyros unless...

"Leyna."

The hushed sound of Thade's voice came from somewhere beside her, pulling her from the thoughts racing through her head. She had to be imagining things. There had been no sound of his footsteps approaching. It was as if he'd already been there, watching. "Great. Now I am hearing things," she grumbled, turning her head toward the noise. Gasping in surprise, she found Thade kneeling at her side, his hand reaching gently toward her shoulder.

"You are not hearing things." He was calm. Serene. A hint of sadness could be heard when he spoke, his hands helping Leyna to a seated position. "I came to speak with you and heard voices coming from your window. You sounded frightened. I feared it was Kael with you."

"If only I were so lucky," she muttered, rising to her feet, dusting the dirt from her dress. Registering his words, she blinked at him in surprise, reminded of her thoughts prior to Thade making his presence known. The aches in her body from the fall were quickly forgotten to the panic she felt. "Kael?" she gasped. "I thought he was in Nesperiti's prison."

Casually observing the area, Thade clasped Leyna's hand, leading her through the trees away from the house. His horse wasn't far away. He was dressed for riding, his black leather boots coming up to his knees. She was surprised to see he was not wearing a cloak, his face fully visible. The elegantly designed frock coat he wore buttoned stylishly up the front with golden buttons, the black fabric of the long sleeves accented by the ruffle of the white undershirt he wore beneath it. "Come," he stated, motioning toward the horse. "We shouldn't linger here to discuss this. The risk of unwanted ears overhearing is too great."

He looked perfect. So perfect that she couldn't convince herself she wasn't dreaming. Knocked unconscious from the fall, imagining him into existence. The only thing that told her it wasn't a dream was how real he felt. Gentle pressure on her hand, guiding her up onto the horse's back behind him. She wrapped her arms around his waist to keep from falling off. It was a completely different feeling to be a passenger on a horse, having no control over where it went or how fast. Thade maneuvered it through the trees at an alarming speed, forcing her to tighten her hold on him.

Leyna couldn't shake her confusion at Thade's unexpected presence outside Zander's house. It didn't make any sense that Feolan would have allowed him to come there alone. Not after the way he reacted to Thade's insistence at accompanying her home that morning. He never would have willingly let him go there. Unless he wasn't aware Thade had left — or was unable to accompany him for some reason.

Why would Thade have come there alone? She shuddered to think what Kyros would have done had he sensed Thade's presence outside the window. Then came the most uncomfortable realization of all. Thade had heard voices coming from inside the house. How much had he heard? Was he aware of Kyros's orders for her to get close to him? To seduce him!

Their pace finally began to slow as they neared another line of trees outside of the city. Leyna recognized the area to be near Thade's home, but still a mile or so off from the tiny neighborhood. Through the woods, she was certain they would reach the backs of the houses, crossing the property lines of his neighbors. She'd never been beyond the front of his home, her curiosity sparked at the chance of seeing it in more detail.

A clearing opened up around them, the ground spattered with color from various wildflowers emerging from the vibrant green grass. Thade signaled the horse to stop, pausing to inhale a deep breath of the fresh air before carefully lowering himself down, offering his hand to Leyna to assist her as well. "I hope this will suffice. Normally I would have preferred to take you to my home, but Feolan was having Lady Diah over for dinner this evening and I feel lately that I am more in the way around them than anything."

"This is beautiful," Leyna observed the area in fascination. "How close to your home are we? It cannot be far."

"Just through the last line of trees over there," Thade motioned with his hand to the group of trees opposite where they had entered. "This is where Feolan and I come in the mornings to train and practice our meditation. It is my favorite part of the day, given that aside from my time here, I rarely have an opportunity to see anything but the walls of the house."

"Feolan seems very protective of you. I must admit that I am amazed he even let you leave without him."

"He does not know I am gone," Thade chuckled. "Feolan has known me since I was still a very young boy. I think he forgets at times that I am not a child anymore, and in fact outrank him. He means well, though. I cannot fault him for it."

Stepping through the luscious grass, Leyna took in the sweet scent of flowers in the air. It relaxed her. Easing her troubled nerves after the fear that had haunted her since the moment she'd seen Kyros outside her door. She felt safe here. And though she knew it was her who should be on guard to protect Thade, she also knew he would never let anything happen to her. "This is another one of those moments where I wish I had good news to bring you. The scenery is far too pleasant for such depressing things."

"The sun will be below the horizon soon enough and the bright colors of the land will fade. I believe the shadows will make it more fitting for whatever you could possibly say. However, I feel as though I should be the one to speak first. You should be made aware of our current predicament."

Leyna stared at Thade, afraid to know what he referred to. In her mind she'd already pieced together the frightening truth. Somehow Kael was no longer in custody. Her fear laid in how he'd managed to get free. "I have gathered, from some things already spoken, that this predicament involves Kael having escaped. Is Feolan safe? No one is injured, I hope?"

"Nothing more than a bump on the head, which Lady Diah has been more than attentive to," Thade chuckled. "I doubt he feels a thing, really. It seems Kael regained consciousness before Feolan could reach the city gates. With the attack being unexpected, there was little Feolan could do to defend himself. Kael struck him, knocking Feolan from the horse, and took off toward the city. I only just learned of it this morning. After tending to Feolan's injuries, I waited for the first opportunity which would allow me to come to you and verify your safety. My fear was that Kael would immediately seek you out."

"He must have gone to Kyros instead. What Kyros did to him afterwards, I am unsure," Leyna frowned. In her mind she could hear Kyros's words. *Kael would never agree to what I am going to ask of you, which is why I had no choice but to make sure he wouldn't get in my way.* How would he prevent Kael from getting in the way? "Kyros alluded to detaining Kael. I just do not know how long that will last. Given the particulars of what Kyros came to me for, I imagine he would not want Kael underfoot anytime soon."

"Maybe you could clarify for me the discussion which took place. I overheard a great deal from my cover outside the window. I admit, only some of it made any sense to me."

"So you heard Kael has told Kyros everything. About his work for you," Leyna sighed. "He told Kyros he believes there is still another spy among them. Not to mention, having told him of the nonsense involving you and me. Kyros has ordered me to get information from you which might expose the other spy."

A curious half-smile passed over Thade's lips, a soft sparkle twinkling in his silver eyes. "Yes. I believe you are supposed to seduce me? Did I hear that correctly?"

It sounded so much more ridiculous when Thade said it. The humor eased the humiliation only somewhat, Leyna's cheeks still flushing with warmth at the thought of discussing the idea with him. "It seems like it would be hard to seduce a man who is already aware of the plan to do so."

"You are welcome to try. I must warn you though, I am not easily seduced. Many a woman has tried and failed." His tone was playful. She'd never heard him speak in that manner before, seeming almost flirtatious.

Peering at him quizzically, she shook her head, laughing quietly to herself. "My only experience with seduction comes from the conversation I had with you and Feolan while in Velorum. The morning you informed me Prince Enaes was coming to Siscal."

"Ah, yes. How to seduce powerful men," he smirked. "Something tells me that our advice would not have been very helpful. If my memory serves me well, it was suggested that you do nothing if you hoped to catch their eye."

"Even if I were a woman who knew how to manipulate my wiles, as you called them, you would be far too clever a man to fall for it."

"You are well on your way to being the most evil kind of woman, then. I shall have to beware your natural charms."

Their eyes met, holding each other's gaze for a moment before dissolving into laughter. "I cannot believe you remember that conversation," she smiled, shaking her head emphatically.

"And you," Thade agreed. "That must have been nearly twenty years ago now. So much has changed since then. Most noticeably, you."

"I am still the same girl I was back then. The only difference is that I wear a skirt now instead of the less than fashionable commissioned pants and jacket of the military uniform."

Making his way out into the center of the clearing, Thade tilted his face up toward the sky, the grey clouds overhead signaling the coming of night, the last light fading away over the grass. "You would have enjoyed the military training in Tanispa," he mused. "I have never found anything quite like it since I was ordered to come to Siscal. The fighters here have always felt lacking to me, in comparison."

"Why did they send you here?" Leyna couldn't hold back the question. She'd never heard him speak of his personal life before the war. He was as much a mystery to her in regards to his past as she was to him.

Calmly, he lowered his gaze, motioning for Leyna to come closer. "A political trade-off. Truthfully, I know little about the details. My mother was the one who handled it all. I had no choice but to go where I was told." Extending his right arm outward, Thade bent his wrist, directing the back of his hand toward Leyna, his stance relaxed. "Come," he smiled. "I will test your senses and reflexes while we discuss how we will deal with this change in our plans."

She stared at him, at a loss to what he was referring. Test her senses and reflexes? She could barely see a thing. He couldn't possibly expect her to spar with him in the dark. And in her dress! She wasn't prepared for any form of test. "I really am not dressed appropriately for – anything," she argued.

"There is no dress code for this," Thade chortled, lightly taking her right arm, positioning it like his own, the backs of their hands and wrists touching. "It is an old training exercise. One which Feolan and I still enjoy to this day. You do not have to move at first. We will start easy."

With a gentle motion, he pressed against her arm, his upper body circling slowly. He kept his center in perfect alignment, shifting his weight back and forth between his legs. She followed his lead, laughing nervously, unsure whether or not she was doing any of it right. "So what exactly is this supposed to do?" she asked, their arms continuing the slow, relaxed circle in the air between their bodies.

"General Cadell called it 'Harmonious Hands.' Similar, in theory, to the way your teacher at the academy taught you blind fighting," he explained, never ceasing the movement between them. "Only with this, you learn to feel your opponent's next move. It is more about evading. Flowing. Less about the power and more about how to manipulate your opponent's momentum against them. My goal is to remain in constant contact with you, staying relaxed, and trying to keep you off balance without utilizing any force of my own."

"It sounds complicated." Leyna found herself distracted by the slight increase in speed from Thade's arm, rocking them back and forth at a steady pace. Suddenly she felt her arm collapse against her chest, halting the motion mid-circle.

Grabbing her arm, Thade shook it gently, noticing the tenseness in her muscles. "Relax. It is like a dance, really. When doing a waltz, when your partner steps forward, you do not move into him, do you?" he smiled. "When the man steps forward, the lady steps back – moving with him. Similarly, if I come toward you, your body should bend with it. Continue the flow. However you can maneuver yourself to avoid it, be it bending or twisting. Let us try again. But this time, do not think about it so much. Tell me more about what happened this afternoon. It will act as a distraction, forcing you to naturally follow the movement of my arm."

They reset their hands in the middle, beginning the slow circle once again. She tried to think of it like a dance. A very strange dance. One where she had no idea what the moves were, but hoping she would be able to react properly to Thade's lead. "Kyros claims he has killed Mikel. If that is true, then I am a free woman. In a way."

"Do you have reason to believe he would lie to you about Mikel's death?"

"No. Honestly, I feel the only thing he told me which was not accurate was his claim that he attempted to speak reasonably with Mikel before taking his life. It seems more Kyros's style to simply walk in and take what he wanted, much like Damir."

"Then you are free, except for the debt Kyros feels you owe him for having released you," Thade nodded. He never missed a beat with their flowing motion, occasionally directing the rotation higher or lower, testing Leyna's reaction to the change. "He blackmails you with that debt to force you into seducing me for information?"

As she opened her mouth to speak, Thade switched up the circle again, aiming the rotation toward Leyna's head. Instinctively, she rolled with the movement, bending her back low to evade it, catching a hint of a smile on Thade's lips as she rose back up, carrying on with the momentum as if nothing had happened. "That is essentially the way of things, yes," she replied. A swell of pride was building inside her at the successful evasion. Afraid of losing her focus, she tried to suppress it. "I just am not sure what that means in the long run. Kyros wants me to spend time with you, though I am not certain how he intends to take me away from Oksuva without creating a scene. She thinks I am still one of her ladies."

"Then she is not aware of her husband's death?"

The thought came as a shock to her. How could Oksuva know? They had only just returned to Siscal the day before. It was possible the news had not yet reached anyone else in their group. With Mikel dead, Oksuva would have no use for her, unless Kyros or Damir insisted on her presence. Though if Kyros kept his word and removed Leyna from the house, Oksuva's opinion mattered little. "No. I believe she is unaware."

"In that case, she will have little to say on the matter if I were to ask you to accompany me to Mialan before the week's end," he stated matter-of-factly. "You can tell Kyros it is part of your plan for seduction, and then you will be free to join me in meeting with the Mialan royals. It originally was supposed to be a social gathering to show the continued allegiance between Mialan and Tanispa, but I have since decided to request a new alliance with them, in preparation for the possibility of a coming war."

Mialan. It had been over two decades since she saw that island last. Slowly, she brought her arm to a halt, staring blankly at Thade through the shadows. "I cannot go to Mialan," she whispered. There was no logical reason she could give him for not wanting to see it again. Over time, the area would have grown. Changed. There was more than likely nothing left of the neighborhood she once lived in with Reina. Even then, it had been run down and dilapidated. Someone would have torn it down.

The lighthearted expression on Thade's face faded away. He looked disappointed, though why it would mean so much to him; she couldn't put her finger on. "Leyna." His voice was calm. Quiet. "What is it about your past that prevents you from doing so much in the present?"

"What makes you think that my reasons have anything to do with my past?"

"Because there is no other explanation," he frowned. "As far as I can see, there is no reason why you would not want to go unless it held some significance to your past which you were afraid I would find out. Or you are afraid to face."

"I am not afraid to face my past," Leyna argued, hearing the trembling in her own tone. She couldn't hide it from him. She didn't understand why it frightened her so much to return to that place. If anything, it might present her with some kind of closure. The thought of trying to face it with Thade there only made it seem that much more impossible. There was no telling how her emotions would react to the memories, and she just couldn't bear the thought of breaking down in front of him.

"We make an interesting pair, you and I," Thade mumbled, turning away from her to gaze off into the darkened trees leading toward his house. "Haunted by our pasts, unwilling and unable to tell anyone anything about it. You might think I could never understand, but you would be surprised just how understanding I might be of your situation. Whatever it is."

"You are haunted by your past?" Leyna asked. A familiar frustration bubbled up inside her. So many people had tried to claim they knew exactly how she felt while she was growing up, but none of them ever did. And how could they? How could he? A man of his position couldn't possibly know what it was like to live in her shoes. "I find it difficult to believe we are as similar as you think. I would ask you to elaborate, but I already know you will refuse."

Thade straightened his back, smoothing out the folds of his coat uncomfortably. "You are right," he said suddenly. "I have no right to ask you to come with me if you have no desire to go. You have done so much for me already that it would be selfish of me to continue to press. I will go alone."

"Alone?" Leyna blinked. "I assumed Feolan would join you if I did not."

"This business runs a little outside and above the typical duties of the Consul. I act as Queen Vorsila's voice here in Siscal. To travel to another country steps outside that rank. Because of this, Feolan will be remaining here to act in my stead in the event that anything is needed in my absence. There is nothing for him to learn by accompanying me."

Damn. He had known exactly how to word it to make her refusal impossible. There was no doubt in her mind he'd done so intentionally. He was a clever man after all. "Why me, then?" she exhaled, her shoulders drooping forward in defeat. "If this trip is so important that Feolan cannot even go, why am I any different?"

He lifted his brow at her, curious. He could tell she was giving in. "Because it happens that the Mialan court is having a celebration during the time I will be there. Coincidentally, that day also happens to be your birthday. For once, since I have known you, I would like to see you enjoy yourself on that day. No wars. No drunken men in taverns. No tedious etiquette lessons or waiting on other people hand and foot. Just you; enjoying being you."

How had he remembered? After all these years, he still recalled her birthday from that admission at Malic's. And this year would mark the sixth that had passed since he showed up on Faustine's doorstep looking for her. "You have turned the tables on me," she said lightly. "I believe it was you who once asked how you could say no to me; and how could I say no to you when you look at me like that? You look miserable." She laughed at the words, breaking the awkwardness. "I will go. Just stop giving me those puppy eyes. They do not suit you. Captain."

"Back to Captain, hmm?" he chuckled. "Then as your Captain, put your arm back up. We still must continue with the final stage of the exercise."

"And what might that stage be?"

"Reading the reactions in my body to predict what my next move will be. We both must try to bypass the other's guard to strike. Whoever is being struck at must register the subtle nuances of their opponent's actions through changes in movement and muscle tenseness to know when and how to block."

"Interesting," Leyna smiled, extending her arm out to connect with the back of Thade's hand. She felt relaxed. For the first time in years, she actually felt free of the burdens which had weighed upon her shoulders. There was only one last thing she needed to do. "I have a stipulation before I will fully submit to your invitation."

Gently starting the circular pattern with their arms, Thade peered at her through the darkness, the silver glow of his eyes illuminating the inquisitive expression on his face. "A stipulation? I am almost afraid to ask what that might be."

"It is nothing too great. I merely request that you pen a letter to the priests in Tanispa," she replied quietly. Thade gazed at her solemnly, immediately aware of her implications. "It is best it be done in a way that prevents Kael from knowing the deliberations have started. That way he will be unable to argue it. And once the decision has been made, it cannot be rescinded."

"It could be rescinded by one person, but she would never do so," Thade nodded. "I have told her enough about you to guarantee that she would never cause you such pain. Though I have to ask — are you certain this is what you want? If so, then I will have it sent by courier before dawn."

"After the most recent news, I could not be more certain." Following the flow of their hands, Leyna found an opportunity to take advantage of Thade's obvious distraction by her request. His body was open. She kept her hand in contact with his while their motion drew nearer to his chest, her hand snapping effortlessly over to strike the flat of her palm into his abdomen. The flapping motion of the energy in her body caused him to puff out the air in his lungs, caught off guard by the impact. "I am also certain that I just won."

The look of surprise on Thade's features quickly faded into a smile. Their laughter rang through the trees, carefree. "You cheated," he grinned, rubbing his stomach. Laughing even harder, Leyna shook her head, folding her arms across her chest.

"I did not. I simply distracted you, which worked to my benefit."

Leyna enjoyed being in his company. They'd always been brought together by business. The casualness of their demeanors in that moment felt foreign to her, yet somehow comforting. It was as if they had known each other since they were kids, a deep kinship that was impossible for her to understand. And she didn't want to waste the moment by thinking too deeply on it.

Their laughter was cut short by the sudden sound of footsteps approaching through the trees. In the darkness it echoed from all sides of the clearing, the location difficult to pinpoint. Protectively, Thade stepped in front of Leyna, listening intently. "Show yourself!" he called out, the authority in his tone reminding Leyna of the war.

"Consul," Feolan's voice rang through the shadows, coming from the tree line near the house. "How long have you been out here? I only just realized you were gone and came looking when I heard voices. Who is with you?"

"Ah, Feolan," Thade laughed, relaxing his guard. "It is Leyna. She was trying to seduce me."

Leyna's jaw fell open in shock, pushing him playfully away from her. "I was not!" she gasped. She could feel the warmth in her cheeks. Her only savior was the cover of the darkness, hiding her flushed face.

"It sounded better than admitting I lost," he chortled. "All is well, Feolan. I was trying to give you and Lady Diah some privacy."

Feolan's grey eyes appeared through the trees, moving closer to them. "If Leyna is here, that would lead me to believe you went into town, like I asked you not to until we could go together. Tonight."

"Of course, yes, Father, I forgot," Thade drawled. "Really, Feolan. You never used to be like this. It is like living back at home with my governess all over again."

"You are starting to sound like your brother." Feolan's words brought the clearing to silence. Crickets chirped faintly in the distance, their song falling on deaf ears.

Brother? He had never mentioned a brother. Come to think of it, he had never really mentioned his family at all. "Sir?" she started, gazing at him curiously through the shadows, the brightness of his eyes dimming at the sound of her voice.

Thade's body stiffened. Any sign of his previous playful demeanor dissipated, leaving him looking grim, moving away from Leyna toward the woods leading to his home. "Very well," he said calmly, avoiding Leyna's stare. "Leyna, I will have the letter you requested sent to Tanispa within the hour. Feolan – if it is not too much trouble, see that Leyna gets back to Zander's safely. I will be in my study."

Hanging his head, Feolan scolded himself quietly. "I am sorry, Leyna," he sighed. "I have known the Consul for so long. We served in the military together in Tanispa almost thirty years ago. I am so used to him behaving like a seasoned veteran and politician that when he does something even somewhat rash, I forget how young he is. I tend to overreact."

"Young?" Leyna asked. She found it hard to think of him being young after having known him for so many years. "How old is he?"

She'd asked Thade that question during the war, met only with his clever device of holding the answer over her head in exchange for her admitting her own age. It almost made her feel guilty for asking about it behind his back. Changing her mind, she opened her mouth to retract her question, her heart sinking at the sound of Feolan's response, her words coming too late to prevent it.

"He will be forty-seven this year."

"Forty-seven?" Something in that number didn't add up. How could he have served in the military nearly thirty years if he was only forty-seven? "That cannot be possible," she argued out loud. "That would have made him not even twenty when he joined the Tanispan military."

"Let us get you back to Zander's," Feolan cleared his throat uncomfortably. "I should not leave Lady Diah waiting too long, and I am sure the Consul will want to speak with me —"

"Feolan," she cut in desperately. "Why do you avoid the subject?

"Because it is not my business to discuss," he stated firmly. "And I suggest you not speak of it to him unless he volunteers the topic himself. Please. I must beg this of you."

"I will not make you beg," Leyna frowned, running her fingers through her hair in frustration. She wished he'd never answered her question. It only made her want to know more about him. But to ask would be out of line. While they were friends, he was still the Consul. To be so forward with him in regards to his own personal life could cause more trouble than she was willing to risk. She valued their friendship too much.

Climbing up on the horse, Feolan situated himself, offering his hand out to Leyna. She hesitated. It had felt so good to let go of everything for that brief time there in the clearing. The thought of returning to the mess she'd left behind at Zander's house was crushing on her heart.

Finally giving in, she accepted his hand. With a firm tug, he helped her up onto the horse, inhaling deeply before digging his heels into its sides, clucking his tongue to signal it into motion. There would be plenty of time to enjoy the escape from her mission come the week's end. Mialan held the painful memories of her past, but it also held an opportunity for her to remember who she was. Eleni did not exist there. And she couldn't wait to leave her behind.

Chapter Twenty

Days and nights held a surreal quality to Leyna, sleeping and waking without fear of the people around her discovering her secrets, or threatening her life. She'd forgotten how far away the places of her childhood were. They bypassed the desert by traveling along the Tanispan border to Carpaen. It added at least two days to their trip, but it allowed the carriage drivers to continue moving through the night without becoming lost in the sands.

Circling the desert avoided the city itself where Leyna had spent so many years learning from Blaise at the academy. While she wanted to regret not seeing it again, she couldn't help but feel relief. She wasn't ready to face it. Mialan alone would be a test for her. Possibly the hardest one she would have to bear. Throughout her childhood she told herself she would never go back to that place. To never again be faced with the memory of that horrible night, the way her mother's body looked, lying there on the floor, covered in blood, broken, life stripped from her bluing lips.

She shuddered to think about it. But it was hard to tell if it was the thought alone which sent the chill through her spine, or if it was the biting sea breeze blowing over her from the water crashing around the ship. Far off she could make out the image of land on the horizon. It was a welcome sight to her sickened stomach. The waves had tossed her around for days, leaving her green and uncomfortable.

It took them just under two weeks to reach the southwestern shore of Carpaen along the coastline. It was like another world to Leyna. She wondered how she and Reina ever managed the journey when they were so young. Her memories were hazy from that part of her past. Vague images of riding in the backs of caravans, begging for help. She never wanted to experience such misery again.

Stars could still be seen, dotting the sky up above. The last remnants of the night she spent awake on the deck. Leaning over the rail, she took in a deep breath, feeling the spray of the water on her face.

"I am beginning to think you never sleep." Thade's voice cut through her thoughts. She wasn't surprised by the sound. For the first time in years she had no need to flinch when someone came up on her unexpectedly. There was no reason to fear him, the way Kael insisted she should. He was harmless. At least to her. She'd seen him fight enough to know he was dangerous to anyone who crossed his blade.

"How could I possibly sleep when there is something so beautiful out here?"

His eyes lingered on Leyna, dimming briefly from the distance in them. Lost in thought. "Yes, I thought the same thing when I laid down last night." He paused. Clearing his throat, he looked away, motioning out over the rail. "The sea – I have always found it relaxing. Peaceful. I rarely have opportunity to enjoy it."

Oblivious to his awkwardness, Leyna nodded in agreement, taking in the scent of the saltwater. "I only recall seeing it once, though I know I must have crossed it at least twice. I do not recall the trip being quite so long."

"It used to be somewhat shorter. Years back, they had to build a new port which changed the distance between the Mialan dock and Carpaen. You have been to Mialan before?"

Oh, why did he have to ask questions? Their trip had been so calm and comfortable until then. She had feared her past feelings for Thade would make it unbearable, but she had found it pleasant. They experienced few opportunities where they were alone together, making it easier to maintain a professional distance and conversation. Throughout the ride to the docks, they shared the carriage with the alternating driver, giving them a place to rest in order to keep their pace without stop. Even when sleeping, the presence of the driver eased any tension she originally felt.

It all came back to her at that moment. Hearing his question. She should have known it would come up. And she couldn't hide it from him now. She had already admitted her familiarity with the area. "Years ago," she dismissed it with a wave of her hand. "So, where does the ship dock?"

Moving to her side, Thade folded his arms over the wooden rail, following Leyna's gaze into the horizon. "It still docks at the city of Avataio where it did before. It runs along the coastline there and pretty far inland. Originally, the docks were further south. There is a peninsula on the outskirts of town. When that neighborhood got to be too dangerous for the regular travelers, they changed the route, moving it closer to the Mialan palace."

"Dangerous?" Leyna asked. Her senses tingled, uncomfortably aware of Thade's presence beside her, their arms occasionally brushing against one another with the rocking of the boat. She felt silly, wanting to move away, yet strangely enjoying the closeness. The innocent touch of his skin. "Did something happen there? It seems odd that one portion of the city would get so bad."

"It was already a poorer section of town. Crime tended to be more widespread, with everyone struggling to make ends meet," he explained. "I was still a young man myself when things came to their height, so I am a little sketchy on the details. All I know is they had some issues with the Ven'shal, and other criminals got a bit bolder in their own right. Robbing people when they got off the ships, stealing from merchants — King Osias decided to shut down their main source of crime by closing the docks and increased his guards at the city gates leading into that part of town. It is hard to say what the place is like now. Whenever I visit, I never venture beyond the palace courtyard."

"You stay at the palace?"

"We both will," Thade smiled, twisting his body slightly to look at her. "You are a member of Queen Nesperiti's court. The Mialans treat their noble visitors with the utmost care and luxury. You will want for nothing while we are there."

Such a funny way to word it. Want for nothing? She wanted answers to her questions. None of which could be given to her by the palace servants. To see for herself what had become of that little neighborhood she once called home. She wanted to know who she was. Nothing she wanted could be guaranteed by Mialan hospitality. Most couldn't be granted by anyone at all.

There was such gentleness in his eyes. He couldn't possibly know the terrible things going through her head. If he knew, he wouldn't look at her like that. She couldn't bear to look at him herself. "I have no experience at court. I hope you will forgive me if I keep to my chambers throughout much of the visit. I would hate to embarrass myself, and even worse, you."

"How do you plan to learn anything about court life if you hide from it?" Thade chuckled, cocking his head curiously to one side.

She glanced over to him, unable to resist. His face was enchanting. "I am not hiding from it," she laughed quietly. "I am sparing you the humiliation. Besides – I do not exactly have the clothing to match the ladies at court. I will look like a pauper in comparison."

"If dresses are your only concern, then you have no need to worry. I will request to have something made for you upon our arrival."

"I cannot let you do that."

"Why not? It could be a birthday present. When was the last time you received one of those?"

"The last time I celebrated my birthday," she sighed. "And before you ask, it was much too long ago for me to remember, so do not pry."

Thade was quiet. Thinking over what Leyna said. He exhaled slowly, turning back to face out to the expanse of water surrounding them. "We have not had a chance to discuss much since we left. I am curious to know if Oksuva has become aware of her husband's demise."

Grateful for the change in subject, Leyna smiled, nodding to the empty air in front of her. "She was about as torn up about it as you would expect. She went out to celebrate with Gislan the night she heard the news."

"Does Kael know where you are now?"

"I do not know," she smirked. The thought amused her to no end. He would be absolutely livid if he knew, though she doubted Kyros would have included him in on the information. "Do you really think he would have allowed me to go away with you – alone – across three countries and a sea? By now I can only imagine he is worked up in a rage over where I have disappeared to."

"Did you tell anyone where you were going?"

Leyna pondered his question. It was difficult to say whether or not Kyros would have told anyone of their plans. "Kyros knows I am with you, but he does not know where. I have maintained a conscious fear of them being able to spy on me through their magic after discovering from Kael that it was possible."

"They would need to have an idea of where you are." Thade was calm. Unfazed by the thought. "The spirits have to know where to look, and they can only go so far. Kael would not be able to find you in Mialan through those means, even if he knew where you were. A more powerful sorcerer might be able to, but I am not certain if this Kyros holds that kind of control. From what I have heard of Damir, he would be the only one I would fear."

"What I do not understand then is — how did Kael know to look for me at your home that first night I snuck out to visit you? He was unaware of my friendship with you. As far as he knew, I had only ever spoken with you that one night when he introduced us."

"He is a jealous man," Thade shrugged. "He most likely went over in his mind the list of men that you might possibly be with in the area, and sent spirits to confirm his paranoia. He knows where I live. It would have been easy enough."

"You know, he has been suspicious of you and me since that night the three of us met in the city? Even before he started dabbling with tainted energy." She'd never thought about it before. In his sobriety, Kael had still made it very clear that he didn't trust her around other men. He all but said that he considered Thade competition.

That evening had been a nightmare. Facing Thade and Feolan with her battered body. Thade wanted so much then for her to leave the mission and come work with him at court. And she'd been so tempted. Tempted by the pleading look in his eyes while they sat there in the dancing flame of the candle, alone in his room, the bed so warm and welcoming to her tired limbs. She'd been swept up by his eyes, his lips — to the point that they had followed her back to her room with Kael. To think she had almost given herself to Kael that night, picturing Thade's hands caressing her skin…

"Leyna, why do you blush so?"

Horrified, she brought her hands up to her face, covering her cheeks under her palms. "I should really get back to my room and start packing," she breathed, turning away from Thade in embarrassment. How could she have let herself get lost in those thoughts again? She'd been doing so well. "The docks are getting closer. I suspect we will be to them within a few hours. I want to make sure I am ready to go when we get there."

From the moment they reached the docks, there was no time for Leyna to think about her embarrassment from earlier on the ship. She had avoided Thade's curious gaze throughout the ride to the palace. Once inside, they were whisked apart, taken to their chambers within the massive walls, bags carried along by several strapping young servants.

It was incredible to her. Never before had she experienced that kind of service, having always done everything for herself. She almost felt bad for accepting their help, but was comforted in knowing that, unlike the slaves of Mikel's home, these men and women were paid for their hard work. Compensation made it all much less barbaric than slavery.

Her chambers consisted of multiple rooms, decorated with the finest silk from the curtains draping the windows, down to the soft blankets outfitting the canopy bed. Everything she could have ever needed was at her disposal. A large vanity situated against the wall boasted a mirror reaching up several feet, reflecting the bright walls and furnishings. The closet looked bare with her minimal array of dresses hanging inside it, the cloth seeming dingy and poor in comparison to everything else in the room. And to think they had been considered some of Oksuva's finest! There was no way Leyna would ever blend in among the Mialan ladies dressed in such outdated and drab clothing.

Against her better judgment, she allowed the seamstresses into the room. Although they hadn't had a chance to speak since she left him on the ship deck, Thade held true to his insistence on having something made. They measured her every which way imaginable, assuring that they would have the garment to her before dinner the following day. That left only the need to keep out of sight for the remainder of the afternoon through the evening. It sounded simple enough, though an excuse to avoid leaving the room for breakfast the next day might be a little more difficult. She could always feign some sort of headache. The girls at Faustine's had used illness to find their way out of most anything they didn't want to do.

There was only one thing on her mind that she wanted to do. It would be dangerous, and a great risk to her own safety given what she'd heard, but the threat couldn't change her mind. She had to get out of the palace and see the city for herself. To see what had become of her old neighborhood.

The servant assigned to her chambers seemed confused by Leyna's request for a sword. She wasn't certain of the directions back to her old home, if it was even still there, but from what Thade had said regarding the neighborhood, it would be foolish of her to go there without some form of protection. Not that it was any less foolish to go there alone. Sword or not.

A horse was being prepared for her while she finished getting ready. Her clothing couldn't be too restricting in case she needed to fight. There would be no corsets or tightly laced bodices. If she could've had access to a pair of pants, she would have accepted them gratefully. But that would have been too convenient. Instead she had to settle for a simple summer dress which hung loosely from her hips, hugging the curves of her upper body while still allowing ample movement. It was far from fitting for a woman of court, but her intentions were not to be seen by anyone in the palace.

Strapping the sword belt around her waist, she adjusted the sheath on her hip, checking the grip and ease of draw. Satisfied, she hurried through the door into the hall, wrapping her cloak around her shoulders while she walked, hoping to conceal her strange wardrobe from view.

She felt like a thief trying to escape the scene of a crime. If anyone recognized her, she risked word getting back to Thade which would raise more questions from him than she was ready to answer. He meant well, which was why it hurt her to think that she was now running about the palace behind his back. No, he couldn't be allowed to know she had left. It would be easier that way. For both of them.

Richly clad men and women meandered through the various halls of the palace. Their pace was relaxed, their eyes glancing over to Leyna in passive disapproval as she hurried by, her face cast downward to the floor to avoid looking at them directly.

Getting through the front door had been her biggest concern, though it proved easier than finding her way through the winding halls. Only the guards were stationed there, nodding to her with curious expressions.

She could hear voices coming from the courtyard outside, distant enough that she was comforted to think they were too far away for anyone to notice her as she climbed into the saddle on the horse, snapping the reins sharply.

Her sense of direction was better than most. She'd always prided herself on it during the war, but now she would have only that to rely on in finding her way to the old docks. Based on where their ship had come to port in comparison to where Thade indicated the bad part of town to be, it seemed easy enough to deduce which way to go. It was just a matter of determining which streets would take her there.

The fading light from the sun would make her task more difficult. There remained enough illumination to estimate at least a few more hours of natural light, but she had no way of knowing how far the old docks were from the palace. The city was large. If she lost her way at all, it would add more time to the travel, costing her precious daylight.

The nicer homes and shops were arranged closer to the palace gates, forming a busier section of town for the upper echelons of society. Further out, the streets were more cluttered with wagons and stalls where the middle classes peddled their wares, calling out at Leyna while she passed. None of it really sank in for her, oblivious to the outbursts and attempts to catch her attention. All she cared about was the city gate which loomed up ahead in the distance. Thade had mentioned something of a gate situated between the poorer neighborhoods and the main streets. She couldn't stop moving. If her instincts were accurate, her destination was close at hand.

The guards made no move to stop her as she approached the gates. Getting out of the city wasn't a concern to the Mialan government. It would be getting back in that would pose a problem. Anyone who left the safety of the city walls did so at their own risk.

Immediately upon passing through, Leyna was aware of the drastic change in scenery. Windows were broken out of most of the buildings, roofs caved in or patched, though some still appeared somewhat capable of functioning. Trash lined the gravel road, the eyes of peasants staying on her as she rode by, their figures wrapped in mud-covered rags. Many of them looked almost angered by her presence. There was no welcome in their gaze.

A shudder ran through her at the sight. What had happened to this place? It had never been anything like the lavish streets of the inner city, but it had been respectable enough for the lower classes to raise their families. There was never any fear for safety when traversing the roads. The citizens had kept the area clean. They'd taken pride in their land. This looked like a completely foreign world to Leyna, dwindling her hopes of finding any semblance of the place she once considered home.

Battered wooden signs pointed to the left toward the old docks. Vague memories floated through her head. There had been merchants back then who set up at the docks. Her mother took her to visit them every few weeks. They sold fruits and vegetables, along with handmade toys and dolls. When she'd been particularly good, Leyna might be rewarded with one, and she had cherished each of them, regardless of the poor design many had been constructed with.

An occasional abandoned wagon could be seen along the deserted docks. She didn't dare take the horse over the rotting wood for fear of falling through into the murky water below.

From there it was only a mile or so to the house she'd lived in. Though the area had changed, she could never forget the way there from the docks. It had been ingrained in her mind even before that fateful night when she led Reina to the ships. No amount of time could erase it.

There had been a walking path pressed down through the grass of a nearby field. They used it to get to and from the docks, avoiding the busy traffic of caravans along the road. Time had taken its toll on the landscape. Most of the earth had been either torn up or overgrown, making it impossible for there to be any remnants of the old path. Steering her horse into the taller weeds, she slowed her pace. She didn't want to risk missing any detail.

Up ahead she could see the familiar outline of a house situated on the other end of the field. Her heart pounded, echoing hollowly through her head. It was still there. The walls still stood, weathered with age, but unmistakable.

Emotions welled up inside her at the mere sight of it. How could she ever have thought she was ready for this? It was like she was a child again, facing the horrors of that night. She didn't want to relive it. But she knew she had to. This was the last place that might hold some proof of her existence. Some reason why she couldn't give up, when the idea of doing so was more tempting than ever. She had failed to get her revenge. The depression hindered her desire to keep trying, but it was still there, deeply implanted in her heart.

A post was dug into the ground outside the back of the house. Reina's father used to tie his horse there when he came home from the docks for lunch. Rohan. The name floated into her mind from somewhere. She could hear Aviden's voice speaking it to her mother. It amazed her it still lingered with her in such clarity.

Tying off her own horse, she stood in silence, frozen. It was as if her feet had rooted themselves into the ground. She hated how afraid she was of this little house. It couldn't do anything to her. Physically. Mentally it held the power to break her down from the inside. It was more threatening than the menacing stares she'd seen on the faces of the townspeople. Men she could fight. The past was untouchable.

Concerned some homeless peasant could have made the rickety house into their home, her hand moved reflexively to the hilt of her sword. Unlike the last time she'd been there, she knew how to defend herself. Things would have been so much different if she could have done so then. If only she could take herself back to that night with the knowledge she had now.

The back door hung at an angle on its rusted and broken hinges. It looked dark inside. Tearing her feet from where they had sunken into the moist soil of the yard, she moved forward. One foot at a time. Each step took every ounce of will she possessed to keep from turning back and running to her horse. She couldn't let herself run. She'd already come so far.

Gently pressing her hand against the dilapidated door, it creaked with age before the corroded hinges gave out, sending the heavy wood crashing to the ground. She felt her heart leap in her chest, choking back a scream. It was just a door. If anything, the noise might scare off anyone else who could be inside.

Stains were visible on the wooden floor. Blood. Leyna had seen enough of it since that night to know what it looked like. Nasha's desperate last words rattled through her skull, seeing the place where her body had fallen, the final breath of life exhaling from her mouth. A part of Leyna's mind had feared her bones would still be there. The skeleton decaying from the elements over time. But it wasn't there. Someone must have found the body and taken it away. She could only hope it hadn't been collected by Damir as a trophy. He may not have succeeded in seeing them all dead, but he'd been victorious over her mother and Nasha.

It wasn't just fear that filled her now. Anger threatened to take her over, nagging at the edges of her mind. Squatting down beside the stained wooden floor, it spoke so much to those repressed memories inside. To picture Nasha handing her that tiny pouch of coins, pleading with her to take Reina and escape to the docks. Closing her eyes to push away the images, Leyna rose back to her feet, taking a deep breath to ease her racing heart.

Her whole body was shaking. She wanted to see more. Details of that night came to her like theatre performers coming to life in her own memories, playing out the graphic scene for her to watch. But she saw it now with the clarity of her adult mind. Things that hadn't made sense to her back then seemed to fit into place.

The layout of the house was simple. There was a closet a few feet from the back door where they kept their coats and shoes. She could already see it, the door ajar to reveal a small trunk on the inside. It was so much smaller than she remembered. She had grown significantly since then. It was doubtful she could fit into it now, even if she found some reason to try.

Making her way to the trunk she ran her fingers along the lid. Leyna lifted it up, finding the task less strenuous than it had been in her nightmares of being trapped inside. Blood still clung to the latch where it had fallen against her. The scar on her back tingled uncomfortably at the memory. Though it came back to her easily, it couldn't prove anything about who she was. Lowering the lid down, she tore her eyes away from the closet. She needed to keep moving. There was still so much to see and the sunlight wouldn't wait for her.

Her feet knew exactly where to go, moving down the narrow hallway toward the front of the house. Several items were missing, though it came as no surprise. It was obvious no one had actually lived there after the attack. No one in their right mind would have wanted it. It was to be expected that things would have been looted.

Bypassing the dining room, Leyna stepped into the living area, bracing herself for the worst. There, at the center of the floor, was the stain she'd been dreading, circles of pooled blood having soaked deeply into the grain of the wood. In her mind, she saw her mother lying there. The blood was everywhere. It flowed freely from wounds all over her body, fresh, deep. Impossible for anyone to have survived.

Slowly, she moved toward the image. It was so real to her. The blue of her mother's lips telling of the blood loss she endured from the wound which ended her suffering.

Kneeling down, Leyna reached out toward the face, her fingertips moving through the image, meeting nothing but the gritty, cold floor.

She wasn't there. She hadn't been there for years. But her spirit felt close by. Lingering in the room with Leyna. She couldn't see her, but sensed it the way she had by the Lake of the Gods.

Warmth from salty tears filled her eyes, winning over the anger that had been building to that moment. It dissipated, replaced by an unbearable emptiness. It had been more than two decades since she'd shed any tears over the loss of her mother. Reina had been the most important thing then, and Reina couldn't see her cry. That would have made Leyna's promises hollow when she assured Reina everything would be alright. But Reina wasn't here now. Leyna was alone with the sadness that had haunted her for every waking moment of her life.

The tears ran in streams down her pale cheeks as she was racked with an uncontrollable fit of sobs, bending forward to bury her face in her hands. She couldn't remember if she had wept to find her mother lying there that night. Now, twenty-six years later, she returned, soaking the blood-stained floor with her tears.

She reached out to where the image of her mother had been. In her mind she could see her hands from those years ago, clutching at the blood-soaked fabric of her mother's dress. Yes. She had wept. Though she had no understanding of death, somehow she had known her mother would never be there to comfort her again. Never would she rise up, take Leyna in her arms, and assure her everything was going to be alright. Nothing was alright. It never had been since that night.

Her tears fell harder, sobs heavier, soaking through her fingers which covered her face. Nothing could cut through the misery now. It was like a flood gate had opened to let years of latent emotions escape. When the sound of someone quietly speaking her name cut through it all, her irrational thoughts sent her into a panic. She could see the man coming toward her as she cried over the corpse of her mother. Kyros. The memory of his name and face rekindled her anger again. He needed to die. Anyone who could do such unspeakable things to another person didn't deserve to live the comfortable life he reveled in.

She was on her feet in a single fluid motion, her hand drawing her sword from the sheath before she could turn to look. Through her tear-filled gaze, she recognized the silver glow of Thade's eyes, staring back at her, no trace of the malice in Kyros's face from that night.

Her sword clattered to the floor as she collapsed to her knees. There was no point in trying to hide from him now. He had seen her there, weeping like a child. Nothing could convince him he'd seen anything different. She lacked the clarity of mind to even begin thinking of excuses. Truthfully, she no longer cared. He would have to accept her loss of control and composure. It was his own fault for following her. If he would have just left her alone.

Words wouldn't form on her lips. A tiny shred of her being wanted him there. She desired to be alone while at the same time she couldn't stand the thought of enduring these memories without someone there. But why did it have to be him? The one person she had tried so hard to hide her inner torment from all these years. And now he was standing in the very house it had all happened in. Staring at her sympathetically. The confusion in his eyes said it all.

She waited for the questions to start. To her surprise, they never came. He was in front of her, kneeling, his arms wrapping around her comfortingly, pressing her head gently against his shoulder. He said nothing, hushing her lamentation while running his hand lightly through her hair.

Thade's embrace was the downfall of her tenuous hold over already wild emotions. Breaking down, she leaned into his hold, her sobs muffled by the soft fabric of his shirt. Silk. Her tears had likely already ruined the garment. But he didn't seem to care.

It was nothing like she'd envisioned his embrace to be, though the circumstances were far from ideal. Everything was wrong. Yet she couldn't stop her tears. The mess in her head made it impossible to dwell on such trivial emotions such as love. Or pride. All that mattered was that someone was there for her. She was grateful for it. This would have been impossible to bear without him. It felt good to simply be held. To let her tears that she'd kept in for so long fall, without being judged. She felt safe with him. As if in his arms, everything really would be alright, the way he whispered to her now.

"It is alright. I am here, Leyna."

Time felt nonexistent while listening to his gentle assurances. The sunlight still glittered through the grime on the windows, filtering in with an eerie shadow along the floor. She knew she needed to collect herself. Maneuvering the streets back into the city would be far more difficult once the sun had set. And she still had so much she needed to do while she was there.

Slowly, she pulled away from Thade, embarrassed at the thought of how she must look to him. Her eyes felt puffy and red from crying. On his shoulder, a large stain from the moisture spread out over the surface of his cream tunic, adding to her humiliation. "I am sorry, sir," she breathed, cut short by a harsh sob coursing through her body. Her hand reached out to touch the damp fabric, retracting quickly at the sound of his uncomfortable laughter.

"It is quite alright," he smiled. Calmly, he wiped his thumb along her cheek, brushing away a stray tear which had escaped through her lashes. "You are far more important. I would dampen hundreds of shirts with your tears if you required a shoulder to cry on."

"Lucky for you, I do not require such," she sighed, her hand lifting to wipe her eyes. "You merely caught me off guard. I am not sure if I should be angry or grateful that you followed me. How did you know where I went? Or that I was even gone?"

Helping Leyna to her feet, Thade brushed the dust from her skirt, seemingly unfazed by her questions. "You have been behaving oddly since I spoke with you on the ship this morning. After I had some time to think it over, I realized a few details which were not entirely adding up. I suppose my curiosity was piqued and I decided to keep an eye out for you, in case you tried to sneak away."

"But I thought you said you do not venture outside the palace courtyard when you visit."

"I do not," he said flatly. "This place is extremely dangerous for both of us. I am ashamed to say I cannot guarantee my ability to protect you if anything happens. Though I assure you I would try."

"You were the Captain of the Siscalian military. I suspect these common thugs would have no chance against you," Leyna chortled.

It felt strange to be standing there with him. Inside those walls, still broken and spattered with blood from the battle that had taken place. It was a gruesome sight. In her head, she could still picture the armored corpses lying scattered around the rooms, their bodies twisted at awkward angles, blood pooling on the floor beneath them. Even throughout the war, nothing had felt quite so grotesque to Leyna as the memory of that night. Walking through the halls with her childlike innocence. Surrounded by death.

"You think very highly of my skills," Thade mused, his eyes observing the room around them somberly. "I would inquire about why you were drawn to this house. Considering the melancholy which remains in your eyes, however, I cannot blame you for not speaking of it."

Her curiosity at Thade's words compelled her to speak. She didn't want to give life to the horrible details that floated through her own mind, but Thade's reasons for following her sparked something inside. What details had he pieced together which didn't quite fit? He'd spoken many times of the lack of cohesion in the details of her past. So why now, after all this time, did he start to question the facts? "What things did not add up?"

Thade glanced over to her in surprise, his eyes blinking quizzically at her. "I beg your pardon?"

"You said you followed me because you realized some details about me were not adding up. Frankly, things have not added up for me in quite some time."

Folding his arms over his chest, Leyna could see Thade's discomfort. He hesitated to speak. Something about the room appeared to draw his attention, his voice distant when he finally managed to form words. "You know I have always told you that I trusted you. Even when Prince Enaes presented me with so many reasons why I should not. Because of that, I have been seeking connections between things you have spoken of in the past and the facts which Enaes laid out. I discovered one. I am not sure why it never hit me before."

"I do not recall having told you anything —" Leyna started, her protests cut short by the grimace that passed over Thade's face.

"Since the day you accompanied me to meet with Prince Enaes during the war, I have suspected there to be some link between you and Iden Evantine," he continued. "Enaes spoke the name of Iden's daughter, Sarayi. Your reaction to the name has always played at the corners of my mind. It was possible your sudden fit of coughing was mere coincidence, but you are not exactly prone to things like that."

Leyna laughed quietly in embarrassment at the memory. Not exactly the best first impression to make when meeting the Crown Prince of her people. "I can't believe you remember that…"

"Ah, but that is not even the largest part of the puzzle," he nodded. "Your birthday. At Malic's. Perhaps it was due to the alcohol that you consumed, but you spoke of a girl you had left in an orphanage in Carpaen. You admitted to being an orphan yourself. Someone had murdered your mother. Tried to kill you. Had I been thinking more clearly at the time, I would have questioned you further on that rather than your age. But then Enaes shared with me the truth of Iden's daughter. She had been murdered. In Mialan. So I thought, perhaps, that I had uncovered the connection. You told me this morning you have been to Mialan. However, I am constantly reminded of the fact that Iden denied Sarayi having any children in Tanispa. He said if she had any children, they would have been fathered by the Mialan man she lived with here."

"So you followed me to see if you could uncover me as a half-breed?" Leyna scoffed. How could she have let so many details slip out over the years? Beyond that, how did he remember them all?

"You do not deny the association with Sarayi?"

It was too much for her to endure. While it seemed a waste of her breath to speak of her past without documentation to back her words, she had to get it out. She needed someone to hear her side of the story before she was written off completely under the false assumptions that she was nothing more than a well-hidden Esai. "Do you want to know what really happened to Iden's daughter?" she snapped. "He used her to increase his own power amongst Queen Vorsila's court. If I knew the details, I would tell you, I really would, but I was no more than five when his plans came to fruition. He forced her to marry a man he suspected to be a practitioner of forbidden sorceries just so his daughter could find proof of his illegal practices and expose him as a traitor. That traitor saw to it that Sarayi paid for ruining him." Stomping her foot down on the floor over the bloodstains, she failed to fight back a new wave of tears which flooded her eyes. "Damir had her murdered because of Iden! And Iden, I am certain, never lost a wink of sleep over any of it."

"Leyna," Thade's voice was quiet, reaching his arm out toward her comfortingly. She pulled away, caught up in the anguish of her story.

"Iden would never admit that I was any relation to him. He knew Sarayi had been involved with another man before she was forced to marry Damir."

She could feel his hands grasping at her shoulders, tugging her toward him again. "Hush, Leyna. You do not have to talk about it if you do not wish to." He hugged her tightly, struggling to maintain his hold while she thrashed about wildly in his arms to get away.

The hatred she felt toward Iden was overwhelming. She wanted to strike out at something, anything, just to feel it break. She wished it could be Iden. But that wouldn't be possible. He was safely in the comfort of his house in Tanispa, enjoying the riches of the court that had been bestowed upon him for the service of his family. Taking the credit for deeds which had caused pain and suffering to Leyna and the death of her mother. And all for his own greed!

Breaking away from Thade, she pushed past him down the hallway, pain showing in his eyes at his inability to calm her. She remembered Kyros chasing after her. Leading him into Rohan's study. There had to be something there. Some document with her name. They paid their taxes like everyone else in the city. He must have recorded her mother's presence there, along with her own. The government required accurate counts of members within the household.

There was more blood in the study than she remembered. A large circle had formed in front of the table beside Rohan's desk. Kyros's. His body had fallen there initially after Nasha found him chasing Leyna. Streaks of the dark stain showed where he'd been dragged away, allowing for Leyna to escape from underneath the table. Adrenaline coursed through her limbs, making it easier to shift the heavy table out of the way, sliding it along the wall to reveal the hiding place she'd sought from Kyros's blade.

Thade followed, standing quietly in the doorway. Watching. Waiting to see if she would choose to disclose any further information. He knew better than to try to stop her.

The only thing that gave her pause was the sight of her own blood staining the floor where the table had been. Kyros's sword had torn through her flesh with every swipe, leaving a larger mark than she expected. She had been so small! Reflexively, she reached behind her back, placing the flat of her palm over the scars she knew were there, raised skin noticeable to her touch from under the thin fabric.

Grimacing, she turned away. She couldn't look at the sight of the blood. The marks on her body meant nothing next to the sacrifices that had kept her alive. Many others shed far more blood than her.

She rummaged through the drawers of the desk in a daze, shuffling through the papers that were there, surprisingly still intact. Something cut into Leyna's finger as she dug through the papers, her arm snapping back painfully. Laughing to herself, she couldn't help but find the humor in the trivial pain.

Curious, she snatched up a slip of parchment from under a heavy metal fragment which looked to be a paperweight of some sort. The parchment was folded over, the crease crisp and defined. A broken wax seal covered the edge along the front. She'd seen it once before, the memory vivid in her mind despite the years that passed. At the time, she'd paid very little attention to it, though now it came back in perfect detail. The same seal had been on the letter announcing Prince Enaes's arrival in Siscal during the war.

"That is the royal seal," Thade's voice came quietly from over her shoulder. She jumped slightly, startled by his approach.

Turning away from him, Leyna opened the parchment, her eyes scanning through the dim light of the room. The sun had sunk below the city walls, no longer casting enough light in the room to make the words on it visible. She needed to think quickly. Sliding her cloak off her shoulders, she laid it down on the floor in front of the desk, piling the loose papers up in the center of it. Eagerly, she moved from drawer to drawer. Having collected every piece she could find, she folded up the corners of her cloak to act as a makeshift bag.

"It is getting dark. If what you say about this place is true, then we should not dawdle."

Thade gave no protest as he followed her through the door of the study. There was no time to waste in getting back to the palace. She wanted to know what was inside that parchment. Something important enough to bear the seal of Queen Vorsila herself.

Reaching down to her waist, Leyna felt the empty sheath on her hip. She couldn't leave without her sword. It belonged to the Mialan palace, but above even that, she didn't dare venture out into those streets without a weapon. The inhabitants had shown their less-than-welcoming nature toward her when she arrived. Under the cover of the darkening sky, there was no telling what they might do. Night was the perfect time for the most ruthless of thugs to show their ugly faces.

She remembered having seen it last in the front room. When she discovered Thade there with her, she'd let it fall to the ground. How perfectly foolish of her. What would she have done if they'd come across someone else inside the home? Their safety would have been left solely in Thade's hands. And while she was certain he was capable of defending them, it still didn't justify putting that kind of burden on Thade. He was the Consul, after all. Once he stepped down from the position of Captain, he was no longer required to participate in battle. It was her job to defend him.

She moved back to the front of the house, searching the floor for the outline of her sword in the darkness. Her heart raced nervously at the realization that it wasn't there. The floor was devoid of anything other than the broken pieces of furniture and plaster along the corners. She cursed under her breath, focusing her energy into the palm of her right hand. A soft blue glow illuminated the room. There was still no sign of the blade.

"Something does not feel right," Thade said calmly, wrapping his arm around Leyna to guide her back toward the hall. "We can come back when the sun returns in the morning if there is more you wish to see, but at this moment, we need to get back to the horses."

Just as Thade finished his sentence, the creaking of floorboards came from the dining area nearby. A hulking outline appeared in the doorway, the light from Leyna's hand glinting off the polished metal of her sword, securely gripped in the figure's right hand. "You classy folks look a little lost," a man's voice stated casually from the shadows. "If you give me all your coins and worthwhile belongings, I might be convinced to give you directions back where you belong."

Leyna was impressed by the lack of fear she felt. At first she'd been concerned, but seeing him, there was nothing menacing about his appearance. Not in the way she experienced from others in the past. He was nothing more than a neighborhood thug, his greasy brown hair matted down on his head, curling up around his slightly pointed ears. Mialan. Her relief came in that instant. When she realized he was not Ven'shal. No other race could carry quite the same intimidating aura as they could.

"If you let us pass, I might be convinced to let it slide that you are attempting to rob us," she replied calmly, tightening her grip on the bundled cloak in her hands.

Whatever happened, she couldn't lose it. She needed more time to go through the papers.

From behind her, Leyna could hear Thade drawing his own sword, stepping up beside her protectively. Laughter rang through the tattered walls. The man was finding them entertaining. "You talk tough for a lady," he chortled.

Ignoring Thade's shouts for her to stop, Leyna moved in swiftly, calculating the openings in the man's defenses. She had more important things to worry about right now than this man's attempts at bolstering his own ego. She spoke tough for a lady? What exactly was that supposed to imply anyway?

The light she'd been creating blinked out of existence, leaving them in darkness once again. With a few well-aimed strikes, Leyna easily wrested the sword from the man's grip, bones twisting and cracking. Painful cries filled the room, but she didn't hear them. All she cared about was that she had her sword back. He would be too distracted to try and press the issue with them any further.

"Come along, sir. Let us get back to our horses before he gets it in his mind to try again."

Extending her palm, the soft light reappeared over Leyna's hand to guide them. She could tell by the expression on Thade's face that he was impressed. Had they not been in such dangerous territory, he might have spoken praise for her actions, but now was not the time. He fell into step beside her, hurrying down the hallway toward the hole where the back door once hung.

Rushing out into the night, Leyna ran her free hand through her hair in frustration, eyes rolling heavenward at the sight of the empty post where she'd left her horse. "This cannot be happening!" she gasped, kicking at the post angrily with her slippered foot. An excruciating pain shot through her leg, reminding her that she wasn't wearing the thick boots she'd worn during the war. Women's shoes were not designed for striking anything with any amount of force.

"Either he untied it, or the nail in the post was too rusted to maintain the hold. If the horse was spooked, it might have pulled free," Thade suggested, never ceasing his brisk walk around the side of the house. He returned a few seconds later atop his own horse, leading it over to where Leyna was standing. "It is gone, and we have no time to search it out."

"I cannot just leave it!" she exclaimed. "That horse belongs to the King."

Inside the house, she could make out the sound of cursing coming toward the door. She glanced back hesitantly, her eyes opening wide at the feeling of Thade's hands lifting her up onto the horse in front of him. "I will buy him a new one," Thade whispered into her ear, snapping the reins to push the animal into a steady gallop.

Her position felt awkward. Never before had she ridden double with anyone on a horse fully saddled. The design was too bulky, steep in the back to disallow for a passenger. In the front, it bore only a slightly raised portion to create the shape of the saddle, giving ample room for a smaller person to ride, while still causing her hips to roll back uncomfortably with the incline.

Thade's arms held her upright on either side where he gripped the reins. It took all her strength to keep from sliding with every pounding step the horse made, her arms clutching the bundled cloak tightly to her chest. Its contents mattered more to her than anything.

They made their way through the dirty streets faster than Leyna anticipated. When they reached the city gates, the guards moved to stop them, their long spears pointed threateningly, preventing them from continuing forward.

"State your name." The command came from a burly guard standing off to the side, his thick mustache curling up in a thin point from under his nose. Leyna recognized him from when she passed through earlier. He had eyed her curiously, but said nothing, letting her go by without question.

"Thade Imri of Queen Vorsila's court," Thade announced, his voice ringing with an air of authority. "I am a guest with King Osias and Queen Adalyn. If you question me, I have my documents."

In a clang of metal, the guards removed their spears from the horse's path, bustling out of the way. "No need, Your Grace," the larger man motioned for them to continue, bowing his head respectfully. "For your own safety, I suggest you not cross through this gate at such an hour in the future. It is not a place for guests of our King."

"Noted." With a hard press of his heels into the horse's sides, Thade signaled it forward once again, keeping a steady walk through the gates, his breath escaping in relief when they reached the other side.

She could sense Thade was feeling the same awkwardness that had come over her immediately upon situating herself on the horse with him. His body was tense. Keenly aware of her presence, the way she was of his. It was the only thing which pulled her from her thoughts of the parchment concealed in her cloak. The scent of his cologne wafted on the breeze over to her nostrils, pleasantly, relaxing her with its gentleness until she was reminded of Thade pressed so closely against her. If only her horse hadn't run away! Most of her discomfort would have been avoidable.

Deep inside, she hated to admit that she was enjoying it to a certain extent. The thought only added to her guilt. It wasn't appropriate for her to think that way. It was better to spend the entire journey back to the palace in uncomfortable silence than to give in to any of the feelings which made it pleasant.

When they reached the palace gates, Leyna found it easier to focus on other things once again, the papers inside her cloak crinkling in her tightly wrapped arms. Thade dismounted, offering the reins to a servant who greeted them near the palace doors. Holding out his arms, he assisted Leyna to the ground, being careful not to disturb the bundle to which she clung.

Leyna started to move toward the palace doors, lost in her own reverie until the sensation of something tugging at her waist drew her back to reality, her eyes blinking in confusion at Thade. His hands were at the clasp of her sword belt, holding her in place easily with his fingers tucked behind the heavy leather. "I do not recommend going inside with your weapon. Perhaps we could give it to the doorman to return?"

"Oh," she breathed, nervous laughter bubbling up inside. "I forgot I was even wearing it. How embarrassing that would have been…"

With an understanding smile, Thade unhooked the buckle of the belt, sliding it out from around her waist. He remained by her side as they moved up the palace steps. The guards stationed at the doors nodded to Thade in greeting, their eyes looking over Leyna curiously. She stood out like a sore thumb. Nothing about her resembled a lady of the court at that moment, her hair disheveled from the wind, dress plain and simple, dirtied from the dust and grime in the house. *They must think Thade is bringing a peasant back from the streets.*

Leaning over to whisper a request to the servant waiting inside the door, he handed the sword belt over to him. Giving a reflexive nod, the man turned away, disappearing down a long corridor, the flames of the elaborate sconces lining the walls flickering as he passed.

Hurriedly, she made her way down the twisting halls which led to her room. There were more people around than before, making her uneasy. Their watchful eyes followed her and Thade. She could see the questioning expressions. No one knew who she was. And to see her in such a state! She would surely be the talk of the palace before the night was over.

Her hands fumbled over the doorknob to her room. When it finally clicked open, she took a step forward, noticing Thade's sudden hesitance to follow. Her composure regained, she was no longer against the idea of having him around while she looked through the papers. If anything, she wanted him there. She didn't want to be alone with the thoughts that were running rampant in her head after returning to that place. They terrified her. At least if she could convince him to stay, she would have someone to ease her mind before she attempted sleep.

"What is the matter, Consul?" she asked. "I do not mind if you come in."

Shaking his head, Thade let his eyes drift over the long hallway on either side of them, his forehead creasing under an obvious mental struggle, though over what, Leyna couldn't put her finger on. "I am not sure that I should," he replied quietly.

Not sure that he should? He was starting to sound like her. They had never stood on formalities of appropriateness before when she'd been concerned over visiting him or Feolan alone. So why was this any different here, this night? "Please?" She gazed at him pleadingly. The last thing she wanted was for him to leave. He was the only person in the world whose company she desired at that moment. And she didn't care if anyone thought it to be scandalous. "I really do not want to be alone right now."

"I suppose I could come in — but only for a few minutes," he nodded. Giving one last glance down the hallway, he moved quickly into the room, exhaling a deep breath at escaping the prying eyes of the courtiers. "I cannot remain for long. I hope that you understand."

"Truthfully, I do not understand." Leyna shrugged, tossing the cloak down on a low table situated in front of an elegant sofa, the polished mahogany surface reflecting the flames of the sconces lighting the room. "You and I have met privately on several occasions over the past few years. I was always the one afraid it would be considered inappropriate and you assured me it was fine. So why now have you changed your mind?"

"This is different," he frowned. Everything about his demeanor had changed from that which he'd displayed before entering the palace doors. He looked nervous, hands fidgeting where he held them clasped in front of him, clenching and unclenching his fingers while absently observing the room around him, avoiding Leyna's gaze. "Courtiers tend to have nothing better to do than insert their noses into everyone else's business. Though the priests are reviewing the request I sent them in regards to the dismissal of your marriage arrangement – until the time that they send their verdict – you are still a promised woman. And while you and I both know that we are merely friends, your betrothed has vocalized accusations of infidelity between the two of us. If any of the vultures in this palace find cause to assume anything intimate is occurring, it could destroy any chance of convincing the Tanispan priests to grant your annulment."

Leyna inhaled sharply with dismay. It had never crossed her mind before then. They were in a different society than in Siscal. And the number of eyes that had witnessed them together in the hallway alone was enough to set her own nerves on edge at the possibility of being denied her separation from Kael. "Maybe you should go, then," she whispered, lowering herself miserably onto the soft cushions of the sofa. The one time she truly needed someone to be there for her, and the mistakes from her past were forcing her to endure the pain alone.

"No," Thade stated plainly. With an air of pride, he knelt down on the floor in front of the table across from Leyna, gently pushing the folded cloak over closer to her. "I have some time. With you having just returned, the chamber servants will be coming shortly to check on you. As long as I am gone before you dismiss them for the night, we should have very little to worry about. Nothing which could not be argued and proven false, anyway."

A smile spread over Leyna's lips to hear him agree with her request. Excitedly, she slid down from the sofa to kneel on the floor, unwrapping the folds of her cloak like a child opening a long-awaited gift. She knew it was likely that the papers inside it would prove nothing. But it was the possibility! The tiny thread of hope that something might give a clue to verify that she existed. And she was not the Mialan half-breed that Iden might try to claim.

Most of the papers were faded. Worthless. Tax documents from nearly three decades past, if not longer. Rohan must have been meticulous with his record keeping. What she wanted to find was that single parchment which had been on her mind from the moment she laid eyes on it. Rohan would have no need to receive missives from Tanispa, and certainly not from the Queen. Leyna clung to the hope that it was something belonging to her mother. Something that had been forgotten about for all these years, lying in the dusty, moldy rooms of that abandoned house.

There among the tattered records of Rohan's finances, she caught sight of the heavy parchment, the wax seal like blood coating the edge of the flap. Snatching it up greedily, she stared down at it, holding her breath. This was it. It could either be her savior, or her downfall. If it spoke nothing to lead her to the truth, then her pain of reliving it all would have been in vain.

In her peripheral vision, she could see Thade's eyes widen at the sight of it. He was intrigued. Seemingly as much as she was.

Rising up from the floor, she began to pace across the room, suddenly nervous. If it contained nothing, she hated the thought of Thade seeing her break down in tears yet again. Her image in his mind was already destroyed enough without making it worse.

She closed her eyes. The thick edge of the parchment was pressed against the flat of her thumb, ready to be opened with a single movement. *Just do it.* She couldn't bear the anticipation. With a quick motion, she opened the flap of the document, afraid that if she didn't move fast, she might lose her nerve. Lifting her right eyelid just enough to let in the light, she squinted at the writing she saw there. It was very official looking. Names were written on it in fancy calligraphy. Signatures.

She opened her eyes the rest of the way, staring down at the ink in bewilderment. A heavy, boldly written title was printed clearly along the top. Certificate of Birth. Could it be? It didn't seem possible. Their departure from Damir's home had been too sudden for her mother to grab any of their belongings.

And now, there it was. She could see her name written on the line. Leyna Evantine. Dated back thirty-five years, nearly to the day. But it was not her name which shocked her the most. Listed as the parents, clearly Sarayi Evantine — and Aviden Diah.

Oh gods. It couldn't be true. How could her mother ever have kept this a secret from Damir? The records were enough to ruin the whole family. Sarayi had chosen to document the true father on the royal birth certificate. All the more reason for Iden to have sought ways of removing the documents from Vorsila's records.

Folding the parchment back up, she pressed it tightly over her heart. Tears were threatening to fall again, but this time they were tears of joy. She had found it. She'd seen it with her own eyes. Leyna Evantine did exist. No one could take that victory away from her. Not even Damir.

Deep breaths. She had to regain her composure before she could speak anything to Thade. Everything felt perfect at that moment. She had her proof. As long as they were alone, she felt justified in finally answering the questions he had been so patiently waiting twenty years to ask. A great weight had lifted off her shoulders. And maybe now, she might receive the answers to her questions about him. He always told her he would reveal his own secrets when she felt it time to reveal hers.

She went over all the details in her head. How could she approach the topic? Would he be expecting it? He seemed distracted by so many other things. Thade was watching her. Clearly curious. Nodding to him, she gave a short curtsy, scolding herself for her nervousness. "Consul."

"You must be nervous," he chuckled, leaning back casually on the floor, propping himself up with his arms. "I can always tell when you are, because you resort to formalities and titles. I think at this moment you can safely call me Thade. I would not be offended. After all, I do believe I am here in this room as a friend. Not your superior in any way."

"Sorry," she blushed. Averting her eyes, she moved over to the sofa. She wasn't sure if she wanted to stand or sit when she told him the news. It was exciting, in a way. To finally reveal all of the things she'd wanted to say for so long. Or almost all of them. There were a few more private matters that could never be discussed. Clearing her throat, she sat down, the movement lacking in any grace, the cushion bouncing under her gentle weight.

His eyes were watching her closely. Something about the way he stared caused her to tremble. She was losing her nerve. What if he was angry with her? She had put them both at such a great risk during the war with her secrets. She couldn't blame him if he resented her in some way for it. They sat silently for what felt like ages. She prayed one of the chamber servants would come through the door, taking away her opportunity to disclose the information. What was taking them so long?

"Fifteen."

The number fell from her lips against her better judgment. She hoped her body was not as visibly shaken as her voice sounded. Watching Thade's face, she searched for his reaction, unsure if he would even understand what she was saying.

At first, his eyes revealed confusion. Fifteen? Such an odd start to a conversation. Random. Then, all at once, his already pale complexion seemed to drain of what little color there was, staring up at her solemnly. "Please tell me that is not –"

"Not exactly," she stammered. Her fingers fidgeted awkwardly in her lap, her head reeling over how to explain herself to him. "The first time you asked me, it would have been eighteen. But you already knew me for a few years before that."

Tilting his head back, Thade gazed up at the ceiling. He looked absolutely wretched. "The gods may never forgive my soul…"

"But you knew I was young," Leyna argued, her guilt growing at the sight of him looking so miserable, knowing it was because of her. "You made it very clear to me that you suspected."

"I suspected you were not old enough to be out in society. I never once imagined that you were – a child –"

"Thade," she whispered. Hearing her voice speak his name only added to the desperation she felt. How could she possibly convey to him that it wasn't his fault? He'd done so much for her. She might not be alive had it not been for him. The military had been her only chance to afford shelter and food. To survive. "I had no choice but to try and fool everyone when I came here. No one in Carpaen would give me a job because they knew how old I was. The only thing I was qualified to do was fight, so the military was my only option. Had you turned me away, I would have likely starved to death in some alley somewhere in the desert."

"You presented yourself in a very convincing way when we met."

"I always thought I looked a fool to you," she laughed pathetically. She could still picture Cady stuffing the folded pieces of cloth down into the bodice of her borrowed dress. And her shoes! She thought for sure she would be discovered when Thade had located her lost shoe under the body of the ghereac.

"You looked young. Never foolish," Thade frowned. "I have never been well-versed in any matter regarding women. Perhaps it was simply my naivety which prevented me from estimating your age more precisely."

"Had you known the truth, would you have turned me away?"

Shifting his eyes down to Leyna's face, he held her gaze steady. "No," he shook his head. "I would have proceeded with things a bit differently and kept a far better watch over you than I did, but I think I would have played the fool all the same."

"And that is what I do not understand," she sighed. "You knew I was violating the rules of both the military and our people, yet you willingly allowed it."

Calmly, he rose to his feet. All signs of discomfort had left him, his posture erect with every deliberate step he took in a slow pace back and forth across the room, his voice calm when he spoke. "Because I violated the same rules. In many ways, you reminded me of myself. I had to assume you had good reason for doing what you did."

"I must admit that I am somewhat aware of your age. All things considered, given the status your family must have, it seems like it would have been far more difficult for you to hide the truth from the military."

Thade paused, glancing over to her sharply. He looked almost angry at first before his features relaxed, exhaling a heavy sigh of defeat. "General Cadell knew my age when I joined the military in Tanispa. He accepted me because he was ordered to do so. Feolan was placed in charge of watching over me until I was of age. As soon as I was old enough, I was sent to Siscal to operate as their Captain for the war. General Matias to this day is unaware of how old I was when I was promoted to my position. Only just past my twenty-fifth birthday."

It explained a great deal in Leyna's mind. Why Feolan was always so protective of Thade. Still, it felt odd to her. During the war in Siscal, Feolan had never been as watchful of Thade as he was now. It was almost as if he'd reverted to the parental role to keep an eye on him in his ventures into politics. "But why did you join the military so young? Or at all — I have been learning that many members of nobility, while they have training in combat, have never actually served in any militant aspect. Fighting is more sport to them than anything else."

"I took an interest in it," Thade replied, his tone short, unwilling to elaborate. "I have also taken an interest in that piece of parchment. Might I inquire of its contents?"

Suddenly remembering the document in her hand, she blinked in surprise, holding it out to stare down at it hesitantly. It was the final piece of the puzzle in explaining herself to him. Once he had read it, he could no longer question the truth of her words – no matter what Prince Enaes might believe he had found. "Oh, this…" she stumbled over her words, shakily rising to her feet. With nervous excitement, she made her way over to where Thade stood, his pacing halted to accept the parchment from her outstretched hand.

She watched his face closely. For some reason she feared what his reaction would be to learning her true parents. He had determined her link with Sarayi, but never had she spoken of her suspicions regarding Aviden Diah. The father of the same woman Feolan now courted.

His eyes opened wide, a contemplative expression crossing over his regal features. "Well," he murmured. "This actually explains a lot… but still leaves a great deal unanswered."

"What does it explain?" she asked excitedly. Her heart pounded against her chest, anxious to hear what Thade had to say about the matter. "It proves to you that I am who I claim to be, at the very least."

"Yes, well – I was unaware that the Duke of Escovul had two children. Serendipitous, really, that both of them ended up under Lady Faustine's roof." Never taking his eyes off the parchment, he continued his pacing again, leaving Leyna to stare at him, following his movements like the hypnotic swing of a pendulum. "When he was killed, it left a lot of questions unanswered. It was assumed to be the work of the Ven'shal, but the reasons were never uncovered. I suppose it is possible it was the same Ven'shal who killed Iden's daughter."

"You talk as if I am detached from the whole picture," she frowned, stepping into his path, forcing him to look her in the eye. "Don't you see? You were the one who told me of it yourself, back when I first started working for you to uncover Oksuva and Mikel's motives. My mother was documented to have been married to Damir Rohld – the same Ven'shal who currently works in conjunction with Oksuva to raise Arcastus from the dead. He discovered that the child he believed to be his daughter was really the child of another man. In his anger, he used his sorcery against us. My mother witnessed it and testified of it, leading to Damir's banishment from Tanispa. Do you not think Damir would have also sought the identity of the child's father to take revenge?"

The relaxed atmosphere was gone, replaced by a tension unlike any Leyna had ever felt in Thade's presence before. "Then how did your mother come into possession of the Queen's copy of the birth record? You do realize this is the reason why Prince Enaes has been unable to verify your identity..."

"I was nine years old when my mother was murdered. All I was thinking about at that time was how to get away from the sword-wielding psychopath who was chasing me through the house," she sighed. "I have no means of knowing anything about this document." Frustrated, she started to turn away from Thade, his hand reaching out to her arm, holding her in place.

"You saw the man that was chasing you?"

"Yes," she breathed, staring down at Thade's hand gripping her arm tightly. "It is the same man who put the scars on my back. It also happens to be the same man who now is blackmailing me into trying to seduce you."

"Kyros? You are certain of it?"

"He still bears the scar left from the blow which rendered him unconscious long enough for me to escape with Reina."

Thade's grip loosened on her arm at the admission. "Who is Reina? The child from the orphanage you mentioned that night at Malic's? Your sister?"

"She is not really my sister," Leyna laughed, hanging her head. "When my mother and I fled from Damir the night he discovered the truth about me, she took us to Aviden for help. He arranged for us to come to Mialan to stay with a friend of his, Rohan. I was young, but I recall him saying something about Rohan's wife having passed away, leaving him with two children to raise on his own. This man was supposed to help us hide from Damir in exchange for my mother helping him with them. Reina was one of his children. Nasha the other. My mother, Rohan, and Nasha were all killed the night those men came for us. I was locked away in a trunk in the closet. Nasha managed to knock Kyros over the head, but she was too wounded. She survived long enough to hand me the coins to make the trip to the mainland. Reina's care was left up to me."

"And you had to leave Reina at the orphanage in order to come to Siscal."

"Yes. We did not have enough money to pay for our room and I was too young to be employed anywhere in town. I was supposed to join the military to save money and return to Carpaen. But she ran away."

"Do you know whatever became of her?"

His question was like a punch in the stomach. How could she possibly explain to him that Reina had been the woman caught with Kael the night Leyna returned from Kaipoi? All of the facts were a tangled mess in her own mind. "She works at Malic's as a barmaid. She recognized me the night I accompanied Oksuva there to meet with Kyros for the first time. Almost ruined my cover."

"Have you seen her since?"

"I have," she replied quietly. Averting her eyes from Thade's, she turned away from him, moving back over to settle herself on the sofa. "When I returned from Kaipoi, she was sharing a bed with my betrothed."

Thade's face contorted into a strained grimace, his legs carrying him quickly to sit next to her. "They know who you are."

"What?"

His statement chilled her through to her very core. It had been nagging at the back of her mind for some time now, but to hear him say it, it became real.

"I think you have suspected, but there is no doubt in my mind, Leyna," Thade's voice was calm and quiet, the only sign of unrest coming from the bright glow of his silver eyes gazing into hers. "You told me Kael was doing some kind of work for Kyros. It is no coincidence Kael chose to bed that particular woman. She revealed her link to you – to the woman that Kyros suspected you to be – and he sent Kael to uncover what she knew. I am removing you from the mission. I refuse to sit by and let them kill you."

"We already went over this, Thade," she argued. "I was going to leave the mission but Kyros has made it impossible. He will hold Mikel's death over my head in order to force me –"

"Then we will have to find a way to hide you from him."

"I will not hide!" she shouted. Her body was trembling uncontrollably. Thade gazed up at her in awe, unsure of how to react to her outburst. "These men killed my family. They intend to attack our Queen and to destroy our people. I *refuse* to stand by and do *nothing* like I did before! I will have a hand in their downfall. If I have it my way, that hand will be the one holding the blade which pierces through their hearts."

A click came from the door to the room, a young woman stepping in, giving a low curtsy to them both without taking her eyes off the floor. Leyna and Thade stared at her in confusion before registering who she was. It had taken the chamber servant that long to arrive? And to appear now. The most inopportune moment. "Is there anything I can get for you, Milady?"

Noticing Thade's presence, the girl shifted uncomfortably. Leyna couldn't imagine what they must look like to her. Her dress was still covered in dirt, her hair tangled in a mass atop her head. Thade remained with his usual poise, though the look in his eyes was all it took for anyone to know that he was less than enthused about the interruption. "I believe that is my cue to leave," he replied, standing up next to Leyna. He turned to face her, pulling her into a careful hug, maintaining an appropriate distance between their bodies. "I understand you seek revenge for what they did to your mother, but you have so much more to live for. To follow that path could ultimately lead to your own demise."

It was nothing more than a soft whisper in her ear. Inaudible to anyone else. "If someone killed your family, would you not desire revenge more than anything? I have nothing standing in my way. My life has been nothing but a lie since I walked out of the door to that house. I do not even have a husband who would care if I never came home again. All I have is my loyalty to our Queen which surpasses all else, but in avenging my mother, I still serve the Queen, and that makes it the most important thing I have to live for."

"You have friends who care about you and a new chance at a family with Lady Diah as your sister. I do not blame you for your desire to kill these men who did this to you, but please — do not feel you must face it all alone. Let me help you."

She felt Thade's arms pull away before she could respond, his head nodding in a brief farewell. Without a word, he turned from her. She wanted to reach out. To stop him. But that would never be allowed inside the palace walls. The courtiers had likely already begun their incessant whispers about the time they had spent alone.

The moment he was through the door, she motioned for the chamber servant to come closer. "I could use a bath," she stated quietly, staring down at her soiled clothes. "If you could prepare one for me, I would be much obliged."

As the woman hurried off, Leyna turned toward the table in front of the sofa, staring down at the piles of letters and documents still resting on the thick fabric of her cloak, half-opened and faded from wear. The certificate! Clutching her head, she let out a moan, flopping down in defeat. Thade still had it.

After the events of the evening, she had no desire to face the questioning stares of the other courtiers too soon, their imaginations still likely running rampant with their assumptions. No. The document would have to remain with Thade for now. She had no intention of leaving her room again for a few days until her presence was required at the party.

Chapter Twenty-One

Another birthday had come. Leyna didn't know exactly what to think of it. For so many years she'd paid little attention to the coming and going of the date, but today felt different, for some reason. She was far away from all of her problems. No one other than Thade and Feolan knew where she was. She had to assume Maeri had dragged the information out of Feolan somehow, but it didn't matter. What mattered was that this year, it was Leyna's birthday. Not Eleni's.

The seamstress dropped off a dress as promised after they had arrived, but Leyna was surprised to wake up that morning to find three more gowns hanging in a row along the closet of her room. All were of impressive design, rivaling even the most expensive outfits she'd witnessed the ladies of the Mialan court wearing around the palace. Gems and pearls adorned them, adding a flash that made no attempt at hiding what must have been a great cost. The hardest decision she had to make was which one to wear for the celebration that night. While the party wasn't actually for her, she considered it to be, determined that she was going to let go of everything and have a good time. She couldn't even remember what that felt like.

Her corset was of the finest make, solid stays unmoving against her midsection. It required two of the chamber servants to tighten. She wanted it to be perfect. It didn't matter that it hindered her breathing worse than anything she'd ever experienced. The corsets Oksuva had loaned her were nothing in comparison.

Of the gowns that had been tailored for her, she chose to go with a deep sapphire blue damask accented with silver weaving. Something about the color pulled her in. It was regal. Elegant. Unlike anything she'd worn before, nor did she ever expect to have occasion to wear again. Tonight she would be a princess in her own mind. Pearls accented the seams of the gown, the silver border splitting open at the waist to reveal a lighter hued material underneath. It was incredibly heavy against her body. There were so many pieces that she wondered how the ladies of the court could ever keep them straight.

The bodice of the gown clung tightly against her upper body, accenting her already slender figure with the aid of the corset. She didn't think it possible to compact her chest any more than it already was. It was no wonder the courtiers were rumored to lead such scandalous lives. Their clothing was an open array of garments designed to flaunt the feminine assets in front of the most powerful men in the country. If the courts in Siscal were anything like it, she could see Teagan looking upon the women as a buffet of unsuspecting victims. Though with the style of dress, perhaps the women were more suspecting than they might let on.

Bustling about the room, the chambermaids meticulously arranged her hair in a mass of shimmering ebon curls forming ringlets along the frame of her face. It hung long around her shoulders. She chose to go without the common headdress the Mialan women would be sure to wear for the party, concealing much of their hair from view under their elaborate hats. Instead, she opted for something that would only accent her hair rather than cover it up. A band of glittering sapphires accentuated by smaller cut diamonds rested like a delicate tiara around the top of her head.

They carefully applied a dark liner around her eyes. In the mirror, she hardly recognized herself under the changes they were making to her features, accenting her high cheekbones, painting her lips in a deep crimson to contrast her pale complexion. The final touches came in various adornments for her ears and wrists, complimenting her long, slender neck with a high-resting choker of silver and sapphires dangling down to splay out over her collarbone.

With a final glance over her reflection, she nodded in approval, content that her scars were concealed under the layers of fabric and fine jewels. It was all far too much. She felt guilty for having accepted the gifts, knowing they had been bestowed upon her by Thade in his attempts to shower her with attention for her birthday. She would have to make sure they were all returned to him before they left for Siscal.

Pearls even adorned the heeled slippers the servants provided as the last remaining piece to the outfit. They matched the gown perfectly. Thade spared no expense in the design of this wardrobe. But tonight wasn't supposed to be about him. Tonight, she intended to keep her eyes open. She couldn't be with Thade for more reasons than she could list, so it seemed only sensible to avoid paining her heart with the truth on her birthday.

No one would recognize her from the ragged girl they'd seen wandering the halls her first night in the palace. Since then, she had kept herself locked away. They would need some time to forget about her presence if she had any hope of being accepted among them at the party.

And tonight she looked like she belonged. She felt like royalty making her way down the hallway to the ballroom, the heavy fabric of her gown trailing elegantly along the ground behind her with every step. The corset worked well in keeping her posture straight, chin held high as she passed the other courtiers still lingering in the halls. She couldn't help but smile to notice the glances of the men, staring at her curiously as she moved by them, an air of mystery surrounding her. This was going to be a fun night. She could sense it.

Tables lined the sides of the grand ballroom, already filled with exquisitely dressed courtiers, lost in conversation. At the head of the room she could see the main table prepared for the host and hostess. They were unmistakable in their position overlooking the room, faces calm and serene underneath finely crafted crowns of sparkling gems and precious metals.

King Osias and Queen Adalyn. They were a sight to behold. He was a broad man, his figure widened by the golden epaulets accenting the shoulders of his finely tailored jacket. His wife complemented him perfectly in her matching gown of gold and white brocade. They looked older, though still young by Mialan standards. Queen Adalyn was set apart from her husband by her long, rich, auburn hair next to his shorter blackened locks. Not quite as awe inspiring as Queen Vorsila had been when Leyna first saw her at the masque, but still impressive.

Her eyes were drawn to the familiar outline of Thade standing behind the table where the King and Queen were seated, engrossed in what appeared to be a very deep conversation with a pretty young woman. Mialan in descent, but undeniably beautiful in her own right. Her auburn hair was worn in an upswept mass of curls which hung gracefully down over her bare shoulders. Her figure was enhanced by the tightly laced bodice holding her in place, delicate golden silk shimmering under the light of the chandeliers dangling overhead, catching the diamonds of the crown on her head with a brilliant flash.

Leyna didn't realize she'd paused to stare until she noticed Thade's eyes glance over to her idly, starting to shift away before quickly turning back in an undisguised look of awe. Content that she had drawn his attention, she averted her eyes casually, smiling her most charming smile at the group of men standing near the wall where she entered.

They greeted her warmly. Not that she expected them to react any differently. Their names held no meaning as they introduced themselves, recalling stories of heroic hunting excursions in attempts to impress her with their displays of overt masculinity. She found it comical the way they behaved. Nothing more than the common soldiers she had served beside in the war, only dressed in clothing worth more than the annual salary of a military man.

It was surprising how much her popularity grew with every dance she accepted. She couldn't remember the last time she laughed and carried on the way she found herself doing. But it all felt empty. Hollow. This wasn't her. It was like an elaborate production to make her seem more worthy of the attention of these men who had never experienced life outside the politics of court. They didn't know what it was like to wonder how they were going to afford rent or put food on the table. And yet she laughed along with them, pretending she was just like the other frail ladies, staring daggers at her from their seats, devoid of any attention. She'd developed quite a crowd around her.

"If you gentlemen would excuse us, I am going to steal this young woman away from you," an airy, feminine voice announced from somewhere nearby. At the sound, the men split apart to form a path, revealing the elegant form of the woman Leyna had seen speaking with Thade when she arrived.

Respectfully, Leyna dipped down into a formal curtsy, unsure of who the woman was, but certain her rank was well above that which Leyna held. In customary fashion for a woman of high standing, she lowered her head, making sure not to bend down more than Leyna. It was a symbol of rank that one never bowed lower than those who bowed down before you. "I am led to believe you are the legendary Leyna that Queen Vorsila's Consul has been speaking so highly of since he arrived."

Ah, even more embarrassing than she thought! This woman knew of her and yet Leyna could recall no name to identify her. "I must admit, I am regretfully lacking in my knowledge of the court. I... I am unsure who you are."

She was laughing. A soft, silvery sound that came like chimes on a gentle breeze. It seemed a good sign, at the very least. She wasn't angered by Leyna's ignorance. "I am Princess Chlora Therborin. You have been a guest in my parents' home since you arrived to Avataio."

Princess? Leyna was absolutely mortified to think that she had been so disrespectful. Lowering her eyes to the floor, she sank down to her knee, directing her words away from the woman in fear of adding to her already irreparable blunder. "Your Highness," she breathed. "I am so sorry. Please forgive me –"

"Oh, there is no need for that," Chlora smiled, motioning for Leyna to stand. "The Consul tells me it is your birthday this evening. I came over to extend to you my family's blessing on the occasion. You will have to entertain us with a dance before the night becomes too late. Something of the Tanispan court. I have always so loved the gracefulness of their movements."

"I could not possibly," Leyna blushed. "This celebration is for your family. I would not feel right taking the attention away."

"Nonsense. It would be an excuse to get the Consul out of his seat. I doubt any of these other men would know the steps."

Leyna couldn't help but laugh at the thought of dancing with Thade. "I am not certain how that would work. I have never seen the Consul dance before. I wonder sometimes if he really truly does know how."

Catching sight of Thade's eyes slowly looking over to them from across the room, Leyna waggled her fingers in a playful wave. He lifted his hand to wave back, the motion short and hesitant, as if he was unsure of whether or not she was actually directing the gesture at him.

"If I insisted, I am certain he would agree to dance with you. Whatever it is you have done, he seems unable to speak of anything but you unless directed toward a different topic. Though inevitably, he finds a way to turn it back to you."

"I find that difficult to believe," Leyna shook her head, unwilling to accept what she was hearing. "Perhaps he would dance with you. I would love to see you perform one of the dances from your court."

Chlora chuckled quietly, casting her gaze over to Thade, almost wistfully. "Sadly, I am not Vor'shai. He would never give me a second look. Quite an extraordinary catch though. My parents tried to arrange a marriage between us, but were politely declined due to heritage."

"Really?" Leyna couldn't hide the surprise in her voice. Marriage? Thade had never spoken of any arrangements or possible matches for marriage. And to a princess? His family must hold a much higher status than she thought. Though he was the right hand of the Queen. It was fitting he would marry into royalty. She had to wonder if he would have been betrothed to one of Vorsila's daughters, if they were still alive.

"He would have been a much better match than the man I am engaged to presently. But such is life, I suppose," Chlora shrugged.

Leyna felt her heart wrench with jealousy at the mere thought of another woman winning Thade's hand in marriage. It was foolish, she knew, but it was out of her control. None of these women were even close to being good enough for him. They were all fake and shallow with their expensive jewelry and low-cut dresses, flaunting their bodies like a party favor. She couldn't bear the thought of him ending up with someone who only cared about his title and money. He would be nothing more than a trophy to dangle off their arm at court. They couldn't possibly love him the way she did.

She fell silent at the sight of a younger lady approaching Thade. Her long brown hair was tightly done up in the back with a clip fashioned of gold and diamonds. She looked cheap, her make-up darker than seemed acceptable next to her light skin and burgundy dress with the bodice cinched awkwardly around her chest. She looked almost desperate to catch his attention. Leyna smiled in spite of herself at the lack of interest she could see on Thade's face.

"Would you do me the honor of demonstrating a dance for us? Please?"

"Hmm?" Leyna mumbled. The sound of Chlora's voice brought her back from her reverie. "Oh," she stammered. "Right — well. That depends on if you can convince the Consul to be my partner. As you said, the other men here likely do not know the steps, and I would look rather foolish trying to dance alone."

Chlora's face brightened, her hand reaching out to clasp Leyna's. "It may take a bit of work. He is stubborn, but we can trick him."

They moved across the floor at a brisk pace, pausing occasionally to accept the greetings of other courtiers along the way. Accompanying the Princess only added to the curious stares, watching Leyna as if they should know who she was but couldn't recognize her face. She felt powerful next to Chlora. Her friendship was a status symbol in and of itself. Many longed to be in the confidence of royalty, but few ever managed to achieve such trust. Leyna knew the only reason Chlora even gave her a second glance was due to Thade's praises.

"The Consul tells me that you lived in Mialan some years back," Chlora chimed in suddenly. Their pace slowed. Her words sounded deliberate. Leyna inhaled a breath, realizing the true reason why the Princess had approached her.

"Really? He told you that?" she said stiffly. "I suppose it is true. But it was over twenty five years ago. Much has changed since then."

"If what he says is true, then I will be sure that you receive a gift before you leave for the mainland. Something for your birthday. It seems fitting."

Leyna opened her mouth to inquire of what Chlora was referring to, the words lost to her. They were already within sight of Thade, his eyes brightening at their approach.

"Ah, Your Highness. Lady Evantine. To what do I owe the pleasure of your company?"

"Your Grace, this lovely young woman has agreed to demonstrate one of the Tanispan court dances for us in honor of her special day," Chlora smiled. Her voice was charming. She was making a great effort to sweet-talk him into submission. "It only seems right that you would be her partner. You are the only Vor'shai here and the dance would be far more graceful and impressive if done by those who created it."

Thade chuckled to himself. He looked at home in the presence of royalty, blending in perfectly, his countenance regal and commanding. He was stunning in his deep blue doublet lined with silver chains and trim to match his eyes. It was secured up the front with silver sapphire-inset buttons which brought out the rich hue of the velvet. Standing next to him, Leyna smiled at their complementing wardrobes. If she hadn't known any better, she might have thought they'd arranged it intentionally.

"Your Highness. You know as well as I that there is little difference between the dances you enjoy here in Mialan and the ones we do back home." He took a casual sip from his wine goblet. "Surely you have others here who would be willing to put on a show for you."

"The only show I desire to see is that of this young lady dancing. If the dances are so similar, then I will just have to recruit another dashing young man to join her. There are plenty around who would not be so rude as to turn her away like you."

Thade looked taken aback by her remark, lowering his goblet from his lips. "It is not a matter of rudeness. I simply am not much of a dancer."

"I do say, Leyna. I believe you may be right in your assumptions that he does not know how to dance," Chlora smirked, linking her arm through Leyna's. "There are plenty of others more suitable for you." Turning, Chlora gestured toward a group of men lingering a few feet away, ignoring Thade's protests from behind. "What say you of the gentleman in the green?"

"He certainly is handsome," Leyna nodded in agreement. "Does he dance well? I cannot have someone stepping all over my feet."

"That is Lord Felton. He is known for having a way with the ladies. A splendid performer, but I would not accept an invitation from him beyond the dance."

"I will not be shown up by Lord Felton," Thade interjected, tipping his head back to drink the last of his wine. "You intentionally threw her to that wolf just to get me."

"And it worked," Chlora smiled. Nonchalantly, she turned back to Thade, offering Leyna's arm to him. "Your family might not have allowed us to marry, but I still know exactly how to get what I want from you."

Straightening his doublet proudly, Thade took Leyna's hand in his, tossing a final glance over his shoulder at Chlora as he led Leyna out to the center of the floor. "That woman is absolutely spoiled rotten. I sympathize for her husband-to-be."

"You did not have to dance with me if you did not want to." She felt guilty for having forced him into it. The wine was affecting her thought processes. Without it, she knew she never would have tried to convince him to do anything. Especially not something which required him to be so close to her. The situation was awkward enough, even without her fluttering heart.

Thade spun her around in front of him. With a nod to the musicians, he placed his right hand at her waist, positioning her with perfect carriage in his arms. "Do not be ridiculous. I wanted to dance with you. I merely did not want to do so with so many eyes upon us. However, I could not very well let her pawn you off on Lord Felton. That man is the Teagan of the Mialan court."

"Sounds pleasant," she grinned.

When the music started, she let herself be swept away by the melody. Thade's frame was flawless. He moved her easily around the floor, leading in and out of the intricate steps of a dance Leyna hadn't done since her time with Lady Faustine. It was a miracle she even remembered the pattern. Her feet stumbled only once, but Thade caught her, hiding the fumble effortlessly.

While pulling her into him again, Thade leaned forward, his voice barely audible over the thrum of the music. "Has anyone ever told you that you are a remarkable dancer?"

"Once," Leyna smiled to herself. It was silly of her, really. Although she'd been put-off by the whole situation at the masque in Tanispa, she had always thought fondly of the dance she shared with the young Prince. His compliment remained with her. Most times she thought back on that night in a poor light, though it meant a great deal to receive such praise from a man of his standing.

"Ah, then I am not the first," Thade chortled. "It does not make it any less true, however. You have the grace of a noblewoman without the pretentiousness which tends to accompany it."

"When you have that kind of wealth and power, pretentiousness only seems natural."

"It is your modesty that makes these men drawn to you." Thade's voice cut off as they broke apart. Leyna twirled by him gracefully, catching his hand on the other side. "But they assume it to be false. A means of gaining their affection. They do not realize you really are genuine – and if they find out, they will eat you alive."

Leyna held his gaze steady, challenging him playfully. "And are you going to protect me from the circling vultures?"

"I would, if I thought you would let me."

What an odd statement for him to make. He would protect her. She knew that to be true. He had told her many times in the past. But what made him think she wouldn't let him? Had she come across so independent that he believed she would push him away? Deny him?

But how many times had she done so already? Numerous. She couldn't even begin to count them. He'd tried so desperately to help her from the moment she returned to Siscal after the masque. He wanted to protect her from Mikel and Oksuva, knowing what they were like, and what being around them would do to her. The risk she was taking. Time and time again he attempted to save her from the terrible things that were happening around them. The lies, the deceit, the betrayal. Over and over, she had denied him. Left him feeling helpless while he watched her continue to fall deeper into it all.

Maybe it was the wine, but the guilt inside her was growing at the mere thought of what she had done to him. After all this time! How could she ever make it right?

She could enjoy this night the way he wished for her to. To enjoy life in a way she never had in the entire time she'd known him. And she was. The night had been magnificent, so far. She felt like a princess, dancing the dances of the Tanispan court. Every man in the room was watching her, wanting to be her partner, and she had no intentions of choosing any of them. She was like one of the maidens in her mother's fairy tales. It would all end when she returned to her room that night. Taking off the lipstick and the jewels which shone brilliantly against her skin. She would go back to being plain old Leyna Evantine. The orphan grandchild of a narcissistic nobleman.

Although the music had ended, the room continued to spin in Leyna's vision. She was approaching drunkenness from the never-ending glasses of wine provided to her throughout the night. There had been a reason why she swore off alcohol the night of her eighteenth birthday. It clouded her judgment and her vision, making it impossible to think clearly. She needed air.

Giving a final graceful curtsy to Thade, she couldn't think about the applause that filled the room. For the first time that night, she was reminded of just how uncomfortable the corset strapped unnaturally tight around her body was. It was a sadistic sort of fashion the wealthy reveled in. They would give up air for the sake of appearing more slender and appealing to the masses. How that made sense, she would never understand.

"Leyna, are you alright?"

"I cannot breathe," she whispered, becoming aware of Thade's presence still at her side. "I need fresh air."

"There is a veranda adjoining the back courtyard which has an entrance through this room," he nodded. "I doubt they would miss us if we stepped out there for a few moments."

Emphatically, she bobbed her head in agreement, letting him lead her through the crowd lining the wall, the voices of courtiers greeting them as they passed. All Leyna could think about was getting to that door.

Her gait was unsteady by the time they reached the arch. Somehow her head was getting foggier with every passing moment. How much wine had she drunk? The amount far exceeded that which she'd consumed at Malic's the last time she willingly consumed alcohol. It baffled her to think anyone could possibly enjoy the feeling.

The courtyard was a welcome change of scenery. A gentle breeze wafted through the well-trimmed hedges, bringing with it a scent of pine and some heavenly floral fragrance. Coming to a stop, she inhaled deeply, staring morosely off into the distance. "How do these people do it?" she asked. "I could not handle the constant parties and socializing, everyone always aware of your personal business. I would go absolutely mad."

"There is a reason why I choose to keep my home outside the main palace of Siscal," Thade chuckled, urging her forward again with a slow and casual pace over the cobblestone path leading through the garden.

Leyna sighed miserably. She couldn't imagine what it must be like. For a single night it was fun to dress in such extravagant clothing and behave like she was on top of the world, but it could grow tiresome. It was an empty existence, without purpose or meaning. How could it be that the peasants likely experienced a far more fulfilling life than those of the courtiers? There was only so much comfort money could bring when all of your friends were just waiting for you to misstep so they could plunge a knife into your back and take it all away.

"I had no idea things would be like this. How do you handle it? It is a far cry from the days we spent at war."

"Yes, it is tedious, that is certain," Thade agreed. "Many times I find myself missing the simple duties of a Captain. As long as my men were well-trained and fully equipped for whatever might come our way, that was all I needed. Now it is a daily struggle to maintain the relations between Tanispa and Siscal. And though that may seem an easy task, it is far from it. Constantly, there are trivial things which, for some reason, hold much more weight than they justifiably should – and those could tear apart the entire alliance with a single misspoken statement. Royalty can be fickle in their feelings toward other governments, and the people that serve under them can be even more so."

"Have you ever considered returning to the military?" It felt a harmless question to ask. Though there was no war waging currently, there was always need for protection from one thing or another.

Thade appeared to consider her question before responding, his expression forlorn. "I considered it in the past, but the decision is not mine to make anymore. I do what I am told. I am grateful for the opportunities, but I miss the freedom. The bond of friendship that built over time in working with others, knowing they would always be there. And in some cases, knowing that they would die for you. One does not find such camaraderie in politics."

"It is harder to take an arrow for someone when the weapons are words."

Thade smiled briefly. He couldn't argue. It was an accurate assessment of the world he lived in now, after the war. "We do have some great memories from then, however. Somehow we all managed to keep our senses of humor despite the stringent lifestyle."

Leyna couldn't help but smile at the thought of days gone by, reminiscing about the nights spent among friends, laughing, simply enjoying each other's presence, grateful for their time together. They were constantly aware that it could be taken away in the blink of an eye. No moment was wasted. "Do you remember that tavern we all visited on our way through the mountains?"

"In Puavi? On our way to Velorum?"

"Yes, that is the one," she nodded, chuckling to herself. The memory remained too humorous for her even now to keep from laughing. "I am amazed Teagan still spoke to me after that."

"For convincing that poor waitress that he was eyeing the bartender rather than her?" Thade grinned.

"Her face was priceless! You cannot deny it," she laughed. Hearing the sound echoing through the garden, she covered her mouth with her hand, eyes darting around the area in embarrassment. "He would not stop bragging that he was so desirable. And she was absolutely smitten with him. I could not just let him succeed. His ego would have been suffocating."

"Honestly, I am not sure he ever discovered who told the girl. I believe he assumed it was Feolan."

"Feolan never would have done it," she shook her head. "He was far too shocked when I did."

"You must admit," Thade mused. "You never really came across as the type to pull such a joke when we first met you. We considered you to be so level-headed and serious. Quick-witted and clever, but never a prankster. Teagan most likely, to this day, would not believe it was you."

"Well, I could not simply be the focal point of everyone else's jokes. A girl has to develop a sense of humor. I cannot count the number of times Teagan claimed that the only reason I was made lieutenant was because the commanding officers thought I was pretty and would make a good distraction against the enemy."

Shaking his head, Thade chuckled quietly to himself. "Teagan had a fear of being inferior. To him, women are objects to be utilized for the pleasures of men. He could never truly see the skill you possessed. But Feolan and I did, as did General Matias and Commander Laoter. Never doubt that your promotion through the ranks was entirely professional and in honor of your hard work, dedication, and skill."

She could feel the warmth building in her cheeks at the compliment. Doubt had lingered in her mind over the years, in fear that there may have been an ulterior motive to her promotion. Constantly, she'd been plagued with the idea that she was hindering the unit because of her age. Holding them back. As a higher ranking officer it would have been easier for them to monitor her, protect her, or keep her out of the battle with other business matters if they so desired. Never had they exercised that power, but the concern had remained nevertheless.

"Well, for a man who felt threatened by me, he certainly did enough to try and gain my attention."

"You were the only woman he ever encountered who would not give him the time of day. It was a challenge to him. In the end, I believe he resented you for it. And in turn, also resented Feolan and me, under the false impression that we somehow had something to do with it."

"I was a child," Leyna laughed. "My thoughts could not have been further from romance. I knew nothing of men. The first time I even really saw a man with his shirt off was the night of my birthday at Malic's." She thought it over, considering whether or not to speak further on the topic. Consciously, she made the decision to keep it to herself, though the wine caused the words to tumble from her lips. "But alas, for this birthday, I do not think I will be seeing you with your shirt off again."

Thade's head cocked to one side in amusement, a faint smirk visible on his face. Leyna felt her insides clench. How could she have said something like that to him? She wanted to duck behind the hedges and never come out.

"I do not think I will be seeing you with your shirt off this evening either, so perhaps it is a loss on both our parts," Thade mused.

Her? Leyna struggled to recall what he was implicating, the alcohol affecting the clarity of her thoughts. She paused in the middle of the path, turning to look at him in bewilderment. "You consider it a loss to miss removing my clothes?"

He opened his mouth to speak, seeming to suddenly become aware of what he'd said. No words came at first, his expression revealing obvious embarrassment, a tint of red forming over the pale skin of his cheeks. "I believe I might have worded that in a manner which I did not intend —"

"I am teasing you," Leyna smiled, pushing him playfully. Deep down she couldn't help but remain curious what had led to such a blunder in speech, but she didn't dare press the issue. "Besides, I am older and clearly more capable of handling the wine. I do not feel intoxicated enough to remove my garments in front of you the way I so shamefully did back then."

"Ah, I thought perhaps it was a new method you were considering in your seduction of me."

"Here is hardly the place," she laughed, rolling her eyes at the remark. Twirling around, she took in the sight of the elaborate garden surrounding them. A gentle scent of flowers grew more fragrant as they moved deeper into the midst of the garden, the colors of the blossoms vibrant in the light of the full moon overhead.

The scene was like a painting. Everything was perfectly in its place. No detail of the garden had been overlooked in the layout, forming a complexity of geometric shapes with the cobblestone paths winding through the trees and flowerbeds. Torches were burning at various points along the way, casting a flickering orange hue along the ground. Overhead, the sky was clear, twinkling stars glittering like diamonds.

She realized, in that instant, just how lucky she was. Through all the hardships, she still had this moment in time. This beauty that many would never see in their lives, and that many others took for granted, never truly appreciating the splendor. Had the wine not relaxed her, she wondered if she would have overlooked it herself.

"Maeri would have loved this place," she sighed. "We should see that she and Feolan have an opportunity to visit sometime."

Leading her to a well-crafted wooden bench at the side of the path, Thade helped her down onto the seat, positioning himself at her side. "They will be rather busy for some time, I suspect," he smiled. "Feolan confided in me that he intended to ask for her hand in marriage while we were away. They will have very little opportunity to enjoy much of anything while planning the ceremony. If all went according to his plan, they will have already performed the engagement ritual by the time we return."

"Marriage?" Leyna gasped. So soon? It seemed only weeks had passed since Maeri first spoke of their attraction. They wasted very little time with the courting process. "I would have expected Feolan to require more time. I heard what happened with his last marriage. It sounded absolutely tragic."

"He has been seeking to move past it. Over the years he has courted many ladies, but none have struck him quite the same as Lady Diah has. I think she will treat him well."

"But what of you? Have you ever been struck in such a way?" Damn her mouth. She was quickly becoming aware again of the reason why she had sworn off alcohol.

He looked thoughtful, contemplating the question. "Not any of the women I have courted, no," he said simply. "But I have a very particular taste in women, I think.

None of the ladies at court possess any of the qualities I so desire. I find them dull. Lacking."

"What is your taste in women that makes it so impossible to find a suitable match?"

"Oh, that is a tricky question," he chuckled. "Most men simply require beauty. They fear free will; the concept of a wife having opinions and carrying on intelligent conversation. But to me – I want my wife to be able to form her own opinions, and to not be afraid to voice them. To stand up for what she believes. I like a woman who is not afraid to take chances. Not frightened of getting a bit dirty."

Leyna laughed quietly at the thought. He was describing a woman she didn't believe existed. With standards that high, he was sure to lead a very lonely life. "I have never heard of a noblewoman who was not afraid of getting a bit dirty. They are not exactly brought up to play rough. That was one thing Lady Faustine strictly forbid."

"That is true," he nodded. "But I detest the thought of sitting around all day, sipping wine, and chattering absently about the weather. I want someone at my side who will challenge me to think. And above all, she has to have an open heart. I cannot tolerate selfishness."

"You will be hard-pressed to ever find a woman who fits that mold." Suddenly uncomfortable, Leyna stood up from the bench. She was feeling the familiar flutter in her stomach at being so close to him. She didn't trust herself. Not with the way she'd already been behaving, against her better judgment. "But there are plenty of beautiful women for you to choose from at least. Even Princess Chlora still seems attracted to you."

Rising swiftly to his feet, Thade turned his gaze heavenward. He was silent for a moment, searching for the words to say, the struggle visible on every gentle line of his face. "The Princess does not fit any of the requirements I have listed, and there are still so many more which remain unspoken. The negotiation attempt at joining her and I was a long time ago, and met with many objections. Several of which were from me."

"I am surprised they did not try to arrange a marriage between her and one of Queen Vorsila's sons. That would have been more advantageous, I assume."

"Yes." He looked bemused by the notion, lowering his eyes to stare at her calmly. "Yes, however, she dislikes Prince Enaes. And given the precarious nature of Queen Vorsila's family line, her other son is not permitted to marry until Enaes has been suitably joined with a wife. Any acceptable woman would be paired with Enaes instead. An heir is far more important to the family than love. Even if Queen Vorsila had not been predisposed to denying Princess Chlora simply because of her Mialan heritage, the arrangement would be a marriage to Prince Enaes – or no one at all."

"That is awful." Leyna was discomfited at the thought. She no longer could blame the young Prince's lack of interest in the women at the masque. Why would he want to risk losing his heart to someone, only to then have her torn away and given to his brother?

"That is also the reason I have been avoiding telling Prince Enaes of your whereabouts."

Leyna's attention was immediately pulled away from her scattered thoughts. What did Enaes's marriage have to do with her whereabouts? "I do not understand..."

"For all you have done for the royal family, Queen Vorsila conceded, even with the question of your family line, that if Enaes desired to take you as a wife, she would allow it. But he does not deserve you."

"Deserve me?" she breathed. "That does not matter. I have no desire to marry him. He is the perfect example of everything I despise in a man. Attractive, yes, but his personality makes him hideously repulsive."

Thade clasped Leyna's hands in his. His gaze was almost desperate. "I could not bear to see you marry someone like him. It is part of the reason why I had hoped to see you out of Faustine's care. I did not want to see you married off to some mindless nobleman to spend the rest of your days as his silent trophy wife. You are an intelligent woman, capable of so many great things! You deserve a husband who will actually appreciate you. Enaes would not. I doubt he understands the concept of love."

They stood silently, locked in each other's gaze. It was all so much to take in. How long had he known? Enaes had no doubt been knocking down his door at every opportunity in search of some clue of Leyna's whereabouts. And Thade had lied to him. To the Crown Prince of Tanispa, he lied about knowing where she was.

But why had he never before told her he felt that way? She'd been unaware he thought so highly of her to risk hiding her from the royal family. It seemed traitorous. And to what reward? If Prince Enaes was not worthy of her, who did he think was?

An unusual tension had formed between them, as if out of nowhere. She didn't understand it. Something in his eyes – the way they glowed so brilliantly at her in the night – swept her away. She thought she would lose herself completely in their depths. It wasn't until she noticed his head move in closer to hers that she realized what was happening. Her entire body trembled in excitement. Nervous. If he kissed her, she didn't know how she would react. But there he was, his lips slowly lowering to her own.

At the last instant, Thade's eyes lifted up to gaze off over her shoulder, narrowly missing her lips with his as he pulled his head away. She was mortified. Had she imagined it?

She wanted it. Every part of her wanted to take him in her arms and press her lips to his. She feared that even thinking about it would lead to a catastrophe with her altered level of consciousness from the wine. In her mind she could see herself doing it. But she had to hold back. She couldn't give in.

"What is wrong?" she whispered.

"We cannot," he replied quietly, his eyes lingering on whatever it was he caught sight of behind her. "It is not right."

"I am not fifteen anymore, Thade."

"Yes. But I have had too much wine. And so have you." Stepping away, he released her hands, putting a gap between their bodies. "I have to be up early tomorrow for a meeting with King Osias before we make our way back to the ship. I bid you farewell for the evening."

"Thade –" She hated how desperate she sounded.

He cut her off with a sharp wave of his hand. "You should stay and enjoy the party. It is still your birthday, after all."

In a graceful maneuver around her, Thade walked away. She watched as he moved down the cobblestone toward the veranda, her eyes stinging with the sensation of tears that threatened to fall. She couldn't cry. She couldn't face the people inside the ballroom again with smudged make-up and puffy eyes. It just wouldn't be proper.

There in the distance, she caught sight of a familiar face gazing out into the darkness from the arching palace doors. Chlora. Had she been what Thade was looking at? It was strange that he'd been so comfortable with her and then suddenly tensed. Something had distracted him. As if he was afraid of something. But what? Of hurting her? Or was he still afraid someone would see them together and start stories of a scandal?

She knew very little of Chlora. From the way Thade spoke, he didn't care for or trust her. To see her standing there watching them – she had to wonder if he was right. For a member of an allied royal house to witness Thade with Leyna could prove disastrous. And they were already teetering on a fine line as it was.

Her heart ached to think about it, watching Thade drifting further away. Chlora was greeting him. The smile on her face was almost devious. What could she have possibly seen? They'd done nothing. But from their distance, it would have looked like much more to the unsuspecting observer. The angle. From the veranda, Leyna's body had obscured the view of Thade's face. It was possible Chlora already assumed more than what was true about what transpired between them. She would have been unable to see that their lips never touched. Though, oh, how Leyna wanted them to!

Thade looked rigid in his motions around Chlora. He was on guard, cautious about every move he made. Leyna could see the discomfort in his mannerisms. By the time he managed to break away to return inside the crowded ballroom, Leyna felt her senses returning, slowly. It was a lot to take in. Whether or not Thade loved her was still debatable in her mind, but he had said a great deal which proved that he cared about her deeply, concerned for her happiness and well-being. That meant more to her than she ever would have thought. It had always been easier to simply assume he saw her as nothing more than a colleague.

And to hear that Queen Vorsila had approved her as a suitable wife for Prince Enaes! It tore at her very insides to think of the possibility. She didn't love Enaes. Nor did she think she ever could come to. He loved women almost as much as he loved the power of his position. Never would he be capable of being true and faithful to a single woman. She knew all too well how much it hurt to be tossed aside by someone she thought loved her. Kael had shown her it wasn't anything she ever wanted to experience again. And with Enaes, it would be a far more public scandal. Everyone would know of his infidelity, whispering about it behind her back, laughing at her, assuming she was completely unaware of his nighttime escapades.

No. She forced the unpleasant daydreams away. She wouldn't let that come to pass. Enaes couldn't be allowed to find her until Vorsila had chosen a different wife for him. Their need for an heir would make it necessary to arrange a marriage soon. Once he was no longer a bachelor on the prowl, she could relax again, knowing she would not be out of line to turn him away if he attempted to proposition her.

Straightening back up proudly, she patted her cheeks self-consciously, making sure no tears had fallen without her notice. This was to be her final night at court in Mialan. She couldn't let a single hiccup ruin her evening. There were still plenty of songs to be danced and people to meet. She would have time to dwell on the intricacies of the unwelcome drama in her life after the party ended and sleep had cleared the fog from her head. With a final glance around the garden, she bid the beauty of the night farewell, hastening her steps back toward the palace and into the fray once again.

The next morning Leyna awoke to the sound of a chambermaid bustling around the room, laying out a gown for Leyna to wear. Her head ached. She had no desire to be roused so early from her slumber, the wine from the previous night having left her feeling ill. "Milady, I'm sorry to wake you, but we must get you dressed," the woman urged gently.

Leyna gazed up at her through sleep-filled eyes, confused by what was being said. Why did she need to be dressed so early? The carriage to the dock wasn't supposed to be called until mid-afternoon. "It is still early," she murmured, rolling over to bury her face in the soft pillows. She didn't want to leave the bed. It was warm. Comfortable. Under the blankets she didn't have to focus on the awkwardness which lingered over her at the memory of the previous night. She didn't want to see any of the courtiers from the party, and most of all, she wasn't ready to face Thade.

"Milady, please," the chambermaid pleaded, drawing the blankets away from Leyna, exposing her to the chill in the room. "The Consul is expecting you. We can't leave His Grace waiting."

Sitting up on the bed Leyna hugged her arms to her chest for warmth, eyes blank from surprise at the woman's words. The Consul? But he was supposed to be in a meeting with King Osias and Queen Adalyn. Unless something had happened. Could

Chlora have gone to them about what she saw in the garden? Leyna quickly rose from the bed, ignoring the cold floor against her bare feet. She needed to get to Thade. If they had somehow angered the King and Queen, he would need her there to explain the truth.

"How long has he been waiting?" she asked, arms lifted to allow the woman to remove Leyna's nightgown, a thin white chemise being arranged in its place.

"Only a few minutes. He asked that you be dressed appropriately for an audience with the King. We have very little time, so we must hurry."

Leyna's mind was utter chaos. Audience with the King? Oh, it must be bad. There was no other circumstance which would merit her presence with the King. None that she could think of, at least. Thade was perfectly capable of handling the meeting on his own. Leyna was of no importance to their discussion.

Inhaling a deep breath, Leyna felt the chambermaid wrap a corset around her waist, attaching the clasps and tugging hard on the laces. The sensation was familiar, yet unpleasant. Her hope had been to not wear another corset for the remainder of their trip, if she had any say in the matter. The time she'd spent at the party was enough to last her a lifetime. Another pull fastened it tighter, restricting her movement, her body jerking with every yank of the strings. "That is tight enough," she gasped, still groggy from sleep. It was too early in the morning to feel so restricted.

"Just a little more, Milady," the woman tugged again, nearly knocking Leyna off her feet. Regaining her balance, Leyna gestured toward the dress laid out across the bed.

"I assure you, the corset is fine. The dress, please. Hurry."

With an obedient nod the woman retrieved the gown. She struggled to pull it over Leyna's head, the fabric heavy and thick, falling in waves of glittering gold around her body. It fit snug to the curves of her figure, the silver brocade accenting the elegant design. Fewer jewels adorned it than that which she'd worn the night before, though the quality of the garment made embellishments unnecessary. Tiny pearls edged the neckline, draping off Leyna's shoulders, adding the only hint of flash to the dress.

Leyna watched in the mirror while her hair transformed under the woman's hands, the tangled mass quickly becoming smooth gentle waves over her shoulders. Simple.

There was no time for anything elaborate. The King would have to be satisfied with what could be managed on such short notice.

"My shoes," Leyna pointed to a pair of gold slippers next to the closet on the floor. She wanted out of the room. Every second felt wasted on useless preparation. The chambermaid continued to style Leyna's hair, reaching for a headdress positioned on the dresser. Shaking her head, Leyna motioned to the shoes again, the gesture more demanding than before. "There is no time. My shoes, please." She snatched the headdress from the maid's hand, discarding it.

A knock at the door caused both women to jump in surprise, eyes shifted to see who was interrupting their frantic attempts to get Leyna ready. In the entry stood a younger blonde woman, bobbing down into a quick curtsy. "His Grace, the Consul, requested I check your progress."

"I am nearly ready. I need only to put on my shoes —"

"Good heavens, you aren't planning to leave the room like that, are you?" the woman gasped.

Leyna stared at her, unsure of how to respond. "There is little time for anything else. Surely the Consul will understand."

"He is in no rush, Milady," the blonde woman smiled, moving quickly into the room. "There is still at least half an hour before the meeting. Let me help you." She collected the make-up trays on the dresser, setting herself in front of Leyna, steady hands beginning to apply the liner to her eyes. "You are attending an audience with the King and Queen. I don't know how they do things in Tanispa, but here it would be rude to show yourself in their presence in such a state."

"It is rude in Tanispa as well. I merely thought our time to be more limited. Frankly, I am unaware of what the hour even is." Leyna had yet to get used to having people doing things for her. It felt strange to have two women catering to her every whim, one painting her face while the other arranged the coif headdress over her hair, the golden veil trailing down low in the back. In a matter of minutes she saw her reflection change from the hastily dressed woman she'd seen there not long before, now revealing the face of a courtier. She could pass easily as nobility with the mask the servants provided her. If the etiquette learned from Lady Faustine would be enough to get her through the meeting without exposing the roughness she retained around the edges of her manner.

Clutching the heavy fabric of her skirts in her hand, Leyna made her way toward the door, drawing in a deep breath, her mind scattered over what she was walking into. If Thade was in no hurry, it gave an indication of there being no immediate concern. But why would he want her with him at the meeting? It didn't make any sense. She held no sway over the Mialan royalty. They barely knew her name. It was unlikely they would care what she had to say.

The hallway was quiet aside from the scant few early risers, dressed and ready for their morning walk or ride around the grounds. Their faces were drawn, fatigued from the late hours they'd kept the night before. Leyna sympathized with them. Her own body longed to still be curled up under the blankets, safely in bed. She wasn't ready for whatever Thade required of her. It would be so simple to feign her headache being more severe than it was and insist upon returning to her chambers. Inside she fought with herself over the idea. An escape would be welcome, but she couldn't do that to Thade. He was counting on her. She would have to steel her resolve and plunge ahead blindly into whatever was waiting.

In the foyer she could see Thade standing near the center of the room. He was dressed in style, much the same as he had been the night before, though significantly more refreshed in appearance than anyone else Leyna had passed that morning. To her surprise his garb again resembled her own, the vibrant gold of his doublet lined with silver cording vertically down the front and sleeves, small epaulets adding a broader shape to his shoulders. His black trousers were barely visible under the high boots covering his feet and legs. A wide golden chain of office rested around his neck, signaling his superior rank to anyone who might happen by. "Lady Evantine," he nodded sharply, bowing stiffly from the waist in greeting. "I was afraid you might decline my request for your company."

"I would be lying if I said it wasn't considered," she replied. Gracefully, she sank into a curtsy before him. All eyes were on them, curious stares directed from every corner where the guards and palace servants stood, whispering amongst each other. Formality was important. Anything more lax would be indicative of a deeper relationship of which they both needed to be on guard to prevent discussions. Leyna worried how many people already knew of Chlora spying on them in the gardens. The thought added to the discomfort she was already feeling, afraid to lift her eyes to meet Thade's.

"I must admit I am confused by the invitation. Your meeting with King Osias was to be in regards to business. I fail to see how my company will do anything but hinder the talks."

"On the contrary, you are quite well-versed in the matters which will be discussed. I can think of no one else more capable of assisting me," a faint smile passed over Thade's lips, offering his arm out to Leyna to accompany him. "That aside, I thought the experience might do you some good. My hope is still to see you at my side on Nesperiti's court. This is a good opportunity to learn."

Accepting Thade's arm, she fell into step beside him. There was a tension between them. A lingering hesitation, reminiscent of that which Leyna had felt in the garden when they parted ways last. Thade was distant. Lost in his own thoughts. It was obvious to Leyna that he was holding back a great deal, though it was impossible to distinguish what. Her head was a tumult of confusion itself without adding to the chaos by trying to decipher what was in Thade's mind.

"I was hoping by now you might have had enough time to consider my offer. You have not yet given me a response in regards to your decision to join me at court in Siscal."

Leyna kept her eyes straight ahead, chin held high, proud. "Now hardly seems the time," she stated quietly. "Ask me again after we are excused from the King."

They paused in their brisk pace, lingering in front of a high-arched door to the left. Guards were positioned on either side, erect, arms pressed tight to their sides. At Thade and Leyna's approach the men gave a sharp pivot, attention focused on Thade. "His Majesty awaits you," one of the guards announced, his fist clenched tightly, crossing over his chest.

Thade ignored the guard, turning to face Leyna, eyes settled sternly over her face. "You give me your word that you will grant me an answer once our business is concluded?"

"We shall see," she mumbled, embarrassed by the questioning stares of the guards upon them. "Please. We cannot keep His Majesty waiting."

Argument was impossible for Thade in that moment. The presence of the guards made speaking openly out of the question, leaving him with no choice but to accept her tentative assurances. "Very well. Gentlemen. If you will."

Obediently, the two men reached for the handles of the double doors, pulling them open to grant entrance into the room beyond. A red carpet spread across the floor. Near the opposite end of the lengthy room Leyna could see two thrones positioned side by side, the regal countenances of the King and Queen instantly drawing her thoughts back to the task at hand. They were there. The throne room of the Mialan royal family. A slight breath of relief escaped Leyna to discover Chlora to be absent. Her personality had come across acceptable for social situations but grating when it came to business. More would be accomplished without her there, seeking to attract attention.

Inside her chest, the pounding of her heart was growing stronger, almost unbearable in its inconsistent fluttering and skipping. Her first instinct was to run. Thade's arm linked with her own was the only thing holding her there. She felt him stiffen at her hesitation, forcing her to take another step forward. Behind them she could hear the doors closing. She was trapped. There would be no escape now.

Their pace was slow. Agonizing to Leyna's nerves. By the time they reached the glimmering gold of the thrones, she feared her legs would give out and send her collapsing to the floor at the feet of King Osias. Reflexively, she went through the motions taught to her by Lady Faustine. It was instinct, requiring little thought to accomplish. Eyes lowered, she sank into a deep curtsy, maintaining the position near the floor at Thade's side until she felt the gentle pressure of his hand signaling her to rise.

"Your Majesties," he bowed again, motioning toward Leyna with a fluid gesture of his hand. "If I might present to you the Lady Evantine. Heroine of Tanispa and newly appointed member of Queen Nesperiti's court in Siscal."

Averting her gaze to conceal the blood rushing to her cheeks at the introduction, Leyna curtsied once again. Etiquette was on her side in hiding her discomfort. The King and Queen would think little of her downcast eyes, assuming it to be nothing more than respect and modesty.

"Yes, we have heard much about you, young lady," King Osias bellowed. With a wave of his heavily ring-adorned hand he motioned for her to rise, smiling broadly. "An impressive display in the art of dance you gave at the celebration last evening. Not since my last visit to Queen Vorsila have I witnessed a performance of such skill." With a wink he set his eyes on Thade, nodding to him in approval. "Your Grace, I must ask that you and the Lady visit again. The women of this court could use a good example from time to time. I fear our daughter's dislike of music has made them forget how important it is."

"I would be delighted to see her accompany me here again. It is my hope I may be able to convince her that her presence at court is more valuable than anywhere else." Thade cast her a sideways glance. "But if you insist it of her, I find it hard to believe she would refuse."

"Then I must insist! You will of course not decline our invitation to Princess Chlora's wedding."

"I would not think of missing such an occasion. Has a date been arranged?"

For the first time since their approach, Osias's smile fell. "I am afraid not," he shook his head, lines of frustration creased along his forehead. "You know how she can be. But we will have a date soon enough. Please, extend our invitation to Queen Vorsila and Prince Enaes as well. The ceremony would not be right without all of our friends there to share in the joyful occasion."

"What say you, Lady Evantine? Will you accept His Majesty's invitation?" Thade raised his brow, inquisitive. His words were deliberate. Precisely aimed in a way which would back Leyna into a corner. Propriety required her to accept. He was well aware of her inability to decline for sake of appearances. And once her word was given, she would have little choice but to follow through.

"I will do my best to be in attendance," she nodded, her voice soft, delicate. It was the closest to an affirmation she was capable of. There was no telling where she would be, or what she would be doing, when Chlora finally settled on a date. Her affections toward the groom had come across as lacking during conversation. It was doubtful she would seek to hasten the vows.

"Splendid." Osias's face brightened once again, beckoning Thade to step in closer. "Now, with formalities out of the way, tell me. What is this business you spoke of in your letter? It sounded quite urgent."

In a sudden flurry of movement at Osias's side, Queen Adalyn rose to her feet, the elaborate crimson skirts of her gown flowing out around her. "Perhaps Lady Evantine and I should go for a turn around the room and leave the business talks to the men," she smiled, offering her hand out to Leyna warmly. "My husband can get rather long-winded over political matters. I would much like to learn a bit more about the mystery woman His Grace has brought to accompany him."

Thade's eyes shifted between King Osias and Queen Adalyn. "With all due respect, Your Majesty, but my hope was to allow Lady Evantine a chance to speak on the matter which I regret to lay before you. Her knowledge is far more vast than my own in regards to the intricacies. The issue is of a larger scale than I prefer to burden you both with, but Queen Adalyn, it might be best if you hear my request as well."

Intrigued by Thade's request, Adalyn lowered herself onto the throne once again, urging him to continue with a silent nod of her head.

"It is unlike you to be so grim," Osias squinted at Thade. Curious. "Whatever the matter is, let us hear it. You know we will do what we can to assist."

"Under any other circumstances I would say assistance is unnecessary, but I cannot assure you with any amount of certainty. It has become known to us that the Ven'shal seek war upon Tanispa."

"War, you say? Were they not banished from your country centuries ago?"

"They were. It is impossible to know how long their army has been building." Thade sighed, the weight of the situation evident on his elegant features. "It grieves me that I must come to you now, as your humble ally, to request your support should these matters take a turn for the worst."

Osias stroked his chin in thoughtful contemplation. "You have reason to be concerned with their army? What intelligence do you have which makes you believe this to be a significant threat?"

"We have witnesses, Your Majesty," Leyna chimed in, shooting Thade an apologetic glance. He had brought her to assist, not to lead. Though she felt Thade had been correct in his belief of her being more versed on the subject than himself. "A group of Ven'shal and Esai have formed a partnership in which they intend to resurrect the old Ven'shal sorcerer, Arcastus, from his grave. Are you familiar with this name, Your Majesty?"

"I am familiar. Continue," Osias waved his hand in an almost dismissive gesture.

Nodding to him respectfully, Leyna pressed on. "If they are successful, and we have received information which indicates they could be so, it would increase the strength tenfold of any army they bring against Tanispa. Not only is our own country at risk, but others could be as well. Those involved are power-hungry. A victory over one government might spark their greed to continue toward another. If we attempt to take them on alone, we risk the safety of all our lands. With your help, our defense might be strong enough to push them back before they have a chance to gain any footing."

Adalyn stared at her husband, horror-stricken at the thought of what Leyna was saying. Aware of his wife's sudden panic, Osias rested his hand gently on Adalyn's arm, reassuring her that everything would be alright. "This is dire, indeed. Lady Evantine, you give a very compelling statement on the matter."

"It is because I feel very strongly regarding it," she stated calmly. "This is a time where we must rely on our friends and allies in order to guarantee the safety of more than just a single race of people. The Vor'shai are not the only ones threatened by Arcastus's return, but with the right preparation, further turmoil can be avoided. For the sake of your people as well as our own."

"Well, it does not take much to convince an old man like me," Osias chuckled, the sound forced under the strain of his own heavy thoughts. "Queen Vorsila has always been a good friend to Mialan. Although it is preferred war be avoided at whatever cost, I could not, in good conscience, turn you away if that is the path the gods see fit to lead us down."

"I assure you, Your Majesty. All precautions are being implemented to deter violence. We hope to avoid war as much as you do. We merely would rather err on the side of caution and make sure our allies are informed and prepared."

"A wise decision," Osias nodded to Leyna, his attention shifting to where Thade remained silent at her side, eyes fixed on her, seemingly distracted. "Your Grace, you may send word to Queen Vorsila that she can count on us. I will make sure our General is informed and preparing his soldiers for action. I trust you will do the same."

"General Cadell has been kept abreast of the situation," Thade cleared his throat, straightening his back to stand proudly before the King. "Your continued friendship means a great deal to us. If there is anything we can offer you in return, do not hesitate to ask."

"You can see that Vorsila and Enaes are at our daughter's wedding. For now, I see no need to ask anything else of your people."

With a smile Thade bowed, stepping in closer to Leyna's side once again. "The Levadis family will be in attendance. You can rest assured. Queen Vorsila would not miss the occasion and you know Prince Enaes would never turn down a chance to see your lovely daughter."

"Ah, flattery! And to think you have already received what you wanted from me. You are a good man, Your Grace," Osias rose from the throne, giving a slight nod of his head in a show of respect. "And Lady Evantine," he added. "Do not forget that you will be expected at the celebration as well. You are always welcome here in our home. Any friend of His Grace and the Tanispan Queen is a friend of ours."

"You are too kind, Your Majesty." Leyna curtsied low, a feeling of relief washing over her. It was almost done. The farewells had begun. It wouldn't be much longer before she and Thade could escape from the throne room. Once free of the King and Queen, her only concern would be getting away from Thade before he could insist on drawing an answer from her.

Standing at her husband's side, Queen Adalyn smiled pleasantly, nodding her head to Thade and Leyna in turn. "Be safe in your travels home. It is a long road."

With one final nod Thade hooked his arm around Leyna's, urging her toward the door. She had to concentrate on her steps. One foot in front of the other. Slow. She couldn't look too desperate to get out of the room. Inside, she was proud of the way she'd conducted herself in front of the Mialan royalty. Lady Faustine's teachings had not gone to waste. At times Leyna feared the lessons would be forgotten due to lack of practice. It was a rare occasion for her to have need of them. Out of Faustine's care, the chances of being at court for any function had been slim – though if Thade had his way, she would find herself tossed into things far more frequently than she was comfortable with. After so many years in the role of a slave, it was an intimidating thought to consider. The constant fear of what the upper echelons would do if they ever discovered the secret of her past work. It was hardly becoming of a woman of any standing.

When the doors swung open into the hallway she quickened her pace, anxious to get away. Slipping her arm away from Thade's, she hurried back toward the foyer where they'd first met, wanting nothing more than to put enough distance between them that he would be unable to call out to her in fear of drawing attention.

"Leyna –"

She didn't acknowledge his voice. They were almost out of the hallway. In the presence of the courtiers in the foyer, she would be safe. Their conversation would have no choice but to cease until whenever Thade managed to get her alone again. And she had no intention of allowing that to happen. Not after the last time. That brief instant in the garden haunted her still. Thade's company now did nothing to ease the hurt she felt inside. Everything was too confusing! It was so much easier when their meetings were only occasional and chaperoned by Feolan. She didn't trust herself in Thade's presence alone. Her feelings were becoming too much for her to control.

From behind her, she could hear footsteps approaching, quick and light. Desperate, she tried to move faster. Their hurried pace was already summoning unwanted glances from the courtiers now filling the palace, refreshed after their previous evening's excursions. Why was he chasing her? She'd hoped he would refrain from doing so in order to avoid the stares now directed at them. Begrudgingly, she slowed.

"Leyna, is something wrong?" Thade asked, coming to stand at her side. She could see him scanning the room, taking in the watchful glances. "Why are you running away from me?"

"Because I already know the question you intend to ask, and I have no answer for you," she stated firmly. There. She'd said it. Now if only he would leave her alone. The topic wasn't one which could be discussed in the company of so many others.

Thade's expression flinched. He was torn by the things he wanted to say and the things he couldn't. She could see the conflict in every thoughtful line on his face. "I do not want to push you, Leyna, but I fail to see why the decision is so difficult for you to make. I thought you were ready to leave the mission. When last we spoke of it, the only thing holding you back was Kael."

"I'm not discussing this here."

"Then let us go somewhere else."

"You have lost your mind," she breathed, resuming her brisk pace toward her room. Where did he think they would go? The eyes would be everywhere. Curious. Waiting for them to do anything which might add to the stories. To disappear somewhere together would only make things worse and speaking openly wasn't an option.

He remained behind her every step of the way. His pace was smoother than before. Less rushed. If she could just get to her room there would be no fear of facing him. Thade wouldn't dare enter her private chambers with her alone. Not after the scene they'd already put on for everyone in the foyer. She could see the door coming into view up ahead. Just a few more steps. Her hand was on the knob, already stepping into the room. Thade reached out for her arm, attempting to keep her in the hallway, unable to manage a firm grip without risking injury to her. He paused, thinking briefly over what to do before stepping into the room after her, closing the door with a loud click.

"You cannot run away from this Leyna. The decision must be made before we return to Siscal. If you are leaving the mission, which I strongly suggest you do, it would be unwise to take you back to the inn where Kyros has given you lodging. We will need to think of another plan."

"Do you have any idea what people are going to say about you being here with me?" Leyna hissed, stepping toward him to urge him closer to the door. "Do you not think they whisper enough about us as it is?"

"Propriety is not worth sacrificing your life."

"You're being overdramatic, Thade."

"Am I?" he questioned, pushing forward to guide Leyna back to the center of the room with nothing more than his body. She was intimidated by him. The closeness between them was unnerving, sending her senses into a wave of panic. "My phrasing perhaps is a bit blunt, but if you think of the position you would be placing yourself in, returning to the mission would be next to suicide. Kyros and Damir know who you are. There is no more cover. No more hiding. The truth is out, and even the most clever of spies has to know when to cut their losses and move on."

"But what if there is more to be learned?"

"You are no use to us dead."

Exasperated, Leyna let her shoulders droop, pained to hear Thade speak in such a fashion. She was no use to them dead? Was that all it was about? Her service to the Queen? "So that is it, then? You want me out of there because I am more useful to you elsewhere?"

She could see the torment in Thade's eyes. "I did not mean that," he shook his head, reaching out to grasp Leyna lightly by her arms. "I want you out of there because I could not bear to see you hurt, knowing that I had an opportunity to prevent it. The suffering you have endured to this point lies on my shoulders already. Do not haunt me with the guilt of an unnecessary death. I care about you too much."

"If it means so much to you, then why do you not order me? Command me to leave the mission. Why is that so difficult for you to do? Anyone else you would not tolerate this without making the decision for them."

"Because I am not requesting this of you as your superior. I ask this of you as your friend. Do not go back there. Let me help you to start the life I should have provided upon your initial return to Siscal. This work was never my intention for you, and you know that. I was against it from the beginning, but you argued for your desire to feel your heart race to remind you that you are still alive. Haven't you grown tired of the wolves yet?"

He was standing so close to her. Inside her chest she could feel the rapid flutter of her heart, breaths coming in short gasps. Why was she so out of breath? She could hear her own voice speaking the words Thade recalled, in the privacy of his study in Siscal. If only she'd known then what she knew now. It all had sounded so intriguing at the time. So exciting. There was nothing exciting about it anymore. Thade had known, even then. He'd argued with her, protesting her insistence. *There are other ways to make your heart race than throwing yourself to the wolves. . .*

Her heart was racing now, though she doubted that had been what Thade had in mind when he'd spoken those words to her. All she could think about now was him. His body. The desperation in his eyes. If her heart beat any faster, she feared her chest would explode. "I think I may have."

Thade drew in a breath, the expression on his face revealing the uncertainty he felt at hearing her answer. "Is it true?" he asked, the words nothing more than a faint exhale from his lips. "You will return to Siscal with me and relinquish the mission?"

"How could I say no to you?" She chided herself silently for speaking what was in her mind. It was impossible to deny him. Whatever hold she once had over him, he now maintained the same power over her. As if he could ask for the world and she would sacrifice anything to give it to him. "What I mean is — I will do it for you. As a friend," she nodded, swallowing hard, embarrassed by the slip of her tongue. "I hate to admit it, but you are right. Staying there is only hindering us at this point. I can learn nothing more from Oksuva, and Kael is too great of a risk. The only person with whom we might still be able to garner information is Kyros, and he will inevitably seek to destroy me. The details he can provide are better left for Zander to uncover. Once he does, I will be there to help you strategize a defense the way we did during the war."

The relief in Thade's eyes was immeasurable. For a moment she thought he might kiss her in his joy, instead leaning forward to lightly place his lips to her forehead. "You have lifted a great burden from my shoulders, Leyna," he smiled, staring at her in admiration. "I am sorry if I was too forceful, but you must know how much this means to me."

"I know," she whispered. At first it had been less obvious, but the look on Thade's face was all she needed to realize how happy he was. It made her heart swell with pride to know that she had brought him such joy. "My belongings remain at the inn in Siscal. They will require me to return there for at least a few moments, but not long. Afterwards, we will have to think of where I will go. Outside of the mission, I have nothing. I have not had anything for years."

"We will think of something on our way home," he nodded, stepping away from her toward the door. "I will send for the carriage now. Have the chambermaid help you pack. We should be on the road before the day grows much later."

Chapter Twenty-Two

The familiar landscape of Siscal brought heaviness to Leyna's heart, reminding her of the dangers inherent to the area. Within the hour she would be at the inn. She feared Kyros would be there to greet her. To demand of her information about her time with Thade. There was nothing to be shared with Kyros. A meeting with him would only end in violence and she no longer desired to face him. She wanted away from him. Away from everything.

Thade remained quiet throughout the trip. He had acquired a constant look of deep and troubling thought, but when she inquired, he dismissed her politely, claiming he was fine. Tired from the journey. She couldn't argue the fatigue she felt herself from the length of the trip, but it was obvious that Thade's troubles went far deeper than that. The awkwardness of their meeting in the garden at the party in Mialan had left a gap between them which made it feel inappropriate for her to try and convince him to open up while their last conversation in her chambers made her heart flutter just thinking about hearing his voice.

Finally, when nearing the ranges of the mountains bordering Siscal, Thade tore his eyes away from the window, taking something from inside his jacket. It was a small box. Some type of wood comprised the shape, the finish worn away in spots, edges chipped. "I almost forgot," he stated quietly. "Princess Chlora asked that I give this to you. A belated birthday present, as it were."

Accepting it curiously, Leyna lifted the lid, peering inside as if afraid the contents might jump out. She found nothing so menacing. Instead it looked to be a ring. Pulling the lid away completely, she gazed down at it, amazed by the beauty of the design. The shape was feminine. Thin silver formed the band, widening at the face to reveal what resembled a family crest.

She glanced over to Thade questioningly. There had to be more to it. Some explanation. "Did she tell you anything about it? I do not understand why she would give this to me."

"It was removed from Sarayi's finger after her body was discovered by the Mialan guards," he replied. "I recognized the crest instantly as that of the Evantine family. They have been prominent in the Tanispan court for centuries. I suggested to her that it would be better cared for in your possession than in some vault, collecting dust in that box. As I was able to confirm for her that you are the descendant of Sarayi, she gave in to my requests and offered it as a gift from the Mialan royal family. In their condolences for your loss."

Holding the ring between her thumb and index finger, Leyna let the light play off the tiny jewels in the design, sparkling like new despite their apparent age. In the back of her mind, she recalled a vague image of the ring on her mother's finger. It had meant little to her as a child. The details were skewed in memory, preventing her from retrieving a solid picture. But this looked familiar somehow. A piece of her mother there in her hand.

She slid it carefully onto her finger. It fit perfectly. Snug. Not too tight for comfort. She admired the skill in the design, miniature diamonds forming the blades of twin crossed swords along the crest. Sapphires created a band around the edges of a shield in the background, floral leaves cascading from the top and sides in graceful waves. It must have been expensive to make, though the cost would have been provided by some distant ancestor. Passed down through the generations of Evantine women. The natural line of the family.

"Did she know anything about what happened that day?" Leyna felt compelled to ask. This ring was a sign that someone had been there. Someone had found the bodies. Perhaps providing a proper burial. It only made sense that they would have investigated the matter. The deaths were too brutal. Too suspicious.

"Enough to add to my concerns about you returning to the inn at all," he frowned. "The guards were able to take one man into custody who admitted his involvement in the assassination. He pled guilty in having participated in the death of Rohan while naming Damir responsible for killing Sarayi. That makes your situation far more precarious."

"I have nowhere to go," she argued. "I have no home – nothing to my name, if I do not at least return there for my things. My only refuge was Zander's house and they all frequent it. I have conceded to leave the mission, but we have yet to determine where I will go. I cannot very well live with you. Society would never allow that, nor would it be wise for either of us, given Kael's accusations."

Thade fell silent again. His forehead creased in concentration, the time passing slowly before he spoke. "When Feolan married his first wife, he purchased a home near mine. It was not in use for very long, given the circumstances, and when they separated, he moved back in with me. His wife remained there for a few months before she moved away to have Teagan's child. The house has been vacant ever since. It is still deeded to Feolan. You can consider it yours."

She didn't know what to say. The thought of having her own home was exciting and frightening at the same time. It would be an escape from the watchful eyes of the others, but there were dangers in staying there alone. If anything happened, Zander wouldn't be there to come to her aid.

"Are you sure? Shouldn't you speak to Feolan first?"

"He will not argue. On many occasions he has discussed the possibility of selling the place. He has no desire to use it any longer. It holds far too many painful memories for him, and with the possibility of he and Lady Diah marrying, he will certainly have no need of it. They would be seeking a new place to start their family."

"I will still need to return to the inn to collect my belongings," she pondered, thinking over the few personal affects she'd brought with her when they came from Dalonshire. None of them were particularly important, but she would not have the money to spend on purchasing a whole new wardrobe right away. And shopping would place her in the public eye, at risk of being seen by Kyros and the others.

"Is it necessary, Leyna?" Thade inquired, the consternation on his face deepening. "Whatever you have there, I could replace for you easily. It would be safer for you to simply return with me until Feolan's home is prepared, and never go to that inn again."

"No, Thade. I will not allow you to spend your money on me. It is bad enough that I accepted the gowns you had made for me in Mialan."

"Those were gifts. There is nothing wrong with accepting them."

"They are gifts of a very high price which I do not deserve," she sighed. Her head ached. Every part of her wanted to go wherever Thade asked, but there was too much standing between them. The rumors which would abound by her spending too much time in his presence. Accepting expensive gifts. Not to mention her own confused feelings toward him. It was best that she not allow him to be so kind, and not grant them opportunities of privacy together. "Do not worry. I will not return them. But if you will hold onto the things I brought along for our trip, I should be able to collect the rest from the inn in a single bag. It will not take long. Perhaps you or Feolan could meet me somewhere? In an hour or so, at most."

"I will not leave the area until you return. It is best you not linger there. Not even for an hour. You should gather your things and be gone from the room before anyone discovers you have returned. And Leyna –" Trailing off, Thade knelt down in front of his seat, pulling out a long case from a compartment beneath it. "Although I will not be far away, if you are concerned about rumors, it would be best I not be seen accompanying you. I want you to take this."

Unhooking the latch revealed a finely crafted saber within an intricately carved and painted scabbard of polished black and silver. It was a majestic weapon. She hesitated to touch it as he offered the scabbard to her, afraid of damaging the craftsmanship. "I cannot take this," she breathed in exasperation. "It must have cost a fortune. I do not want to risk ruining or losing it."

"It is only taking up space under that seat," he argued. "Take it. I will feel more comfortable letting you go back there if I know you have a weapon. That dress will make defending yourself hard enough as it is without also having the disadvantage of being unarmed."

She allowed Thade to set the scabbard on her outstretched palms, her eyes trailing down to the flowing skirt of her dress. It was less restricting than the ones designed for court, but the excess fabric was a tripping hazard for even the most skilled of fighters. "I do not intend to be at the room long enough to draw attention."

Her eyes shifted past Thade in confusion as he began to unclasp one of the belts around his waist. It was exquisitely designed, like everything she had ever seen him wear, silver shimmering in the light streaming through the carriage windows. Unfamiliar diamond shaped blue gems were set along the center of it in rows. Painstakingly detailed, etched lines connected between each stone, twisting in a complex geometric pattern over the surface.

Aloof, he handed the belt to her, releasing it quickly before she could try to give it back. In a fluid motion, he moved over to his seat again. "You are a bit more slender around the waist than I am, but I believe your hips will support it well enough."

"Are you saying I have fat hips?" she chuckled, turning the belt over in her hand to inspect it more closely.

"Your hips are perfect – in a very practical way, that is." Thade's face scrunched up awkwardly. "I am sure they are just fine."

Leyna laughed quietly to herself. Something about seeing Thade squirm was enjoyable. He was always the perfect image of calm. It was entertaining to think she had the ability to break his concentration, forcing him to consider his words more closely, his face turning away to shield the faint pink hue on his cheeks.

When the carriage came to a stop, she was surprised to find them so close to the inn, the entrance visible through her window. It was a risk for them to have ventured so far into town together. But Kyros was aware of whose company she was in. The only person who stood to be angered by it was Kael, and he hardly seemed important enough at the moment to concern herself with. Over the last month, she'd come to realize just how much more pleasant life was without him around. It was hard to imagine how she ever thought she could spend the rest of her life with him.

Wrapping the belt around her waist, Leyna pulled the clasp as far as it would go, making sure the scabbard was securely in place at her side. Thade was right about it being somewhat larger than desired, but it would serve well enough. She hoped to have no need of it, wanting to be in and out of the inn within a matter of only a few minutes, leaving again without drawing notice to her arrival.

"I still am not comfortable letting you go in alone. At this point I am willing to risk being seen if it guarantees your safety –"

"No," she shook her head, opening the carriage door to step down onto the familiar gravel of the street. It was too dangerous to risk. Just knowing Thade would be near was enough to give her the confidence she needed. It would only take a few minutes to pack. There was no need to put Thade in danger over a few personal affects. "Don't worry about me. Keep an eye on the inn. I will be out shortly."

Before he could say anything else, she closed the carriage door, separating them. With a casual wave, she stepped away, moving toward the building and turning her back on the horses. Whether Kyros was aware of her being in the company of Thade or not, she didn't want to think about what would happen if they were to meet face-to-face. It was best she not linger around Thade in any way that might draw attention to his presence.

Walking away from the carriage brought a sense of loneliness to her heart. In Thade's company, she'd felt alive. Capable of doing anything she put her mind to. It had been easier to speak of coming here when he was sitting there at her side. Now that she was back, she felt the familiar tug of unease in her stomach, twisting and churning, growing in intensity. She thought she would surely vomit. A part of her wanted to run back and climb into the carriage with Thade again, but she couldn't allow it. She was already here. What was so frightening about seeing her room one last time?

Hurrying into the inn, Leyna made her way up the stairs, pausing outside the door to get up the nerve to go inside. It had been so long since she was there last. It was unsettling to think of what might be waiting for her. No one else had any reason to be there. Kyros arranged the room for her own personal use. He was the only person she had need to be concerned of, and he had no way of knowing when she would be returning. Fear hung over her at the thought of seeing him again. After being back in that house where he'd first tried to take her life, she hated to consider facing him now. The image in her mind was more intimidating. Frightening.

Pushing the door gently inward, she heard the hinges creek under the movement. The scent of dust filled her nostrils. It was stagnant. Musty. Nothing like she remembered. Even before the housekeepers managed to make it appear lived-in. It seemed they had left the room uncared for in her absence. Despite the thickness of the air which gave the illusion of emptiness, there was something out of place about the room. Something that didn't quite sit with her senses.

"Hello?" she called out. The sound of her voice echoed through the walls eerily. No one answered. Not that she expected anyone to. Her nerves and imagination were getting the better of her. She needed to just get in, gather her things, and get out.

Closing the door slowly, she moved in, quiet, cautious. If anyone was watching for her return, she didn't want to advertise her arrival. But the uncomfortable feeling refused to subside, no matter how she reassured herself that there was nothing to fear.

Hand on the hilt of her sword, she made her way across the darkened room, tiptoeing lightly. She'd become accustomed to living with many other people. Out of respect for the others, she was used to moving about silently, making as little noise as possible. For some reason she was almost surprised to find her room vacant and unvisited. Kyros, at the very least, should have come looking. She didn't want to consider the possibility of Damir having called for the others to meet again. And if he had, would they have gone without her?

Of course they would have. She was a liability, particularly if they had discovered her identity. The only reason for them to have not killed her yet was if they felt she had some other use. They would toy with her until her convenience wore out. Death would follow quickly once they lost interest.

At the window she carefully slid the curtains back, making sure not to move them too quickly. A faint glow from the setting sun filtered into the room, allowing her to get a better look at her surroundings.

"Going somewhere?"

Kael's voice was almost unrecognizable to her ears. It was slow. Menacing. No sign of the caring man she'd met all those years ago. This was the voice of the monster inside Kael's skin, gazing at her calmly from the bed. "Kael," she gasped, stumbling backward in surprise. "What are you doing here?"

"Now, Eleni — what kind of greeting is that for a wife to give her husband?" he asked. Effortlessly, he stood and made his way from the bed to where she was standing by the window, grasping her chin gruffly between his fingers. "You smell like him. And to think some part of me didn't think you would actually run off the way they told me you had. Kyros grants you your freedom and you so willingly run to whore yourself to the Consul? I'll have you know, I have put a stop to that nonsense."

"It is nothing like you think. There is nothing between the Consul and I. We traveled together as friends. Kyros could never force me into dishonoring myself, the way you would."

"The way I would?" he huffed. "What exactly is that supposed to mean?"

Jerking her face away from Kael's hand, she stepped backward, glancing uncomfortably around the room. "You had no qualms with crawling into bed with another woman when Kyros asked."

"That is different!"

"How is it different?" she snapped angrily. "You have been to bed with at least two other women, that I am aware of, and yet you tell me it is different? You still think that is acceptable? I am your betrothed —"

"That's right. And it is time that you started to act like it." Grabbing her roughly by her bicep, Kael pushed Leyna backward into the open closet, pressing her hard against the wall. A cloud of dust leapt up around them as they disrupted the area. "From here on, you are never to speak to that man again. Do you understand me? He or his man servant."

"You cannot control who I befriend any more than I can control who you sleep with. Now get your hands off me." Leyna tried to pull away, unable to move.

"I love you, Eleni. You may think I am being unreasonable, but I do it for us. Because I do not want people thinking that my wife is a whore. I should have that man's head for touching you."

"He never touched me!" she shouted, pushing at Kael futilely with her free hand. "You have no right to accuse me of these things. I have wanted only what was best for you, to cleanse you of that awful magic which taints your soul, yet you continue to go against my wishes, and for what? To defy me? To prove to me that you do not have to do what I ask? Do you really care that little about yourself?"

Kael's hand connected hard against her cheek with a crisp smack, turning her head to the right. Losing control, Leyna brought her own hand up in retaliation. Her palm narrowly struck at his face as he caught her wrist in a crushing grasp. "You would strike me for denying you that man's company?" he smirked.

"I strike you because you struck me," she hissed. "I am not some slave girl you can push around. You promised I would be more than that to you."

"Well, I was wrong. It seems you are nothing more than a slave. But a slave that is my wife, and therefore you will do what I tell you."

Struggling against his grip, Leyna tried to lash out at him again. She was furious. No longer did she feel any pity. She hated him. Every part of her wanted nothing more than to draw her weapon and separate his head from his body, freeing her from his madness and releasing whatever was left of his tortured soul so that he might find some solace in the afterlife.

He held her firm. The look on his face revealed that he was enjoying watching her fight against him, gloating silently at his superior strength. "Tell me, Eleni," he mused. "Was all this worth it? Does his higher rank really make his bed that much more desirable to you? Do you think you could ever be something more to him than a prostitute? He could have any woman at court, all of which are far prettier and wealthier than you. You could never be good enough."

His words stung beyond the physical. She believed for so long that she would never be good enough for Thade. It pained her to think of it, knowing that she had let her guard down on their trip to Mialan. Foolishly, she'd let herself think that night in the garden that there was a chance he might share the feelings she held for him. But in the end, he had walked away, blaming it on the wine. And maybe he was right. Maybe it was nothing more than their intoxicated minds forgetting who they were, and who they were with — blinded by the beauty of the night.

"I already told you," she spoke through gritted teeth. "There is nothing between the two of us. We are only friends. Now release your hold on me this instant."

"Or you will what? Show me, Eleni. Don't hold anything back. Show me your true feelings toward me."

"What do you mean?"

"If you despise me so much that you will continue to defy my requests, then take your blade. You must have brought it for a reason."

Leyna gazed at him in disbelief. "You wish to fight me?"

"It seems you wish to fight me."

Kael released his hold on her wrist, watching her rub at it painfully with her other hand. For the first time, she became aware of the weapon, looking out of place strapped around his waist. She had never known him to carry a sword. It was almost as if he had expected to fight someone. "Have I drawn my blade?" she asked, gazing up at him sadly.

"I will say this," he replied calmly. "If you strike me down, you may do whatever you want. Until then, you will do what I ask of you. Or rather, what I tell you to do."

"So the choice is to either kill you, or give up my freedom?"

"Is that so much to ask?"

Bowing her head, she heaved a sigh. To fight him would be suicide. She was out of practice and out of her element. He had her cornered already. But giving in was out of the question. She was leaving the mission to assist Thade. He was counting on her. Their people were counting on her. "I cannot do what you ask of me."

"Then you are willing to kill me?" he arched his brow curiously at her.

"No, I don't want to fight you! You are trying to get under my skin so that I will draw my weapon, but I will not."

She was surprised to see him step away, placing distance between them, allowing her a chance to escape. The expression on his face was one of utter confusion. He was struggling with something in his mind, it seemed. Whatever it was, it pained him greatly, his forehead creasing under the strain. "I love you, Eleni. You know that I do."

"I don't know that anymore, Kael," she shook her head. His feelings for her had ceased to be clear since the night of Mikel and Oksuva's anniversary party. "I think you may have loved me at one time, and I you, but you have changed. I don't think you know what you feel about anything anymore."

"I will never stop loving you. That is why I must do everything I can to keep you from slipping away. Never will I let you go, no matter how much you try to defy me. If it means I have to kill the Consul in order to have you for myself, then I will. I don't care what Kyros has asked of you."

"You have no choice but to let me go." For a moment she second-guessed speaking of her plans. He was unstable. It was dangerous to add salt to his already clearly burning wounds. He had to know, though. It would be more treacherous for him to hear it from someone else. "A request has already been sent to Tanispa for review by the priests to annul our engagement. It was a mistake. I was still trying to find who I was and you were struggling against your own guilt for your betrayal and the pull of the sorcery inside you. If only we could have waited –"

"You what?" The rage in his eyes frightened her. There was no color left in them at all, the white now coated in a thick blackness, concealing the softness she once saw there. "You went behind my back in search of an annulment? Is that where you have been for the last month? Arranging for your freedom so that you could be with that man?"

She wanted to scream. Why would he not let go of his silly notions about her and Thade? He was obsessed with the idea and nothing she said was doing anything to rid him of it. "It has nothing to do with the Consul!" she screamed, pulling at her hair desperately with her hands. It was all she could do to keep from lashing out at him. She couldn't let that happen. "I tried, Kael! I was frightened by what you were becoming, but I offered to stand by your side and help you to fight it. All you did in return was fall deeper. You accuse me of affairs which I have never had, while you betray yourself."

"I have seen the way you look at him. I saw the change in his eyes the night I introduced you. Can you honestly tell me that if he were to kiss you, that you would push him away?"

"I –" her voice broke at his question, thinking of the garden in Mialan. They had received no word back from the priests then in regards to the decision of her annulment. And yet she had wanted Thade to kiss her. Her heart had longed for it. As his face came closer, her desire had grown until it was almost unbearable. She'd made no move to stop him. Thankfully, he managed to stop himself.

It must have been the wine. If she had been in control of her senses, none of that would have happened. She would have prevented the inappropriately flirtatious words which inevitably led to their being so close in the first place from falling from her lips. Yet still, she couldn't say with any certainty that she could convince herself to push Thade away if he moved to try again, even in her sober state.

"Your hesitance says everything I need to know."

"Kael, no," she argued, moving forward in desperation. Why had she paused? The answer had been right there on the tip of her tongue, waiting to assure him that she held no feelings for Thade. But it was a lie. Just like everything else he thought he knew about her. "He has no reason to want me, so there is no reason for you to concern yourself with it."

"Then tell me what you do when you are alone with him. What is it that you occupy such lengthy spans of time with?"

Her eyes followed Kael's hand idly tapping against the hilt of his sword. He was staring at her, unflinchingly, his inky black eyes still managing to reveal the unspoken accusations running through his mind. "I cannot really say." How could she tell him that they discussed his failure? His spiral into the depths of the sorcery they fought to destroy. If Kael learned the idea of the annulment had been Thade's, there would be no stopping the rage that would ensue.

"You cannot, or will not?" He scoffed. "What is the great secret that you refuse to tell?"

"There is no secret, Kael," she lied. "Thade and I are friends. Our conversations deal with trivial things and hold no importance in the matter of you and me."

"You are on a first name basis with the Consul now?"

Damn him! He was trying to get her to slip up. But what could he possibly be hoping to learn? She had done nothing wrong. "What do you want me to say?" she gasped, exasperated by his persistence in his claims. "If you think I am going to fumble over my words and reveal some great secret, I am sorry, but there is none. I have nothing to hide."

"Let me wager a guess, then," he said with a smirk, pacing casually across the room, his hands clasped behind his back. "You left the country together, alone. Prior to that, I had already confronted him with my suspicions regarding his nighttime conduct with you at his house." His eyes widened as he turned back to face her, pointing his index finger at her sternly. "I have it!" he shouted. "You are pregnant with his child, aren't you? This last month you went away to seek a place for you to spend your confinement once it became too noticeable to hide from me."

"You have got to be joking!" she choked on her own breath at the madness of what Kael was suggesting. "This is exactly why you and I cannot ever be married. Your jealousy is making you insane. It is ludicrous that you would even think such a thing."

In a swift motion, Kael covered the space between them, drawing his hand back. Before she could defend herself, his fist drove hard into Leyna's stomach, dropping her to her knees, gasping for air. "That would also explain your sudden decision to go behind my back to seek the annulment." He picked her up gruffly by her hair, holding her in place while his knee delivered another blow to her abdomen. She coughed painfully, clutching at her stomach. "Oh, I'm sorry. Am I jostling the baby?"

"You've lost your mind," she exhaled, trying to regain her composure in fear he might strike again. "I already told you why I sought the annulment. It is because you are unfaithful and unreasonable – and above all else, you are insane! Foul magic has warped your mind irreparably, and frankly I no longer feel anything but pity for you."

Releasing his hold on Leyna, she heard the sound of his sword being pulled from its scabbard, sunlight from the window glinting off the blade. "Get up," he snarled. "I will see you dead before I see you in the arms of another man."

"I am not going to fight you, Kael."

"Draw your blade or die, you whore!" he screamed, spittle flying from his mouth. He looked wild standing there in the sparsely furnished room. His hair was tousled, teeth bared menacingly as he positioned himself in a fighting stance. "You no longer have an option. If you want to walk away from me, then you will have to do it over my corpse."

Reluctantly, she reached down for the sword hanging at her side. She had no chance in defeating him here. Not while he was so filled with rage. His unstable mind made him an even deadlier opponent, lacking any fear of death. Unfortunately for her, the situation was to his advantage.

If she fell at the hands of Kael, Thade would hold himself accountable for having let her go in alone. She hated the thought of putting him through such anguish. He already suffered so much because of her over the years. All she could do now was defend herself. With any luck, escape might be possible. If she could hold him at bay just a little longer, she could send some signal to Thade through the window. Kael would be no match for the two of them together.

Seeing Kael's blade descending upon her, she drew her sword in a fluid motion with her right arm. Instinct remained in her favor for battle. Survival had been something she'd grown accustomed to fighting for, and the body could muster unnatural strength when faced with the possibility of death.

Their swords clashed with a loud scrape of metal on metal. He was stronger than she remembered, bearing down on her ruthlessly. She could see the look of a killer in his eyes. A madman. He moved with incredible temerity and speed, gripping his sword in both hands, swinging almost wildly. Very little semblance of technique could be seen through his strikes. It was hard to defend against. There was no method to his madness, Kael's movements sporadic and unpredictable.

Through the rush of the battle, Leyna was grateful for the superior design of the saber Thade had provided her. With the power of Kael's strikes, the blades she used during the war would have shattered into pieces, leaving her vulnerable. This weapon was lightweight enough for freedom of movement unlike any other she had wielded. She found it easy to maneuver from side to side, blocking his blows easily.

With a high feint, Kael lured Leyna's sword arm up, grabbing it securely in his free hand. The impact of his elbow across her face sent her reeling. She felt as though she was falling, but somehow she was still on her feet, held firmly in place by Kael's uncanny strength. Not since her fight in Mikel's arena had she felt physical pain to such severity. The strikes from his elbow came repeatedly, snapping her neck to the side with every blow.

The sudden pain in her leg came unexpectedly. A grotesque snap echoed through the room around them as Kael drove his foot hard into the side of her knee, her screams filling the air, shrill and panicked. She crumpled to the ground in a heap. Her fingers barely managed to maintain their grip on her sword, tears of agony streaming down her cheeks. She needed to stand up. There was no way she would be able to hold onto the fight much longer if she remained on the ground. She would be at his mercy with such limited range of motion.

In one final surge of strength, she forced herself back to her feet, crying out at the pain shooting through her left leg. It was excruciating. Adrenaline was the only thing keeping her from collapsing to the ground in defeat. Fierce and defiant, she lunged at Kael, most of her weight distributed on her right side, pushing through the pain to force him back, disarming him in his state of shock at seeing her determination. His sword clattered onto the floorboards a few feet away, leaving him in confused awe.

The distraction lasted only seconds before he sprung into motion again. He charged forward in blind rage, driving his shoulder into her chest, knocking her hard to the ground on her back. The impact sent her own sword tumbling from her grasp as he straddled her body, his fists pummeling mercilessly at her face.

Protecting her head was the only thing she could think about in that position. Her hands moved up to guard her temples, absorbing much of the impact with her arms. She squirmed under his weight. He was more balanced than Mikel had been when she'd fought him that last afternoon in Dalonshire, and the injury to her leg would make it more difficult to maneuver to freedom. Thrusting her hips upward, she tried to throw him off, desperate for a single moment of peace. Her attempts to unbalance him only added to his uncontrolled rage. With immeasurable strength, he pried her arms away from her head, pinning them down to the floor. Once unhindered, he slammed his head forward into hers, his crown and her nose connecting with a sickening crunch.

Blood filled her mouth, coppery and bitter. She didn't even feel the pain as their heads collided again. She was barely clinging to consciousness. A deep cut had opened on Kael's forehead, his hand lifting up to dab at the blood curiously. "Are you going to force me to kill you?"

"Do what you will," she whispered haggardly. "I gladly accept death if my only other choice is to submit to you."

She could barely feel his fingers wrapping around her slender neck, tightening, pressing hard against her throat. As she started to gasp for breath, she noticed Kael's expression falter. A trickle of air passed through her lungs. Just as she felt the cold chill of death creeping over her, Kael suddenly pulled away, rising to his feet in a frantic motion.

He looked frightened in that instant. A hint of the man Leyna had once known could be seen through his abyssal eyes, gazing down at her in horror. "You brought this on yourself," he gasped, his fingers running desperately through his disheveled black hair. "If you would have just done what I asked of you, none of this would have happened. We could have been so happy together, Eleni."

Kael moved over to the door. Leyna could hear the sound of his fist connecting with the wall, splintering the wood under the force of the blow. She couldn't move. Her spirit felt as though it was floating above her body, watching everything, detached. Was she dead? Is this what it felt like to die? There was no pain. The eyes on her body stared emptily up at the ceiling, almost seeming to peer through her airy form looking down from above.

Through the fog of her mind, she heard Kael say something about a doctor. He was standing over her again, talking about getting help. But what good would any of it do if she was already dead?

She didn't want to die. Panic filled her. No. She couldn't die. Not yet. There was still so much that needed to be done! Thade was waiting for her. Somehow, she needed to get back to her body. It wasn't time for her to die. Damir was still out there, preparing to wage war against her people. They needed her help.

Swimming through the empty space, she drew in closer to her motionless form lying on the floor. Her chest rose, ever so slightly, trying to filter air into her lungs, previously deprived under Kael's grasp. Yes! She was breathing. She was alive, though barely. But barely was enough.

With one final surge of power, she dove back down, willing her body to move. Her eyes blinked. Good. It was a start. She was conscious, at least. Now if she could just get her limbs to move.

In her mind she could see Thade's face. Regardless of whether or not she would ever be good enough for him, he was the reason she found to keep going. He needed her. The Queen needed her. Revenge felt trivial at that moment. There were other reasons why Damir needed to die. Why Kyros couldn't be allowed to live. They stood to kill more than just a single family. They would exterminate an entire race if given the chance.

Her fingers twitched. She started to come back from her reverie, pain flooding her senses once again. She had to look beyond it. Kael was still there, his fingers pressed against the side of her neck in search of a pulse. There was a commotion coming from the doorway but her head wouldn't cooperate to turn and see what was creating the stir. Kael rose to his feet in a swift motion. Everything was out of her line of sight, her ears only catching bits of conversation passing between Kael and someone else. Another male, the sound of the new voice cutting into her vague consciousness with a familiarity that she couldn't deny. Thade.

"I knew you wouldn't be far off," Kael chuckled. The concern that had been visible in his voice only moments before dissipated almost instantly. "I had come prepared to fight you tonight. It was really only unfortunate chance that I was forced to raise my hand to her. How fortuitous that fate would bring you here for me to finish as well."

"Stand aside, Kael. I came for her, not you."

"You think I am going to just hand her over to you? My own wife? Have you lost your mind?

"There is no one here who fits that title for you." Thade's voice was eerily calm. He was coming closer, the creak of the wooden floor signaling his location for Leyna's dimmed senses. Desperate, she gathered every ounce of strength she could manage, her neck rolling to the side to bring the two men into view. Kael was moving away from her toward his fallen sword. His distraction granted Thade an opportunity to cross the room to Leyna's side, falling to his knees in a rush, eyes open wide at the sight of the injuries she'd sustained.

"Leyna! Can you hear me?"

At the sound of the name being spoken, Kael froze, gazing blankly into the distance. Leyna could feel Thade's hand lightly brushing over her face. With a gentle sweep of his fingers he tucked a blood-soaked strand of her hair behind her ear, staring into her eyes as if willing her to move. To blink. To give any sign of life.

It took too much energy to speak. So many words came to mind that she wanted to say, but no sound came. She could sense Thade's anger rising as he took in her battered appearance, his eyes turning on Kael with a ferocity she'd never seen there before. He was positioned like a barricade protecting her from further advances. She admired the honor Thade showed in his desire to defend her. So many men she encountered over the years wouldn't have thought twice about risking their own life for the sake of a woman. But she didn't want him to fight Kael. The thought of anything happening to Thade was more painful than the sensation already coursing through her body.

Seeming to regain his composure, Kael cocked his head to one side, peering curiously at Thade through his blackened eyes. "Despite what you may like to think, or who you are convinced she is, I know my own wife when I see her, and she is lying there on the floor behind you. Hand her over to me and I will not go to Queen Nesperiti to inform her of your vile behavior."

"By the hand of Queen Vorsila Levadis herself, that woman you refer to is not your wife, nor will she ever be. For nearly three weeks now, you have been a single man. And this woman is free of you. I suppose this suffices as your official notification of annulment."

Leyna felt her heart crash inside her chest. She was free? The decision had come sooner than expected, but when had he heard the news? And by the Queen? She feared it was nothing more than a ruse to fool Kael into submission. It was too good to be true.

"Well, she must have her claws sunk deeper into you than I thought. The only way a decision would have been reached so quickly is if you had something to do with it. An abuse of power. I wonder, what reward were you expecting?"

"Other than seeing a good woman rescued from a life with a man who does not deserve her? I smell the stench of your treachery from here. You are a disgrace to your people."

"I dedicated my life to my people! I risked everything to get the information you required and this is how you repay me? You steal my wife? Defile her? You humiliate me and then insult me further by calling me a disgrace? You are a no good scoundrel. You don't deserve the power you hold."

With an eerie calm, Thade rose to his feet, moving to clench his fingers around the neck of Kael's shirt, jerking him forward. "You accuse me of defiling her? Look at what you have done before you cast accusations! You treat her like she is nothing more than a slave. An animal! She is not so low as to deserve such treatment. If you were any bit a man, you would have treated her like a goddess."

Unfazed by Thade's firm hold on him, Kael laughed, pushing roughly to break away. "You are going to school me in how to treat a woman?" Lifting his sword, Kael aimed the tip of the blade at Thade. They held each other's gaze, unflinching.

"You dare draw your blade on a man of our Queen?"

"I intend to do more than simply draw it." Kael lunged forward with his sword, a scowl crossing his features as the blade met with only empty air, Thade's body twisting easily to avoid the blow. Thade moved with incredible precision, stepping forward to apply pressure at various points of Kael's body with an intricate weaving of his hands. The tips of his fingers struck Kael's neck and chest, causing him to gasp for breath.

Unable to maintain his grip on the sword, it fell from Kael's hand, landing on the floor with a clatter against the wood.

"Get out of here," Thade pushed Kael backward, a dull thud accompanying the sound of his body collapsing to the floor in a breathless heap. "If you show your face anywhere near her again, I will have you arrested, the way you should have been the last time I saw you. For your deeds, you are hereby declared a traitor and are forever banished from Tanispa."

Clutching at his chest Kael clambered to his feet. "I'm not done here," he snarled. Wildly, he reached out for Thade, gripping his doublet to try and throw him to the ground. Thade stood firm, stance solid, unmoving.

"The longer you insist on fighting me, the less time there will be to seek a doctor for her," Thade said through gritted teeth, grabbing Kael's wrists in his hands to twist them outward, locking them in place to apply an awkward pressure to the joints. "Do you want to be the one responsible for her death? The woman you claim to love?"

"Let the whore die," Kael winced at the pain under Thade's grasp. Desperate for a means of escape, Kael thrust his knee upward, driving it into Thade's stomach to release his hold. "If I kill you, it will serve to not only defend my honor that you have insulted, but it will also guarantee you and your people stay out of Damir's way. At least they appreciate the effort I have invested into our work."

Thade recovered quickly, seemingly unshaken by the blow. Like an impenetrable force he moved forward, a flurry of punches raining down upon Kael's disoriented form, forcing him back, further away from Leyna. "That was all I needed to know," Thade replied calmly, delivering one last strike to the side of Kael's head, the knuckles solidly driving into his temple, rendering him unconscious.

Falling limply to the ground, Kael lay there, unmoving. Thade paid him little attention as he rushed back to Leyna's side, scooping her into his arms with the utmost care, not wanting to hurt her, unsure of the extent of her wounds.

"Is he dead?" Leyna gasped, managing to find her voice through the pain and confusion.

Relief flooded over Thade's features to hear her speak. "Do not worry about him," he replied, stepping over Kael's body toward the door. "Let's get you out of here first."

Out of there? But her belongings were still in the closet. And the sword! Exhaling a sharp breath, she scanned the room frantically for the saber that had fallen from her hands when Kael knocked her to the floor. It couldn't be far from them. She'd heard it clatter over her head.

Struggling against Thade's grasp, she fought to lower herself to her feet, not ready to leave. Her own limbs worked against her efforts, preventing her from breaking free. "Your sword," she groaned. It took all of her strength, pointing her index finger toward the fallen blade near the window. "And my clothes. It's all still here. I didn't have time —"

"Hush," Thade quieted her, moving swiftly toward the saber where she directed him. With a fluid sweep he retrieved the blade, showing no difficulty in maintaining his hold on Leyna, hurrying toward the door before she could protest. "We cannot worry about your belongings. We must hurry. He will regain consciousness sooner than I would like."

She wanted to argue. There were so many things she wanted to say, but her mind was slowed from the agony flooding her. The movement alone exacerbated the pain throughout her body, waves of discomfort a constant reminder of her injuries. She just wanted it to stop. To her relief it did, her vision fading as Thade carried her through the lobby and out into the night.

When Leyna started to regain consciousness, she was painfully aware of an uncomfortable pressure and stiffness in her left leg. Someone was leaning over her. The cloudiness of her vision was persistent, casting shadows over everything around her. Vaguely, she detected a subtle perfume. "Maeri?"

"Hush, Leyna," Maeri breathed. "Just relax. You are safe now."

"Leyna?" Feolan's voice was louder. His anger was evident, the sound of his heavy footsteps coming closer from the other side of the room. "Why did he do this to you?"

"Darling, please. I just told her not to speak. She needs to relax."

"I was under the impression that Kyros left town and had taken Kael with him, given Zander's last report."

Left town? Kyros hadn't mentioned anything to her about leaving. "It is difficult to explain," she coughed, straining to open her eyes to let in more light. "Where am I?" Nothing Leyna did allowed her to see the details of the room. She could feel the soft cushions underneath her, and see the white ceiling overhead, but her head hurt too much.

"We are at the Consul's home," Maeri replied quietly. "You are in rough shape. I don't think it would be wise for you to go anywhere else for a while. Your leg — was badly broken. Of all the things I actually paid attention to in Faustine's lessons, you are lucky I remembered wound tending. The bone is set, but if you aren't careful, it won't heal."

"Where is the Consul?"

"He is here," Feolan nodded. Leyna could feel his hand patting the back of hers, reassuringly. "He was rather upset by your condition when he arrived back here. We thought you were dead at first. You showed no signs of life; and those bruises around your neck —"

What an odd thought, to imagine Thade being so bothered by her injuries. During the war, they had witnessed far more gruesome sights than a few broken bones and minor lacerations. "I never took him to be the squeamish type."

"Well, that was not quite what I meant — Ah, Thade. She is awake." Feolan's hand moved away, followed by the sound of his footsteps across the floor, growing fainter.

She could hear them speaking in hushed tones, the exact words inaudible. If only it didn't hurt so much to move! She wanted to sit up and assure them she would be just fine. After all, she was alive. That meant she would still be able to help them find a way to defeat Damir.

"We should be prepared, then." Thade's voice sounded hard. Angry. "Kael is foolish enough to look for her, and this will no doubt be the first place he comes."

"Sir, you cannot seriously be thinking of fighting him. We cannot take risks like that," Feolan argued. "If he insists on combat, then I will see to his terms, but you are not to draw your weapon."

"Feolan, no," Maeri pleaded. They were all away from her now. Caught up in their own personal emotions over the situation. Leyna hated the thought of the burden she'd become on her friends. It wasn't supposed to be like this.

But Thade was right. If Kael desired revenge, his first thought would be to come for her. And his jealousy would point him directly to Thade. Unless he sought to strike at them in some other way. Kael had the means of wounding them in ways beyond the physical — and she didn't doubt his ability to carry through.

Grimacing from the pain, Leyna tried to prop herself up on the cushions, her strained groans catching the attention of her friends still arguing on the other side of the room. "Thade," she winced. "If he comes here, he will try to kill you."

Thade moved swiftly over to her side, leaving Feolan staring after him in protest. "Am I the reason he did this to you? I must know."

Leyna laughed miserably. To think on his accusations seemed ridiculous. She didn't know how to put them into words. "I doubt he knows why he did it. His reasons were convoluted and inane. He has somehow convinced himself that I am having your child."

"Leyna, are you pregnant?" Maeri asked innocently, moving back over to stand beside the arm of the settee.

Thade and Leyna both glanced over to Maeri in confusion. "Of course not, Maeri," she breathed irritably. "The man has lost his mind. You and I both know what is required to lead to that condition, and I certainly have not been doing that with the Consul." She thought over her words uncomfortably, realizing the awkwardness of her statement, her cheeks flushing with warmth.

"My child?" Thade whispered in disbelief. "Are you telling me Kael did this to you because of some asinine idea his unstable mind fabricated?"

"It is even worse," Leyna sighed. "I had to tell him about the request for an annulment. He now believes I am trying to leave him so that I can be with you — and that we were off for the last month seeking a place for me to hide away once my supposed pregnancy becomes too noticeable."

"I have never seen anyone fall this far before. This insanity. There is no basis for the claims he makes."

"He is likely threatened by you, sir," Feolan shrugged, his eyes moving cautiously over to the door. "You are far more pleasant company for his own wife-to-be than he is. In a perfectly innocent way, of course, but he knows nothing of your long standing friendship. You have everything he desires to achieve in life. Wealth, status — he is blindly convinced you will take away the only thing he cares about."

"If he cared about her, he would not have done this," Thade scowled. "Better men than him have been imprisoned for less. This is unacceptable."

Leyna shook her head. The events of Thade's confrontation with Kael were coming back with more clarity, a shiver coursing through her spine at the memory. She could see the blank look in Kael's eyes as he stood over his sword, hearing Thade call out a name as he reached Leyna's side. A name Kael likely knew but to that point had not expected Thade to speak. No longer did an attack on Thade's home seem imminent. The revelation of her true name would bring a new wave of danger much larger than anything Kael was capable of on his own.

"He knows who I am." Nothing else felt necessary to say.

Realization dawned on Thade's face after a moment of silence, revealing his guilt and frustration at his mistake. He cursed under his breath, averting his eyes from Leyna. "I said your name. How could I have been so foolish?"

"You used her name in Kael's presence?" Feolan blinked in disbelief. "Did he say anything in response? Surely he must have been confused —"

"He has heard the name before. Damir and Kyros are aware of it, and have likely shared the information with Kael," Leyna cut in, not wanting to see Thade beat himself up over an honest mistake. She couldn't blame him for losing his head. "Kyros has indicated his familiarity with my identity, but suggested me to be oblivious to it. Unaware of my own past. I was so young back then. It would make sense for Kyros and Damir to believe me to have been taken as a slave when I left Mialan and forgotten myself."

She knew Feolan and Maeri would be confused by her statement, but she couldn't focus on them right now. There were things she was curious about. Things Thade had spoken of to Kael which had yet to be explained to her in any detail. She wanted to know about his claims regarding her annulment, while at the same time she had no desire to discuss it in the presence of Maeri and Feolan. If she was going to receive bad news, she wanted as few witnesses as possible. "Thade," she whispered quietly, the sound of his name immediately drawing Thade's attention back to her. "I would like to speak with you in private — if that is not inappropriate of me to request."

"It is not inappropriate at all," he replied calmly, glancing up to Feolan with a stern gaze. "If you and Lady Diah would step out for a few moments. It is a pleasant evening outside. Perhaps you could enjoy a bit of a walk."

"Sir, I don't think —" Feolan started, his protest cut short by Thade's interjection.

"That is an order, Feolan," Thade's voice was commanding, reminding Leyna of the days she served under him in the war. Feolan knew better than to argue with a direct order.

"We will be in the study, then," Feolan stated, casting a final look of concern at the two of them. Begrudgingly, he put his arm around Maeri, pressing her in the direction of the hallway, his gaze lingering over his shoulder at Thade as he disappeared down the hall.

Thade's eyes remained on the shadows, waiting for the sound of the study door closing before letting his gaze slowly move back to where Leyna remained lying on the cushions in front of him. "I apologize. Giving orders is not something I enjoy doing, but at times I have little choice. Feolan dislikes leaving me unattended."

"I cannot blame him," Leyna smiled. Letting her muscles relax into the softness of the settee, her pain eased with the release of the strain she'd been exerting. "Under any other circumstances, I wouldn't have minded their company, but the matter I wish to ask you on is a bit personal and I am not ready to discuss it among everyone quite yet."

"I suspect I already know what you refer to, though given that I have been wrong in the past, I will let you ask rather than assume," he nodded.

Leyna felt her mouth twitch in a half-smile, her nerves starting to get the better of her at the thought of asking the question weighing on her mind. The possibility of being free of her engagement was almost too good to be true. She feared hearing him confirm it to be nothing more than a clever trick used to get under Kael's skin. "Is it true?" she asked hesitantly, unsure of how else to begin. "Am I released from my bond with Kael?"

Thade gave a knowing nod, unsurprised. "It is true. My only regret is that I was unable to reveal the news to you in a more pleasant fashion."

"But when?" Leyna breathed, unable to hide her relief. "How did you hear? I thought you were still awaiting word on the priests' decision when we departed from Mialan."

"I must admit, I was surprised by the swift response as well. There is a confession I must make to you, however." Thade's eyes settled on Leyna, watching her closely to see her reaction. "The request was never sent to the Tanispan priests. I directed the courier to deliver the letter to the hands of Her Majesty personally. In my mind, I believed our chances of success were greater under her deliberations than those of anyone else. Not to mention, she would be more open to hearing my arguments in your defense than the priests. Knowing I would be in Mialan, she had her decision sent to me there. I received it in the morning when I awoke after the party. I thought to give you the news as a home-coming gift when we arrived to Siscal. I now know I should have told you sooner..."

"No," she interrupted, struggling to lift her hand to silence him. "What matters is that it is done. I couldn't care less about how I learned of it or when, as long as I know. I was afraid you were only saying it to anger Kael."

"In a way, I was." Thade frowned. "All I could think about was how to hurt him the most for what he did to you. I did not think you were awake to hear what I was saying and I knew the news would hit him hard. In truth, when I think over my actions last night, I do not believe I was thinking at all." He was staring at Leyna, gazing at her with concern. His motions were graceful, confident, moving around the arm of the settee to situate himself next to her on the cushions.

The familiar guilt came over her that she couldn't escape whenever he looked at her that way. "I am so sorry," she whispered. "You are too good to me. Anyone else would have given up on me years ago for all the trouble I have caused."

Gently, he brushed his thumb over the skin of her forehead. The cut there seemed to catch his attention, distracting him momentarily, his voice distant. "I cannot imagine what you must be going through right now. You handle everything with such poise and strength that I have never witnessed before. If you need to talk about anything, or to let out your frustrations, please do not feel you must put on a façade in front of me. I worry that you bottle it all up simply to give the illusion that you do not need anyone to help you."

Leyna smiled up at him warmly. "There was a time when I admit I did so, but that is no longer the case. This is not the time for me to do everything on my own. You need my help just as much as I need yours. I will have time to wallow in self-pity over my personal mistakes after the threat of war has subsided."

Nodding his head, Thade moved from the settee, grabbing a blanket from the back of the chair across the room to cover her. "Try to get some sleep, then," he replied, his voice solemn and quiet. "We will have much to discuss when you are rested. There were some interesting developments while we were away, and I believe there will be plenty of work to be done in a very short amount of time if we are going to have any hope at beating our enemy."

Chapter Twenty-Three

The courtyard of Queen Nesperiti's palace brought back painful memories as Leyna allowed Thade to assist her down the path, winding through the lush grounds toward the entrance. He had fashioned a crutch to help her gain some mobility while her leg healed. She was unaccustomed to the device, finding it difficult to manage at times. Even broken, her own leg was far easier to utilize than a padded stick could ever be. But she was not allowed to put weight on the injury for at least a few more weeks.

It was embarrassing, entering into the palace in her condition, the looks of distaste she received from the other courtiers. An injury to the extent of hers was unusual for a noblewoman. Her gait was awkward and slow, being careful not to accidentally set the base of her crutch on the hem of her gown, afraid of tripping and sending herself and Thade both tumbling to the ground. What a spectacle that would be!

They were to meet with the Carpaen ambassadors with word on Tanispa's request for an alliance. Queen Nesperiti had granted her favor in the matter, left with little option for decline given the assistance Tanispa had offered during Siscal's most recent war against Namorea.

As a show of courtesy, Nesperiti had granted them use of her palace to conduct their business with Carpaen due to Leyna's inability to travel through the desert. Long distances would be too difficult until the bone was healed, and their time was limited. It was impossible to know when Damir and Oksuva would begin their march on the Vor'shai. More than two weeks had already passed since Leyna and Thade returned from Mialan and still there was no word from Zander. Leyna couldn't help but fear the worst.

Throughout the years she lived in Carpaen, Leyna had never seen the royal family. Occasionally, they would pass through the city of Eykanua to visit the academy, but her duties always prevented her from laying eyes on them. She couldn't deny her curiosity, but there would be no sating that today. Their meeting would be with Emperor Rad-nor's ambassador to Siscal. Leyna could only hope that the Emperor would be sympa-thetic to their plight and have sent good news.

"I am not certain I am ready for this," Leyna whispered, leaning heavily on her crutch, Thade's hand gently resting on her shoulder in case she stumbled. "My appear-ance is far from appropriate to be doing any kind of business. Especially to the degree of importance as ours."

"The Carpaen ambassador is a good man. He will think nothing of your injury. My only concern is whether or not you are in any pain. Are you comfortable?" Thade asked.

His question made her laugh. Comfortable? Her lungs were restricted by a damna-ble corset cinched tightly around her midsection, the flowing cornflower blue skirts of her gown constantly in the way of her crutch with every step, muscles tensed, agitating the fractured bone in her leg. "I'm not certain that is the word I would use to describe my current state, but if it eases your mind, then consider it to be so."

Thade stared at her, a grimace crossing his elegant features. "When we reach our destination, I will request a chair for you. There is no need for you to stand throughout the meeting."

"Do not worry about me, Thade," she smiled. It was sweet of him to show the concern he did, but she felt it was misplaced. As if he somehow blamed himself for the injury and sought exoneration in tending to her every whim. "We should not keep them waiting," Leyna motioned Thade forward down the hall. "They are expecting us."

Nodding his head Thade resumed his slow pace at Leyna's side. She was grateful for his knowledge of the palace layout. Without him, she would be lost. The halls were more intricate than any other she'd seen, branching off at strange angles to create corridors leading deeper into the center of the building. The human nations enjoyed extravagance. Large numbers of people around them at any given time, adding to the appearance of importance.

Upon reaching the door of the meeting room, Thade allowed himself to step away from Leyna, opening the door for her to enter. He barely let her take more than two steps inside before he was beside her again, guiding her forward to the center of the room. A large table was situated there, the high-glossed finish of the surface reflecting the dancing lights from candles on the chandelier overhead.

Two men were seated at the table. At Thade and Leyna's entrance, the men rose to their feet, stepping around their chairs to bow in cordial greeting. "Consul Imri, I presume?" one of the men stated, lifting his head to give a dashing smile.

Leyna drew in a sharp breath at the sight of him, overcome with a strange happiness to see his face. It had been years since she'd seen it last, though she remembered every detail, hindered only by a slight grey to his sun-bleached hair and several added lines around his eyes and mouth. The complexion of his face retained the deep tan that she recalled from her youth. An effect caused by the amount of time he spent in the hot desert sun.

Their eyes met, recognition quickly forming over the man's expression. "My heavens, Leyna? Is that you?"

"Blaise," she said, excited to see him. Though their last meeting had been far from enjoyable, time changed a great deal between the two of them. Twenty years had come to pass since that day at the Academy when Blaise fought to prevent her from leaving Carpaen. Now there was no fear of him. Only a deep nostalgia at seeing the familiar face of an old friend. "I had no idea you had any interest in politics. Are you no longer teaching at the Academy?"

Seeing her struggle forward with her steps, Blaise intercepted her, arms wrapping around her in a warm embrace. "My time there is scarce, these days. My recent promotion to the position of Emperor Radnor's Steward has come as a welcome relief to these old bones of mine. I'm not as young as I used to be. The long days teaching are a bit much anymore. You, however – I didn't think it possible, but you are even more beautiful now than the day you left Eykanua. Time has treated you better than it has me, that's for sure," he chuckled. Pulling away he held Leyna's arms lightly, looking her over appraisingly, forehead creased with sympathy. "Alas, you seem to be injured. Still playing rough, are you?"

"As rough as they will let me, these days."

"That's my girl," he grinned, patting her arm approvingly. "Ah, but where are my manners? Have you met Henri?" Blaise gestured toward the other man still standing near the table, his face contorted in confusion, similar to the expression now evident on

Thade's as he made his way to Leyna's side. The man shared the same bronze complexion as Blaise, though significantly less lined with aged. Light brown waves of curly hair sat over his shoulders, brushed neatly, resting on the high collar of his rich blue doublet. "Henri is Emperor Radnor's ambassador here in Siscal."

Moving forward Henri bowed to Leyna, taking her hand gently in his to kiss the back of it. "A pleasure, Miss —?"

"Evantine," Thade cut in. His voice drew the attention of both men, as if suddenly reminding them of his presence. "Lady... Evantine. She is a respected member of Queen Nesperiti's court."

"A Siscalian Courtier? For some reason I was under the impression you would be in Queen Vorsila's court by now. The Tanispan Prince indicated that to be the case, anyway." Blaise raised his brow inquisitively in Leyna's direction. "You must be good friends with the Tanispans, at least, if they are allowing you to accompany their Consul on business. Do, please, have a seat. There is no need for rigid formalities. We are among friends, here."

Thade wasted no time in helping Leyna to one of the elegant cushioned chairs at the table, making sure she was comfortably settled before situating himself next to her. He recovered from the initial surprise at Blaise's warm greeting, watching the two men take their seats across from him. "With the Emperor's Steward in attendance, it leads me to believe my letter was received?"

"Yes, it was," Blaise cast an apologetic glance to Henri. "I'm sorry. I know I said I would merely be observing, but that was before I knew who we were meeting with."

"I take no offense, Your Grace."

"Good good. Now, the Emperor and I spoke and he was inclined to offer assistance, but ultimately left the decision to me based on the statements heard here today. Perhaps you could explain a little about the situation which has brought us together?"

Hesitant, Leyna looked over to Thade, unsure of whether it would be appropriate for her to speak. It was Thade's role to do the negotiating for Queen Vorsila. Leyna's company was supposed to be for no other reason than experience in diplomacy. She met his gaze, steady, both saying nothing in response to Blaise's question. With a nod of approval Thade motioned her to speak, relinquishing the floor. "Well, it is complicated," she started. "We have reason to believe that the Ven'shal intend to wage a second war on Tanispa. If they are able to acquire an army of the size we fear, the threat could bleed into Carpaen and Siscal. With this in mind, we feel it is imperative to give warning of the impending attacks and seek out the assistance of our neighbors."

Blaise stroked his chin, thoughtful. "I see. Well, I certainly understand where that would pose a problem. What exactly is it you require of the Carpaen military? You know well enough our preference at neutrality."

"I do, which is why I was afraid to hear the news of Emperor Radnor's decision. After all, he chose to allow the Namiren soldiers to set up war camps on his land while they attacked Siscal." Leyna's tone held more bitterness than she wanted. The Carpaen government's unwillingness to assist in the war against Namorea had caused countless deaths which could have been otherwise avoided. Siscal might have lost the battle if not for the Tanispan army coming to their rescue. A part of her still resented the Emperor's passiveness.

"My dear, such venom I hear in your sweet voice. What reason do you have to speak so?"

"It was not intended, Your Grace," she stated calmly, chiding herself for the acidity of her statement. Now wasn't the time to let her past issues boil to the surface. It was important the meeting remain amicable.

Mouth open wide, Blaise gave a nod of understanding, his hand reaching out to rest lightly atop Leyna's on the table. Taken aback by the gesture she pulled it away, staring at him in confusion. "I think I understand," he frowned. "I heard what happened to you during the war. You don't blame Carpaen, I hope. If anything the fault lies only on those who allowed you into the regiment. We both know you shouldn't have been on the field in the first place."

At her side Leyna could feel Thade tense, clearly bothered by Blaise's accusations. Flustered, Leyna tried to distract from the topic, anxious to direct conversation back to the issue at hand. "No fault lies on anyone in that other than myself. The past, how-ever, holds no bearing over our current predicament. Carpaen maintained neutrality then, but this war will be different. It will be closer to your borders, and the chances of it stretching into Emperor Radnor's lands are very high. The Ven'shal will fight, and they will kill innocent people in Carpaen. I must implore you to see the severity of this threat."

"Consul, what say you of the situation? You appear put-off. Should Carpaen have reason to be concerned? Is the situation really so dire?"

"Lady Evantine speaks the plain truth of the matter," Thade stated, a faint strain evident in his voice. "Carpaen has more reason to be concerned than Siscal. The landscape of your country is more agreeable for war. Fewer mountains. Less creatures in the wild due to the number of cities you boast. Not to mention easier access to the Tanispan border by means of the river. The Ven'shal will without doubt find Carpaen the perfect target to begin their march."

"That is a compelling argument, indeed. One which I will be sure to pass on to the Emperor." Blaise looked Leyna over, his gaze scrutinizing, a vague smile curling at the corners of his lips. "I give my consent, not only because the Emperor was already pre-disposed to the thought, but because I desire to help Lady Evantine. Henri will write up the necessary documents. My only request is for a brief audience with the lady, if I may?"

"She is giving you audience presently. Is that not enough?" Thade mused.

Blaise snorted indignantly. "I shouldn't have to specify my meaning. The request was for privacy, if I might be so bold."

Rising from her chair Leyna struggled to steady her balance. The crutch wasn't far off, her hand grasping for it to provide support for her injured leg while Thade immediately stood to assist her. "Leyna, what are you doing?" he whispered. "You are under no obligation to grant his request."

"It will only be a moment." Leyna directed a smile at Blaise, gesturing toward an open area of the room. "I cannot give absolute privacy, for many reasons which I'm certain you understand, but I can offer you my undivided attention. If you will walk with me? I am a bit of a cripple these days."

Blaise hurried around the table to take his place at Leyna's side, stepping between her and Thade, oblivious to the hesitance Thade gave in releasing her. "Of course. Please excuse us, gentlemen. I will not keep the lady's company from you for long."

Aware of Thade and Henri's watchful eyes, curious by Blaise's actions, Leyna struggled to manage her steps alone, not wanting to rely too heavily on Blaise for support. The situation was awkward enough without adding the humiliation of being unable to stand on her own. Content that they were out of earshot of the others, she turned to face him, no longer sure if she'd made the right decision in allowing them privacy. Instantly upon looking in his eyes she was returned to that day in the academy when she first explained her intentions of leaving for Siscal. He'd been less than pleased with the idea. By now she assumed his infatuation with her had ended, but there was no telling what his emotions had shifted to.

"Leyna." Blaise paused, shaking his head in disbelief. "I can't believe it's really you."

"I'm a bit surprised by you as well."

"I thought I would never see you again. Your departure was so sudden. Why did you never come to say goodbye?"

Struck by the question, Leyna gazed at him, a grimace crossing her features. How could she explain it? He would never understand the discomfort he'd caused her when they discussed her plan. At the time she'd been too young to grasp the extent of her wild idea and her desperation caused his arguments to fall on deaf ears. The rumors rampant through the academy regarding his feelings for her had done nothing to benefit his chances at talking her out of going. Even with the best of intentions, his words were hollow in Leyna's belief that they were meant for nothing but his own gain in keeping her close. "I knew you would try to stop me," she sighed. Defeated. "It was wrong, I know. I should have come and given at least some mild assurances of my safety, but – I was young, Blaise. I cannot be held accountable for the flaws of my inexperience. All I can offer you now are my sincerest apologies."

"But you never came back. You never wrote –"

"You know the military well enough to be familiar with how it works," Leyna argued. "As long as the war raged in Siscal, there was no chance of my returning to Carpaen."

"Yes, but I never expected them to actually accept you." Exasperated, Blaise cast his eyes to the ceiling. He breathed in deeply to try and regain his composure, lowering his gaze to look at her once again. "I waited, day after day, for word from you. Somehow I thought they would turn you away for your age and leave you with no choice but to write for me to bring you back to the academy. Had I known they would be foolish enough to employ you, I never would have let you walk away. It was ludicrous. The chances of your plans succeeding had been laughable. The first word I received was the day I heard of your brush with death while protecting the Tanispan Prince. Ever since then I have been kicking myself for ever letting you go."

"You wanted me to fail?"

"No, I wanted you to realize that you needed me..." Blaise let his voice trail off. He looked hurt. Pained by the memories her presence brought over him. "You have always been stubborn, Leyna. Telling you that your idea was insane would never have convinced you to stay. I knew you would have to see for yourself. And once you discovered the truth, I wanted to be the one you came to. I would have done anything for you, and you know that. I – I wanted to marry you."

Averting her eyes, Leyna brought her hand up to cover her mouth. Her stomach wrenched to hear him say the words. She'd been so young! Never had she thought his emotions ran so deep. Blaise had been an attractive man in his younger days. Capable of winning the hand of any girl in Eykanua if he desired. So why her? His little orphaned pauper.

And worst of all was the truth in her own heart. She'd never reciprocated those feelings for him, nor did she believe it to ever have been possible. Even if forced to return in humiliation and defeat, his dreams would never have come to fruition. At least not in love. The dire circumstances of her and Reina's situation might have forced her to concede in union, but never could she have loved him.

"Blaise, please," she whispered. "You must understand something. It would be wrong of me not to give you the truth, after all this time. And while I dislike the thought of hurting you, in the end I feel it will give you the closure you require, in my telling you that I have never felt the way toward you which you profess to have felt for me."

"You were young. I believe it was possible for your heart to change."

"While I respect you and am forever indebted for the kindness you bestowed upon Reina and myself, I must insist that it never would have been so. You must understand, Blaise. The gods took us in the directions they intended us to go, and chose for our paths to never cross again until time no longer allowed us to be anything more than friends. Please accept my regret for having caused you pain, but I assure you it was never intended." Leyna's lips parted to speak again, breath caught in her throat at the sight of Thade and Henri positioned only a few feet away. When had they approached? Her face flushed, the tips of her ears heated with the burning humiliation of what might have been overheard. At the sudden change in Leyna's countenance Blaise was alerted to the others, casting an agonized glance to the floor to avoid their stares.

"I'm sorry, Your Grace," Henri started, moving forward with a hesitant step. Blaise waved him into silence.

"Don't. It's unnecessary."

"If you will excuse my intrusion, then. I never would have thought to interrupt but the lady looked distraught and I feared for her well-being." Thade came to Leyna's side, staring down at her with concern. "Are you alright?"

"I am quite fine, though a little tired," she stated quietly. Her emotions were surprisingly calm. It eased her mind to finally have the opportunity to explain herself to Blaise. Whether it pained him or not, he deserved to know the truth. To not torment himself any longer about the choices which brought her where she was in life. Leaving Eykanua that day was the best decision she ever made. A life spent in Carpaen with Blaise would have been lacking everything she desired, and he would have learned over time that his love was misplaced on one so young. It was best for them to part now as friends than to have inevitably parted ways long ago in hatred.

"Consider it forgotten, Consul," Blaise forced a smile, lifting his eyes to give a polite nod. "I believe we were nearly finished, as it is. As far as business, I maintain my word that Carpaen will offer whatever assistance Queen Vorsila requires. My only stipulation is that you take good care of Lady Evantine. She deserves to be treated with the highest regard."

Thade returned Blaise's nod. Leyna could feel the pressure of Thade's arm around hers tighten, pulling her in closer to him protectively. "You have my word that the Lady will be well looked after."

"Good," Blaise replied. "If I hear of any harm befalling her, I will be very displeased." With a deep bow, he lowered to his knee before Leyna, gently kissing the back of her hand. Quickly, he straightened, his attention toward Thade more precise and formal. "Milady. Consul. I look forward to being of assistance to you in the future. It has been a pleasure. Henri, come. We have work to do before I return to Carpaen."

Without a word Henri followed Blaise toward the door, their progress halted as he gave one final pause, turning back to address Thade. "Oh, and Consul?"

"Yes, Your Grace?"

"Do give my congratulations to Lord Feolan on his upcoming nuptials. I only recently learned of his betrothal."

"It is a very recent event, indeed," Thade nodded. "The betrothal ceremony was only a few weeks ago. I am sure Lord Feolan and his wife-to-be would be pleased to have you at the wedding."

"When is it to take place?"

"Two weeks from tomorrow. At the chapel in the eastern corner of the city."

"I regret business will have me detained. With my felicitation, you will also have to pass along my apologies for being unable to attend. It may be for the best. I'm not particularly fond of weddings myself."

"That is a sad thing to hear. Marriage is a most joyful occasion."

Blaise laughed, the sound bitter and hollow. "For some," he stated flatly. "Good day to you both."

Leyna and Thade stood in silence while the men made their way out of the room, a loud click of the door leaving them alone. She prayed Thade wouldn't ask any questions. It was embarrassing enough to know that he had overheard any part of her conversation. To be forced into explaining it would only injure her worse.

A quiet intake of breath signaled Thade's attempt at speech, cut off by a sharp raise of Leyna's hand. "Before you say anything, please do not ask about my past with Blaise. I assure you there is nothing to it of any importance."

"I was not going to pry."

"But you are curious. I can tell." Leyna looked up at him, the warmth returning to her cheeks. How could she think of being with any other man when standing at Thade's side? If only he knew! "He was a good friend of mine when I lived in

Carpaen. You must have been aware of our familiarity. Blaise was the man Prince Enaes spoke with when he inquired of my name at the academy in Eykanua."

A look of understanding passed over Thade's features. "Ah, yes. I suppose I never made the connection before. Truthfully, I paid little attention to the names Enaes gave. Enough to retain them, only. There must have been more than a mere familiarity to have raised such a profession from him."

She wanted to crawl under the table and hide behind the elegant chairs. He'd heard Blaise's admission. It hurt her to think of him being aware of the words which Blaise spoke. Thade had done so much for her in achieving the annulment of her previous engagement, while also hiding her from Prince Enaes's attempts at seeking her hand. And now this? Another man eager to have her. How awful it must make her look in Thade's eyes! "Do you think less of me for it? I lack any understanding of why he would feel that way for me. When last Blaise and I were in each other's company, I was only fifteen. If I did anything to spark such emotions in him, it was not by any intentional means. To hear him say those things to me now, I am — shocked. Words cannot describe how much so."

"It seems you have stolen the hearts of more men than I thought," Thade stated, his tone quiet. Detached. "What torment it must be for them all."

"The only torment right now is that which my leg is causing me," Leyna sighed. She didn't want to discuss the past anymore. What was done couldn't be changed. The only thing she could do was try and move beyond it. They had Carpaen's support. Right now, nothing else mattered. "I should get home to rest. The doctor wouldn't be happy to know how long I have already been on my feet."

At her request Thade seemed to revive from whatever reverie he was lost in. Composed, he gave a slight nod, helping to guide Leyna toward the door. "Of course," he said calmly. "I am supposed to help Feolan with some last minute details on the wedding. We should be headed back before it gets much later."

The chapel yard was quiet and peaceful. Devoid of the bustling city sounds that Leyna was accustomed to when not in the privacy of her home. She'd spent the better part of the last few weeks alone due to her injuries, propped up on the dingy cushions of an antique settee in the house she'd come to call her own. Feolan was more than willing to let her take it on. One last thing he needed to worry about while preparing for his marriage to Maeri.

Even through the turmoil of the impending war, he and Maeri managed to find joy in each other. A celebration of any grand scale was out of the question under the current circumstances, but they were content with a private ceremony to exchange their vows until such a time when they could make it a larger affair. They had arranged for the priest at the chapel to join them, with Thade and Leyna acting as their witnesses. Never had Leyna seen either of them as happy as they looked that morning while gazing with admiration into each other's eyes. It had been absolutely breathtaking to watch.

A part of her still grieved over her own failed union with Kael. She tried to console herself that it was not meant to be. The gods would have found a way to help them work through it if they really were intended for each other. From the start, everything had been against them. And now, there was no recovering from the things which had happened. In the eyes of the Queen, it had never happened. She was free of the bonds placed over her that day in Dalonshire when she so foolishly accepted his proposal. That was a mistake she did not intend to make again anytime soon.

She was tired of everyone helping her. For years she'd been forced to care for herself and now, with everyone constantly at her side trying to do things for her, she was having a hard time adjusting. After the marriage ceremony, she'd sent them all away to discuss the plans for the afternoon. The bridal evening. Feolan and Maeri had found a new home they would be moving into, leaving Thade to his privacy. Slowly, they seemed to be taking over the little neighborhood. They were all within a few blocks radius of one another, making it easy to gather for meetings, though she was not allowed to leave her home without one of them there to watch her. A guard was positioned outside her door to ensure her safety — and to prevent her from wandering off without Thade or Feolan knowing. It was too dangerous. They never failed to mention it.

Their list of allies was growing rapidly. Mialan willingly agreed to the allegiance with Tanispa while talks with Carpaen and Siscal had secured both prominent human nations as allies. Prince Enaes left not long after she and Thade had departed for Mialan, making his way deeper into the southern regions of the world, engaging in talks with countries Leyna never knew to exist before then. It surprised her just how little she knew of the very world she lived in. Her life had been sheltered from so many things.

Talks with the Namiren King Galidric had been attempted. As expected, the ambassador was turned away without an opportunity to state his case. Their hope was that in securing allies with as many other military forces as possible, the lack of Namorea's support would prove a minor setback. Nothing worth losing sleep over. If the Namirens sided with the Ven'shal, they would pose little in the way of a threat. The Vor'shai defeated them once before. It would take very little to force them out of the way again.

Leyna gazed at the altar in the little chapel, the sight of it depressing with its simplistic beauty, decorated with flowers and candles to symbolize the ceremony that had taken place there. She wanted to be happy for them. And in most ways, she was. Her only downfall was the sadness she felt for herself. Maeri deserved to be happy. She'd found a good man in Feolan. In the Vor'shai tradition, he had chosen to take the name of Diah as a symbol of his loyalty and love for the family of his new bride. It was all so disgustingly sappy and romantic.

Arranging her crutch under her arm, she clumsily lifted herself from the pew, easing her way out into the aisle. The hard wood of the device was uncomfortable, but it was better than being stuck in bed all day. At least this way, she was able to enjoy some fresh air from time to time, albeit under the constant watch of her appointed bodyguard. That silly bone couldn't heal fast enough. She felt ridiculous hobbling around like an invalid.

A tiny glass door was sitting open, leading out to the chapel gardens. Bird song floated in from outside, soothing and melodic, calling to Leyna in a cheerful tune. The path was laid with well-packed dirt, easy enough to handle on the crutch, without the risk of it sinking into the soil.

"At last I have beaten you at your game of hide-and-seek. Well played, Lady Evantine. Well played."

Reflexively, Leyna lifted her hand from the crutch, covering her mouth in awe at the sight of Prince Enaes standing in the garden. Leaning casually against an ivy-wrapped post at the center of the courtyard. Dismayed, she watched her crutch fall to the ground, unsure of what she should do. Etiquette urged her to kneel at his presence. Kneel! The thought was comical to her. In her condition, to take a knee would prove a humiliating display.

Enaes pushed himself away from the post, his strides easy and confident, crossing over to where Leyna remained. She stood frozen in shock, eyes watching the Prince in almost horrified silence. Bending down, he retrieved the crutch, looking over it curiously before offering it to her. "You are injured? My Lady, what happened?"

"An unfortunate riding accident," she lied, taking the crutch back, uncomfortably avoiding his gaze. "I will be done with this thing in a few days, and good riddance to it. How did you find me? I did not see you come into the chapel."

"That is because I never entered the chapel. The garden path connects to a side street behind the far wall. Convenient really." Enaes's chin rose up proudly at his own brilliance. "A courier from my mother met me a few days ago while I was on my way north from talks with the Tuniron King. Imagine my surprise to learn that Lord Feolan was to be married! But then — I began to think."

What a new and exciting experience that must have been. She tried to hold back rolling her eyes at Enaes's words, irritated by the pompousness of his tone. "And of what did you think?"

"I recalled that my darling Leyna had a long history of friendship with Lord Feolan from the stories I heard of the war," he smiled. "I thought — surely she will be present for the ceremony. Though, I must say I am surprised to find so few in attendance."

"Impending war makes celebrating anything a bit more difficult. A more traditional ceremony will be conducted in Tanispa once things have settled."

"That is all well and good, but it is not the ceremony I am concerned with. They could have been married in a horse stable for all I care." Enaes waved dismissively. "All I cared about was your presence. And I have found you."

His hand lightly caressed the skin of her cheek. She couldn't focus on it. Something felt wrong. Out of place. "Do your guards know where you have disappeared to? These are dangerous times."

"My guards are currently distracting the Consul and the bridegroom. I have been waiting far too long for this moment to let them take it from me."

"You should not be here," Leyna shook her head, shuffling away from him nervously. Her crutch made the feat more difficult, nearly causing her to fall into a bed of blooming larkspurs.

Grabbing onto her arm, Enaes prevented her stumbling. "On the contrary, this is the one place I should be. My mother has been lecturing me for years to choose a bride and never have I found anyone to be worthy of that honor other than you. Their fair faces pale in comparison to your beauty and strength. I have chosen you to be my Queen."

Of all the times to not be wearing a corset! It would have given her a means of feigning loss of consciousness at his request, buying her a brief moment to escape her required response. Though that would only prolong the torture. Had any woman ever declined a royal proposal before? Faustine's teaching had not prepared her for this. To deny his request seemed traitorous, but to accept would be dishonest. "Your Highness," she breathed. "This is hardly the time and place to discuss such matters."

"If I let you slip away, it may be another six years before I see your face again," he stated. She couldn't look past the desperation in his eyes, the way he stared at her, begging her not to run away. It made his words feel strangely genuine. "I must know you will be mine. You are all I have thought about since you left me there on the dance floor at the masque. My dreams have been haunted by your eyes. The softness of your skin. These visions have led me to you. However, I must say, the image in my mind did not do justice to your beauty."

"I have never heard of you to speak such flattery about anyone but yourself. How can you be so certain I am the one you desire? You know nothing about me."

Enaes's expression faltered at her insult. He regained his composure quickly, moving in closer until they were standing face-to-face, Leyna's arm still held gently in his hand. "You wound me, Leyna. I admit that my past has been dotted with mistakes and foolishness, but those days must come to an end. I need a wife with whom to rule Tanispa when my mother decides it is time to relinquish the throne. You are the only woman I desire to have at my side."

"Your Highness," she frowned. He wasn't going to give in. Enaes was too accustomed to getting what he wanted. Denying him would only stoke his voracity. Inside she knew her unattainable nature was the only reason he desired her the way he did. She was the one woman who denied him. The one he could not have, and therefore he wanted her more than anything. "Being near me is dangerous. Have you no knowledge of the work I have done in the years since you saw me last? There are people who want to see me dead. If they find you here with me, they would have both of our heads without blinking an eye. You need to leave. Now."

"I will not leave without you!" Enaes insisted. In his passion, he caught her up in his embrace, his lips pressing against hers. She was too surprised to push him away. The ground she treaded was uncertain and frightening. He had the power to force her to do most anything, regardless of her protests. To oppose him could be her downfall.

She stood, unmoving, refusing to take an active role. Nothing could make her feel for this man anything other than the respect required from his heritage. Her heart belonged to someone else. Even if that man denied her, no prince could force her to change that.

Slowly, Enaes leaned his head back, his eyes staring deeply into hers. She remained rigid in his arms. Almost cold in her steady gaze. "What must I do to make you love me?" he asked.

A harsh laugh sent chills down Leyna's spine from somewhere behind Enaes, ringing through the peaceful garden, silencing the birds with the menacing sound. "Oh, I have been asking her that question for some time."

"Kael," Leyna spat the name like poison on her tongue. There was no time to think on Enaes's proposal. She needed to get him out of there. Kael couldn't be allowed near him.

Kael chuckled, his blackened eyes and cruel grin appearing from behind a line of bushes near the back of the garden. "I hope you don't think I came here looking for you, Leyna." He threw his head back, the evil laughter ringing through the trees, louder than before. "We were following him. The fact that *he* led us to you is purely a delightful coincidence."

Us? Her eyes darted around the garden, the muscles in her body tensed and on guard in preparation for an ambush. Kael may be foolish in many ways, but she knew he was smart enough to know not to try attacking the Prince of Tanispa alone. "If you want him, you will have to go through me."

"That could be very easily arranged, Eleni. Or is it Leyna?" Kael stroked his chin thoughtfully. "I have been hearing some very interesting things about you lately. As much as I would love to believe that you are nothing more than an orphan sold into slavery, I am not under any such delusion. My blade can cut through you easily enough, regardless of who you are."

"Leave this place, scum," Enaes cut in, his voice calm and commanding. "If you do as I say, then I will not have my guards separate your head from your body."

Kael's shoulders shook under his silent laughter. He looked too confident. His strides casual, hand resting idly on the sword hilt at his waist. "Your guards? If any of them survive, they will be a bit too wrapped up in their own troubles to care about the orders you bark."

The crunch of gravel sounded from all around them, growing louder until Leyna could see the source creeping out from behind the trees and bushes. The men were well-concealed physically, masks covering their faces apart from an opening which revealed the blackened eyes within. She'd never seen so many Ven'shal in one place before, other than the pathetic guests of Mikel's useless gatherings. Only a handful, but more than enough to overpower her and Enaes.

Fighting was out of the question. Her leg would not tolerate the strain. At most, she could try to hold her ground, utilizing her crutch to keep them at bay, but that would do little good for Enaes. They needed help. It didn't matter how skilled Enaes might be, she would be no good to him. He would be at their mercy.

"We cannot fight them," she hissed quietly into Enaes's ear. "If I can lure them close, you might be able to break through to the street."

Men were closing in, circling them, preventing any chance of escape back into the chapel. Panic rushed through Leyna at the thought of Thade and Feolan out front. *My guards are currently distracting the Consul and the bridegroom.* If Kael had arranged an attack on the guards, they would go after Thade.

She saw the opening they needed for Enaes to escape. "Now!" she shouted, thrusting her crutch forward into the chest of one man. Enaes drew his sword, slashing at another, leaping through the gap.

In a rush, their attackers scattered, taking chase after Enaes as he moved swiftly toward the back of the garden. Leyna tried to run after him. She needed to find a way to keep the men back, but they were too quick. With her focus on the Prince, she suddenly felt her arms caught up behind her, holding her in place. "You have no idea how pathetic you look right now, do you?" Kael laughed, kicking her crutch away from her.

"Run, Enaes!" she cried out. It didn't matter what happened to her anymore. All she cared about was that the Prince made it to safety. She struggled against the hold of her captor, unable to break free. These men were strong. Well-trained. They reminded her of the Sanarik during the war, ruthless and cunning. But far more powerful than any of the Sanarik had ever been.

Enaes was surrounded, battling against their blades valiantly. She was surprised by his skill with the sword, though she knew she shouldn't be. The royal family had plenty of time to spend mastering the art of combat. Enaes had fought beside the Tanispan military when they came to Siscal years ago. There was just far more riding on this battle.

Renewing her efforts to break free, she kicked her legs backward, nearly striking Kael, the blows ill-aimed in her desperate attempt. His eyes flashed angrily, stepping out of the way just in time to avoid the attack. Kael released his current hold on Leyna, stepping around to wrap the fingers of his right hand tightly around her neck, more in a show of dominance than an attempt to cut off air. Disgusted by the sight of him, Leyna spat the saliva from her mouth, striking him in the face.

"You are a feisty one," he scowled, wiping the spittle away from his face, nose wrinkled in distaste. "After all the time we spent together, to think that I never knew. Kyros told me there would be one way to verify your identity, but how embarrassing it was for me to admit that you had kept your body so well-hidden from me. So I remain curious. The truth of your name and affiliation with the Consul explains the scars that I have seen on your chest and arm over the years, but thought to be nothing more than old wounds from your previous masters. Arrows. It makes sense now. Why you were so afraid of the bow when I was teaching you."

Kael chuckled, sliding his hand away from her throat to the lacey neckline of her bodice. He tugged down at the edge with his index finger, revealing the scar that had been only partially concealed by the fabric. Kael smirked at the sight. With a gesture of command, one of the other men approached from out of the foray on the Prince, forcing Leyna to the ground, pressing her face painfully into the dirt. "Kyros believes he may have left a mark on the girl Damir seeks. So tell me, Leyna. Will I find anything interesting?"

His words fell on deaf ears. She was desperate to see Enaes, to know he was alright. Metal against metal clashing told her that the battle continued, but she couldn't see who was winning. She was unaware Kael had continued speaking until a blinding pain shot like fire across her back, pulling her to reality once more.

In her distraction, no scream came from her at the pain. Her teeth gritted. She couldn't give him the satisfaction of hearing her cry out. Leyna could feel Kael's hand brush the skin of her back. Air was somehow reaching it, stinging slightly from her right shoulder down to just above her left hip. "It is fortunate for you, but unfortunate for me that this means I cannot kill you. Death will have to wait."

Pressure was building in her core. The energy pulsed, strong, vibrant, coursing through her veins in a way she'd never felt before. It was invigorating. She didn't understand what was happening, but it was like some force within the earth was empowering her, filling her with a tremor-like electricity crackling along her skin. Focusing it inward, she drew the newfound strength to the central point of her abdomen, holding it there, waiting. It felt as if some ethereal force was lifting her. Urging her to get back to her feet.

She thrust the energy outward, bathing the garden in an eruption of blinding light. The hands released her. She felt free. Alive. The power continued to flow through her limbs, helping her back to her feet with a surge of strength, as if the energy alone moved her. The way she experienced while submerged in the Lake of the Gods. But there was no time to question what was happening. She needed to get to Enaes.

Limping, she dragged her injured leg, ignoring the pain from her altered gait. Enaes was still fighting. She could hear the swords, her vision gradually recovering from the flash. Without fear, she threw herself into the middle of the battle, aware that she lacked any means of protecting herself against the flurry of blades raining down on Enaes. Her strength surprised even her as she grabbed onto a Ven'shal thug, picking him up and tossing him to the ground behind her. She needed to get through these men. She needed to get to Enaes so he could escape.

"Enaes, run!" she shouted, gripping the shirt of another assassin, throwing him down into one of the flower beds. Blood trailed over the path from injured fighters. She couldn't see Enaes well enough to know the condition of his health, but she could see movement from the midst of the crowd.

In mid-stride, she collected a discarded blade from one of the fallen assailants. The flow of energy through her system eased the pain in her leg. While stiff, it felt refreshed. Rejuvenated. She had the element of surprise by her entering the fight. They were focused on their target, pushing him back against the wall, surrounding him. With relentless force, she continued forward, thrusting her blade at the men. Without need of her crutch, the numbers were less intimidating. She parried their attacks, drawing attention away from Enaes to grant him a moment of reprieve. One by one she cut them down. Enaes was in sight now. Almost within reach, stumbling back from the unyielding opponents pressing in on him.

Rushing to his aid Leyna fought off the thugs. They were falling, some easier than others, but defeated all the same. Only a few more. Kael was shouting something behind her but she didn't pay any heed. With his men dead, she and Enaes would be able to take Kael down easily. Turning to the last Ven'shal standing, she drove her blade through his back, thrusting it upward while twisting the hilt savagely. Using her foot she kicked him from her sword, discarding his body in a bloody heap on the ground.

As the man fell she caught sight of something at the edge of her vision. Enaes wasn't moving. A harsh cough escaped him, hands grasping at some object protruding from his abdomen. Leyna stared at him. Unwilling to register what she was seeing. In Leyna's eyes, everything was moving in slow motion, his body doubled forward, blood quickly filling his mouth, trickling down his lips as he collapsed to his knees.

Gradually, the scene began to sink in. She'd been too late. She was right there, fighting by his side, and yet somehow she'd missed it. Somehow she'd moved too slow. The dead thug's blade had torn through Enaes before she could stop him.

"No!" she screamed. Over and over the word came out, meaningless in her panic, but somehow reflexive, an outlet for the horror and pain which overwhelmed her senses. "No, no, no..."

Awkwardly, she knelt down before Enaes, her injured leg extended out to the side. Adrenaline continued to mask the pain, but the dull throb she felt through the length of her leg told her that she had overexerted it beyond that which was allowable for it to heal. It didn't matter to her. Enaes was covered in blood, his hands clutching at the handle of his enemy's blade. He struggled to remove it, his progress stopped by Leyna's gentle touch.

"Wait," she whispered, leaning over to tear off a large strip of fabric from her skirt. "We need some kind of tourniquet or you will bleed out before I can get you to a doctor. Can you hold this?"

His fingers trembled as he accepted the material. He was shaking. And yet he remained calm, even in the face of his own death.

She doubted her abilities to tend a wound the size and severity that this looked to be. It seemed pointless. The wound was too great. But she had to try. She needed to give him some kind of hope at least.

Tightening her fingers around the hilt of the sword, she inhaled, pulling it back hard, throwing her weight behind the effort in fear that the sword would stick and aggravate the wound. Once it was free, she grasped the fabric from Enaes's limp and bloodied fingers, leaning in to wrap it around him. Tears filled her eyes. This was all her fault. If he hadn't been so caught up in finding her, he never would have come there. He never would have left his guards.

"Do you weep at the thought of my death?" he asked quietly, his voice cracking from the pain. She gazed at him, misery drawn on his face.

"Of course I would weep at your death. But you are not going to die. We are going to get you out of here."

Her fingers fumbled desperately over the knot she was attempting to tie in the thick fabric. Enaes's hand lightly caressed her cheek, a strained smile forming over his paling lips. "Knowing that I am in your arms makes death not seem quite so frightening."

"You are not dying," she argued, tears of frustration and pain streaming down her face as she fought to get back to her feet, his body like deadweight to her arms. "I need you to help me if you can. Lean on me. We need to get you out of here."

Suddenly, Enaes's eyes opened wide with shock, his body pitching forward against her under some great force. Gasping in surprise, Leyna wrapped her arms around him, fighting to keep him up but losing the battle, crumpling down to her good knee under the weight. There behind him she could see Kael's cruel eyes staring down at them. Laughing. His laughter rang through the garden walls, his hands still wrapped around the handle of a large dagger dug deeply into Enaes's back. "And to think – you could have slept your way to a crown," he smirked coldly.

"You bastard!" she shouted, clinging desperately to Enaes's limp body dangling from her arms. "I will see you burn for this, Kael."

"Do you think that frightens me?" Kael asked, tilting his head curiously to one side. Fiercely, he grabbed onto Enaes's lifeless form, tearing it from Leyna's grasp and throwing it unceremoniously onto the gravel path. "The only reason you are still alive is because Damir requires it. He has a special death in mind for you. I expect he will be ecstatic to learn that you are exactly what we thought. Regardless, you and I both know you don't stand a chance against me. I have your blood on my blade to prove that."

With calm and precise movements, Leyna pulled the dagger from Enaes's back, the crimson liquid staining the weapon, thick and dark in the sunlight. She took in steady breaths, her chest rising and falling slowly. The strange energy flowed through her limbs once more as she stood up. Everything fell into slow motion, the way it looked when she witnessed Enaes collapsing to the ground from his mortal wound. She felt in control. Powerful. Moreover, Kael looked weak to her now.

She could feel the blade of the dagger in her hand. Her fingers clutched it, tightening to ensure a firm grip. As if guided by an invisible force, her arm lashed out at Kael, raking the tip of the dagger across his throat, narrowly escaping the full strike as he stumbled backward in awe, wiping at the blood visible over the wound.

"And I have your blood on this blade," Leyna stated calmly, holding the dagger up for Kael to see, the thick liquid pooling in the groove. "The gods have witnessed your treachery. But it will be by my hand that you receive your punishment."

"Whatever helps you sleep better at night, darling." Kael's voice was casual and uncaring, but the look in his eyes revealed a hint of uncertainty at what he saw there, burning in Leyna's gaze. "There will be time for dealing out punishments later. Right now there is much to be done. Arcastus wakes. We will see then whose treachery is worse."

Turning on his heel, Kael disappeared around the corner from where he had come. Leyna wanted to run after him, to make him pay for what he had done, but the energy was leaving, her body drained. Exhausted. Pain was beginning again in her leg, worse than the dull ache she'd experienced before. Whatever had been allowing her to function during the fight was wearing off faster than she could gather her thoughts. Falling from her motionless hand, the dagger dropped to the ground, forgotten.

The area looked like a war zone. Bodies lay broken and battered over the ground, blood spilling onto the vibrantly colored flowers circling the path. Shock was beginning to set in, taking over her senses to render her motionless, consumed by the horror of reality. Enaes was dead. He had died in her arms. She'd witnessed the moment of his passing. The moment that she failed to protect her Queen's son.

There must have been *something* she could have done to prevent it. Where had she gone wrong? She should have seen the attack coming, the way she'd seen the Sanarik loading their bows that day in Queen Nesperiti's courtyard. Her time out of training had left her weakened and vulnerable. It was unacceptable! Dallying with the court and fraternizing with the enemy to gain information was not where she belonged. She was needed on the battlefield, practiced and prepared for the war that was coming. Thade would argue it — but then, that was before their Prince had been murdered.

Thade. Oh, how would she tell him? How could she tell anyone what happened? It would be the greatest tragedy in Leyna's lifetime. The Queen would be furious to know they had failed to protect her son. The heir to her throne. She had already lost so many children at the hands of the Ven'shal. Vorsila would not hesitate to declare war against them now.

Breaking through the shock, Leyna was suddenly painfully aware of the excruciating fire burning through her injured leg. Her crutch would be useless. She needed to get Enaes's body out of here, and that couldn't be done while balancing her own weight on that clumsy stick.

With a strained groan, she gritted her teeth, hoisting Enaes up into her arms. Leyna cursed her weakness. During the war, she dragged many of her fallen soldiers from the battlefield, never thinking twice about their weight. Her arms felt like mush. She needed to find the quickest route to the front of the chapel. If Thade and Feolan were even still there.

Oh, gods — what if they are dead too? No. She wouldn't think about that. She needed to focus on getting Enaes out of the garden. It was backtracking, but going through the chapel would be the shortest route.

The pain got worse with every step. Enaes's weight combined with her own was too much for her injured leg. She feared it would snap again, from the pressure. Just a little further. The chapel was only about four steps away. Three. Two. One.

Moving into the chapel, Leyna noticed the main door leading out onto the street was open. Some kind of commotion could be heard through it, but she couldn't make out what was being said. The voices sounded concerned. A little frantic. She could make out Feolan's voice. Calm. Soothing. Leyna feared the worst when she heard Maeri's frightened responses. She was near hysterics over something. *And they didn't even know...*

She couldn't take any more. Why was the door so far away? It had seemed a much smaller room when they gathered for the ceremony. Now it loomed before her like a mountain, feeling impossible to reach the summit. There was no choice but to keep going. Clutching Enaes tightly in her arms, she felt him slipping. She adjusted her grip to hoist him up further, afraid of dropping him.

At the frame of the chapel door, Leyna felt her balance falter, stumbling against the edge. Her legs forced her body forward into the street. All eyes turned toward the clatter of her feet scraping over the gravel, her muscles giving out from the exertion and sending her collapsing in defeat. She couldn't keep going. Her body was exhausted beyond limits, emotionally drained and confused. Her hands continued to hold tightly to Enaes's body, not wanting to let it go. She couldn't maintain her grasp for much longer. The weight seemed to increase with every passing moment, pulling her down with it. Giving in, she lowered him to the ground, bending over him, tears of fear and exhaustion streaming down her face.

She lifted her head the most she could manage, searching the crowd for the familiar faces of her friends. She needed to know that they were alive and safe. Footsteps were approaching quickly from her right, their rhythm skidding to a halt in front of Leyna. Turning her head, she saw Thade's confused eyes staring back at her in a flash of brilliant silver. He looked as though someone had just struck him in the stomach. His jaw fell agape in horror, staring at Enaes's body in her arms, blood still trickling over his blue lips.

In an almost drunken stupor, Thade stumbled forward, sliding over the gravel to his knees in front of Leyna. She feared he would have fallen if one of the guards at his side had not extended an arm to steady him. He knelt in shock for a moment, hands clutched desperately at the sides of his own face. Slowly he reached out. His whole body trembled, moisture welling up in the corners of his eyes, lingering. Taking the corpse of Enaes from Leyna, he pulled him in tightly to his chest, clinging to him in agony. "Enaes, you fool," he whispered, rocking back and forth on his knees. "What were you thinking? Why?"

Leyna couldn't bear to watch the pain she saw there in Thade's eyes. It was worse than seeing the sword pierced through Enaes's body, crushing her heart into little pieces. The guilt was paralyzing. Thade begged the question of Enaes's corpse. Why? She knew why. It was because of her. He was thinking about her, and he foolishly ignored the possibility of danger. She had warned him! She tried to get him to leave, but he was inexorable. Stubborn until the very end.

But noble. Honorable. He had been so brave in his final moments. Convinced of his love for her.

She didn't dare tell Thade the name of the assassin yet. He would blame himself for having not killed Kael when he had the chance. He could have easily struck him down rather than rendering him unconscious, but he'd been merciful. There had been no way of knowing then what he was capable of. What Damir and Kyros would use him for. Doing their dirty work so they could keep their hands clean.

Through her guilt-stricken thoughts, she became aware of Thade's eyes on her, watching her, struggling to hold back the emotions that continued to threaten his gentle features. "Leyna," he whispered. Swallowing hard, he paused to try and maintain his composure. "What happened? Please, tell me what happened."

The others were gathering around now. Maeri was behind her, looking her over for injuries. Leyna's dress was covered in blood, most of it belonging to Enaes. Dirt was caked to her face from where she'd been held down at Kael's command. She must look an absolute wreck.

"Kael," she grimaced, covering her face shamefully with her hands. "He had men with him. I tried to save him, but there were too many. I had no weapon and Kael knew I would be worthless on this stupid leg –"

"Leyna, it's not your fault," Maeri sighed.

"Yes it is!" Leyna shouted miserably. "He was there because of me. I told him it was dangerous and insisted he leave, but he wouldn't listen! If it had not been for me, he would still be alive."

Feolan moved around to Leyna's side, propping her arm around his neck. "We need to get you up. You are going to hurt your leg worse," he frowned, nodding to Maeri to help him lift her off the ground. "A doctor will need to have a look at your back as well. It looks bad."

Her back? The pain there was so trivial in comparison to everything else. She'd forgotten all about it. Bringing her attention to it made her consciously aware of the draft fluttering over her skin there. Her bodice dangled by the remaining laces, exposing the marks she'd hidden for so long. Kael had seen them. He would know now that she had never been a slave. Kyros and Damir had likely told him, but there would be no doubt now that Leyna had no questions regarding her identity. She would be exposed as a spy. Working against them all along.

"My back is fine," she argued. Frustrated, she tried to pull away, succeeding only in toppling back to the ground with a cry of pain at her injured leg giving out from under her.

Thade's grimace deepened to see her lying there in front of him. The guards looked on, hesitant, unsure of what they should be doing. They had failed in their job of protecting Enaes. But how could she blame them? Enaes was crafty. In the end, it had been his downfall.

While Feolan and Maeri struggled to help Leyna back to her feet, Thade rose gracefully, arms still wrapped tightly around Enaes's lifeless body. "Close off the chapel grounds," he ordered to the guards. "When his body is secured, we will do a thorough investigation of the area. No one is to be allowed in or out until the search is concluded. Understood?"

One of the guards bowed low in response, his eyes directed down to the ground out of respect. Following his lead, the others did the same, holding the position for a long moment before hurrying off to take up watch at the doors.

"There is another entrance off the garden," Leyna added quietly. "It is how he got inside."

"You heard the Lady," Thade nodded toward two of the guards sternly. "Find the secondary entrance and secure it. Do not move until Lord Diah and I return."

It was strange to hear that name. Memories sparked in her head, causing her to flinch involuntarily at the thought. The joy of the occasion had been destroyed in an instant. Blood spatters stained the white fabric of Maeri's dress from where she'd rubbed against Leyna. Feolan appeared dusty and sweat-covered from some unknown struggle. Now was hardly the time to ask him about what happened before she arrived.

Stopped in the middle of the street, Thade kept his eyes locked straight ahead in the distance, his hold remaining firm on Enaes. "What was his reason for seeking you which required him to trick his guards into leaving him alone?"

Leyna stared at him. It wasn't a question she was prepared to answer. "He —" she stammered, searching for the right words. "He came to ask for my hand in marriage."

"And what was your response? Did you accept the proposal?"

She tried to look past the disbelieving stares of Feolan and Maeri at her side. They would have to remain dumbfounded. She had no desire to explain it to them right now. "I gave no response other than to urge him to leave, insisting it was not the time or place and warning him of the dangers."

"Very well," Thade mumbled quietly, moving past her toward the carriage. "Feolan, Maeri… if you can help her to my carriage, I can take her from there. You are in no way required to give up your plans on account of this unfortunate accident."

"We will accompany you," Feolan nodded. Leaving the painful sight of the chapel, he and Maeri began to guide Leyna over to the carriage behind Thade, giving no hesitation at leaving their bridal coach empty. "There will be plenty of time for us to spend together. Right now, we are needed by our Prince."

Chapter Twenty-Four

Sleep was impossible in the nights that followed Enaes's death. When Leyna closed her eyes, all she could see was the look on his face while she held him in her arms, his fingers brushing her cheek, smiling through the pain. It haunted her. He died believing he loved her, and that misguided love led to his demise.

Conversation between her and her friends had seemed hollow as well. There was nothing to be said. Only one child remained as heir to the Vor'shai throne. It frightened Leyna to think what would happen if something were to befall the young Prince. Vorsila would be left with nothing. No claim to the throne for the Levadis family. She would be forced to relinquish the crown to a new line upon her death, changing the course of Tanispa's future to break ties with the old royal line of the past.

Thade left for Tanispa immediately upon completing the inspection of the chapel grounds. It had fallen on him to bring the terrible news to the royal family. It was a tragedy. All of Tanispa would be in arms over the death, demanding that justice be served on the assassin. War would be on everyone's lips.

And they would get what they wanted. It was imminent. Kael had spoken of Arcastus waking. If there was any truth to his claims then they would be in for a fight beyond anything Tanispa had faced in centuries. Not since the war against the Ven'shal during Queen Nalashi's reign. Leyna couldn't imagine what a fight of that degree would be like. Her experience with war only stretched to her knowledge of fighting the Namirens and Sanarik in the mountains of Siscal. The Ven'shal would pose a far greater threat than Namorea ever could.

Even worse, there had been no word from Zander. No one had seen or heard from him since before Leyna and Thade left for Mialan nearly two months ago. Whatever Oksuva and Damir were up to, there was no way to know. Leyna feared Zander to be dead. If anything happened to him, she knew the guilt would eat away at her for leaving him with those monsters alone.

Slowly, Leyna stepped out the front door of her house, instantly blocked by the guard standing firm in her path. Her crutch was battered. Pieces of the wood were splintered from the fight against Kael's men, making it difficult to maintain her weight over it. Cautious of her safety, the guard lightly held her arm, helping to act as support. "I am not leaving," she stated calmly, noticing the disapproving look in the guard's eyes. "I just want to see the road by the Consul's home."

"You shouldn't be seen outdoors, Milady. You know the orders of the Consul and Lord Diah."

"I am tired of the scenery inside. There is little to entertain within the four walls of my room. I only ask for a moment. A brief breath of fresh air to cleanse the dust from my nose."

Begrudgingly, the man released her arm, making no move to step away. The heavy plate armor covering his body looked awkward and uncomfortable. Leyna sympathized for him. He would be stationed outside her door for the remainder of the night until his relief came in the morning. She shuddered to think of how miserable such a job must be.

For over a week Leyna had kept watch for Thade's carriage to return. There had been no time frame given for his trip. Feolan expected him to be gone for no less than a month, the Queen requiring his assistance in preparations for the funeral and mourning process. Thade would need to accept her visitors on her behalf while she grieved in solitude. Leyna's heart ached for him to return. She was lost without him. No one to go to when she felt she would be driven insane from the nightmares. Maeri and Feolan had moved into their home, offering her to come stay with them if she would be more comfortable around people, but she couldn't bring herself to accept the invitation. They were newlyweds and would be wanting their time alone together. She had burdened them all quite enough over the years.

A clattering of horse's hooves in the distance caught Leyna's attention, moving closer to the quiet little neighborhood. The sky was already darkened for the night, rain pouring down from above, residents inside their homes tucked in for bed. Whoever was approaching was coming quickly, already near the path leading to where she was standing outside her house. She recognized the familiar face of Zander, disheveled from the wind and water blowing through his hair. Excited to see him alive, she waved her hands to get his attention, not wanting to make too much noise in fear of disrupting the quiet of the neighborhood. Noticing her there, Zander called out for the horse to stop, rearing back with a loud whinny before settling irritably under his command. "Leyna," he breathed, dismounting in a single leap from the horse's back. "Is the Consul home? I must speak with him immediately."

"Zander," she started to speak, realizing it was possible Zander had not heard of the news. "The Consul has been gone for over a week. He had to return Prince Enaes's body to the Queen."

"Body?" he blinked. "So it is true. What happened?"

"Kael assassinated the Prince. Things have been an absolute mess."

Scanning the area, Zander seemed to take note of the house behind Leyna for the first time since his arrival. With a sharp glance at the guard, he gave an inquisitive look in Leyna's direction. "Is this where you stay now? If so, then we should go inside. I have no way of knowing if I was followed."

"I'm supposed to be indoors anyway," she muttered. Motioning toward the door, she signaled him to go inside, lingering behind only long enough to catch the displeasure on the guard's face before stepping into the house, closing the door to leave the man outside. "Zander, you look like something is troubling you. We have been worried, not knowing where you have been."

"We have been on the western coast of Tanispa for over a month now," he sighed, flopping down tiredly on the old settee in her front room. His whole body relaxed into the worn cushions. Exhausted. "It is worse than we thought. Damir was successful. Arcastus lives. We are looking at the start of a war that I'm not sure we can win. And if they see me, they will kill me. Just like they did to Oksuva."

"Oksuva is dead?" Leyna gasped. Through the surprise in her voice, she realized it was no great shock to her. Damir was not the kind of person to tolerate an outside partner. He was using her for the amulet. Once she handed it over to him, he no longer had any need for her. "What about Gislan? Did she escape?"

"They had no reason to kill her. She required nothing from them out of the deal other than to be guaranteed safety during the war. They let her live under the stipulation that once they won, she was to disappear so they wouldn't have to deal with her anymore. Me, however, they took issue with simply because I am Vor'shai."

"What made them think you would be any issue?"

"Arcastus wanted the blood of a Vor'shai in order to seal the ritual which bound his spirit back to his body. I think they suspected I might disagree with that."

Leyna limped around the room, settling herself in the tiny wooden chair situated in front of a small desk near the front. Thoughtfully, she leaned forward, resting her chin in her hands. "And I suppose Kael is too far gone to fit that requirement?"

"Kael is the one they sent to bring back the blood. They wanted someone of importance to the Vor'shai people. He insisted he could bring them the blood of Prince Enaes. How could Damir and Arcastus turn that down?" Zander shook his head. "When Kael returned, I didn't expect him to have actually done it. I mean – to kill the Prince? A part of me wanted to believe Kael maintained some semblance of the loyalty he once held for his people. I suppose I hoped he was playing some game with them. But if Enaes is dead…" a grimace passed over his features at the thought. "My god, Leyna. Do you realize what this means?"

"It means a lot of things. To start, Arcastus will be gathering his strength now and there is nothing we can do about it. Secondly, our Prince is dead. Queen Vorsila has but a single heir left to maintain the throne while at the same time she is on the brink of war. Our people have taken a hard hit and Arcastus will take advantage of that to strike us while we are down."

Zander was quiet for a minute, letting everything sink in. She couldn't imagine what he had been through over the past few weeks. What he had witnessed. Things were falling apart around them. For so long, they'd had the whole thing in control, prepared for a fight against Mikel and Oksuva. With Damir in the picture, it changed everything. He was impossible to predict. They couldn't know what he was planning to do next. And with Arcastus awake, it would only get worse.

"But what can we do?" he frowned. "Our job was to prevent this from happening. I was confident we'd succeed. My plans didn't extend into how to handle failure."

"You saw the ritual. Maybe that will hold an answer. What of the amulet? Can you tell me anything about that?"

Heaving a sigh, Zander rose from the settee. He looked tired. His eyes drooped from fatigue. Little of the sparkle remained in them, once so optimistic over the thought of beating Damir at his own game. "I know it is important enough that they keep it under constant watch," he explained. "Kyros had imitations made of it. One of them carries the real one while the others hold the forgeries. It served as the source of power – almost like a conduit of energy – for the ritual. Their guard over it would lead me to believe it still holds significance to Arcastus's strength. The problem would be determining which one is real, and how to get it from them."

"But would Damir trust anyone else to protect the real amulet?"

"He has to," Zander shrugged. "For Damir to wear it would be too obvious. It would be expected."

"Or maybe he assumes we would think it too obvious and therefore kept it for himself."

"Possible, I suppose. But I think he gives his enemies more credit than that. Damir is well aware of the fact that the Vor'shai are not fools. They beat the Ven'shal once before. One misstep on his part, and we could beat them again."

Leyna watched as Zander took a step, preparing to begin a slow pace across the room but stopping, too tired to put forth the effort. "Who then would be the least obvious choice? I would say whoever was the weakest amongst them, but Damir wouldn't risk that. If the weak link was discovered, it would be taken too easily."

"It must be Kyros or Kael."

She stared back at him in confusion. Kael? How could he not be the weakest of the group? He was still in the process of falling to insanity. Any link he still had with the Vor'shai would make him a threat. "You place Kael at a higher rank than Oran? He seems so weak in comparison. I would have expected him to be the bottom of the barrel."

"If you think about it, Kael has the potential to become as great a threat to us as Damir." Zander moved over to the settee to casually rest his hand against the back of it. "A fallen Vor'shai has knowledge of the way our magic works, as well as the way of the Ven'shal sorcery. They have manipulated the energy in the same ways that we have, and therefore would be more capable of countering it. That energy never leaves them, it just gets distorted. Damir has even shown signs that a Vor'shai using their sorcery can bypass some of the negative effects Ven'shal magic is said to carry. It has always been destructive to the life around it, drawing the energy from the planet itself, stealing it, using it up. Damir has demonstrated a skill and control with the magic which disproves that."

"So Kael's familiarity with our ways makes him more of a threat?"

"In more ways than you can imagine," he frowned. "His familiarity with us — you and I — and the Consul as well. He will be more prepared."

Leaning on her crutch, Leyna returned to her feet. She couldn't sit still. It was so infuriating! Their own friend and ally turned against them. Murdered their Prince. He worked with the very forces that intended to destroy their entire race. The same race he once swore to protect. To think that she had thought to marry him! He fell too quickly for her to catch, and it hurt to know that she might have been able to help him. If he would have just let her. But he didn't want to be saved. Not enough to fight back on his own.

"What will you do now, then?" she asked quietly. "Without being able to watch them, we are removed from any further knowledge of their plans. They know where you live — they could come for you at any time."

"They could come for you as well. And they intend to, I'm sure." He gazed toward the window, distracted by something. "I need to find a way to help our cause that will keep me out of their sights," he nodded. "The military has seemed a viable option. Not here in Siscal, but in Tanispa. If they will accept me. But what about you? I would think it would be harder for a lady of the court to just disappear."

"Yes," Leyna sighed. He was right. The thought crossed her mind on many occasions over the past few weeks. Until she was healed, the military was out. And to simply leave, even to rejoin the military in Siscal, would draw unwanted attention from Queen Nesperiti. Possibly spark her ire. Nesperiti had been gracious in extending a court position to her. To throw it away so soon would come across as an insult. The Siscalian Queen preferred to keep her nobles and soldiers separate. "I have a responsibility here and until I can find a means of escaping it without destroying my reputation, I am stuck."

He couldn't argue. Politics were much too dangerous to play games with when it came to positions under a king or queen. "Very well then," he said calmly. "If the Consul is gone, then I believe it is safe to assume that Feolan is acting in his stead for the time being? I should speak with him before I leave for Tanispa. Perhaps I could request he put in a good word for you about a leave of absence from the court here."

"That will not be necessary. However, if you are looking to speak with him, he and Maeri have moved into a house not far from here. The one with the large tree in the front, about a block away."

"They moved in together?"

"Well, that is what husbands and wives tend to do after they are married," she chuckled.

The look on Zander's face was priceless. His jaw hung open, staring at her in shock. "Married? When did they get married?"

They moved closer to the door while speaking, Zander's expression remaining fixed in awe. "Not long ago. Be sure to give your congratulations to them. They are the new Lord and Lady Diah, now."

"I should have known she would find someone like him," Zander smiled, shaking his head in mild disappointment. "If she had remained available until the war was over, I might have pursued her myself."

A twinge of jealousy caused Leyna to cringe at his words. Men loved a well-trained lady. Maeri was the epitome of what men wanted. Beautiful, smart, delicate – in need of protection. Maeri had been brought up to nurture, not to fight. Why would a man have need of a woman who could take care of herself? It challenged their masculinity.

In the back of her mind, she pondered what her life would have been like if she'd conducted herself in the same way as Maeri. The men would have taken a greater interest, but her days would have been less fulfilling. She preferred to leave her mark on the world with her deeds rather than fend off the affections of every man on the court. That said something for her. After all, the Prince had sought her to be his wife. How many ladies could say that?

"Well, she is not available, so it looks like you might have to keep your eyes open for someone else."

"What about you, Leyna?" he flashed her a charming grin. "We could have dinner before I become a military man."

Opening the door, she rolled her eyes at him. "Goodbye, Zander," she chuckled, tapping the door with her hand to signal him out. "Keep in touch. Maybe we will see each other again soon."

"Your loss," he shrugged nonchalantly. Pulling his shoulders back, he moved past Leyna through the door, strutting proudly out to his horse. "The offer stands in case you change your mind."

"I don't think I will."

"That is unfortunate, Milady," he gazed at her, the smile fading from his lips. "All joking aside, I do wish things could be different. It has been a pleasure working by your side these past years. You are possibly the strongest woman I have ever had the honor of meeting."

His tone was serious. Like a final goodbye from someone who expects to never be seen again. He was going off to war. Reality had a harsher sting than she was comfortable with, recognizing for the first time that it was possible he might die on the battlefield. They all could. This war had so much more riding on it than the fight against the Namiren army. Her people stood to lose everything.

Words didn't feel appropriate at that moment. What could you possibly say to someone you might never see again? Farewell seemed empty. Impersonal. Silence was all she could manage without fear of tearing up. She scolded herself quietly. *You are getting soft. Next you will start weeping like the other girls at Faustine's.*

Modestly bowing her head, she sank into a graceful curtsy, favoring her injured leg. She was grateful for the cover of her skirt to hide the awkwardness of her movements. As he climbed up onto his horse, Leyna couldn't bear to watch him leave. She couldn't think it might be the last time she would see him. He was a strong fighter. He would make a great soldier, and they would arise victorious over the Ven'shal the way they had before.

Leyna toyed with the end of her crutch, admiring the carving work she'd taken for granted in it all the other times she looked at it. The doctor assured her the bone was healing fine. She would need to be careful not to do anything too strenuous, but the walking device was no longer necessary for her to get around.

It had been several days since she heard any news from Feolan. Zander wasted no time in getting out of Siscal, and with good reason, knowing Damir would come looking for him. Zander was a risk to Damir and the others. He'd witnessed the return of Arcastus. It seemed sloppy work that they let him get away.

Maeri came by to check on her every day. She and Feolan worried about the way she sat around the house, alone, lost in thought over the impending war. They feared she would blame herself somehow. To that point, she still refused to discuss the events in the chapel garden that day. There was no need to unleash her feelings on her friends when they already had so much on their minds. Her guilt was better dealt with alone, where no one else had to know the way it ate away at her. Blaming herself for Enaes's death.

She jumped at the unexpected knock on her door, nearly dropping the crutch on the ground. Maeri. Her visit was later today than usual. She tended to come at midday, bringing food to make sure Leyna was eating properly. The sun had already begun to sink to usher in the coming of evening and Maeri had not yet come. Something must have delayed her.

Rising up from the settee, she slowly made her way over to the door, hesitant to put much weight on her healing leg. It was still sore to use, but the improvement was significant from the pain which hindered her in the past few weeks. Just to be free of the crutch was a wonder in itself.

She opened the door, her normal greeting for Maeri prepared, lips curled up in a forced smile, hiding her troubled thoughts. Before she could open her mouth to speak, her eyes blinked in surprise at Feolan's face there at her door instead of Maeri's, his expression solemn and drawn. "Feolan," she breathed. "I thought you were Maeri."

"No, I told Maeri I would check on you before I came home. My business simply took a bit longer than expected."

"That is fine. Please, do come in —"

"I cannot stay," he cut in. "Thade has returned. He sent me here to request your presence."

Her heart fluttered in her chest. Thade? He was back? "Yes, of course," she nodded emphatically, reaching for the cloak hanging on a stand near the door. The coming winter had already put a chill in the air. It was depressingly fitting for the mood that had fallen over them of late. "We should not keep him waiting then."

"*You* should not keep him waiting." Feolan's tone was distant. Worry filled his eyes, the way he gazed at her in the dimming light. "I will not be joining you. He desires your company in private, but I must warn you – he is in a very troubled state of mind over the stress of the past few weeks. Think carefully about what you say to him."

Private? The fluttering in her heart intensified at the thought. Something wasn't right. It was unlike Thade to call for her in this manner. Over the past year they'd spent a few occasions in private company, but never had he directly requested it. And to deny Feolan's presence… she shivered at the thought of what might be wrong. "I see. The look in your eyes has me worried. Is there cause for alarm?"

She was already out the door, pulling it shut behind her. Feolan shook his head. "No alarm. Not yet, anyway. I will accompany you as far as his door though you really should not be walking too much."

"My leg is fine," she argued. "The distance is not far. You should get home to Maeri. I will be alright, I promise."

"I am not comfortable leaving you –"

"Feolan, please. You worry more than you should about me. After all the battles we fought by each other's side, I would like to think you have a bit more faith in me."

"I have faith in you, Leyna. But you have changed since I first met you. We have all changed. Even the Consul. None of us are the same as we were back then, and I recognize that those changes open us up to more than I like to admit." He looked pensive. Leyna could see something was troubling him that he wasn't saying. "I just do not want to see you get hurt."

Lightly, she patted him on the arm, hoping to give him some reassurance. What did he think was going to happen to her between her house and Thade's? The distance wasn't enough to leave her vulnerable to the extent of his concern. "If it will ease your mind, you are welcome to remain here and watch me until I reach his door. From the corner, you would have a clear view of the path from here to there."

"No," Feolan shook his head, offering his arm out to assist Leyna in her steps. "While I respect your independence, we have suffered enough loss. I refuse to risk your safety on account of your stubbornness. Besides, you know the Consul would be very displeased with me if I failed to see you to his door as requested. I only ask that when you leave, one of his guards accompany. If you would do me the favor of coming by to visit my wife and I after you leave this meeting, I have some things I would like to discuss with you."

Giving in to his insistence Leyna allowed Feolan to help her across the gravel, wishing she'd been more prepared for this audience. She felt under-dressed for a meeting with the Consul. Friends or not, he was an important man. At times she tended to overlook that fact, but his absence had put things into perspective, reminding her of his close relationship with the Queen, and her family; or what was left of it.

Two well-groomed guards stood on either side of Thade's door as Feolan and Leyna approached, eyeing her suspiciously. The one on the right peered questioningly at Feolan, moving to block the door. "Lord Diah, we have direct orders about not allowing unknown visitors."

"Lady Evantine is far from an unknown visitor. She is expected. I don't recommend keeping her out in the cold." Feolan held the guard's gaze, the man's hardened expression softening at the sound of Leyna's name, stepping to open the door. Before it could swing inward, the motion was stopped by something inside, a somber looking Thade appearing in the doorway.

"Thank you, Officer. I will handle this from here. Lord Diah," Thade nodded to Feolan. "Your assistance is appreciated. Go home to your wife. I am sure she is waiting for you."

"Of course, sir. I beg you though; please see to it that Leyna does not leave here alone."

"She will not leave here alone. Now go. I have kept you long enough."

With a final hesitant glance Feolan offered Leyna's arm to Thade, turning away to make his way down the street toward his house. Thade waited for him to be a distance away before addressing the guards again, the tone of his voice authoritative and firm. "You are both excused."

"But sir, we were told —" the guard stammered uncomfortably. Thade held his hand up, gesturing for him to be silent.

"I know what you were told. My word outranks your previous orders, so I suggest you gentlemen find another location to stand for the night."

Hesitant, the guard bowed his head in acknowledgment. "As you wish, sir," he mumbled, clearly uneasy with the new orders. The men awkwardly glanced between each other and Thade, gradually working their way down the steps to the road. Thade watched with a stern eye until they had mounted their horses. Content they would continue as directed, he moved out of the doorway, motioning for Leyna to come inside.

He was dressed in what appeared to be mourning attire. A heavy gold chain draped over his shoulders — a chain of office Leyna had never seen him wear before — extravagant gemstones encircling a crest in the center. His doublet was of the finest quality. Black velvet accented in gold over the shoulders and buttons securing it tightly down the front. It was tailor-made to fit him perfectly, down to the length of his sleeves and height of the collar around his neck.

No smile passed over his lips as he ushered her inside, closing the door behind her, his hands double checking the lock. His appearance was eminent. Regal. It commanded immediate respect from any who crossed his path, sending Leyna reflexively into a deep curtsy, her eyes lowering humbly to the floor at his feet. She thought to say something, but it felt out of place.

Reaching out his hands, Thade caught her arms gently, raising her back to her feet. "Leyna, please. Why do you greet me so?"

"It felt appropriate," she said quietly, her eyes shifting to his nervously. He sounded sad. It was all she could do to keep from taking him in her arms to assure him everything would be okay. But she couldn't say that. She had no way to know whether anything would ever be okay again.

"I beg you to look me in the eye the way you always do," he frowned. "We are equals here in this house. Friends. Titles mean nothing between us right now."

At his pleading tone, she nodded in understanding. How could she deny him when he looked at her with such silent desperation? His silver eyes made him broodingly handsome. Sexy, in a way she hated to admit even to herself. This was hardly the time or place to admire his form – though there was much for her to admire.

Straightening her posture, she stepped away from Thade's hands, fidgeting with her own against the clasp of her cloak. "Feolan made it sound as though something was terribly wrong. I must admit I was a bit surprised to hear that you requested my presence without his."

Thade turned away in a blur of shimmering black and gold. Casual yet strong. "I have not had a moment of peace since I left for Tanispa. I desired a bit of privacy before I forget what the word means."

"Then I should not bother you – unless you need someone to speak to." Hesitantly, she moved further into the room, leaning against the back of the settee. They'd shared so much in this very room. *If the walls could talk...*

So many things had changed since her first visit here. And now they stood, so close yet so far away, separated by some grim barrier which made Thade feel like a stranger, stiff and closed off. "There are some things I must discuss with you, and I cannot do so with all those eyes and ears prying into my business. I want to be able to speak openly. Do you promise that you will not hold back anything, no matter how much you think it might offend me? I ask only for your honesty."

"My honesty is all I have ever given, Thade."

He turned around to face her, the melancholy expression on his face deepening at the sight of her eyes. "I do not know how best to say this, so I must come right out with it before I go mad." With long strides, he moved closer, pausing a few paces from the settee, holding her solemn gaze. "Tomorrow I am returning to Tanispa. Once I depart, I will not be coming back to Siscal – and the harsh truth I have come to realize is that you and I may never see each other again."

The words were like a sword piercing through her chest, impaling her heart, savagely tearing it to pieces. Never see each other again? Her mind wouldn't accept it. She couldn't imagine a life without Thade being there, waiting in this place for Leyna to come with the latest news of her excursions. He was the only person who really knew her. Who understood her. She had bared everything to him until there was nothing left to hide.

Except the way she felt about him.

Caught up with grief at the thought of losing him forever, she covered her mouth with her hand. Her throat contracted. Tears threatened to fall, and she wasn't sure she would be able to hold them back. She wasn't sure she wanted to. What sense was there in hiding it now? After tonight, anything she said or did would be nothing but a memory for him while he traveled back to Tanispa.

Giving in to the emotion, she let the tears fall from her eyes. He looked startled by her reaction. His hand reached out as if to touch her arm reassuringly, but he seemed to decide against it, holding his ground, staring at her, grimacing. "In all the years we have known each other, I have only witnessed you weep once. I regretfully am not prepared with how I can console you. This is rather… unexpected."

"You have been my closest friend for all these years and you did not expect me to weep at the thought of losing you? Do I come across so heartless? If so, I have made a terrible error in expressing how much your friendship has meant to me. And now, it seems it is too late for me to rectify my mistake."

"Then we both mourn our failure," he replied. Slowly, he took a step toward her, offering his arms, as if afraid she might pull away if he embraced her. "I have many regrets about things I should have said or done over the years. A part of me took for granted that we had all the time in the world. But I see now that I was wrong."

"Why must you go away?" she sobbed. "What requires you to leave without promise of return?"

"My family commands it." He grimaced at her unwillingness to come to him, his arms dropping back to his sides. "They granted me a single day to tie up loose ends and say my farewells. That is not enough time for me to do it."

"Then do not go back!" It was irrational. She was no longer thinking coherently. They were on the brink of war! What good would it do to take their best soldier away?

Thade winced at her outburst. "If you could give me a reason to defy them, I would. The gods know I have thought on it harder than I should."

She couldn't hold herself back any longer, stepping toward him, covering the distance that had been opened to her before. It was out of line, but she didn't care. She needed to hold him. To feel him close. Part of her hoped she would discover him to be nothing but an apparition, that she would find herself once again in her own home, suffering from a nightmare sparked by the fear of losing her friends to the war.

But he was very real, his muscular chest firm and strong against her. It felt good. Comforting. She didn't want to let him go. Fear lingered in the back of her mind that he would push her away. It was surprising to her that he didn't. Instead, he slowly lifted his arms, wrapping them around her gently.

She stood, lost in his embrace, inhaling the sweet scent of his hair and skin where her head was cradled against his shoulder. No words could express the emotions she felt rushing through her body at his touch. Why had she never told him before how much she cared about him? Maeri had told her to, but she'd foolishly disregarded the advice. And now she clung desperately to him, soaking another of his shirts with tears.

Vaguely, she became aware of Thade's hands moving to pull her arms away from his shoulder. The movement was gentle. Soft. Nothing like the disgusted shove she expected. His hand lightly tilted her head up. She didn't fight it, trusting him completely. Their eyes locked, staring at one another in silence, losing themselves in the moment. Suddenly, his lips were pressed against hers, his eyes opening briefly to gauge her reaction in fear of what she would do.

Confusion filled her. Her body tingled all over, heart racing, thoughts unfocused. All she could think about was his mouth. It was nothing like Kael's hard passionate kisses. She felt like they were slowly melting together, becoming a single entity. When he finally pulled away, she didn't want it to stop, leaning forward eagerly for more.

"Was I too — am I out of line?" His voice was barely above a whisper to her ears.

How could he even ask? It felt so perfect! What could possibly be wrong with something that felt so right? "No," she said quietly, gently resting her hand around his neck. "Actually, I was hoping that maybe you would... do it again?"

For the first time since she arrived that evening, Thade smiled. Fondly gazing down at her, he gave in to Leyna's urging hands, drawing her into him again, slow and soft.

He was everything she had imagined him to be and more. It was too easy to melt into his arms, clouding her senses with the pleasure the act gave. She was afraid of the lack of control she felt over her body. Her chest fluttered almost uncomfortably, anxious, wanting more, but a nagging voice in her mind told her she could not. It wouldn't be right.

"Run away with me." Thade said without warning. He was staring into her eyes. In their depths she could find no sign of jest in the suggestion.

"Run away with you? Thade —"

"I thought about you the entire trip here from Tanispa. If I cannot take you with me, then we will go somewhere else. Away from Siscal." His tone was growing more excited with every word. "We can find a priest who would marry us and escape from this all."

This couldn't be happening. She thought her chest would explode if her heart beat any faster. "Are you asking me to marry you?"

"You are the only woman I desire to have as my wife. If you will have me, then yes — I am asking you for your hand in marriage."

"I — yes," she breathed, overwhelmed with happiness. "I will follow you to the end of the world and back if you ask me to."

"And I may have to ask you to," his words came out in a relieved exhale, pulling her in closer. "You are the only reason I could find worthy enough of defying everything. I was afraid you would not feel the same."

"I was willing to give my life for yours back then." Fumbling over the clasp on her cloak, Leyna released it, letting the heavy fabric fall to the floor around her feet. The bodice she was wearing swept low across her chest. Laces held it firmly in place, accentuating her upper body while exposing the scar over her breast. She took Thade's hand in hers, touching his fingers to the imperfection there. "I would do it all over again if that was what it took to prove the feelings I have held for you all these years."

She could see he was captivated. His eyes saw nothing but her. "I would never allow that to happen again," he said softly, his lips lowering to gently kiss the skin of her neck. "I regret that it took something so terrible to make me see how much you meant to me then. It took me all this time to understand what I was feeling, and everything has stood between us since the gods brought us back together at the masque. I feared I would lose you."

It sounded strange to her. At the masque? Through her clouded thoughts, she knew the words didn't make sense, but she didn't care. Every inch of her was distracted by the light brush of his lips against her neck, his arms holding her tightly. She couldn't focus on words with his hands tugging at the laces of her bodice.

When the cords gave way, she felt Thade's sharp intake of breath as the heavy piece of fabric loosened, held up only by the pressure of their bodies pressed together. She couldn't help but blush at the thought of him seeing her so exposed. In her dreams, she'd been more comfortable with her figure, free of the scars. She felt like a monster, her only disguise the piece of her dress which now dangled precariously, threatening to reveal everything.

His fingers brushed lightly over the imperfections on her back that had plagued her for so long. "No one will ever hurt you again. I give you my word," he breathed.

By pure instinct, her hands moved to the buttons on his doublet. They were well designed. Sturdy. It was difficult to get them loose, though she felt compelled to do so quickly. She was becoming more and more aware of her uncertainty at the situation. Not in whether it was wrong or right, but in her lack of knowledge, stumbling through the motions in hopes that she would do everything right.

Only the top few buttons had come free under her curious fingers when he stopped her. "I am not very experienced in how to handle a situation like this," he said suddenly.

"Neither am I," she smiled, nervous at the admission. They laughed quietly at their own awkwardness.

The laughter eased the tension between them as Thade slowly guided her around the settee, keeping her held tightly to him, carefully lowering her onto the cushions. As the weight of his body descended upon her, she felt like she should be stopping him. So often she had denied Kael, but this was different somehow. There was no question of her feelings for Thade. This was what she wanted. And though nothing else in her mind had any clarity in this moment, her feelings remained the one thing she knew for sure.

It was Thade who pulled his head away from hers, concern passing over his gentle features. "What am I doing?" he exhaled, leaning back on the settee away from her. "This was not my intention. I apologize —"

"Why do you apologize?" she asked, her breath heavy from the rush of emotions.

"This is exactly why Feolan hesitated to allow me to meet with you alone. I am not thinking straight." Noticing Leyna's crooked bodice and confused expression, Thade's cheeks flushed with color, his hands moving to adjust the fabric back over her. "He has become aware of my feelings for you over the years. We work so closely together, it was impossible to hide it from him. Knowing that I called you here to tell you goodbye, he feared what might occur. That I would not be able to resist you. And he was right. I am not in control, the way I should be."

"Do you think less of me for not stopping you?" The thought horrified her. Had she let him down? It all felt so right, but now, looking back on it, she'd given in to actions unbecoming of a lady. She should have stopped him.

Thade shook his head, the somber look returning. His eyes could still be seen glancing over her body briefly, shifting away by sheer force of will. He wanted to be near her. She could see the effort it took him to remain at a distance, rising up from the settee to begin a nervous pace. "I could never think poorly of you, Leyna. I should not have behaved so. After all, it was I who argued your innocence to the Queen. I would be wronging you terribly to let that happen."

Pressing her bodice against herself tightly, Leyna sat up on the settee, gazing into the depths of Thade's brightly shining eyes. "The gods have brought us together." His pacing halted. Thade was entranced by her every movement, hanging off her every word. "We have fought through the trials and managed to find ourselves here together, against the odds. In my mind, we are husband and wife in every way but on that little piece of parchment in the Queen's library. And we will have that soon enough once we leave here. But if you are not comfortable, then I will not press the matter. I cannot fault you for it. I only hope you will not fault *me*."

She wanted to go to him. To take him in her arms, just for the sake of holding him the way she'd longed to for so long. It didn't matter whether they did anything beyond lying in each other's arms. They would have their whole lives together after this night.

At the sight of her struggling to stand, Thade moved to her side, supporting her with his hand. "You are right," he said, his voice soft and calm, no longer showing the signs of uncertainty he exhibited before. Leaning in, he pressed his lips against hers again. His strength impressed her as he lifted her easily into his arms from the settee. "But my wife-to-be deserves better than this uncomfortable thing."

"Are you sure?" she whispered. The fluttering in her heart was returning. Wilder than before. Without a word, he nodded his head, eyes twinkling in the dimming light of the room from the setting sun outside, holding her to him as he carried her away down the hall to his room.

Leyna's eyes fluttered open, taking in the sight of the room around her in wonder. She'd been afraid to fall asleep. That she would awaken the next morning only to discover it had all been a dream. But there was no denying now that it was in fact very real.

Thade's arm was tucked under her on the bed, his bare chest exposed from under the soft satin sheets, rising and falling from the gentle inhale and exhale of his breath while he slept. Her head was resting on him, her body pressed up against his under the blankets. It was heaven to her. A gift from the gods after everything they had suffered.

When the sun came up, they would be gone. None of the troubles would matter to them anymore. He would be her husband and everything would be perfect. It seemed too good to be true. And in a way, she knew deep down that it was.

Panic welled up inside of her at the thought of what they had done. Not at the idea of having given herself to Thade, but at the fear of what he was giving up by running away with her. What she was letting him throw away! It was selfish. If she loved him, she should tell him that his responsibilities were vastly more important than her. Their people needed him. And while she knew nothing of the reason his family called him back, she could only assume it was something beyond the scope of anything she could imagine. Who was she to take him away from it?

"Oh no," she breathed. How could she have let this happen? She had unwittingly become the very evil creature Feolan claimed all women to be those years ago. Thade was willing to give up everything to be with her. If he had not been distracted by her, he never would have thought to turn his back on his responsibilities. She couldn't let him do it. The risks were too great. He was the Queen's Consul, after all. He could be charged with treason for leaving – and what would be the punishment for such a crime? They would certainly have him banished, or worse – killed.

Calm yourself. She laid her palm against Thade's chest, trying to force the thoughts out of her mind. *Stop overreacting. You are just confused by everything that has happened. That is normal.*

If only she could believe it! She wasn't confused. Everything made perfect sense. She finally had the one thing she wanted – and she had to let him go. They could not be together. Not like this. Whatever his reasons for desiring her, he would move past them. He was going to have to. They couldn't spend their whole lives running.

There were things she needed to focus on as well. She couldn't fight Damir if she was at the other end of the world. Eventually, they would both start to resent each other for the things they had left to be together. It would be unbearable. Worse than the pain that seared through her heart at the thought of leaving him now.

At least now they would leave with a part of each other. She would never forget him, and she prayed he would never forget her.

Afraid of waking him, Leyna carefully lifted her head from his chest, sliding noiselessly from the bed. His muscles twitched at the disappearance of her weight against him. She froze at the sight, holding her breath as if it would somehow prevent him from opening his eyes. He looked so peaceful lying there. She needed to get out of his room before she changed her mind and crawled back into the safety of his muscular arms.

It was too early in the morning for her to worry about being seen by anyone in the neighborhood. Gathering her clothes from the floor, she dressed herself as she made her way back to the front of the house. Her body was trembling. So many new emotions to take in. Tears were filling her eyes even as she told herself she wouldn't cry. This was for the best. No matter how much she repeated it in her mind, it didn't make it any easier to cope with. How could something that felt so perfect be so wrong for them?

Not even taking the time to clasp her cloak over her shoulders, she hurried out the front door, quietly closing it behind her. She couldn't chance him waking up before she had time to get back home, and the walk would be slow on her injured leg.

Feolan. Oh, gods! How could she have forgotten? She promised him she would come visit him when she left Thade's. But there was no time for that now. She just needed to get inside the safety of her house and then maybe the pain would go away. She could try to convince herself that nothing happened. Her heart would crumble if she didn't think of something.

Her pace was nothing more than a hobble along the gravel road. Afraid of being seen in the soft light of the morning, she tried to keep close to the remaining shadows cast by the houses, a pained grimace locked on her face with every step. The guard was stationed outside her door, moving toward her in confusion to see her, limping along the street without anyone else around. She was grateful for his support. His arm linked with hers to guide her the final steps, helping her through the front door.

"Milady, what are you doing out alone?"

"I have to leave," she breathed, desperate for air after her torturous walk. Remaining in that house wasn't an option. When Thade awoke, he would come to find her. And what would she tell him? How could she explain why they couldn't be together? It pained her to think of what he might say. How he would feel about her desertion.

Without Thade and Zander, there was nothing she could do in Siscal to benefit her people. Her position on Nesperiti's court offered nothing. To sit around and sip tea with Feolan and Maeri, never knowing what fate may befall their friends and country. She didn't know where she was going, but it was obvious that she would have to leave Siscal. Perhaps Carpaen? Blaise had assured the military's assistance in the war. If they would accept her, it would allow her to fight against the Ven'shal. While Tanispa's army would be preferred, the chance of running into Thade on the road was too great. Carpaen was her best choice for now. She could determine where to go once she was safely across the border into the desert.

Stumbling through the house Leyna pulled out her bags, throwing clothes into them, not caring whether or not the fabric was wrinkled or torn in the process. There was no time! All that mattered was getting out of there before Thade or Feolan found her. The guard hurried around the room to keep up with her. "I can't allow you to leave. You know my orders."

"I don't care about your orders. You have no idea what is going on," she gasped. "I need to borrow your horse. The faster I can get away from here, the better."

"The Consul will have my head —"

"Tell him I hit you. He might believe that," she cut him off. Defiant. Nothing was going to stand in her way. Feolan and Thade knew her well enough to be aware of her stubborn nature. There was no fear of punishment for the guard if she left against his wishes. The only way he would be able to prevent her departure would be to physically hold her back, and he wouldn't dare lay a finger on her.

Letting her eyes trail around the room, Leyna shook her head. Items remained scattered about. Decorations. Nothing of importance. Anything else she needed there would be a way of replacing once she reached Carpaen. Clothes would be enough to get her through until then. Once she joined the military, the dresses would be of little consequence anyhow. Bags clutched tightly in her hands, she made her way through the front door, footsteps clambering along behind her from the desperate approach of the guard.

"Milady, stop."

"Stay by the door as you are commanded to do," Leyna stated firmly. With a heave she threw the bags over the back of the guard's horse, climbing easily into the saddle with only a mild grunt of discomfort at her injured leg. "Your horse will be at the stable in town. I'll get my own from there. I apologize, but you must understand, I do this because I have no other choice."

Her heels dug hard into the horse's sides, signaling it to move, a hard snap of the reins sending it into a gallop. She ignored the protests of the guard behind her. Why wouldn't he be quiet? The sound of his voice would wake everyone in the neighborhood.

A biting chill from the wind whipped through Leyna's hair. She wasn't dressed for a long ride in the current temperatures, but there would be time to worry about warmth later. If the guard's shouts had woken Feolan or Thade, he would direct them to the stables in town. She would have to find a fast way out of the city. The concern lay in the difficulty of getting through the gates. Since the assassination of Prince Enaes, Queen Nesperiti had placed guards at every entrance through the city walls. Check points to investigate the travelers passing through. She feared an attempt on her own life, which Leyna knew was the last thing the Ven'shal would be concerned with. Queen Nesperiti meant nothing to them. The heightened security was only an added headache.

Impatient, Leyna reached the western gates. Keeping close to the city wall, she edged her way toward the entrance, relieved to find the gate easily approachable. At the mention of her name, the guards gave no hesitation to let her in. Sometimes it helped to be important. She couldn't help but smirk to herself as she hurried into the city streets, moving as fast as the horse would allow.

The strain on her injured leg caused the discomfort to slowly turn into a dull ache as she dismounted, securing the horse to a post. She cursed silently to herself as she stepped into the stable. If she wasn't careful, the fracture would be exacerbated, leaving her worthless for several more weeks before she could join the military in any country. Through gritted teeth she gave her order to the stable boy. Her body was frozen from the cold. Jaw clenched to prevent her teeth from chattering. The walls of the barn provided only minimal warmth as she was led over to a chair, awaiting a horse to be brought out for purchase.

Dazed, she stared off into the distance. Everything felt wrong. It was incredible how she'd managed to turn her life upside down within the single hour since waking in Thade's arms. She didn't dare allow her mind to wander over the previous night. Tears threatened to fall, the moisture only adding to the chill already built around the skin of her face. In the chaos of her mind, she wasn't sure which was more painful. The ache in her leg or the thought of Thade waking up to find her gone. Covering her face in her hands she tried to wipe the tears away, replaced by more, coming faster. Hooves clattered across the ground of the stable. Her horse was coming. Now wasn't the time to lose herself in a weeping fit.

Hurriedly, she paid for the animal, wasting no time in climbing onto its back, free of any saddle. She couldn't worry about proper riding etiquette. It wouldn't be long before she was on the road to Carpaen. The weather would be warmer there. With any luck she would be able to travel through the night. If she got off course, it would be in the hands of the gods to take her where she was intended to go.

A line was beginning to form at the gates leading out of the city when she reached them. Nervous with anticipation, Leyna fidgeted, silently urging the guards to move faster. If Feolan and Thade came looking for her, they would be sure to pass this way. She was in danger of being caught until she was beyond the walls and into the mountains. Her familiarity with the area allowed her to maneuver the smaller wooded trails to reach the desert without having to stay on the road. Finding her amidst the trees would be a greater feat. One which she doubted Thade or Feolan would be able to do. Especially not if she managed to get a head start.

Through her scattered thoughts, a voice floated on the breeze, reaching Leyna's ears to send a shiver down her spine which jarred her worse than the cold. It wasn't directed toward her, but she recognized it. Kael. He was nearby. Closer than she was comfortable with. Afraid to look over her shoulder, she kept her head down, face pointed toward the horse's mane. Maybe he hadn't seen her.

There was someone else with him. Another man. That voice was quieter, but distinguishable as that of Oran Bedrick. The words were broken through the noise of the street, but she could make out pieces of what was being spoken between the two men. They were coming from Zander's house. Kyros was waiting for them somewhere. An amulet. Worried about the guards at the gates. Slowly, Leyna lifted her head to peer over her shoulder. She needed to know how far away they were. If they were able to hear her speak when she reached the guards, Kael would take chase. He was the last person she wanted a fight with right now. Not after last night.

Behind her in line she could see a single carriage and two horses separating her from Oran and Kael. Good. It would provide enough of a gap that Leyna could be well down the road before they came after her. Sitting up straight on her horse, she tried to give her most casual smile to the guards. She couldn't let them see the troubled look in her eyes. They would ask questions and stall her. Right now, she needed to get out of the city. Fast.

"State your name."

"Leyna Evantine. Member of Queen Nesperiti's Court."

"Reason for leaving?"

"I am visiting the Emperor's Steward in Carpaen," Leyna stated, her tone hushed. The voices behind her had quieted. The lack of noise in the street was nerve-racking As if everyone around had stopped to listen to her speak. "He is expecting me to arrive as soon as possible. I am in a bit of a rush."

"When will you be returning?"

Leyna lowered her head, exhaling heavily, the fog of her breath billowing in the cold air around her. "In a month's time," she lied.

"Hey!"

Her heart sank in her chest at the shout coming from behind her in line. Casting the guard a desperate look she motioned toward the road ahead. "Am I free to pass? Please?"

"Very well." With a clinking of metal from his armor, the guard stepped out of Leyna's path, clearing the way.

She gave a loud click of her tongue to urge the horse onward. Fingers wrapped tightly in the mane, Leyna leaned forward, picking up speed on the road. Commotion sounded from the gates, shouts echoing through the street. It didn't take long before she was aware of a second set of hooves pounding along the road, quickly gaining on her.

At her side she could see another horse in her peripheral vision, the rider snapping the reins, calling out for it to move faster. "Stop!" Kael ordered. Roughly, he veered toward her, forcing Leyna's horse to step off the road. Focused, she forced her horse to move faster, heels digging into its sides, breaking away from Kael, though only by a few inches. She couldn't focus, the cold air blowing in her face. If she was unable to get away from Kael, her plans would be ruined. He would chase her through the desert if given a chance. She had to think of something, but her thoughts were a jumbled, confusing mess.

Kael was coming up on her side again. Gathering himself, he leapt from the saddle, lunging at Leyna, his body slamming into hers with the force of a ghereac, sending her toppling to the hard ground. Crying out, Leyna felt herself rolling over the grass with Kael's arms wrapped around her, coming to a halt with him on top, pinning her to the ground. "Get off me!" she screamed, rocking her body back and forth, throwing her weight against him to try and break away.

There was no enjoyment in Kael's eyes as he stared down at her, struggling to maintain his grip. "Damir wants you. I'm not missing an opportunity to bring you to him."

On the ground there was little she could do against him. Blaise had taught very little in the way of fighting from her back. It was her biggest downfall in combat. As long as Kael kept her pinned there, she had few options to work with, her legs useless under the weight of his body, arms locked to the ground over her head.

Flashbacks from her last fight with him at the inn did nothing to ease her troubled thoughts. If he took to hitting his head into hers again, it would be over. There was no means for her to defend against it. She needed to keep him distracted. At least until she could think of a way to break free. With a continuous motion she rocked her hips from side to side, dragging them further across the ground as Kael moved to stay on top of her.

From around his neck something glinted in the light. An amulet. The golden chain was thin but sturdy, what looked to be a large medallion hanging from the front. Four gems of a deep blue were situated in a square, set around a larger yellow stone on an otherwise flat surface. It looked old. Well cared for, but wearing from age, the shine from the metal lacking in its polished finish. The gems were the only thing about it which still sparkled in the morning light.

Could it be the amulet Zander spoke of? He never described it. Somehow she hadn't expected to ever see it. And now, for it to be so near. If she could just get her hands away from him, close enough to touch it. To rip the chain from his neck. It was more important than her freedom, on the off chance that it was the real thing; an authentic relic of the ancient Ven'shal. The key to Arcastus's new life.

Renewing her efforts to break her hands from Kael's grasp, she fought hard, but to no avail. He was stronger than she remembered. No doubt empowered by some form of magic she had no knowledge of.

"There is something tragic and beautiful about watching you try to fight against me," he smirked. Leaning his head down, his face hovered just over hers, the stench of his breath invading her nostrils. "I saw it the first time we fought. And you felt it too, so don't tell me you didn't. You wanted to kiss me just as badly as I wanted you. It makes me wonder what would have happened if Mikel hadn't interrupted us."

"Nothing would have happened." She strained against him. Her eyes were focused on the amulet. It dangled, tauntingly, almost lying against her chest.

Easily, he forced her to remain still, the size of his hand enough to cover her slender wrists with one arm, leaving the other free as he stroked the side of her face, the sensation warm, like electricity coursing through his fingertips. "I hate that I still love you," he murmured. Inhaling a breath, he sniffed at the side of her neck, taking in the smell of her skin. "I still want you, even though you reek of that man's bed."

His lips were upon hers. Hot and moist – like some animal mauling her while she was helpless to stop it. In her frenzy to get away she felt her confusion at Kael's words. Did he know about her and Thade? How could he? No one could possibly be aware. It was nothing but Kael's usual jealousy, assuming her relations with Thade to be of a more intimate nature, the way he always did. The difference now was that it was true. But she didn't have to answer to Kael. What she did with anyone was no longer any of his business. Renewing her efforts, she fought against his hold. Desperate to get his mouth away from hers, she forced her lips apart, biting down hard on the flesh of Kael's tongue, his head lifting in pain-filled rage.

"Stop moving!" His free hand came across her face, the palm connecting with a solid smack. Her head reeled at the sting. She couldn't see anything other than the sky overhead, Kael's mouth moving down over her neck, his hand tearing at the loosely tied laces of her bodice. "I don't think you struggled like this against the Consul. If it makes you feel any better, just imagine it's him. You might even enjoy it."

"Who do you think I was envisioning every time you ever touched me?" she spat. There was venom in her tone. It would infuriate him, she knew, to think that he had never been good enough, and while there had been times where she'd allowed herself to enjoy Kael's presence over the years, the underlying truth was undeniable. It was always Thade that she wanted. Kael was nothing but a substitute in her heart for the one thing she thought she could never have.

He stopped moving, the darkness in his eyes flashing wildly as he looked down at her. His chest heaved with every breath. The fury was building, rising up inside him, until he couldn't take it anymore, his hands clawing at her bodice, no longer able to focus on the laces. "You whore!" he shouted. "You made me believe that you loved me!"

"I did love you!" Her hands were free. In his haste to get at her clothes, he forgot about her arms, leaving them unguarded. Even with the feeling of her bodice quickly loosening, all she could think about was the amulet around his neck. She needed to get it. There at his chest, she could see the chain. As her hand reached for it, she saw a moment of panic in Kael's eyes, his upper body shifting away from her, to avoid her grasping hand. He was too slow. Her fingers caught hold of the medallion, cool and hard to the touch. It thrummed with energy unlike anything she'd felt before. Old energy. The power in it was immeasurable to her inexperienced mind, but no knowledge was needed to feel the darkness it contained, to know it was pure evil.

Suddenly, Kael lifted from her, his arms grasping at the medallion still clutched in Leyna's hand. She couldn't maintain her grip. The gems cut through her skin like knives at the force of it being ripped away. A scream came from her lips at the sensation of the pain. Bright light streamed from the medallion, bursting outward to envelope her outstretched arm until it had consumed every inch of her body, wrapping her in a cloak of white energy. A shroud of shadow followed the light, fingerlike tendrils shooting over the surface, unable to penetrate the shield around her, dissipating in a puff of grey smoke.

Quickly, Leyna got to her feet, her progress hindered by the pain in her leg, reminding her of the injury. The impact of her fall had no doubt done damage to the bone, but she didn't care about the discomfort. Something had happened when she touched the relic. The real thing! Damir had foolishly given it to Kael. If he only knew the ways Kael had misled him, he'd have been struck down, yet instead, he was rewarded for his errors by being given the most potent piece of the puzzle they needed to succeed in their ridiculous war.

The expression on Kael's face told her he was aware of the mistake he'd made. In coming there, he jeopardized everything he was working toward. Quickly, he struggled to regain his composure, a mask of confidence over his uncertainty. "I wish I knew why Damir insists he be the one to take your life," he snapped, tucking the amulet into his shirt, protectively. "If it wasn't for that, I would kill you right here and now, instead of playing games trying to bring you in alive."

"You are nothing but talk, Kael," she replied. "Even now, you barely contain your own fear. I think, deep down, you know you cannot win. Damir will fail and you will fall with him."

"You talk tougher when you aren't lying on your back." The smirk on his face was insufferable. Angered, Leyna moved forward, her hand balled into a fist, knuckles colliding hard with his left eye. In a fit of rage Kael pushed her back, snatching her arms in his hands, the tips of his fingernails digging deep into the skin. She tried to hold her ground but he was too strong. Her body slammed hard against the trunk of a wide tree. The collision was unexpected, causing Leyna's head to snap backward into the rough bark. Stars spun around her head at the impact. While the pain didn't quite register in her mind, she couldn't escape the vertigo.

Her hands came up reflexively to fight against his grip. She needed to get away from him. It was foolish for her to have struck at him once she'd managed to get to her feet. That had been her chance to escape. To find her horse and get to it before Kael could come for her again. It was too late now. She would have to create a new opening if she wanted to get away.

Oh, how she wished she was a better fighter! In her mind she saw everything she should be doing, to free herself from his grasp, still held in his clutches against the tree. Envisioning it wasn't enough. The openings were there, but she lacked the strength and skill to reach them.

During the war, she never stopped to think about whether or not she could or couldn't achieve the upper hand in the fight. She just went for it. This was no different from that. What was there to lose in trying? Her fingers curled, her hand pulling back. A hard strike to the nose was all she needed. If she could lift her arm enough.

An exasperated curse erupted from Kael at the feeling of her palm slamming against the bridge of his nose. He stumbled backward. This was her chance. Wild with panic Leyna limped, pain racing up her leg with every step. She could see her horse. It wasn't far. If she could just get to it before Kael recovered his senses.

The horse reared back nervously at Leyna's hasty approach, almost striking her with its front hooves. Stepping back, she waited for it to settle, lightly offering her hand out, hushing it in soothing tones. She could hear Kael's footsteps. Content that the horse wouldn't jerk away from her touch, Leyna grabbed onto its mane, swinging her leg over its back, already in motion before she was settled in place. It wouldn't take long for Kael to find his own mount and take chase again. Continuing on the road was out of the question. Although she hated the thought of returning to her house, it was the only thing she could do. Fighting Kael alone wasn't possible. She had no weapon and the injury to her leg would only weaken her more. The guard would be an extra pair of hands to fend him off until she could find a better means of protecting herself.

She could already see the fork in the road which led toward her house. Images of all the horrible outcomes of her return flashed before her eyes, sickening her. She could picture Thade running out into the street after her, unarmed. Kael brandishing his sword. She would be powerless to stop a fight between them.

No. She wouldn't let it happen. Thade wouldn't allow himself to be taken down so easily. And what if he had already left to look for her? He and Feolan might already be in the city, unaware that she had long since left.

Her heart ached as she rode past Thade's house. To her surprise, the front door was standing open. At the speed she moved, it was impossible to see if anyone was within, but she couldn't focus on Thade right now. Her house was getting closer. Relieved, she could see the guard stationed outside the door. Running up to meet her on the horse, he helped her to the ground, calling after her as she rushed out of his reach, eyes locked on the door. She'd left her sword inside. If she was going to have any chance at fighting Kael, she would need a weapon.

Through the reflection in the front window she could see Kael leaping from his horse behind her. Frantic, she tried to move faster. Why did her leg have to hurt so badly? Dragging it, she stumbled forward, hands reaching for the door. A hard yank on her hair caused her to snap to a halt, crumpling to the uneven ground. She barely rolled out of the way in time, Kael's foot stomping down, grinding on the dirt where Leyna had been only moments before.

Climbing back to her feet she could see the guard grab Kael's shoulder, distracting him, though only briefly. With a gruff shove Kael forced the man back, moving after Leyna once again. His hands grabbed onto her neck, firmly lifting her into the air. She screamed, arms flailing about in her attempts to get away. The weightlessness of her position was frightening. She wanted down. There was no way for her to strike him successfully.

Suddenly, Leyna felt herself flying through the air. Splintering wood surrounded her as she collided with the front door, coming to land over the remnants of the shattered fragments. Kael was on her again, picking her up to throw her against the desk in the front room of the house, causing it to slide with a loud scrape across the floor. She was desperate for anything to use against him, but at least she was standing again. Grasping at the vase on the desk she threw it toward Kael, the glass breaking upon impact with his arms.

Across the room near the window Leyna could see her sword leaning against the wall, sheathed in its scabbard. Her eyes came to rest on it just as Kael followed her gaze, both of them running toward it. Leyna was closer, but hindered by her injured gait, the two reaching the wall at the same time, crashing into the window above. Glass fell to the floor around them in jagged pieces. Seeing the opportunity, Leyna reached for one of the broken sections still in the frame. She wrapped her hand around it, paying no attention to the pain as the edges sliced through her palm. Snapping it free, she pierced the tip into Kael's shoulder, her own pained cries filling the room, blood pouring from her hand over the smooth surface of the glass, a thick crimson color spilling forth to stain Kael's shirt from the wound she inflicted on him in the process.

Blinded by his desire for revenge, Kael attacked through the pain. The glass remained in his shoulder, Leyna's hand knocked away by his swinging arms. With a few quick movements he swept her legs out from under her, both of them skidding along the hard wood floor, Kael on top, a maniacal laugh bellowing from him. "I don't have any more time to play these games, *Leyna.*" He spat the name, his disgust evident. "Haven't we done this enough for you to realize you can't win against me?"

Leyna flinched at the sight of her guard appearing over Kael's shoulder, brandishing a wide fragment of wood left from the door, bringing it down hard over Kael's head. It broke into smaller pieces, shards flying in every direction, Kael's body slumping forward with a pained grunt. The guard lifted him from atop Leyna, a loud crash echoing through the room where Kael was flung through the window, landing outside on the street. The guard wasted no time in following after him, the sound of their fight continuing, distant to Leyna's ears. Her head was swimming. For a moment she could breathe, taking in the chaos around her. The room was in shambles.

From the open doorway Leyna could hear someone speaking, the sound coming closer. Rising on her elbows she tried to focus on the man coming toward her. "Leyna, are you alright?" Feolan's voice was small and hollow. He looked wretched.

What a sight she must be to him! He was already helping her to her feet, looking her over carefully in search of injuries. Blood stained the front of her dress and continued to flow freely from the laceration on her hand. At the sight of it Feolan tore at his own shirt, ripping a piece of the fabric to create a bandage for the wound. "Is he still outside?" Leyna gasped, peering through the window to see what had become of Kael. In the distance she could see a horse disappearing down the road, her guard slowly making his way back toward the house.

"He would be a fool to attack again with three of us against him. I think you're safe for now," Feolan nodded, gently holding her arms to stare into her eyes. "Are you alright? Where were — what did he do?"

"I do not want to think about what he did or did not do. Please," Leyna sighed. The tension in her muscles finally began to ease, her shoulders sinking with exhaustion. "Thank you for coming. I was afraid everyone would be asleep."

"I have not slept." Feolan lowered his hand away from her. Hesitant. Something continued to trouble him. "I was waiting for you to come speak with me after you left the Consul's home last night, but as it turns out, you did not."

He'd been watching for her? Why did everyone suddenly take such an interest in her doings? But then — she had to wonder — why did she care? It was irritating before, but never had it made her quite so uncomfortable and angry as she felt now. *Maybe because this time you are guilty.* She hoped Feolan wouldn't see the confession there in her eyes.

He looked ready to speak, but remained silent. His hand slid into the pocket of his vest, drawing out a somewhat wrinkled piece of parchment, a hardened wax seal over the edge sending a shiver through Leyna's spine. The royal seal. Her birth certificate? Had he retrieved it from Thade somehow?

"You are an adult and free to make your own decisions, but I fear that even you have no idea what fire you play with." Holding the parchment up, Leyna realized the seal was unbroken. The wax was brighter than the document uncovered from that dusty drawer in Mialan. "I would not question your meeting with him last night, were it not for the fact that he told me his only intention was to give you this letter and bid you farewell. As the letter was not in your possession this morning, I am sure you can see where that makes things rather curious."

"There was much to discuss —"

"I spoke with him, Leyna. There is no need to deny anything. I do not judge."

Her face burned, flushed with color at what Feolan knew. A nagging feeling tickled the back of her thoughts. Thade told him? Surely, Thade was aware that she'd snuck away while he slept, and yet he did not come looking for her? With a grimace, she clutched her chest, eyes averted from Feolan's scrutinizing gaze.

Why did she care? The whole reason she slipped away was so she wouldn't have to face Thade to say her goodbyes. So why did it hurt her so badly that it had worked?

"Leyna," Feolan said quietly, his hand hovering over her arm, unsure of whether or not he should touch her. "I know what must be in your head, but I assure you that he is thinking of you. It is my fault he is not here right now. I practically had to chain him to the seat of the carriage to get him to leave. As it turns out, he was under the impression he was not returning to Tanispa this morning."

"He has gone?"

"Yes. The guards saw the carriage off not long before I saw you ride past his door."

The pain already building in her heart increased. Why did she have to be so foolish? They could have been together, even now, riding off to find a priest. Instead, she had to be responsible. For the first time in her life she'd given in and done something reckless, and she now had to live with the regret that she gave it up, but only after she'd done just enough for it to haunt her forever.

"I see," she whispered. What more was there to say? The last thing she wanted right now was a lecture from Feolan about why what she and Thade did was wrong. She knew that already. Her own conscience was hard enough on her without Feolan's help.

"Do you have any idea of the repercussions you would have faced if he had not returned to Tanispa?" Feolan asked suddenly. It was not what Leyna expected. "You could have been considered a traitor. The Queen would have been within her rights to have you executed in order to guarantee his presence at court. While she has never been the type to rule at such an extreme of force, there are other punishments you could have endured, and that truth is the only reason he agreed to go instead of coming to find you this morning."

"Perhaps you are missing the fact that I left because I recognized the importance of his duties in Tanispa," she sighed in defeat. "I could not let myself become the same evil creature you and Thade claimed women to be during the war. He told me then that I would turn into that one day, but I never intended... I never thought I would do that to him."

Feolan took her uninjured hand in his, pressing the parchment against her palm. "It's the ones who do not purposely use their charms that are the most dangerous. I must admit, your charms nearly reeled me in as well, at one time. Knowing what I know now, had it been Thade who kissed you that day at Malic's, things would have been much different."

Blinking in disbelief, Leyna snapped a glance at Feolan. "I am confused. How did I nearly reel you in? Your words do not make sense."

"Oh, Leyna," he chuckled, shaking his head. "You are a beautiful woman. I knew the night I saw you at the masque that Thade was in trouble. I was swept up in the surprise at seeing you – the way you had changed, and grown – it is surprising that a young man like him was able to hold his feelings back for so long. And you know," the soft chortle grew into an awkward laugh. "When you and Zander left that first night, he let it be known he was not pleased that I had kissed you. I knew then to give up any foolish ideas."

"That explains a lot, I suppose. Maeri came to me and asked about the two of us. Whether or not there was anything between us. It seemed so strange at the time, but I assured her there was nothing. I am sorry if I caused you any trouble. I had no idea…"

Feolan motioned for her to stop. "I love my wife. Nothing I felt toward you was ever more than fleeting. Do not fear that there was ever any awkwardness to it. Once we left Tanispa from the masque, my head cleared, and I was reminded of who you were. You and Thade have always been like my own adopted children. It is trivial and unimportant now." He tapped the parchment in her hand curiously. "This letter comes from Queen Vorsila. You may want to open it."

Distracted by the talk of Thade, the envelope had slipped her mind. She made her way over to the crooked desk, prying gently at the wax, afraid of damaging the letter. It was tedious work, but finally the edge pulled away and she drew the folds back. While she read over the elegant calligraphic script, she felt something sting at her shoulder, wincing in pain, to find Feolan standing behind her with a bloody shard of glass in his hand.

"You will need stitches, I believe."

"I am too busy for that," Leyna frowned. She waved dismissively at him. It was too much to take in at once. First the night with Thade, then Kael's attack, Feolan's lectures, and now this. Queen Vorsila requested her presence in Tanispa? What could she possibly want with her?

Fear threatened to send her into a panic at the possibilities which came to mind. Did she blame her for Enaes's death? But it wasn't her fault. She knew that. Thade had been the one to relay the news to the Queen. He wouldn't have placed any blame on her, would he? And worse, with her actions of the past night, what if Vorsila found out about what Leyna had done? Would she be held accountable? Tried for treason the way Feolan spoke? With a grimace she closed the parchment, rising from the desk in a stiff motion, favoring her injured leg. She had no choice but to go and face whatever consequences there were. The Queen had summoned her. To refuse would only make things worse.

"When first I left this morning, my intentions were to find my way to Carpaen. It would seem the gods are diverting my path."

Feolan gazed at her, the solemn expression steady on his face. "Carpaen?"

"I am worthless here in Siscal," Leyna frowned. "As a member of court, military service under Queen Nesperiti's army would be difficult to achieve. And though Zander chose to enlist under the General in Tanispa, I could not very well go to the same country where Thade will be. It would only cause more trouble. Carpaen seemed the most likely place to settle. The Emperor's Steward is an old friend of mine. He could have been called upon to assist in placing me among the ranks there to fight against our enemies. Now, even more than before, I have no choice but to leave Siscal. Kael knows where I stay and he will tell Kyros. He claims Damir wants me brought to him. This tells me that the attack this morning, while unexpected, only foreshadows more to come."

"I wish there was something I could say which might change your mind, but I know well enough that it would be useless to try." Feolan shook his head, motioning for Leyna to sit. Taking his direction she lowered herself onto the chair once again, allowing him to inspect the cut on her shoulder. "If you insist on leaving this instant to meet with the Queen, at least allow me to stitch your wounds and see that you are properly tended. Your hand will infect quickly if we do not at least get it cleaned. I will have you know, however, that I am not keen on letting you make the journey alone. At least allow a guard to accompany you."

Leyna chuckled miserably to herself. She was tired of guards. Tired of being watched over like a child. How would it look to Queen Vorsila if she arrived in Tanispa with someone looking over her shoulder? Appearances were too important among her own people. And Leyna was far too proud to allow the Queen to think her weak. "I will concede to your assistance with the wounds, but as for accompaniment, I must decline," she stated calmly. Her mind was made up. Nothing Feolan could argue would make her consider differently. "Kael and Oran were on their way to meet Kyros, from what I understood. They will be distracted for now. By the time they are even aware of my having left Siscal, I will already be across the Tanispan border."

"Very well," Feolan nodded. "We must hurry to my home to gather the things I need to tend your injuries. Maeri will want to see you as well. All I ask is that you promise to be careful, Leyna. The threat of war is all around us. No country is safe. Especially for you."

"Trust me, I know. I have considered it already and will be on my guard," she smiled. It was the smallest gesture she could think of to provide any comfort to Feolan. He would worry about her no matter what she said and guarantees of safety were impossible to offer. Fear clutched tightly around her heart but she had to push through it. She couldn't let her emotions ruin her chances at defeating Damir. Next time they attacked, she would be ready for them. And Kael wouldn't get away so easily.

Chapter Twenty-Five

It felt strange to be back in Tanispa. Years had passed since the last time she saw Sivaeria, the countryside bringing back memories of her days with Faustine. She slowed her pace as she rode her horse into the courtyard of the palace, not wanting to set off the guards, knowing they would be on alert for an attack. One couldn't be too cautious when it came to the Queen.

A taller Vor'shai man in a military fashion doublet stood near the entry gate, the deep burnt umber glow from his eyes watching Leyna curiously as she passed. With every step her horse took toward the palace doors, he moved in closer, following her, his movements like those of a large stalking mountain cat. She could see him approaching out of the corner of her eye. Not wanting to create a scene, she brought the horse to a halt, dismounting carefully to avoid tearing her skirt.

"What is your business here, miss?" As he came nearer, his eyes scanned every part of her. He was looking for weapons. She could tell by the way his gaze lingered where knives and swords might possibly be concealed, nodding in approval to find her noticeably unarmed.

She dipped into a formal curtsy before him, favoring the tired and aching leg which had grown stiff and sore from the long ride. "My name is Leyna Evantine. I come on request of Queen Vorsila. In the satchel on my horse you will find the letter with Her Majesty's seal, if validation of my word is required."

Upon hearing her name, the man stepped in closer, his gaze more scrutinizing than before. It was an uncomfortable feeling. He presented himself with an air of nobility and power, though the sword at his side — and the dagger hidden in a small sheath around his boot — looked more like a fighter. Military perhaps. Of very high rank, judging by the exquisite detail of the scabbard on his hip. The gemstones adorning it glittered in the sunlight, matching the gold lining of his doublet.

The doublet resembled that which Thade had worn the day he came to Siscal to say his goodbyes. But she couldn't think about him right now. Blood already started to flush a pink hue into her cheeks.

"*The* Leyna Evantine, hmm? From the stories I have heard, I always pictured you to be... sturdier."

"Sturdier – Sir?"

"Much larger than you are," he nodded with a smirk. "How ever did a frail feminine figure like yours survive three poisoned arrows?"

"Do not let my appearance fool you, sir. I may be slight, but my will is strong. You might be amazed at what that can do for a person when the impossible is put before them."

He held her steady gaze in silence for a moment before giving one last approving nod. Stepping back, he pressed his right hand over his abdomen, bowing to her respectfully. "General Cadell of the Queen's Royal Army. I was beginning to think Leyna Evantine was a myth, after all these years of elusion. It is an honor to make your acquaintance." With a sharp snap of his fingers he signaled for Leyna to rise. "I will announce your arrival to Her Majesty."

As she stood up, she was aware of the other guards around the grounds eyeing her curiously. There weren't quite so many men stationed around the gates when she last visited. It was like a small military fort between where she stood and the road.

Keeping up with Cadell's long, fluid strides proved a difficult task for Leyna's hindered gait. Occasionally, he would come to a stop, never looking back at her, merely waiting for the sound of her footsteps to grow closer before resuming his march forward.

Following the General inside, Leyna noticed the palace halls to be devoid of the crowds that had clogged them the night of the masque. Only a few courtiers wandered about, lost in their own affairs, oblivious to Leyna as she limped through the high-arched front doors and into the brilliantly lit foyer. The vaulted ceiling loomed elegantly overhead with its extravagant chandeliers.

Outside a massive gilded door, Cadell motioned for her to wait, disappearing inside. Her heart was racing, almost painfully, unsure of what to expect when he returned, afraid of being instantly grappled by strong arms, and dragged off to a cell in the darkest and dankest prison.

Time dragged by in the silence of the empty hallway. Nervously, Leyna fidgeted, nibbling on her lower lip, fingers clenching and unclenching. By the time Cadell reappeared, she had worked herself into a panic, nearly fainting in fear of his possible impending assault. She closed her eyes, bracing herself.

Cadell was a very intimidating man. It was no wonder he was in charge of arguably the greatest military in the world. Every strand of his long brown hair was perfectly held in place, showing off his sharp features and distinctly pointed ears. His muscles were well-defined even while concealed under the flattering shape of his doublet, broad shouldered; well-built for a man of their race, which tended to be more slender than most. His outward appearance, even at peace, screamed power to everyone around him. She was afraid to see what he was like on the battlefield.

The sound of his footsteps came to a stop in front of her. He said nothing. At his lack of communication, she forced herself to open her eyes, finding him staring at her, amused. "You look as though you expect to be maimed."

"If you only knew the week I have had…" Embarrassed, she shook her head, deciding against speaking any further. She was more curious about what he had to say of Queen Vorsila's decision to meet with her. The letter had not specified a time. Given the Queen's busy schedule, Leyna feared the meeting would be put off until another day.

"Well, it would seem your luck has changed," he said. His tone perpetually sounded vaguely sarcastic, yet deep and monotone. With another snap of his fingers he motioned for Leyna to move. Like some animal trained to obey the gesture, Leyna followed at his heels through the imposing door. She struggled to conceal her limp. It would never do to let them see her injury if she had any hope of convincing them to let her join the military there.

Queen Vorsila's proud form at the head of the room took Leyna's breath away. Just as she'd been at the masque those years ago, power radiated from her, even at this distance, though no mask shielded her regal features from view this time. Her lips were painted a deep shade of red, a dramatic effect against the pale, flawless white of her skin. The silver in her eyes shone like diamonds from her doll-like face, giving the appearance of a porcelain statue, erect, waiting, vigilant for whatever might cross her path. She was dressed in a heavy gown of black damask fabric hanging in delicate folds to the floor from her slender waist. The black pearls adorning her nearly translucent complexion told Leyna that she was still dressed in her mourning attire, a rim of redness visible along the edge of her eyes as Leyna approached.

Respectfully, Leyna lowered herself to the ground in a deep curtsy, her eyes diverted away from Vorsila's.

"Your Majesty, I present to you the Lady Leyna Evantine." Cadell's voice was surreal to Leyna, speaking her name with such authority, as if she were of some great significance. It made her want to laugh out of pity for herself, though her nerves prevented it.

"So this is the woman I hear so much about? You are quite right, General. Much more petite than I expected." Her voice was like silk, every syllable of the old Vor'shai language rolling from her lips, soft and dulcet, yet somehow commanding of attention. "Stop groveling like a peasant girl. Stand up so I can take a look at you."

The train of Vorsila's gown trailed along behind her as she moved gracefully down the stairs to circle around Leyna, inspecting her. Leyna tried to maintain her standing posture. Lack of poise would be displeasing to the Queen, and she needed to look perfect.

Cadell took a position near the steps where Vorsila had descended, arms folded, back straight. Leyna felt on display for them both, the way they stared at her, curious, judging. When Vorsila reached the stairs again, she kept her chin jutted out proudly. "So calling you here was all I needed to do in order to get you to creep out of the shadows? Not that word could have reached you, the way you were being hidden away from us. And do not think I am not aware that we were being toyed with in regards to your whereabouts."

"Your Majesty, I assure you the fault is entirely mine —"

"Hush, dear, do not lie to me," Vorsila raised her hand sternly. "It is noble of you to try and take the blame, but the culprit has admitted the deed to me. He and I had a very long discussion on the matter."

Her heart jerked in her chest at the thought. Thade admitted to the Queen that he intentionally misled them? Was that why they called him back? She remembered her thoughts after Thade informed her of Enaes's search for her. His desire for marriage. The deed was traitorous. She couldn't bear the thought of him being punished because of her.

"I must beg of you to pardon him," she pleaded. In desperation, she sank back down to her knees, bowing low at Vorsila's feet. "I will endure any punishment in his stead, as it is only because of me that he thought to do such a thing."

Vorsila looked down her nose at Leyna. The corner of her mouth twitched as if to smile, though it faded before it could fully mature. "Punishment?" she laughed, a sound like chimes ringing in a gentle wind. "Child, I would not punish him. I cannot blame him. I loved my son as dearly as I loved all of my children, but it was not unknown to me how foolish Enaes was. I dreaded the day some poor unsuspecting woman would be bound to him. He needed a lady who was not smart enough to see through him. If I *were* to pair you with one of my son's, it would have been his brother. You are far more suited to him, I think."

His brother? The young Prince? He would be heir to the throne now – and under great pressure to choose a wife, to save the dying Levadis line. *Oh gods...* What if that was what she intended this meeting for?

Uncomfortable with the thought, Leyna rose slowly to her feet, straightening the fabric of her dress out of nervousness. Her eyes remained downcast. "So the Consul is not being punished for it?"

"The Consul?"

"Yes, Consul Imri."

"Imri?" Vorsila pondered. "Ah, yes, of course. The Consul. Former, now. But no, I would not punish him. He has been punished enough, I believe. I do say, he speaks very highly of you. Were he anything like my poor Enaes, I might be inclined to think that you had him under some sort of witchcraft. Or already had your claws scratched into his back." She paused to look Leyna over carefully, watching every tiny detail of her face. "But you are not that kind of girl, I hope."

Vorsila's eyes burned into her, calm, waiting for a response. Leyna shuddered to realize the hidden meaning behind Vorsila's words. She swallowed hard, thinking of that last night with Thade, lost in the passion. But it was not a deed like so many women had done with Enaes. It wasn't a quest for power, or hunger for a lift in status by finding her way into his bed. They intended marriage. And it pained her to think of the love she still carried for him in her heart. "I am not, Your Majesty," she replied quietly. "The Consul and I were very dear friends, but I would not let myself come between him and his duty to you and our people."

"Why does it pain you so to speak of him?"

Leyna inhaled deeply, her eyes meeting Vorsila's, heart racing. "I beg your pardon?"

"Oh, please," Vorsila waved dismissively. "Your broken heart is practically palpable. It all but bleeds on my floor. Tell me, Evantine. Was it really me you came here to see, or did you travel all this way in hopes of catching a glimpse of his face?"

Seeing him? The thought never crossed her mind, though it set her heart on fire to consider the possibility. He would be at court. It was reasonable to think that he could, even now, be somewhere within the palace, standing in the same maze of hallways that she traveled to reach this throne room. But she could honestly say that he wasn't her purpose in coming there. Her purpose lay in the hands of Vorsila and Cadell.

"In truth, I came here in hopes of requesting something of Your Majesty."

Brow raised in curiosity, Vorsila stepped back to stand at Cadell's side, arms folded over her chest. "Something of me? Do share, then. Your personality intrigues me, so I will indulge myself in hearing your request."

Straightforward felt the best approach with a woman like the Queen. "I came to beg entry into your forces against the Ven'shal."

A sparkle flashed in Cadell's eyes at Leyna's words. He and Vorsila glanced between each other, her expression thoughtful. Contemplative of the idea. Leyna hoped it was a good sign.

"To clarify, I assume by 'forces,' you refer to General Zerne's men?"

"That is correct, Your Majesty. I desire to serve in your military endeavors to fight those whom surely plot against our country as we speak."

"What do you think, General? You have the floor to speak with the woman, if you like."

Cadell stepped forward, his sharp features hardened as he looked her over once again the way he had upon her arrival. "You have prior military experience, from what I hear?"

"I do, sir."

"Trained at the academy in Carpaen before that?"

Surprised by his knowledge of her past, Leyna nodded to him. Enaes had done his research well – though she wondered now if he had sent certain others to do some of the work for him, if not all of it.

Boldly reaching for the neck of her dress, Cadell tugged downward on the lace, revealing the scar there for Vorsila to see. "Your Majesty. This mark here is the reason your son lived. That kind of loyalty and service cannot be taught. Not even my best men have had opportunity to show it the way this woman has. She certainly has potential."

"Well, then," Vorsila shrugged. "I do say, though, I have never before witnessed a duchess serving in the military."

"Duchess, Your Majesty?" Leyna blinked at her in confusion.

"Yes," Vorsila stated plainly. "I had requested you to come here in order to properly bestow upon you the title which is rightfully yours through birth. I was recently shown documentation which verified the family heritage my son searched for so diligently over the years. Upon the death of your father, the one Aviden Diah, his properties and titles fall to the hands of his children. As further records show that the heir of Count Iden Evantine and the Duke of Escovul were rightfully married at the time of your birth, by right, you are his first born, regardless of this terrible scandal."

"But what of his daughter, Maeri Diah?"

"What of her? She is married to my Consul. Her rank is secure in his," Vorsila glanced over to Cadell, clearly amused by something. "My law and word is final, and the title has been passed to you. Though, if the military is your wish, we may be able to work something out. I think it might even be beneficial if the new Duchess of Escovul kept a low profile in the public eye for a period of time."

All Leyna could think of was Thade. He was the only person who could have passed any of this information to the Queen. It explained the reason he conveniently continued to forget returning the birth certificate to her. It was no accident he wandered off with it the night she found it in Mialan. His intention was always to bring it to the Queen and restore her name. She wanted to be angry about it, but the shock was too great to break through.

"I still do not understand," she shook her head, confused by Vorsila's words. "You said that Count Iden's daughter and the Duke were married at the time I was born. That cannot be accurate. Sarayi Evantine was the wife of Damir Rohld."

Cadell chuckled, his hands folding firmly behind his back as he turned to face Vorsila. The Queen smiled at him, her expression shifting to Leyna in a look of sympathy. "You poor child. He said you were a bit lost to it all."

"Lost to what, Your Majesty?"

"The truth," she said. "That helpful little document listed the name of a priest I happen to know quite well. He was more willing to discuss the matter than the Count. He was the one who married your parents. It was quite the scandal. No wonder your grandfather sought to cover it all up, not that it will save him when I have the time to deal with the matter. His daughter was married when she exchanged vows to that traitor Rohld. The bond was null and void. The priest admitted to a bit of tampering to get the divorce through when the Duke was set to marry the mother of his next child. None of this matters, of course. You should not concern yourself with it. These crimes do not reflect on you. The question now is… what to do with you."

The silence in the spacious room was a deafening roar to Leyna's ears, awaiting Vorsila's decision. A title meant nothing to her. She couldn't defeat Damir by gallivanting around at court with some flashy position and grand estate somewhere in the country.

Motioning for Cadell to come closer, Vorsila leaned in to whisper something to him, the words spoken between them inaudible to Leyna. When they finally stepped apart, Vorsila turned her stern gaze to Leyna, the elegant features devoid of any expression. "Cadell has an opening for a new Captain that we have yet to fill. He is willing to extend the position to you, under a few stipulations."

"Captain?" Leyna gasped. "Your Majesty, I do not think —"

"Are you going to reject his offer? He is not likely to make it again and an insult such as that could result in his dismissal of your request altogether."

Leyna glanced over to Cadell, shaking her head quickly. "No – no, I am not rejecting it. I simply… was not expecting anything of that… caliber. To be honest, I feared outright rejection."

"Young lady, I owe you my son's life. You have my eternal gratitude," Vorsila replied, her tone calm, revealing a hint of the sadness that Leyna could see hidden in the depths of her silvery eyes. "I am being more open and generous than I would to any other woman in your position. Consider this a test. I will let you know when I feel you have shown enough. Now are you ready to hear the conditions or shall we end the negotiations?"

"I am listening, Your Majesty." She was flattered by the Queen's seeming affection. But she spoke of gratefulness in saving her son, when it was also she who failed to protect him. Did she not know about her presence at the time of Enaes's death?

With a quick gesture, Vorsila signaled Cadell to step forward.

"You will dedicate every waking moment to your training with me over the next few months," he stated. His tone made it clear there was no room to compromise. "When you are ready, I will introduce you to the troops. Until then, you are to be invisible unless you are directed otherwise by either myself or Her Majesty. No one at court is to know of your military status. Do you understand me?"

"Yes, sir."

"And last but not least," he glanced over to Vorsila, acknowledging her with a respectful nod before continuing. "For the time, you are not to be anywhere near Her Majesty's son. Do not speak to him, do not look at him, and by whatever means possible, keep enough distance between you both that communication is not even considered. Your association and known identity with our enemies makes you a danger. We cannot risk the last remaining heir to the throne being killed in any crossfire aimed at you. Are we clear?"

"I am, sir — but what if he approaches me? Would it not be uncouth, to say the least, for me to ignore him?"

"These orders come from Her Majesty. Her word stands above any other order you receive. If he approaches… you walk away. Leave the aftermath to us."

"As you command, sir. Your Highness," she bowed to Cadell, turning to dip into a low curtsy before the Queen.

She could barely contain her excitement. Her plan had worked! She was in, if she could master the training Cadell challenged her with. It would be nothing like the regiment in Siscal. There was no doubt in her mind about that.

"Then the matter is done," Vorsila nodded. "And not a moment too soon. I have other business I must attend to. I leave the poor girl in your hands, General."

Bowing to her, Cadell snapped to attention, waiting for Vorsila to return to her seat on the throne before moving to usher Leyna out of the room. Their progress was halted by the sudden sound of Vorsila's voice ringing through the air after them.

"And General — do see to it that one of our physicians takes a look at that limp of hers. Those doctors in Siscal are quite lacking. We cannot have our Captain hobbling about like an invalid."

"Of course, Your Majesty," Cadell agreed, looking Leyna over with a smirk. "Come, girl. Let us get you out of that dress." He paused with a wink, stepping in front of her to leave her staring after him in confusion. "No Captain of mine is going to be caught prancing about in women's clothing on my watch. I will have you fitted while we wait for the doctor to arrive."

"Focus!" Cadell shouted, his hands moving in quick succession. Jab, cross, hook, his feet gliding over the floor to push Leyna back. His fighting prowess was above any other Leyna had seen before. Speed and timing, not to mention his impeccable technique, made him a force to be reckoned with. It amazed her that she somehow continued to stand toe-to-toe with him in their current bout, though she could only assume he was going easy on her.

Block and counter. Never be pushed back. That was easy for him to say. He was built like a rock.

They traded strikes back and forth, Leyna's hands aiming for the points Cadell had taught her to focus on. Always a vital or vulnerable target. If the technique used didn't serve to end the fight in some way, then it was a waste of time and energy. He stayed close to her, his lead foot maintaining constant contact with hers, either in front or behind. When she shifted her stance, he moved with her, never losing his point of contact.

Finally breaking through her guard, Cadell caught her arm as she threw a punch, gripping it between his hands at her wrist and just below her elbow. A hard jerk startled her, breaking her focus, Cadell's hands moving forward rapidly. They paused at the last second, his knuckles aimed at her throat while his other hand tangled into her hair, rendering her effectively helpless.

"What went wrong? Do you know?"

"I hesitated, sir," she replied calmly.

Cadell nodded in agreement, his hand releasing her hair. "You are a skilled fighter, and over the past few weeks I have seen you improve immeasurably," he stated. "Most of your opponents will not be an issue for you. I have faith that you are capable of cutting through them effortlessly. My concern is for the more seasoned warriors, and trust me, they will have a few. It is inevitable. Even the weakest armies will have a few gems."

Taking her arm, Cadell repositioned Leyna as she had been before he closed in on her for the win. He gripped her wrist and forearm in his hands, the look in his eyes questioning and intense. Leyna understood. "I should have come in with my free hand. With your arms down, your head is open," she said.

"Possibly, but it could be a false opening," he nodded. "Look at the rest of my body. There are a few things which work to your disadvantage in this position. Can you tell me what they all are?"

"You have control of it," she frowned. Her eyes scanned over his hold on her, discouraged.

At her statement, he shifted his grip on her forearm to just over her elbow, the application of pressure there causing her to double forward, guided by his every whim. "That is one thing, yes. If I have a hold on you, chances are great that I will not give you an opportunity to take another strike. From here I could easily finish you. You're off balance, unable to kick or sweep, and your free hand is now out of range for defense. Freedom is not impossible, but difficult." He allowed her back up, repositioning his hands to their original placement. "What did I do which caused you to hesitate?"

The match played over in her mind, vivid in detail. She remembered that brief second of disorientation. "You did something. I flinched," she mused. It was simple, now that she thought about it. Nothing more than a mere tug on her arm, but executed in a way that blocked her mind from recognizing what was happening until it was too late.

"Very good," he smiled. "You can disrupt the thought process of your opponent. A simple, sharp, and precise pull or strike can take them out of their thoughts, breaking their focus for that split second, which is all you need to get in and finish it. But there is one final thing at this point, and a few points prior even, that you failed to take note of."

"Other than my arm?" She peered at him, quizzical. There was nothing else that stood out to her. He nodded, a knowing smirk gradually forming over his lips. At her continued confusion, his front leg snapped into motion near her foot, her eyes opening wide in shock at the sudden lurching sensation as her body fell backward, a simple buckling of her knee sending her crashing to the floor with a dull thud.

Staring up at the ceiling in a daze, Cadell's face appeared in her vision. His hand extended out to help her up. "Watch my feet. Just because I am using them to stand on does not mean I cannot use them to put you off yours." His strength alone picked her up off her back, her feet positioned in front of him again. He slid his foot forward into his stance, demonstrating where she had gone wrong. "My leg is set here for a few purposes, all of which are intentional," he nodded. "The knee is turned in to protect the groin, and my foot is slightly hooked behind yours. This gives me control over your leg that you most likely are not thinking about. I can sweep your foot, or check your knee, or both. Either way, you are going down."

"Has anyone ever told you that you're a very frightening man?" Leyna chuckled, moving away before he could take her down again.

"You do not become the General of the Royal Army by being a pushover," he chortled softly. "However, you hold your own against me better than most. I am impressed, to be honest. The last time I had a pupil that learned as quickly as you I believe was when the young Thade came under my tutelage. One of the best men I have had the pleasure of training. A few more months, and you might give him a run for his money."

Leyna concealed a grimace at the mention of Thade's name. Almost a month had passed for her in Tanispa and there remained no sign of him. Not that any free time had been granted since her acceptance into Cadell's ranks. She'd spent no time at all in her chambers at court. Arrangements were made to have Reina found and brought to the rooms for protection while Leyna took refuge in the Captain's Quarters of the barracks. Upon waking each morning, she was met by Cadell, spending the day, apart from lunch and dinner, in training. The thought of seeking Thade out never crossed her mind.

"The last time I saw him fight, he took down his opponent with incredible ease," Leyna smiled through her misery at the thought of Thade's easy victory over Kael. The calculated strikes he'd utilized reminded her now of Cadell's methods, unlike any of the techniques they taught during her time with the Siscalian military. It came as no surprise to her that Cadell's men were as feared and respected as they were.

He took note of the change in her demeanor, the smile fading from his face. A glass of water sat on a small table near the wall, his hand motioning toward it, glancing to Leyna inquisitively. "Thirsty?" he asked. "I will allow you a brief break. Orders came from Her Majesty this morning which I must pass on to you."

Water. The word alone was refreshing, her throat dry and parched from the workout. Brushing the dust from her pants, she moved over to the table to snatch up the glass and drink it down in a few swift gulps. "Orders? Has there been some news regarding the enemy's movement?"

"They are closing in," he nodded. "We have multiple units on guard at the perimeter of the city as well as the borders of Carpaen and Siscal, which have already suffered a few attacks. Arcastus and Damir are said to have men coming from both directions. But that is not quite what I meant."

"It does not involve the impending attack?" He was acting strangely. Something about the news made him appear discontent. Perhaps unhappy with the decision of the Queen?

"Queen Vorsila insists that the plans for the masquerade ball will continue – against my counsel, of course. It is set to take place in a week from tomorrow evening. Even worse, she requests that you put in an appearance as the Duchess."

Leyna frowned at the thought. "That is a terrible idea on many levels. I must advise against it..."

"I did advise against it, but it is out of my hands. Seems there are some people at court who are questioning your existence and Queen Vorsila wants you to make their acquaintance."

"But if the Prince is there, would that not directly conflict with my orders to maintain distance from him?"

"I will be at your side to ensure you remain a safe distance from His Royal Highness." Cadell frowned, the lines on his face deepening in concentration. "Her Majesty has conceded that your presence cannot be a lengthy one at the party. I need you to be prepared in case of an attack –"

"Which is bound to occur. It is the perfect opening for our enemy."

Cadell nodded to her in agreement. "I know. And the Queen knows. She is prepared for it, but she feels that cancelling the party would send the people into a panic. It is set to be in honor of the late Prince Enaes. A memorial of sorts. I recommend you attend in whatever attire you can which allows you to wear most of your uniform underneath. If anything happens before we are able to excuse you from the party, you need to be able and ready to lead the men with me."

Her heart was pounding. Deep inside, she found herself excited at the chance to be free of her training for an evening, to experience the grandeur of court. But then she remembered all the reasons why she'd hated it in the past. "You and I should not be so distracted. Could these introductions not wait until a more appropriate time?"

"Our Queen told me her reasons, all of which I cannot argue, but none of which I can share," he explained. "Your presence will be nothing more than a brief appearance. Enough to circulate word of your attendance, at the very least. I told her I could not allow you out of your duties for more than a half hour's time, which she understands. Whatever articles of your uniform you are unable to conceal under your dress will be kept in one of the council rooms just off the hall leading to the main ballroom. After your time at the party has ended, you are to report there, finish dressing, and head to the watch tower at the gates. Are we understood?"

"Yes, sir."

It was an absolute mess! Her head reeled at the thought of leaving her post for any span of time during such an occasion. They needed to have someone to watch in her place until she could get back to her duties. Someone she could trust to handle any situations that might arise in her absence.

"Do we have any lead commanders?"

"I have commanders, yes. Why?" Cadell asked, squinting at her, curious by her question.

"I need to have someone I can trust watching over things while I am otherwise engaged. You know these men better than I do."

"I leave the choice in your hands. It is the job of the Captain to appoint duties in situations like this. We can arrange a meeting with the commanders if you desire to better acquaint yourself with them."

Leyna sat the empty glass down on the table, her body held up by her arm resting lightly on the edge. There was not enough time to get to know any of those men well enough to present a responsibility so great. She was certain they were all worthy men, or Cadell would not permit them the titles they carried, but that didn't mean they would perform the same for her. They hardly knew her, and it was no secret that some of the men were somewhat put-off at the idea of taking orders from a courtier.

"There is a soldier within the ranks, or at least there should be, who goes by the name of Zander Tercsin," she said suddenly. Her face brightened at the thought. "Do you know this man?"

Cadell pondered over it. "Yes, the name does – ah, I see. Of course. Do you trust him?"

"With my life," she nodded in affirmation.

"He has a good history from the reports of his work over the years," Cadell mused. "His fighting is clean and efficient. If you feel he is capable of the job, I can extend a promotion to him as a commander, but he will be under your authority. If he behaves dishonorably, his actions will reflect on you and will be taken into account when determining whether or not you should fall to the repercussions of it."

"He will not behave dishonorably. I can think of no one else for the job."

"It is done then." Cadell wrung his hands, a sharp motion of his head signaling Leyna to move. "I will meet with him and brief him of his orders when we finish here tonight and threaten him with death if he tells anyone at court your identity. That should do the trick." He held his face stern for a moment before flashing a quick wink in Leyna's direction.

Leyna chuckled to herself at the thought of Zander's face in hearing a threat from Cadell. He wouldn't turn down the promotion, and he didn't dare cross the General. Moving out onto the floor, she readied herself for another round, her body already screaming at her with exhaustion. "He will prove a worthy commander. I feel confident in that."

"He'd better. Now ready yourself. There is still much for you to learn if I am going to have you ready for a war in a week. Do not expect to be sleeping tonight."

Chapter Twenty-Six

Her dress fit awkwardly over the waistband of the uniform pants. To hide the legs from view, Leyna borrowed pins from the seamstresses, securing the ankles up and away from the satin slippers she wore over her feet. The neckline was designed to sit high around her neck, the sleeves long and lacy, concealing the thinner fabric of the shirt she wore underneath. Zander's fingers tugged on the bodice laces, pushing the extra material of her shirt down inside. "Women," he smirked with a hard yank of his arms. "If you were only a man, this situation wouldn't be nearly as complicated."

"Just get it tied and presentable enough that I can get this over with," she grumbled. Her hands ran along the smooth silken fabric. She wished the circumstances allowed her to appreciate the fine garment more, but it was nothing but a costume now, hiding her true purpose for a brief time.

A detailed mask stared up at her from the small table at her side, purple amethyst stones glittering radiantly around its eyes. The gems were evenly spaced to create a dramatic slant over the opening, smaller stones lining the edges down along the cheek and up to the forehead. At the temple, the mask extended stiffly outward, decorated on both sides with flowers formed of silvery silk. Gently, she lifted it to her face, the shimmering ribbons fluttering down over her shoulders, colorful and elegant, accenting the deep mauve tone of her gown.

Zander finished securing the bodice with one final jerk, his hand playfully slapping Leyna on the back, nearly causing the mask to fall from her grasp. "There. You almost pass as a lady."

"For the next thirty minutes, she had better," Cadell's voice rang out across the room from where he stood near the door. His uniform was the traditional black and gold design of Tanispan military attire, though the trim shone brighter than normal. A pair of gold and ruby cufflinks sparkled in the light of the room. "Commander, you know the plan. As soon as the Captain and I exit this room, you are to report to the watch tower near the front entrance of the palace. If a tree so much as bends in a peculiar fashion, you are to come and notify us immediately. Are we understood?"

"Yes, General." Zander's smile disappeared from his lips without a trace. He knew better than to become too relaxed around Cadell.

"Captain," Cadell turned to Leyna, looking her over closely. "Not bad." His fingers tapped the surface of the mask dangling from his own hand. It was simple in design. All gold, with a thin, roped trim around the edges. Intricate black geometric patterns filled the empty space around the eyes and molded cheeks, bringing out the colors of his uniform as he slid it over his face. "The Queen and her son have already entered the ballroom and taken their seats. We will make our entrance, mingle briefly, dance a single song if necessary, and find the exit. You are not to leave my side."

"Very well. To the tower then, Commander," Leyna nodded to Zander. "We will see you soon."

Zander's heels snapped together in a sharp motion, his hand giving a crisp salute. Without further direction, he turned away, moving swiftly from the room.

Leyna was far too distracted to focus, barely aware of her and Cadell passing through the door into the hallway. The people passed by as if in a dream, blurred images in her mind, their voices a droning hum with no clear words amongst the noise. People bowed and curtsied to her like royalty. Even with a mask, they recognized the unmistakable uniform of Cadell at her side, addressing him by his title.

The ballroom brought back memories to Leyna, standing there again, colorful masked faces surrounding her from one end of the room to the other. Music wafted through the air with a gentle melody while couples danced, smooth and graceful, across the floor. At their approach, the crowd near the arched entry stepped to the side. They formed a path down the center of the floor, opening the way for them to the exquisite thrones at the head of the room, where Queen Vorsila and the Prince sat, somber and rigid in their mourning attire. They wore matching blackened masks, golden knot-work the only splash of color aside from their pale skin.

His interest clearly piqued at Cadell's arrival, the Prince's head cocked to one side, peering down the aisle to where Leyna and the General stood. Courtiers flocked to them, lavishing them with compliments and pleasantries in hopes of garnering favor.

The attention left Leyna uncomfortable at the thought of all the eyes upon them. Questioning and curious. They all wanted to know who she was. Cadell was the most powerful man in all of Tanispa, aside from the Prince, and his affairs were always of public interest.

Leyna found her gaze wandering over the feathered faces in the ballroom. It was an occasion which demanded the presence of anyone who held significance in the Tanispan court. Her heart fluttered to think on the possibility of Thade being there, hidden amongst the mass of people, unbeknownst to her under the cover of his mask. Would he even recognize her if they crossed paths? She didn't know what she would say to him if he did. There was just too much. Too many words left unspoken that morning before she slipped out of his arms.

Would he be angry with her? He must have understood her reasons for leaving. Feolan spoke of the same fears when he came to her after seeing Thade off to Tanispa. There was just too much risk. And though it hurt her to walk away, nothing she felt now would compare to the pain of knowing she was the reason he was banished for treason, or worse. No. It was better this way. And it was better if she ceased her incessant search for him amongst the strangers.

"You look lost," Cadell mumbled to her under his breath.

She glanced over, pulled from her reverie at the sound of his voice. "I am being watchful. That is significantly better than lost. One cannot be too cautious at times like these."

Halfway down the aisle, Cadell redirected them off the open path, into the tightly packed throng around the dance floor. Leyna followed his gaze toward the thrones, noticing the Prince to be on his feet. Queen Vorsila positioned herself in front of him, her thin form petite and frail next to her son's muscular build. Something appeared to be wrong. Leyna couldn't see their faces due to the masks, but their body language suggested a disagreement of some kind, the Prince's gloved hands clenched into fists. After a moment, they both returned to their seats, the Prince's eyes staring hard into the crowd.

Men came by to offer their praise upon Cadell for his work with the military in preparation for war, their conversations shallow and empty to Leyna's distracted mind. They occasionally would inquire about the Captain's position. Had it been filled and by whom. He was evasive with his responses, informing them that it was assigned and that the Captain was well-prepared for any impending attacks, and they shouldn't worry themselves.

She didn't feel prepared. How could she be prepared for anything when she was packed into these ridiculous clothes, trapped in the middle of the ballroom by a group of people who had no idea of the danger they could be in. She needed to be outside with the unit, ready to give orders if an attack came. Ready to fight.

A quiet voice managed to find its way to her ear amongst the cacophony of noise filling the room, her head perking up in surprise at the familiar sound. "You are still in Tanispa?" Feolan asked, barely audible over the din. "Maeri and I thought for sure you would disappear and we would never see you again."

"How did you know it was me?"

"The rumors abound in regards to the mystery woman in the company of General Cadell." Feolan glanced over to the General before continuing. "Whispers say it's the new Duchess of Escovul. Maeri and I are familiar enough with that title to assume."

Hesitant to speak, Leyna let her eyes hover on Cadell, curious if he was aware anyone had approached. He appeared caught up in a deep conversation with a taller gentleman dressed in a perfectly tailored suit of deep green damask fabric, their faces turned in toward each other. Satisfied that he was distracted, she tilted her head closer to her shoulder, hoping Feolan would be able to hear. "The only reason I am here is because Queen Vorsila commanded it. Were it not for that, I would be occupied by far more important matters."

"A certain someone desires to know of your health and well-being. Perhaps you could give assurance to be passed on, as well as for my own concern."

"A certain someone?" she asked. Her heart pounded against the inside of her chest. "Might that someone be who I think it is?"

"He returned to Siscal in attempts to see you again a few days after you departed," Feolan's eyes scanned the room, his head coming back to pause next to Leyna's ear once again. "You can imagine his panic to find the front door of your home broken in, the window shattered, and blood stains spattered about. I explained the events the best I could. Of course, all I was able to tell him was your intended destination at the time, but that you left no word of your plans beyond that."

"And since then, have you seen him?"

"I have not spoken with him, but he is here this evening."

A pull at her arm told her that Cadell was ready to move, the other man stepping away from the crowd. Horrible timing. She just needed a few more minutes... "Your Grace, it is about time for us to demonstrate your skill at a single waltz before we find our way to the exit." He started to move away, his eyes shifting suddenly to take note of Feolan standing so close to Leyna's side. "Why, Consul. I did not notice you there. Sadly, I must take the Lady away."

"Would it be possible for me to steal her for a dance this evening?"

"I am afraid not," Cadell shook his head sternly. "She is not to be out of my sight." Leaning in, he added quietly to Leyna, "Nor were you supposed to be speaking with anyone."

"A waltz then," she nodded with false cheerfulness. "Consul, if you please, pass along that I am well and I give my deepest regrets for my inability to say more."

Before she could wait for a reply, Cadell pulled her away, guiding her stiffly out onto the dance floor. The musicians began a soft, graceful melody, signaling the start of a new dance. With the poise only an aristocrat could possess, Cadell bowed deeply, his hand offered to Leyna in expectance. Following his lead, she sank into a formal curtsy, her slender hand daintily resting atop Cadell's.

There was no denying his incredible partnership as he swept her into the dance. He knew the steps, leading from one move to another, never breaking frame or rhythm. It was a flawless rendition of the dance, though her head was in the clouds. She couldn't think about the music. Thade was there. Feolan made no indications of his presence being merely assumed. *I have not spoken with him, but he is here this evening.* Had he seen him? Would he go to him and pass on the message? But then, Thade would be aware of her attendance, if he was not already. He would look for her. She couldn't let that happen. They needed to finish the dance and get out of there before things grew any more complicated than they already were.

Leyna became aware of Cadell's sudden distraction, his eyes drawn toward the head of the room, an expression of concern visible around his deepening frown lines. "We may be exiting sooner than expected."

"General? What is it?"

"The Queen has signaled us to the door. I suggest you move quickly."

Out of the corner of her eye, Leyna glanced over to Vorsila, her crimson painted lips curled downward in a discontented frown. The Prince was nowhere to be seen, his throne empty, the elegant plumes of his mask lost among the sea of people moving around the room. Leyna barely had a chance to take a step when she caught sight of Zander's familiar form pushing through the crowd, his unmasked face causing him to stand out among the guests. They recognized the military uniform he wore. The concern lay in why he was approaching Cadell with such haste.

People were moving, separating for the Prince who was now visible, steadily nearing the dance floor, his eyes focused straight ahead, unaware of the women batting their eyes at him as he passed. Cadell urged Leyna forward, his hands pushing her to move toward the door. "Meet up with the commander. We will meet after you get changed and you can brief me on the situation then."

"Sir –"

"Do you understand?" Cadell's teeth were gritted, his eyes narrowed at her, almost threatening. Nodding her head, she let him shove her toward the crowd, immediately regaining her balance to fall into step at Zander's side.

"You look worried, Commander. Speak," she stated calmly. She didn't dare meet any of the curious stares aimed at her through the crowd. No one could be allowed to know what was going on. Her rank in the military couldn't be made obvious, Leyna's body language attempting to look less authoritative while moving out of the room with Zander.

It took them mere moments to reach the hallway. The corridors were less congested, making travel easier through the twists and turns which led to the chamber where their evening had begun only a short time ago. Waiting until they were out of range from any curious bystanders who might overhear, Zander launched into his report, holding the door open for her to slip inside. "An enemy unit is approaching the palace."

"The palace?" Leyna gasped. "How did they get by the border patrols? They were not supposed to yet be within Tanispan lands."

"We do not yet know. There is no mistake, though. Reports show them to be only a few miles off. They will be upon us within the hour. There is little time to prepare."

Struggling with the laces on her bodice, Leyna felt her frustration building. There was no time for this! She should already be dressed and standing at the tower. "It is knotted," she huffed, her fingers clenching around the thick ribbons. With a hard yank, the loops holding it in place snapped at their seams. The dress was ruined. Though it made little difference.

Zander already had her uniform doublet in hand as she slid the bodice off, helping her arms through the sleeves over her shirt. While she secured the buttons, Zander unfastened the pins from her pant legs, the clatter of the metal against the floor where he tossed them the only sound in the room other than the hurried rustle of fabric. Her armor waited for her off on a table not far away. It took several minutes for her to put it on, the breast plate thin and light in comparison to the armor she was accustomed to in Siscal. Her gloves allowed for ample movement of her fingers and wrists. Better for the use of the sword now attached at her hip. After a final glance over her inventory and arsenal of weapons, she was content that everything was in order the way it was intended.

"I will make my way to the unit out front so word can be passed along to the outer legions. You are to brief the General of the news, tell him of my location, and then get yourself prepared to guard the palace at all costs. Make sure the men here are ready. It is your duty to keep these walls safe for the Queen and her son. Understood?"

"I never knew you could be so bossy —"

"I will be worse if Damir breaks through the palace gates. Are you clear or not?"

Their eyes met in silence, Leyna's gaze hardened by the threat they were facing. She needed him to be serious. There was a time for lightheartedness, but this was not it. She was his Captain. If he couldn't pull himself together, then there was no chance of protecting anyone.

"I'm clear, Captain," he replied calmly, snapping to attention with a crisp salute. She cast him a grateful look as she walked past him, fastening her helmet in place, her legs seeming not to move fast enough to carry her to the door.

When the door opened, she found Cadell standing outside it, his mask discarded on the floor at his feet. The Prince was there with him, still concealed under a shroud of feathers and silk. "Ah, Captain. Do we have a report?" Cadell greeted in concern. Leyna said nothing, her hand raising to snap her fingers at Zander commandingly, never pausing in her determined strides toward the front doors of the palace. There was no time for her to explain it to Cadell. One of them needed to be with the troops, and at this moment, that someone was her.

Scattered gasps could be heard from the courtiers who saw her making her way down the halls. There was no use in trying to hide the imminent danger from them. It was inevitable that Cadell would order everyone from the ballroom to see Queen Vorsila and the Prince escorted to a shelter somewhere inside the palace. The party was over. They just didn't know it yet.

Outside the air had a chill to it. It smelled like rain, mingled with something which set her mind on edge. Fire. Smoke was coming from somewhere, and close. Too thick to be any further away than a mile, two at most. The familiar feel of war surrounded her. Frightening and yet exciting. Every inch of her body felt alive with the thrum of danger, the need to destroy the enemy, and restore her people to peace.

Her boots gave off a dull thud with every step she took up the watch tower stairs, pounding over the stone in determined strides. At her approach, the soldiers said nothing, only offering her a handheld telescope to observe the distance, their expressions grim from under their helmets. She didn't need help to see the orange glow on the horizon. The fighting had begun.

"Captain, what is the status?" Cadell's voice cut through the stunned silence of the tiny room. Handing him the scope, she kept her focus directed toward the light in the distance.

"The attack has begun. I will ride out to the front-lines to direct defense. It is where I should have been in the first place. Is the Queen safe?"

"The commander secured her in the shelter below the palace – Amand," Cadell motioned firmly to one of the soldiers positioned at the window. "See that our horses are saddled and ready. I don't care what you have to do, just see that it gets done. The Captain and I need to be riding in less than five minutes."

With a sharp salute, the man hurried from his post to the stairs, his footsteps gradually fading into the distance.

Though her outward appearance was calm, Leyna's insides were screaming. The Namiren soldiers had always displayed faults in their abilities to fight and plan attacks. Their most devastating allies had been in the Sanarik, and even they had their flaws when they came against a skilled defender. But these men who led the attack now — she knew them too well. Kael was strong and intelligent, despite his ridiculous obsession with her. Kyros had no such point of weakness, nor did Damir. Damir would be a formidable opponent. His magic was strong, beyond that of any Leyna could imagine. The Namiren soldiers had nothing of that caliber during their supposed crusade.

Cadell had known that from the start. He trained her in the ways of their own magic during her lessons, showing her how to counter the things Damir's men might throw at them. But there was only so much preparation they could do without knowing the extent of Arcastus's strength. Leyna's body shivered to think on it. *Stay focused.* She couldn't let herself get discouraged before they even had a chance to get going.

Behind Cadell another figure appeared whom Leyna was not expecting to see, her heart jumping in her chest in fear. The black mourning doublet of the Prince, though covered by very finely crafted armor over his chest, face, and limbs, made him look out of place among the uniforms of the soldiers around him. Why was he there? Cadell should have been escorting him to a shelter, not into the middle of the battle itself!

In her confusion, she shook her head to clear her thoughts. She needed to think about the troops. Cadell was the General. All she could do was trust that he knew what he was doing. She gave a brief nod to the Prince, ignoring his presence beyond her short acknowledgement. "General," she stated quietly, hoping the Prince wouldn't overhear. "Why is the Prince here and not with his mother?" She couldn't move beyond the burning question. If Cadell intended to ride with her to the front-lines, he couldn't possibly bring the Prince along with him. It was foolishness for him to be there as it was.

"Because I have no authority to command him not to be," Cadell snapped. "So I suggest you help me keep an eye on him."

She could feel the eyes of the Prince on her, watching her, taking in her every move as he stepped forward. It was disconcerting. He was tense, standing there at Cadell's side. As well he should be. He was a damn fool to have come out there.

"Amand is taking too long. I am going down to the horses," she announced, brushing past Cadell to reach the stairs. There was no point in standing around in the awkward silence. They were wasting precious time that could be spent at the front-lines.

It was surreal. The way the wind blew across her face outside the watch tower, tossing about what little bit of hair protruded from underneath her helmet, the scent of smoke and fire wafting across her nostrils. It smelled of war. And even worse, it smelled of death. A strong stench brought upon the wind which smelled of decaying flesh. But that couldn't be possible. An odor that strong would require corpses to be lying out for days. Leyna had walked through enough week-old battlefields, collecting the bodies of fallen friends, to know the difference. This assault was fresh.

Out of habit, she grabbed onto the saddle situated next to the horse's feet, not yet having been placed on its back while Amand scurried about to ready Cadell's horse. It was better for her to do it herself. She could never get used to having all of the soldiers under her thumb to do her bidding. As long as her arms and legs functioned, she could manage the menial tasks on her own. The men were soldiers after all. Not slaves.

She was already on her horse when Cadell and the Prince appeared through the door of the tower. She didn't dare leave without Cadell, but he moved so slow! How could he be so calm and detached? Had he seen battle so many times that it really had so little sway over him? Either that, or he was simply a master at disguising his own fears. Some might think the same of her, the way she conducted herself in this situa-tion. The truth was that she was simply too busy to waste time worrying. It would do them little good to work themselves into a frenzy. That was a reaction only the court-iers and townspeople had the luxury of exhibiting. The soldiers looked up to their superior officers and it would be almost a crime to let any of them see the uncertainty which flooded Leyna's mind.

Calling out a command, Leyna directed Amand to send word to Varik, the Cavalry Commander. They needed his troops to reinforce the front-lines. The Prince would also be safer among the group than if the three of them rode separately. Any enemies they encountered along the way would need to get through them all first to get to him.

Their intentions of being on their way so quickly were not realistic in Leyna's mind. Preferred, yes, but not plausible, regardless of what Cadell said. They couldn't afford any mistakes caused by haste. She lost track of time while waiting for Varik to arrive, heart pounding at the sight of his men gathering around them, the clattering of horses' hooves over the ground signaling their approach. "Commander Varik," she greeted him with a steady voice. "Have your best men come to the front. We must keep His Highness guarded on all sides. Everyone else will need to be on the lookout. There is no word yet on how close the enemy has managed to come, if they have breached our defenses."

Varik looked proud atop his horse, armor gleaming in the light of the moon overhead. His long black hair was pulled back, hanging down under his helmet. She could see his stern, glowing eyes, their deep green color flecked with tiny hints of yellow. Without hesitation, he did as Leyna commanded, directing his lieutenants to gather on either side of her and Cadell, blocking in the Prince between them. Once in formation, Varik took his place at the front of the unit, his arm clinking against the metal of his hauberk as he motioned for his men to move forward.

"Captain, you know our enemy best. What can you tell us about their strategies?" Cadell asked, his voice carried away on the wind as they galloped along the countryside toward the firelight in the distance.

Leyna shook her head in frustration. "I know nothing of their strategies. Commander Tercsin had more opportunity to learn of their methods than I. All I can tell you is not to underestimate them. They are all well-trained fighters and their leader, Damir, wields magic with great skill. As far as Arcastus, I do not even know what he looks like, but if rumor serves true, he will be unmistakable, and his power immense."

At her side, the sudden whinny of a horse cut her off. The man next to her tumbled from its back, nearly trampled underfoot. There was a whistle coming from somewhere in the air. Instinctively, Leyna lifted her right arm just in time to deflect an incoming arrow off the surface of the vambrace, somehow managing to catch it at an angle to prevent it piercing through the armor. The unit came to a halt, shields raised protectively over them as a flurry of arrows rained down from overhead.

"Sanarik!" she hissed. Their arrows were unmistakable. The flights were perfectly cut for ample speed and accuracy, the points arranged of two heads combined into one for greater damage upon impact. They were fortunate one of the Sanarik had fired early. As the last of the arrows plummeted to the ground, Leyna shouted out to the troops, praying they would hear her through the startled cries of the horses. "Commander, direct some of your men to the east. They cannot be far. The rest of us need to move before the next volley. And fast. Keep your shields up and do not stop."

In an instant, the group split off under the commands of Leyna and Varik, pushing forward through the open fields to the battle ahead. Knowing the Sanarik, they would not be found in a single mass like most enemy forces. She couldn't risk the entire unit being compromised by their tactics. The number of Sanarik soldiers would be minimal, but scattered, and without any light to give hint of their hiding places, they would be a threat. To remain there with the Prince would be like delivering his head to the enemy on a silver platter. The men left behind would create enough of a distraction to allow them to get the Prince out of range, and to get to the troops.

"Those bastards gave us a run for our money back in Siscal," Cadell grunted, coming up from behind Leyna. "What in the blazes are they doing with the Ven'shal?"

"Getting revenge for their defeat," she stated. "If their presence here is any indication, I would not be surprised to discover that they have also recruited the Namiren army."

The smell of smoke and decay grew stronger as they closed the distance. The ground was littered with bodies of fallen Ven'shal soldiers. The Tanispan forces evidently doing well even without reinforcement. Swords clashed. Shouts and commands echoed from somewhere, though by whom and to which side of the battle, Leyna couldn't place. It was utter chaos.

How had they let this happen? Scouts had been stationed all over Tanispa, in abundance around Sivaeria to prevent exactly this. Either Damir and Arcastus found a way to sneak past the scouts, or someone let them through. Cadell's men were too good to be outsmarted by such drastic proportions. It wouldn't happen again, though. She would see to it.

Sword drawn, Leyna plunged into the battle. The number of enemy soldiers came as a shock to her, given how many fallen they had passed. For years, the Ven'shal were believed to be in hiding, their numbers greatly decreased from the war during Queen Nalashi's rule, but it was evident now that somewhere, they never ceased to flourish, gradually building up their army once again. Among the dark colorless eyes of the Ven'shal fighters were the taller figures of the familiar Namiren race, their armor polished and shining under the orange glow of the flames behind them.

Her stomach sank at the sight of the fire consuming the land. Grass burned brightly, the line of fire spreading from one end to the other to crawl over the trees and plants along the forest borders. There was something unnatural about it, the color a little too bright, too precise in its direction of travel. It was being controlled somehow. Allowing the enemy forces to pass through unharmed into the battle while preventing the Vor'shai from penetrating into the waiting troops. A Ven'shal tactic no doubt. However, it seemed to Leyna that the constant control over the fire would be a strain on whoever maintained it.

A hard blow from the side knocked her from her horse, the impact with the ground forcing the breath from her lungs painfully. She should have been more prepared for it. She scolded herself through gasps for air, somehow managing to roll over onto her back, blade raised to block the attack of the Ven'shal soldier bearing down on top of her. With grace, she maneuvered around the strikes. The tip of her sword found its target, blood pouring from the wound as he collapsed to the ground.

Her foe finished, she started to turn away, ready to take on the next who tried to best her. Before she could move, something caught her attention. A grey light poured forth from the ground, covering the body like oil, seeping into its eyes, mouth, nose, and ears. The corpse trembled and twitched. Reflexively, Leyna stepped back.

A burst of blackened light lifted the body to its feet, eyes glowing with supernatural energy, fists clenched. Leyna was stunned by what she saw in front of her. This couldn't be happening. She saw him die!

The fist connected with her helmet hard, sending her tumbling backward off her feet. He was strong. No. Not he – It. Whatever was empowering it was increasing its strength tenfold. In a display of incredible agility, Leyna rolled over her shoulder, absorbing the impact of the fall and climbing to her feet.

Her sword seemed suddenly worthless. She skewered the heart for a second time, then slashed its throat for good measure. It did not seem to notice. It showed no indication that it even felt the pain.

Baffled exclamations of other men all around her suggested that she was not the first to discover the phenomenon. The eerie light resurrected each corpse. A renewed army, unaffected by their weapons. It was terrifying. How could they beat something that couldn't die? Something that was already dead.

In a final effort to deflect her opponent, Leyna sheathed her sword, relying only on her hands and feet to defend against this... creature. The thought of touching it made her shudder. It radiated evil. Like the spirits Damir had risen from the graves in Kaipoi...

Those spirits had been intangible. Non-corporeal beings. It had been a testament to Damir's power, but she doubted his ability to animate these corpses. They were too complete. Too strong. Damir spoke of it taking time and effort to restore life after he struck down Yasar. No, this had to be the work of a far stronger sorcerer. But she'd managed to affect the specter that attacked her in the cemetery that night. Perhaps the same method would prove effective now.

Steeling her mind, she focused on her core. If she could force out the magic which animated the creature... But would she be strong enough? There was no time to worry. She had no choice but to try. That was all there was to it.

With a jolt, she directed her energy outward, her hand wrapping around the neck of the moving corpse. She needed to find an area of the body not covered by its armor. Skin-to-skin contact. And it appeared to be working. The legs and arms ceased their striking, slowly becoming a wild flail, until it was nothing more than an occasional twitch of the muscles. The dark aura crept from the eyes, small at first, then increasing to a wave of shadow pouring forth from its eyes and mouth, open now in a silent scream. Finally, the twitching halted, the corpse going limp and slumping to the ground as the last of the darkness faded away.

She stared at it, unmoving, dark. The unnatural light gone. *It is dead. An empty shell.* She'd managed to push out the sorcery, but how long could she maintain that kind of power, and against how many other monstrosities? She placed her heel on the corpse's head, applying all her weight to crush its skull, making sure it wouldn't stand up again.

Around her, the battle continued on, the eerie corpse puppets starting to push her men back. The fire was weakening, no longer reaching toward the sky with the same ferocity she'd witnessed upon their arrival. A new wave of living soldiers marched over the line where it had been. They faced a combination of living and dead, and her men were still struggling in their attempts to cut down the dead ones. They weren't ready for fresh foes.

She needed to think fast. Sorcery of this sort required assistance from some outside force to be sustained. The spirits in the cemetery under Damir's control had been raised from the ground by the dark shadow which covered the grass, killing it. He had somehow sucked the life out of the earth itself to pull forth the spirits. *Look down*, she ordered herself silently. If that were true, then the ground she stood on now should be dead.

Cautious of the enemy still pressing forward, Leyna crouched down, hand outstretched to the grass covering the field. Her fingers sank into blackened earth covered in an ashy film of what, at one time, had been living plant life. *How does this help us?*

Why couldn't she think? The pounding of feet over the land signaled the rapid approach of new soldiers. They would be upon them in seconds, and each one that fell would only rise back up if she didn't find some way to cut down their numbers. They would overrun Tanispa with sheer mass alone. All of her magic training under Cadell had been in war tactics. How to bend odds to her benefit in battle, strengthening her resolve, steadying her aim, and anything else she could do to take down an enemy. But this was different. She needed to pull the energy out of each corpse. All at once. Counteract the sorcery somehow.

She pictured Feolan in her mind. Years ago he had taught her how to use this magic for the first time. To quicken the bloom of a flower in the forests of Velorum while waiting on the Namiren troops to march through. There was something in that lesson which felt important to her now. But she couldn't simply restore the grass. It would only replenish their source of power to raise more dead. No. There had to be another way. Another means of feeding that energy into the ground.

And then it came to her. Take it back. It made sense. If she could put her energy into the plants to help them grow, there must be a way to draw their energy back out of the animated corpses and return it to where it came from.

The soil felt soft and grimy under her knees, her palms flattened against the ashen surface. She hated to admit that she knew nothing about what she was preparing to attempt. There was no saying it would even work. *Just do it. Try something. Anything.*

Centering her energy, she felt a circuit form between herself and the earth. Gradually, every beating heart that stood upon the ground thrummed in her ears. Their pulses radiated through her body. She knew their exact location on the field. She felt the ground, cold, but not entirely lifeless. But there were also pockets of emptiness, almost sucking the life from her spirit through the connection. *Fight back. Pull it back.*

There were too many of them for her to focus on all at once. She needed to start small. The stronger pull of the dead soldiers closest to her. Sinking deep within herself, she fought against the flow of energy, feeling it start to reverse. Whoever was controlling it was too distracted by the numbers to fight against her small, pitiful attempts. With every pull Leyna exerted, a weaker pull tried to take it back, like an invisible game of tug-of-war. She felt it getting closer. More powerful. She was winning, but she was tiring. The strain was too much for a single person to take on alone.

It was no excuse. *Keep going!* It couldn't be much longer. She could feel it, the ground thrumming with energy once again, the way it had before being stripped of life. The blackened surface was slowly sprouting anew. Green. Life was forming again. And the dead were growing weaker. Their strikes were less precise, groggy and ill-timed, until finally they started to fall, collapsing to the ground in broken heaps of what remained of their bodies.

Through her connection with the ground Leyna could sense the strain on her body lessening, assisted by unseen forces which told her that others among her men had discovered the same strategy. Enemy troops continued to march on them, however. Drawing her sword, she stood, her eyes searching the chaos for Cadell or the Prince. They were supposed to be watching him. If anything happened to the Prince...

She wouldn't think about it. If she found Cadell, she would find the Prince. Cadell wouldn't leave his side. Not at a time like this.

Their numbers were still sizable enough that the battle was far from over. They couldn't afford to fall back to regroup with the enemy so close to the palace. They needed to push the enemy back, out of Sivaeria, and put a larger distance between them and the Queen. Cadell's army was strong enough to do it. To hold their ground. They just needed to survive this fight.

It felt like hours before she finally reached the center of the battle. She cut down soldier after soldier, removing their heads after they fell. Then, she saw it, recognizing the familiar helmet of the General easily cutting through the lines of enemies. Hordes of undead pushed in around his unit. The eerie glow radiated from every orifice and wound as they attacked, savage and crazed. Cadell boldly dropped his weapon and extended his hands forward, a bright flash of light shooting forth from his palms, knocking the rotting soldiers off their feet to grant him a moment to regain his composure and breath.

At his side, Leyna finally saw the grand markings of the Prince's armor, piercing the eye of one corpse as it began to rise. She was uncomfortable with the thought of the Prince fighting in this battle. It wasn't his place. Maybe his siblings before him had the luxury of representing their kingdom in war, but not him. There was no one left if he fell to the enemy. And the devastation it would cause Queen Vorsila would be immeasurable. They couldn't risk losing the royal heir on account of his inability to recognize his own importance.

Approaching from behind a new corpse that challenged the Prince, she gripped her fingers around the bare skin of its neck, a blue light pulsing forth through her arm into the dead flesh, coursing through it until the body gave way, collapsing at the Prince's feet. The Prince's weapon lowered at the sight of Leyna standing there. His silver eyes flashed brightly from under his helmet, grateful for her assistance, but unable to speak before she turned away, throwing herself back into the heat of the fight.

Almost from nowhere, a ghastly figure appeared in front of them, troops from both sides stumbling backward to give him space. Unlike the other soldiers, he wore no helmet or armor. Scars marred every inch of skin across his face and hands, bone visible under layers of torn flesh. The glow of his yellowed eyes looked sickly. Evil. Full of menace. He was an impressive, grotesque sight. Pale skin, shimmering in the moonlight, an aura of shadow and light surrounding him, cape billowing in the wind. Leyna feared that her overuse of energy might be causing her to hallucinate.

"I think we found the lich," Cadell muttered, his arm extending out across Leyna's midsection, pushing her back behind him. His eyes shifted over to the Prince, content to see him taking a position behind Cadell and Leyna. "Your Highness, I recommend you keep cover from this one. Do not leave our guard."

Unwilling to hide behind Cadell, Leyna stepped forward once again to his side, peering through her helmet at the disgusting creature standing in the center of the field, the fighting halted in awe of his approach. Arcastus. The name burned in her head, her eyes locked on him in disbelief. "You will forgive me if I don't bow and grovel at the feet of your prince," the lich rasped. "I have a bit of a bone to pick with his family."

Cadell's fingers tightened around the hilt of his sword. It was doubtful the blade would have any effect against this creature, but habit prevailed in the sense of security the weapon gave, just to know it was there at the ready.

"Mescavis did not act on behalf of our people. You are mistaken —"

Arcastus laughed, a horrid, rattling sound, his yellow eyes flaring briefly against his scarred and rotting flesh. "He was a Vor'shai, the same as you. He served the same

Queen as every other damnable member of your race. The same Queen that banished my people, forcing them to live in exile like criminals. I may not have fought back then, but I will be the one to finish what started those years ago."

With a wave of his hand, Arcastus released a pulse of energy through his fingertips, aimed at one of the Vor'shai soldiers. It exploded over his armor, wrapping him in a veil of shadows, constricting around him, crushing organs and bones. His body went limp, suffocated under the pressure, the tendrils dropping it carelessly to the ground. It took no more than a moment, but felt like an eon to witness.

At the fall of the corpse, the sound of clashing swords could be heard, striking up the battle once again. Arcastus took a step forward. His hideous eyes were focused on them, shifting between Leyna and Cadell. He sought a strategy. She could read it on what was left of his face. He wanted the Prince, but they stood between him.

Cadell seemed the obvious choice for the attack. Take down their leader – the strongest warrior – then the Prince. Break their spirit. They were the most vulnerable points to the will of the Vor'shai people. With every step Arcastus took forward, Cadell and Leyna moved back, forcing the Prince to move with them, guarded by their bodies.

She watched his eyes. If he thought to strike, it would be telegraphed through them. A brief flash or dim of the yellow glow caused by the fluctuation of energy within. She could only hope her reflexes would allow her to move quickly enough to intercept the attack.

There was no conscious thought in her head when the flash erupted in his eyes, exaggerated by her imagination. The world around her moved in slow motion as she elbowed her way in front of Cadell, the hollow sound of his voice shouting at her ringing in her ears. She leapt into the air, sword raised. Her intended strike pattern flashed in her vision. Bash the side of the head with the back of her fist, slice the torso from neck to naval, throw him to the ground with a burst of energy, and remove his head with a sweeping motion.

Before her plan could come to fruition, the impact of shadowy fingers against her chest knocked the wind out of her, obliterating all thoughts of her attack. Tumbling backward, she felt Cadell lose his balance under the force of her body colliding with him. His hands grasped Leyna under her arms to hold her up, nearly causing them both to fall into the Prince.

In that instant, she felt her body go numb, lungs seized, unable to breathe. A black film passed across her eyes, but soon dissipated, air whistling into her lungs with a harsh wheeze. She was alive. Her chest felt as though a boulder had crashed down atop her from above, but she was alive. It didn't seem possible. Not with how easily Arcastus demonstrated his magic before.

When she steadied herself on her feet, she could see the brief look of confusion in Arcastus's eyes, narrowed at her angrily. Lunging forward, he plucked her from Cadell's hands. "Why aren't you dead?" he hissed.

"I could ask the same of you," Leyna huffed. His hand was crushing her neck at the sides, fingertips digging into the skin, their skeletal shape piercing through the flesh. *Focus.* She knew he could kill her easily, but something was stopping him. He was too distracted to think about breaking her neck. Fortunate for her.

Gathering her strength, she brought her elbow hard across his face, her nose wrinkled in disgust at the feeling of the flesh squishing against her armor, bones snapping and popping grotesquely at the force. He threw her down to the ground with a cry of pain. Smoke rose from his fingertips where they had pierced her skin, his features twisted in a grimace of agony.

Free of his hold, she scrambled to her feet. By instinct, she drew her arm back to strike him again. He evaded with surprising agility, side stepping, distancing himself from her.

Another wave of shadow shot from his other hand, impacting her armor, enough force to knock her to the ground, but deflected once again, leaving behind nothing but a painful chill through her body, lungs gasping for air. Desperately, she climbed to her feet. She needed to get at him again. Around her, the animated corpses fell to the ground, ceasing their movement at Arcastus's distraction. But how could she kill him? They knew nothing about him. He was already dead, and her energy would not be enough to force his spirit from his body. His resurrection was different from that of the fallen soldiers. It would take more than a simple magic trick to take him down.

"Fall back!" Arcastus commanded, the raspy voice echoing through the open field. His men tried to break away from the Vor'shai soldiers, the front line finding it impossible to escape.

"Keep fighting!" Leyna shouted. They wouldn't stop until the last of the Ven'shal soldiers no longer stood. At least the ones they could get to before a retreat was completed.

Swallowed up in a cloud of shadow, Arcastus disappeared from view. Leyna spun around hesitantly, unsure of what to expect from him. Was he really gone, or was it some kind of trick to distract her? To leave her vulnerable for another attack.

"Captain!" Cadell's voice suddenly reached her ears. How long had he been calling for her? "Retreat, Captain. Let the men take care of the last of them."

"We need to get the Prince out of here," she stated firmly. "There is no way to know that they won't come back again, and he made his target very clear."

She moved toward Cadell, securing her sword in the sheath at her hip. He cut her off, his finger extended to poke at her armor. The tip of it passed through where the metal once had been. Leyna winced in pain at the pressure of his touch against the tender skin of her midsection. "You are done fighting, Captain. At least for now. Commander Varik will oversee the men and arrange them to take watch over the perimeter in case of any further attacks. I will see the Prince back to the palace and order camp to be set up a few miles out. You are to return to the watch tower and wait for me there. Do not deviate in your course for any reason. Do you understand?"

"Yes, General," she sighed, frustrated by the orders. Why would he send her away? There was still so much that needed to be done.

"Then I suggest you get moving," he pointed sternly in the direction of the palace. "Find your horse and get it to a run. You are in no condition to risk an attack by any stray Sanarik on the way, and I am not losing you or our Prince tonight."

Chapter Twenty-Seven

Rounding the last stair to the top of the watch tower, Leyna tossed her helmet angrily down on the ground, her fists clenched in frustration. How did they possibly think they would be able to defeat Arcastus? His magic was virtually unknown to them.

"What the hell happened to you?" Zander asked from somewhere inside the room.

"We are fighting a war. What do you think happened?" she snapped. There was no one around to hear the informal address. And at that moment, she didn't care if it was overheard or not. "Arcastus is raising his fallen troops against us. How are we supposed to win when we can't keep the dead down?"

Zander moved over to her side, his hands unfastening the armor from around her body. He pulled the hauberk over her head, holding it out to examine more closely. A large hole had been burned through the breastplate. Streaked and charred. Leyna's eyes blinked in surprise at the sight of it. "You look like someone raised *you* from the dead. I'm not teasing. You look awful."

"Thanks," she grumbled, snatching the armor back from his hands. What could have caused so much damage? And how could she have survived it? "It must have been Arcastus," she mused. "I do not recall it feeling as if he struck with such force, however. Not enough to do this."

"Those marks on your neck —"

"Why are you asking so many questions? I am alive. That is all that matters. We need to focus on how to beat this... thing."

"No, we need to focus on your injuries. Why did you come here and not the infirmary?"

"I am hardly scratched," Leyna sighed. But the pain was beginning to set in. The rush of the battle made it nonexistent, adrenaline pumping through her veins to keep her moving. All she wanted to do now was sleep. To close her eyes for a week. Maybe everything would be better when she woke up.

Noticing her start to sway on her feet, Zander guided Leyna to a chair next to the window. Careful not to hurt her any more than she already was, he tilted her head gently to one side, examining the marks there on her skin. "These look bad, Leyna. You have lost a significant amount of blood."

"I am fine. Just a little tired," she gestured for him to move away. "I am only waiting here until the General returns and then I plan to get back to the troops and make sure everything is in order."

"Then while you are waiting, you can let me clean up some of these cuts. You may be my Captain, but you are also my friend."

"We do not even have proper bandages —"

"Hush," he chuckled, pouring a cup of water out of a jug in the corner of the room. "I can make do with what we've got."

There was no sense in arguing. She knew Zander well enough to know that he wouldn't back down if he had his mind set on it. At this point, she no longer cared. Her body ached and burned. The pain in her neck was excruciating and she was convinced at least one of her ribs was broken. Arcastus's magic was more potent than she wanted to admit.

Breath caught in her throat at the pressure of a small cloth being pressed against the side of her neck. Against her will, tears filled her eyes at the pain, her teeth biting down on her lip in attempts to fight them back. She'd experienced so much worse in the past. This was nothing, or at least that was what she kept telling herself. The look on Zander's face was all she needed to know the wounds were worse than she thought, but she didn't dare ask him for the truth. It was easier to just pretend it was a mere scratch.

"Let me guess; Arcastus did this?"

"How did you know," she grimaced. A miserable laugh tried to escape her lips, stopped by the discomfort it caused with the strain of her neck.

"You forget that I've seen what that man – thing – looks like. The bruising is consistent with a hand, but the punctures are from something thinner and sharper. I assume his bony grip would dig in a bit more than any of the others."

"I didn't see any of the others. While that may be a blessing in disguise, it makes me wonder what they are up to. I fear them to have another army stationed somewhere that we do not know about and will miss until it is too late."

Rewetting the cloth in the tiny water cup, Zander started to dab at the wounds again, his forehead creased in concentration. "Is the battle still going? I wouldn't recommend you going back out."

"No," Leyna found herself bemused at the memory of Arcastus's face before he retreated. There had been something there. Confusion mingled with pain, and what looked to be a touch of fear. No, not fear. Uncertainty. Whatever it was, it shook his confidence significantly. Enough to send him away to regroup. "Something must have spooked Arcastus. He and I were fighting and he suddenly just – stopped. He ordered his men to fall back. We were just finishing off the last of those remaining when I headed back here."

Footsteps from somewhere down below caught her attention, her voice trailing off. She didn't want Cadell to see how severe her injuries were. The man had enough on his plate as it was without having to deal with her foolishness. She hoped whoever it was would simply pass the tower by and leave them in peace.

To her dismay, the sound grew nearer, echoing off the walls of the stairwell leading to where Zander and Leyna sat, frozen, anxious at the thought of who might be coming. A breath of relief escaped Leyna's lungs at the sight of Cadell's face rounding the corner of the stairs. While she wasn't ready to face him quite yet, he was a welcome sight in comparison to other possibilities.

His features were twisted, almost angry at first, his brow twitching to see Zander standing there at Leyna's side. "Commander Tercsin. If you would excuse us."

"With all due respect, General, I would prefer to stay here with the Captain –"

"Perhaps you misunderstood, Commander," Cadell glanced over to Zander with a stern expression, eyes narrowed. "That was an order. Take up watch at the base of the tower. Understood?"

"Clear as day, General," he muttered, letting the bloodied cloth drop into Cadell's hands. "The Captain needs a doctor. I suggest she see one soon. I will be guarding the door."

Giving a final salute, Zander turned away from Cadell, his eyes lingering on Leyna apologetically, not wanting to leave her in the condition she was in. In a huff, he made his way to the stairs, looking straight ahead to avoid eye-contact with Cadell as his gaze followed him to the stairwell.

His attention remained on the empty corridor, seemingly lost in his own thoughts. Leyna watched him carefully. He wasn't the type of man to be easily distracted. "General, is something troubling you?"

"Are you out of your mind?" he asked, his attention turning from the stairs to focus intently on Leyna. "Is there a reason you are so utterly reckless with your life and safety?"

"I do not understand..."

"You could have been killed, Captain. Did you think about that before you threw yourself in the line of fire?"

She flinched at the emotion in his voice, uncertain of whether it was anger or shock that thickened it with a sense of disapproval. "I was under the impression it was my job to protect you and the Prince, no matter the cost."

"Your job is to stay alive," he replied, his tone sharp. "Let me worry about protecting the Prince. Your survival is crucial. Do not be so foolish as to think it is not."

"How is it that my survival is so crucial when you are the one who is needed to lead this military to victory? They have taken orders from you long before I was ever offered this position. If you were to die, I think it would crush their spirit. You mean everything to these men. I am nothing more than a replacement that they've known for only a few months; and seen only a dozen occasions at best. My death would change nothing to them whereas yours would ruin them."

Steadying his breath, Cadell stared down at the bloody cloth in his hands as if only just realizing what it was. With a quick glance, he eyed the marks on Leyna's neck. His feet carried him to her side in a single, fluid stride. "What has you convinced that you have nothing worth living for?" His voice was calmer, a hint of concern in the inflection despite the determined look on his face while dabbing at her wounds. It was obvious to Leyna that he lacked experience in conversation beyond combat strategy and defense tactics.

"Cadell," she started, afraid of how he would react to hearing her speak to him by name instead of his proper title. His brow creased briefly, almost immediately, but he did not interject. "My closest family was murdered and those of my kin who remain deny my name. The man I love is not allowed to be with me and I will most likely never see him again. But that does not mean I have a death wish."

He paused in his work with the cloth, his eyes searching her face suspiciously. "It is odd to hear you speak of love. Might I inquire who the gentleman is?"

"No. It holds no bearing on the situation at hand," Leyna waved dismissively. The last thing she wanted was to bring Thade's name up in their conversation. Queen Vorsila had hinted at enough during their meeting in regards to Leyna's feelings toward him. Elaboration didn't seem necessary. Especially not with a war raging outside their walls. "Right now we need to focus on what we learned of our enemy during this battle. I have no experience fighting against corpses."

"My hope was that you might be able to share some insight to possible weaknesses."

"Truthfully, the one you should ask is Commander Tercsin."

"Yes, you said that before," Cadell frowned. "Were you not closely associated with them for a time? Did you learn nothing of them over the years you spent in their company?"

"In all honesty, I learned little of the men who matter." Leyna's voice trailed off with a sharp intake of air as Cadell dampened the cloth once again, pressing it against the wounds on her neck. She didn't think it was possible, but somehow the pain was increasing. Worsened by her fatigue. "I was with them for over six years, but only the past year brought anything of use. If you want names, I can tell you those, but not much beyond."

"Then tell me the names. Who are the men that work closest to the lich?"

Leyna sighed at the thought of the men Cadell requested her to identify. He was bound to recognize them. At least a few. Damir was a known traitor to Queen Vorsila.

It only seemed appropriate that Cadell would be familiar with him. "The main associate of concern is the man you may know as Damir Rohld. His right hand man is called Kyros, and below him is Oran Bedrick. Their newest recruit is a fallen Vor'shai by the name of Kael Hadaren. A former employee of Consul Imri."

"Yes, I recall the name," Cadell nodded. Tossing the cloth aside he peered at the marks on Leyna's neck, brow furrowed with concern. "While you are rather beat up from the fight, I think the question on everyone's lips is in regards to your ability to withstand the lich's magic. You saw what it did to our other soldiers. Is there a secret you know of which grants you immunity?"

"General, I will be honest with you. When it comes to my survival tonight, I am possibly more confused than anyone. I have gone over and over it in my head and nothing makes any sense."

"So you know nothing of Arcastus?"

Shaking her head, Leyna gave a slight shrug of her shoulders, wincing from the pain the movement caused. "I never saw him before tonight. Consul Imri was already in the process of removing me from the mission before Arcastus was resurrected. That is why I suggest speaking with Commander Tercsin. To my knowledge, he was present for the ritual which revived the lich."

Cadell stood silently for a moment, taking in what Leyna was saying. His expression hardened briefly, as if hesitating, a hand reaching out toward Leyna's neck, retracting again before making contact with the skin. Stiffly, he turned away, moving toward the window overlooking the street below. "Tercsin!" he called out, his voice echoing loudly through the room. Once the ringing of his voice ceased, Leyna could hear the sound of footsteps coming up the stairs, Cadell's rigid form turning back to face her again. "We will hear what he has to say on the subject, then."

When Zander appeared around the corner, Leyna could detect the concern in his expression, their eyes meeting to gaze at one another. He looked relieved to see her still seated, back straight, seemingly safe for the time being. "Is everything alright, General?" he asked, his brow raised, inquisitive.

"For now, though I don't intend to waste much more time, given the Captain's injuries. I'm going to ask you a question and I want you to speak plainly. Were you present during the ritual of resurrection performed on Arcastus?"

Made nervous by the question, Zander glanced over to Leyna uneasily. "I was present, yes, though I assure you my hand played no part in it."

"I'm not worried about your hands," Cadell stated, motioning Zander to step forward, closer. "I want details. Anything which might help us against him in battle. The Captain says you are the one to speak with on the matter."

"Quite frankly, I didn't understand much of what was going on. I lack familiarity with the Ven'shal magic, as we all do," Zander shrugged. "All I know is that the initial ritual involved an amulet provided to Damir by an Esai known as Oksuva. It was an ancient relic which belonged to Arcastus. He imbued it with some unknown magic before his death which allowed them to recall his spirit into the corpse. However, once the body was revived, he was severely weakened by the state of decay the flesh was in. He demanded the blood of a Vor'shai to further the ritual and restore his strength. My assumption would be that the blood and the amulet have something to do with his power, but what exactly, I'm not sure."

Leyna's head lifted, a thought crossing her mind which she realized had yet to be revealed to Zander. "Kael has the amulet," she said quickly, starting to stand but finding her progress halted by Cadell's hand pressing her back down onto the chair.

"Kael?" Zander blinked in surprise. "You know this for a fact?"

"I'm certain of it," she breathed, the expansion of air in her lungs causing a sharp pain to cut through her left side, reminding her of the damage done to her ribs. "Before I left Siscal I had an unfortunate meeting with him outside the city gates. While we were fighting, I saw the amulet."

"How can you be sure it wasn't one of the forgeries?"

"Because something happened when I touched it – "

"Both of you, stop," Cadell ordered, directing their attention back to him. "What about this amulet? You suspect there to be forgeries of it? To what benefit would that cause for them?"

Zander's nervous expression softened in understanding at Cadell's questions. "Yes, I should explain that better," he chuckled. "The amulet is without doubt a key to Arcastus's power. In order to protect it, Kyros had imitations made to help deter notice from the original. I wasn't sure which of them took possession of the actual relic once the ritual was complete. When Kael returned with Prince Enaes's blood, they removed it from Kael's sword and placed it inside a hollow gem. This somehow sparked Arcastus's gradual recovery."

Something about Zander's explanation caught Leyna's attention. Kael's sword? He had to be mistaken. Enaes had been killed by the dagger Kael wielded. "I assume by sword, you refer to the dagger Kael used to kill Prince Enaes."

Cadell and Zander glanced over to Leyna, surprised by her statement. "How do you know about the dagger?" Zander took a step forward, his curiosity building. Cadell held out his hand, stopping him from coming any closer.

"Captain, you were present at the time of Enaes's death?"

She suddenly doubted the idea to have spoken anything out loud on the subject. In the back of her mind she'd always assumed Cadell to be aware of her presence in the garden at the time of Enaes's assassination. The look of confusion on his face was enough to tell her that she had assumed incorrectly. "I – well. It is complicated," she stammered. "Regrettably, I was witness to the murder, yes. I did everything I could to save him. My blade was a mere second too slow. If I had been just a little faster..."

"Captain, you are not on trial here." Cadell rested his hand gently on her shoulder. "Perhaps you should answer the commander's question. What involvement did this dagger have in Prince Enaes's death?"

"The dagger is what ultimately took his life, but I recovered the weapon. The only blood on Kael's blade –" Leyna's eyes grew distant. She didn't want to think about the possibilities. "Zander, you never answered me. Was it a dagger, or Kael's blade from which the blood was removed?"

"It was intended to be collected from the dagger but it was misplaced. The only blood Kael presented was from his personal sword, as I said." Zander's confused expression deepened at the horror on Leyna's face. "Leyna, what is it?"

Leyna clutched at her stomach, hunched forward in her seat. This couldn't be happening. Why would Kael do something so foolish? Passing her blood as the

Prince's? Arcastus couldn't possibly know the truth. Though it would explain a number of mysteries which had come to her attention since that day in the chapel garden. The reaction the amulet had to her touch. Her seeming resistance to Arcastus's magic. But could it really be? Something so trivial as a few droplets of her blood? "Oh, gods," she breathed. The position of her body aggravated the discomfort of her wounds, though she couldn't focus on it anymore. What did physical pain matter when there was a chance her very existence was empowering their enemy?

Vaguely, she became aware of Cadell kneeling in front of her, staring into her eyes, fearful that her injuries had taken a turn for the worse. "Captain, are you alright? Captain!"

Terrified by the thought, Leyna lifted her gaze past Cadell to stare pitifully into Zander's eyes. "It wasn't the Prince's blood," she whispered, shaking her head in disbelief. "The blood on Kael's sword was mine."

Zander's mouth fell agape at Leyna's words. "Yours?" he gasped. "Leyna, how is that possible?"

"I told you, Zander. I was there. I was attempting to fend off Kael and his men so Prince Enaes could get away. During my fight with Kael, he cut me with his sword." In her mind Leyna could hear Kael's voice with perfect clarity. *You and I both know you don't stand a chance against me. I have your blood on my blade to prove that.* "He must have panicked when he realized the dagger was left behind. Arcastus was expecting him to bring the blood of the Prince, but all he had was mine. If you were Kael, would you want to admit your failure to a creature like Arcastus?"

"And even if it wasn't the Prince's blood, it was still from a Vor'shai. Arcastus would never know the difference," Zander stated in realization. "Leyna, this might be a good thing for us."

"How exactly is this a good thing?" Leyna scoffed, allowing Cadell to gently lift her shoulders back, easing the pain in her side.

Amused by the notion, Zander slowly moved over to where he'd discarded Leyna's damaged armor, lifting it up to display it before her and Cadell. "Arcastus believes the donor of his ritual blood is dead. Clearly, your link to him weakens his magic against you. A blow to the degree which created this kind of damage would kill any normal soldier. Yet you survived. I can't explain why, but you can't argue it to be true."

Cadell's brow creased, thoughtful by what Zander was suggesting. His eyes lingered over the burnt hole through the hauberk, glancing over to take stock of Leyna's injuries once again. "We will need to investigate this further," he nodded. Noticing the distress in Leyna's eyes, he patted her shoulder reassuringly, a half-smile passing over his lips. "If Arcastus knows nothing of this little secret, we might have the upper-hand yet. Let's not fret over it until we find out what this means, exactly."

The sound of feet thudding along the stone caused them to turn their attention toward the stairs, muscles tensed at the sight of Commander Varik's form appearing around the corner. Straightening his back, Cadell stared at Varik sternly, arms folded across his chest expectantly.

"I'm sorry to intrude, General, but I thought you should be aware. The last of the men have returned from the field. Camp is nearly completed and they are preparing to rest for the night."

"Very good," Cadell nodded. "Head down to the camp and make sure everything is in order. I must see the Captain to the physicians before we join you."

"Yes, sir." Varik gave a sharp salute, hurrying back down the stairs to leave the three of them alone once again.

"Tercsin, your information might prove rather useful. We will discuss it more later but for now if you will help me get the Captain standing. She needs to be seen presently by a doctor."

"I am fine, really," Leyna argued, hoisted to her feet by the two men gently grasping at her arms from either side.

Cadell's brow raised sharply in Leyna's direction, signaling for her to be quiet. "Let me do my job, Captain." He cut in, silencing her protests. "The war has begun. We need you to be on your feet and ready to fight. You won't do anyone any good in your current condition."

Defeated, Leyna gave in to Cadell's insistence, feet shuffling along the floor toward the stairs under his and Zander's guidance. She didn't want to fight him any longer.

Her body ached. Pain coursed through every limb, a constant reminder of the night's battle. Yes. A doctor would be good. She could worry about Arcastus once the thought of breathing no longer seemed like such a chore.

Months passed for Leyna in a blur of fighting and death, their supplies and soldiers slowly depleting under Arcastus's ever growing numbers. The dead collected from the field were revived by his magic with increasing efficiency. Every wave was harder to force back than the one previous. Arcastus was stronger than ever, showing no sign of tiring.

After almost a year of ceaseless fighting, Leyna couldn't help but feel the weight of defeat hanging heavy over their men. Morale was lower than ever. War was now widespread across the land, preventing Siscal and Carpaen from sending aid, leaving Tanispa to call on the unseasoned reserve from Mialan for support. But she couldn't focus on the negative. As long as she and Cadell were alive, they would continue to fight. Arcastus wouldn't find them so easy to break.

The lich himself had been in hiding since the first night. Never showing his face on the battlefield. His continued presence, however, was undeniable. From the shadows, he lurked, manipulating the dead to rise and fight, strong enough now to even turn their own fallen soldiers against them.

Their work was never done. Leyna felt her body growing tired of the daily struggles, though unable to sleep. When rest did come, she was roused by the calls of the watchmen, signaling a new wave bearing down on them in the night. It came as a surprise to her when the attacks came to a sudden halt, leaving them in peace for several uneasy days.

"Are you sure it is such a good idea for the men to be drinking when we are overdue for an attack?"

"Relax, Commander," Cadell elbowed Zander hard in the bicep, nearly knocking him over from the force. "We have plenty of soldiers on watch. These men have been at war for months without reprieve. They've not seen their wives and children or any semblance of normality since this all started. The least we can offer them is a single chance at remembering the good things in life – otherwise, they might forget why they are fighting for it."

Adjusting her helmet on her head, Leyna cast an unsettled glance in the direction of the tent, arms folded across her chest in an attempt to create warmth from the chill in the air. "My only concern is in the Prince's presence here. If the enemy is keeping watch, they might be inclined to arrange an ambush simply to get at him. Arcastus made his goal very clear. His being here now is just asking for trouble."

"By all means, you go in and tell the Prince he is not allowed to be here," Cadell chuckled. "Let me know how that goes," Despite his jovial demeanor, Leyna could see the attentiveness in his gaze, his eyes sweeping the area around them in a constant search for signs of anything out of place.

"Jesting aside, shouldn't he be out trying to find a bride and provide an heir rather than making small talk with drunken soldiers?" Zander swirled the water around in the bottom of his mug, oblivious to the unamused glances being cast at him from Leyna and Cadell.

"His presence is good for morale," Cadell argued. "It makes the men feel appreciated. In the past I have seen some start to feel as if the royal family had forgotten them, and it can lead to complacency and in worst cases, revolt. We cannot risk either of those right now."

"Zander is just bitter he is not inside drinking with them. Personally, I think a full night's sleep would be more beneficial to us all than wine." Tilting her head back, Leyna gazed up at the stars overhead. They were a beautiful sight to behold after so long neglecting their presence. There was so much she found herself taking for granted these days. So many little things that she tended to forget in her hurry to keep the troops equipped and on guard. Time didn't allow for admiration anymore.

In the inky darkness, the stars twinkled brightly, accenting the full moon hanging in the midst of them all. If she had a paint brush, she might have felt compelled to put the image to canvas and preserve its beauty forever. But by morning, the sight would be forgotten once again, lost to the bustle of battle preparations.

The sound of approaching footsteps from outside the tent drew Leyna out of her reverie, head tilting back further to see who or what was coming. An upside-down image of Varik filled her vision, a smile crossing over her lips. He looked looser than usual. A side effect of the wine.

"What brings you away from the party, Commander?" Cadell raised an eyebrow in Varik's direction, clearly curious by his approach. Varik gave a crisp salute in greeting, his body language revealing an obvious discomfort at interrupting them.

"The Prince is requesting to speak with you and the Captain, sir."

"The Captain and I are rather busy. Perhaps another time."

Varik shifted uncomfortably on his feet. "I was instructed to inform you that he is not merely asking."

Cadell chuckled quietly, his hand patting Leyna on the back. "Looks like he is pulling rank. In that case," he glanced over to Varik, his smile fading. "The Captain remains busy. I, however, will be along in a moment."

Leyna looked up to Cadell, nervous at the thought of disobeying a direct order from the Prince. "General, are you sure that is wise?"

"I will deal with it." Taking his place at Varik's side, Cadell motioned for her to remain seated. "Besides, someone must maintain the watch while the soldiers are distracted. Keep an eye on the perimeter."

Her mouth hung open in unspoken protest, knowing it was a waste of breath to argue with him.

Varik's expression revealed his own uncertainty at Cadell's directions though he didn't dare speak out against the decision. "Come with me, then," he replied quietly.

Leyna's eyes followed the men as they walked away, her stomach queasy. Distracted, she motioned for Zander to follow, beginning their rounds along the perimeter of camp.

"So, what is it?" Zander smirked, breaking into Leyna's thoughts with the sound of his voice. "The General doesn't want you to ensnare the Queen's final son with your beauty?"

"If it were that superficial, Cadell would not risk angering the Prince over it."

He shrugged. "Nothing seems worth the royal wrath to me."

Leyna sighed in frustration, unsure of how she could possibly explain it to him. Would he even understand? His own presence near the Prince could be just as dangerous, if not more so, than hers. "Tell me something, Zander," she mused, straightening her posture. "Has Cadell ever let you anywhere near the Prince?"

"No," he stated in a matter-of-fact tone. "But I am not the Captain and the Prince has never directly ordered an audience with me."

"What about the night of the masque? Did he not leave you in charge of seeing the royal family to safety?"

"The Prince refused to leave the General's side. They argued for a while and the next thing I knew, they were leaving. After making sure the Queen was secured, of course."

"You and I are a threat to the Prince's safety," she sighed. "Our enemies know us and have reason to come after us in retaliation. I personally was ordered by Queen Vorsila to stay away from her son. She and Cadell do not want to risk him getting caught in the crossfire. I imagine you might discover them to have a similar fear about you."

"Then why did they let you come here?" he asked. "Why did they allow you to join the military and offer you such a prestigious position when it would only draw the enemy's attention to you? Something just feels out of place to me."

"I like to think that I am being rewarded for my years of loyalty," Leyna said defensively. Zander did have a point, though. Many things felt suspicious. And while there were logical explanations, they didn't quite clear up the holes.

They continued in awkward silence, lost in thought over their own lives. It was incredible to think how far they both had come over the past few years. When they met, neither of them could have guessed that in over half a decade they would be sitting where they were, leading the military of their people, and locked in the most important war Tanispa had endured in centuries. It was a massive leap from their trivial role as spies in the company of Gislan and Oksuva. Two people who, while pivotal in setting things into motion, turned out to be no real threat themselves.

"Why did you come to Tanispa?"

"What?" His question confused her. Why wouldn't she come to Tanispa? The course of action was in no way curious, in the same way it made sense for Zander to have come. They were Vor'shai. Their people needed them.

"I thought you were staying in Siscal to help Feolan. I mean, you were on the court and had your home, and a perfect position to help our Queen from a safe distance. You never really told me why you gave it all up."

"I didn't give it up." She folded her hands in her lap, her eyes focused ahead into the darkness. "It was taken from me. There was an – unexpected event – after which I was already planning to leave Siscal when Kael happened upon me at the checkpoint by the city gates. He followed me back to my house, removing any safety that location might have once offered me. In the end, I was presented with a formal request from Queen Vorsila for my presence in Tanispa. When you add everything up, there was little reason to stay and no choice but to go."

Zander cast a glance in her direction out of the corner of his eye, his brow raised inquisitively. "Unexpected event?"

She frowned. It hurt to think about. The constant attention required of her for the war kept her mind too pre-occupied to dwell on it. Now, all of those feelings rushed over her ten-fold. "It's really complicated, Zander. I would rather not get into it."

"Ah, but you've already mentioned it. Courtesy now requires you to explain."

Biting her lip, discomfort welled up inside at the thought of speaking anything to Zander about Thade. How could he even understand? He knew nothing about the depths of her past relationship with Thade, even prior to the business which had crossed Leyna's path with Zander's. He would think she was being foolish to cling to her emotions the way she did. "It was nothing," she lied, turning away in hopes that Zander wouldn't see the truth in her eyes. "I should not have said anything."

Paused in his steps, Zander removed his helmet, extending his arm to prevent Leyna from moving away from him. "Leyna, look at me," he stated. She tried to avoid his gaze, but he made it difficult to look away, positioning his face in her direct line of sight. Reaching out his hands Zander unhooked Leyna's helmet, revealing her face. Her cheeks flushed with warmth, fingers lashing out to retrieve her armor.

"Whatever it is makes you blush. It troubles you. I can tell. We are friends, Leyna. You can tell me."

Chiding herself, she paced the ground in front of him, her eyes occasionally shifting in the direction where Cadell had gone. Why couldn't he come back? An interruption would force Zander to let this foolishness go. "Commander, return my helmet," she stated firmly, teeth gritted from embarrassment.

"If I return it, will you tell me what is troubling you?"

"Perhaps." She ceased her pacing, tapping her foot impatiently. "We are in the middle of a war. You would deprive me of protection? I suggest you don your own helmet as well unless you want to leave both our heads open for a Sanarik's arrow."

Begrudgingly, Zander handed her helmet back, replacing his own over his head. "I worry about you, Leyna. Most women could talk a man's ear off with their personal affairs but you — I don't know. You've always kept them bottled up. I don't mean any disrespect by inquiring, I just want to help. As a friend."

"What do you want me to say?" Leyna snapped, roughly positioning her helmet over her head once again. She was angered by his persistence while at the same time she couldn't blame him. Her behavior was suspicious enough without constantly avoiding his questions. "Does it change anything if I were to tell you that I am in love with the former Consul? That prior to my coming to Tanispa he and I — admitted our feelings for one another?"

"Admitted your feelings? Oh my god," he breathed in disbelief. "Did you sleep with the Consul?"

"I told you, I don't want to talk about it."

With a harsh exhale, she moved away from him, wringing her hands uncomfortably. None of this was his business. Why couldn't she have just told him no? It would have spared her from his bewilderment which now left him stammering at her in shock. They had a perimeter to keep safe. Now wasn't the time to discuss her private business. Nor was it in any way polite to speak of Thade in such a way while he wasn't there to defend his own actions.

After a moment of shocked silence Zander quickly caught up to Leyna's hastened pace, peering at her through the darkness. They were moving out of range from the lights burning around the tent. Most of the camp was deserted, the men having gathered around the Prince. It was a relief to Leyna knowing that the chances of their conversation being overheard were slim.

"Leyna, wait," Zander puffed, grabbing onto her arm to try and slow her steady stride. "Does this bother you? Why are you so angry? Do you regret it?"

The question stopped Leyna in her tracks. Did she regret it? No. Certainly not. Amongst the pain and confusion, that was the one thing she knew without doubt. It was impossible to regret that night with Thade. And she would do it all over again if given the chance. "I have no regrets," she stated quietly, eyes locked ahead in the distance. "It is just — complicated."

"If you don't regret it, then what is there for you to be so embarrassed about? Is it because you are a woman and society puts so much pressure on the idea of being virtuous?" Zander rolled his eyes. "Is that image enough to make you ashamed of being in love with him?"

"Why is everyone suddenly so interested in my personal affairs?" she asked, not wanting to discuss the matter any further. Zander had a point. It was just too disheartening for her to admit it. "First Cadell and now you — next thing the Prince is going to be demanding I give him details so they know how severe my punishment should be for involving myself with a man whose private activities are supposed to be approved by the Queen. Or so I have learned."

Zander gazed at her, a look of understanding visible in his eyes. "So that's what you're concerned about," he said softly. "You aren't embarrassed that you did it; you're afraid of what the Queen will do if she finds out. Frankly, I wouldn't worry about it. No harm came from it. It's not like you're pregnant or anything."

Covering her face with her hand, Leyna's shoulders heaved irritably. Leave it to Zander to find a way to make an already awkward situation more awkward. The fear of a child never crossed her mind over the months that passed after that night with Thade. It was a bright side to be considered, at the very least. Undoubtedly, a child would've made things far more complicated than they already were. She should be grateful their ties were able to be severed so easily.

But poor Thade. He had no way of knowing anything about her after that night. All of those concerns; did they haunt him? In the time that passed, there were so many things that could've happened... "It is not fair," she whispered, her thoughts voiced aloud in the darkness.

"What's not fair?" Zander peered at her quizzically. The sound of his voice caused her to blush, realizing her mistake at speaking the statement.

"Nothing," she waved dismissively. "I was just talking to myself."

He moved over to her side, hesitant, his hand resting lightly on her shoulder, tensed in preparation to pull away if she showed any sign of anger at his touch. "He is a lucky man to have your love, and a fool to let you go."

"He didn't let me go. I left him," she grimaced at the memory. "He asked me to marry him. We were going to run away together, but I couldn't let him do it. I couldn't bear the guilt – or the fear in knowing the danger I would be putting him in. They would have labeled him a traitor for deserting the Queen. And I... I could've been executed, simply for luring him away. So I left. He and I have not seen each other since."

"And yet both of you are in Tanispa. So what is stopping him from seeking you out now? You're a duchess, for goodness sake! There is nothing preventing him from making you his wife. No title or status separates you anymore."

"Hush!" she hissed at him. "Watch what you say. You never know who might be listening."

Deranged laughter filled the air around them, chills shooting up Leyna's spine. Her heart felt as if it stopped inside her chest, the blood running cold in her veins. She spun, seeking the location of the sound, unable to see anything but shadows cast by the tents and trees of the deserted camp.

Instantly, Zander's hand settled on the hilt of his sword. The confusion in his eyes was evident, his gaze darting from shadow to shadow, searching the darkness for the intruder. "Show yourself!" he shouted at the emptiness.

Several darkened shadows appeared from amongst the surrounding trees, a distant horn blowing a warning from the watch towers. A bit late on the call. Leyna stepped backward, gripping her sword in preparation for battle.

A tendril of black smoke crept along the ground at Zander's feet. Nervously, he backed away from it, unable to create more distance. "Stop running, you coward," Kael's voice floated on the breeze. "Imagine my surprise to find both of my targets together. And unguarded. I'm amazed how lazy you Vor'shai get when given a few days off."

"You should think about who you are calling a coward when you're the one hiding," Leyna called out, taunting him, praying he might show his face. A practitioner of Ven'shal sorcery was a deadly foe already, but with the element of surprise, they had almost no chance.

"I'm not hiding," Kael laughed, the sound echoing from all directions. "You just aren't looking hard enough."

Shadows moved about in front of them, dancing back and forth in the gentle wind. The finger-like smoke could be traced to one of the images, drawing Leyna's attention to the source. Directing her energy through her hand, Leyna projected a bright white light at the slithering tendrils, the shape dispersing in a cloud of grey smoke. In the flash, the shadows brightened, illuminating the faint outline of Ven'shal soldiers concealed within them. Stealth tactics. She cursed under her breath for never having considered it before.

The other figures were closing in on them. Blades drawn, Zander and Leyna stood their ground, unsure of how to fight something they couldn't see. The darkness would make the attacks of their foe more difficult to follow. But not impossible. They couldn't make themselves invisible. As long as there was some hint of their movement, there was a chance to defeat them.

It was strange to see Zander's sword slicing through the air, seemingly at nothing, a clang of metal against metal erupting upon contact with the twisting shadows. A shape was coming toward Leyna, fast, agile. It closed in with incredible speed, writhing in the wind created by the motion. As she sent a flash of light up from her palm, the figure flinched, revealing the vague image of Kael, granting Leyna an opening to strike. Her elbow shot upward, a loud crack emitting from his jaw as she connected with his chin. His distraction allowed Leyna to follow with a hook to the face, surprising herself at the power it possessed, Kael's body twisting at a strange angle under the force.

She couldn't lose the advantage she'd gained in throwing the first strike. He was off his guard, off balance, distracted by the pain. Now was her chance to keep him down.

There was no way to know how quickly the other soldiers would be able to reach them to provide assistance. The horns were still sounding in the distance. Leyna could only hope the attack would snap the soldiers back to sobriety.

In a flurry of blows, she pushed Kael back, meeting little resistance. A hint of what almost looked to be concern crossed his sharp features now fully visible without the cover of the shadows, lost in his distraction, the blackened surface of his eyes narrowed at her menacingly. "Someone learned how to fight —"

Leyna gritted her teeth as her knuckles collided with his temple. "I used to care if you got hurt." Another blow to the other side of his face. "But now you can rot with the rest of those corpses, for all I care. You are dead to me."

Her knee rose up to meet his stomach, caught in his hands before it could reach its target. Pushing down, he lunged at her, meeting nothing but empty air as she stepped out of the way, his own momentum carrying him forward, down to the ground. "Well done," he spat, climbing to his feet with a smirk. "You should know better than to think you can beat me though, Leyna. If you give up, this could be a lot less painful."

"And you should know that you can't kill me," she evaded another lunge, her heart racing.

"I'm not here to kill you." Kael's laughter cut through the night air again, louder than before. "Arcastus wants you. Alive. I'm just here to escort you. It's your choice whether you go willingly. Either way suits me just fine."

From the camp, Leyna heard the din of jovial conversation fall silent. It wouldn't be long now. If she could only hold out for a few more seconds, Kael would be out-numbered, forced to surrender. "Do you really think I'd let you win that easily?" she snapped.

Suddenly, the ground slid out from under her feet. The impact of the fall knocked the wind out of her lungs, an attempted scream caught in her throat. Pressure around her ankles bound them together. Something was dragging her. Pulling her along the grass, away from Zander.

She'd let him distract her. How could she have missed the attack? She should've known he would try something. The grip on her ankles felt like hands, but cold. Like ice against her skin. Kael moved along in front of her, the tendrils of shadow leading from his fingers to the ground. The same magic he'd used in attempts to go after Zander. If she could get a clear shot at them, it would be easy enough to break free of their hold.

She flattened her palms against the grass, clearing the scattered thoughts from her mind. She needed to focus. There was plenty of time to devise a plan before he could get her far enough away to present any real danger. If she could concentrate, she could manipulate her own force against him.

A thrum of energy tingled down the length of her arms and into the rich Tanispan soil. She felt the grass pulse, responding to the urgency of her command. Infused with new vigor, the blades of grass began to grow, gradually at first, then twisting into thick tendrils of green. They found purchase, pulling taut, Kael's upper body pitched forward under the sudden tension, breaking his own connection on the shadowy shackles binding Leyna's legs.

She rose to one knee and drew her sword. "I won't be taken without a fight," she stated, her voice calm despite the pounding heart in her chest. "You'll find me a better match than before."

Angrily, Kael swept his hands across the vines holding him captive, splitting them under the force. Uncertainty remained on his face, no longer confident in his ability to defeat her with the same ease as before. "Maybe I should seek out your beloved Consul to use as leverage against you. I imagine you would give yourself up if you thought it would save him."

"He would defeat you just as easily now as he did the last time. You couldn't catch him if you wanted."

The sound of his sword sliding from its sheath was less threatening than Leyna remembered. She was more prepared now. More skilled in her technique, thanks to Cadell's training. This time would be different. And she hoped quicker.

He came at her with a frenzy of swings in an attempt to dazzle her and open her guard. They were easy to parry, none aimed toward any vital targets. He was afraid of landing a blow that might end her life. His hesitance was her advantage. He couldn't kill her, but she was all too eager to end his life. And he was aware of it.

His guard was solid. There was no doubt he was a clever fighter. But even the most talented swordsmen were bound to make mistakes. Fatigue would be her best weapon against him, if her own endurance could hold. She needed to wear him out.

Holding the sword over her head, Leyna blocked another strike as it descended, Kael's strength forcing Leyna to her knees, arms trembling under the strain. He wasn't getting any weaker. There was no sign of him even being winded from the exertion.

She needed to be patient. Wait for an error. Once it came, timing would be essential to her victory. He was sure to notice any hole in his defense and correct it quickly. Leyna realized her best chance would be deception. If Kael thought he was winning, his overconfidence might cause him to get sloppy. *Make him think he is stronger.*

Sinking lower, she embellished the struggle. An arrogant smile spread over his lips.

Her conscience attacked at the most inopportune moment. The opening was there. Waiting for her to strike. Kael's defense was failing, focused more on maintaining his strength in pushing Leyna down. But why couldn't she move? Guilt? For the man he used to be? There was no use in mourning the fate of the monster that stood over her now. Any semblance of the old Kael had died alongside Enaes in Siscal.

As if moving of their own volition, her arms took advantage of Kael's distraction in his seeming victory. She redirected Kael's sword to the ground, side stepping, thrusting the tip of her blade deep into his abdomen. She felt the pain. Though only in her mind, she cried out from it, driving the sword deeper still.

There was no pain in Kael's eyes. Despite not wanting to face him in that moment, she couldn't look away, her insides clenching. "You actually did it," he wheezed. He sounded impressed. Almost relieved at the cool metal piercing through his body under her hands. Slouching forward, he inhaled, the gurgling noise wretched to Leyna's ears, her only distraction being the sound of his whispered voice. "I was afraid you wouldn't do it."

Afraid she wouldn't do it? He wanted to die? No. She refused to accept what she was hearing. "I won't let you put that guilt on me, Kael," she breathed.

"Finish it," he hissed. A dull thud at her side signaled Kael's sword falling in defeat. Shaky and pained, his fingers wrapped over Leyna's hands on the hilt of her weapon, trying to push it in further. "Set me free." His voice was a desperate pleading gasp. "Do it!"

The sound of movement came from behind Kael. Too quiet to be the troops coming from the tents. In her mind, she was transported back to the chapel garden in Siscal, cradling Enaes in her arms. It was a horrible sensation. Her imagination was in control, seeing an armor-clad figure rise up from over Kael's shoulder. It held something in its hand. A dagger. The same dagger which dealt the final blow to Enaes under Kael's control. *This isn't happening...*

Kael's body lurched forward in a solid jerk from the impact. She saw his face, then Enaes's, unable to focus on reality. The life was fading from the eyes of the man now lying, deadweight, in her arms, sinking down on top of her. "Kael," she shook him desperately. "Kael!"

The figure behind him wasn't fading. But it wasn't Kael's foggy shape in her head. The armor of the Prince glistened a brilliant silver in the moonlight, his hands sliding away from the dagger protruding out of Kael's upper back.

It wasn't in her mind. Oh, god, it was real!

Through the surreal images playing before her eyes, the sound of footsteps grew closer from the distance. A few at first, rapidly growing to a louder, collective clatter of armored men racing to pull Kael's body off of her.

She wasn't thinking clearly. There was some detail — one of great importance — that eluded her. *Think!* Her eyes darted over the area, straining her memory for what it was. They were carrying Kael away. No! They had to stop! "Put him down!" she shouted. She tore free of the hands holding her, checking her for injuries, oblivious to their presence.

Doing as commanded, the soldiers paused in confusion. She was in front of them instantly, clawing at Kael's neck. The amulet. She needed to find the amulet. If it was allowed to be lost, then Kael would've died for nothing. It didn't have to be in vain. Providing them with the amulet would be a great help to his people. In death, he could find some form of redemption. Her fingers closed around the chain there against his skin. She had it! The key to unlocking Arcastus's weakness.

The round medallion slid out from under Kael's bloodied collar, landing heavily against her hand. There was no flash of light or swirling shadows the way she'd witnessed in Siscal when she saw the amulet for the first time. It was thick. Gaudy. The gems were larger, the surface dim and unreflective in the light. "No," she exhaled, clutching it tightly in her hand until the edges cut into her palm. "It's fake! Damn you, Kael, why did you do this? Where is the real one?" she shouted, fists pounding against Kael's chest.

Leyna was distantly aware of someone pulling her back to her feet. She was in a panic. The feeling of frustration was overwhelming. Why did he have to say those things? It would've been so much easier to cope if he'd just continued to be his usual evil self. The one she'd come to expect over the years. And the amulet! Who had the real one?

Another pair of strong arms was pulling her in a different direction. "Your Highness, you need to get back to the tent." It was Cadell's voice coming from somewhere close by. They were his hands holding her yet she was vaguely aware of a pair of silver eyes watching her as she was being dragged away. The Prince. Cadell was taking her away from him. "Zander, Varik – see that the men clear this body out of here. His friends might come looking for him. Set up a perimeter. We need to be ready."

Everything was slowing down again, her senses gradually returning. How could she have let her emotions run away like that? It was one of Cadell's first lessons in their training. Emotions could be the fine line between life and death in combat. And why now, of all times, did those old feelings resurface in her mind? She hated Kael. It didn't make sense not to hate him for all the pain he'd caused. He killed Enaes! He was a traitor. And she almost let him live.

"I can walk on my own, General," she stated, her voice trembling slightly from the adrenaline still coursing through her system. Cadell traveled – rapidly – putting distance between them and the men. He was anxious, seemingly desperate to get her as far away from the Prince as possible.

"I will not release you until you are safely inside your tent," he said firmly. "I failed to protect you once this evening. I refuse to make the same mistake again."

He was rougher than normal as he pushed her through the flap of their tent, securing it as best he could behind him. She reached up to her helmet, pulling it off, the metal clanging to the ground at her feet. "He wasn't trying to kill me."

"No? Because it certainly looked that way when I arrived."

"He was not allowed to kill me. Arcastus ordered him to bring me alive."

"To kidnap you?"

"Yes."

"Why?"

Leyna's mouth hung open, speechless. She had no answer. It sounded ridiculous, even to her, despite the fact that she was the one trying to argue it. "I don't know," she sighed in defeat. "Why did you let the Prince come there? The intention might not have been to kill me, but he could've been killed without Kael blinking an eye."

"I think you are falsely under the assumption of my control over the Prince being greater than it is."

"But are you not capable of being persuasive enough to convince him to remain safe?"

"He heard the name of the man attacking. There was no convincing him of anything."

Unhooking the clasps on her armor, Leyna began to slide out of it, anxious to be free of the unnecessary weight upon her shoulders. "What difference does the name make when the Prince's life is at stake?"

"Do you not think he knows the identity of the man who killed his brother?"

The words came like a punch in the stomach. It made sense. How could she blame him for wanting revenge? She harbored the same feelings toward Damir. Over the years, she'd risked her own life countless times on the off chance of striking him down, but she wasn't the last remaining heir to the royal throne.

"How did he come into possession of the dagger which killed Prince Enaes?"

"It was found at the scene of Enaes's murder," Cadell frowned. "If we're lucky, his insistence to fight will lessen now that he has avenged his brother. The death of one so close to the heart of our enemy will almost certainly guarantee a large scale attack, and soon."

"Good," she nodded. It was exactly what she wanted. To draw out the men working for Arcastus. And if they were lucky, it would draw the lich out as well. "I want

Arcastus. I failed to prevent his resurrection, but I intend to be the reason his soul departs this world forever."

Cadell looked prepared to argue at first, his features tensed, eyes narrowed. After a moment, they started to ease. "You remind me of the young Prince, you know that?" he said. The look on his face gave the impression of irritability while his tone masked a hint of pride at her determination. "You have the mind of a soldier, the heart of a queen for her subjects, and the stubbornness of a mule. May the gods have mercy on Arcastus's soul when he realizes what he has gotten himself into by challenging you."

Chapter Twenty-Eight

Leyna sat in a chair positioned near the front of the command tent, eyes directed down at the floor, concerned. Thoughtful. Zander and Cadell stood facing one another a few feet away, Varik's slender figure perched at the door, guarding the entry in case anyone happened by. The same questions hung on everyone's lips, but it was Cadell who chose to speak first.

"Kidnapping is an odd war strategy. There has to be a reason why Arcastus would want the Captain brought to him alive."

"Maybe he is starting to suspect something," Zander shrugged. "After Leyna's first confrontation with him, even the most confident of warriors would start to second-guess whether they had all their plans in order. Given Kael's history with her, it seems foolish to me that they would send him to bring her back — unless it was done as a punishment. Maybe he admitted the truth and was sent to correct his error."

Cadell stroked his chin, contemplating Zander's suggestion. It made sense, though Leyna found it hard to believe it was so simple. If there was a concern of Leyna some-how getting in the way, it seemed more likely that Arcastus would demand her brought before him dead. A live prisoner was too much of a risk.

"Maybe," she stated quietly, lifting her eyes from the floor without meeting the curious stares of the others. "But why alive? Why not dead? I would be less trouble-some to his plans if I was simply — removed."

"Not if he fears what your death at this point would do to him." Zander came to stand at Leyna's side. "The ritual was intended to use the blood of a slain Vor'shai. Arcastus is a skilled sorcerer, but what if he wasn't prepared for something like this? Have we considered the possibility that even Arcastus has no idea what this blunder means to his magic? He would want to investigate more thoroughly before doing anything drastic. For all we know, Leyna's death could weaken him. Maybe even kill him. There is no way to be certain what the connection involves."

Cadell's eyes were fixed on Leyna, curious. Intrigued by the possibility. "Or do you think his intention was to remove her from the fight altogether? To keep her hostage. If she is a threat, it would make sense for him to find some way of eliminating her from the battlefield without striking her down."

"There is no way to guess their intentions. These are madmen we are dealing with. Our rational minds could never sink to their level," Leyna leaned back in her seat. It was frustrating. She wanted the answers as much as the others, but she realized how impossible it would be to obtain them. Without someone who understood the ways of Arcastus, they would accomplish nothing but guesswork, and assumptions would never get them anywhere. "The bottom line is that this changes nothing for us. I will not be removed from the fight simply because of a failed attempt at abduction. I need to be out there alongside the troops. If you take me off the field, then Arcastus wins either way."

Cadell folded his arms across his chest. He made no excuse for argument. Leyna knew he understood her point. They couldn't afford to lose their captain at a time like this. Not with the possibility of increased attacks. One of the enemy generals was dead. They had the upper-hand. "We need to be more careful then," he nodded. "If they tried once, they are bound to try again. Our goal is to be ready for them the next time. We will keep more men near you. Try not to stray far when we charge."

"That is not a promise I can make, General. You know how hectic things get on the field," Leyna clucked her tongue, discouraged. She was supposed to help the Tanispan soldiers, not hinder them more than they already were with their falling numbers and weakness against the growing army of undead.

"At least assure me you will try. I will attempt to keep close to you as well. Our number one priority should be to keep you out of their grasp. We still don't know what usefulness your association will be, but if there is any chance that it will benefit us, we need to be attentive. Beyond that, we don't want to risk losing one of our best fighters."

"You know I will try," she said calmly, forcing a smile of reassurance for the sake of Zander and Cadell. They were worried about her. And with good reason. She was worried about herself. There was no way to know what Arcastus would do if given the chance. Kael's oversight had left her in a very sticky position. One that she wished could be avoided. "I will be prepared if they come for me again. If I notice anything out of the ordinary, I will find my way back to the rest of the troops and take cover among their numbers. For now, that is all I can offer."

"And that's all we can ask," Cadell gave an approving smile, clapping his hand firmly over Leyna's shoulder. "I'm not about to let them take you from us."

Cadell's prediction of increased attacks proved accurate over the next few nights. Arcastus's men came in waves, with still no sign of their leader. His absence on the battlefield left Leyna feeling uneasy. They were plotting something. The attacks were a distraction, though she could only guess what their actual plan was.

The enemy focus moved away from the surrounding countries, centering on Tani-spa with a ferocity unlike anything seen before in the lifetime of the soldiers. Whatever Arcastus's intentions were, he made no attempt to hide his interest in Sivaeria. Fewer armies marched on Carpaen and Siscal, leaving more of the neighboring militaries able to send reserve troops to aid the Vor'shai. But the Ven'shal numbers were growing. Strengthened by the ever rising corpses which fought on Arcastus's side. Not even the Queen could have expected their power. It was disheartening to Leyna, her experience in the military having always been on the winning end, but now failing at every attempt against the Ven'shal.

She couldn't allow herself to think on the negatives at that moment. They were under attack. Line after line of Arcastus's men poured onto the field, straining the endurance of her soldiers, leaving them winded and in need of rest. It would only be so much longer before the Tanispan troops would start to fall back. The Sanarik fought from the shadows, cutting down Leyna's men with relative ease, unpredictable in their attacks. Worse, the Namiren warriors were stronger now than before, second only to the power of the Ven'shal sorcerers leading the army forward.

Leyna's arms and legs carried her on mechanically. Block, parry, thrust. It was unending. The Ven'shal kept coming. Persistent. Her eyes burned from lack of sleep, but she had no choice but to keep fighting. She longed for just a glimpse of the enemy leaders. They would be the weak point. Without Arcastus, the resurrection of the dead would cease. Their numbers would finally lessen. But was it too late? Were their own troops depleted too greatly to come back from the loss?

A figure stood ahead of her, dressed in armor different from the other Ven'shal soldiers. His hauberk gleamed silver in the light of the moon overhead, standing out amongst the blackened surfaces of the usual enemy uniform. He seemed to take notice of her, beckoning her forward. There was no time to guess at his motives. Get in and get out. Cut him down and move on to the next, the same as any other enemy. Sword drawn high, she prepared to lunge, finding the motion stopped by a pair of strong hands wrapping around her, arms pinned to her sides.

She struggled under the hold. Her movement came to an awestruck stop as the figure she'd been targeting removed his helmet, a pleased smile crossing over his lips to see her there. "Well, hello my darling little Eleni," Oran's voice exaggerated the sweetness in his tone. "Or what is it now? Leyna?"

Her efforts to free herself resumed, more desperate than before. Though she refused to let Oran see it, she feared what would happen if she couldn't get away. There was no telling what Arcastus wanted with her. And knowing the nature of his ways, she didn't want to risk finding out. She'd given Cadell her assurances that this wouldn't happen. How could she have missed their approach?

"Going so soon? Ah, but there is someone who wants to see you."

It wasn't Oran who spoke. The whisper came from closer, pressed to her ear, sinister in its familiarity. Fear rushed through every corner of her being in recognition. Kyros.

A shadowy black veil crept over her eyes, disrupting her vision. Slowly she felt the tendrils of the perverted energy wrapping around her, squeezing tight over her arms and legs, restricting any movement she attempted. *You are stronger than him. Just get away. Break his grip.* It was one thing to think it, but a completely different matter in following through. Kyros was stronger than Kael twice over, if not more. Who was she fooling? She was blinded and helpless. Escape was futile.

This was no game, the way it had been when she first met Kyros, following Oksuva around like a puppy. He knew her weaknesses and was unfazed by her strengths. She could feel them dragging her along. Direction was lost to her under the blackened film which covered her eyes, leaving her unable to see anything. Her hands were empty. The weight of her sword no longer in her grasp. Cursing silently, she realized that it had fallen from her fingers when Kyros took hold of her. Even if she broke free, she would be defenseless.

Before she could gather the strength to fight the darkness, she felt them come to a stop, her hands bound tightly by something cold, yet soft. A creaking accompanied the sensation of her ankles being wrapped by a thick rope, the scent of bark filling her nostrils. Tree roots. Her assailants were using the earth against her, forcing the living base of the trees to uproot from the ground, bending to the will of their commands, acting as rough shackles to hold Leyna in place.

"I fail to see what good I am to you," she scoffed, her eyes blinking as the veil of shadow slipped away, revealing Kyros and Arcastus standing only inches from where she was bound. They were in a thicket somewhere, dense trees blocking her view of the battlefield. A tangle of roots held fast to her legs, her wrists bound by a thin tendril of shadow extending out from Arcastus's hand.

"You aren't any good to us. You really would be much more useful dead, and you should've been, but someone failed me," Arcastus rasped. His skeletal features hadn't improved from the last time Leyna saw him. For the first time, she caught sight of his hands, the bony tips of his fingers clicking together while he manipulated the magic binding her. "This battle has gone on for too long. But now, I intend to finish things. However, not until I've done a bit of experimenting on you."

The thought sent chills down her spine. Experiments? She failed to see what he could possibly want with her. Though she preferred not to die, it seemed most beneficial to Arcastus for her to be dead. Toying with her beyond a direct execution felt like a waste of time on his part.

Grabbing onto her bound hands, Arcastus dragged the blade of a knife along her right palm. It happened so fast. She barely had a chance to register the pain, watching the blood trickle from the wound. At the sight of it, Arcastus stepped away. "Collect the specimen, Kyros. You know I can't touch it."

"What exactly are you hoping to prove?" she snapped, attempting to jerk her hands away from Kyros, the bindings holding her in place.

Kyros laughed. He pulled a vial from inside a satchel wrapped around his waist. Holding it up to the light, he checked it for imperfections, satisfied with the smooth, clear glass. In a fluid motion he gathered some blood from her hand, flicking the outer surface of the cylinder with his fingernail.

She needed to know what they were doing. Whatever it was, it related to her intimately, far more so than she was comfortable with. Every minute they kept her was another she should be out with her troops.

There had to be some way of breaking free, the shadowy shackles still linked to Arcastus's hands from where he stood at Kyros's side, heads tilted together in contemplation over the vial. They were distracted. If she could just get her legs loose.

She needed to overcome the magic manipulating the roots. The shackles were draining her. Something in the link between her and Arcastus was drawing energy from her body. Invigorating him.

Fight it. You are stronger than he is. Another lie. An unconvincing one, at that. Arcastus was the epitome of the ancient Ven'shal. Powerful, strong — and evil. A part of him in life might have once shown compassion for Mescavis's loss, but those days were far behind. His decaying form now only thought of death and destruction. Negotiating any compromise would be out of the question. Her only option was to outwit him.

Closing her eyes, she tried to ignore the murmuring conversations of the men. Maybe she could reverse the flow of energy, like with the grass that first night against Arcastus's undead soldiers. It was her only chance at regaining enough strength to overpower them. She drew the last of her energy inside herself, holding it, centered in her core. The sensation of the connection with Arcastus was sickening. Her body rejected it, pushing much of the power away even as she drew more inward.

After several long moments of silence, a soft creak reached her ears from below. It was working. The roots budged, if only a little. She had to go slow, or risk being noticed. Bit by bit the tree receded. It was hard not to lose concentration in her excitement over the success. Her legs were mobile again. A single high step would set her free of the restraints. But not yet. Timing would be everything.

Her curiosity about what Kyros and Arcastus were doing grew with every passing moment. There was a small flame on the ground, Arcastus's raspy voice chanting some ancient incantation. It was the blood they were concerned with. Her blood. Her body was nothing more than the vessel. It seemed to her advantage. The less attention they paid to her, the better.

Arcastus's voice trailed off. Whatever ritual he performed was almost complete. They would return to her soon. She prepared to run. The shadows around her wrists might still pose an issue, but she didn't fear them as much; though there was a definite difference between these bonds and those which Kael conjured. Focus was the key. She couldn't let him tap into her own energy and use it against her.

"It will take a few moments," Arcastus explained to Kyros nonchalantly. "This will tell us the extent of the connection. If I feel any adverse effects when her heart stops, we will know she must be kept alive. At least until we can devise a permanent solution."

His tone grew more and more irritated as he spoke. There was a clear hatred over the predicament. Leyna couldn't help but find the weakness in Arcastus's plan to be convenient. It was almost as if it had been arranged for her benefit.

Could it be? Kael's final words echoed in her mind. He wanted to die. The sorcery was too strong for him to overcome — and yet there were signs that it was wavering. Some fragment of the old Kael had been present in the moment of his death. Many times she'd witnessed flickers of it. An occasional internal struggle.

Arcastus was coming closer, the stench of death surrounding him, suffocating Leyna's senses. She couldn't focus on her own thoughts anymore. All she could see was his cadaverous form, flesh dangling from bones. The least grotesque parts of his body were the black pits of his eyes, tinted with their yellowish glow. They weren't quite like Kyros's. A swirl of shadow danced in the sockets, like some sliver of his tortured soul. "It will all be over soon, my dear," he said with a skeletal grin. "Damir would've loved to see you in these final moments. You should consider yourself lucky. If he had his way, your death would be slow and painful, with days of torture. Unfortunately, I don't have that kind of time."

"Neither do I." Leyna felt the sticky texture on her palm where the knife had opened the skin. Blood. Arcastus said he couldn't touch it. He was close enough for her to reach, even in her bindings. She didn't know what would happen, but it was her only available weapon, her sword long since abandoned on the battlefield.

Her palm shot out across Arcastus's face, the blood smearing over his decaying flesh. The feeling was disgusting. It was all she could do to keep from retching at her fingers dragging over the slimy skin. Smoke erupted from him under her touch, pained wails echoing through the dense copse. His hands lifted to his face, his spectral hold on

Leyna broken, releasing her from the shackles. She leapt from the roots, clashing into Kyros with her shoulder and sending him sprawling, his sword landing at Leyna's feet.

That was too easy. Something isn't right. She pushed the thoughts away in frustration as she scooped up Kyros's fallen weapon. She needed to get back in the open where the troops could help her, but she had no inkling of where she was. All she knew was that she couldn't remain with Arcastus and Kyros. Together they would be impossible to confront alone.

Running as fast as she could, she pushed through the thick trees blocking her path. In the distance the sounds of battle waged on. *Follow the sound.* She couldn't be far. She was across enemy lines, without doubt. Getting through the mob would be a challenge if she had any hope of reaching her men. *Don't look back. Keep your eyes ahead.* Kyros was right behind her. She could hear his breath with every step under the strain of their rapid pace. If she could just get into the thick of the fighting. It would be easier to hide on the battle field.

To her surprise, the armored soldiers of the Vor'shai came quickly into view. Either Kyros hadn't taken her far, or her men were pushing them back. It would be easy to cut through them without Arcastus reviving the fallen Ven'shal. With his attention distracted, the enemy would not be replenished. And there she was – their brave Captain – running away.

Kyros was closing on her. The sensation of something cold and sharp pierced into her right shoulder, sending her to the ground, the weight of something heavy sprawled on top of her. It was the worst position for a fight with someone as skilled as Kyros. Never give your enemy your back. Cadell stressed it to her, repeatedly, and yet she did it. Unintentional, but still foolish. She was at his mercy.

Laughter filled the air around her. Haunting, evil. If it wasn't going to be the last thing she heard in life, she might have feared the nightmares it would cause. Bracing herself for the impact, she closed her eyes, her breath held.

She heard someone shout. The weight lifted from her back, cutting the maniacal cackle short, replaced by an abrupt silence. Was she dead? Had he killed her?

She screamed at the feeling of a blade being tugged from her shoulder. Not dead. The pain was a good sign. If only she could move her right arm. Her attempts were excruciating, a searing fire coursing through every nerve, every tendon, every ligament, straight through the muscles down to her fingertips. Grasping the shoulder, she fought back the desire to panic. Shock was starting to set in. It clouded her mind, chest heaving. Now was not the time to hyperventilate. The enemy was still close. But where? What stopped him from taking her life?

Through hazy vision she saw an outline of Kyros in the darkness, his lithe form twisting and turning to evade the attacks coming at him, the opposing blade catching the light of the moon overhead. Arcastus preferred the nighttime charges despite the difficulty it lent in sight distance. She had to squint to focus on the figure confronting Kyros. There was no mistaking the Prince's armor. He'd come to her rescue? It was her job to protect him, not the other way around...

With her mobile hand, she fumbled blindly over the ground to find Kyros's sword. She needed to get to the Prince. Kyros would surely kill him, and it would be all her fault! It couldn't have fallen far.

The scent of decay in the air caused her heart to race. Arcastus was coming. He must have seen them. "Damn it," she breathed. How could she fight Arcastus without a weapon? Her magic would be child's play in comparison to his. And the thought of touching him in hand-to-hand combat made her shudder. There must be another option.

Rising to her knees, her leg bumped against something hard on the ground. A blade. Someone had dropped a short sword. It was thinner than most military issue, but strong. Durable. The metal was covered in a dark liquid along the tip. Blood. *Oh god, it's my blood.* She tried to reach for it, crying out in agony. She couldn't grip it. Her right arm was useless.

There was no more time to waste. The stench was growing stronger, closer. In a fluid motion, she grabbed the weapon with her left hand, adjusting the grip awkwardly with her fingers. Of all the moments to fight off-handed, it had to be now?

As she spun on her knees to face Arcastus, her blade thrust outward, meeting resistance immediately. In awe, she watched Arcastus's skeletal legs come out from under him. They cracked upon impact with the ground. Agile and swift, she rolled to her feet with the momentum.

The wails escaping Arcastus's thin, rotting lips sent chills down her spine. Soldiers stopped to find the source of the sound, covering their ears from the shrillness of it.

The blade protruded from his abdomen. It seemed a superficial wound for a lich, but something about it caused him great suffering. He was paralyzed on the ground, smoke rising from the wound, the metal burning into the sallow skin barely covering his bones.

He was vulnerable. It frustrated her to realize she was at a loss on how to kill something like him. Did he have a heart? Vital organs? There was nothing to him but skin and bones under a heavy cloak of black, velvety fabric. In her delirium from her own wound, she couldn't help but laugh at the cliché of his appearance. All he needed was a wand and he would look like an evil wizard character straight out of one of the fairy tales she used to love when she was a child.

Snap out of it! The world around her spun in circles, out of control. Arcastus was recovering. Through her blurred vision, she could see him clutching at the sword, pulling it free with some effort. Leyna tried to stop him, but her limbs were uncoordinated. Arcastus lunged for her, their bodies toppling to the ground in a heap, the rancid scent of his corpse almost choking her with its pungent aroma.

Her blood. She needed to find a way to use it against him the way she had in the clearing. It had been on the blade which she'd picked up from the ground, causing the insufferable wails which had escaped Arcastus upon contact. The blow to his stomach wasn't enough to kill him. He was already dead. Mortal wounds would do nothing to keep him down. Desperate, she pressed her hand against the laceration on her shoulder, feeling the blood coating her skin from the gash. Trying to keep Arcastus away from her, she extended her blood-covered palm over his face, her own cries mingling with Arcastus's from the pain she felt, as if her skin was on fire. Tendrils of smoke rose from where his blood mixed with hers against his rotted cheeks.

A loud groan echoed from off to her right. The sound of clashing swords came to a sudden halt, leaving the field in near silence for the first time since nightfall. Looking up, she saw Kyros's body slumped down on the ground, run through with a sword still clutched in the hands of the Prince. A bright light erupted from around Kyros, splitting off into three beams scattered in different directions across the field. One of them met with Arcastus, surrounding him in a brilliant glow, illuminating his form as well as something else which hung from his neck.

The medallion. Through the light which covered Arcastus, Leyna could see the details in perfect clarity. Unlike the first time when she'd observed it, two of the corner gems were broken, shattered. The center gem pulsed, sporadic, a flash of light flickering from inside. Next to it, a tiny, clear, pearl-like gem, radiated with a soft, reddish hue, the color inside undulating in synchronization with the center stone. As the light faded from around Kyros, Leyna could feel Arcastus seem to grow stronger from his position atop her, renewing his efforts to strike at her with the sword.

The stones. They were linked somehow; one with each of the men responsible for Arcastus's resurrection. The first for Kael, and the second now shattered at Kyros's death. *That means the central gem must be for their leader.* It had to be destroyed. As long as the stone was intact, Arcastus would survive. But he was so strong. Her muscles shook with every effort she made to fend off the attacks.

Footsteps pounded over the ground from all directions around where Leyna and Arcastus struggled against one another. With the last of her energy, Leyna thrust her hand upward against Arcastus's chin, his neck snapping from the pressure, bones cracking as his head tilted at an unnatural angle. There was no time to think about getting the amulet from him. In her brief opening, Leyna rolled out from under Arcastus, struggling to regain her footing, the world still spinning rapidly in her vision. Through the confusion, she could make out the sight of Ven'shal soldiers rushing forward to aid Arcastus, coming in waves. She had to get away. Someone was at her side, dragging her in the opposite direction from the incoming enemy troops. Shouting for a retreat.

All she wanted to do was sleep. Her right arm was numb, heavy. Deadweight from her shoulder. The sensation of darkness coming over her felt unnatural. Not the usual woozy feeling from loss of blood. She was beyond shock. Mentally, she couldn't register the motion of her own body, feet stumbling along the uneven ground toward the camp. Her head was floating. Every beat of her heart came slower than the next. Thud. Loud inside her ears. Another step. Thud. Her brain was losing oxygen from the languid pulse.

What is happening to me?

She attempted to speak words out loud, but couldn't hear her voice. No one was responding. But wait – voices came from somewhere. They were close. Right overhead. She was lying on the ground now. How did she get there?

Thud.

In a brief moment of release, she felt the world slip away from her, the voices gone, leaving her with a feeling of peace before her body shut down, the resounding beat of her heart ceasing, giving way to absolute silence.

Chapter Twenty-Nine

The physicians in the tent scurried about at the sight of Thade holding Leyna's lifeless form in his arms, long strides carrying him over to a hard, flat, surgical table near the back of the area. His helmet had been discarded on the field, dirt and blood smeared across his cheeks and forehead. An agonized look filled his eyes as he laid her down. "Help me get this armor off her," he commanded. "She is dying. Do not waste time just standing there."

A doctor came to his aid, removing the helmet from over Leyna's head. Seeing her face, Thade's body stiffened, a pained grimace contorting his elegant features, even through the grime which covered his skin. The doctor pressed his fingers against Leyna's neck in search of vital signs. "Pulse is absent," he called out to the nurses.

"Come on, Leyna," Thade breathed, patting the sides of her face gently. "Come back to me. You have been through worse. Do not leave me like this. Not like this."

"Your Highness, it will be easier for the doctors to tend her if you step away," Cadell's voice came hollowly from the entrance. He looked ragged. His own pain at seeing Leyna lying there was evident on his usually stern face. "Come. Stand over here by me."

"I am more help at her side than yours. If the doctors need assistance, I am perfectly capable of providing it."

"You are too emotional, Thade," Cadell shook his head. "You are not thinking clearly enough to be of any use here."

Thade's fingers moved over the straps of Leyna's armor, helping to remove it from over her blood-soaked shirt. His hand moved to her wrist to seek a pulse. He found nothing. Her heart remained still. Unbeating. "Why was no one with her?"

he shouted. Without thinking, he tore the remainder of the fabric over the wound on her chest, exposing the injury for the doctor's to examine. "You assured me when I discovered her under your care that you would never let her out of your sight," he yelled to Cadell. "This is exactly what I feared would happen! I should have fought harder to have her removed from military service, but I foolishly let you and my mother convince me to leave it be."

"Your mother gave me orders, and I followed them. You know her word is higher than even yours. What would you have me do? Disobey the Queen?" Cadell's voice trailed off, dejected.

Medical staff continued to bustle about the table, cleaning the wound on her chest. Once covered by a makeshift bandage, she was turned over, the laceration on her back visible through the torn material. "Queen Vorsila insisted our focus needed to remain on the war efforts," Cadell continued. "And I find it difficult to disagree. Had it been up to you, she never would have been allowed to fight."

Pushed out of the way by one of the doctors, Thade watched the nurses working. Diligently cleaning the wounds, keeping watch over her vitals every few moments. There was still no response. "Of course I wouldn't have let her fight," he snapped. His eyes remained locked on Leyna, unable to tear them away. "And for this very reason! Because those men would single her out. Did you not take into consideration any of the information I sent you over the past several years? They know her. The head of this all is the very same Damir Rohld who killed her mother. There was never any doubt that he, at the very least, would come for her. And still you let this continue."

"We need her," Cadell said through gritted teeth. Grabbing onto Thade's arm, he pulled him aside, away from any possible eavesdroppers among those surrounding Leyna's body. "You said it yourself, in your own reports from Siscal, that she was one of the best fighters in your unit. One of our most loyal subjects. And she knows the enemy. We cannot afford to lose her. The men respect her. They trust her. They look up to her. We are too far into this now to take her away and none of this will mean anything at all if we do not win this war. Think like a prince and not a man with a broken heart. Your people and their safety must come before all else. Do not make the same mistakes your brother did."

"And what good will she do us if they cannot revive her?" Thade grimaced at the thought. "She will have died without ever knowing. I will lose her without having even one last chance to tell her how I feel, and all because of this ridiculous deception arranged just to keep her in this battle. My mother may have the peoples' interest in mind but she fails to consider her own son."

Tensed and rigid, Cadell let Thade's words linger on the air between them. He watched the doctors hurry about the tent, calling out orders to the nurses, gathering their implements to suture Leyna's wounds, the constant shouts announcing the continued lack of life signs from her. He sighed. "Do not make this any harder than it already is."

There was nothing to be said in response. They watched in silence, waiting for some word on Leyna's condition, both anxious and admittedly frightened of the possible outcome. Her body had been without a pulse for far too long. Any other soldier would have been pronounced deceased long before now, but something kept the doctors going, the nurses finishing the sutures and tending to the wounds.

When they finally moved away, Thade took a step forward, his fingers reaching tentatively out to Leyna's slender arm, pale and lifeless against the white surface of the table. "Your Highness," one of the doctors stated calmly from the other side of the table. "She appears to be alive, but lacking any vital signs, which I must admit has us all rather confused. Many of us have checked and double checked, and sense a flow of energy inside her. Whatever is causing this suspended state in her can only be some form of sorcery. But without knowledge of what it is, we cannot fight it."

"Will she live then?" Thade questioned.

The doctors glanced at each other, hesitant, their uncertainty obvious under Thade's inquisitive gaze. "From what we can tell. It is difficult to say. We can't judge any length of time for its duration. For all we know, she could remain comatose for years, or could wake in moments. We have nothing by which to say, and that leaves me with very few answers to the questions I'm sure you have. I've never personally seen anything like this before."

"But she has no pulse. Will that not cause damage to her?" Cadell asked, moving to Thade's side, his hand resting on his shoulder. "Surely there must be more we can do to keep her stable."

"The energy flow tells us that the body is still functioning. Something other than the heart is pushing blood through her system. We simply need to keep watch in case it ceases to do so, though at such a time, it would stand to reason her heart would resume the work."

"And her arm?" Cadell added. "The injury looks severe. Will she be able to use it again?"

Heaving a sigh, the doctor checked again for a pulse on Leyna's neck, pausing to think over his response. "If a more skilled physician, perhaps one of those on Her Majesty's staff, were to perform some work on it, there would be a possibility of recovery. With only the equipment available to us here – no. She would lose all use of it."

"Then Her Majesty's physicians will be contacted," Thade stated firmly. Cadell glanced over to him, curious, but not daring to speak a word in protest. It was unusual for the Queen's personal physicians to treat someone outside of the royal family. The gesture would look strange to anyone who caught word of the order.

"Are you sure about this, Your Highness?" he asked.

Thade stared ahead a moment, his eyes never blinking. "As far as I am concerned, she is to be treated like a member of our family."

"As you wish then, sir," Cadell nodded. He turned toward the door, pausing in thought. Slowly, he spun back around, his gaze shifting over to where Thade remained standing at Leyna's side. "Perhaps the orders should come from you. It would be best if you were not here when she wakes up. I will stay with her."

Grabbing a small stool from the side, Thade positioned it next to the table, settling himself onto it proudly. Every action was deliberate. Silent and intentionally disregarding Cadell's suggestion.

Cadell took another step forward. "Your Highness –"

"I believe it is your duty to see to the troops and make sure they are being directed appropriately for defensive measures in case of another wave of attacks," Thade stated swiftly and without emotion. "If they are doing as required, you can take a few minutes to return to the palace, check on my mother, and see that the physicians are notified of their immediate departure for our location. I will sit with her."

"Thade, I do not recommend this."

"I do not care what you recommend. I will not leave her side until I know she is out of danger. Think positively, though. If I am here, I am not on the battlefield."

Fists clenched, Cadell drew in a deep breath, words forming on his lips but never spoken. His own guilt kept him quiet. He watched Thade, ever vigilant, his hand clasped over Leyna's, an occasional shift of his weight to lean forward, squinting for any sign of life in her. Obvious pain crossed over Cadell's face at the sight, his brow furrowed. "And what will you do if she awakens? It does not change the fact that she cannot see your face."

"Let me worry about that," Thade replied quietly. "You have your orders, General."

Hollow sounds filled Leyna's head. Some like voices, others the clink of metal against metal, or stone. It was a mess of nothingness to her. Thud. *Was that her heart? It was so loud inside her ears, echoing through every corner of her head, painful and overwhelming. She ached. As though she'd been at Malic's Tavern for days guzzling the most disgusting bottle of ale.*

Thud.

There it was again. The strange voices were less distant than before. They were close. Something poked at her. She thought to push it away, but her body showed no response. It came again, longer this time, yelling something in gibberish to someone else. Two people were poking at her, prodding her.

A softer, gentler pressure, squeezed at her hand. At least she thought it was her hand. She realized she had no concept of where anything was on her body. It was detached from everything inside her head. Other than the occasional pressure of whatever surrounded her, she felt nothing. She could move nothing.

It was different from when her mind was detached before, when Kael nearly killed her in Siscal. Things were visible then. The pain in her body had been gone and she'd looked down upon it from above; no connection to it at all. But now, she felt the pain. An uncomfortable tingle spreading throughout her. Why couldn't she see? It sent panic through her. She wanted to know who was touching her. Who was holding her here?

There was no memory of how she'd gotten to this point. No comfort from the fear. Was it Arcastus? What happened to him? Vague images in her mind sparked the memory of a fight. She'd been fighting him. But who won? Her arm — she couldn't use her arm. Then how did she fight him?

Questions raged in her head. With a final, reverberating thud from her heart, suddenly the world sprung to life around her, in a flitting second of bright light and noise. Gasping for breath, she saw a crowd of people leaning over her. One face looked surreal among the others, seated at her side, his features drawn, skin pale, darkened circles under his eyes from lack of sleep. Even through her confusion, she recognized him. Thade. He was there.

She tried to reach out to him, finding the task impossible. The lights faded away. Another wave of panic came over her. Was she going under again? No. The sounds were still there. Voices spoke in loud tones over her, shouting orders to others. Their words finally made sense in her mind. It was her they were talking about. Vital signs returning. Abnormal. What was abnormal about them? Her lips wouldn't move to form the sentence.

When the light returned to her again, she found the same crowd of faces around her, though the one she sought could no longer be seen. Thade was gone. But why would he leave? He wouldn't have left her. Maybe he'd never been there. Could she be hallucinating?

"Thade..." her frail voice came as nothing more than a cracked whisper. She wanted to shout it! It was like a nightmare. Unable to move her body and unable to scream. She couldn't get away from any of it.

Close your eyes.

Had someone spoken the words to her, or was she imagining it? The voice had been her own. Too loud to be any of the people around her. Her thoughts were becoming more indistinct, sleep taking over again. Yes, close your eyes, *she urged silently.* This is just a dream. There must be a way to wake up from it.

The light disappeared around her, the voices fading, slowly, gradually becoming the incoherent din she'd heard before. She was tired. All she wanted was peace and quiet so she could get some sleep, drifting off into unconsciousness once again.

Leyna opened her eyes to the light of the sun filtering in through the walls of the tent, heralding the coming of another day. They all blended together. She spent them the same, waking up in her bed, allowed only to stand for a brief time before Cadell would guide her back to rest, afraid of aggravating whatever had caused her initial fall on the battlefield. There had been little time to explain anything to Cadell during the intensive therapy the physicians put her through to improve the function of Leyna's injured arm. She was aware that fighting continued around her, but she was disallowed from entering the fray. And it would remain that way for some time.

"You are making good progress in your recovery," Cadell smiled down at her from beside the bed. Leyna blinked her eyes, still trying to focus on her surroundings.

"Am I?" she mumbled. It was a silly question, but she didn't care. She was still half-asleep. Intelligent conversation didn't feel like something she was capable of quite yet. Not so early in the day. "Why are you looking at me like that, General? Is something wrong?"

He chuckled, shaking his head in amusement. "No, nothing is wrong. I was merely hoping to have a chance to speak with you before the physicians arrive for your treatment. They do have a tendency to keep you occupied. I could use input from my Captain, however. If you are feeling well enough."

"I suppose that depends on what the input is that you desire. I don't feel very useful for much at the moment."

Cadell reached behind him to pull forward a stool, situating it at the side of the bed. Leaning forward, he checked the wrappings on Leyna's shoulder, nodding in approval to find them clean and well secured. "I have been curious about what happened the night you fell. How you ended up fighting the very man we explicitly decided you would do everything in your power to avoid. Your mysterious condition has baffled the best doctors in the country. Is there any insight you could provide in regards to it?"

Sinking back into the uneven mattress of her bed, Leyna sighed. She didn't know what to say. Everything from that night remained a haze in her mind. Flashes of images, but nothing more. "It all happened so fast," she frowned. "I was fighting... and then there was something. Oran. I saw him and went to strike, but was stopped by someone else. Kyros took me away somewhere. There was no chance for me to get away from him. I guess I let my guard down."

"They took you away?" Cadell stared at her.

"I couldn't have been gone for long. Kyros took me to Arcastus." Leyna shuddered at the memory. She could still smell his stench, sickening her. "They were doing something. I could not understand everything they were saying. It is a bit of a blur. All I know is that they cut my hand. Collected my blood in a vial. There was a small fire on the ground. Arcastus did something with the blood, chanted strange words over the fire. When he was done, he said something I thought sounded odd. Something about whether or not he would feel any pain when my heart stopped. I suppose I wasn't thinking much on it at the time."

"How did you get away? Did they let you go?"

"No," Leyna sighed quietly to herself. "Arcastus made mention of not being able to touch my blood. I decided to try and see what would happen if he did. When he and Kyros returned to me after the strange ritual, I had already managed to loosen my bonds. My hand was still bleeding from where Kyros cut it, so I smeared it across Arcastus's face. It certainly distracted him. Long enough for me to get free at least."

"Distracted him? Can you give me more detail?" Cadell asked. "Anything at all?"

Leyna nibbled her lip, thoughtful. The images were jumbled in her mind. It was difficult to know in which order any of the events occurred. "I think it burned him," she murmured. "I remember there being smoke. He was in pain. I am not certain exactly what it did to him. I just know that it did – something."

Rising to his feet, Cadell began a slow pace across the floor. "So your blood caused him pain. Do you think it weakened him at all? Did you notice anything else? This is the closest any of us has been to him. Whatever information you can provide will be crucial."

"I believe it could have weakened him, yes. At the very least, pained him enough to create a significant distraction. My concern lies with the medallion," Leyna sat up in the bed, favoring her injured arm. It still hurt. Despite the work done by the physicians, the healing process was frustratingly slow. She wanted it to be better. Pain-free. The troops needed her back on the field. "The Prince took down Kyros. At the moment of his death, I saw a strange light seep from him, split in three directions, one of which came to settle on Arcastus. When it did, Arcastus seemed to grow stronger.

My concern is what this could mean if any of the others are slain. If this is a transference of power, somehow."

"You think they are linked to the amulet."

"Yes. I feel that is the one detail I can say with any certainty," she nodded. "I saw the amulet with my own eyes. There are four stones, one in each corner. My assumption is that each one represents the four responsible for Arcastus's resurrection. Damir, Kyros, Oran, and Kael. There is a central stone, which I believe to correspond with Arcastus. Beside it is a smaller clear pearl. That one, I suspect, contains my blood. Kael and Kyros are both dead. When I saw the medallion around Arcastus's neck, two of the corner stones were shattered."

Cadell paused in his pacing. He stared into the distance, taking in what Leyna was saying. "So we have to determine what this means, exactly. What happens if Arcastus is killed while the last two remain alive? Or is that even possible? Perhaps Arcastus can only survive if those who revived him live. In which case, we would need to strike down Damir and Oran..."

"There is no way to know for sure," Leyna argued. She didn't want to think of the possibility that Arcastus might be invincible as long as Damir was alive. "For all we know, the stones could simply be a circuit."

"But you are connected to this in some way."

"To Arcastus, yes. Kyros had no reaction to my blood. I don't know the details, but it would seem my power is only over their leader."

Cadell's frown deepened. "That is certainly something which will have to be taken into consideration in our plans. Either way, it is undeniable. If you have any advantage over Arcastus, we need to have you with us when we go into battle." Casually, he made his way back over to the bed, tapping at Leyna's shoulder lightly. "The doctors say you should be recovered in a few more weeks. Once they give the clearance, we will have to begin devising a plan of attack. The longer we sit back and wait, the more of our men they cut down, leaving us heavily depleted in numbers. Even now, we are at a strong disadvantage. I am hoping to hear word from our other allies soon. If we are going to prepare for a full-on offensive, we are going to need as much help as we can get."

Leyna and Cadell were distracted from the conversation at the sound of someone approaching outside the tent. The flap opened to reveal one of the Vor'shai physicians, medical bag in hand, a soft smile crossing over his gentle features to see Leyna sitting up. "Are you ready for your treatment?" he asked, letting the flap fall closed behind him. Cadell stepped away from the bed, allowing the doctor to stand at Leyna's side.

"I suppose so," she mumbled, casting an apologetic glance over to Cadell. "We will think of something," she assured him, grimacing at the sensation of the doctor beginning to shift her injured shoulder, checking her range of motion. "I don't care if we have to smear my blood on the blades of every soldier in our army. Arcastus will be taken down. One way or another."

Leyna woke with a start, sitting up in her makeshift bed on the ground of the tent. Her heart raced, pounding inside her chest, almost painfully. Breathless from being suddenly yanked out of her dreams. It was the same dream she'd suffered from since first awakening in the medical tent.

It was impossible to know if it was real. The images were clear in her mind, yet foggy. Just distant enough to seem like a figment of her imagination. A painful vision of Thade's face there at her side. But she knew it couldn't be true. In the time since she arrived in Tanispa, she'd yet to actually see his face. To think he would've known she was there, and that he would come to her side — it was too much for her to bear. She wanted it so badly but reality had a painful way of rearing its ugly head.

Rubbing her temples to clear her thoughts, Leyna slouched forward with nothing more than a minor pang of discomfort to remind her of the injury in her shoulder. The Queen's physicians worked miracles on the damage to it. They had been strict on her recovery process, however. No fighting. For weeks it had been so. While she wanted to be out there, beside her men, another part of her couldn't fathom the foolishness of returning to battle in her condition. Her reflexes in her right arm would be off, slower than normal, unable to deflect attacks, leaving her vulnerable to further injury.

Outside the sky was dark. Somehow she'd lost most of her afternoon to sleep. There was little else for her to do while confined to her tent. Cadell rarely let her out of his sight, which proved useful to Leyna. Any meetings he required with the other commanders took place there, in her presence, allowing her to remain up to date on plans and news of the ongoing battles.

Cadell believed Damir and Arcastus were plotting more carefully for their next assault. Arcastus had to be more cautious than before. He knew Leyna was aware of his weakness. It would be a downfall to him in any battle unless he came prepared. He and Damir would have to be more wary. Their attacks came fewer and farther between. Ambushes were more common. Sanarik were spotted throughout the area, their arrows aimed at the watchmen of the Vor'shai army. More and more Namiren soldiers fronted the waves which followed, costing them men while giving the Ven'shal plenty of opportunity to tend their wounded and recruit amongst their ranks. A reckoning was coming. And it would be greater than anything they'd experienced to this point in the war.

Leyna became suddenly aware of Cadell's absence. How strange for him to step away, for more than a brief time. He insisted on being by her, every waking moment, and while she slept, keeping watch from where his maps spread over the table on the far side of the tent. "I am sure he just stepped outside for a minute," she mumbled, slowly rising up to her feet.

Her pants were wrinkled, hanging loosely from her hips at the lack of a belt. Sleep-wear for women was hard to come by in military uniform. She found herself longing for the cotton nightgowns provided by Lady Faustine. To feel like a girl again. She couldn't remember how it felt. For over a year she knew nothing but the hard strides of battle, or watching men down their spirits around a hardwood table, covered in mud and sweat. Wrinkling her nose up in disgust, she pushed the image from her mind, her steps hesitant as she drew nearer to the entrance of the tent.

Peering through the flap, she turned her head from side to side, concerned to find Cadell nowhere in sight. *This isn't like him...* Stepping back inside, she hurried to tuck her shirt into her pants, scanning the area for where her belt might have been placed. Something wasn't right.

In her rush, she moved over to the map table, taking note of a bottle of ink resting on top of a thick piece of parchment. Words were scrawled over the surface of it. Cadell's writing. His penmanship was unmistakable. "Royal orders require my presence elsewhere. The time will be brief. Remain in the tent. I will have a guard posted. You will be safe."

Relief flooded over her to read his words. He was safe. Probably better that way. She wasn't in any state of dress to be seen wandering around the camp. Not to mention the danger it would pose to her. *Idiot.* She patted at her waist, realizing she had no weapon.

Leaning over the map table, she pushed the bottle of ink away, moving the letter to the side. Tiny markers had been placed to represent new watch towers. Positions the Sanarik would find more difficult to reach. The downfall was the distance. They were deeper afield. More isolated than the original posts. If they located any sign of a threat, it would take longer for the news to reach the camp.

Time was everything when it came to their enemies. In the extra minutes it might take a guard to send a warning to her and Cadell, the Namiren soldiers would already be upon them. A closer location needed to be found for new towers.

Her finger traced over the map, following the river which ran along the eastern border of their camp. It was too wide to cross without boats. The center was deep and the rapids just south of their location could be deadly to an unskilled pilot. But how could it be used to their advantage? If no attack was expected from that direction, it seemed pointless to set up a watch – unless they were up high enough to get a good view of the surrounding woods and fields. With a quality spyglass, they could have a decent range. At least out to the hills along the Sivaerian border.

From somewhere outside, she caught the sound of soft footsteps approaching the tent. Her head snapped up, alert. Through the material of the flap, an outline of a figure appeared, hunched over, stopped in front of the entrance. It stood there. Perfectly still. Listening for something.

Quietly, she moved out from behind the table, careful not to make too much noise. Not that it mattered. The flickering light of the candles inside the tent would surely create a shadow on the wall. They were likely already aware of her presence inside. "Who is there?"

At the sound of her voice, the person tapped against the flap, their head turning to scan the area around. Searching for anyone who might have noticed them. It was too suspicious. Cadell needed to get back. Now.

"Leyna."

The whisper was far from threatening. Something about it was familiar and warm. Her dream flashed back in her mind, the hazy image of Thade seated there beside her, his eyes filled with pain. It couldn't be him; in her dream or in reality. Her legs carried her toward the entrance without thinking.

Her fingers undid the buttoned flap, staring hard at the person she now let step through the opening, fastening the entrance back in place behind them. "Who are you?" She couldn't see his face. The cloak he wore covered him from head-to-toe, candlelight unable to reach his features from under the thick fabric. Hesitantly, she made her way around the figure, stepping away from the door to the center of the tent, keeping distance between them.

She nearly fainted to see the hands reach up to the hood, the material sliding away to reveal the man hidden underneath it. A gasp escaped her. It couldn't be true. Her mind was playing some awful trick on her. Or she was still sleeping. A cruel nightmare.

"Do not cry," Thade whispered at the sight of Leyna's anguished expression, moving forward to sweep her into his arms. "I did not want to startle you, but it seems I have done so anyway."

"Is it really you?" Her hands pressed against his cheeks and around his face in disbelief. "How did you —"

Gently, he pressed his lips against hers, easing her shocked protests. She wanted to stay there in that moment, in his arms, forever. It was too good to be true. She wasn't yet convinced of the reality, finding it too easy to believe it was all a dream. One from which she didn't want to wake. She'd forgotten what it was like to lose herself in his arms. His scent, his kiss, his embrace — everything told her this wasn't her imagination. He was really there. After all this time, she had him back.

"I'm so sorry," she grimaced. It hurt her to think of the pain she'd caused him when she left. At the time it made perfect sense, but now — now it felt cruel. Heartless. How could she have walked away from him after telling him that they would spend forever together? She'd made no efforts to seek him out while in Tanispa and yet here he was. He'd found her, and she was ashamed. She felt as if she had somehow failed him.

Shaking his head, he softly clasped her face in his hands to lift her gaze to meet his own. There was no anger there. No disappointment. Only pure joy at having her in his arms again. "Do not apologize, Leyna. I understand why you did it. Never once have I held it against you. I only wish things could have been different. I shouldn't have been so foolish." He leaned in to kiss her again, seeming not to want to stop. "I was so afraid of the possibility of you getting hurt that I almost made things worse for both of us. This way, the way things are now, there is still a chance for us."

"I did not want to be one of those women you and Feolan talked about. If I had stayed I would have put you at risk. I could not live with that."

He chuckled quietly to himself, despite the mood. "You worry too much. Feolan and I spoke in jest. Even in love, we still make our own decisions. I find it hard to believe you were taking advantage of me in any way."

Warmth built in her face. She felt foolish. How could she have been so afraid of letting him love her? But what would the Queen say if she knew he was there with her now?

"I must admit, I am a bit confused in regards to your position under Her Majesty now that you have returned to Tanispa," she said suddenly. The question fell from her lips, one that had danced around in her head since she'd arrived there. "You lost your title as Consul. What exactly is your current station?"

The smile on his lips wavered. "That is a bit more difficult to explain. I would prefer to focus on you. I am not the one who nearly died. How are you feeling?"

"I feel discouraged," she sighed. "Kael is dead. And though I should be happy about it, I am not. I am no longer certain he was truly the evil person I believed for so long."

"He nearly killed you, Leyna. He was abusive and unfaithful, and a traitor to our people. What in all of that makes you think him not to be evil?"

She stepped away from Thade's embrace, covering her face with her hands. "Inside, I think there was still a part of him. The real Kael, unable to break free of the magic. Things he did... They were too foolish. Too convenient for us. I suspect some part of him intentionally made the mistakes I once dismissed to be pure ignorance."

"What mistakes?" Thade asked. Calmly, he led her over to the makeshift bed on the ground, motioning for her to have a seat. "I must admit, once I left Siscal to bury Enaes, very little information regarding you and Zander ever reached me."

Taking up one of the blankets, she wrapped it around herself, clutching it tightly. The winter chill felt suddenly harsher than before. Thade sat, watching her intently, his body scooting closer to her at the sight of her shivering. "The first happened the day of Prince Enaes's murder," she said. "I wasn't aware of it until well after the fact. The dagger Kael used to kill Enaes – Zander told me Enaes's blood was used to help Arcastus regain his strength. But I took the dagger. And Kael never came back for it. Instead he presented Damir and Arcastus with his own sword, which had *my* blood on it. Not Enaes's."

"And they accepted this?"

She lowered her hands away from her face thoughtfully. "He convinced them the blood on the blade was Enaes's. Kael must have known this would cause trouble for them, as long as I was alive. Some part of him knew it and did it anyway."

"You believe he purposefully left us that advantage?" He grimaced at some unknown memory, draping his arm around Leyna's shoulders. "Did your link to this ritual have anything to do with whatever caused your sudden illness? We thought you were dead. You were without a pulse for days. No sign of breath – I sat by your side, praying the doctors were right and you would just… wake up."

Leyna gave in to the warmth of his body, her head resting on his shoulder. He leaned forward, gently kissing her forehead. "Perhaps," she replied, not wanting to break the calm of the moment with words.

"Cadell tells me Kael's intentions the night he died were to kidnap you. Do you know why?"

"I do now," she laughed quietly, miserable at the thought. How could she have let them put her in such a position? Cadell had built her up from a competent warrior to a superior captain, yet she fell so easily into their trap. Her drive to kill Oran made her blind to Kyros's approach. Cadell would be disappointed if he knew. "It took them a while to act once they discovered what happened. The blood used in the ritual was supposed to come from the Prince, dead. Arcastus didn't know how to proceed with a loose end of that nature. They were unaware of the effect my death would have on him, and therefore were unwilling to kill me."

She didn't want to discuss any of this right now. For the first time in over a year she had Thade there with her and still everything had to be about the war. Just once she wanted to forget Arcastus and Damir, and all the terrible things they'd done. Or planned to do. She'd devoted most of her life to fighting him, and for what? All she wanted was a chance at peace before Cadell returned with further orders.

"Did he do something when he attacked you?" Thade asked, squeezing her tightly, as if apologizing for the conversation. He had no more desire to discuss it than she did, but it was necessary. He needed to know what happened, if only for his own peace of mind.

Tilting her head back, she sighed, realizing the futility in trying to avoid the topic. There would be time to discuss matters outside the war once she'd appeased his curiosity. "No, he did not. Honestly, I think he wanted me to kill him. He practically thanked me after I ran him through with my blade, but it was the Prince who finished the job. Not that I blame him for wanting to kill the man responsible for his brother's death. It was closure he deserved."

"There is something I am missing, then," he mumbled to himself, seeming oblivious. "We still have no idea what caused your odd comatose state."

"Kyros and Oran tricked me during the battle," Leyna frowned. She hated to speak it out loud. And to Thade, of all people. "I am not proud to say I let myself become distracted and was unable to break away in time to avoid being taken to Arcastus." She shifted her eyes away from Thade, embarrassed. "I am no more certain now of what they did than I was then, but they took my blood again. While I was arranging my escape, they did something with it, and Arcastus spoke of seeing if he felt any adverse effects. All I can assume is whatever ritual he performed was intended to kill me. Or nearly kill me, I suppose."

"How did you get away?"

Leyna recalled the fight in her mind, details coming back with more clarity than before. "My blood. Arcastus said he could not touch it. It seems to hurt him."

Her eyes drifted over to the entrance of the tent, afraid to find Cadell standing there. "Do not worry," Thade said suddenly. "He will be gone a while longer."

"It is just — if he finds you here..."

Lightly, he placed his fingertips on the side of her chin, guiding her face back to him. "This moment with you is worth any punishment. I can no longer blame Enaes for so foolishly straying from the safety of his men just to see your face. I would do it a thousand times over at the risk of death to hold you in my arms. Nothing will change that."

"I think everyone values my life far more than I do."

"Cadell is not unreasonable," Thade brushed a stray hair away from her face. "He allowed me to remain at your side when you were sick. At least until you awoke. He feared your shock at seeing me there."

"Then what makes you think —"

Thade's lips against hers prevented her from saying anything else. She didn't want to push him away anymore. Letting go of her worries felt indescribable. What did it matter if Cadell returned? She wasn't ashamed of her love for Thade. Cadell was already aware of the way she felt about him, from her own admissions, and she no longer cared who else knew.

Desperate to hold him, she gave up fighting back the emotions which welled up inside. Seated beside him on the bed, she pulled him in closer, feeling only a mild discomfort from the injury in her shoulder, not caring about the pain. It wasn't enough to keep her from Thade. Not after what they'd been through to see each other again.

It didn't take long for the chill to disappear, their bodies emitting warmth to distract them from the cold lingering in the air despite the stove which heated the tent. The thin mattress lacked the comfort of the bed at Thade's home in Siscal, but it mattered little. They were taken in by each other. Unaware of anything around them. Leyna lost herself in Thade's embrace, neither one willing to let the other go until they found themselves under the blankets, tangled up in each other's arms, ignoring the uneven surface of the makeshift bed. They lay there, cradling one another, the thumping of their racing hearts the only sound.

She clung to him. It was too hard to think about living without him for another year, or longer, if the war persisted. And after it ended, how long would it take for

Queen Vorsila to give her blessing? It was absolute torture. The tightness of his embrace told her he felt the same.

They laid there in silence. No words could properly express the feelings they both fought to keep inside. It was heart-wrenching for either of them to think of him going away. Though it was only fair. She'd left him before, and now he would be forced to repay the favor, leaving her there in an empty bed, praying it hadn't been just a dream.

"I have very little time," he whispered.

She pulled him to her, tighter, laying her head tenderly against his bare chest. "You could just stay here. I, for one, would not complain."

Thade chuckled quietly at her words, his eyes staring up at the dull grey color of the tent overhead. The candlelight was dimming, the wick nearly burnt out at the base. From outside, they could hear the boisterous voices of soldiers passing by the tent, making their way back from some unapproved nighttime social call somewhere in the camp. "It must be later than I thought," he frowned. "I rather hoped to have more time with you."

"I would beg you to stay, but I suspect Cadell would not approve," she sighed, a pain piercing through her heart at the sensation of Thade's body sliding out from under her embrace. Reflexively, she tightened her hold, unable to keep him in her grasp as he rose to his feet, gathering up his clothes.

She watched him in the dim light, admiring the curve of his muscles, the way his clothes fit perfectly over his figure, elegant in their simplicity. She wanted to go to him, but she knew their farewells would only be more difficult if she did.

Securing his cloak over his shoulders, he knelt down on the bed beside her, leaning in for one final kiss. As he pulled away, she heard his name tumble from her lips, almost desperate in the sound. "Thade —"

He blinked, his motion to turn away halted. "Yes?"

The words she longed to say were on the tip of her tongue. Did she dare to speak them? They'd haunted her every second since she'd seen him last, regretting never having said them before. Now was her chance to make it right. "I love you."

His face almost seemed to melt at the sound of the words, his lips turning up in a soft smile. In that instant, Leyna couldn't remember having ever seen him so happy. Her own heart felt about to burst from the flood of emotions coursing through it. His fingers gently moved through her hair, fondly gazing down at her where she lay on the bed, blankets pulled up tightly around her. Leaning in, his lips paused next to her ear, the sound of his breath sending shivers through her, the words he spoke no more than an airy whisper, but filled with more sincerity than anything she'd ever heard before.

"I love you, Leyna."

Her throat felt tight, the surge of emotions bringing tears of happiness to her eyes. Their gaze met one final time before he forced himself to his feet, pain evident on his face. They both knew there was nothing else to do other than accept their duties and the distance it required between them. To disregard it would bring more suffering than a single farewell now, which brought with it the chance of another meeting.

At the entrance of the tent, he turned back once more, the hood of his cloak pulled up to conceal his features. "I will see you again soon. I promise." With that, he was gone, leaving Leyna with the heavy weight of loneliness at her side in the bed.

Leyna opened her eyes the next morning, her arm draped over the bed where Thade had lain, inhaling the traces of his scent on the pillow. The usual nightmares had left her. For the first time in weeks, she slept restfully, content, her heart filled with joy at the thought of seeing him again. He'd come for her. That simple fact eased any fear she may still harbor of his feelings after she'd left him in Siscal. He loved her. That was all she needed to know to be assured they would see each other again.

She became aware of another presence in the room, the soft sound of fingertips drumming on the table pulling her from her reverie. Embarrassed, she clutched the blankets around her body tightly, sitting up to face Cadell who was seated, his posture casual, watching from a chair behind the map table.

"Good morning, Captain. You slept well?"

"I slept fine, thank you," she replied begrudgingly. Her fingers fidgeted over the blanket, uncomfortable with him seeing her in such a state of undress, despite the cover the sheets provided. "You were out rather late, General. I admit, I was expecting you to return before I retired for the evening."

He shrugged, nonchalant in his movements. She recognized the uniform he wore to be the same he'd been dressed in the day before, his hair somewhat tousled about on his head. Aside from the minor signs of disarray on his person, he looked otherwise calm and rested, a curious sparkle in his eye which served only to make the smirk on his face more unnerving. "I thought I should give you a bit of privacy."

"Such as the privacy you offer now?"

"I will turn away, if you would like to dress yourself, Captain. Though I recommend a different choice of sleeping attire in the future," he remarked.

Leyna caught what she thought to be a wink from Cadell as he turned in his chair, leaning back against the table with his arms propped behind his head. Awkwardly, she climbed out of the bed, keeping the blankets close while she gathered her pants and shirt, pulling them on quickly. "You are acting strangely, Cadell," she stated, her arms folded over her chest. "I am getting the impression you are hiding something from me."

"On the contrary, I should ask what you are hiding from me." He spun on the seat, his elbows resting on the table, his chin positioned thoughtfully in his hands as he looked her over. "Do you really think I would leave and not keep track of who came and went from your presence? Your safety is my largest concern, and currently a direct order for me to maintain it. I am merely finding amusement in your attempts to pretend your evening was uneventful."

Lowering her arms back to her sides, she shifted her feet, uncomfortable with his words. He knew? If he was speaking the truth, it made no sense for him to be so casual. So accepting. "If you know so much, then why do you toy with me?"

"Leyna —" Cadell straightened in the chair, the smile on his lips fading. "I need you to understand the severity of this situation. Come," he gestured toward the empty stool across the table, "have a seat."

Hesitant, she made her way over, situating herself on the stool Cadell indicated. She was afraid to say anything, concerned that he didn't know nearly as much as he seemed to. He was a clever man. It was difficult to say whether he was manipulating her for information, or if he truly knew of Thade's visit.

"What do we need to discuss?"

Cadell tapped his index finger against the surface of the map, deep in thought over his next words. He stared at her silently for a moment, giving a slight nod before he started to speak. "I know about Thade, Leyna. I know he came here last night. I'm the one who allowed him to do so. But that detail must never leave this tent. No one can know he was here. I would lose my head over it. You may think I jest, but I cannot be any more serious."

"If it was such a risk to you, then why did you allow it?" Leyna squinted her eyes at him in disbelief.

"Because I owed it to you both," he frowned. "I have intentionally kept you apart since the day you arrived in Tanispa. Not by my own decision, but by royal order. I cannot say I disagree with the reasons, though when he heard our plans for an attack on the Ven'shal, he came to me, pleading to let him see you. I couldn't deny him."

At first she was taken aback by the thought of Cadell having purposefully kept her and Thade separated. At the same time, the truth about the previous evening caused Leyna to laugh in spite of herself. She'd been so worried about Cadell coming in and finding them there. It explained Thade's lack of concern. "He knew you weren't coming back."

Cadell chuckled. "He also stayed longer than I anticipated. But I cannot say I blame him. If I could see my wife again for a single evening, I would stay even longer."

Her cheeks burned with warmth. She couldn't remember the last time she'd felt so flustered, eyes averted from Cadell's, uneasy at the thought of him knowing so much of what transpired. It was unladylike, to say the least. She feared losing his respect. Of everyone she'd come to know in Tanispa, she was fond of Cadell the most. She respected him more than anyone else in the military. He was a strong and fierce leader, yet understanding, with a compassionate side none of the other soldiers seemed aware of, and he made sure to keep it that way. Their work being so closely linked, she'd come to trust him as a friend. To think of damaging her image in his eyes was disheartening.

"Please, do not think less of me for my actions," she said quietly, her eyes remaining cast down to the ground. "You must understand, the feelings he and I share are not superficial. When we parted ways in Siscal, he'd asked for my hand in marriage…"

Glancing up, she saw Cadell's eyes open wide, for only an instant, immediately returning to his usual, steadfast gaze. "I could not think less of you for any of this. However, his intentions of marriage do make things a little different. Did you accept this proposal?"

"I did, but — it is confusing. I feared what would happen if he did not return to Tanispa, so I left. Until last night, he and I have not seen each other since we agreed to the marriage."

"We shall have to wait and see then," he leaned back in his seat, legs propped up on the table, lost in thought once again. "For now, we need to focus on the plan I have laid out. I've been in talks with Queen Vorsila's ambassadors for some time now, and we finally received word back on some very strong allies. With their help, our forces will be strengthened, and I think now is the time for us to initiate a strike against the enemy instead of waiting for them to come to us."

"You want us to storm the Ven'shal army?" The thought was ludicrous in her mind. She searched his face for any sign of humor, discovering nothing but determination in his eyes.

"Before Prince Enaes died, he embarked on a trip to the jungle regions in the south, and while there struck up a bargain with the people of Tunir. They have a strong, well-trained military, and their people are some of the best to have by your side in battle. They recently agreed to send aid. We expect them to arrive within the week." Cadell paused. "But it is our second ally which has my confidence built a bit higher."

"And who might that be? I thought we already were utilizing every source we had."

A smile passed over Cadell's lips, devious in design. "Have you ever traveled to the lands north of Tanispa? Up into the tundra and arctic regions of Ethrysta?"

Leyna shook her head, amused at the thought of anyone traversing the lands in the north. There was nothing there but frozen ground and bitter cold snow. Most people would succumb to death in such climates. "I was not aware there was anything there worth seeing."

"There is a race of people who dwell there known as the Ovatai. Hunters. Fierce fighters. More cunning than even the most insidious Sanarik. They are, to our fortune, long time allies of the Vor'shai people, though we rarely have need to call upon them, and never have they called upon us." Cadell tapped the map with his index finger, smiling. "But they have agreed to send some of their warriors here. Once the Ovatai and the Tunirons reach us, we will have an army fit to bring down the Ven'shal. We have received intelligence that Damir, Oran, and Arcastus are within the camps. Now is our best time to strike."

"And if the attack fails?"

"Then we will all perish." Cadell's eyes dimmed dramatically. "Failure is not something we can allow to happen, but the longer we sit here and let them build their army, the less our chance of survival is. Our troops are not getting any more plentiful or healthy. Truth be told, I cannot recall the last time our numbers were in such decline."

She pondered over his words. There was merit to what he said. To continue waiting for the Ven'shal to attack would be foolish. But to stage an assault against them… it was a frightening concept. They would need every man and woman capable of fighting. "This leads me to one question, I suppose," she said suddenly, reaching up to rub her injured shoulder. "How does any of this have to do with why you let Thade come here last night? You told me this plan was discussed with him prior to your agreeing to do so."

"You will be at my side in the front-lines of the attack. I shouldn't need to elaborate any further for you to understand the danger you will be in." Cadell stood up from his chair, pacing the ground slowly, his hand thoughtfully stroking his chin. "I can't keep you out of the line of fire, nor do I suspect you have any desire to quit now when we are so close to victory. I simply cannot guarantee your safety. That alone was reason enough for me to grant you both one chance to speak before I take you into the fray again."

"And if we win? Will he and I be allowed to see each other?"

"If we win, the war will be over, and Queen Vorsila will be free to grant her approval, which would allow you both to do whatever you please."

"Then I suggest we get our men prepared," she said firmly, rising from her chair with an air of authority. "We don't have much time to get the details worked out before the other troops arrive. I will call for the commanders to join us. We will not sleep until we have every point covered."

Chapter Thirty

The day was upon them sooner than Leyna expected. The Vor'shai camps were flooded with troops of varying races, all clad in their traditional armor, in preparation for what the night would bring. Once the sun sank below the horizon, they would make their move. The Ven'shal tended to wait until the dead of night to launch their attacks, so a strike at dusk would find them unready.

While the ally troops poured into the camp, Leyna and Cadell remained inside their tent, tense and anxious, awaiting the arrival of leaders from the other armies. General Matias took on the job of briefing the Mialan and Carpaen commanders of their roles in the fight, leaving Cadell and Leyna to welcome the Tuniron and Ovatai leaders and work out the final details of the plan.

"Try not to wear a path in the ground, Captain. We cannot have these men thinking we tend toward nervous habits."

Leyna paused, realizing only then that she'd even been pacing. "I apologize, General," she sighed, dropping down into a chair next to the mapping table. "I am not entirely certain what to expect of these people. How do I know what is appropriate etiquette toward them when I know nothing of their kind?"

"I trust you will know what to do when the time comes. Just — try to avoid staring. Both cultures can be a shock to the senses to witness for the first time. For you to see them both simultaneously, I would hate to see you look like a fool." Cadell chuckled to himself at the thought. "If it makes it any easier, consider it like a meeting with foreign royalty. Treat them the same as you would Queen Vorsila, and there should be no issues."

"I have seen many disturbing things. I doubt a pair of men will throw me off my senses to such an extreme."

"You really haven't seen these people before then, have you?" Cadell's brow rose in her direction. A glint of amusement could be seen there, a smirk tugging at the corner of his lips. "Let me tell you about the first time I ever laid eyes on one of the Ovatai. I was a young man, not yet old enough to serve in the military myself, and my father was at court with Queen Nalashi. Though the reason for their presence escapes me now, two Ovatai warriors were guests of the Queen. I nearly soiled myself at the mere sight of them."

Covering her mouth with her hand, she tried not to laugh out loud at the mental image of Cadell wetting himself over something so seemingly trivial. "I find that hard to believe," she grinned, unable to contain it.

"Just don't let them see any change in your face when you meet them," he replied, his tone stern, no hint of the humor from only moments ago. "The Ovatai are fierce warriors. Very primal. Some believe them to be an ancient line of Vor'shai, though it is hard to know whether there is fact to the claim. The only thing which gives it any merit is their ability to utilize a form of magic very similar to ours, but in a far different manner. Their agreement to assist us comes as a surprise to me, really. They do not involve themselves in the affairs of other countries. I suspect they only do so because of our dire predicament, and our defeat would only lead to an inevitable war between the Ven'shal and their people anyway. Better to take the enemy out before the blood spills on their own soil... or ice."

"And the Tunirons? What is so intimidating about them?"

"They are human, but more fierce than any you have ever seen. Much like the Ovatai, their lives are a constant struggle for survival. The wildlife in the jungles is unforgiving and merciless, and they rarely leave it. Many of their fighters won't speak our language. Any directions will have to be given to their General, whose name I loathe to say I cannot completely enunciate in the correct fashion. Uttae?"

"That's not a name, it is a grunt," Leyna chortled. "I just enjoy hearing you say it."

Cadell laughed, a cough escaping him at the sound of someone approaching outside the tent. Stiffly, he rose to his feet, snapping for Leyna to do the same, his hands sliding over his uniform jacket to make sure it was free of any wrinkles or dust. The flap of the tent came open, Zander's face appearing before motioning two men inside; or at least what Leyna thought to be men.

The person on the left held an animalistic appearance, his arms long and lanky, yet muscular, the tone of his body revealing his impeccable strength and agility without requiring any motion. His hands were large, Leyna's eyes staring at the long digits on each, similar to those visible on his bare feet. His complexion was unblemished ebony, the only color coming from the stark white of his eyes against his skin, their rich, deep, almost black irises staring hard at Leyna as he entered. The smooth surface of his bald head shone as if waxed, catching the light of the torches set up throughout the room.

The man on the right couldn't be more opposite. He stood erect, his posture flawless and proud. Long, snowy white hair hung like a mane down from his head to his waist, blending in with his porcelain-fine skin. His eyes were like icy blue lakes, vibrant in their glow. Just below his piercing gaze, a soft layer of hair resembling fur covered the skin on the rest of his face, down his neck, and all over the remainder of his body. Longer tufts dangled from his forearms and calves, protruding out from his white gloves and boots made of some animal hide unfamiliar to Leyna's eyes. He was tall. Several inches stood between the top of Leyna's head to his chin. His body was lean and muscular, sharply pointed wolf-like ears twitching like a cat with every sound.

"You are the General of the Vor'shai, no?" The white haired man inquired, his words like silk in a very formal Vor'shai dialect, distracting Leyna from her own awe while trying to decipher the accent. She felt lost in her own language, amazed that anyone still spoke in such a way.

"Chief Okivra. We are in your debt for your assistance," Cadell stated calmly, yet genuine, utilizing the modern Vor'shai structure while bowing low to each of the men in turn. At the curious raise of the other man's brow, Cadell switched to the language spoken between Carpaen and Siscal, finding it better suited for the man's ears. "General Uttae. We are honored by your presence. I am General Cadell, and this is Captain Leyna, one of our most skilled soldiers."

"She is a woman," Okivra said in his broken language, his nose wrinkled in what Leyna could only interpret as disgust.

Her expression fell, struggling to maintain her composure at the sexist remark. There was nothing wrong with being a woman, and she wasn't afraid to tell him so. It was her promise to Cadell to treat them with respect which stayed her tongue.

"Do not let her gender fool you. Her combat prowess rivals that of any man among our troops."

"No wonder you lose." Okivra turned to face Cadell, ignoring Leyna's presence entirely. "My warriors are instructed to take orders from no one but me. I trust our battle methods over yours."

As Okivra continued to speak, the flow of his language began to catch on in Leyna's mind, becoming less broken with every tiny nuance she discovered. She would've been impressed were it not for the disrespect he showed to her, and now Cadell. How could they organize an attack with a man unwilling to hear their plan? The Vor'shai were familiar with the terrain and the enemy. It was foolish for these people to push forward without any understanding of what they were up against.

"I trust you will lead them to victory. We will do our best to follow your example," Cadell bowed low to Okivra, his eyes cast to the floor, the white of the Chief's boots turning to move swiftly out of the tent without any other word. Straightening his shoulders, Cadell nodded politely to Uttae, returning to the southern language once again. "I apologize, General. If you like, I can review our attack plan with you. Modifications can be made if you disagree on any points. We are not here to give you or your men orders."

Uttae grunted, white teeth shining from under the dark color of his lips. The way he stared at her left Leyna uneasy, unsure of how to react to his strange mannerisms. It was hard to focus on anything with his abnormal form distracting her from her own thoughts. "General," she cut in. "I think it may be best if I start rallying the men together and making sure the commanders are aware of the details. In case there are any last minute questions."

Cadell looked surprised, his expression easing to one of understanding. "Very well. Do not stray far. You know my orders. I will find you momentarily."

With a polite bow to Uttae, Leyna hurried from the tent, hoping her departure didn't appear too desperate. These men were crazy. Unnatural. In her mind, Uttae couldn't look more out of place among their people. He was like a starved ghereac sizing her up for a meal while Okivra was willing to write her off as useless simply because of her gender. Her? A female Vor'shai? The foundation of their race? Could the Ovatai really be so ancient in their views as well as their language?

"Hold up there, Captain."

Spinning around quickly, Leyna's fists clenched, her breath drawn in sharply at the sight of Zander coming up from behind. She released the tension in her hands, extending her fingers long at her side. "I need to calm down."

"I thought you and the General were meeting with the foreign powers?" Zander smirked. "Did things not go well?"

"The General failed to mention anything about the Ovatai Chief being a pig. The nerve of that man! No wonder his people live in seclusion. I cannot imagine anyone ever wanting to associate with someone as pompous and self-centered."

"Well, as the Chief, he is guaranteed to have a wife, which means he will or has already been breeding. There are most likely little chiefs running amok. You'll just have to prove that you're better than him. What did he do?" Zander looked her over carefully, content to see a smile form on her lips at his comments.

"He doubts my ability to fight based solely on the fact that I am a woman."

Zander laughed. The sound echoed through the camp, his head thrown back toward the sky. "Are you serious?"

"Of course I am serious," Leyna slapped his arm. "When Cadell advised him I was one of the unit's most skilled soldiers, he insulted him by saying that was the reason we have been losing."

"Oh, he sounds like a prize," Zander chuckled. "Leyna – Captain –" he emphasized the title, looking around to make sure no one overheard his blunder. "In my knowledge of his people, the Ovatai have some of the most frightening female warriors of any race on Myatheira. He may think his people better than ours, but he certainly can't discredit you simply on the basis of your being a girl. To do so would insult every woman in his ranks."

Leyna folded her arms across her chest. "I can be just as frightening as any of their women."

"Then show him. He agreed to bring his men to help, so he can't be all bad."

"Just mostly bad. The scoundrel," she scoffed. "I pray all his children to be female."

As she spoke, the flap of the tent came open, Cadell and Uttae emerging from inside. Uttae moved away, deeper into the camp, Cadell scanning the area, coming to notice Leyna, a look of relief flashing in his eyes. "I was worried you might have wandered off somewhere."

"I did my duty and kept her in one place, sir," Zander smiled. "Wasn't easy, though."

"Never is, with her," Cadell nodded, his hand resting firmly on Leyna's shoulder. "Don't let that man get to you. He's not as mean as he comes across."

"Oh, yes, certainly. He seems absolutely pleasant. We should have him for tea sometime after the war."

A shiver passed through her with a sudden whip of the icy breeze. She couldn't imagine living somewhere so bitter cold every day of the year. Maybe it would freeze her heart as well to be that miserable. Constantly fighting for survival against the elements as well as the arctic creatures lurking about — the Ovatai life was not something she could ever understand, nor did she have any desire to. All that mattered was whether or not they could help defeat the Ven'shal.

Rubbing her arms gently for warmth, she sighed in defeat. It was useless to remain angry over a comment which meant nothing to her in the end. They would go into battle, and when all was said and done, the Ovatai would depart and his opinion would no longer matter. She was the Captain of the Vor'shai military. They needed her to be focused on the fight, not her pride.

"The sun will be setting soon. I didn't have a chance to call together the commanders and go over the plan a final time…"

"Don't worry about it, Captain. They know their directions," Cadell said. "You should take this time to get yourself prepared. Empty your thoughts of anything which might distract you from our goal. We need you to be ready. And I need you to be clear-headed and focused on whatever needs to be done to keep yourself alive. And Commander," he added, turning his attention to Zander. "You know your orders. Protect her at all costs. If all goes well, this will be the last time I put her in this situation."

"I put myself in this situation, General. I know what I am getting myself into. There is no need to risk the lives of others to protect mine when I am fully aware of the risks."

"That is enough, Captain," Cadell interrupted, his tone firm and decisive. "You know where I stand on this. I will accept no arguments from you. Now go. I will finish the briefing with the commanders and then come back for you. Amand is stationed right outside the tent. Do not leave it, and if anything happens, he will make sure word reaches me. Until then, I suggest you get your head on straight. It's going to be a long night."

Under the dusky violet sky, Leyna and Cadell directed the troops forward, the crunch of snow under foot louder than either was comfortable with. The Ovatai were already ahead of them, skulking easily through the white landscape, everything about their bodies seamlessly blending in with their surroundings. Sanarik watchmen were stationed all around the enemy camps. Their positions were unknown, hidden amongst the trees, but not well enough to slip past the notice of Okivra's men who seemed to simply sniff them out.

The air was silent. Leyna could hear nothing of the Ovatai attacks, her eyes blinking with surprise to see a bright flash of light appear up ahead, an indication of a successful approach, the area cleared of any and all enemy scouts. Trees littered the landscape, more densely than the battlefields of so many attacks before. A common strategy of the Sanarik was to maintain camp within the protection of nature. Plenty of places to hide while their arrows could seek their mark.

Overhead, the Tunirons found the treetops to be home. An occasional creak from above hinted to their otherwise stealthy presence, easing toward the camp, weapons strapped to their backs, prepared to be drawn at the first opportunity. Leyna was amazed by the ease with which they maneuvered through the branches, having never seen anything quite like it before. "Whatever happens, promise me you will take care of yourself. I fear I will not be able to keep my eyes on you as well as I would like," Cadell whispered.

Leyna nodded, not wanting to respond aloud in fear of exposing their position to the enemy. Hand gripped firmly around the hilt of her sword, she held it up in front of her, a slow count starting in her head. It was almost time. Burnt wood scented the air around them. They were getting closer, voices audible through the trees, though too muffled to decipher the conversation. It was still early for the enemy to be positioning themselves for their regular attack. If luck was on Leyna's side, they would be without armor and weapons upon the initial strike, leaving them vulnerable for the first wave of soldiers to cut through.

Slowly, Leyna lifted her blade into the air, high over her own head, like a beacon to the troops awaiting their command. When the moment felt right, she let a soft wave of energy pulse from her hand to the sword, a gentle blue light coursing over the edges of the blade, giving the signal for them to charge.

In a rush of movement, the first wave cut through the final line of trees leading to the camp. Leyna and Cadell held their ground, anxious, listening intently to the sound of chaos erupting only a few feet ahead. The element of surprise was on their side. Screams of the unprepared Namiren soldiers echoed through the trees. The first wave would be the easiest. Once the soldiers had scattered from the camp, the Ven'shal fighters would be alerted to the impending attack. They would put up more resistance for the next charge.

Once their presence was known, it would be only a matter of time before the fallen enemy would start to reawaken under Arcastus's control. A special unit of Vor'shai soldiers were in wait of the dead to rise. They were to find their way onto the battlefield and, under cover of the other allied fighters, take to the ground, replenishing the energy into the soil to weaken the animated corpses.

The sky continued to sink into darkness. There was an ominous sensation about it. Thick and unnatural. No matter what came, Leyna was determined to face it honorably. If death found her on the battlefield, her only regret would be for the life she would never live in Thade's eyes. But there was no other death more respectable than that of a soldier, fighting for their Queen. She couldn't let her desire for revenge cloud her thoughts. This was about more than that. They were fighting for their freedom and peace. Such things outweighed the festering anguish of an orphan girl.

"The first wave has scattered them. The enemy will regroup and come out swinging." Cadell drew his sword, tilting the blade from side to side, the light of the moon reflecting off the flawless surface of the metal. "We can do this. We just need to fight smart."

In a show of respect, Leyna held out her own blade, the sides of their swords meeting with a soft clink of metal against metal in the darkness. "We are Vor'shai," she smiled. "We always fight intelligently."

Cadell smirked, raising his sword into the air. It was up to him to give the final signal to disperse into combat. They listened for what felt like hours, when Leyna knew it couldn't have been more than a few minutes. Several at most. The clambering of footsteps could be heard clearly in the distance, swift in pace, moving directly toward them. Before Cadell gave the signal, a cool chill came suddenly at Leyna's side, her head turning to find the snowy figure of Okivra next to her.

His gaze met with Cadell's, a flash of unspoken communication visible in their brightly glowing eyes. With a nod, Cadell's blade burst to light, his own legs carrying him forward into battle with the roar of the troops. Leyna's muscles tensed in preparation to follow, her progress halted by Okivra's strong arm outstretched across her chest, preventing her from moving.

"Wait."

She couldn't disobey the command. The way he spoke told her there was reason behind his actions. Reasons he would never take the time to explain to her, nor did they have time for her to even ponder over the possibilities.

When the last of the men had charged into the battle, he lowered his arm, motioning for her to remain with him. Carefully, they crept forward through the snow, making their way closer to the line of trees between them and the enemy. She refused to let on her discomfort in his position at her side. Did he not think she was skilled enough to enter the conflict?

"Come with me," he stated. "The heart of the enemy lies in wait on the other side of the battle. We will take the fight to them."

He was asking her to fight at his side? She couldn't hide her disbelief as she fell into step beside him, not wanting to risk lagging behind when granted such an honor. How he knew where anyone was within the enemy forces was a mystery. *Perhaps they scouted ahead during the initial attack.*

They were running at an angle around the camp, just outside the battle. Occasionally they paused, Okivra's ears twitching, listening, pinpointing the location of something Leyna couldn't see. He drew an elegant, finely crafted longbow from his back, an arrow coming to meet his expectant fingers without any effort to utilize the magic to call it from his quiver. Leaning back, he aimed high, exhaling a cold, foggy breath at the moment of release. Leyna was in awe over the speed with which the arrow took flight, helped along by the wind. A sharp crack of branches overhead followed the shot, a pair of Sanarik soldiers falling limply to the ground with a thud at their feet. Leyna inhaled sharply, taken aback by the sight. *Two soldiers with a single arrow?*

Okivra wasted no time in continuing on, paying no more attention to his victims other than a disgusted snort at the blood staining the snow.

Leyna was aware of the battle somewhere to her left. She was being led deeper into the trees, a small path guiding them closer to a different segment of the enemy camp. Around her, she realized other Ovatai warriors had taken up position on all sides, their movements so subtle she couldn't be certain her eyes weren't playing tricks on her.

Lights flickered from a small clearing not far ahead. There was another camp within the trees, though it was hard to tell how heavily guarded it was from their position. Okivra gave little time for pause as he broke through the tree line with Leyna at his heels, her eyes opening wide at the sight of the Ven'shal soldiers standing ready on the other side.

They took to fighting instantly upon seeing the Ovatai bearing down on them, attacking from all angles, high and low, blood spray covering the ground in seconds. She couldn't focus on her uneasiness around Okivra. The soldiers were stronger than any others she'd encountered during the war.

Unlike the usual men under Arcastus's charge, these troops were more skilled with their magic. Tiny bulbs of electricity shot from their hands, connecting with Leyna's armor in solid hits, her balance compromised briefly while she struggled to regain control over her body.

A second wave stormed her and Okivra from deeper into the camp. Leyna's heart pounded wildly in her chest, overexerted from the constant barrage of attacks, not ceasing in their ferocity for even a second to grant her some reprieve. *There are too many of them. I can't keep going like this.*

The thoughts had barely completed in her mind when an ear splitting scream pierced the air from beside her, Okivra's body leaning forward under the strength of his battle cry. All around them, the wind picked up in a frenzy, the dead leaves clinging to the trees tossed about, howling with intensity, pushing the soldiers away like rag dolls. Leyna stood in utter shock. Never before had she seen anything like this magic. The strength of it was devastating, and the control Okivra demonstrated was even more frightening.

Among the enemy troops, Leyna could see a familiar figure, blackened eyes settled on her, a smirk curled around Arcastus's decaying lips. He stumbled only slightly from the force of Okivra's energy, composing himself quickly to draw a sword from its sheath.

Arcastus was hers. Narrowing her eyes, Leyna took a step forward, cutting through the enemy to get to where he was. This was how it was intended. Had Cadell known where Arcastus would be? Was that why he had Okivra take her there? None of the other fighters would stand a chance against the lich. Leyna was their only hope in bringing him down. But Cadell never would have approved of her coming there without him. Unless he believed Okivra to be a better help in the battle.

At Leyna's approach, Arcastus sent a wave of blackened energy toward her, blasting against the heavy metal of her helmet, knocking it from her head. The force was disorienting. Her neck snapped backward from the impact, tiny specks of white light dancing in front of her vision while she tried to regain her senses. Sword gripped tightly in her hand, she made the first move. Lunging toward him. Arcastus blocked easily, their blades meeting in a flurry of strikes, one after the other, his skill impressive. He tended to hide behind the power of his perverse magic. But it was essentially useless against her. And he knew it.

"I learned something about you during our last encounter," he laughed, bearing down on Leyna again with his weapon. She parried, countering, meeting with nothing but empty air as Arcastus evaded, stepping out of the way. "It seems I can kill you," Arcastus lunged again. "I will take great pleasure in doing so."

With incredible strength Arcastus brought his bony fist across Leyna's face, the strike cracking her jaw painfully. A coppery taste rolled over her tongue. Blood. Her entire mouth burned from the blow, though there was no time to dwell on it. Arcastus had given her an advantage without realizing his mistake. Head snapping to face him, Leyna spit the thick substance from her mouth, listening to it sizzle upon meeting Arcastus's face. It distracted him enough for her to charge again, forcing him back, off balance.

Flailing wildly, Arcastus's sword sliced across Leyna's right arm, striking close to her still-healing wound from their last battle. She flinched to see the blood soaking into her shirt, fearful that he would aggravate the injury, leaving her unable to use her dominant hand. Content that his move was more accident than tactic, she thrust forward again, sending him tumbling to the ground.

It all felt surreal, yet familiar. They were back where they had been in their last fight, only this time she wasn't at any disadvantage from Kyros's meddling attacks. Forcefully, she bashed the hilt of her sword against the side of Arcastus's head, repeating the blow, again and again, leaving him unable to focus, losing his hold on his own blade. Leyna pressed the metal of her sword against the laceration on her arm, coating it with a layer of her blood. If she was going to take advantage of his distraction, she had to act fast.

Satisfied with her work, Leyna drove her blade deep into her mark, thrusting it into the lich's neck. His agonized wails filled the air, only briefly, cut off by a sudden gurgle which sent him into silence. Leyna stared at him, afraid of what might happen. He couldn't be dead. A man of his power would never fall so easily.

Yet there he lay. Still. Unmoving. A film of light began to build up around his corpse-like form, shooting into the air and splitting into two directions. Astonished, Leyna stumbled backward, unsteady on her feet. What had happened?

Frantic, she scanned the area in search of where the light had gone. One of the beams had been close. But there was no way to know which one of the remaining two was hidden nearby. Oran would never stray far from Damir. Not at a time like this. He was weak. If Arcastus was dead, Oran would turn to Damir for direction.

Revenge nagged at the back of Leyna's mind, though there was more reason for seeking Damir out than her personal vendetta. He was stronger than Oran.

All around her on the field, Leyna could see the undead soldiers falter, trembling, their bodies collapsing to the ground. They lay still for no more than a moment before wobbling back to life, slowly regaining their footing to take a stance against Okivra's men. Something was continuing to manipulate them. Restoring their life. Damir. It was the only explanation.

"You know your way with a sword well enough. I understand not why your General insists you be treated like a child," Okivra scoffed. His eyes burned into Leyna's, the icy blue thrashing about in waves from the excess energy contained inside.

"So that is why you brought me with you. General Cadell requested a babysitter for me? I assure you, one is not necessary. Feel free to go about your business as you desire." She was angry at the thought. Furious. They would accomplish nothing so long as Cadell continued to treat her like some fragile doll. His intentions were good, but they were insulting.

Turning away from Okivra, she threw herself back into the fray, her arms mechanically performing the motions of battle. Enemy troops were coming for Arcastus's body, but she couldn't let them take it. Not yet. Forcing them back, she tried to reach him, tearing at the throat of his corpse. The amulet was gone. She cursed to herself, searching the area for any sign of Damir. He would be the one who held the medallion. They would never have allowed it in Oran's grasp. She had to find him. With the medallion in her possession, she could find a way to finish this.

He had to be somewhere in the midst of all these soldiers, pouring forth from even deeper in the woods. Their numbers seemed never-ending, many wearing armor clearly damaged from previous battles, no doubt healed and revived by Damir. If it was in fact him, his skill with Arcastus's magic had grown significantly since the night in Kaipoi. He was an eager student under Arcastus's tutelage. Possibly more deadly in battle than his master. There was no telling what the effects of Arcastus's death would have on him. She hated how little she knew about the enemy and their rituals. If she hadn't been so wrapped up in her own personal dramas, she could've taken the time to discover more of their secrets, but the time for that had come and gone. All that was left was to focus on the present – and find him.

A cool breeze whipped through the trees. There was something unnatural about it. She shuddered hard, her teeth chattering. It was then that she noticed a soft tendril of black smoke lingering on the air in front of her. Taunting her in its subtlety, the wind twirled it in circles around her body, looping again and again, faster with every new rush. She tried to back away but found her legs rooted in place. Eventually the shadows broke away, shooting off in the direction of a new line of trees, almost seeming to beckon her forward to follow it.

It was a trap. Some kind of magic to lure her away from the others. Yet she felt compelled to follow. To see where it would lead her. *What are you thinking?* It was foolish to even consider it. But she wanted to. She *had* to. Damir was out there somewhere, and he would be looking for her. If there was any chance this magic would lead her to him... No. She couldn't. The stress of the battle was making her foolhardy.

Her eyes drifted over the area to where Okivra continued his valiant charge, his gaze moving to glance in her direction between foes. He was still watching her. It was humiliating to think that a man of his status and rank had been asked to keep an eye on her. *Get away from him. Find Damir.*

"You are going to get yourself killed," she muttered to herself, her fingers clenched tightly around the hilt of her sword. Her conscience was torn. She wanted to follow the smoke, but she knew it was wrong. The inky tendril rose up, coming to whorl around her once again before moving back toward the trees, tempting her.

With a groan of frustration, she waited for Okivra to look away before darting off into the trees. Silently, she chided herself for what she was doing. It was beyond ridiculous to be separating herself from anyone who might come to her aid in the event of the worst. And the worst was a guarantee where Damir was concerned. Their history made it impossible to think he might show any mercy to her.

From somewhere up ahead she could hear the snap of twigs breaking underfoot. Someone was there. Not far away. It didn't move with any great speed, though in the cover of the trees, a hasty pace wasn't necessary. They were concealed from the other fighters. No one would know where they were. Against her better judgment, Leyna continued to follow, led deeper into the woods by the smoky fingers. Eventually she found herself in a small clearing. The tree cover remained thick around her, though a break in the foliage allowed her to make out the figure of a man standing there. Waiting for her.

"Oh, my dear, I didn't think you would come."

Damir's voice sent shivers coursing down her spine. It had been so long since she'd heard it last. Awakened by the sound, nightmares from her childhood sprung to life in her mind. The time had come for her to face the demons of her past. "You don't know me very well at all then, Damir."

"I know you better than you think," Damir said calmly. The swirling tendrils of shadow writhed in the soft wind, wrapping lightly around Damir's body before dissipating into nothingness. "I know why you're here. I know what gets under your skin, and who to hurt if I want to make you suffer. You were hard to find at first, but now you are an open book."

"You are nothing to me, and you never were," she snapped.

"And you were never anything to me other than the bastard child of a whore."

Leyna's eyes flashed in heated anger at his words. "My mother was not a whore."

"No?" he laughed. His legs moved in a casual pace toward her, the light of the moon illuminating his pale features in the darkness, the abyssal depths of his eyes staring through her, filled with malice. "And where is your father now, hmm? Oh – that's right – dead."

"Because you killed him," she spat, her hand clenched into a fist at her side. He deserved so much worse than anything she could possibly do. "You can't get under my skin, Damir. Do not waste your energy."

"Oh, I think I can." He was enjoying every second of this. She could see the spiteful pleasure written on his face. "I could tell you a few things about your mother that I'm sure you don't know."

"Leave her out of this."

Holding out his hand, Damir sent a wave of black energy toward her, the tendrils wrapping around her waist. Leyna tried to back away, finding her footing compromised by a thick root jutting up from the ground, her fall broken only by the support of Damir's energy holding her in place. He sneered at the sight of her, stepping in closer. Extending her arms out, she tried to strike at him, his fingers clutching at her right hand, twisting it backward to wrench her mother's ring painfully from her finger. She cried out, snatching at him, desperate to get it back.

Sliding it onto his hand, he held it up, positioning it in front of Leyna's face, a curious expression distorting the amusement in his eyes. "I meant to take this from your mother's corpse the day I killed her. A souvenir, if you will. A constant reminder of the family who would pay for their betrayal." Gruffly, he brought the back of his hand across her face, the gemstones on the ring slicing at Leyna's skin, a trickle of blood building at the surface. "An oversight, really, that it was left behind."

Leyna struggled against her shadowy bonds in vain. He was strong. More than she remembered. She chastised herself for coming there alone. She'd been a fool to think that she stood a chance. "You will die for what you've done," she hissed, increasing her efforts to break free.

He laughed quietly at her empty threats. "I was surprised to finally find you," he continued, ignoring her heated glare. "I thought it would be simpler than it was, I admit. You gave me a bit of a run for my money. I had even given up, but then you fell into my lap. And now…" Damir held the ring up. Examining it. In the thick of the trees, the break in the branches overhead allowed the moon to shine just enough light to reveal the blood left behind on the gems from where it struck Leyna. "You will die just as easily as she did."

"You will find me harder to kill. I don't intend to go down without a fight."

"Oh, I hope you put up more of a fight than your mother did. I have been looking forward to this moment for too long for it to be wasted. Your death will be a blessing to the others. One less tramp in this world. And don't think I don't know about your escapades with the Vor'shai Consul. Your former husband told me all about it. I can't say I'm surprised. You take after your mother in more than just your looks."

The sight of Damir wearing her family's heirloom disgusted Leyna. Horrified her. She tried to hide her discontent, not wanting to give him the satisfaction. "Give me back the ring."

"I'll fight you for it," he smirked, lightly caressing her cheek. Leyna slapped his hand away, angry and repulsed at the thought of him touching her. At his laughter, she resumed her attempts to break free of the spectral bonds, finding them sturdy. Unbending. "It is a shame you are so beautiful," Damir smiled to see her struggle. "Your mother was also. It was the only reason I agreed to marry her. If I didn't want you dead so badly, I might be tempted to try and corrupt you instead."

Just being near him made her feel tainted and dirty. To see his face there made her want to scream, lash out at him, to make him know the hatred she carried for him. In a hurried motion, she brought her hands up, pushing hard into his chest to knock him backward. To her dismay, he held firm.

In retaliation, he pushed her back, sending her stumbling over the uneven ground, nearly falling under the force, breaking the link with his shadowy hold. Her chest hurt where his hands connected. The strength of his arms was immense. Unnatural. No one could be that strong. "You think you can fight me, brat?" he said through gritted teeth. He moved forward, closing the distance between them again. "Do you think you are strong enough to defeat me? Your mother thought that, and look where she is now."

Leyna's hand rose up to reveal her sword swinging toward him. "Maybe I'll surprise you."

With incredible speed, Damir deflected her blade, his fingers clutching her wrist tightly, digging the tips into the skin, the weapon forced from her grasp. Her features twisted into a painful grimace. His grip was solid. No amount of prying could release the hold. Laughter filled the trees around her at her failed attempts. He was enjoying watching her futilely trying to get away.

"If you would only accept that I am superior, I might be swayed to let you live. You could be my slave. I hear you make an excellent one."

Using her free arm, Leyna brought the back of her hand across Damir's face, interrupting his rant and snapping his neck to one side under the impact. He gave no pause at the strike, his own hand clenched tight, knuckles driving into her cheek, leaving her disoriented. The blows kept on, punch after punch, his grip on her wrist finally released to press down on her shoulder, his knee rising to knock the wind out of her lungs.

He pushed her back with each strike. Closer and closer to one of the wide tree bases, face twisted into a menacing scowl. She couldn't regain her senses long enough to counter him, the pain in her body flaring with every blow, feeling herself forced against the tree, no longer able to retreat. Each punch precise, he brought his fists to one side of her face, then another, only stopping to admire his work as the vines from up above crept down to wrap Leyna's arms in place, pinning them against the rough bark.

"You might be right. You might be stronger than your mother." His voice was steady, unaffected by the exertion of his attacks. "But I am stronger now than I was when she tried to fight me. Which doesn't say much for your chances of survival, now does it?" He drove his fist hard into her stomach.

"Do you think you can hurt me with your constant mention of her death?" she asked, struggling to breathe.

He smiled. Confident, he stepped in closer to her. "It doesn't bother you to think of the things I did before I killed her?" He took another step, his body pressed up to hers. She could feel his breath against the skin of her neck. Involuntarily she shuddered, unable to break free of the vines. "The way I broke all the fragile bones in her body?" He whispered into her ear. "The way my blade slid easily through her, the same way it will you. Will you scream just as she did? Screams of agony at the pain of death? I reveled in hers before I snapped her pretty little neck."

Leyna was surprised at the calm that came over her. Anger boiled up in the back of her mind, yet she pushed it away. They were lies. She knew it, somehow. He wouldn't break her. She refused to let him. "I fail to see why you are so confident in your victory," she spat. "Even if you manage to kill me, your other men have fallen. Arcastus is dead. You have lost."

"Lost?" he cackled maniacally. "On the contrary, child, you have helped me to succeed. Kael's incompetence might have been Arcastus's weakness, but to me — it was an opportunity. And you played into it all quite nicely."

She stared at him, mouth agape, unwilling to believe what he was saying. It couldn't be true. She had done nothing which would benefit Damir. "You lie!" she shouted angrily. "I killed Arcastus."

Damir struck her again, his fist sinking hard into her stomach, knocking the wind out of her. "Yes, you killed Arcastus. And for that, I thank you. I wasn't sure how I was going to pull that off myself. But with your help, I don't have to. Admittedly, I doubted you to be capable of it, but when I saw you fighting him out there — I was impressed. It seemed only fair for me to help you out a little. Guide things along."

Idly, he let his fingers trace along the chain which hung around his neck. Leyna recognized it instantly. The amulet. He had it. If she could just get free... "You did not help me. I watched him die. You were nowhere around."

"Did you really think the great Arcastus would fall so easily?" Damir clucked his tongue, shaking his head in exaggerated sympathy. "A shattered stone at the right moment weakened him. I saw you draw your blade back for the killing blow. It was my chance to see Arcastus dead. To possess the power which once was his. And now, I have the strength of the others. My hope was to kill Oran before I found you, but I couldn't wait any longer."

Leyna's head reeled. It had all been part of his plan. "No," she whispered in disbelief. "I will not accept that."

"We make a good team, you and I. It is a shame I have to kill you."

A surge of energy pulsed through her limbs at his words. Small at first but quickly growing to an ache in her muscles, the way she'd felt in the chapel courtyard at the thought of Enaes being defeated by Kael's men. This was stronger than even that.

Building until it culminated into a bright flash of pure white light, guiding her to snap through the vines with little effort, her hands pressed tightly to the sides of Damir's head, slamming her own hard into the bridge of his nose.

She gave him no chance to regain his balance, her fists pummeling, pushing him back. Bringing her leg up, she drove the heel of her foot into his midsection, his figure flailing while tumbling to the ground. "You are a murderer and a traitor," she snapped. "No one will mourn your death. Your soul will burn forever in Sytlea's abyss."

From around Damir's neck, she caught sight of a soft yellow glow. It was unmistakable. The perfect circular shape, reflecting the colors of the shattered gems, like a kaleidoscope. Her hand shot out. It needed to be destroyed. They'd made a terrible error in allowing it to fall into his hands.

Damir's eyes opened wide, reaching up to clench his hand over hers, keeping her just out of reach. "I don't think so," he growled.

They wrestled over it, Damir's strength returning to press her back, straddling her on the ground, his free hand connecting in a fist to her body. She heard a snap and knew instantly it was a rib. She refused to let up, her elbow knocking into the side of Damir's head. With a grunt he tipped to the right. Leyna took advantage of his poor balance, rolling over to position herself on top of him once again, the knife edge of her hand delivering a strike to his throat, his fingers releasing their grasp over hers, giving her leave to snatch the medallion.

The chain around Damir's neck was stronger than Leyna expected. It took her two strong yanks to snap, Damir's hands returning to reach for it, his fingers brushing over her skin just as she tore it away. Leyna fell back from her own momentum. She paused to stare down at it in awe. The central stone was split into several pieces while the red swirled pearl next to it remained intact. A hard crack from the third corner gem caused her to jump in surprise.

A stone for every person involved in the ritual. Arcastus in the central location. Four others surrounding. Kael, Kyros – Oran. A smile passed over her lips. "You are all that is left," she said softly, her tone revealing her content at the realization. "Oran is dead. It is between you and me now."

"And you are a fool to think you can end me. Do you realize what that means?" Damir laughed, the sound less intimidating than it had been before. A soft glow crept along the ground, wrapping itself around his legs, seeming to seep into his skin. "We are all linked. When Arcastus died, his power was transferred to Oran and myself. If Oran truly is dead, it only serves to relocate the entirety of Arcastus's magic into me. I am nigh indestructible now."

With a sudden burst of newfound strength, Damir pushed her backward, forcing her to the ground. In a fluid motion she rolled onto her knees, slamming the face of the amulet into a nearby tree. Leyna ground the corner gem into the rough bark, her palm twisting hard to dig it deeper. To her dismay, the gem remained whole, no sign of damage evident at all over the surface. "No one is indestructible," she muttered, rising to her feet while stepping away to place more distance between her and Damir. "I will find a way to kill you."

"It is impossible!" he shouted. "Face it, Leyna. You've failed in everything. To avenge your mother, to save your people. Everything and everyone you love will be destroyed, your land burnt and overrun by the very race you thought you could beat. I almost wish I could keep you alive so you could witness the fall firsthand."

Leyna frantically pondered her options. Arcastus had been injured by her blood when Damir claimed to have broken the central gem. It was strengthened by his state of health. She needed to wound Damir, wear him down, weaken him.

Thoughtfully, she slid the amulet into a pocket of her shirt under her armor, a casual look on her face while she scanned the ground for her sword.

"Yes, I think that would be a bit of entertainment, don't you think?" he continued blithely. "To see the death of everything you hold dear? I could start with your beloved Consul. You can die knowing that he'll be with you soon – after I've satisfied myself with torturing him thoroughly."

"You will not touch him!"

Damir's head tilted back in raucous laughter. "So, now I see how to hit a nerve with you!" In a blur of motion, he moved to stand in front of her, his laughter cut off abruptly as he stared curiously into her eyes. "I think you honestly believe you love the bastard. The truth is – you are nothing more than a nighttime fling to him. A whore–"

Frustrated, Leyna brought her knee up into Damir's groin, his voice trailing off at the pain, doubled over on the ground. "You know nothing about him," she spat.

Her sword wasn't far away. Taking a step she tried to reach for it, finding her legs caught up by Damir's hands, pulling her down to the ground with a heavy thud. Leyna kicked outward with her feet, unable to break free of his grasp. He crawled over to her, arms wrapped tightly around her waist as he lifted her, rising to his feet. In a surge of strength he threw her across the clearing, her back jarring painfully upon making impact with one of the trees. Crying out, she tumbled to the ground, agonized tears filling her eyes.

He was too strong. With Oran dead, there was nothing stopping him. She had no control over him. No means of weakening him the way she had Arcastus.

Before she could stand, Damir was on her again, gripping her by the arms to slam her against the tree a second time, her skull cracking hard along the surface. Through Damir's laughter, he threw her down, her body skidding along the uneven ground, coming to rest near the center of the clearing.

Through the haze of her jumbled thoughts, she could see the reflection of the moon flash over something amidst the grass. Her sword. Groaning from the strain on her battered body, she reached for it, feeling the tips of her fingers graze the hilt, struggling to drag it closer. She hurt everywhere. The thought of standing only added to the excruciating discomfort, but she had no choice. She had to try and find a way to weaken Damir. Injure him. It would take a miracle for her to accomplish in her condition. His endurance would surpass her own.

Lifting her eyes to the sky, she prayed silently for help. She needed guidance and strength. "Mother, if you can hear me, I need you with me now," she whispered, a sting of tears forming in the corners of her eyes. "I cannot do this alone."

A feeling of peace settled upon her again, like that day in the Lake of the Gods. It all came down to this. Whatever was meant to be would be, and only fate knew what was in store for her. Victory or death. There could be no in between.

She heard the sound of Damir's blade being drawn. Lowering her eyes, she saw him over her, eyes flashing with untapped power. A predator's snarl escaped his mouth as he charged. Leyna gathered the last of her energy to pull herself to her knees, spinning around to face Damir, their swords meeting with a loud clang through the small clearing.

They traded blows in perfect time, neither able to break the guard or concentration of the other. Leyna's lungs burned from the strain while Damir kept his breath even, effortless. There was too much riding on her success. No matter how exhausted she felt, she had to press on.

Her arms and legs screamed in pain and fatigue. It wasn't working. He wasn't getting any weaker from the battle. She feared he was growing stronger, faster, refreshed after every clash, while she was failing fast. Time no longer made sense. It felt like hours to her tired muscles. The speed with which he attacked was enough to wear down even the most skilled of warriors, forcing her to react with the same intensity.

Damir delivered a hard blow to the side of Leyna's head with the hilt of his sword, dropping her to the ground, her head swimming. This was it. Her arms no longer reacted to her urges to lift the blade. She was vulnerable. Open to whatever Damir chose to do. "I'm sorry, mother," she breathed. "I tried. I wasn't strong enough. I have failed you."

"You'll have plenty of time to talk to her soon enough."

His final blow came as if in slow motion. She braced herself for the strike. For the instant the world would cease to be. She could see Thade's face, her heart breaking to think of losing him. She didn't want to die. This wasn't how things were supposed to end.

A thrum of energy wrested her arms suddenly. It felt like tiny fingers at first, taking on the sensation of hands clasping over her own, fighting against her uncooperative limbs, tightening her grip on her sword. Some outside presence wrapped itself around her in an invisible cloak, the only sign of its existence the softly glowing aura which radiated over the surface of her skin from head-to-toe.

What is happening? She no longer felt in control over her own body, yet she still sensed the unnatural calm. Damir was getting closer. The tip of his sword thrusting toward her. At the last second, her body lowered, the strange ethereal hands lifting her arms. In that instant she felt her pain subside. Nothing more than a dull throb through the bruised and broken bones she'd endured under Damir's assault. She was on her feet again, though she wasn't sure how she'd managed it. She watched the sword in her hand lash out at Damir, a look of surprise in his eyes to see her pressing on in the battle.

Leyna's arms and legs moved with increased precision and speed. Every strike Damir delivered, she countered, advancing on him with a barrage of movement to dazzle his already confused senses. In a final effort, she saw her opening. Ducking below Damir's powerful swing, she dropped to her knees, the blade of her sword piercing through his armor, driven upward into his chest.

He let out a surprised puff of air, the weight of his body bearing down on top of her, pitched forward under the unexpected blow. With a hard jerk, her hands twisted the sword inside him, his convulsions adding to his weight, impossible for Leyna to fight any longer, her back pressed into the cold snow underneath her, the strange energy dissipating almost as suddenly as it had come.

The amulet. It was there within her reach, if she could just get the strength to move her arm. He was so heavy! She could hardly breathe under his weight.

"Leyna!"

Someone was coming. But that didn't matter. She needed the amulet. As long as the gem remained intact, there was a chance for him to reanimate. Any moment he could jump back to life. There was no telling what the magic would do. Arcastus's power was in him with nowhere to release itself.

Slowly, she felt the cool metal against her fingertips. So close! It was right there… in her grasp. She struggled to pull it from inside her pocket, her eyes looking it over fearfully. The final stone remained in one piece, though a tiny flaw could be seen in the center. A weak point.

Movement from Damir's body sent a wave of panic through her. *He's not dead!* She gasped, frantic to find a way to destroy the stone. Resting her thumb over it, she closed her eyes, the last of her energy focused from her core into the gem, a flash of light bursting from her fingers. The tip of her thumb pressed through the stone, a wince of pain crossing her face as tiny fragments pierced her skin.

She waited, holding her breath. Damir was still again, blood seeping from his gaping wound to cover her hands, staining the snow with its deep crimson shade. *It worked.* She couldn't bring herself to believe it through her exhaustion. *It worked! Damir is dead…*

"Leyna!"

The voice came again. She couldn't locate the source from where she was lying. Something about it struck her as odd. Familiar. It was Thade, distinct, desperate, growing increasingly louder, the echo of it bouncing around in her aching head. But it wasn't possible. Her imagination had to be playing tricks on her. Hallucinating from the strain of the battle. Thade was not involved in the military of Tanispa. He wasn't present for the battle.

Damir's body lifted, air rushing into her lungs in grateful gulps. She wanted to pick up her head, to see who it was that came to her rescue, but the otherworldly light had left her, along with any hope of regaining the use of her muscles without more rest. If she could just close her eyes and sleep for a moment…

"Leyna, wake up!" Thade's voice came again. Closer this time. He was right by her side, her body being lifted from the snow, arms pulling her to his chest. She couldn't see anything. Her eyes refused to open while her conscious mind struggled to maintain control over her head, fading in and out of awareness.

She couldn't remember ever having felt so physically and mentally exhausted. Her body was shutting down, slowly, sleep winning the battle she waged in keeping it going. Cool fingers pulled at her eyelids, opening them enough to let in the moonlight which shone down on her from above. There in the soft glow was the familiar silver light of Thade's eyes gazing down at her sadly.

"Thade?" she whispered. Her voice was hoarse. Strained. "What are you doing here?"

At the sound of her words, Thade lifted her head up higher, his fingertips pressed against the center of her forehead between her eyes. A soft light transferred through him into her. She started to feel her senses clearing, her energy returning enough to allow her to hold her eyes open on her own.

There was no denying Thade's presence there beside her. He was real. No part of her imagination could create something so believable. The muscles on his arms were firm where they held her to him, cradling her. His hair was matted down with sweat, a helmet discarded off to his side, just barely in Leyna's vision as he sat her up to look her over with concern. He was clad in full armor, prepared for battle, the surface of it nicked and scratched, several gouges torn from it, speckles of blood spattered about. At his shoulder was the royal crest; the same clasp worn by the Prince when he joined her and Cadell on the field.

"Why are you wearing the Prince's armor?"

His eyes widened, an expression of pure misery forming over his elegant features. "Leyna, I can explain —"

"Your Highness, we need to get her out of here."

Okivra. What was he doing? *Your Highness?* "Thade, what is going on?"

Another pair of strong arms took her from Thade's embrace. She was lifted up high, the white of Okivra's hair seeming to glow in the dark around his face. He was taking her through the trees where she'd found her way to Damir. The other Ovatai warriors were around them, creating a shield against attacks which might come from unseen foes amongst the trees. Over Okivra's shoulder, she could see Thade behind them, the forlorn expression never leaving his eyes.

They were getting closer to the initial point of their attack. Bodies littered the ground, many of which appeared to be of her men combined with fallen soldiers of the Mialan and Siscalian armies. The enemy uniform was scattered about with increased frequency, outnumbering the loss on the side of the Vor'shai.

"What happened?" Cadell's voice sounded pained, just outside of her line of sight. "Most of them just suddenly dropped. Our scouts can't find any sign of them anywhere."

"Damir is dead," Thade announced. "The soldiers kept alive by his magic likely died alongside him. The Sanarik are not unintelligent enough to stick around when they know they are losing. If we are lucky, the rest of their living troops have retreated."

Embarrassed at her weakened state, Leyna tried to regain her strength, not wanting to be seen by her men being carried about in the arms of Okivra like some pathetic child. "I am fine to stand on my own," she argued.

Okivra's right eye twitched oddly. Without hesitation, he released his hold on her, setting her down on her feet. He snorted in amusement at her trembling legs, barely able to hold her up without her hand reaching out to brace herself against his sturdy chest.

From her new view, she could see Cadell, his arm covered in blood, limp at his side. "Commander Tercsin, see that the Captain is returned safely to the camp for the doctors to look over. Varik, you come with me to see the Prince out of this place before any lagging Ven'shal decide to take a shot at him."

Tercsin… Zander. He was alive. Leyna heaved a sigh of relief, the exhale of air nearly causing her to collapse to the ground. Okivra's strong hand grabbed onto her arm, holding her up. "My men and I will follow your Captain. In her condition, watching her is necessary now."

Hands were pushing her along toward the horses left outside the perimeter of the enemy camps. Despite her exhaustion, she didn't want to go. She wanted to see Thade. There were so many questions still to be answered. "Thade," she called out, turning back. "What is going on?"

"Now is not the time, Captain," Cadell stated firmly. "We will discuss this later. Do as you are told and follow Chief Okivra. That is an order."

She could see Thade watching her. His legs moved him forward a step, held back by Uttae's immense frame stepping in to block him. *Your Highness.* She couldn't get the words out of her mind. Thade was the Prince? It couldn't be. It was impossible.

"The horses are right over here," Zander's voice could be heard from somewhere nearby. Lost in her own thoughts, she no longer cared what they did with her. Everything was too confused, too garbled by the chaos of what was happening around them, unable to think clearly enough to bring the details together with any cohesion.

Fatigue was returning, the last of Thade's extended energy fading from her limbs. She was being lifted onto a horse. *I can't control this thing,* she thought distractedly, her upper body slumping forward. Zander climbed up onto it behind her, guiding her back against him. "I've got this," he said quietly, taking the reins around her to hold her in place with his arms. "You just get some sleep. I have a feeling you are going to need it in the next few days."

Chapter Thirty-One

Every inch of her body ached where she lay, her eyes slowly opening to take in her surroundings. The bed she was in provided too much comfort to be the tattered mattress in her tent. There was no bite to the air from the cold winter wind. Not even a cool draft. It was warm and relaxing, tempting her to close her eyes and drift back off into sleep.

When the memories of the battle crept into her head, she felt her heart start to race, the fear and confusion that had plagued her after Damir's death rushing over her once again. A reminder of all the things that didn't make sense. The things that didn't quite fit in the big picture. *Your Highness...*

Sitting up in the bed, Leyna held her head in her hands, unable to think straight. They addressed Thade as the Prince. But how could that be? The royal name was Levadis. He was Thade Imri. Was he some kind of decoy? A false prince on the battle field to distract the enemy from the real one? It was possible. It seemed devious enough for Cadell to try. That had to be it. It was the only explanation which made any sense to her.

She had been stripped of her armor. The heaviness of it no longer hindered her movements, reminding her of her state of health during the last conscious thoughts in her mind. Bandages were bound about her arms and legs. Someone tended to her wounds. And her clothes — they were clean. Fresh. Her frayed field uniform traded in for a thin, soft nightgown of shimmery grey silk lightly brushing over her skin. Frantic, she clutched at her right hand, remembering the sight of her mother's ring on Damir's finger. To her surprise, she could feel the metal against her skin. Someone had retrieved it for her. Or maybe she was imagining it all...

Movement on the right side of the room caught her eye, her head snapping to see what, or who, was there. She was surprised to see Cadell quietly stepping into the room, his arm arranged in a sling on the outside of a well-tailored velvet tunic, the deep forest green shade bringing out the ruddy glow of his eyes. "Ah, you finally wake. I am happy to see that."

"Where am I?" she asked. It seemed a most logical question, yet at the same time foolish. They were inside a room, filled with exquisite decorations, and any comfort she could ever ask for. She'd been brought back to the palace of Queen Vorsila, but why? There was still so much to be done on the field.

"You are in your quarters, Your Grace."

Leyna peered at him through her long lashes. His behavior was confusing. Your Grace? Why would he call her that? "What happened to Captain?"

"We are beyond that title here in these walls. And given the circumstances, I believe we are beyond that title in most places." He closed the door behind him, careful not to make too much noise. "There are others still waiting to see you when you are up for company. I do not want them to catch wind of you being awake quite yet. How are you feeling? Is there anything I can do for you?"

"You can tell me what is going on," she frowned. "I think at this point, I have a right to know everything."

"You do, yes. And I fully intend to explain, but before I can, I need to show you something. If you feel up for a bit of a walk."

She eyed him, suspicious of what could be going through his mind. How could she be certain of his honesty now after so much had been kept from her?

Careful of her lack of balance, Leyna scooted to the edge of the bed, her feet getting a feel for the floor, steadying herself before rising up to center her weight. She wobbled slightly. Other than the aches and pains in her joints, she felt surprisingly well. Healthy. Energized by the much needed rest. And on an actual bed! For the first time in over a year she remembered how it felt to wake up without discomfort.

With hesitant steps, she made her way to a wardrobe situated near the opposite wall from where Cadell stood. There had to be something inside it. Anything would do to cover up her nightgown to allow her a stroll, so long as it did not take her far from the room. Her energy was not reliable enough to guarantee long, strenuous walks.

Inside the wardrobe she found only a few items. They looked familiar, yet foreign. Garments fashioned of fine silks, damask patterns, and elaborate brocades. It had been well before the war when she'd seen them all last. The contents of her bag packed the day she left for Tanispa.

There at the far left was her old cloak, the fabric worn, but suitable for what she needed it to do. Removing it from its hook, she draped it over her shoulders, her fingers easily able to secure the clasp, making sure her body was completely covered before pulling the hood up over her head. "I hope you are leading. These walls are nothing but a maze to me."

Cadell gave a sharp nod as he stepped away from the door he was standing near. "We will have to take the servants' corridor in order to get past those waiting outside this room. Make sure you put on some shoes. It is still cold outside."

"We are going outside?" Leyna gawked at him in surprise. In the snow? What could he possibly need to show her that required them to trek through the freezing wind? To argue would be pointless, however. In a quick grab, she pulled a pair of fashionable high-ankle slippers from the wardrobe, sliding them onto her feet while trying to keep pace with Cadell through a smaller door not far from the bed.

He guided her down the twisting hallways. No words being passed between the two of them until they reached another door, unremarkable from the side they approached. With his free hand, Cadell turned the knob, a flood of light filling the darkened corridor from an open window somewhere on the other side. Stepping through, he motioned for her to follow. Not wanting to be lost in the dark hall, she moved through the opening, her eyes taking in the sight.

A large bed sat against the wall to her left, the frame crafted from a sturdy wood, painted with golden trim on high canopy poles reaching up toward the ceiling. The silken curtains were drawn back, the blankets untouched, perfectly in place, as if no one had slept there for quite some time. Paintings of well-dressed men and women whose faces looked foreign to Leyna decorated the walls. The colors were vibrant, the detail immaculate, an uneasy feeling coming over her at the sensation of being watched by the people within the frames. "Where are we?" she asked quietly, afraid of disturbing the peace of the empty room.

"These were Prince Enaes's quarters before he was taken from us. We are merely passing through them to get to our destination."

Leyna shuddered to think of being in the room of a dead prince. It felt wrong, somehow. An invasion of his privacy. She couldn't help but to be astonished at the cleanliness of it. A lack of dust on the surfaces. The maids certainly kept the place up rather well for the occupant of the room, as if they anticipated one day for him to return. But that would never be so. Another casualty in an unnecessary and brutal war.

When they stepped out of the spacious rooms, she exhaled, unaware that she'd even been holding her breath. It was a relief to be back in the main hallways of the palace. The royal wing lacked the hustle and bustle of the courtiers, no one around to see them making their way to a large arched door at the end of the hall, stepping through to the blowing wind outside. She'd expected to find herself in a massive courtyard of some kind, designed for the royal family to seek solace from their busy days and nights. Instead, it opened out into an expanse of now frozen and dead gardens, barren of any color other than the glistening white coating of snow over top the trellises.

Cadell continued, his pace slowed to allow Leyna a chance to catch up with him. It was difficult not to be distracted by the sights. They were entering into a stretch of trees, a well traveled path cut through them, lacking any sign of prints in the snow to indicate anyone to have passed through recently.

Up ahead, Leyna could see a clearing of some kind, the snowfall lessened by the branches overhead which created a slight barrier around the area. As they approached, Leyna became suddenly very aware of what the clearing was. Her blood ran cold, a shiver coursing through her spine at the sight of the tall, elaborate headstones lining the whitened ground. A cemetery. Given the location, she could only assume it was not one which was generally open for the public to visit on a whim.

She continued to follow Cadell, finally coming to pause in front of a grave still decorated with trinkets and farewell gifts. It sat within a group of closely gathered sites, the names carved into the surface of the stones in a fancy calligraphic script. Staring down to the one at her feet, she grimaced at the sight, guilt rising up inside her. Prince Enaes Levadis.

Her eyes were drawn to the other stones in morbid fascination. It appeared to be a family plot, another grave similar to Enaes's situated to the right, bearing the name of the eldest Prince, Thade's voice still clear in her mind speaking of the tragedy involving the Levadis children over the years, the name of Prince Ehren floating across her memory.

In the center of the small headstones rested two, much larger graves, only one of which bore any carving to indicate who was buried beneath it in the frozen ground. King Ehren Imri Levadis. Leyna glanced over to Cadell, unsure of what to say. *Imri.* A name ingrained forever in her head.

"The Imri family was of the highest noble ranks in Tanispa during the time when Queen Nalashi was seeking a husband for her daughter, Vorsila. Ehren was a fine gentleman and he was quite smitten with the Queen's daughter, as it was. Negotiations were swift and the two were married. Ehren, within tradition, took the Levadis name upon entering into the royal family. Upon his death, shortly after the birth of their youngest son, Vorsila named the child in memory of his father. Thade Imri Levadis."

"This unmarked grave – is this intended for Queen Vorsila?" Leyna gazed at the blank stone, a perfect match to the massive carved statue at its side, a mirror image of the design, simple, yet elegant, with two doves perched on the top of an arch linking the stones together.

Cadell nodded in solemn appreciation. "When she leaves this world, she will finally be reunited with her lost children and her beloved husband. I think even now she grows weary of the heartache the loss of so many loved ones has caused. She has yet to fully recover from Enaes's death. I doubt anyone could blame her for her misery."

To the other side of the blank stone was another, smaller marker, the image of a rose carved over the Levadis name. It bore no first name, only a single date to denote both birth and death. Beyond it marked the resting place of Princess Amari, though her grave appeared simple next to the two smaller stones to its side, adorned by two tiny cherubs resting atop, their fingers outstretched toward one another to create a small arch across the gap to touch in the center. Kadri and Kaelin Levadis. The twins Thade had spoken of so long ago. Murdered at what was believed to be the hands of some Ven'shal assassin.

"Why did you bring me here?" she asked, suddenly uncomfortable at being surrounded by death on all sides.

Cadell brushed his fingertips over the letters in King Ehren's name, his expression filled with thoughtful contemplation. "Look around us," he replied quietly. "Every person lying in rest in this plot bears a single name, linking them all, dating back to the first Vor'shai Queen, Kaori Levadis herself. The Levadis name is timeless among our people. But it is in danger of dying. The Ven'shal have seen to that quite successfully in the murders of the only daughters born to Queen Vorsila and her husband."

A cold wind whipped through the clearing. Leyna let her eyes take in everything around her, a heavy weight on her shoulders to think of what Cadell was saying. If Thade married within the Vor'shai, by tradition, he would take on the name of his wife. Vorsila would see her family name removed from the throne. She would lose everything then. A failure in a line of the strongest Vor'shai family in history. "What does this have to do with me?"

"It has everything to do with you, Leyna," he sighed. "There was more behind the Queen's decision to keep distance between you and her son than simply his safety during the war. She fears his marriage. While an heir is important to her, she recognizes that the only means of attaining one from a son would cost the Levadis family the throne. She is a proud woman; one with many years still left ahead of her. She would rather seek a new husband and attempt to give birth to an heir of her own than watch the family name die with her son's wife. Part of her hope was that he would lose interest in you while separated and she could continue to seek a match for him with a family who would willingly defy the tradition and take the Levadis name in marriage. But the nobles are power-hungry people. Such an agreement is not likely to be met inside the Vor'shai."

"Are you saying she would give up the purity of the family line by marrying him to a woman of some other race simply to keep the Levadis name in power?"

"The thought was discussed, but she turned it down as well. Her options are few. My fear is that she will not give her blessing for your union with her son. Your grandfather is not exactly unknown among the court." Cadell shifted his injured arm uncomfortably. "There is more to a royal marriage than a simple engagement. If Prince Thade were to request your hand, in a more official capacity than you say he did before, negotiations would be opened between Queen Vorsila and the Evantine family. Iden would never agree to the marriage without securing his own name for the throne."

Covering her face with her hands, Leyna tried to hold back the tears threatening to fall from her eyes. It couldn't have all been for nothing. Things were supposed to be better after the war. He'd assured her of her approval to be with Thade in the event of a victory, and now he was rescinding the promise? This couldn't be happening. She'd come so far and in the end it would be her own blood that destroyed her. Her own kin.

Iden would be the cause of her misery in life the same as he had done to her mother up until her death.

"I thought her acceptance of me for marriage into her family was already given. Is it not true she gave her blessing for Enaes to seek my hand?"

"She didn't expect him to actually find you, and even more so, she did not expect her other son to fall in love with you."

"But I am an adult," she argued. She winced at the pressure of her hands against an unknown injury on her face, lowering her arms back down to her sides in exasperation. "I am perfectly capable of negotiating my own terms! The Evantine family denied my existence. Do you honestly believe I have any desire to maintain their last name were I to marry?"

"The bride cannot negotiate her own terms."

"And what if the bride had no family? Would she simply be denied marriage because there was no one else to negotiate?"

"I do not speak in hypotheticals, Leyna." Cadell's tone was more firm than before, settling Leyna's rising anger in fear of upsetting him. "All I can tell you is the way things are. Either Iden agrees to relinquish rights to his family name on the throne, or Queen Vorsila does. And they are both stubborn enough to prevent the marriage from happening."

In silence, she stared down at the lines of graves. There had to be some other way. If it weren't for Thade's ancestors, they would not be in this predicament. Why couldn't he have been from some other family? A genuine descendant of King Ehren's original line of the Imri name would still have granted them more freedom simply for him not being heir to the throne. It was funny to think back to when he was just the Consul — and how impossible she felt a relationship between them would've been. In that position, the blessing of marriage might have had a better chance than it did now.

"There has to be another way," she mumbled out loud, lost in her thoughts. "There must be someone other than Iden who could speak on my behalf."

"With your parents no longer alive to handle the matter, it defaults to the next of kin, whoever holds the highest station, that being Iden. I am sorry, Leyna. There is no other way."

"No." Her eyes brightened, a devious smile crossing her lips. There was one hope. One loophole they may be able to take advantage of. "I do have another relative. Do these rules require them to share the Evantine name?"

Cadell looked her over, curious to what was going through her mind. "I suppose that question has never been raised before. Explain?"

"Aviden Diah," she blurted out excitedly, unable to hold in her emotions. She paused, inhaling deeply to regain some semblance of composure.

"Lord Diah is no longer with us —"

"I know," she laughed, nervous about the response her idea would receive. "But he had another daughter. A half-sister to me. She is my next of kin, and by proxy, her husband is as well. One of higher rank than Iden. Queen Vorsila's Consul to Siscal. Feolan Diah."

Turning to face him, Leyna tried to decipher the look on his face, almost sick with fear of him denying her the last chance she had at happiness. Feolan and Maeri would without doubt negotiate in her favor. If Cadell could find a way to bend the rules, ever so slightly, it would prove beneficial to everyone — except Iden. Not that he deserved any recognition for his behavior. He was a disgrace to the Evantine family. If her grandmother was still alive, she'd be appalled at what he was doing to it. What he had already done to it.

His brow rose, thinking over her words with careful consideration. She watched him, holding back the urge to reach out and shake the answer out of him. "You make a valid point," he mused. "I must say, though it would complicate matters on one end, it would certainly ease them on the other. But I cannot say with any certainty whether it would be allowed. That call would be up to Her Majesty to decide."

"So there is a chance?" she asked, gazing at him hopefully. His features softened to see her looking at him in such a way, a smile spreading over his mouth.

"There is definitely a chance."

Unable to keep her excitement in, she wrapped her arms around him in a joyful embrace, feeling him flinch at first before lightly patting her back with his uninjured hand. "You will argue for me, won't you?" she pleaded. "You know how much he means to me. I would forever be in your debt."

"You would owe us nothing," he chuckled, wincing as he pulled away, his free hand rubbing at his wounded arm. "If anything, we would be doing you a great injustice by denying you. Keep in mind, Prince Thade would not be here now if it had not been for your heroics back in Siscal. Queen Vorsila nearly lost both of her sons in a single instant, prevented only by your bravery. And that does not count any of the many things you have so selflessly done and sacrificed during your time in service here. I will be sure to remind Her Majesty of such, in case she has forgotten, though I doubt she has. Such deeds are never overlooked by her."

"When do you think we will know of her decision?"

"Soon enough," he nodded. "Once you and I are healed, she spoke of throwing a bit of a celebration in our honor. A way to re-introduce you to the court and to see you are properly praised and recognized for your deeds, now that the war is over and your service no longer requires any form of secrecy. I will do my best to guarantee you an answer that night."

"Then heal up quickly," she smiled, resting her hand over Cadell's injured arm. "My heart cannot handle waiting much longer."

Offering out his good hand, Cadell motioned for her to take it, his head nodding in the direction of the palace. "And it will not have to," he replied. "I suggest you have a seamstress begin work on a gown for the party. All eyes will be on you that night. We must make sure you look your best."

Over the next few weeks, Leyna could hardly stand the anxiety she felt in regards to the possible outcomes of the celebration. Invitations had been sent, the whole of Tanispa set to gather in the Queen's ballroom. By the time the night arrived, she suddenly found herself trembling from nerves. Afraid of what people would say. How would they react to her? And if Queen Vorsila's answer was no, there was no way to know how she would take the news. Poorly, but the humiliation would be the worst. Everyone would be witness to her denial. It was all too much to think about.

The seamstress was finishing the final touches to her dress, making sure everything was perfect and in place, every piece fitting the way it was intended. It had been a long time since she'd felt the discomfort of a corset, but she found it difficult to mind. Tonight she was a lady. It was a small price to pay.

Folds of a gentle soft-blue fabric fell from her slender waist, cinched up tight under the corset and the laces of the gown. A kirtle of a rich sapphire hue was visible through the cut of the top layer, accented by a delicate white lace along the edges. A silver chain draped around her waist, hanging down elegantly in front of the skirt, the links interspersed with tiny, glittering sapphires to catch the light. The bodice showed off her curves, tasteful in design. A sapphire blue ribbon stretched from a silver and gem-studded brooch at the center of the chest, wrapping down at an angle to her waist and around her back; a splash of color against the softer shades.

The neckline was lower than Leyna was used to. No attempt was made to create a mask over her scars, the skin exposed over the collarbone, off-the-shoulder sleeves of white lace delicately resting over her upper arm. Long trailing lines of fabric hung from the elbows, regal in its length and grace, nearly reaching the floor when her arms lowered to her sides.

"Are you sure it is not too much?" she asked hesitantly, her posture erect while the seamstress tied the final bow at the base of the bodice. "I feel overdressed."

"You cannot be overdressed at your own party, dear," the woman smiled. "Now have a seat so I can finish your hair. The General will be here any minute to escort you and we still have much to do."

She did as she was told. If she didn't do something, she was going to go mad from the anticipation. She couldn't remember ever having felt so nervous before in her life. It was worse than the fear she'd felt walking to the final battle of the war. How could it be that she was more afraid of the Queen than she was of an enemy bent on seeing her dead?

Across from her, she could see the reflection of herself, watching her hair transformed under the woman's expert hands. Her long ebon locks hung down her back, only the front pulled up in elegant ringlets, held in place by a clip of silver and sapphires, tiny strands of gem-adorned chains hanging down in the back. The colors of her ensemble brought out the deep glow of her blue eyes, accented by the make-up lining the edges of her lashes, a stark contrast to her pale skin, cheeks rosy from the blush as well as her own nervous excitement, matching the pink of her full lips. She was ready. At least in costume. She couldn't be certain her mind was ever going to be truly prepared for this night.

"You look stunning, Your Grace," Cadell's voice came from the doorway, a servant leading him into the room. He was dressed in his usual formal attire, the military colors suiting him well. "Are you ready for our party? I expect it will be a very long evening."

"I am not sure I would use the term 'ready,' but at the very least, I cannot think of anything else necessary to do before we head down to the fray." She rose up from the chair, smoothing the fabric over her midsection. The corset was already making breathing difficult. "I do not do well with this. You will need to appear twice as masculine in order to make me look feminine by comparison."

"That hardly sounds like a concern," he smirked. Through her nervousness, Leyna couldn't help but laugh at him, moving over to stand at his side. "The crowd is already gathering," he added. "Chief Okivra and his wife were arriving when I stepped through to come here. It must be quite an occasion for him to make the trip south a second time within only a few months."

"That does nothing to make this any less stressful," she nibbled her lower lip. "Let us just get this entrance over with. I cannot stand the anticipation much longer."

He flashed her a knowing smile as they moved through the door, their elbows linked. She knew him to be the type of man who didn't enjoy large gatherings. They were in very similar situations regarding a celebration in their honor, forcing them both to endure the crowd. *It is only for one night,* she tried to calm herself. *After tonight, things will be different, one way or another.*

She knew better than to try and convince Cadell to tell her anything regarding his discussions with the Queen. He was impossible to read. His guard was up, prepared for her watchful gaze, intent on not giving anything away before the proper moment. It was frustrating to her. The night had arrived and still she would be forced to wait.

They paused outside the door of the ballroom, Leyna's heart fluttering uncontrollably inside her chest. She was trembling. Cadell could sense it, his hand reaching up to rest over hers gently. "You will do fine," he whispered, nodding politely to the doorman. "We are ready, sir, if they are prepared for our entrance."

Trumpets sounded from somewhere nearby as the door opened, announcing their arrival. Everything went silent inside the room, save for a single voice calling out their names in a booming shout. "Her Majesty's General Cadell Zerne and his Captain, Her Grace, the Duchess of Escovul!"

"I cannot do this," she breathed suddenly, pulling back against his arm. She needed out of there. Her breath caught in her lungs, the sensation of hyperventilating sending her into a panic at the sound of their names announced to the room. Everyone was waiting for them. They would be watching. Iden was sure to be in attendance, and well aware of who she was. It was too much.

Cadell held her firm, preventing her from getting away. "You have no choice, Leyna," he said quietly. The doors were opening wider, revealing them to the crowd inside. Frozen in place, Leyna stared out at the faces.

It was an incredible sight. All of these people kneeling for her. The little orphan left with nothing, and here she was, attending a gathering in her honor, celebrating her, with the entire kingdom anxious to look upon her face. It was breathtaking. She would have remained there, agape at the crowd, if Cadell hadn't urged her forward, guiding her through the path created for them down the center of the room. Only for royalty had she ever seen such a silent and respectful display upon arrival to this room.

Queen Vorsila rose to her feet upon their entrance. For the first time, Leyna could see Thade's face, standing proudly at the Queen's side, unobstructed by the mask they all were accustomed to seeing over his features at public gatherings. There was no longer any need to hide him. He was the Crown Prince, heir to the throne. The last surviving child of the Queen. She couldn't hide his identity forever out of fear of the Ven'shal.

Leyna couldn't take her eyes off of him. His doublet matched her dress in color, the rich sapphire blues lined with a lighter cording around the shoulders and waist. A crown of twisted silver and gold rested atop his head, diamonds sparkling in the light of the chandeliers. It was a drastic change from his casual appearance while in Siscal. Little details of the past fell into place when she thought back on them, surprised by the fact of it having taken so long for her to figure out who Thade was. There were so many hints. So much that should have given him away, but she'd been so oblivious.

Music once again started to play throughout the room, the guests rising to their feet to return to their conversations. A single face stood out to her amongst the crowd, his blue eyes wide and staring, locked on her every move. His features looked familiar, though she knew not from where. At first glance he resembled someone she'd seen before, but if she looked too closely, she lost the memory, unable to grasp it long enough to determine who he was. He was moving through the crowd now, the distance between them growing shorter with every step until he was before her and Cadell, his arms open wide to her in greeting.

"My dear Leyna. I thought I would never see you again."

Straight-faced, she remained still, her arms down at her sides. "I beg your pardon?" she asked. A knot in her stomach tightened. On the man's right hand was a ring similar to the one she wore on her own, the gems glittering to show off a crest carved into the surface. *Iden?*

"Do not tell me you have forgotten your grandfather," he chuckled. His arms opened wider, waiting for her to accept his embrace.

She continued to stare at him, making no move to show any sign of pleasure at his presence before her. He was the last person she wanted to see. And it was no secret his display of affection was for his own benefit, not hers. "Of course I have not forgotten you. But your memory of me does tend to be a bit fleeting. You remember me now, but you forgot me before — how long until you forget me again?"

"I never forgot you," he frowned. "How could I forget my own granddaughter?"

"You forgot me because it was not convenient for you to recall me at the time. I mean about as much to you as your own daughter did, and that says very little of your affections. It is best you lower your arms, because I have no desire to play your games simply to better yourself."

Iden blinked in surprise at her. "You think you are too good for your own family now? Has your position and accomplishment all gone to your head? You forget who worked to bring honor to the name you bear. A bit more appreciation is expected."

"I suggest you leave the lady be for now," Cadell cut in, stepping between the two of them. "Her Grace has more pressing matters to attend to. This is her party, after all."

"Our party, but yes," she nodded. "This discussion is for another time. It would be uncouth of me to tell you exactly how I feel about you in front of all these people."

Moving to turn away, Leyna gasped to find herself face-to-face with a muscular chest, the velvety material of the doublet giving off a soft sheen in the light. Slowly, she lifted her eyes to see who blocked her path, her heart nearly stopping in her chest at the sight of Thade standing so close to her. "If you gentlemen will excuse us. I have need of an audience with the lady."

"Of course, Your Highness," Cadell bowed.

The other people in the room no longer mattered to her. Their voices faded away into nothing but a background noise, ignoring the stammering protests of Iden as she fell into step beside Thade, their arms linked, posture formal, keeping a distance between their bodies while they maneuvered through the crowd.

He guided her toward the head of the room. Fewer people gathered near the thrones, creating a space at the wall where they could stand without fear of interruption. Leyna was aware of the eyes on them, curious ears straining to hear what was being said for the sake of adding to the local gossip. The courtiers loved their rumors. They thrived on it. *Let them think what they wish*, she thought, dismissing their prying stares. *None of them matter. Especially not now.*

"I did not think you would be allowed to speak with me," she said softly, her eyes shifting nervously to the floor, afraid to meet his gaze directly.

"Let them try to stop me," he smiled. With a gentle touch, he lifted her chin with his hand, his head tilted to stare deeply into her eyes. "Why do you suddenly look so afraid to be near me?"

"Because you are the Prince, Thade," she exhaled. "Why did you never tell me? I feel like an absolute fool."

Clasping her hands in his, Thade shook his head with a disheartened grimace. "You are not a fool. There were so many times when I wanted to tell you. And most of them I nearly did. But I feared you would treat me differently. That you would be afraid to be yourself around me, the way so many others are when in the presence of someone of my station. The way you are right now."

"No," she squeezed his hands tightly in hers. "I am just thinking over all the times when I should have figured it out. I see the resemblances now between you and your family. Your eyes – they should have been the definitive clue. Tell me, Thade. Did you know it was me when you asked me to dance at the masque all those years ago?"

He chuckled to himself, a hint of red rising in his cheeks. Shaking his head, he smiled back at her, the sparkle in his eye nearly causing her to swoon. He was unbelievably handsome in that instant. It was hard not to just wrap her arms around him in front of everyone in the room, not caring what any of them thought of her. Somehow she managed to restrain herself.

"Would you believe me if I said no? You changed so much during the time we were apart. When I saw you off to Faustine's that day in Siscal, you were still a child. The girl I asked to dance that evening was very much a woman. When you spoke to me, however – a part of me suspected. I longed to keep you for another waltz, but my brother, in his usual fashion, stole you away from me. Had you not left so suddenly, I very well may have lost my disguise that very night; to you as well as Feolan."

"You mean to tell me he was unaware before that night as well?" She found it hard to believe Feolan was left out of such an important detail in Thade's life. His strange behavior throughout their trip back to Siscal made sense, however. It must have come as quite a shock to him, the same as it had to her when she'd finally figured it out.

"Outside my immediate family, Cadell was the only other person aware of my identity. It was that way for years. Admittedly, Feolan's knowledge of the truth made things easier between us for business. There was a level of trust that otherwise never would have been achieved."

"And yet you still chose not to tell me that night in Siscal?"

"I wanted to – but my head was not clear. I was so afraid of losing you forever, all I could think of was how to keep us together," he explained, the sadness undeniable in his eyes. "I knew there was a strong chance my mother would deny the marriage; and even if she agreed to it, I could not imagine putting you in the same danger as my family has faced for years. Constantly in fear of our lives, and our children – do you have any idea the horrible things I feared might befall them? I just wanted us to be happy, and my very birthright would have made it impossible."

"So when exactly were you going to tell me?" she asked, her tone stern. She wanted to know. She deserved to know. "Were you just going to keep it a secret and then, one day when we were old and grey, simply 'oh, by the way, I happen to be the Crown Prince of Tanispa.' What a great surprise that would be."

"I had made up my mind before I fell asleep that I would tell you as soon as we awoke the next morning. But you were gone."

She fell silent. How could she possibly be upset with him over something which meant so little now? His reasons were understandable. And there was no way for her to know how she would've reacted to the news back then. So much had changed since that night. She hated to think that she would have denied him simply because of his position, out of fear that he would turn out like his brother Enaes. Her respect for the royal family was greater now than it had been then.

There was only one detail which continued to confuse her. He was willing to give up everything that night, just to be with her. To leave the throne and all the power behind. It amazed her to think of the sacrifice. Was she really worth that much to him? "You were willing to leave all this behind for me? To give it all up in a single night – in a single decision – without any regret?"

"I would give it up even now if you asked it of me, Leyna. You need only say the word and I will walk out this door with you and never return, if it is your desire."

"No," she shook her head, amazed at what she was hearing him say. She could never allow him to do such a thing. After all the work they did to save their people, she couldn't then be the reason it all fell apart. "I would never ask that of you, Thade."

"Then my request still stands, the way it did that night," he said suddenly. She stared at him in disbelief as he knelt down on the floor in front of her, his hand gently taking hers. He gazed up at her, his eyes glowing brightly, seeming to plead with her silently. "Will you share all of this with me, Leyna? As my wife? My Queen?"

Her hand lifted to cover her mouth in awe. This was the last thing she expected. How could she possibly respond? Everyone in the room was watching, including the Queen, the sound of the hushed whispers in the crowd amplified through the silence. "I think I might faint," she breathed, fanning herself frantically. Damn that corset. All she needed was a single full breath in order to calm her racing heart before it burst from her chest in front of the entire city of Sivaeria.

A fearful look passed over Thade's eyes at her reaction. He continued to gaze up at her, expectantly, waiting to hear her response, afraid of what her silence might mean. She watched him, unable to take her eyes from him. It meant everything for her to say yes. And if she did, how could the Queen possibly deny them in front of her entire kingdom?

"Yes," she smiled, a soft laugh escaping her lips at the sight of the relief in Thade's eyes.

In a blur of motion, Thade rose to his feet, catching her up in a fierce embrace, her feet lifted from the ground as he spun them around, pausing only to draw her to him in a tight hold, pressing his lips to hers. Everything around her disappeared, feeling nothing but his kiss, his arms wrapped around her tenderly. It wasn't until he pulled his lips away that she thought again of her conversation with Cadell, the fear returning to her eyes in place of the happiness.

"What is it?" Thade asked in concern. "Is something wrong?"

"Your mother," she said quietly. "What if she does not allow it?"

"Do not be ridiculous," a soft voice chimed from behind Thade, the slender figure of Queen Vorsila taking shape at his side. "The Lord and Lady Diah were more than generous during the negotiations. How could I possibly refuse an offer like that? At this point, it mattered little if you said yes or no to the proposal. The choice was made for you."

Relief washed over her to hear the Queen's words. It had worked! They were able to bypass Iden's greed. All of the pain and suffering of the years all came down to this point, and it was more than worth the joy she felt. She would endure it a hundred times over just for that moment.

Excitedly, she took Thade in her arms again, finally feeling as if things were falling into place where they belonged.

Iden's voice cut through the crowd, breaking the applause of the courtiers. The cheers trailed off, their eyes turning to face him as he approached the Queen. "I expect we will be needing to go over the standard marriage procedures. It is an honor to share this happy moment with you and your family."

"Ah, you," Vorsila rolled her eyes. "I nearly forgot about you."

Thade pulled Leyna in closer to him, his body turned slightly to keep himself between her and Iden protectively. "In case you have not heard, the lady is already spoken for. Negotiations have been completed and closed."

"That cannot be," Iden argued. "With all due respect, I am her guardian. She cannot be married without my consent."

"You should have thought about that before you lied to the General when he came to you inquiring of the existence of your granddaughter and before you involved yourself in the theft of documents from my personal records. Such deeds relinquished any rights you had over this woman. Her next of kin has been contacted. Your fate, however, will be in her hands at this point. If I were you, I would pray she is a merciful queen," Vorsila smiled. "Now step back before I have you removed from my home. If you cause any trouble this evening for my son or his betrothed, I will not be so merciful."

Cadell appeared from behind Iden, his hands firmly grasping the man by the arms to escort him away. Content, Vorsila turned back to Leyna and Thade, her arms outstretched to Leyna with a smile.

"Thank you," Leyna whispered, afraid of hurting the Queen if she pressed too hard against her frail form. "This means more to me than you know."

"I owe you my family," Vorsila nodded, stepping back to offer Leyna's arm to Thade once again. "Now you two enjoy the party. I have wedding plans to attend to and I expect grandchildren immediately. No excuses." She turned to Thade, her index finger pointed at him sternly.

"Yes, mother," he chuckled. Gently, he leaned in to kiss Vorsila on the cheek, his attention turning to Leyna with a warm smile. "Come, Milady," he said, taking Leyna's arm in his. "I am saving all of my dances for you this evening... and every other evening after that."